THE SHADOWS OF BABYLON

by
Julie Daubé

AmErica House
Baltimore

First printing

ISBN: 1-59129-131-3
PUBLISHED BY AMERICA HOUSE BOOK PUBLISHERS
www.publishamerica.com
Baltimore

Printed in the United States of America

To my husband Alex,
a true patriot and a constant source of inspiration.

To those who have given their lives in defense of America's freedom.

ACKNOWLEDGMENTS

I am indebted to a number of people who helped to make this book possible. My husband Alex offered invaluable support and editorial assistance. His help with the action scenes was immensely valuable.

Several people provided significant help in shaping the final product. My grateful professional acknowledgment goes to:

Joan Phillips, for being the first person to read *The Shadows of Babylon* and for her excellent editorial advice; Sharon Glidden Cole, for her encouragement and proofreading; Pamela Fogle, for creating the cover art; my brother, John Grundmann, for brainstorming ideas for the design; and Debbie Bernardo, for her photography skills.

Most writers have had a mentor at some time or another. In my case, it was Dr. Roger Dupré, who gave me much-needed constructive criticism in developing my characters and whose advice changed the course of this novel.

My heartfelt thanks go to the following individuals whose commitment to truth, freedom, and justice has been an inspiration to me: Officer Jack McLamb, Sheriff Richard Mack, Captain Joyce Riley, Colonel Bo Gritz, Dr. Len Horowitz, Ms. Sharon Biggs, Mr. Bob Capiello, and Mr. Frank St. George.

In addition, I am grateful to those whose prayers helped make this dream a reality, including my family, my friends, and my colleagues.

Special thanks go to John Shoemaker, Executive Producer of Hot Talk Radio, KKCS AM, and Chuck Baker, host of the Colorado Springs talk show, "On the Carpet," for allowing me to discuss *The Shadows of Babylon* with their many listeners.

Finally, I would like to thank my father, Henry Grundmann, for teaching me the values of liberty, integrity, and godliness that made America great.

PART I

THE SHADOWS LENGTHEN

"The day of the Lord will come like a thief in the night. While people are saying, 'Peace and safety,' destruction will come on them suddenly...and they will not escape."
(1 Thessalonians 5:2-3 NIV)

CHAPTER 1

Matt Lanyon fought his way through the congested traffic, past the supermarkets, singles bars and boarded-up storefronts that lined the main drag of Hempstead Turnpike. Frustrated, he sighed. Typical Long Island—even on a Saturday morning you get stuck in traffic. Still, this was a bit much. He scanned the road for signs of construction work or an accident. Nothing. Then, he noticed a large sign on a decaying telephone pole:

"WORLD PEACE RALLY AT EISENHOWER PARK, SATURDAY, SEPTEMBER 20, 9 A.M. - 11 A.M."

So, that was it. He suddenly remembered his wife Gina yacking about a rally this weekend, something to do with the new constitution everyone was talking about. She had wanted to go, but it was their anniversary and they had already made special plans that Matt wasn't about to change. Besides, he didn't like the idea of adopting a new constitution, and had made that very clear to Gina. Then again, it might be interesting to hear what the other side had to say. He glanced at his watch. Good. Still time to catch at least part of the rally and make his appointment at the Bureau of Controlled Substances. The parking areas all looked jammed, so he pulled into the Home Depot parking lot across the street and parked there.

Walking toward the park, he heard the sound of a helicopter overhead. He looked up at the black, unmarked chopper as it hovered above the trees. A strange uneasiness came over him. It was the same kind of helicopter he had seen while hiking near the old, abandoned Army base out at Montauk Point last summer. What had troubled him then was that the helicopter had appeared to be following him. He had heard rumors that some top-secret government experiments were going on at the base, but he didn't believe them. He had never put much stock in "conspiracy theories." Yet he couldn't dismiss those black helicopters. It seemed they were everywhere these days. One of his coworkers recently said that relatives of his out west had seen more than a dozen of them flying in formation, and had heard of people actually being chased by them. Of course, the choppers could belong to the military, or even the police, but why wouldn't they have any markings? And why would they be following people for no apparent reason? Matt didn't like to think of himself as one of those "conspiracy nuts" the media was always making fun of, but the thought of mysterious, unmarked helicopters flying around filled him with a vague sense of apprehension. They formed part of a picture he found increasingly foreboding. He felt the same way about all the cameras he saw at intersections to catch people running red lights.

He smiled. *Guess I'm getting paranoid.*

Matt reached Field 6 where the rally was being held. Hundreds of people were sitting on lawn chairs or blankets, while others stood in clusters holding banners promoting world peace, love and brotherhood. A bunch of teens were proudly waving the UN flag. In the center of the crowd television cameras surrounded a stage. To his right stood a middle-aged, heavy-set woman holding a poster with the words, "END HATRED AND OPPRESSION: SUPPORT WORLD GOVERNMENT!"

Matt smiled at her. "I see you're a big supporter of the new constitution."

"Of course. Aren't you?"

"I'm not so sure," he said. "I do know a lot of people who are in favor of it, but it sounds like a pretty drastic step to me. For one thing, I'd like to know more about the wording of it."

She handed him a pamphlet. "Here's some information. I think the UN is still working on the final draft, though."

Matt looked at the pamphlet and frowned. A world constitution! He never would have thought such a thing possible, at least, not in his lifetime. But a lot had changed since he was a kid growing up during the Cold War. The collapse of the former Soviet Union was a major unifying event. Trade barriers had all but vanished. Still, not everyone was as gung-ho for world government as the people here. He recalled the controversy that had erupted when the President gave his support to the World Constitution in his last State of the Union Address. Heated arguments broke out on Capitol Hill, with "right-wing" congressman and senators—as the media referred to them—vowing to do everything in their power to oppose this new step toward world peace. Despite the conservative opposition, ballot initiatives calling for a constitutional convention had passed in the required number of states that would be choosing delegates this November. Matt didn't really pay all that much attention to the news these days, but Gina loved filling him on all these developments...no matter how much he tuned her out.

"Well...what do you think?" the woman asked when Matt was silent.

Scanning the pamphlet, Matt saw that it consisted mainly of slogans supporting world peace, but with little substance. "Hmm. Do you know if American citizens will have a say in all this? Will we have any input into how this constitution is worded?"

The woman smiled broadly. "But don't you see? We won't be just American citizens anymore. We'll be citizens of the *world*. Think about it!"

Matt was silent. The whole idea just didn't sit right with him, even though most New Yorkers seemed sold on world government. But he didn't feel like getting into a debate right now. "I'll try to give it some thought," he said politely.

Turning his attention to the group on the platform, he noticed several government officials, including his congresswoman, one of those bleeding-hearts who claimed to represent the "common people" yet never answered any of the letters he had sent her. He was surprised to see members of the clergy as well.

Startled out of his thoughts by some loud cheering and whistling, Matt looked in the direction of the commotion. A long, black limo had pulled up, and a throng of people surrounded it, including reporters frantically snapping pictures, as the back door opened. Matt expected a rock star to emerge, but he groaned when he saw who it was. With a huge smile that appeared frozen onto her face, Senator Serena Conlin was escorted to the stage. Matt watched with disgust as she waved to her admirers.

How blind can people be? Then again, why should he be surprised? Her own husband had betrayed the American people by selling military secrets to China in exchange for campaign contributions, yet he had been one of the most popular presidents in the nation's history.

He was just about to turn and leave when he saw the senator approach the mike. The woman next to him gushed like a schoolgirl. "Isn't she wonderful? Such a humanitarian!"

Matt recalled that the senator was a vociferous animal rights activist who had introduced a bill to legalize infanticide of children born with congenital diseases. "Oh, she's something else, all right," he said.

A hush came over the crowd as Senator Conlin began to speak. Matt started to walk away, but found himself strangely captivated by her voice. He decided to stick around.

"Good morning, fellow citizens of the world!" she said.

The crowd let out a cheer.

"I can't tell you how happy I am to see so many of you gathered here to support this noble cause." She smiled radiantly, and Matt, who had never seen her in person, suddenly understood why so many people were drawn to her. There was some indefinable quality she possessed that almost mesmerized him.

"Less than a year ago," she continued, "the entire world became united under a common economic system. Now, we are ready for an even greater challenge. The time has come to recognize that we are one human family and to unite under a common system of governance. Think about what this would mean! An end to war, prejudice, and division. The fear of nuclear disaster would be gone forever! The United Nations has created a document that will make all of this possible—a world constitution. It already has been ratified by the European Union, the Russian Federation of Independent States, Japan, and Canada, whose citizens are eagerly awaiting us to join them in this bold and courageous step toward world peace. Naturally, there are those who may have reservations about adopting a new constitution. However, it can no longer be denied that the United States Constitution has become outdated. It was written for another time, another generation, by men who thought themselves superior to other races, and to women." She paused dramatically. "Are we going to let a piece of paper written by dead white men stand in the way of world peace?" she asked.

She was answered with a resounding "NO!" and more clapping.

Her tone suddenly became harsh, and Matt felt disturbed by the words that followed. "Sadly, there are some people in this country who are opposed to unity, peace, and brotherhood. These people are guilty of the crime of hate! The World Constitution would ensure that they could learn to live harmoniously in our global community. New, more effective civil rights laws would be enacted to protect us from those who spread hatred and bigotry."

A cheer went up from the crowd, and the senator paused briefly before continuing. "If you want to live in a world of peace, love, and brotherhood, then I urge you to support the Constitution for Federation Earth. Our future depends on it!"

The crowd went wild. Those who were seated jumped up from their chairs, clapping furiously. Some were shouting, "We love you, Serena!" The woman next to Matt had tears in her eyes. He had to admit, it all sounded good. Especially after the turmoil of the past year. He remembered how shocked everyone had been when the federal government was officially declared bankrupt and the Stock Market crashed, precipitating a worldwide depression. He shuddered as he recalled the images on the nightly news...businesses gutted by fires...violent gangs turning cities into war zones, just to fill their own bellies...women and children, their homes repossessed by the banks, huddled in dilapidated buildings. Martial law had been declared and mandatory curfews instituted. Then there was the day the bank repossessed the house he and Gina had bought only a year earlier, forcing them to move in with Gina's parents, whose house was paid off. It was also the same week his dad lost the family business and Gina heard that the newspaper she worked for was in financial trouble. What a nightmare! To add salt to the wound, Matt had never gotten along with Gina's father, and had fallen into a deep depression at the thought of being dependent on his in-laws. There were times when he had almost gone out of his mind with despair. He could see how the prospect of world peace would be attractive these days. But something in his gut told him that scrapping the United States Constitution would be a fatal mistake.

Suddenly a huge video screen lit up the stage, and a hush came over the crowd. He knew he had to get going, but he wanted to see this new attraction. On the screen, the planet earth appeared in a view from outer space, and a loud, commanding voice rang out through the crowd.

"For over two thousand years, our planet has been divided by war, religion, hatred and intolerance."

Images of violence burst onto the screen. Crusaders from the Middle Ages marched off to battle, carrying flags with the sign of the cross. Men dressed like pilgrims laughed gleefully as they burned terrified young women at the stake. American settlers rode into Indian villages, setting fire to wigwams and gunning down squaws and their children.

"Even today, our world remains divided. Flag-waving patriots, along with extremist religious groups, continue to spawn hatred and violence." The scene shifted to the city streets, where men and women carrying pro-life banners and Bibles stood in front of an abortion clinic, their heads bowed in prayer. The scene flashed abruptly to an angry-looking man wearing a preacher's collar and shouting hysterically, "Renounce your evil lifestyles or we will destroy you! The judgement of God is upon you!"

Boos and shouts of anger came from the crowd. Matt stared at the screen, a sick feeling in his stomach. Although he wasn't religious by any means, he knew his brother John and his sister-in-law were, and it bothered him to see people like them associated with hatred and fanaticism.

"Only one thing can save us," the narrator said. "We must unite under a world government to purge these forces of hatred and strife from our planet. We will never have world peace without world law!"

The crowd clapped and cheered wildly, waving their banners with a zeal that Matt found strangely unnerving. A few people were chanting, "World peace through world law!" The video continued. Glancing at his watch, Matt realized he was almost late for his appointment. He stuffed the pamphlet into his back pocket and headed to his car.

As Matt drove toward Westbury, he thought about the country's depression and its effect on his life. His parents had lost everything, including the construction company that Matt was supposed to inherit. He was bitter. At first, he had hoped to start his own business, but now it looked as if he'd never be able to save enough. No matter how careful they were, Gina and Matt barely managed to save anything because of their tremendous tax burden. And it was impossible to get a loan these days. But what disturbed Matt the most was the change in his father. Once cheerful and optimistic, he had become sullen and withdrawn. Like everyone else who had lost their life's savings, his parents had become totally dependent on the government, and his father hated that almost as much as losing his house. Though the Social Security fund had gone bankrupt, Matt heard that the federal government had borrowed heavily from the International Monetary Fund to revive the system. But the income Matt's parents received was barely enough to live on. It infuriated him to see them going without heat just to put food on the table. He had written a few strongly worded letters about their plight to his representatives, but they merely assured him that they would "keep his views in mind." He knew that his brother was helping their parents out financially, but didn't seem interested in trying to change things politically. Typical Christian, Matt thought. All he does is pray and read the Bible.

As Matt pulled into the lot in front of Nassau County's newly constructed Public Safety and Welfare Center, he tried not to look at the boarded-up, decayed buildings nearby that had once been flourishing businesses—a grim reminder of the death of prosperity.

He pushed open the heavy glass door and looked at the directory near the elevator. Bureau of Controlled Substances, second floor. He still wasn't sure why he had been summoned here, but he knew that the BCS didn't fool around. They played a major role in the war on drugs and were determined to keep drug dealers out of business. Matt had tried to settle this over the phone but was told he had to come in person. Still, he figured there must be some mistake. Even if he wanted to buy drugs, it was now virtually impossible to do so.

Once Matt entered the office, he groaned; even with an appointment he had to wait in line. Finally he stood before the information counter. A short, plump woman with a face like a bulldog glared at him. "Next!" she shouted.

He showed her his summons. "Room E," she said. "Next!"

"Wait a minute. Where's Room E?"

She rolled her eyes. "Look at the directory! You can read, can't you?"

"Now just a minute—"

She ignored him. "Next!"

Shaking his head in disgust, Matt walked away. *And to think my taxes pay her salary!*

He eventually found Room E, but there was another long line in front of the room. Everyone had the same appointment, it seemed. It was finally his turn, and he entered the small, dingy room. Drab, gray paint covered the walls, and the windows looked like they hadn't been cleaned in years. Behind a desk sat a middle-aged man in a blue uniform, looking somewhat bored. Matt handed him the summons.

"I got this letter—" Matt began.

The man looked over the letter. "Gimme your card," he said gruffly.

"What?" Matt was a bit confused.

"I need your debit card."

"What for?"

"There's a question here about possible illegal use of your card."

Somewhat startled, Matt gave him the card, and the man swiped it through a machine. "I'd like to know what this is all about," Matt said.

"Hold on a minute." Matt waited while the computer flashed a long series of numbers onto the screen. "Okay, here's the problem." The man pointed to one of the transactions. "Last month you made an illegal purchase with your debit card. It says here you ordered two quarts of sulfuric acid from an out-of-state company."

Matt stared, taken aback. He realized that the cleaning chemicals he had ordered were impossible to find in New York, but he didn't know they were illegal. And he couldn't believe that anyone would check into his purchases without his permission. "Since when does anyone have the right to check up on what I buy with my own hard-earned money?" he asked.

"The point is, you bought something illegal. Also dangerous. You got a permit for those chemicals?"

"No." Matt frowned. "Why would I need a permit for sulfuric acid? I've been using that stuff to unclog drains all my life, and so did my father. Since when do I need a permit for it?"

"Well, the Controlled Substances Act of 2000 had a bunch of new chemicals added to it. So, since you don't have a permit for that stuff, you're going to have to turn them in and pay an automatic fine of 1,000 debits."

Matt almost slammed his fist on the desk. "I can't believe this! I don't have that kind of money." A debit was the equivalent of one Eurodollar.

"It's either that or forfeit the privilege of using your card. You have five days to turn in the chemicals. And, we're perfectly willing to work out a payment plan for the fine. But if you fail to comply, we'll close your account and you'll face criminal charges."

"Criminal charges? Over a simple mail-order purchase?"

"An illegal purchase." He handed Matt a slip of paper. "You can turn in the chemicals at any of those addresses. In the future, you'd better be more careful about chemical purchases. A lot of substances require a permit now."

"This is ridiculous! How am I supposed to know that a chemical I've been buying for years is suddenly illegal? Did the BCS bother to tell anybody? And who gave you guys the right to check into my purchases?"

"Ignorance of the law is no excuse, Mr. Lanyon. We do whatever is necessary to protect the public from dangerous substances. And we have the authority to investigate illegal purchases."

"Boy, Orwell wasn't that far off, just a few years early," Matt said. "What's next—hidden cameras in my home?"

He sounded impatient. "Look, just cooperate and there won't be any trouble."

Realizing that nothing could be gained by arguing with him, Matt turned and left the building. It's not that the chemicals were all that important to him, it was the principle at stake. As far as he was concerned, his privacy had been invaded. And the prospect of having his account closed was not something to be taken lightly. Without cash, people depended on their debit cards for everything, even to buy necessities like food. He couldn't understand why the government would close his account over something like this—it seemed so drastic. Not long ago, he would have been able to order the chemicals by simply mailing a check to the company, and no one would have bothered him. He suddenly realized that government agencies now had the power to keep track of every purchase made. This idea frightened him. True, he had bought something illegal, but he didn't like the fact that his purchases were being monitored. He wondered how many others were being targeted.

Up until how Matt had liked the convenience of using one card for all financial transactions. He never dreamed that the new system would be abused. For years he and Gina had been using credit cards and ATM cards for almost everything. Even most supermarkets had a debit card system. When the depression hit, world leaders championed the universal debit card as the only way to end the depression, along with money laundering and other crimes. Drug dealers would be forced out of business, and it would be impossible to buy illegal weapons, since all transactions would be electronically recorded and could be checked. But Matt figured that those who were determined to get a hold of illegal weapons would find a way to do so. And after what just happened to him, he sure didn't think it was worth giving up freedom in exchange for apparent security.

When he arrived home, he found Gina in the living room with their neighbors from the apartment next door, Ben and Elsie Weiss, along with their teenage grandson, David. Ben, who reminded Matt of his grandfather, wore square-rimmed glasses with thick, black frames. He had taken a fatherly interest in Matt since he had started doing odd jobs for them. David, tall, gangly, and dark-haired, also wore glasses.

Gina got up from the couch. "Hi, hon. Ben and Elsie came by to wish us a happy anniversary. They even brought us some apple strudel! Wasn't that sweet of them?"

Matt smiled as Gina walked toward him. Wearing snug blue jeans and a red sweater that accentuated her trim figure, she had high cheekbones, wavy reddish brown hair, and long, delicate lashes slanting over her large, brown eyes. She was quite a catch. And with his rugged build, fair hair and blue eyes, he knew they made an attractive couple. In his aggravation earlier, he had almost forgotten about their anniversary. He decided to put the whole incident out of his mind.

Matt eyed the strudel on the coffee table. "Thanks, that was really thoughtful of you guys." He reached over and patted Ben on the shoulder, and as his eyes fell on the series of numbers engraved above Ben's wrist, Matt felt a chill.

Apparently Ben didn't notice. "Oh, don't mention it," he said, and his brown eyes twinkled. "We couldn't forget your anniversary."

"So, how did your appointment go?" Gina asked a bit apprehensively as Matt sat on an easy chair opposite the couch.

"Let's talk about it later." He wanted to change the subject. "Hey, did you guys hear about that big rally at Eisenhower Park this morning? I passed it on my way to Westbury."

"I heard something about a rally on News 12 this morning," Elsie said. "I think it was about that new constitution."

David brightened. "Yeah, my Global Studies teacher keeps talking about it. She says it's an important step to achieving world peace."

Ben frowned. "I'm not so sure about that, David. It'll take more than a new constitution to do that. A piece of paper can't change human nature."

David looked surprised. "You mean you're against world order?"

Ben waved his hand contemptuously. "World order! Humph!"

"My teacher says it's the only way to end war and oppression," David said earnestly. "She said we'll destroy each other if something isn't done to ensure world peace."

Matt chuckled. "You sound a lot like the people at that rally."

Gina looked puzzled. "Matt, you told me you didn't want to go to the rally."

"Well, I was curious." Matt briefly described the speech and the video, then went and got the pamphlet out of his pocket. He showed it to Ben, who read it silently.

Ben looked troubled. "It's just as I thought. This is nothing but anti-American propaganda. You can bet the UN is going to use this so-called World Constitution to bring America—and the world—to its knees, all in the name of peace and brotherhood. It's what some of my own misguided countrymen seem to want...peace at any price, never mind the consequences." He let out a sigh. "That's the problem with people today, they're willing to accept any solution to the latest crisis without ever thinking of the consequences. I saw that happen in Germany." Elsie's frail hand clasped Ben's, and her deep brown eyes were full of compassion.

"But wouldn't it be great if the democracy we have here could be worldwide?" Gina asked. "That's what the new constitution is all about. For centuries, there's been inequality, fighting, and racial conflict all over the world. The World Constitution will end all that."

Elsie looked doubtful. "You really think it's that simple?"

"Well, obviously it will involve some adjustments," Gina said. "But I can't think of any better way to bring peace to this world. Just one look at the news is enough to prove that something needs to be done. The Middle East is a mess, and it's one of the areas that hasn't adopted the World Constitution yet. Those greedy OPEC nations! They keep insisting on more power in the World Parliament before they agree to adopt the Constitution. And the Israelis are—" She stopped, and there was an awkward silence. Matt glared at her, annoyed by her blunder.

Ben laughed good-naturedly. "What? Too uncompromising? Too strong-willed? I, for one, don't mind, as long as they don't give in to all this nonsense about a world constitution. The Israelis have given up too much land already—and now the UN wants them to give up their national sovereignty? It's crazy!"

"But isn't peace more important than national sovereignty?" asked Gina.

Matt forced a smile. "My little crusader." He didn't like the fact that Gina supported the World Constitution but figured it was useless to try to change her mind; she tended to be pretty stubborn when she was set on something. "But Ben and Elsie didn't come here to talk politics all morning. And I'll bet David finds this talk pretty tedious."

"No, I've really been getting into politics lately. In Global Studies, we do all kinds of neat stuff like role-playing and group projects."

"It's great to see a young person so enthusiastic about school these days," Gina said with a smile. But Matt noticed that Ben didn't look too pleased.

"Oh, I wanted to ask you something, Matt," Ben said suddenly. "Elsie and I were wondering if you're still interested in cleaning out the pipes in our kitchen. I know you do good work, and I'd rather have you do it than that idiot superintendent who doesn't know what he's doing."

Matt hesitated. He hadn't wanted to talk about the incident at the BCS, but the chemicals he had to turn in were the ones he'd planned to use to clean the clogged pipes. Now he'd have to use something less effective, unless he managed to get a permit for them. Reluctantly, he explained the situation to Ben. "Of course, I'll still do the job. I'll just have to use a different kind of chemical, which might not work as well. Sulfuric acid is the best thing for clogged pipes."

Ben gave a whistle of surprise. "This is something! So, now the government is keeping track of what we buy."

Matt smiled ruefully. "Yeah, sounds like something out of *1984*, doesn't it?"

"What's *1984*?" asked David.

"Oh, it's a famous book about totalitarian government," Ben replied. "Much of it was based on the Nazi regime. I'm sure you've heard the saying, 'Big Brother is watching you.'"

David looked puzzled. "No. What does it mean?"

Ben's brow was furrowed. "Hmm. I'm surprised you've never heard it. That book should be required reading in every high school. It's about a government that controls every aspect of people's lives. The people are under constant surveillance by the government, and they're told that their leader—Big Brother—watches everything they do. So, when people say, 'Big Brother is watching you,' they mean that the government is watching us, or keeping track of us. Kind of like what happened to Matt today."

"But isn't that what the government's supposed to do?" David asked. "I mean, they have to make sure people don't break the law, right?"

Ben looked thoughtful. "Why don't you read *1984*? It will show you what can happen when a government gets too powerful."

Matt wondered why Ben didn't tell David about his experience as a Jew living in Nazi Germany. Then, he figured it was too painful to talk about, especially to his grandchildren, whom he probably wanted to shield from such horrors.

"Okay," David said. "I'll take it out of the library. It sounds interesting."

Gina laughed. "You better be careful, Ben—you might scare David with all this talk of totalitarianism. Anyway, I doubt that anything like that could happen in America."

Matt looked at her in amazement. "Wait a minute. What about what just happened to me at the BCS? Don't you find that just a little bit frightening?"

"But it's their job to protect us. Sulfuric acid can be pretty dangerous in the wrong hands. I mean, what if some psychopath got a hold of it and used it to hurt someone?"

"Gina, knives and baseball clubs are deadly in the wrong hands," Matt said. "Does that mean we should outlaw them? Or force people to get permits for them?"

Gina rolled her eyes. "Now you're being silly."

Elsie laughed, as if trying to lighten the tension. "Listen, it's your anniversary. You two don't want to get into an argument now, do you?"

"No, you're right," Gina said with a sigh.

Ben looked at his watch. "Boy, where did this morning go? Elsie and I have to get going—we're taking David shopping for a birthday present. He turns seventeen tomorrow."

"Well, happy birthday," said Matt. Everyone got up, and Gina went to get the Weisses' coats.

"I'll be in touch about cleaning those pipes," Matt told Ben.

"Great."

After they had left, Gina began clearing away the coffee cups.

Matt picked up the tray of strudel. "So, you really see nothing wrong with the fact that a government agency can keep track of what we buy now?"

"Well, I don't like the idea. But I can understand their reasoning. I just hate the thought of criminals having access to dangerous chemicals. But I guess they went a little too far by checking into your account."

"You bet they did. I wonder what's next."

"What do you mean?"

Matt followed Gina into the kitchen and placed the tray on the counter. "I never realized how this debit card system could be abused. It gives the government a lot more power. I mean, if they wanted to, they could ban any product and they'd be able to keep track of anyone who bought it. You know, sulfuric acid has been perfectly legal for over 200 years—where the hell do they get off banning it?"

Gina began washing the cups. "This really has you worried."

"Naturally, I'm concerned. You know, they threatened to close my account if I didn't cooperate."

"That is pretty drastic."

"I wonder if there's anything I can do about this."

"Like what?"

He thought for a moment. "Maybe I'll write a letter to the paper or something. People should know that this kind of stuff is going on."

Gina's eyes lit up then. "You know, this might make an interesting story. Maybe I'll do a little investigating, see if other people have gone through anything like this. I'll mention it to Ken." Ken Hughes was managing editor of *Island News*, the paper Gina worked for.

"That's a great idea!"

They finished cleaning up and headed back to the living room. Matt hunted through the pile of clutter on the end table for the TV guide. There was a science fiction movie he wanted to tape later. "So, you ready for our outing?"

The Planting Fields Arboretum in the town of Oyster Bay was one of their favorite places. Filled with beautiful trees and lush green meadows, it had once been a palatial private estate that was donated to the town. It was even more special because Matt and Gina had their wedding pictures taken there.

"Oh, I almost forgot to make reservations for dinner tonight," Gina said suddenly. "I better do that now." She leaned over to kiss him on the cheek, then disappeared into the kitchen to make the call. They planned to have dinner at their favorite restaurant, a French bistro on Sunrise Highway. Gina was quite a wine connoisseur, and the restaurant had an extensive wine list. Matt usually just had a couple of beers, though tonight Gina would most likely insist on champagne. He hoped they had enough in their account for such a lavish evening.

In a moment or two Gina joined Matt in the living room again.

Matt had just finished timing his show. "You ready to go?"

"Sure."

They were just getting their coats when the phone rang. "Let the machine pick up," Matt said.

They both waited, but as the caller began his message, Gina hurried to the phone and picked it up immediately. Matt groaned as he listened to her end of the conversation. "What? In the hospital? Sure, I can get there…no, it's not a problem. I'll get over there as soon as I can." She hung up and looked over at Matt. "I'm sorry, honey, but there's a big story breaking and the reporter who was covering it got hurt. He's in the hospital. Ken figured since I'm right in the area—"

"Gina, this is the one Saturday you've had off in months."

"Matt, you know how important my career is to me. I have a responsibility to my editor and to the public."

He rolled his eyes. "Give me a break."

"What's that supposed to mean?"

"Forget it. Go do what you have to do, but don't expect me to wait around for you to get home. I'll see you later—maybe." He grabbed his jacket and stormed out of the apartment.

* * * *

Gina fought the urge to cry as she fumbled with her car keys. Why was it that today of all days, this had to happen? She wanted to run out after Matt, but that would just make him think he was right. Besides, she had a story to cover. She had worked very hard to get where she was, and she didn't do it by letting other reporters beat her to a story. She grabbed her coat and purse and went out to the parking lot. Matt was nowhere in sight. She sighed. Why does he have to act like a child when he doesn't get his way?

As she drove along Newbridge Road, Gina focused on the details of the story. Ken hadn't told her very much, something about a riot and an arrest. Yet she found herself thinking of Matt and the disappointed look in his eyes. Things were so different now. When she first met him, he was almost as ambitious as she was. She remembered all the overtime he had put in as a carpenter for his father's company, and he never seemed to mind. And he had been equally proud of her accomplishments. But in recent months, Matt's attitude had changed, and now he seemed to resent her career. Something in his personality had also changed, but she couldn't put her finger on it...something in his manner...she didn't know. She tried to clear her mind of the nagging questions that she found increasingly difficult to ignore.

She arrived at the Nassau County Jail just as a prisoner was being dragged roughly out of a squad car. Reporters and camera crews were pushing their way toward him. Blood trickled down his face from a gash on his forehead, and his dark gray hair was matted with sweat. She took a few shots of him, then looked around to see if any others had been arrested, but saw no one else. *Strange for a riot*, she thought. Just one man arrested? She looked at him again. He appeared to be in his mid-fifties, and had a slender, almost frail build. Gina was struck by his peaceful expression and air of dignity. Then she noticed his collar. The man was a priest! Somehow this startled her. She had heard of priests being arrested before, but only at those radical anti-abortion demonstrations she detested. She hurried inside and spoke to the sergeant at the information desk. He told her that the priest—Father Flannery—was taken to the county jail because the judge had decided he was too dangerous to let out on bail. He had been charged with hatespeech and disturbing the peace. She was also startled to learn that the riot had taken place during the rally at Eisenhower Park; Matt must have just missed it.

When Captain Harris finally arrived for a press conference, he was very harried and spoke brusquely. He didn't give many details, just reiterated what Gina had heard from the sergeant. After the hurried press conference, Gina and the other reporters asked for permission to interview the priest, as well as the arresting officers.

"I'm afraid that's out of the question," the captain said emphatically.

The reporters looked baffled. "But why?" asked Gina.

"Security reasons."

The reporters all began firing questions at once. Captain Harris was adamant. "Look, I'm a very busy man, and I have a jail to run, so I'll have to ask you all to leave."

Gina left reluctantly. As the door closed behind her, she felt like the possibility for a good story had closed as well. She had the basic facts, but there were missing pieces. And she couldn't understand why the captain was so eager to get rid of the reporters. She wondered what the priest could have said to incite such rage.

* * * *

A heavy rain pelted the streets of Manhattan as Gina made her way toward

Park Avenue. Far fewer people walked downtown, and there was an air of gloom on their faces. Most of the buildings still wore scars from the looting and fires that had raged during the depression riots. With insurance companies having gone bankrupt, few people could afford to rebuild the businesses they had owned. The government was financing a series of rebuilding projects in the city, but there was a long waiting list. Most people had grown tired of waiting and had applied for welfare benefits. What would those poor people do without a safety net? She frowned, thinking of Matt. *If he had his way, they'd all be out on the streets begging.* Why couldn't he see that in times such as these, people depended on the government for their very survival?

It wasn't long before she arrived at the headquarters of the Council for Global Unity, or the CGU, which had sponsored the rally. She stared in disbelief at the boutiques, elite shops, and upscale restaurants along the tree-lined sidewalk of Park Avenue. Glancing at the cars in the private garage adjacent to the entrance, Gina noticed that they were all brand new luxury models—Mercedes, Lincoln Town Cars, BMWs—a rare sight these days. These people must be fairly wealthy. The building, a stately residence dating from the 1940s, resembled an aristocratic hotel. Its understated elegance surprised Gina, who had never seen the Council's headquarters before and had expected something a bit more ostentatious. She also noticed that there was no sign in front of the building to identify the organization.

She walked through the revolving glass doors and across the marble floor toward the reception area. Rich, dark paneling covered the walls, and porcelain vases held exquisite arrangements of tiger lilies, tea roses, and purple irises. On the back wall she saw a bronze relief sculpture of the planet earth. Beneath the sculpture were the Latin words, *Novus Ordo Seclorum*. A man was sitting behind a marble counter. "May I help you?" His voice was courteous yet firm. He wore a black suit that accentuated his broad shoulders, and looked somewhat like a secret service agent.

"Yes, I'm a reporter from *Island News*, and I'd like to speak to someone about the rally at Eisenhower Park earlier today." She had tried to do this over the phone, but couldn't seem to get a hold of anyone who could answer her questions. She had called the hospital to find out if Mike Casey, the reporter injured in the riot, was able to receive visitors. But she was told he had a mild concussion and was too disoriented to answer any questions.

"Just a moment." He picked up the phone on his desk. "There's a reporter here who has some questions about that rally held today on Long Island.... Certainly. I'll send her up." He hung up the phone. "You can go up to suite

202, but first I'll need to see some I.D. And I'll also need to search your bag."

She was just a bit startled at that. "Is there any particular reason?"

"We have many government officials coming and going here. It's simply a security measure."

A few moments later Gina knocked on the door to suite 202. She was completely flabbergasted when she saw who opened the door. "You're Serena Conlin!" she blurted out, and then felt mortified for her child-like exclamation. But she could hardly contain her excitement at meeting one of her own heroines.

Serena Conlin smiled almost indulgently. "I guess my secret's out," she said with an infectious laugh. She extended her hand, and Gina was struck by the senator's natural warmth.

They exchanged pleasantries, and Serena led Gina to a small sitting area. She took a small tape recorder from her handbag and briefly surveyed the room. A luxurious mahogany desk, neatly organized, stood in one corner, and gleaming wooden file cabinets lined the wall. Paintings of scenes from classical mythology hung on the walls. The most striking one depicted the River Styx and Charon, the gnarled Boatman who led souls across the river to the Underworld.

"I understand that the riot was started by a priest named Father Flannery. What did he do to instigate the it?" Gina asked.

"The man was practically insane," the senator replied. "After our presentation, he forced his way onto the stage and demanded to be heard. Naturally, I have always respected people of deep religious convictions, so I didn't want to discourage him. Perhaps that was a mistake." There was a slight pause as Serena's expression changed. Her dancing blue eyes suddenly became cold and lifeless. "What is it that priests are supposed to represent, Ms. Lanyon? Brotherly love, compassion, kindness? I heard none of those things in his diatribe. Frankly, his hatred and intolerance shocked me. He said that a religious war is raging and he will not rest until the enemies of his so-called 'God'—homosexuals, feminists, atheists, Jews, and everyone else who doesn't happen to subscribe to his brand of Christianity—are destroyed."

"That's pretty strong stuff." Gina couldn't believe that a priest, a man of God, would say such things. She thought of his peaceful countenance as he was taken into custody. Appearances certainly could be deceiving. "At what point did the riot begin?"

"Well, everything happened so fast, it's difficult to remember it all clearly.

But some people in the crowd began to challenge him. That's when he went crazy. He became hysterical, screaming that they should all be put to death. Shocking as it sounds, he was actually promoting genocide against those he deemed to be 'sinners'! The next thing I knew, people were throwing things at him. I don't know what would have happened if the police hadn't come when they did."

"Did he put up any kind of a fight when he was arrested?"

"He was very agitated and kept threatening the officers with violence." Serena paused, then looked at her watch. "I'm afraid that's all I can tell you, Ms. Lanyon, as I have an appointment soon. I hope I was helpful."

"Oh, yes, thank you very much for your time. It was an honor to meet you."

"The pleasure was mine," Serena said with a smile.

* * * *

The newsroom was buzzing with activity when Gina arrived. Huge, glass partitions divided reporters frantically typing away to get their stories ready for the next morning's edition. Gina sat at her desk. She knew she had to finish her story by the end of the day, but she hoped to get home early enough to salvage at least part of the afternoon. As she began typing at her computer terminal, her worries about Matt drifted far away. She was startled when she heard Ken's voice. "How's that story on the riot coming?" he asked.

"Pretty good. I couldn't get much at the jail, but guess what? I got an interview with Senator Conlin. It turns out she's a member of the Council for Global Unity, which sponsored the rally. I think I have enough for a fairly good story. I just wish I could have talked to the priest who instigated the riot."

Ken raised his eyebrows. He was in his late forties, with salt-and-pepper-colored hair, hazel eyes, and a lean, haggard face. He expected a lot from his staff, but had earned their respect because of his fairness and ability to encourage them to do their best without intimidating them. "Why couldn't you talk to him?"

"I'm not really sure, actually. The captain said something about security. I guess it's just not his policy to allow prisoners to be interviewed. At least, not anymore."

"That's strange." Ken wore a puzzled expression.

"Why?"

"Because just last month Captain Harris let one of our reporters interview Jake Farrel, convicted of killing his wife."

"That is strange. Harris was the one who refused to let me interview Father Flannery. And he wouldn't let anyone interview the arresting officers, either."

"Hmm. Maybe I'll give him a call."

* * * *

Something told Ken there was more to this story than a simple riot, but he wasn't sure how to handle it. Especially if the CGU was involved. That was a group most editors had learned to treat with respect, if they wanted to keep their jobs. Still, he was dying to find out why Harris didn't want Flannery or the arresting officers to be interviewed. That was very strange indeed.

Sitting at his desk cluttered with unedited copy, he picked up the phone. He waited, chewing on the end of his pencil, until the call went through. "Captain Harris? This is Ken Hughes, managing editor of *Island News.*"

"Yes, Mr. Hughes, what can I do for you?"

"Well, I'm kind of curious about something. One of my reporters was over at the jail this afternoon doing a story about the riot at Eisenhower. She told me you wouldn't let her interview Father Flannery, who allegedly started the riot."

"That's right."

"Is there any particular reason?"

"Look, it's just not my policy to allow prisoners to be interviewed." He sounded annoyed.

"That's very interesting. Because just last month, you allowed one of my reporters to interview Jake Farrel." There was a long pause. "Is there a reason for the sudden change in your policy?"

"This is an entirely different situation. Father Flannery is a violent man. I can't take any chances."

"Farrel is a violent man, too. Didn't he attack the officers who apprehended him? I heard it took three or four officers to subdue him." When Harris didn't answer, Ken continued. "Listen, I don't want to give you a hard time. I'd just like you to level with me. If you don't want anyone to interview Father Flannery, I won't press you. But I'd like to know your reasons, off the record, if you prefer it that way. I'd also like to know why the arresting officers are off-limits to the press as well. It doesn't add up."

Harris sighed. "Oh, I might as well tell you. You'll probably never leave me alone if I don't. I got a call from the Governor. She kind of 'suggested' that I shouldn't let reporters interview the priest or the arresting officers, said it would upset people to hear the stuff he was saying. I don't know why it was so darn important, but I figured I should cooperate. But listen, Hughes—if anyone asks you, you didn't hear this from me."

"Sure," Ken said absently. He was wondering how to pursue this story. They both hung up, and Ken sat at his desk, staring into space. He knew this had the makings of a great story. He recalled that the Governor belonged to the Council for Global Unity, and that members of the Council tended to stick together. They were also a close-mouthed group. Membership was by invitation only, and all those who joined were required to take an oath promising not to reveal anything that was said during meetings closed to the press. Possibly, the Council was covering something up. Why didn't they want anyone to interview the priest? He knew they had to have a reason. It couldn't just be their concern with his violent rhetoric. Still, he had to be careful. It was dangerous to tangle with the CGU—or so he had heard.

He thought suddenly of his father's old friend, Bruce Evans, who used to be the editor of a major newspaper in Washington, D.C. Just over a year ago, Ken had run into Bruce while attending a seminar there. He vaguely remembered him saying something about the Council, some off-handed remark that suggested something sinister about the organization. He tried to recall what it was. They were sitting in an outdoor café on Massachusetts Avenue, under the shade of a Ginkgo tree, and Bruce was telling him how much he had admired Ken's father, who had passed away while Ken was still in college. But what had he said about the Council? He couldn't remember. On a hunch, he picked up the phone and dialed Bruce's number.

After a bit of small talk, Ken broached the reason for his call. "What do you know about the Council for Global Unity, Bruce?"

There was a brief pause. "Why do you ask?" Ken detected an edge of bitterness in the man's voice.

"Well, I got the impression the last time we spoke that you don't think very highly of them."

"That's an understatement." His tone indicated his eagerness to talk about the Council.

"Would you mind telling me why? It might help with a story one of my reporters is working on."

"Let's just say I made the mistake of trying to investigate them. Not too many people know a hell of a lot about them, Ken—and they want to keep it that way. They tried to squelch a story one of my reporters was doing on them. It was an exposé documenting their influence over the State Department. Apparently, no one can get appointed to the State Department unless the directorate of the CGU approves. Anyway, the owner of the paper I was working for warned me not to print the story or I'd be fired. Well, I held off on printing it, but decided to do some unofficial investigating on my own. That was a mistake."

"What happened?"

"My career got destroyed. Oh, I was given a choice, all right: retire, or get blacklisted. I chose the former. Freedom of the press. What a joke!"

There was a pause as Ken tried to digest what Bruce had just said. He had known that the Council exerted a great deal of influence on the media, but this was worse than he had imagined. "I don't know what to say, Bruce, that's...outrageous. How could they get away with something like that?"

"Because the scoundrels control every major newspaper in this country. Ever look at their membership roster? No? Well, I did. Guess what? Members of the Council own every corporate newspaper in the country—not to mention the major news networks. So, that means they control the establishment news media. And that's not all. Did you know that the trustees and presidents of the most prestigious universities in America are also members? That means the Council also controls education. Apparently they have a virtual stranglehold on the nation's most influential teaching colleges. Ken, take my advice. If you want to stay in the newspaper business, don't tangle with the CGU. It just isn't worth it."

"I'll keep that in mind."

"You know, I'm glad your father isn't around to see what's become of the newspaper business." Bruce sounded wistful. "He was a first-rate newspaper man. Always printed the truth, even if it ruffled some feathers—heck, even if it was downright dangerous."

Ken was nonplused. What should he do? Years ago when he started studying journalism, the answer would have been simple. His father had warned him that being a journalist involved some tough choices. "There are a lot of people who don't like reporters snooping into their dark, dirty secrets," he had said. "Some of those people are very powerful. I know from my experience as an investigative reporter. But there's no point in being a journalist if you're afraid to print the truth."

At the idealistic age of eighteen, Ken had been accepted to a prestigious journalism college on the East Coast. He felt ready to take on the world and was eager to challenge the establishment. But after four years of journalism college, he knew better. He had discovered that he'd never make it if he weren't willing to compromise his honesty. As a staff writer for the college newspaper, he had often felt frustrated when the editor changed his stories around—especially if they put the school administration in a bad light or failed to promote the politically correct ideology so pervasive at most universities. He had even spoken to the faculty advisor of the newspaper, an associate professor of journalism. What she said opened Ken's eyes to the dark and ugly world he had entered when he decided to pursue his dream. She told him he had a bright future, but he may not go as far as his potential if he didn't cooperate with the senior staff. Ken knew what she meant; if he didn't tow the line, he wouldn't have any chance for a promotion on the staff. Of course, there were ways to fight such censorship. But he would have made a lot of enemies that way, not a good way to start a career in journalism. And he would need recommendations from his professors and the editor of the school paper to get a job at a newspaper someday.

For a while, he had even considered giving up journalism. But he just couldn't throw his dream away. So, he decided to go along with his editor, at least for the time being. Once hired by a major newspaper, things would be different, he told himself. But now, as he sat at his desk in the office where he had worked for so many years, he wondered if he was really any different from the cowardly journalism student he was in college.

He thought about the members of the CGU and the mysterious power they wielded. No one talked much about the Council. Although there was an official headquarters in New York, Ken had heard that many meetings took place in private drawing rooms of stately hotels. Most high political leaders, including the President of the United States, were members. For years they had remained in the shadows, and few people knew of their activities. In fact, most Americans had never even heard of the Council. Years ago his father had hinted of a sinister organization that controlled the destinies of nations. Could this be the same group?

Ken wondered why an ordinary priest would be of any concern to them. Maybe Gina could look into his background, or question his superiors. That way she could get some information about him without shaking up the CGU. He went out to speak to Gina. Passing his father's portrait hanging on the wall, he quickly averted his eyes.

* * * *

The late afternoon sun cast long shadows across the marble table in the Meditation Room of the CGU's New York Headquarters. A cool autumn breeze drifted in the partially open window, but the sounds of the city streets were barely audible. Several dark figures dressed in armor guarded the door and the windows, their swords unsheathed as if prepared for battle. If the humans seated at the table could have seen these sentinels, a shriek of horror might have echoed through the room.

Watching their charges, the guards couldn't help staring at the third eye above and between each human's earthly eyes. Though no mortal could see it, the guards knew its significance: it was the mark shared only by those special few who had been directly touched by the Prince of their world.

The one called Serena Conlin leaned forward. "Ashtar has contacted me. He says the time is soon." Her eyes seemed to possess a life all their own, as if some unseen entity were looking out at an alien world. She was among the Master's most useful vessels, and it was known that she was under the authority of some very powerful princes.

The man to her left looked at her with small, darting eyes. His name was Frank Maguire, editorial director of the CGU's flagship magazine, *Global Affairs*, and the owner of several major publishing houses. "I just got a message from Raffal," he was saying with an air of self-importance. "He said the same thing. We're now on the verge of the next step in the spiritual evolution of humanity."

"But we must proceed carefully," Serena said. "We must avoid the mistakes of our predecessors."

The one called Frank spoke gruffly. "You're right. We can't take any action unless we have specific orders. The Third Reich was a disaster!"

A woman seated across from Serena spoke next. She was Nadine Chung, owner of a major software company that specialized in Internet technology...which easily could be used to serve the Master's ends. She was also a Communist spy who had gained access to many of America's military secrets through her close relationship with the previous administration. "No it wasn't!" she almost spat. She looked at Frank with contempt, and the guards savored the discord they sensed in the exchange between the two humans. "After all, it paved the way for world government by making the people so fearful of a third world war, and we have fueled that fear to bring about the current situation. Your faith is weak—He is not so easily thwarted." Her thin lips curved slightly upward as she leaned back in her chair. "I heard from

Leiru last night. He told me that the Teacher is about to emerge."

"And the world will look to him...and embrace the light." All eyes turned in the direction of the man seated at the head of the table. His name was Oren Reinhardt, chairman of the CGU. As always, he was impeccably dressed, and his cold, gray eyes possessed an almost hypnotic quality that even the sentinels found unnerving. "I received the same message from Apollyon. But not everyone is ready." At the name of Apollyon the invisible inhabitants of the room shrank back in fear; he was among the most dreadful of princes and it was said that he could crush nations between his fists.

A striking-looking woman sat at Oren's left. Her ebony hair fell in long waves down her back, and her high cheekbones and olive skin gave her an exotic appeal. She called herself Tria, but no one knew her real name. Descended from European royalty, she was quietly using her fortune to buy political favors for the Council. "True," she said in a slight British accent. "The Awakening is happening. But the final stage of spiritual evolution cannot occur until the Cleansing is complete."

The sentinels fought to contain their excitement. The very purpose of their existence was about to unfold...the battle they had been anticipating for the last two thousand years. They would finally get their revenge on their Enemy by destroying his followers once and for all!

Frank's voice had a nervous edge. "But is the time right? The Nazis failed because Hitler wouldn't follow orders. I didn't get any instructions about the Cleansing yet. Did any of you?"

Serena sounded suspicious. "What are you afraid of, Frank?"

"Look, I'm not afraid, I just want to be sure—"

"Perhaps he's having qualms about what needs to be done," said Tria. "Perhaps he is afraid to accept his duty."

The guards perked up at this. They had orders to monitor this group for any signs of weakness.

"I just don't want us to act prematurely," Frank said defensively.

A smooth voice at the other end of the table broke in on their argument. "Then we'll wait." Jack Denning leaned back casually in his chair, smoking a pipe. The mild, almost gentle expression in his soft brown eyes concealed a heart of darkness. Loose folds of skin hung under his chin, and he had a slightly paternal air. A retired general of the United States Army, he was National Security Advisor to the President of the United States, and had been recruited into the Master's service nearly twenty years ago when he joined the Council. Ever since the President took office, Jack had been his most trusted advisor. The guards knew that he worked very closely with the people in this room, known among themselves as the Circle, who comprised the directorate of the Council for Global Unity. "Our superiors will tell us when it's time to begin," Jack was saying. "In the meantime, we've got to work on getting that constitution ratified. There are still some influential people in this country who are opposed to it."

Serena smiled. "Don't worry. They'll be taken care of."

The unseen guards smiled with her.

CHAPTER 2

"A situation has come to my attention that has me very concerned."

Beth Lanyon cringed. It was bad enough to be summoned to the principal's office, but to hear something like that almost made her heart stop. Was she going to be fired? She inhaled deeply in an effort to relax. "What is it?" she asked, her mouth dry and hoarse.

Dr. Calahan was about to respond when the phone rang. "Excuse me one moment," she said.

Beth looked around the office while Dr. Calahan took the call. A huge poster above the principal's desk featured a group of smiling children of various nationalities. The words, "CELEBRATE DIVERSITY," were emblazoned across the top. Next to that was a similar poster with the mandate, "CHILDREN FIRST!" Beth glanced at the books on the desk: *A Course in Miracles*, the *Bhagavad Gita*, *The Aquarian Conspiracy*, *Chariots of the Gods*. Filled with occult themes and references to Eastern mysticism, the books were required reading in many courses, yet the Bible was off limits. And the seminar on multiculturalism she had been forced to attend earlier today was nothing but an attack on Western culture and Christianity. She shook her head. This was diversity?

Dr. Calahan hung up the phone. "I realize you're probably eager to get home," she said, "but this is something that really can't wait." She looked at Beth with an expression of severity. "I've been examining some of your lesson plans, and I must say that I'm concerned. Can you explain why you haven't been following the new Global Studies curriculum?"

Beth hesitated as she tried to put her thoughts together. She had made no secret of her objection to the federally mandated curriculum when it was presented by her department chairman last year, but he had simply lectured her about the necessity to retain federal funding. "I'm sorry, Dr. Calahan, but I just don't feel comfortable with it," Beth said. "For one thing, it's filled with distortions and even blatant factual errors. How can you expect me to teach something which I know is a lie?"

Dr. Calahan shook her head. "Facts aren't important anymore, Beth; attitudes are what really matter in today's progressive society." She glanced down at her notes and frowned. "It looks as if you haven't even mentioned the concept of spiritual evolution in any of your lessons."

"That's because it's a lie," Beth said. When she saw the look on the principal's face, she wondered if she had gone too far. The last thing she needed was to be out of a job. There was just no way she and John would make it on one salary. As an assistant professor of English, he made even less than she did.

But instead of getting angry, Dr. Calahan smiled at Beth as if she were a child incapable of understanding something that was obvious to a more advanced mind. "Oh? Tell me, Beth: did the *Bible* tell you so?" She rolled her eyes, and Beth's face flushed. It was okay to make fun of Christians, but if the principal had mocked the Torah, the civil rights activists would have pounced on her.

"Actually, I don't even have to read the Bible to know it's a lie," Beth said. "All I have to do is look at history. Do you see any evidence that mankind is evolving spiritually?" When the principal didn't answer, Beth went on, "Look at the last century. How many wars have been fought? How many innocent people have been slaughtered by power-mad dictators? Look at Hitler, Stalin, and Castro. If you look at the facts, the idea of spiritual evolution just doesn't hold up."

"But we're in a new age now, Beth," Dr. Calahan said. "Up until very recently, humanity wasn't quite ready to take the next step in spiritual evolution. But a shift in consciousness has been taking place. For the first time in history, people all over the world are working together, trying to find a way to coexist peacefully. The common monetary system is evidence that humanity *is* becoming more united. Besides, Hitler was the product of nationalism, which is finally being exposed as a hindrance to world peace. I'm surprised that as a teacher of history, you failed to realize that." Dr. Calahan spoke in the complacent tone of an adult explaining a simple truth to a young child.

"But Hitler was also influenced by Social Darwinism, which is the logical outgrowth of evolution," Beth said. "As a matter of fact, Hitler's entire philosophy was based on the concept of spiritual evolution. He believed that the Aryan race was evolving spiritually toward godhood, and he saw the Jews as an obstacle to the German people's spiritual evolution. That's why he slaughtered millions of them—along with anyone else who stood in his way." She thought of something else. "Besides, isn't it a violation of the separation of church and state to teach spiritual values in a public school?"

Dr. Calahan frowned. She didn't like being challenged, and it was clear she was losing the argument. "As I said earlier, Beth, a great deal has changed recently, and schools need to change with the times. The U.S. Constitution is out-dated. If all goes well, we'll soon be under the World Constitution. It's up to us to prepare our students to become world citizens. In order to do that, we need to teach certain spiritual values."

Beth was about to respond, but Dr. Calahan cut her off. "I didn't call you in here to have a philosophical discussion," she said. "I just want you to know that you are responsible for covering the entire curriculum, regardless of how you feel about it. I hope I won't have to speak to you again."

After her meeting with the principal, Beth sat in the Global Studies resource center, looking through the chapter headings in upcoming units. She had hoped to get away with skipping some of the material, especially that which she knew to be inaccurate—or an outright lie. What particularly bothered her was the glowing description of Communism as practiced in Red China, where thousands, maybe millions, of Christians were being murdered for their faith. She had pointed this out to her chairman last year, but he told her that they had no choice. Under Achievement 2000, the federal government had assumed total control of the schools. All local school boards and state education departments had been replaced by a national board of education. Any school official who refused to follow a mandate handed down by the board would face disciplinary action, and the school would risk losing all federal funds.

Beth skimmed through the pages of the curriculum guide. "Gaia: The Earth Spirit...Evolution: our salvation." Christian missionary work was listed as an example of civil rights' violations while forced abortions and infanticide were defended as legitimate solutions to overpopulation. She put her face in her hands. *How on earth can I teach this stuff?*

She flipped through the pages of the next unit, "Achieving Global Consciousness." Four words on the top of a page caught her eye: "The Dangers of Fundamentalism." She read the description carefully: "This chapter is designed to teach students about the common truths underlying all major religions. Students will learn that all roads lead to God, however they conceive Him/Her. They also will learn how to recognize the dangers of Christian fundamentalism and the religious right."

She looked at the section at the bottom of the page, and her mouth dropped open. One of the suggested activities included a role-playing scenario in which a group of Christians armed with assault rifles barge into the classroom and demand that the students convert to Christianity or be killed. She slammed the book closed. Then she bowed her head, and prayed for wisdom. She knew she would need it.

* * * *

"Hey, it's been a long time," Matt said with a smile as he entered his brother's cozy, upstairs apartment. A large, panting basset hound lumbered into the foyer and jumped up on him.

"Down, Cleo," John said as he gently pushed the dog away. Matt patted her on the head, and she waddled into the living room.

They sat on the couch and John placed a bag of chips on the coffee table. Cleo approached hesitantly, shoving her long snout onto Matt's lap. He pushed her away, and she curled up under the table. "So, is Beth out garage-saling?"

"Not today. She's at some kind of meeting at school."

Matt raised his eyebrow. "On a Saturday?"

John shrugged. "I think it's a workshop or something. Anyway, there's a good sci- fi movie coming on soon and I thought you might want to see it."

Matt smiled. "Ah...you know my weakness."

"We can order a pizza, if you want."

"Sounds good to me."

"What do you want on it?" John asked.

"Pepperoni. Oh—and mushrooms too."

John called the pizza place, and Matt put his feet up on the coffee table, something he wasn't allowed to do at home. He felt glad that he had decided to come over; it was better than stewing about Gina all day. Then again, he could be in for one of his brother's sermons, and that wasn't exactly fun. He still couldn't fathom the change that had come over John after high school. All of a sudden, he started babbling about Jesus, the Bible, and eternal life, topics that Matt had no interest in whatsoever. He couldn't understand it— John had always been carefree, almost wild. He loved to play pranks at school and was never one to take life very seriously. But suddenly, he had become a different person, and Matt found the change unsettling. Whenever John got started on religion, Matt changed the subject or made some kind of joke. It was a survival tactic.

After ordering the pizza, John went to the refrigerator. "Want a soda?"

"Got any Killian's Red?"

"Sorry."

"McSorely's? Foster's Extra Bitter? Black & Tan?"

"Nope."

Matt was shaking his head. "Don't you have *anything* dark?"

"This isn't the Road House, you alkie!" John said playfully.

"Oh, man, I haven't been there in years!" The Road House was a pub where Matt used to hang out with his old drinking buddies. He had also met Gina there. She had come there to use the phone when her car broke down one night, and he had bought her a drink while she waited for the tow-truck. On a dare from his friends—who had said she was way out of his league—he had asked for her phone number. The rest, as they say, is history.

"Would a Bud Lite kill you?" John asked.

Matt rolled his eyes, but he was smiling. "Oh, great! Only wimpy, down-stream beer on tap here. Okay, bartender—since I'm desperate—I'll try to choke it down."

"Anyway, it's the pizza that counts."

"What? Are you crazy? Pizza without beer? You must be some kind of degenerate!" Matt enjoyed the silly banter—it reminded him of old times.

"Yeah, well, I'm Beth's degenerate—and she likes me just the way I am. The pizza will be here in a forty-five minutes." He returned with their drinks. "So, how've you been lately?"

"Oh, not bad." Matt reached for the bottle John gave him. "I had an interesting morning, though."

"Really? How so?"

Matt told him about the rally and the problem with his debit card. John listened intently, but didn't say much. "Can you believe that?" Matt asked when he had finished.

"I take it you're pretty upset."

"Of course I am! I can't believe this could happen in a free country! I just wish there was something I could do about it."

John looked at him cautiously. "Have you tried praying about it?"

Matt smirked. "I should've known *that* was coming. Look, John, I'm not like you. I believe in taking action, not sitting around waiting for God to do some kind of miracle. I don't know. Sometimes I think I'm the one who's crazy. Most people seem to think this kind of government crap is perfectly acceptable. Even Gina." His tone was bitter.

"Is there a problem between you two?"

Matt looked down at the table. He was surprised at how upset he still felt. "Well, it's our anniversary. We were supposed to spend the day together. But she went off on some assignment, and I don't know when she'll be back. I kind of told her off, so she may not be in such a hurry to get back, anyway." There was a long pause. "It's funny. Gina's career never used to bother me. I mean, I always knew how important her job was, and it never seemed to be a problem. But now, I resent it when she has to cancel our plans to cover a story. Maybe my priorities are changing. It used to be so important for us to get ahead, to make more money—or should I say debits," he added. "But now, I wish Gina and I had more time together. And, I'd like to start a family soon."

"How does Gina feel about that?"

"I don't think she'd be thrilled with the idea."

"Have you two talked about it?"

"I kind of hinted about it a few times, but she always changed the subject."

The movie was starting, so they both turned their attention to the TV. Matt hoped to forget all about his problems with Gina.

The door opened suddenly, and Matt turned around. "You're not going to believe this!" Beth said as she slammed the door behind her.

John immediately got up from the couch. "What's wrong, sweetheart?"

She tossed her purse onto the kitchen counter. It took several moments before she even realized that Matt was there. "Oh, hi, Matt. Sorry about my outburst." She looked at John. "I just had a meeting with the principal."

"Oh, that explains it," John said. "I can see how that would put a damper on your day."

Matt got up from the couch. "Listen, if this is a bad time for me to be here, maybe I should leave."

"No, it's okay," Beth said. "It's not like I was fired or anything. But I probably will be eventually, if I don't quit, that is."

John looked at her with concern. "What is it?"

"It's a long story. I don't want to interrupt your show."

"Don't worry about it." Matt pointed to the TV. "It looks like it's been preempted by some news bulletin."

"What's it about?" Beth asked.

"Just more trouble in the Middle East," Matt said. "What else is new?"

"We might as well turn it off," John said. "You want some pizza?"

"Okay." Beth went to the kitchen cabinet to get a plate.

Matt listened politely while she told them about her meeting with the principal. "You should see the list of suggested activities," Beth said. "One of them involves giving extra credit points to the student who thinks of the most reasons why fundamentalist Christians are a threat to society. Can you believe that?"

"The world sure does hate us," John said. "Now more than ever, I think. Still, Jesus told us to expect this. In fact, it's going to get even worse." He turned to Beth and smiled. "And we both know what that means, don't we?"

"What are you smiling about?" Matt asked, mystified.

John looked at him intently. "Matt, we could very well be living in the most exciting time of history since Jesus walked this earth. All this is just another sign that we're nearing the end of the world."

"Well, that's something to celebrate." Matt laughed. "Hey, let's break out the champagne, we're all going to die! John, you have a really strange way of looking at things sometimes."

"Believe it or not, Beth and I are looking forward to the end of the world," John said.

"That's right." Beth was smiling now, too.

"Am I missing something? I mean, most people aren't too thrilled with that prospect."

"Ever read the Book of Revelation?" John asked.

"Let's see...that's the book with the beast and the dragon running around wreaking havoc on the world, right?"

"Hey, that's right." John sounded surprised. "So, you're familiar with it?"

"I saw a TV special on it a few years ago. I think it was on the Discovery Channel. It was a show about end-of-the-world prophecies or something. But it was pretty far-fetched."

"Why do you say that?" asked Beth.

Matt tried to remember the details of the program. "Well, the show talked about the Antichrist. It said he'll be able to do all kinds of miracles. You know, bring fire down from heaven, stuff like that."

John appeared to be choosing his words carefully. "And, you don't believe the Antichrist will do those things?"

"Listen, I have a hard enough time believing the miracles that *God* did in the Bible. Besides, it doesn't make sense. How can someone evil be able to do miracles? Where would he get that kind of power?"

John smiled knowingly. "That's a good question."

"So, what's the answer?"

"Why don't you read the Book of Revelation and find out?"

Matt laughed. "Oh, I should have known that was coming. You've been trying to get me to read the Bible for years now."

Beth chimed in then. "Matt, this is probably the most exciting time to start reading it. So many things happening in the world today were predicted in the Bible thousands of years ago!"

"Yeah? Like what?"

"If you want to find out, you'll just have to read the Bible for yourself," John said.

"So, that's all you're going to say?" Matt was smiling. "Okay, let's say I decide to read the Bible. Can you at least tell me where can I find all these predictions that are supposedly coming true?"

"Try the Book of Revelation. I should warn you, it's one of the more difficult books. But, it's very exciting." John smiled. "In fact, it's kind of like a sci-fi fantasy novel."

Matt perked up at this. "Really?"

"You'd be amazed at some of the creatures that appear in Revelation," John said. "Ten-headed beasts, weird monsters that come up from out of the ground. There's even a scene involving an asteroid."

"You mean like in the movie *Armageddon*? Cool!" By now he had forgotten all about his pizza. "Are there any other parts of the Bible that deal with stuff like that?"

"There are plenty. In fact, there's one book that describes people having their skin melt right off them—which could indicate some sort of nuclear holocaust. That's one of the most amazing things about the Bible, it foretells events that would have been completely unheard of during the time it was written. Its writers were way ahead of their time."

"But how could they have known about that stuff?"

"Because the Bible was inspired by God," John said. "There's no other book like it. In fact, did you know that the Bible has been the number one bestseller, throughout all of history?"

"No, I had no idea," Matt said. "I hate to say it, but I always thought the Bible was for wimps."

"Why did you think that?" John asked.

He thought about this. "I guess it's all that stuff about turning the other cheek. Especially when I look at what the government's been doing, and how Christians seem to be going along with it. Like at Beth's school. I can't help wondering why you guys aren't fighting this stuff."

"It's not easy, Matt," Beth said. "Unfortunately, we're in a minority." Her green eyes brightened suddenly. "I just thought of something—there's bound to be some parents who don't want their kids exposed to the trash I'm supposed to be teaching. I could call them, maybe set up a meeting."

"Now you're talking!" Matt said. "But why stop there? Why not complain to the government? You can bet that if more people had opposed Achievement 2000 to begin with, it might not have passed."

John sounded bitter. "Oh, and who should we complain to? Senator Conlin? She's the one who wrote the bill introducing Achievement 2000."

Matt threw his hands up. "So, that's it? You're just giving up?"

"To be honest, Matt, I really don't believe our representatives care what we think anymore. They just have their own agenda."

Matt felt annoyed by John's fatalistic attitude. "They might care if more people voiced their opinions. In fact, I think we should try doing something to oppose this new constitution. I just wish I knew what we could do. I mean, do we write to our congressmen and senators, or what?"

"I'm not sure political action is going to solve America's problems," John said.

"Why not?"

"Because America's problems are spiritual, not political."

"Look, you're not in favor of this world constitution, are you?"

"Of course not," John said. "But without a spiritual regeneration, America is lost, with or without a world constitution."

"But don't you want us to be a free country?"

"There are different kinds of freedom, Matt. I think that some Christians get so concerned with political freedom that they forget about the importance of spiritual freedom that comes from a personal relationship with Jesus."

"Here we go again," Matt muttered.

"Matt, we're certainly not in favor of a one-world government," Beth said. "We're just looking at it from a different angle. There's a spiritual dimension to the New World Order that's even more dangerous than its political aspects."

Matt didn't feel like getting into this right now. "Well, tell that to Gina. She thinks this whole idea of world government is great. She says it's the only thing that'll guarantee world peace."

John smiled. "Well, I'm sure you'll do your best to convince her she's wrong."

Matt chuckled. "Are you kidding me? That'll be almost as hard as getting me to read the Bible!"

* * * *

When Gina arrived home, Matt was sitting on the couch with his feet up on the coffee table, drinking a beer and watching a stupid comedy. He didn't look at her.

She sighed. What a perfect anniversary. Maybe if she apologized, they could at least salvage the evening. She sat down next to him. "Matt, I'm sorry about this afternoon."

"Whatever," he said tonelessly.

"Can't we just forget about this? It's our anniversary. We can still go out tonight, you know."

"How generous of you to make time for me."

"Matt, this isn't the first time I've had to work on a Saturday. I'm a reporter. That goes with the territory. I thought you understood that."

He softened. "Maybe I'm getting old-fashioned. I just hate competing with your career. We haven't spent much time together lately, between both our jobs. I thought it would be nice to spend the whole day with you for a change. But I guess your career was more important."

"You know that's not true, you're the most important part of my life." She kissed him gently on the lips. "I'm sorry if I made you doubt that."

He shrugged. "Maybe I'm just insecure."

"Well, don't be. Now, are we still going out tonight?" she asked with a smile.

"Sure." But his eyes were filled with sadness.

* * * *

Before she went to bed that night, Gina noticed a story about the riot on the ten o'clock news. She saw a brief shot of Father Flannery being taken into custody. A reporter was saying that he was involved in the "right-wing anti-peace movement." Two witnesses stated that the priest was extremely violent. The Bishop of the Diocese of Rockville Centre officially denounced Flannery's actions, calling him a hatemonger whose racists views did not reflect the thinking of the Catholic Church. He also went on to say that Flannery's actions were in complete defiance of the Pope, who supported the World Constitution. Gina switched channels to look for footage of the riot, but couldn't find any. That was weird. Reporters kept quoting the priest's "hateful diatribe," but not one station had televised it. Gina couldn't understand it, especially since Matt had told her about all the camera crews he had seen at the rally. Something just didn't add up.

* * * *

"Sorry—we don't want any reporters around here!"

The stooped little woman with white hair almost slammed the door in Gina's face.

Gina stood her ground. "Please, I just want to talk to him for a few minutes."

"The pastor doesn't want any more bad publicity."

"Can't you just tell him I'm here? If he doesn't want to see me, I'll leave."

The woman rubbed her frail, veined hands together. "I really shouldn't. I could get in trouble."

"Look, you don't have to tell the pastor about this. Just tell Father Flannery."

"Tell me what?" asked a friendly voice with a faint Irish brogue. Gina peered in the doorway and recognized Father Flannery.

The old woman was almost in tears. "Oh, dear!"

"I'm sorry I startled you, Mrs. O'Leary." The priest smiled at Gina. "You're here to see me, I take it?"

"She's a reporter!" Mrs. O'Leary blurted out.

Father Flannery brightened. He offered Gina his hand. "I'm Father Flannery, as you've probably guessed. And don't worry, I'm not as dangerous as they say." His eyes had a mischievous twinkle.

Gina was taken aback by his jaunty, easy-going manner. "I'm Gina Lanyon, from *Island News*. I heard you were out of jail."

"Yes, I just made my escape. Some of my more supportive parishioners managed to scrape the funds together to pay my bail. For a while I thought they were going to hold me indefinitely. The bail was set so high, I suppose they figured a priest could never afford it."

"But why? It's not as if you've been accused of murder or anything."

"The judge claims I'm a threat to public safety."

"Would you mind if I asked you a few questions, Father?"

"Not at all. We'll go into the study. Would you care for some tea, or perhaps some coffee?"

"Coffee would be fine." They entered the study and sat down in two checkered easy chairs in front of a large, stone fireplace. Mrs. O'Leary brought them a tray of coffee and cookies, then left them alone, shaking her head ominously as she left the room.

"Poor Mrs. O'Leary," said Father Flannery with a sympathetic smile.

"She's been on the phone all morning, dealing with angry parishioners who believe the so-called news reports. The pastor wants to have me transferred. In fact, he made it clear that he doesn't feel comfortable having me here at all, even for the time being. So, I may have to stay with my sister and her husband, until I get my transfer orders. The way the diocese feels about me right now, it could be Siberia!"

Gina couldn't help laughing. He was completely different from the image portrayed on the news. The media also neglected to mention that he was no ordinary priest; he was a popular radio talk-show host who had developed quite a following among conservative Catholics. As soon as Gina heard he had been released on bail, she called him to set up an interview. When the parish pastor refused to let her talk to him, she decided to pay the priest a surprise visit.

"So, what would you like to know?" he asked.

Gina turned on her tape recorder. "First, I'd like to know how the riot started."

Flannery rubbed his chin with his long, slender fingers. "There's something I think you should know. But most people probably won't believe it, in light of what happened."

"What is it?"

"I was invited to speak at that rally."

Surprised, Gina asked, "Why would you be invited to speak there, since you're opposed to everything the rally stands for? I don't understand."

"I didn't, either, to tell you the truth. A few weeks before the rally, I got a phone call from a member of the International Coalition of Churches." For just an instant, his voice took on a harsh note. "They were working with the Council for Global Unity, helping them to line up speakers from local churches and synagogues. I told the caller very emphatically that I was opposed to world government, and that I had no intention of supporting any constitution written by the UN. He said they simply wanted to give me an opportunity to share my views, and to learn a little more about their perspective. Naturally, I thought this would be a great chance to get the truth to the public." He leaned back in his chair, his hands behind his head. "I had been told that I'd have a chance to share my views, even if they were contrary to those expressed at the rally. Quite frankly, I was surprised, but I accepted the invitation."

"What did you say in your speech?"

"I began by talking about the founding of this country, and the Bill of Rights. I wanted to explain that the Bill of Rights is essential to preserving our freedoms, and if we adopt a new constitution, we risk losing those freedoms. Well, in the middle of my speech, a young man in the audience interrupted me. He asked how I felt about the gay rights legislation passed by Congress last year. Although I'm not in favor of the legislation on constitutional grounds, I didn't feel it was the appropriate time to debate that particular issue. But the fellow was pretty insistent that I answer the question, and some other people in the crowd demanded that I answer it. I explained that the Constitution guarantees all Americans—whether homosexual or heterosexual—the same fundamental rights, and that the Constitution limits the government, not the people. I also said that so-called gay rights legislation grants homosexuals special privileges at the expense of other people's rights. As an example, I mentioned that some Catholic schools have been forced to hire homosexual teachers, which is a violation of religious freedom." He paused, slowly shaking his head. "I suppose I opened a can of worms, because someone else in the crowd began to accuse me of hating homosexuals, simply because I'm a Christian. I tried to explain that as a Christian, I love all people, no matter what their sexual preference, even though I may not condone their behavior."

"That's all you said?" It didn't sound inflammatory enough to start a riot.

He smiled ironically. "Not exactly. You see, someone else in the crowd asked me if I believed that homosexuals are going to hell."

"*That's* a loaded question."

"I'll say."

"So, what did you say?"

"Well, I decided to set the fellow straight—no pun intended—about a rather unpopular notion called sin."

"Can you remember your exact words?"

"Hmm. I said that all people are sinners, and that the punishment for sin is an eternity apart from God. Therefore, we all need to repent and accept Christ's forgiveness. I also I told the fellow that if he sincerely wants to know the truth about hell, he ought to read the Scriptures, because I wasn't about to deliver any sermons on that topic just then. But the crowd started goading me. It was obvious they were trying to draw me into an argument. When they accused me of being against world peace, I said that if they think a piece of paper written by the United Nations could legislate world peace, they were seriously mistaken."

Gina remembered what Serena Conlin had said. "Did you say anything about putting unbelievers to death?"

He looked startled. "No, certainly not! I did say that there can never be lasting peace until the forces of evil are destroyed when Christ returns to establish His Kingdom. I also said that we're in the midst of a spiritual battle for the soul of this nation."

"That's pretty strong language. Don't you think that kind of talk could promote violence?"

"Violence against whom?"

"Against...those who don't share your beliefs."

He smiled. "What I find interesting is that my speech did promote violence, only it was directed against *me*. But it shouldn't be surprising."

"Why not?"

"Because the truth hurts. Why do you think the Jews murdered the Old Testament prophets? Because they told they truth! Why did so many people want Jesus crucified? Because He was telling them the truth. They couldn't admit that they were sinners in need of a Savior, so they nailed Him to a cross. That's why I infuriated the people at that rally, Gina. They were nice and comfortable in their sins, and they didn't want to be reminded that someday they're going to face a righteous God who ultimately will destroy evil when He returns to this earth to judge the nations."

Why did he insist on bringing Jesus into this? "So, when did the riot start?" Gina asked.

"At some point, someone in the audience called me a homophobe, and then people started shouting all kinds of epithets at me. I was being called a racist, a Neo-Nazi, and a white supremacist. I was shocked, because I didn't say anything to suggest I was a racist. Suddenly, people were throwing things. It was pure bedlam. I tried to duck, but I got hit by a bottle. And before I knew it, *I* was being arrested!" He was silent then, and Gina thought about her interview with Serena Conlin.

"Did you say anything about feminists or atheists?" He shook his head. "Did you attack Jews in any way?"

"None whatsoever. Why did you ask?"

"I was just wondering." Then she thought of something. "You said a member of the ICC, or International Coalition of Churches, invited you to speak at the rally?"

"That's right."

"Did you receive anything in writing?"

There was a touch of irony in his voice. "Actually, I received a letter from the honorable Senator Conlin. Since I didn't express much enthusiasm during my conversation with the ICC's representative, she extended a personal invitation."

Gina's mouth dropped open. "Do you have a copy of her letter?"

"I certainly do. Would you like to see it?"

"I'd love to," she said. He left the room and came back a few moments later with the letter. Gina read it, mystified. Serena Conlin hadn't said anything about Father Flannery having been invited to the rally. She studied him. There was nothing about his manner or appearance that suggested he was capable of violence—or even hatred. Yet the major media had portrayed him as a hatemonger. "What are you being charged with?" she asked.

"I believe they're calling it a hatecrime." Father Flannery shook his head. "Freedom of speech is apparently a thing of the past."

"I'll be the first to agree that what happened to you certainly doesn't sound fair. But we need hatecrimes legislation to protect minorities from crimes that are motivated by bigotry and racism."

"I realize that such laws are well-intentioned," said Father Flannery. "And I certainly don't condone violence against minorities, or any innocent person, for that matter. But can't you see that it's a violation of the Bill of Rights to label a certain kind of speech as a crime? Why, our Founding Fathers would be outraged to see this happening in America! And I've never heard of people who make fun of Christians being charged with a hatecrime. There's obviously a double standard here."

"You've got a point. But you have to admit that in general, fundamentalist Christians tend to be pretty intolerant of people who refuse to accept their brand of morality."

"If you mean that we refuse to condone immorality, then you're right. That's the problem with this country—people who have moral convictions are labeled intolerant."

"So what are your plans now?"

"Well, until I get my transfer notice, I plan to continue fighting this new constitution. Of course, it's going to be more difficult, now." He shook his head. "If you ask me, the timing of this whole thing is very convenient, at least for my opposition."

"Why is that?"

"Have you heard about my radio show?" She nodded. "Well, apparently it's been very successful in alerting Catholics and even some Protestants about the dangers of the New World Order—or the Global Village, which has become the more fashionable label for world socialism these days. And,

I had just been invited to speak at various parishes across the country about this issue. But after all the negative press I've gotten, my radio program has been canceled, and the bishop has ordered me to cancel my speaking tour. It seems my arrest has made things a lot easier for those who might see me as a threat to their agenda."

"What are you saying? That you think it was a set-up?"

"Well, I certainly can't prove it. But I'm not one of the ICC's favorite people, so it seems kind of strange that they invited me to speak at a rally they were helping to organize."

"Why? What have they got against you?"

He was silent for a moment, as though wondering how he should phrase his answer. "Let's just say I started asking too many questions about them, and they're not too happy about what I found out."

Gina was intrigued by his somewhat cryptic answer. "What did you find out?"

He looked troubled. "It's something that you might have a hard time believing. But I never trusted them before, and now I trust them even less."

"Is that all you can tell me?"

"What I can tell you is that the ICC doesn't like opposition. They've been able to exclude traditional Christian churches from membership in their organization and have labeled nonmember churches as being on the fringe and hate-centered. They have publicly denounced my radio program on many occasions and have even stated that programs like mine should not be allowed on the air." He sighed. "In retrospect, I was rather foolish to agree to speak at their rally. I guess the chance to reach such a great number of people was too much for me to pass up. Frankly, the possibility that it might be a set-up just never crossed my mind."

Gina turned off her tape recorder. "Well, thank you for your time." She wished he would tell her more about the ICC. She had the impression that there was much more to this organization than he was telling her.

"Don't mention it." They both got up, and Flannery looked at her curiously. "Tell me something. How do you feel about the prospect of a one-world government?"

"I think it's a great idea." She spoke confidently, almost defiantly.

"Have you thought about what it would mean?"

"Of course I have. It would put an end to war, for one thing. And it would stop dictators from oppressing innocent people. Human rights violations would be a thing of the past. Don't you see how important all that is?"

"And who's going to rule this world government?" he asked quietly.

"The World Parliament, of course, in conjunction with the UN."

"A long time ago, a man by the name of Benjamin Disraeli said something very revealing. He said, 'The world is governed by very different personages from what it is imagined by those who are not behind the scenes.'"

Her tone was deliberately condescending. "Sounds like one of those conspiracy theorists."

Father Flannery smiled at that. "Really? Do you know who Benjamin Disraeli was?"

Most likely some right-wing wacko. "The name does sound a little familiar. Who was he?"

"He was the Prime Minister of England some time ago. I'd say he was in a position to know who's really in control of things. Wouldn't you?"

Now she felt embarrassed. "Okay, what's your point?"

"Just that you may be surprised—and disturbed—if you knew the kind of people who are really in control of the UN—and our own government, for that matter."

"Oh, really? Just what do you know about the UN that the rest of the world doesn't know?"

Instead of giving her an answer, he asked, "How much do you trust the United Nations, Ms. Lanyon? Enough to rule this entire planet?"

"Look, it's not as if the UN itself will control everything. Representatives from every country will have a say in how the government is run. But in any case, I think we have to trust the UN if this whole concept of world government is going to work."

"How much do you know about the UN?"

"They played a major role in Desert Storm. And they've been helping underdeveloped countries achieve sustainable development."

He shook his head sadly. "For a reporter, you know surprisingly little about the UN. Just what they want you to know."

"Well, what exactly do you know about the UN that I don't know?"

"Just a moment," he said, and went into the study again. When he returned, he held a clipping from an issue of *Life* magazine. He handed it to Gina. It was a photo of a bullet-riddled Volkswagen. Inside the car she could see a dead woman and child. A man splattered with blood raised his head, a look of anguish on his face.

"The woman and child in that photo were murdered by the United Nation's 'peace-keeping' forces," the priest said bitterly. "It happened in 1961, in

Katanga, which used to be the Belgian Congo. The Katangans wanted self-government, they didn't want to become part of Patrice Lumumba's communist dictatorship. Lumumba had taken over the Congo after the Belgians had liberated it. He started a reign of terror against the Katangans, murdering and torturing innocent men, women and children. All the people wanted was to restore freedom to their country. Do you know what the UN did? They sent their so-called peace-keeping forces, along with American troops, to assist Lumumba. UN planes bombed Katanga's schools, churches and hospitals, and UN 'peace-keeping' troops machine-gunned school children, civilians, and Red Cross workers who were trying to help the wounded. I realize that was considerably before your time, and the media glossed over that atrocity. In fact, the *New York Times* actually supported the UN's military action against Katanga." His eyes blazed with anger. "But tell me: do you want to embrace a government conceived by a group of people who have no regard for your life or liberty?"

Gina stared at the photo, shocked that the UN—the world's last, best hope for peace—could have been behind such carnage. "I admit, it's a horrible thing. But it happened a long time ago. A lot can change in over fifty years."

"Oh, really? Are you aware that in June of 1993, UN troops opened fire on unarmed Somali women and children? It was in *The Washington Post*. And I suppose you've seen the front page photo published in the *Village Voice* of UN peace-keepers roasting a Somali teenager over an open fire?"

"That sounds a little far-fetched."

"Oh?" He showed her the clipping, and she drew back in horror at the gleeful expressions on the faces of the UN soldiers as they dangled a helpless youth over an open flame. "That photograph was published in June of '97. The reporter who covered the story had originally been doing an exposé on sexual harassment of female employees at UN headquarters. During her investigation she was told, 'If you think it's bad here, you should see what goes on in peace-keeping operations.' Interestingly, she found that the abuses of UN peacekeepers were widely reported in foreign newspapers, but ignored by American newspapers." He looked at her intently. "So, do you still trust the UN?"

"Look, I realize that these are terrible abuses, and something should be done to make sure they don't continue. But that doesn't mean we should abandon the ideal of world government. The UN should be reformed—"

He looked incredulous. "Reformed? Tell me something: once the nations of the world give up their sovereignty—and their military might—to the

UN, who will be left to reform it?"

She couldn't think of an answer.

"It's also true that the UN has financed tyrants who committed some of the worst human rights violations in recent history. Even Osama bin Laden received UN funds for his terrorist acts against the American people. Were you aware of that?" When she didn't respond, he said, "I didn't think so."

She shook her head. "How can you expect me to believe that an organization committed to world peace would finance terrorism? It's preposterous." Gina stuffed her tape recorder into her purse. "I should get going." They both walked to the front door.

"It was nice meeting you," said Father Flannery. "And thanks for being willing to hear my side of the story."

"Thank you for answering my questions," she said. Then she went out to her car. She wished she could somehow explain away everything Father Flannery had just told her.

* * * *

Patrick Flannery watched Gina as she drove away. Sighing, he went back inside. He took the tray of coffee and cookies and returned them to the kitchen. The oatmeal cookies, which were still warm from the oven, hadn't been touched. He took a bite of one, savoring the taste of raisins and cinnamon. That woman certainly knew how to bake. Then he washed the coffee mugs and put them away. Most other priests in the rectory would have let Mrs. O'Leary clean up in the study, but Father Flannery liked to save her the trouble.

It was quiet in the rectory this morning. The other priests were attending to their duties, but the pastor had instructed Patrick to remain inside today. He felt a dull ache in his throat at the way his former friends, brothers in the Lord, avoided him now.

He heard the phone ringing, and in the next moment Mrs. O'Leary was calling him. "Telephone, Father!"

He went into the office and picked up his line. "Yes?"

The masculine voice on the other end practically bubbled over with excitement. "You're not going to believe this!"

Patrick smiled. "Calm down, laddy. Take a deep breath, relax."

"Relax? Who can relax? You know that story we were working on? Well, we can finally go public. I have the evidence, all the evidence we need!" He let out a whoop of joy.

Patrick took a deep breath. This was almost too good to be true. "How did you manage that?"

"With a little help from a very unlikely source—the FBI!"

Patrick shook his head. "Laddy, why on earth are you blabbing this over the telephone?"

There was a long, sickening silence. "Oh, man! I just didn't think, I was so excited—"

"Never mind that now." He looked at his watch. "When can we meet?"

"A couple of days."

"Why the delay?"

"I've been away. There are some things I need to take care of."

"All right, we'll meet at the usual place." He gave a date and time. "Will that work?"

"Yeah, no problem."

* * * *

"Something strange is going on," Gina told Ken as she sat opposite his desk later that afternoon. "My contact on the Nassau County PD won't even talk to me about Father Flannery's arrest, and Senator Conlin seems to have lied to me. On top of that, I spoke to Mike Casey. Remember he was injured during the riot?" Ken nodded. "Well, he said that Father Flannery wasn't the one who started it. He said that there were some very vicious people in that crowd, and that they were the ones who started it. In fact, Mike was shocked when he found out that Flannery was even arrested." Gina waited for a response, but Ken didn't say anything. "You know, Father Flannery thinks this whole thing might have been a set-up of some kind."

"Well, that's just speculation," said Ken. "And you can't write a story based on speculation. Besides, Mike had a concussion. It's possible he doesn't remember things too clearly."

"Maybe. But what about all that other stuff?"

He started shuffling through some papers. "What other stuff?"

"Ken, a United States senator lied to me. That's not something to gloss over."

"Gina, it's her word against the word of a man who was charged with hatecrime. Besides, Senator Conlin is extremely popular—and very powerful. I don't think it would be wise to pursue this."

"Are you telling me you're afraid?"

He ignored this. "Anyway, I thought your next big story was going to be on debit card abuses."

"You're right. I suppose I should focus more on that."

She went to her terminal and sat down. All her instincts told her she was on to something big. Why would someone like Serena Conlin go out of her way to discredit a Catholic priest? There had to be a reason. She sighed, thinking of all the worthy causes the senator supported. Reproductive freedom, animal rights, the environment, not to mention world peace. It was hard to believe she would be involved in something underhanded. Of course, her husband wasn't exactly a paragon of virtue. But Gina had always admired Serena for rising above his infidelities. Her supporters believed she could very well become the next president of the United States.

Gina took a sip of her coffee, which was now cold. She found it increasingly difficult to ignore the nagging doubts in her mind. She wished she could forget what Father Flannery had told her about the UN, but it certainly wasn't easy. How could an organization committed to world peace be guilty of such atrocities? It just didn't make sense.

When she saw that her voicemail light was blinking, she picked up her phone to check if there was a message from Senator Conlin. After playing all her messages, she hung up with a sigh. Why was Ken so afraid of her? Why wouldn't the senator return Gina's calls?

Only one answer made sense—the woman had something to hide.

CHAPTER 3

Matt was looking forward to a nice, peaceful evening in front of the TV. He had just settled down on the couch when he heard a knock at the door.

As soon as he saw Ben's ashen face, Matt knew something was wrong. His stomach lurched. Elsie! "Ben, what happened? Do you need help?"

Ben threw his hands up in the air. "It's Anita, that crazy daughter of mine. She won't let me see my grandsons anymore!"

"What? That's terrible!" Matt knew that Ben's grandsons meant the world to him. How could Anita do this to him?

"Elsie's there now, trying to straighten things out." He put his face in his hands. "Matt, what am I going to do? What if I never see David and little Josh again?"

Matt put his hand on Ben's shoulder. "It'll be okay," he said, not knowing what else to say. "Listen, why don't you come inside and we can talk about it?"

"Oh, I don't want to bother you. I'm sure you'd like to have your dinner."

"No, it's okay. Gina's probably working late, so I was just going to have some cereal."

"Well, in that case, would you like to have a sandwich with me? Elsie bought some fresh cold cuts at the deli today."

"Sounds great," Matt said as Ben ushered him into the apartment. It was about the size of Matt and Gina's, but the furniture was much older and somewhat worn. The hardwood floor was immaculate, though, and the kitchen fixtures sparkled.

Matt had never seen Ben so upset before. His eyes had a strained expression and his hands shook as he reached for a plastic bottle of prescription medicine—his heart medication. Matt immediately felt concerned.

"Have a seat," Ben said after swallowing the pill. Matt sat down at the table while Ben began puttering around in the kitchen. He brought out a pitcher of iced tea and two glasses, along with a loaf of Jewish rye and some pastrami. "Emotional blackmail, that's what it is," Ben muttered as Matt fixed himself a sandwich.

Matt was eager to dig into his pastrami sandwich. "Listen, maybe you should start at the beginning." He figured he could eat while Ben launched into his story.

"You remember it was David's birthday recently?" Matt nodded. "Elsie and I bought him some clothes at the second-hand store. But I thought it was time he learned how to use a gun. He's practically a man now, Matt. And his father walked out on them a few years ago. That makes him the man of the house. And little Josh is ten years old. I want David to be able to protect the family if someone breaks in. Is that so terrible?"

"No, of course not," Matt said between bites.

"Anyway, I invited him target shooting next Saturday. And I told him that if it was okay with his mother, I'd let him have one of my rifles, as a belated birthday present. Naturally, I told him it should be used only for target practice or self-defense, and that often the mere sight of a gun is enough to scare off a criminal, so he probably would never even have to use it at all. But Anita went crazy when he asked her if he could go to the range with me! She's terrified of guns—no wonder, with all the propaganda she's heard on the news. And since she knows my guns aren't registered..."

"She's even more upset," Matt finished.

Ben nodded. "She said I can't see David or Josh again unless I get rid of my guns. All of them!" There was a long silence. "Matt, what am I going to do?"

Matt didn't know what to say. He knew that Ben had a pretty extensive collection of firearms and could see how he would be reluctant to part with any of them. But he just couldn't believe that Ben would let anything come between him and his grandsons. "I don't know, Ben," he finally said. "Maybe she just needs some time. I'm sure she'll come around eventually."

"Hmph! I wouldn't be too sure. She just doesn't understand. Would you believe she told Elsie she doesn't think anyone but the police and the military should have guns?"

"That's a little extreme," Matt said. "My dad always owned guns, and he taught John and I how to use them. We used to go target shooting a lot. And once, my dad even used a gun to hold off a burglar. No one was hurt, thank God. Someone had broken into our house while Mom and Dad were out one night, and he was still there when they got back. Luckily, Dad was able to get his gun and hold the burglar at gunpoint, while Mom called the police. I don't know what would have happened to them if Dad hadn't had his gun. Burglars don't like being surprised by the owners of the house they're robbing—and this one had a knife strapped to his leg."

He suddenly thought of something. "You know, Ben, maybe Anita would lighten up a little if you didn't have quite so many guns. You don't actually need that many, do you?" Matt wasn't sure how many Ben actually had, but he thought it was at least a dozen.

Ben's voice rose an octave or two, and Matt was taken aback. "So what if I don't need that many? The point is, I have a right to own as many guns as I want. It says so right in the Constitution, in the Second Amendment. Even without the Second Amendment, I'd still have that right."

Matt figured Ben was going a little senile. "But without the Second Amendment, how can we possibly have the right to own a gun at all?"

Ben smiled faintly. "Ah, so you think the Constitution is what gives us our rights? Is that what you think?"

"Of course. Where else would we get our rights?"

"Tell me something, Matt: do you think our Founding Fathers believed they got their rights from the Constitution?"

Matt thought about it. "I guess not. I mean, they wrote it themselves."

"So, if our rights don't come from the Constitution, where do they come from?"

Matt shrugged. "You got me."

"And you do believe you have the right to keep and bear arms, correct?"

"Yeah..." But suddenly he wasn't feeling very confident about his answer.

Ben shook his head. "Amazing! Here's someone who believes he has the right to keep and bear arms, and he doesn't even know where that right comes from!"

By now Matt had forgotten all about his sandwich. "Okay, then where does it come from?"

"Let me ask you this, Matt: in a dictatorship where there's no Constitution or Bill of Rights, do the people still have the right not to be oppressed by their government? Did the Jews in Nazi Germany have the right to life even though Hitler said they didn't?"

"Of course they did!" He wondered how Ben could even ask such a question.

"So, what it boils down to is whether rights exist apart from the government. You see, Matt, our Founding Fathers believed that rights are something we're born with, not something that the government grants us. Because anything the government gives us, it can also take away."

"Wow...I never thought of it that way."

Ben was smiling indulgently. "Most Americans today haven't." Then his face clouded. "Unfortunately, it was the same misconception about human rights which allowed Hitler to murder six million Jews, along with anyone else the Nazis deemed unworthy of life or liberty. I'm afraid our own government is heading down the same path the Germans turned down when they embraced National Socialism."

"What do you mean? Are you saying that the German people actually supported Nazism?" That was hard to believe.

Ben nodded. "Believe it or not, the Nazi party was voted into office by millions of Germans from all levels of society, and it was no secret what the Nazis had planned for their country. Hitler outlined his political philosophy in his book *Mein Kampf*, which sold more than a million copies, I believe. The German people saw him as a savior."

"Were they *insane*? Or just plain stupid?"

He shook his head sadly. "Far from it. When Hitler came to power, Germany was renowned for its great intellectual achievements, so much so that it was even called the land of poets and philosophers. The German people were not a bunch of primitive barbarians, Matt. They were decent, educated, law-abiding citizens—and they allowed a handful of thugs to take control of their country. I saw it happen. No one did anything to stop it, not until it was far too late."

"What about the Jews? Didn't they try to stop it?"

"Matt, would you believe that we Jews actually *allowed* Hitler to do what he did? He never could have taken us to the deathcamps if we hadn't given him the power to do so."

Matt couldn't believe what he was hearing. "But how is that possible?"

"How is it possible?" He sighed deeply, and Matt wondered if he would be able to continue. "How is it possible that a madman like Hitler was able to take control of one of the most enlightened, civilized, educated countries in the world? It was because the German people, including the Jews, had no understanding of the concept of inalienable, God-given rights. We had been brainwashed for generations to believe that the good of society outweighed the rights of the individual. That's why we gave up our guns." He put his face in his hands. "Idiots! We were idiots! How could we have been so foolish?"

Matt was trying to digest everything Ben had just confided in him. "So, what you're saying is that Hitler was able to exterminate the Jews because he had taken their guns?"

Ben nodded. "Now you understand why I won't register any of mine. That's how it started in Germany. First, they made us register our guns—

then they confiscated them!"

"Really?"

"Of course—how else could the Nazis make sure we couldn't resist when they came to take us to the deathcamps? It didn't even start with the Nazis; before Hitler came to power, there were strict registration laws under the Weimar Republic. The Nazis simply used the existing registration lists to confiscate everyone's guns. Most of us would never even consider buying an unregistered firearm to begin with. We were so brainwashed that we believed only criminals would own such guns. Ironically, the real criminals were running the government, thanks to our own ignorance. America seems to be heading down that same path."

"Are you sure?" In spite of his concern about how powerful the government was becoming, Matt found it hard to believe something so horrendous could happen here.

"Remember what happened during the recent depression? They put a ban on ammunition sales and ordered people to turn in their handguns."

"Yeah, but the ban was temporary," said Matt. "They banned handguns to cut down on all that gang-related violence during the depression riots. Believe me, I'm no fan of gun control, but I can understand why it might be necessary in certain circumstances."

"Aha! Your statement is symptomatic of the very political philosophy which created Nazi Germany in the first place."

Matt was startled. "Huh?"

"Your willingness to accept limitations on your right to keep and bear arms for the so-called public good is what allows dictators like Hitler to disarm and murder their victims. Since it's usually done piecemeal, the average person doesn't even notice his rights are disappearing. One law here, another there, all in the interest of safety and security. Eventually you have an outright dictatorship, without a single shot being fired! It's the same pattern I saw in Nazi Germany. Look at Stalin, Castro and Pol Pot. They all used gun control to ensure no opposition to their murderous schemes. It's happening in America today. Oh, sure, they make it sound like it's for our own good—they want to protect us from violent crime, they say. That's exactly what Hitler said. But you and I both know that if a criminal wants a gun, he's going to get one, whether he has to buy it on the black market or steal it. Meanwhile, honest, law-abiding citizens like you and me can't defend ourselves against these hoods—or the government, if it decides to overstep its bounds. Tell me something, Matt: do you feel safer now than you did before handguns were banned?"

Matt thought about the recent break-ins occurring in the neighborhood. People in the apartment complex had started installing expensive alarm systems that they could barely afford. "Not really."

"I have a friend who just retired from the police force," said Ben. "He told me the ban on handguns had no effect on cutting violent crime. They tried that in Chicago, and guess what? The homicide rate went up, especially handgun slayings. Look what happened when they banned guns in Australia—armed robbery increased by nearly 40 percent. Did you know that? Get this, Matt: my friend says handguns were hardly ever used by the gangs during the depression. Most of them used knives and clubs."

"I didn't know that."

He nodded. "And now it's outrageously expensive to buy ammo, thanks to that insane 500 percent sales tax on it. But does that stop criminals? No, it only makes it impossible for poor people like me to defend myself and my wife against criminals." There was a pause as Matt tried to digest what Ben had just told him. "By the way, Matt, did you know that the United States Gun-Control Act of 1968 was taken almost word-for-word from the Nazi gun-control law of the 1930s?"

"What?! Are you kidding! That's pretty incredible."

"There are a lot of incredible things happening in this country. The problem is, most people don't care. Have you heard about all those no-knock raids? Last year some poor fellow in Denver was murdered by a SWAT team looking for drugs—and it was a case of mistaken identity! All you have to do is watch shows like *Cops* and you can see we're turning into a stinking police state. David taught me how to use the Internet at the library, and I've found dozens of Web sites exposing all of this, but most people simply don't care until it affects them personally. That's the same way it was in Nazi Germany. When their neighbors started disappearing in the middle of the night, most people looked the other way. Then they wondered why no one was there to defend them when the Nazis came after them."

Matt hardly felt like eating anymore. "Man, I feel like a fool for turning in my handgun! It was registered, so I figured I had no choice. Usually, I try not to give in to the government when it violates my rights. Still, I don't know. The idea of owning an illegal weapon—it kind of felt like I'd be going too far. I figured as long as I could keep my shotgun and carbine, I didn't mind giving up my handgun."

"You know, if we Jews had kept our so-called 'illegal' weapons, we would have had a fighting chance. But, like you, we didn't want to break the law. Look where it got us." He picked at his sandwich. "I wish I could make Anita understand all of this, but she just won't listen to reason. That's exactly what's destroying this country."

"But it's still possible to turn things around, right? I mean, it's not as if we've lost all our rights. After all, we still have the right to vote."

Ben shook his head. "It's just a matter of time, Matt. Even if we don't adopt that new constitution, our own is practically meaningless now, because the people no longer understand or defend it. The right to vote can easily be taken away, along with all our other rights, if we have no means of defending ourselves against a federal government that's growing increasingly contemptuous of our rights. Look at what's happened to the Second Amendment—it's been effectively destroyed. No one bothers to fight any of this. Too many Americans are wrapped up in their own petty concerns, and couldn't care less that the freedom their ancestors fought and died for has mostly been traded away—all in the name of 'safety.' The safety of a locked cage!"

Matt was silent as Ben finally began eating his sandwich. He knew that Ben was right. But he also knew that he didn't want to give up; he wanted to do something about it. The question was, what could he do? What could anyone do now? Part of him wished he could ignore the truth—like most Americans who had their heads in the sand. But he couldn't pretend everything was okay.

Ben suddenly got up from the table and returned with a stack of papers which he put down in front of Matt. "I think you should read what our Founding Fathers had to say about the right to keep and bear arms. This is the stuff they won't teach in the public schools anymore!"

Matt started skimming through the quoted passages Ben had placed in front of him. One of them, written by Thomas Jefferson, seemed to leap out at him. "'The strongest reason for the people to retain their right to keep and bear arms is, as a last resort, to defend themselves against tyranny in government.'" Another quote by George Mason, America's first Supreme Court Justice, caught his eye. "'To disarm the people is the best and most effectual way to enslave them.'" There were many more, including some by George Washington and James Madison, as well as Supreme Court cases stating that the police have no legal obligation to protect citizens from crime. What struck Matt most were the quotes by murderous dictators calling for gun control, including Josef Stalin: "'If the opposition disarms, well and good. If it refuses to disarm, we shall disarm it ourselves.'"

"I never heard any of this before. I mean, I always believed in the Second Amendment, but I had no idea how important it was to our Founding Fathers."

Ben nodded. "As you can see from those quotes, they believed that the right to keep and bear arms was the foundation of all our other rights. It was supposed to be the last check on government tyranny, once all peaceful means of keeping the government in line had failed or been taken away. You know something, Matt? If our Founding Fathers were alive today, the media would portray them as dangerous radicals and potential terrorists."

"You really think so?"

"All you have to do is read what they said about the Second Amendment. Why, their views on freedom and the Constitution would be considered subversive by today's government. Just look at the modern day spiritual descendants of our founders—the patriots, constitutionalists, gun rights advocates. Look at how they are portrayed in major newspapers and TV news: as right-wing wackos."

"You know, you're right."

Matt was startled out of his reading when the door opened and Elsie entered the apartment.

Ben got up immediately. "What happened? Did you talk some sense into her?" asked Ben as she took off her faded wool coat.

She shook her head sadly. "I tried to get through to her. But I think she needs some time. She's very upset—" She forced a smile when she saw Matt. "Oh, hello, Matt. How are you?"

"I'm all right. Listen, I'm sure you two need to talk, so I'll get going."

"There's no need to rush off," said Elsie. "Would you like some dessert and coffee? I made a cinnamon babka this morning."

"No, thanks. Gina should be home soon." He patted Ben on the shoulder. "I hope everything works out."

"Thanks, Matt," Ben said. But he didn't sound very hopeful.

* * * *

Matt was still trying to absorb everything Ben had told him when he heard Gina come in. He had the ball game on, but wasn't really paying attention. How could he focus on a petty sport when his entire country hung in the balance? If only he could make Gina understand. He longed to talk to her about the things that burned in his heart and woke him up in the middle of the night. But there had always been a gulf between them, and lately it seemed to be widening.

Gina sat down next to him. "Who's winning?"

He turned off the TV. "I don't know if I care anymore."

She looked surprised. "What's wrong?"

"Somehow I doubt *you'll* understand."

"That's a nice attitude." She got up and went to the kitchen.

She was pouring herself a glass of water when Matt came and stood behind her. He put his arms around her waist, leaned his chin against her shoulder. "I'm sorry, babe," he said.

She let out a sigh. "It's okay. I just wish you'd talk to me once in awhile." She turned to look at him. "Is that so hard?"

"I want to, Gina. Believe me."

"Then why don't you?"

"Because I'm tired of fighting."

"Matt, I don't want to fight, either."

"I know, babe," he said in a soft voice. He sat down at the table and put his face in his hands. How could he even consider raising a family with Gina when they saw things so differently?

She sat down opposite him. "Something really is bothering you. What is it?"

"It's something Ben told me," he said with effort.

"Ben? What did he tell you?"

"Just some stuff about Nazi Germany. Stuff that makes me wonder..."

"About what?"

"Gina, are you sure you should be supporting this World Constitution?" The question came out of the blue, and he could see that she was taken aback. It wasn't something they had talked about much.

"Of course I'm sure. I still don't see why you don't."

"Because I don't trust big government. I never did. Our own government has been out of control for years. What makes you think a one-world government will be any better?"

"Look, we have to give it a chance. Besides, I think you're blowing this all out of proportion. The new government will be a democracy. The way you're carrying on, you'd think it was going to be a dictatorship."

"A democracy can become a dictatorship very easily. All you need is a big enough mob, and everyone's rights are up for grabs."

She folded her arms. "I'm sure that wouldn't happen."

"Gina, what guarantee do we have that it won't? Do you really think it's worth scrapping the U.S. Constitution and Bill of Rights over a flimsy pipe dream? Besides, how much do you know about the World Constitution? Have you actually read it?"

"Not in its entirety. But I'm sure—"

"What? What are you sure of?"

"I'm sure it won't be a dictatorship."

"Why not?"

"Because...people wouldn't let that happen. They wouldn't stand for it."

"Oh, really? Look at what Americans are putting up with already. Gun control, quotas, federal forfeiture laws, roadblocks, cameras on street corners. Who knows what's next?"

"But those laws are there to protect us, Matt."

"That's the problem with this country, everyone wants Big Brother to protect them. The stupid sheep are so desperate for security they don't realize they're throwing away their freedom. That's what happened in Nazi Germany. And you know what Ben said? He said that gun control doesn't protect people from criminals at all. It only protects criminals, robbers and governments alike."

"That's ridiculous. And if you're concerned about criminals, look at Ben. He's got a whole stockpile of guns!"

He wanted to bang his head against the wall. "Gina, he lived under the strictest kind of gun-control laws in Nazi Germany. He saw firsthand what happens when only the government is allowed to have guns. In fact, the Nazi gun-control laws made it possible for Hitler to disarm the Jews and anyone who opposed him. And guess what? Ben told me that our own gun-control laws were based on Nazi gun-control laws."

She rolled her eyes. "That sounds a little extreme, Matt."

"It does sound shocking, I'll admit. But I'm sure Ben knows what he's talking about." He thought of something else. "And what about all those federal forfeiture laws? Don't tell me you think the government has the right to seize innocent people's property?"

"Of course not. But in those cases we're not dealing with innocent people. Sometimes the only way the government can put drug dealers and child pornographers out of business is to seize their property. Or freeze their accounts."

"But Gina, many of the people they've gone after *are* innocent. Look at that new DWI law which allows the police to seize the cars of people who are simply *accused* of drunk driving. What kind of justice is that?"

She shrugged. "Maybe that's the price we have to pay to live in a safe society."

"But wouldn't you rather live in a free society?"

"Of course I would, Matt. I just happen to believe that too much freedom can be dangerous. I mean, do you honestly believe that people should be free to hurt themselves and others by abusing drugs and alcohol?"

"No. But I don't think the government has the right to ignore the Bill of Rights just to stop a few drug dealers, either." Something else dawned on him. "My dad once knew a charter pilot who went bankrupt after the government seized his plane, all because one of his passengers was a convicted cocaine dealer. But the pilot didn't know anything about it! It's guilt by association. And what about those no-knock searches where innocent people are killed by government agents? It's been all over the Internet lately. Does that sound like justice to you?"

"Matt, I'd be careful about believing everything on the Internet. Ranting about government corruption only makes things worse. It can push someone who's unstable over the edge. Anyway, I'm sure most of those anti-government horror stories on the Net are exaggerated, Matt."

He shook his head. "Great. You're just going to believe what you want to believe. What a wonderful trait for a journalist!"

She put her face in her hands and sighed. "Let's just drop this subject. It's obvious we don't see eye to eye on this issue. I don't feel like arguing about it."

He threw up his hands. "You know, you do the same thing every time you can't win an argument—you either change the subject or drop it altogether. You just can't admit when you're wrong."

"I don't want to talk about this anymore. Can't you give it a rest?"

This is what he got for trying to confide in her. "Yeah, I'll give it a rest. I wouldn't want you to have to admit you're wrong!" Grabbing his jacket, he walked toward the door.

"Where are you going?"

"To get away from you for awhile." Cursing, he slammed the door behind him.

Gina jumped up from her chair and followed him out the door. "Matt, wait!"

His tone was like acid. "Why don't you go write some more of your liberal trash? Obviously, it's more important to you than our marriage!" He felt a strange satisfaction when he saw the stricken look on her face.

A dull ache rose in Gina's throat as she reached for a bottle of wine in the back of the refrigerator. After she poured the Chardonnay into a long-stemmed glass, she stood staring at it for quite some time. She took one sip. Then walked slowly into the bedroom and flopped down on the bed. She reached for a stuffed bear Matt had given her long ago. Staring up at the ceiling, she wiped away the tears that slid down her cheeks.

* * * *

Matt didn't know what to expect the following evening when he entered the employee lounge. Especially when he saw that all the chairs and tables had been removed, and a bunch of cushions had been placed in a large circle. A few people were already sitting on them. The smell of sandalwood wafted through the room, and the soothing sounds of the surf, mingled with New Age flutes and synthesizers, came from the CD player in the corner.

Not wanting to feel left out, he sat on one of the cushions and waited expectantly with the others. His muscles ached from working on the loading dock all afternoon, and his light blue work shirt was stained with sweat. He couldn't wait to get home and let the tension drain with a hot shower and a beer. And not necessarily in that order.

Still, this was kind of nice. He closed his eyes as the music carried him away. Everyone seemed to have gone into a relaxation mode. His coworkers spoke in hushed tones. The petty aggravations of work were forgotten.

He dimly became aware of a soft, female voice. He opened his eyes. Hugging her knees to her chest, a young woman sat in the middle of the circle. She wore a flowing electric blue skirt, black leather boots, and a rainbow-colored top. Short, copper-colored hair framed her oval face, and her piercing violet eyes gave her an exotic allure. Around her neck hung a silver chain with a crystal ornament.

Her expression had a far-away, almost mystical quality. "There's a power that lives within all of us," she said. "It caused the stars and the sun to give forth their light, and the first cell to divide. It brought us out of the slimly depths to become the highest form of life on this planet, the crowning glory of the world! It will once again absorb us into itself, as we achieve oneness with the cosmos. It is this power that makes us divine."

There was a long pause as she allowed her words to sink in. "In cosmic consciousness," she said, "our world can be explained as a flow of spirit-energy, which is awareness. In the coming weeks you will learn to awaken the divine power that is your birthright. You will become aware of who you really are and where your destiny lies. You will never again be the same: not only will you be more satisfied, productive employees, but you will become global citizens, able to function at optimal efficiency in our newly emerging, global society."

Matt glanced around at his coworkers to see if they appeared as uncomfortable as he was with all this metaphysical jargon. But they were all listening attentively, almost hanging on her every word.

The woman smiled. "What I'd like to do now is give each of you an opportunity to share a little something about yourselves. We'll start with me. My name is Gail Jordan. I have a Ph.D. in environmental philosophy. I teach feminism and environmental ethics at Stony Brook University."

Matt groaned inwardly. Another one of those touchy-feely airheads.

After everyone had a chance to talk, Gail spoke in a solemn tone. "You are about to embark on an exciting journey, the most significant journey of your lives! In the next few weeks, you will discover a whole new universe, a dimension that lies beyond your senses. You will learn to access its secrets. But that's not all. By applying the scientific principles learned in this class, you will arrive at self-actualization, the highest form of consciousness. You will be empowered to achieve your own godhood as you learn to recognize and use the divine power that already lives within you. There's nothing you can't accomplish when you tap into your higher selves. If you can dream it, you can achieve it!"

While everyone else was obviously enthralled, Matt rolled his eyes. It sickened him that the Department of Labor mandated this nonsense.

How he sat through the next half hour without screaming he didn't know. At a few parts he wanted to speak out and argue, but was afraid of how his coworkers would react. They seemed to be loving it. Maybe it was all in the delivery.

"What'd you think?" asked a big, burly man after the lecture had ended. He had reddish hair with a long beard, and his arms were covered with tattoos.

Matt shrugged. "I don't know. It all sounds kind of mystical, if you ask me."

"What's wrong with that?"

"I'm just wondering how practical this course is going to be. Some of that stuff sounded..." He was groping for the right word.

"What?"

"I don't know...weird. I mean, do you really believe ordinary people like us can be gods?"

"I kind of like the idea. But I don't like having to give up more free time. I don't have enough time with my kids as it is. I missed my son's Little League game to be here tonight."

They walked toward their cars, and the man immediately lit a cigarette after looking around to see if anyone was watching. A recent federal law had banned smoking in all public places, even parking lots. "See you tomorrow, Matt."

"So long." Matt headed toward the second-hand Buick his father had given him after Matt's van had been repossessed during the depression. The van had been his most prized possession, and he hadn't been able to save enough for a new one. With taxes sucking down over 60 percent of people's salaries, who could save anything these days? Fortunately, Gina's car was paid off at the time, so at least they had one car that was running decently. The Buick seemed to spend most of its time in the shop, probably because of its age. With 206,000 miles on it and an engine that had been rebuilt, Matt figured he was lucky it was running at all.

It wasn't until he got home that he remembered the fight with Gina. He had forced himself not to think about it. But another night on their lumpy sofa sure didn't thrill him. Besides, he had been pretty hard on her. Too hard, probably. One of them had to give in sooner or later. It might as well be him.

She listened quietly to his apology, and he hoped he sounded sincere. "Am I forgiven?"

She looked down at his lap. "Sure."

He cupped her chin in his hand. "Then why the long face?"

She shrugged. "Just tired, I guess." She looked at her watch. "It's pretty late. I have to be up early tomorrow." She got up and walked out of the room without looking at him.

Sighing, he turned on the TV. He switched channels, but saw nothing he wanted to watch.

He leaned back against the cushions and stared up at the ceiling. Life was supposed to be better than this.

* * * *

Gail had everyone sitting on the floor again, their legs crossed in what she called the lotus position. She turned on the CD player. A mixture of

Native American flutes, soothing synthesizers, and Celtic chanting filled the room.

Matt felt the tension drain from his body...until Gail started talking. "The Hindus tell us that all the universe is Maya, or illusion. There is no objective reality; what your brain interprets as reality is merely a creation of your own mind. Therefore, your own mental powers can alter your perception by visualizing something different. Reality can be whatever you want it to be!"

Matt looked around to see if anyone else found her assertion as ridiculous as he did, but everyone was looking at her attentively. Some of them were even nodding their heads in agreement. "But that doesn't make sense," Matt told her. "How can reality be what I want it to be?"

Her eyes shone with excitement. "Through the power of your mind, Matt! You can't even begin to imagine the untapped powers of the human mind. We all have the capabilities of God!"

"But if that were true, we wouldn't have all the limitations we have as humans. We wouldn't get sick or grow old—"

She smiled. "Ah! That's because most of us haven't yet learned to draw upon the powers of our Higher Selves."

"But reality *can't* be whatever we want it to be. There are physical laws—"

"Laws are figments of our minds, Matt. The great shamans of indigenous cultures have known that for centuries."

"Wait a second. What about the law of gravity? Is that a figment of my mind?"

She smiled. "In essence, all the truths we cling to are but shadows."

"Okay, so if I decide the law of gravity isn't real for me, I can walk off the edge of a cliff without falling to my death?" he asked.

A couple of people snickered, but Gail said, "Even greater things can be done by those who learn to use the divine power within. You must learn to awaken that power, Matt. You must suspend your doubts. Just imagine what we can achieve by tapping into our higher selves—we can all be as gods!"

Matt refused to be mollified by inane platitudes. "Look, you say that nothing is real, right?"

She nodded. He got up and walked over to the pot of steaming hot coffee water. "What if I pour this pot of boiling water on you?" he asked. "If nothing is real, then you won't feel any pain, right?"

She didn't say anything, and a murmur came over the rest of the class. "Well? Care to put your philosophy to the test?"

There was a long silence, and Matt figured he had her. But she said calmly, "Those who demand proof will be forever disappointed, for they will never be able to ascend to the higher levels of consciousness in which all things are possible to those who believe."

Matt rolled his eyes; she sounded like Obi Wan Kenobi! "Yeah, right."

"Matt, you must understand that perception *is* reality. If you expect me to get scalded, then naturally that's what will happen. However, I do find it disturbing that you would want to pour boiling water on me just to prove a point. Do you enjoy watching people suffer?"

"Of course not! All I want is some proof—"

"Proof? But how can there be proof when there is no objective reality?"

Smiling, he went back to his chair. "Don't worry, you've proven my point pretty well, actually."

She turned to the rest of the class. "You can all learn something from Matt tonight. The hostility that consumes him is a sickness of the soul. In order to attain higher levels of consciousness, you must learn to overcome such negativity. Clearly this is something Matt has not yet learned to do."

"Maybe you should learn to deal honestly with people's objections instead of attacking those who disagree with you," Matt said.

Her face flushed, and he knew he had won. But he was disgusted that no one else had challenged her.

* * * *

Matt heard the soft, urgent whispering as he drifted off to sleep that night. An icy chill swept through him. He was standing on the edge of an abyss. Something unspeakable was at the bottom. Waiting for him. The ground underneath his bare feet crumbled, and he felt himself falling into the swirling blackness below. He threw out his arms, tried to grab something to hold onto.

The scene shifted. He was running through a swamp, slipping and sliding in the mud. Something was chasing him. He knew it wanted to kill him.

Three shadowy figures pounced on Matt's bed. They cackled as they watched him writhe around in the blankets. One of them whispered in his ear, *"You're worthless, Matt. No one cares about you. We're going to kill you! You've given us that right."* They knew he couldn't see them, even if he had been awake. That suited them fine. They had strict orders not to allow this one to become aware of their existence.

Matt tossed and turned. Somehow he sensed he was asleep, but he couldn't wake up. A vise of terror gripped his heart. Soon he could hardly breathe. Tears filled his eyes. *Help me! Oh, God, help me!*

Another figure appeared in the bedroom. The brightness of its garments nearly blinded the creatures tearing into Matt. They fell backwards, screaming in agony and terror. One of the enemy's generals!

Recovering from their initial fright, the three creatures drew their swords and lunged at the intruder.

Swords clashed above Matt's head, sending sparks flying through the room. The three creatures were no match for their enemy. They dug their talons into his powerful arms, but he sent them sprawling backwards into a heap. They looked up at the towering figure whose sword was poised to strike them. It landed on all three of them, and searing pain sliced through them. To a human, the blow would have been fatal.

Whimpering and cursing, the creatures slunk out of the room, disappearing through the wall.

The silent figure approached the bedside and gently touched Matt's forehead. His breathing gradually relaxed.

In the distance he saw a gigantic Cross, almost towering into the sky. Matt stared at the tormented face of the Man who hung from its beams. Blood trickled down from torn flesh beneath a crown of thorns, but the Man's eyes gazed into his with a look of infinite compassion. Peace, safety, love—all these emanated from the Man. Matt vaguely remembered that something was after him, but somehow he knew it could never come here. This place was very special. Matt would have been content to stand there forever.

The scene changed again. He was staring into a black void. He also heard a loud, insistent knocking. A voice whispered softly, *"Matt, open the door...open the door."*

He sat up in bed with a start, his heart beating wildly.

Gina gently touched his shoulder. "Are you all right?" Her voice was filled with concern, her eyes gentle and tender. He was drenched in a cold sweat. What on earth was wrong with him?

It took a moment before he could respond. "Yeah, just another nightmare."

"That's the third nightmare this week!"

Matt lay back down, and Gina put her arms around him. He couldn't seem to stop trembling. "Do you want to talk about it?" she asked.

"No. I'd rather forget it." He gently disengaged himself from Gina's embrace, and slowly got out of bed.

"Where are you going?"

"Think I'll watch a little TV. I doubt I could get back to sleep right now."

As he moved into the darkened hallway, he suddenly had a strange feeling that he wasn't alone, that *something* was watching him from the shadows. *This is nuts.* He switched on the hall light and felt somewhat better. Then he settled onto the couch in the living room, aimlessly switching channels. He shook his head at all the advertisements for those mindless psychic hotlines. There was nothing on that he really felt like watching, but he kept the TV on because the silence frightened him. He finally settled on a late night talk show. But somehow, he couldn't seem to concentrate. He felt a nameless dread that he just couldn't shake, and the thing that frightened him most was that he didn't know what was causing it. *The unknown.* That was always what Matt had found most frightening. He remembered being afraid of the dark as a child because he couldn't see what might be lurking in the shadows. It was also what frightened him about the prospect of death, not being sure of where he would wind up in the afterlife. If there even was one.

He walked over to the bookshelf and hoped to find something to take his mind off his strange anxiety. As he glanced at the titles, he noticed a Bible among all the hardcover books. *Must be the one John gave me.* He took it from the shelf and sat down with it. *There's bound to be something in here to cheer me up.* He randomly flipped through the pages, but didn't see anything in the Old Testament that held his interest, so he started skimming through the New Testament. He stopped in Revelation, and began to read.

Some passages filled him with hope and comfort. But then there were scenes of horror. He saw a picture of a world laid waste with famine, disease and natural disasters of a magnitude Matt couldn't even imagine. Earthquakes. Oceans filled with blood. Stars falling from the heavens. The sun would turn black and the moon blood red. And yet...parts of it really didn't seem that far-fetched. Today plagues like AIDS and Ebola, not to mention nuclear disasters, were realities. Could these be a hint of what was to come?

What if John and Beth were right about the end of the world being near? *Maybe I shouldn't be reading this so late at night.* But something wouldn't let him put it down. He started skimming again, and stopped in Ephesians, chapter six. A passage caught his attention: "'Put on the full armor of God so that you can take your stand against the devil's schemes. For our struggle is not against flesh and blood, but against the rulers, against the authorities, against the powers of this dark world and against the spiritual forces of evil in the heavenly realms.'" He shuddered as he remembered his dream and the thing that was chasing him. He continued reading: "'Therefore put on the full armor of God, so that when the day of evil comes, you may be able to stand your ground....'"

He closed the Bible as the words began to sink in. So, Christians were called to battle the authorities and powers of this world. *But if that's the case, then why do so many cave in to those powers? Why don't John and Beth stand their ground? What's wrong with them?* He read the passage again. "'Our struggle is not against flesh and blood.'" So, was it a spiritual battle? And what were the heavenly realms?

Whenever John talked about the Bible, he made it sound so simple, so cut and dry. But Matt had the impression that this book was far more complex than his brother had led him to believe.

He wanted to read more, but was starting to feel drowsy.

As he padded back to the bedroom, a surprising thought occurred to him. Christianity definitely wasn't for wimps. Based on what he'd read tonight, Christians were in for quite a battle.

That was something Matt certainly didn't feel ready for.

CHAPTER 4

Overlooking the placid waters of the Long Island Sound, the Reinhardt mansion stood like a castle built into the lush, green hillside. It was known that Oren didn't spend much time at the old family estate; he traveled extensively, meeting with international bankers and financiers, the editors of the many newspapers and publishing houses he owned, the numerous politicians who owed him favors. An invitation to the Reinhardt estate was an honor reserved for Oren's most esteemed associates. Kyle Beaumont looked around in awe; this was his first invitation here, and he felt privileged indeed.

Sipping Oren's best brandy, they sat in front of the crackling fire with Serena Conlin, who had also been invited to dinner. She wore a black cocktail dress that clung seductively to her slim figure. The crystal chandelier above them sparkled like diamonds, flooding the room with soft, intimate light. Throughout the evening Kyle wondered why he had been invited here; he knew there had to be a reason, and a good one at that.

Oren handed him several newspaper clippings, and Kyle frowned as he read them. This was all they needed right now. But Oren smiled complacently; his eyes gleamed like polished steel. "What do you think?" Oren asked.

Kyle couldn't understand how Oren could be so calm; these editorials could ruin everything. "This is serious, Oren. What if the people get all fired up about this issue? We could be finished!"

"The problem can easily be rectified," Oren said. "All I have to do is buy the paper."

"Does the owner want to sell?" Kyle asked doubtfully.

Oren appeared to think for a moment. "No, I don't believe he does. But he can be...persuaded, I'm sure. In fact, I seem to recall that he took out a substantial loan from your bank during the depression."

Kyle Beaumont smiled; now he understood why he had been invited here tonight. "Ah, that will make things considerably easier." He looked at the clippings again. "We can't let the public get stirred up about the debit card system when we've worked so hard to finally have it put in place. It's taken us years to get where we are today. Without a cashless monetary system, there's no way to control those who resist our plans to have global taxing authority. And if the public fights us on this, they'll never accept the next phase—"

"*Island News* is a relatively small paper," Serena pointed out. "We can bury it if we need to."

"Yes, but it's in a critical area of the country," Kyle said. "We can't afford to lose support for our plans now, especially on the East Coast which we've always counted on for most of our support. Maybe we should do some damage control."

Serena sipped her brandy. "I think the best plan for now is to ignore the debit card issue. People forget these things very easily. As long as the big corporate papers ignore the issue, it will be dead by the time the next Hollywood scandal hits the front pages."

"What about this Flannery?" Kyle glanced at one of the articles. "Isn't he that big-mouthed priest on the radio?"

Oren smiled. "Not anymore. His show was canceled."

Kyle wasn't satisfied. "Well, I hope he hasn't done too much damage. I understand he's been pretty influential among Catholics, and we can't afford to lose any ground there."

Serena's expression clouded. "You're right. We need the Catholic Church on our side, much as I hate to admit it."

"We already have the Vatican in our pocket," Oren insisted.

"The Vatican isn't enough." Serena spoke scornfully. "We need the support of Catholic believers. Their zeal for world peace has been a tremendous asset to us. If people like Father Flannery succeed in turning large numbers of Catholics against our cause, the support of the Vatican will be worthless."

Oren appeared unperturbed. "Don't worry. Those rallies that we've televised by satellite across the nation should help gain support from the delegates at the convention. Once we get the constitution ratified here in the states, we can start putting pressure on China and the Middle East. It's just a matter of time."

Kyle doubted it would be that easy. "But how is the UN going to get China to give up its nuclear missiles to a global military force?"

Oren held his brandy snifter up to the light. "Negotiations are already underway. The premier of China is on our side. He knows that world government is essential for the final triumph of world communism. He secretly plans to take control of the government once it is established." Oren smiled darkly. "We will, of course, continue to feed that hope."

Shadows within shadows, circles within circles, powers within powers.

How Kyle loved the ways of this world! Those in the outermost circles rarely suspected the existence of the inner circles—but Kyle knew. And Oren had just admitted him—without actually saying it—into the center of the shadows of power! That seemingly offhanded remark about the secret plans of the Chinese premier—nobody in Kyle's circle knew that, or even suspected. It would terrify them. These people really controlled the world!

Kyle Beaumont smiled, feeling something like a tiger after a large, satisfying meal. He was an important member of the CGU, but few people in the Council were privileged to have such information. But Kyle had worked hard for the Council, and had earned that privilege. He had been particularly helpful in influencing some key conservatives in Congress to support the World Constitution.

Oren's next words filled Kyle with an exhilaration that almost made him giddy. "So, that's how things stand now, Kyle. We're very close to obtaining our goal. Soon—the world will be ours."

* * * *

Ken Hughes sat at his desk. He had a ton of work to do, but couldn't seem to concentrate. Things were moving too quickly. Delegates were being chosen for the Constitutional Convention, which was set to begin meeting in January. He heard from the wire services that a group of patriots from Pennsylvania had picketed the capitol in Harrisburg on Election Day; apparently they believed that the ballot initiative calling for a convention had been rigged, and they wanted to protest this manipulating of the polls. But they were arrested because they hadn't been able to obtain a permit, even though they had applied for one well in advance. The newspapers called them "right-wing extremists" opposed to world peace and hinted that they were capable of violence. It was also said that they were affiliated with the "subversive" Patrick Henry Society. Ever since Ken could remember, the Society had been ridiculed and attacked by the media, much like Father Flannery was. But Ken had several friends who were members, and he knew that they were patriots concerned with preserving the American Constitution. He shook his head, disgusted by the deception he saw among his own colleagues.

Ken also had been startled to learn that several public officials who had been vehemently opposed to the new constitution suddenly decided to support it. One was a conservative United States senator, another was a Supreme Court Justice who had sworn to do everything in his power to see that

Americans remained under the protection of the United States Constitution. When Ken called the senator to ask why he had changed his mind, he said that after considerable thought, he felt it was his public duty to support any effort toward world peace. The Supreme Court Justice was unavailable for comment. Several days after he endorsed the World Constitution, he committed suicide.

Since the riot at Eisenhower Park, local news commentators had begun clamoring for stricter hatecrimes legislation, and soon the cry was echoed by newspapers across the country. Ken recalled the President's eloquent, impassioned speech denouncing such crimes and reminding Americans that the Constitution for Federation Earth included stronger civil rights laws and strict penalties for hatecrimes. When Father Flannery applied for a public forum appearance on the local cable Public Access Channel, his application was denied. He and some of his supporters wrote letters to *Island News* about this, but none of them were printed—and Ken felt terrible. The paper's new owner had fired the letters editor and had replaced him with one of his cronies, who was totally dedicated to world government. On top of that, the new publisher announced at the morning news meeting that all current employees would be put on a six-month probationary period. Any staff member who did not abide by the new owner's policies would be fired.

After the meeting, Ken had returned to his office in silence. He had been particularly distressed to discover that the new owner was Damien Whitaker, the brother-in-law of Oren Reinhardt, a staunch supporter of world government.

Ken wondered why Jared Cohen, whose family had owned the paper for decades, would sell the newspaper when it meant so much to him. He remembered the look on Jared's face the previous day—the face of a broken man. Something must have forced him to sell, but what? Ken looked at the portrait of his father, and wondered how he would feel if he could see what had become of the newspaper business. Maybe he wouldn't be all that surprised. He had always warned Ken about the pressures in this business to compromise his honesty and integrity. He obviously knew what he was talking about.

During the meeting Damien had told Ken to run a series of articles supporting the World Constitution, and reminded the letters editor not to print any letters that opposed it. "We have a civic duty to support this constitution," the publisher said when Ken objected. "If you have a problem with that, then I suggest you start looking for a job at another paper, if you can find one that meets your outdated standards."

Ken knew he didn't have much choice. There were no more independent newspapers anywhere in the tri-state area, and he knew that most of the corporate papers were owned or at least controlled by people affiliated with the CGU or other organizations which were opposed to everything America had once stood for. Sometimes he felt like quitting, but he couldn't afford to lose his pension, and he wasn't eligible for retirement yet. The term "between a rock and a hard place" now held new, personal meaning for him. The depression had wiped out all his savings. He had invested substantially in the stock market, and had lost everything. He was putting two of his three children through private colleges, and had taken out a loan to finance their education. If he lost his job, then his boys would have to transfer to government-funded state colleges, and he didn't want that to happen. He knew that the state colleges had the same political agenda, and he wanted his children to be independent thinkers. He also believed that the quality of education at the few private colleges remaining in the country was far superior to that of the state colleges. He wanted the best for his children, and he was determined to give it to them, even if it meant staying at a job he was quickly coming to despise.

* * * *

Bill Rodriguez surveyed his surroundings. Beyond the little general store, evergreens and pines dotted a seemingly endless tract of land leading up the blue ridges of the Pocono Mountains in Northeastern Pennsylvania. He walked up three rickety wooden steps, glanced at the list in his hand, then pushed open the door.

A plump woman of about forty-five or fifty stood behind the counter. Her frizzy blonde hair was tied back in a short ponytail. She glanced up from her magazine and smiled. "Hello."

"Hi there." Bill took a basket and headed straight for the dairy case. He grabbed a half gallon of milk and a carton of eggs. Next he turned to one of the shelves and reached for a package of Wonder Bread and some canned soup.

He placed all his groceries on the counter and he reached into his pocket for his debit card and handed it to the woman. She ran it through the scanner and waited for the approval. She frowned. "I've never seen this happen before."

"What's wrong?"

She eyed him suspiciously. "It says your account has been closed."

His heart almost stopped. "What?" He didn't know what else to say.

"Your account is closed. That's all it says."

He cursed. This was the last thing he needed right now. "It doesn't say why?"

She looked at him as if he were some kind of criminal. "No. But I saw something on the news about this. They say this only happens to drug dealers and terrorists. You know, people who are breaking the law. That's how they catch them."

He fought to remain calm. "There must be some mistake. I haven't done anything illegal. I've never even gotten a traffic ticket!"

"Well, you must have done something."

Her words jarred him suddenly. "I think I know what the problem is." There was a sick feeling in the pit of his stomach.

"In any case, you'd better get it straightened out."

"Gee, that could take time. I really need these groceries now." He pointed to his watch. "Listen, I'll trade you my watch for the groceries—"

Her eyes widened. "Are you crazy? I could get in trouble for that! Bartering is against the law."

"Who's going to know? There's no one else here!"

"I'm sorry, mister, but I can't take any chances. All I need is to be closed down by the government. You'll just have to go straighten this out first if you want to buy any groceries here. There's a number you can call, but you'll probably have to go in person before they'll reopen your account."

She handed him back his card, and he put it in his pocket. Frustrated, he left the store.

He drove along route 590, carefully negotiating the narrow twists and turns in the mountain road. He was anxious to get back to the cabin where he had been staying since his apartment had been ransacked. If only he hadn't run out of food!

The scenic road wound along the Lackawaxen River. He pulled around a sharp curve in the road, past a huge, red barn. *How do I get myself into these things?*

The droning of helicopter blades invaded his thoughts. He listened, then froze. The sound was coming closer, too close. He looked in his rearview mirror. A large, black helicopter was flying right behind his car, closing on him!

The chopper had no markings, and was painted completely black. Bill pressed hard on the gas. His speedometer needle shot up to sixty. The chopper was still gaining on him. He kept his foot on the gas pedal. Now he was doing seventy.

He looked in the mirror again, but couldn't see the chopper. Yet the roaring blades sounded louder than ever. *Must be right on top of me. Let's see how fast you can go!* He pressed his foot to the floor.

Tires screeched as he maneuvered the tight curves of the high mountain road. A blur of trees and bushes flew past him. He tried to keep his eyes on the road. He glanced in his sideview mirror. The chopper was behind him now, but moving to the side instead of directly in back of him. It couldn't get too close because of all the trees. He nearly lost control of the jeep as his sideview mirror exploded into pieces. They were shooting at him!

How could he escape from a helicopter? There were no mountain tunnels that he knew of in this area. The trunk took a few hits as he careened wildly from side to side. A couple of times he nearly had a head-on collision with a car in the opposite lane. The rear window shattered and a bullet punched through the passenger side door, sending the window handle spinning past his nose out of the car.

"Crazy!"

Terrified, he hit the brakes hard and sharply pulled the wheel to the right, barreling into the forest. The copter sped past him overhead as the jeep bounced violently over the rough terrain. He had to slow down to avoid hitting trees and boulders. Fortunately, there was a small path between the trees, which made it somewhat easier to maneuver the jeep. He could still hear the chopper somewhere overhead, but could barely see it through the leafy canopy.

As he came to a deep ravine surrounded by tall pine trees, he realized that this was his chance. He stopped the jeep and jumped out, then climbed through the underbrush that led down toward the bottom of the ravine, which was completely hidden by trees and huge boulders. He decided to wait there, hoping desperately that the chopper would leave him alone.

This was the deepest part of the woods, he wouldn't have been able to get any farther in his jeep. He doubted the pilot could see his jeep from overhead.

He found a somewhat flat, moss-covered rock and sat down heavily. It was very dark here, almost like twilight due to the dense, interlocking branches far above which allowed little light to reach the forest floor. The sound of the chopper faded; they must have given up. But they had gotten close enough to see his license plate, so it wasn't safe to drive the jeep anymore.

He didn't feel safe enough to leave this secluded place yet, so he sat silently and tried to collect his thoughts. It was amazingly quiet here, as though a blanket of silence hung heavily over the forest. His mind was having trouble accepting the change. Only minutes ago he had been deluged with the sounds of rifle fire, screeching tires and the deafening beat of chopper blades. Now this. It was like jumping out of hell and landing in paradise—a very weird but gratefully embraced experience. He was actually beginning to relax. Still, he knew that his life was in terrible danger. But how did they find him? How could they have known he was in the Poconos, on that particular road, at that exact moment?

Suddenly, he froze. Off to the left something was moving through the bushes. It sounded like it was about forty feet away—he couldn't tell if it was coming toward him. Remaining motionless, he tried to see through the small pine trees. He cursed. These bushes that hid him so well also made it nearly impossible to see anything else. The sound seemed to be moving somewhat parallel to the path he had taken and away from him—almost. It sounded like more than one person but he couldn't hear any talking. Trouble! If they continued on that course it would bring them across a narrow opening through the bushes where they could see him! Panicking, he looked for a place to hide. It would be risky moving behind another bush—the twigs and leaves he might step on would give him away. The rock! It might just be big enough to hide him! Carefully, he got behind it and stretched out on the mossy area there. Lying down made him undetectable from the gap ahead. They were almost there. He moved his head slightly to the right where he could just barely see through the gap. There! He let out a sigh of relief. Deer. Three of them. "Man, I don't need this aggravation."

He closed his eyes and just lay there on the soft moss for a minute, regaining his composure.

His mind returned to the problem at hand. How had they found him? He had taken every precaution to avoid being found. He was staying at a friend's cabin and driving a borrowed jeep. Could they have bugged him or his jeep? Then, it hit him.

"Of course! They traced me through my debit card somehow."

It would have taken only a matter of seconds. They had probably called the store and gotten a description of his jeep from the saleswoman, who must have seen him drive away. If that were the case, she could have told them what direction he was heading in. Unless...could the card have some sort of tracking device inside it? He rubbed his chin. In any event, he had been tracked, and the government agents who were after him had assigned a helicopter in the area to look for him.

But why was the helicopter black, without any insignia? Most likely it was probably a police or military helicopter, but why no markings? And why would they shoot at him? Had the government gone crazy?

Bill was exhausted, but he knew he couldn't stay in the bushes forever. And it wasn't safe to go back to the cabin, they might find out he was staying there.

He climbed out from the underbrush and began walking back toward the road. He figured he'd be safe as long as he didn't walk within view of the main road. Yet as he neared the road, he heard the sound of a helicopter again; they hadn't given up after all. That meant staying in the woods.

He felt in his jacket for his knife. At least he'd be able to defend himself from any bears. There were even rumors of wolves in this area. He hoped to find a house where he could use someone's phone to call his contact. Even if it was tapped, he had to take that chance.

It was almost nightfall by the time Bill found a phone. He had gotten lost in the woods near the sleepy little town of Rowland, but had finally found the road again. When he came to a general store, he decided to take a chance and make a collect call since he could no longer use his debit card.

Bill waited while the operator put the call through. "Hank," he said, relieved to hear a familiar voice. "You're not going to believe what just happened!"

He said as little as possible, just enough to make it clear that he didn't feel safe returning to the cabin.

Hank had suggested a rendezvous point where they could meet in case of trouble. "You know where to go. You can ask someone for directions if you have to, but be careful."

CHAPTER 5

The little white church, with its soft, manicured lawn and stained glass windows, could have been the subject of a quaint picture-postcard. But not tonight. An angry mob surrounded the building. Carrying signs scrawled with blasphemous epithets, they shouted curses at the small group of frightened churchgoers who stood huddled together in the parking lot.

Gina looked for Father Flannery, whose urgent phone call had brought her here. Maybe he was inside. But the crowd was pressed against the front door. No one could get past, though a few tried. They were spit at and kicked, then roughly shoved to the sidewalk. Pale and shaken, they limped away, while the crowd jeered.

Gina turned to Phil Walsh, a staff photographer. "These people are animals!" she said.

"No kidding!" He was busy snapping pictures, but wouldn't get very close.

The church was in a quiet neighborhood near the North Shore of Long Island. Up the street was an old clock tower, and a little stream wound its way behind the well-kept Victorian houses. A nearby lake surrounded by willow trees and ferns reflected the last rays of the setting sun.

Gina glanced at the posters in blood-red letters: *CHRISTIANS ARE HATEMONGERS...CHRISTIAN BIGOTS GO TO HELL!* Those carrying the signs were wearing black leather jackets with some sort of symbol painted on the back. It looked like a globe with a triangle in the middle. Could they be gang members?

She looked around for other reporters or camera crews, but the street was deserted except for the mob and a little cluster of churchgoers who lingered nearby. Some of them appeared to be praying, others were singing hymns. "Phil, keep taking pictures. I'm going to try to ask a few questions."

"All right, but be careful." Gina was surprised at the effect this scene was having on Phil, a seasoned news photographer who had probably seen more action than she had. His face was white.

Walking along the sidewalk behind the church, Gina heard the faint sound of a child crying. A woman was huddled behind a tan station wagon. A little boy clung to her, his face buried in her lap. He couldn't have been more than three or four years old.

Gina approached them cautiously. "Are you all right?" Suddenly, the story no longer seemed so important. The woman, who appeared to be in her early thirties, looked up, startled. Disheveled dark hair tumbled past her shoulders.

"I think so," she stammered.

"What happened?"

She pointed at the crowd and shuddered. "They tried to hurt my little boy. They're like...like animals. Why are they doing this?"

"Are either of you hurt?"

"No, we got away. I had to kick one of them—he grabbed my son..." She shook her head in disbelief. "We ran as fast as we could."

Gina sat down next to her on the curb. "So, you were trying to get into the church?" The woman nodded. "Is there anything I can do to help?"

"No. Thank you," she said with a weak smile.

"Listen, I know how upset you must be right now. I don't want to bother you, but I'm a reporter, and I'd be very grateful if you'd answer some questions, if you feel up to it."

She nodded, stroking her son's dark brown hair. He looked up at Gina with wide, frightened eyes. "Go ahead," the woman said.

"What's your name?"

"Angelina Martinez."

Gina asked about the mob outside the church, and Angelina's voice shook with anger. "They came to protest our meeting tonight. But this isn't a protest—this is an attack!"

"What meeting?"

"Christians for Constitutional Liberties. When we got here, that gang was blocking our entrance to the church. Some of them were lying in the street out front, so we couldn't even get our cars into the parking lot."

"Do you know anything about these, er, protestors?"

"Not really. They keep yelling terrible things at us. Hateful things!" She shuddered again and pulled her son closer, as if trying to shield him from their hatred. The crowd was chanting, "Put an end to hatecrime—get rid of Christian slime!"

"Tell me a little about your organization."

"Basically, we want to preserve the rights guaranteed by the Bill of Rights, especially religious freedom. We fear that the UN Constitution is going to destroy religious liberty in this country."

"What makes you so sure?"

Angelina took a pamphlet out of her handbag. "Look at this. This is what the UN Constitution says about religious freedom."

Gina read the pamphlet. "'Article 1. No one shall be subject to coercion which would impair his/her freedom to have a religion or belief of his/her choice. Article 2. Freedom to express one's religion or belief may be subject only to such limitations as are prescribed by law and are necessary to protect public welfare and morals or the fundamental rights or freedoms of others. Article 3. No one shall be permitted to engage in harassment, threats and/or intimidation in manifesting his/her religion or belief.'" She looked at Angelina. "What's so terrible about that? It sounds reasonable to me."

"Perhaps it does. Until you think about what it really means. What if I tell a sinner he won't go to heaven unless he trusts in Jesus? What if the UN sees that as a threat or intimidation?"

Gina recoiled at Angelina's words. "No offense, but I'm not sure I agree with labeling people who don't happen to share your religious beliefs as sinners. And the whole concept of hell is pretty judgmental. Besides, isn't it better to let people make their own decisions about such things? Why push your beliefs on others?"

"People already have the freedom to make their own decisions about God. They are free to accept or reject Him. But shouldn't believers have the right to tell others about the hope they have in Jesus?" When Gina didn't answer, Angelina asked, "Do you want to live in a country where it's a crime to tell people about God?"

"No, of course not."

"Look at Article 2," said Angelina. "It actually says that freedom of religion can be subject to government restrictions. I came to America to get away from such oppression!"

"I understand that, but the restrictions are supposed to protect the public welfare."

"But what if the UN decides it's bad for the public to be exposed to religious beliefs or ideas? They could use that as an excuse to ban all missionary activity. In fact, we fear that's exactly what the UN plans to do."

Gina shook her head. "I just can't believe that." Still, she recalled the *Life* Magazine photo Father Flannery had shown her. Already, seeds of doubt had been planted in her mind. She pushed the image away.

"I wouldn't be so sure, if I were you."

"Well, thanks for answering my questions." Gina glanced over at the crowd. She could hear glass breaking and people screaming. "Hasn't anyone called the police?"

"I think so, but they're taking their time getting here."

"Maybe you two should get out of here," Gina suggested.

"My house is just around the corner. But I'd have to pass that crowd to get there. I'm afraid someone would follow us. I think we're safe here."

"Well, be careful," Gina said as she got up.

"Thank you," Angelina said with a warm smile.

As Gina headed back toward the crowd, someone grabbed her arm. Startled, she whirled around. She heaved a sigh of relief when she saw that it was only Phil. "Don't get too close," he warned her. Some of the protestors were picking up rocks and glass bottles, and began hurling them at the church.

"This is insane," said Gina. "Who *are* these people?"

"I think they're after that Father Flannery. They keep shouting for him to come outside."

"Well, he'd be crazy to do that."

One of the ringleaders raised his voice. He had dark hair and the coldest eyes she had ever seen. An ugly scar ran across his cheek. "We want to talk to you, Flannery! If you come out and face us, no one will get hurt."

An elderly man suddenly approached. He had a leathery, wrinkled face, and spoke in a soft voice. "Please, leave us in peace. We've done nothing to harm you. Neither has Father Flannery. Please go, before someone gets hurt."

The thug grabbed him by his coat. "Yeah, and what if we don't go? What are you going to do about it, old man?"

"I'll pray for you. I'll pray that Christ will forgive you." Gina drew in her breath as the man was pushed roughly to the ground. His glasses fell off, and the punk stomped them to pieces.

The door of the church opened, and Father Flannery came running outside. He roughly pushed aside those who were blocking the entrance, and his eyes blazed with anger. "That's enough!" he shouted. "Leave that man alone! I'll talk to you, but for God's sake, leave these people alone!"

The scar-faced man smiled, his eyes filled with pure hatred. "So, you finally have the guts to face us."

The crowd closed in on the priest. Two of the men pinned his arms to his sides. Gina stared in horror as she watched the leader. He had picked up a brick and was approaching Father Flannery with a gleam in his eyes.

* * * *

Lying on the floor with a cushion under his head, Matt closed his eyes and let his mind go blank. After several weeks he actually found himself looking forward to Gail's course. He couldn't deny that he was more relaxed than he had been in a long time, mostly from applying the exercises he was learning in the class. Maybe eastern mysticism had something practical to offer after all.

He drifted along with the music while Gail counted down to what she called the "Alpha" state, the lowest level of consciousness. "You are walking down a long corridor," she told the class in a soothing voice. "Suddenly you find a door. Open it. What do you see?"

Matt wondered vaguely if he had been hypnotized. He actually saw the door she described—he was really standing in front of it! He reached out to open it, then stopped. Something told him this wasn't a game. Once he opened this door, there was no turning back.

Almost as if she sensed his thoughts, Gail said, "You mustn't be afraid. Behind the door lies your every desire. Power, wealth—love. You can have anything you wish. What is your heart's desire? It is waiting for you behind the door." For some inexplicable reason, Matt suddenly was terrified of what he might find there.

"You must suspend all doubt," Gail said. "Allow no outside authority to hinder you. Do not be distracted by feelings of guilt or shame; such notions are solely the inventions of your mind. Even if you believe in God, you must not allow Him to stand in the way of your desire. Take the first step in reclaiming your own godhood—open the door!"

It was an invitation Matt couldn't resist. He slowly turned the handle.

He was inside a room flooded with soft candlelight. In the corner he saw a brass bed covered with pale satin sheets. A woman with flaming red hair lay across the mattress. She gazed deeply into his eyes and smiled. Somehow, she looked familiar. He was startled when he realized who she was. The boss's secretary, barely out of high school. Usually she wore her hair tied back, but now it fell down her shoulders, wild and free.

Matt had always thought she was cute, and he might have fantasized about her now and then. After all, who wouldn't? But this was different—this was real! Or was it? The images were so vivid he wasn't sure anymore.

She held out her arms to him. He hesitated, thinking of Gina.

"She doesn't understand you, Matt. Forget about her..." The young woman rose from the bed and walked toward him. The scent of her perfume filled his senses. He reached out to take her in his arms.

Suddenly he felt the presence of something unspeakably evil. He opened his eyes and drew back in horror. Something was staring at him, just inches away from his face. It had bright green eyes and the most ghoulish expression he had ever seen. And it was *real!*

He squeezed his eyes shut. *God, please make it go away!* He opened his eyes again and it was gone. He was shaking uncontrollably, but no one else seemed to notice—everyone seemed to be in some sort of trance-like state. What the hell was going on? Taking a deep breath, Matt tried to calm down, but his heart was pounding violently and he was drenched in sweat.

When the class ended, he hurried out to the parking lot where Gina was waiting for him. She had to pick him up because his car was in the shop again, and was likely to become a permanent fixture there. Maybe they could catch a movie or something. Anything to get his mind off his stinking job...and that horrible creature.

When Gina was a half hour late picking him up, Matt felt mildly annoyed. But after an hour had passed, he became concerned. He decided to call the newsroom, hoping that she was just running late.

He slammed down the receiver after being told she had left an hour ago to cover a story. *Of course! Always her job!* That's what came first. It was a chilly evening, and Matt shivered in his light-weight denim jacket. Everyone else had gone home, so he couldn't get a ride. He couldn't really afford the fare for a taxi, and the nearest bus stop was a couple of miles away. And he wasn't even sure the buses were running at this hour. Then he recalled that John lived only a half hour away. Maybe he could give him a ride home.

* * * *

Horrified, Gina stared at the thug who was holding the brick as the crowd closed in on Father Flannery. She turned to Phil. "This has gone too far— I'm calling the police!"

Minutes later she stood in a phone booth around the corner. "Why haven't you sent anyone over here?" she asked the operator. "These people are extremely violent! Someone's going to get hurt!"

"We're very busy down here, miss. We don't have time to check out every hysterical call from religious fanatics."

"Well, I'm not a religious fanatic. I'm a reporter from *Island News*, and if you don't get here soon, there's going to be an ugly front-page story about it in the paper tomorrow!"

"All right, lady, we'll send someone right away."

"Make it fast!"

When she arrived back at the church, Father Flannery was still being held by the thugs. "Can't keep your mouth shut, can you, preacher?" the man with the scar said. "You have to keep shoving your bigoted views down everyone's throat. We warned you not to come to this meeting, but you didn't listen, and now we're gonna have to teach you a lesson."

Someone punched Father Flannery in the abdomen. He reeled backwards, clutching his stomach, while the crowd laughed. Another blow came at his jaw and knocked him to the ground. Blood trickled down from the corner of his lips. Somewhat dazed, he looked up at the man holding the brick. "Better say your prayers, preacher!"

Gina saw the brick moving toward his head. Before she knew what she was doing, she found herself running forward. "Stop it! Leave him alone!"

She was about to tell them the police were on the way when Phil grabbed her by the arm. "Are you crazy?" He looked incredulous. One of the thugs turned in their direction. Smiling maliciously, he began to walk toward her. "Let's get out of here," said Phil. He dragged her along with him as he sprinted away from the crowd.

Gina's foot hit a broken bottle, and she stumbled to the ground. Someone grabbed her from behind, and her heart raced as she tried to pull herself free. She looked ahead for Phil, but couldn't see him anywhere. She began to panic as her arms were pinned behind her. "Let me go!" she screamed as she tried to wriggle free.

Someone was pulling her toward the center of the crowd. "Looks like she wants to share the preacher's punishment," a hoarse voice said.

"Yeah—let's knock their skulls together!" another piped up.

The hoodlum loomed over her with a sadistic smile.

In desperation, she kicked him hard between the legs. He emitted a startled yelp as he crumpled to the ground. Gasps came from the crowd when they realized what had happened. Someone roughly pushed her to the ground and began kicking her in the ribs.

It was only then that she became aware of the sound of police sirens. A squad car pulled up, and the rioters began to scatter.

Dazed and in pain, Gina just lay there for a time. Finally, she mustered the energy to stand up, and hobbled over to Father Flannery. She helped him to his feet. "Are you all right?"

He coughed. "Yes, I think so. Just got the wind knocked out of me." His expression was grave. "You may have saved my life!"

"What do you mean? I almost got killed myself!"

"Yes, but your intervention stopped that, er, creature. long enough for the police to arrive. Actually," he said, looking at the moaning figure on the ground, "you have one heck of a kick."

Gina looked in disgust as the police officers ignored the dispersing crowd and started walking toward Father Flannery, who was still bleeding from the blow to his chin. They sent *one* squad car for a violent mob? Most of the rioters were getting away. One of the officers, a tall, wiry black man in his mid-forties, spoke to Father Flannery. "Are you hurt badly, Father?"

"I think I'll survive."

The officer pointed toward the man lying on the ground. "This the guy who hit you?" The priest nodded. The officer pulled the criminal to his feet, cuffed him and took him away.

The officer returned a moment later. "We'll need a statement from you. Would you mind coming down to headquarters?"

"No problem," said Father Flannery.

"You guys sure took your time getting here," Gina said, delicately feeling her ribs and wincing. She didn't think anything was broken, thank God. She only wished she had gotten a look at the animal who kicked her—she would love to be able to press charges!

"Look, it's not our fault." He sounded genuinely sorry. "We came as soon as we got the call. I wish they had called us here sooner. I have friends who go to this church!"

Gina looked at the church. One of the stained glass windows had been shattered, and pieces of broken glass littered the front steps. A few frightened people stood outside, huddled together, their faces pale.

A man in his early sixties approached, looking at Gina and Father Flannery with concern. "Are you two all right?" he asked.

They both nodded, but Father Flannery was still breathing heavily. "I'll have to go make a statement, but I'll be back later." He patted the man on the shoulder.

His frail-looking hands were shaking. "I'm so sorry this happened."

Father Flannery smiled reassuringly. "We all have some battle scars. You have yours, as well." Almost as an afterthought, he turned to Gina and introduced her to his friend, Reverend Dalton, the senior pastor of the church. He invited Gina to join the congregation for a word of prayer, and she agreed, mainly because she hoped to interview him later.

Pushing open the heavy oak door, she stepped inside the church, followed by Phil. "Where the hell...where did you disappear to? I could've used some help!" she shouted.

Phil looked sheepish and shrugged. "Angry mobs scare me. I tried to get you away from there. What was I supposed to do, go up against those cretins all by myself?"

She glared at him for a moment, then noticed a telephone on a table in the lobby. "Here," she said, roughly handing Phil her tape recorder, which included some of her earlier observations and her interview with Angelina. "Call the newsroom and get a rewrite on this. I'm going to ask some questions, maybe interview the pastor. Tell them they can go with what I have so far, but if they want more, they'll have to wait. And tell them about the attack on Father Flannery and me!"

"Right," said Phil, and quickly headed toward the phone, looking glad to get away from her for the moment.

A hush filled the church as the small group of believers sat down in the wooden pews. Gina sat in the back, hoping to be inconspicuous. She looked around. Behind the altar was a beautiful stained glass window depicting a golden cross against a background of indigo, violet, royal blue, and red. A long crack ran down the center of the window, possibly from one of the rocks thrown at it. The dim lighting had a soothing effect. She looked at the pew-rack in front of her, which contained a few worn Bibles, a leather-bound prayer book, and some hymnals.

Standing in front of the altar, the kindly looking pastor addressed the congregation. "I'm sure this has been a traumatic experience for all of you," he said in a soft voice. "I know you're all pretty shaken up right now, I know I am. But at times like these we need to turn to our Lord, who told us to expect persecution and suffering. We must remember His promise: 'When these things begin to take place...lift up your heads, because your redemption is drawing near.' Let's pray, shall we?"

Gina sat with her head lowered as she listened to his prayer. She was somewhat startled when he prayed for the "poor, misguided souls" who had attacked them. "Open their eyes and their hearts, dear Lord, and bring them to repentance. Bring them to the Cross, Jesus. Show them that they are lost without You. Show them how much You love them, Lord. And help us to forgive them, as You forgave us." She would have expected a minister to heap words of judgement and condemnation upon those monsters who had attacked his congregation so viciously. But his voice was filled with love and compassion for them.

"Under the circumstances," he said when he had finished, "I think it best that we postpone our meeting until Father Flannery can join us. And I'm sure you'd all like to get home, so I won't keep you any longer. But you're welcome to remain in silent prayer for as long as you wish. I'll be here by the altar if anyone has a need they'd like me to pray for."

Gina got up, hoping that Dalton would be willing to talk to her for a few minutes. She saw Phil standing in the back, and she turned around and walked in his direction. He looked a little uneasy as he saw her approaching. "I'm going to try to talk to the pastor," she said. "Did you call in the story?"

"Yeah. But they have to clear it with the publisher before they run it."

"Well, is it going in tomorrow's edition?" Gina asked.

"They didn't say."

"I'll be back in a minute." She went to talk to the pastor while Phil sat in one of the pews in the back.

Reverend Dalton told her that Father Flannery had received threatening phone calls warning him not to go to the meeting. He had called the police and asked for protection, but was told they couldn't do anything unless the callers took action.

Gina shook her head. "I've never seen anything like this before. Those people were like...monsters or wild animals...almost inhuman. I haven't been that scared since I can remember."

He looked at her sadly. "If they only knew Jesus," he said, "they could never do such things. You're not going to believe this, but I used to know one of the young people in that mob."

"Really?"

"Yes. He and his parents live down the block from here. He's always been such a decent boy, used to shovel people's walks in the winter." He shook his head, mystified. "Of all people."

Gina thought about how the gang members had scattered so quickly when the police arrived. *They were such cowards*, she thought. Typical bullies. They only attacked when they sensed fear or weakness.

"Well," the pastor continued, "I suppose anyone can fall in with a bad crowd, even Christians sometimes. To quote from Proverbs, 'Bad company corrupts good character.'"

She didn't like being preached to. "Thank you for your time," she said, "but I should get back to the newsroom."

Just as she was getting into Phil's car, she remembered that she was supposed to pick up Matt from work. She slammed the door roughly and cursed. Matt certainly wouldn't be happy with her tonight.

* * * *

When John and Matt walked into the kitchen, Beth was putting a tray of ziti in the oven. "Dinner will be ready in about a half hour. Sorry to make you guys wait, but I got a late start because of a faculty meeting after school."

"That's okay." Matt frowned. "If it weren't for you guys, I'd probably still be standing outside waiting for Gina." He sat at the kitchen table with John. Cleo nuzzled their legs under the table.

"How did the meeting go?" John asked.

She sighed. "The usual indoctrination." She poured iced tea into three glasses and sat down at the table with them. "It really has me frightened."

"Why? What's going on?" asked Matt.

"We had a guest speaker this afternoon. She was telling us about the global curriculum the UN plans to implement once the new constitution is ratified. There's going to be a global educational bureau that will control what all the schools teach. We're supposed to work on preparing our students for the new curriculum." She shook her head. "It sounds more like brainwashing to me. The speaker said we're supposed to 'wean our students away' from the values of their parents. You know, I'm beginning to hate this job. I just wish more teachers would fight this stuff. But they all go along with it like sheep." She took a sip of her tea.

"I wish you Christians would fight it more," said Matt.

"It's not as if I haven't tried," Beth said. "I called some parents to set up a meeting with the principal last week. Unfortunately, most of them caved in when they heard their kids won't graduate without this new curriculum. So, I tried something daring. It may even get me fired if the principal finds out."

This sounded interesting. "What?"

"I told the class I was going to teach them something very controversial, and it was up to them to decide if it's true." She smiled. "We had quite an interesting discussion. One student even used the Bible to debunk moral relativism."

"What's that?" asked Matt.

"It means there are no absolutes," John said. "That way, people can decide for themselves what's right and wrong."

"What's wrong with that?"

"For one thing, it was a main tenet of Nazism," Beth said. "Think about it, Matt. Would you want a dictator like Hitler deciding what's right for our country?"

"Actually, that seems to be the direction we're heading in," Matt said. "And I'd like to do something to stop it."

Beth frowned. "It can't be stopped until people realize there are moral absolutes. When they decide for themselves what's right and wrong about all aspects of life, then dictators become the norm. Look at Communism. It totally rejects all absolutes, and the innocent are oppressed and subjugated."

"Hmm. You have a point there. So, how did the discussion turn out?"

"Well, the other kids started making fun of the girl who referred to the Bible. But then I told them about the great thinkers in history who believed in God's Word. I even mentioned that some of their baseball heroes are born-again Christians! The kids were flabbergasted. We wound up having an intense discussion about the Bible's influence on books and even movies. After class, I heard a few students talking about starting a Bible study after school." Her eyes shone with excitement. "Isn't that wonderful? God took a seemingly impossible situation and turned it around."

"Good for you," Matt said. "I have a question, though. Will your students be free to discuss the Bible, or have an after-school Bible study, if this World Constitution is adopted?"

Beth's face clouded. "Probably not."

"So why don't you guys do something to stop it?"

"Like what?" asked Beth.

"Well, you could organize a letter-writing campaign at your church. You're bound to find other Christians who are against this world-control-of-everything crap."

Beth brightened. "That doesn't sound like a bad idea."

But John looked wary. "I don't know if that's the answer, Beth."

Matt rolled his eyes. "I just don't understand you, John. Why won't you fight this?"

"I just want to be sure I'm fighting the right battle. Matt, don't get me wrong, I'm not saying I support one-world government. But there are more important things at stake than the political aspects of all this. Beth and I both believe we could be living in the end-times. But we don't think God wants His people to get distracted by political battles right now. We need to focus on the spiritual battle—the battle for people's souls. We should be sharing the gospel instead of getting entangled with politics."

"Does the Bible say that Christians can't get involved in politics?" Matt asked.

John considered. "Not in so many words. But I think when Christians get overly concerned about politics, they start to lose sight of the Kingdom of God. I don't want that to happen to Beth and me."

Beth got up and opened the refrigerator. She took out a head of lettuce and some tomatoes, which she placed on the counter. Then she turned to Matt. "You know, Matt, when Jesus came, most of the Jews rejected Him because He didn't deliver Israel from the political tyranny of Rome. He could have done so, but He didn't—because our salvation was more important than mere political freedom."

"Yeah, yeah, I've heard all that before. But just because Jesus didn't come to save the Jews from Roman oppression, does that mean we can't oppose political tyranny today? I mean, isn't that doing God's will?"

"Not if it means shifting our priorities," said John.

Matt shook his head. "Can't you have more than one priority? And have you ever thought about what kind of a future you'll have if this constitution gets ratified? Think about it—once we do away with our Constitution and the Bill of Rights, the UN will be able to worm into every aspect of our lives. Have you thought about what that will mean to your future—and your children's futures? You are planning on having children, aren't you?"

For an instant, John's expression clouded. But he didn't say anything.

"If you ask me," Matt went on, "people like you are part of the problem. It really gets me that so few of you Christians are willing to stand up for yourselves. What really bothers me is that some of the mainline denominations are embracing this World Constitution. Gina tells me that her parents are big supporters of one-world government, mostly because the Pope likes the idea." He shook his head. "How can religious people be so blind?"

John looked thoughtful. "It's interesting you should say that. Did you know that Jesus accused the Pharisees, who were the religious leaders in His day, of spiritual blindness? And believe it or not, the Antichrist is going to use religion as the bait to deceive the whole world into following him."

"I don't get it. Wouldn't the Antichrist want to do away with religion?"

"Not if he wants the whole world to worship him," John said. "In fact, his most powerful henchman will be a religious leader of sorts, a false prophet. The Bible says he'll do miraculous signs and wonders that will astound the entire world. Basically, the Antichrist will be the central figure of a false religion unparalleled in all of history. It will have all the trappings of divinity, yet none of the substance."

"And all this is predicted in the Bible?"

"It sure is. You're familiar with the Book of Revelation, right?" Matt nodded. "Ever heard of the Whore of Babylon?" John asked.

Matt grinned. "Sounds like someone I used to date back in high school." They all laughed. "Actually, I have heard that phrase before. Wasn't that Jezebel?"

"No," John said. "You're thinking Old Testament."

Matt drew back in mock embarrassment. "Well, pardon me. Not everyone is as up on this Bible lingo as you are."

John smiled. "Sorry. Anyway, the Whore of Babylon, otherwise known as Mystery Babylon, appears in the Book of Revelation. She symbolizes the false religion of the end-times, which will be based on humanism and the occult."

"So she's not a real prostitute," Matt said.

"Right," said John. "She's called the mother of prostitutes because she'll seduce the entire world, at least those who reject Christ, into committing spiritual adultery by forsaking God's truth and following after everything that man has to offer instead."

"The Bible also says that she'll be drunk with the blood of the saints," Beth said, "which means that those who reject her false religion will be martyred."

Matt suddenly thought of something. "Is that what the fall of Babylon is all about?" He was certain he'd seen that expression somewhere in the Bible.

"You're very close," John said. "The fall of Babylon refers to the coming judgement of the false religious system and all its followers. You can read about that in Revelation chapter 18 or 19, I believe."

Though religious gobbledygook usually turned him off, Matt found all of this pretty interesting. "Okay, so how does the Antichrist fit into all this?"

"Initially," said John, "the Antichrist will form an alliance with Mystery Babylon. He'll have the political power but she'll have the religious power. In a way, they'll both be using each other. But ultimately, the Antichrist is going to demand that the whole world worship him. Anyone who refuses will be put to death."

"And you guys are still looking forward to all that, huh?"

Beth laughed as she finished slicing the tomatoes. "Matt, what we're looking forward to is the return of Jesus. You see, all those other terrible things have to happen before He can return."

Matt shook his head. "Wonderful!"

"By the way, have you started reading Revelation yet?" John asked.

Matt made a wry face. "I should have known that was coming. Actually, I did skim through some of it. I didn't like what I saw, though. I still can't figure out why you and Beth are so thrilled about it all."

"You must have just read the negative parts," John said with a smile.

"Yeah, I'd say famine, plagues, and natural disasters are pretty negative." He sipped his tea. "I don't know. You guys are all psyched up about the return of Christ, but I just can't get excited about things like that."

"Why do you think that is?" John asked quietly.

"Who knows? I'm just different from you, that's all. I mean, you see all this as something wonderful and exciting, and I get scared just thinking about it."

John was looking at him intently. "Did you ever think that maybe you feel that way because you're unsure of where you'll stand with Jesus when He returns?"

Matt was silent. This was one area he definitely didn't want to get into. "I don't know. This whole thing gives me the creeps. You know, I've been having nightmares lately. Sometimes almost every night."

John looked troubled. "Really? What about?"

"Weird stuff. They don't make much sense. Half the time it doesn't even seem like I'm asleep. You guys are going to think I'm nuts, but sometimes I actually hear voices at night...and I feel this frightening presence of evil." He thought about the hallucination he'd had earlier—if it *was* a hallucination. "Sometimes I even feel like someone—or something—is watching me. Isn't that crazy?"

"When did these nightmares start?" asked John.

"It's strange, but they started around the same time I started that stupid awareness course at work. Have you taken it yet?"

John nodded. "I tried to get out of it, on the basis that it conflicts with my religious beliefs. But they don't accept any excuses. I even spoke to a lawyer about it, and he said it would be pointless to fight it. Apparently the Supreme Court fully supports this practice. They claim the government has the right to mandate the course because it's for the 'common good.' At least, that's their justification for it. Anyway, the Bible exhorts us to obey those in authority, so I really had no choice."

Matt frowned. "What did you mean when you said the course conflicts with your religious beliefs?"

"Well, the whole awareness craze started out as a type of sensitivity training seminar. It was supposed to make everyone more tolerant. But nowadays, that means throwing your religious beliefs out the window. In fact, when I took the course, the instructor opened the first session by throwing a copy of the Bible on the floor and telling the class, 'There are no absolutes. Whatever your beliefs—whether you're a Christian, Jew or Muslim—forget about them.'"

Matt recalled that Gail had said similar things. He started to tell John some of what he had learned so far.

John shook his head ominously. "So, basically you're all being brainwashed into believing you can achieve your own godhood?"

Matt nodded. "Pretty much. Gail keeps telling us that God is within us, that we could do miracles if we just learned to tap into our potential or whatever. It sounds far-fetched, but I think it's harmless. It's basically just positive thinking."

"Well, I'm not sure how harmless that is," John said. "The basic premise of the course—that you can be your own god—denies the very foundation of Christianity. If we can be as gods, then why do we need the Bible, or Jesus for that matter? As a matter of fact, that's exactly how Satan tempted Eve to eat the forbidden fruit, he told her that she and Adam would be equal to God, knowing good and evil. And then, there's all that guided imagery and visualization you described—the attempt to get you into an altered state of consciousness. It's dangerous, to both Christians and non-Christians."

"How come?"

"Well, we're dealing with the spirit world here. Has your teacher talked about spirit guides yet?"

"Yeah, she said we're going to meet them during the next class." Matt laughed suddenly. "The whole thing sounds like something out of a science fiction movie!"

"Do you know what a spirit guide is?" asked John.

"I'm not really sure. Gail said they're 'ascended masters' from a higher plane of existence. It's all nonsense, if you ask me."

"I wouldn't be too sure, if I were you."

"Why? What do you think the spirit guides are?"

John looked directly into Matt's eyes. "They're demons," he said quietly.

This was too much for Matt. He burst into laughter. "Oh, come on, John, you've got to be kidding! No one believes in demons anymore. That stuff went out with the Dark Ages."

"The Bible says that demons are real," said John.

He thought about the creature he had seen earlier and how real it had appeared. But the thought that it could have been a demon was something he didn't even want to consider. It must have been his imagination playing tricks on him. "Yeah, well, the Bible says a lot of things. That doesn't mean we have to take it literally."

"Well, what about the devil? Do you take him literally?"

Matt shrugged. "I guess so. I mean, I never thought much about it."

"And what about angels—do you believe they're real?"

"I'm not sure."

"The Bible says the Angel Gabriel appeared to Mary to tell her she was going to give birth to the Messiah. Do you believe the Angel Gabriel was real?"

He hesitated. "Well...yeah."

"And what about God? Do you take God literally?"

"Of course. What's your point?"

"The point is," said John, "you do acknowledge the existence of the spirit world, right?"

"I guess." The conversation was making him feel uncomfortable. "So what are you getting at?"

"Well, if God has angels at his command," said John, "isn't it possible that the devil has certain evil beings at his command? After all, Satan was originally an archangel named Lucifer who led a rebellion against God. When he was cast out of heaven, the angels who rebelled with him were also cast out. The Bible says that one third of all the angels in heaven had joined Lucifer in his rebellion against God. Don't you think it's possible that these fallen angels are helping the devil today, trying to lure people away from God?"

Matt considered this. "I don't know. The whole concept of demons sounds pretty far-fetched to me. And what makes you so sure these spirit guides are demons—or that demons even exist, for that matter? What proof do you have, aside from the Bible?"

John looked over at Beth, who had been very quiet during the conversation. She sat down next to John, who gently squeezed her hand, and smiled weakly. "Maybe I should tell him about my experience," she said in a soft voice.

"You sure you're up to talking about it?" asked John.

She hesitated. "I think so. After all, it was a long time ago."

"You're sure?"

She forced a smile. "Yes."

Matt was curious. "What's this all about?"

She took a sip of iced tea, and her hands trembled slightly. She put down her glass. "I guess John never told you I was once heavily into the occult."

Surprised, Matt shook his head. "I thought that stuff was off-limits to Christians."

"I wasn't a Christian at the time. I had no idea what I was getting involved in. I was trying to fill a void in my life, I guess. My mom died when I was just a toddler, and my dad was an alcoholic. He was pretty abusive. By the time I got to college, I was contemplating suicide. That's when I got into spiritualism. I enrolled in a course called Modern Spirituality. It told me everything I wanted to hear. And, that's how I got hooked.

"The teacher claimed there was no death, that our loved ones who had died had simply moved on to another plane of existence. One of the topics covered was how to contact the dead. By the end of the course, I was obsessed with the desire to contact my mother. So, I bought a Ouija board." She shuddered. "That was a mistake!"

"But it's just a harmless game, isn't it?"

"Some people think of it as a game," Beth said. "But it's more than that. Much more."

Intrigued, Matt asked, "So, what is it?"

"Essentially, it's a doorway. It allows access into the spirit world. But human beings aren't supposed to make contact with that world. God specifically condemns it in the Bible."

"But why?"

"Think about it, Matt," said Beth. "In our limited, human perception, we'd have no way of knowing whether the spirits we contacted were evil. God never suggests the possibility of contacting good spirits through such means. For instance, God has angels at His command, but nowhere does the Bible say humans can summon angels. Only God can do that."

"I get it. If you try to contact a spirit being, you'd be leaving yourself vulnerable to the influence of evil spirits. Assuming you believe in that sort of thing."

"Right. And that's what happened to me." She took another sip of iced tea.

"Wait a minute. You're telling me you actually contacted evil spirits?"

"They didn't seem evil at first. I trusted them."

"How come?"

Her expression became troubled. "Because...they knew things. Things that no one else could know about me. Things I had done, and said. They also knew about people I knew, about my father, and the abuse." A tear glistened in her eye, and she wiped it away. "They were very specific, particularly about aspects of my life that I'm not very proud of. It was kind of scary, but it did lead me to trust them. I figured if they knew so much about me, they could be trusted. They weren't always accurate, but I was pretty amazed by the knowledge they seemed to possess."

Matt was fascinated. "So how did you figure out they were evil?"

"It's hard to say, really, because I didn't even want to consider the possibility that there was such a thing as evil spirits. But some of the encounters were terrifying. Sometimes I could feel a distinct presence of evil that almost paralyzed me. The room would get dreadfully cold, even in the middle of June. Once while I was using the Ouija board with some friends, the planchet flew off the board and smashed into a mirror. It really freaked us out."

"Man, this sounds bizarre!"

"Wait. It gets worse." She sighed deeply. "I started hearing a woman's voice occasionally. I thought it might be my mother, but I wasn't sure. I asked the Ouija board to reveal her identity, but the spirits said she was unknown to them. They told me the only way to find out who she was would be to enter into an altered state of consciousness...which would enable me to encounter this disembodied spirit on the astral plane. Through meditation I went into a deep, trance-like state. When I opened my eyes a beautiful woman was standing before me. She looked like an angel. She told me she was an Ascended Master who had gone through hundreds of incarnations since the time of Christ, and in her last incarnation she had been my mother. She called herself Ariel..."

"So, you actually contacted your mother's spirit?" Matt asked when Beth was silent.

Beth shook her head vigorously. "She wasn't my mother; she was masquerading as my mother. That's how demons deceive people—by posing as departed loved ones. Ariel told me I had a destiny to fulfill and that she would help me by teaching me the secrets known only to Ascended Masters such as Buddha and 'Jesus,' but she wasn't referring to the Jesus of the Bible.

"Before I realized it, I was doing everything she told me, even experimenting with mind-altering drugs like LSD in order to achieve a 'higher' state of consciousness. I wanted to learn more about the spirit world, so I read extensively about Eastern mysticism, and even got into astral projection.

I actually saw things that were happening while I was out of my body."

"How do you know they were really happening?"

"Once I saw a terrible car accident. DWI." She shivered. "Everything was so vivid—even the mangled bodies which I saw being pulled from the wreckage. The next day I was watching the news—and I saw a report on the very same accident!"

There was a faraway look in her eyes as she continued. "The deeper I got into spiritualism, the more obsessed I became. It was like a hunger that could never be satisfied. But I still felt as if something were missing from my life. I vaguely remembered that my mom used to read Bible stories to me before she passed away, but Ariel warned me not to read the Bible, she said it was filled with lies and distortions. That didn't sound right to me, but I wasn't sure why. Something told me to pray to Jesus for guidance. A week later, Ariel...changed."

"What do you mean?" Matt asked when she paused.

"She became hostile. She started saying horrible things, blasphemy, mostly. Things I can't even repeat. I began to suspect she was evil, so I asked God to reveal her true nature." Beth smiled faintly. "I didn't realize He would take my request so literally. The next time I summoned Ariel I had the most frightening experience of my life."

Matt was nearly on the edge of his seat as Beth described what she had seen. "She was standing in a field surrounded by a beam of light. Her arms were outstretched, and I had the most intense awareness of love I had ever experienced. I also had a feeling of oneness with God and the universe. As I walked toward her, I remember thinking, how can someone so beautiful be evil? Just as I was about to reach out to her, the skin started peeling off her face. I could see bones and rotting flesh. She turned into this ugly, demonic creature!"

"What?" Matt could hardly believe what he was hearing.

"Her hair turned into slithering black snakes, and her eyes became blood-red. She was making this awful hissing sound..."

She broke off, shivering, and John put his arm around her. "I screamed and the scene faded away. I was so upset that I went to a psychologist, who claimed that the vision was a manifestation of my inner fears, which were caused by low self-esteem. But I couldn't get that image out of my head. I also started having more horrible visions. They centered mostly around dead things, like decaying flesh or dead bodies. Once while I was walking through the woods near the campus, I saw dead animals all over the ground.

Occasionally, I would see a severed arm or head floating in my room at night, and glowing red eyes looking in at me from the window. I thought I was going insane. I kept hearing voices all the time, saying vile and disgusting things. Once, when I was about to enter a Christian bookstore, a voice threatened to kill me. It was terrible. I even stopped using the Ouija board, but that didn't help."

Her voice had a slight tremor. "I knew I couldn't live like this anymore. I started to fantasize about killing myself. Sometimes, I even heard voices encouraging me to do it. And one night, I decided to follow their advice."

Matt was startled. "You attempted suicide?"

"I figured that even if God existed, He would never accept me because I had broken His laws. I got in my car and planned to drive into a tree or over an embankment. I'll never forget that night. A thunderstorm was brewing. As I drove through the pouring rain, I suddenly became terrified at the thought of dying and possibly going to hell. I asked God to reveal Himself to me. I told Him I wasn't even sure if He existed, but if He did, I wanted to know Him.

"When I got back to my room, I kept hearing voices telling me that God didn't love me, my life was worthless, so I might as well kill myself. My roommate was out that night, so it would have been the perfect time. I could have used her prescription sleeping pills. I was about to swallow the entire bottle when I heard someone knocking on the door, and the voices suddenly stopped." Matt felt a chill when Beth told him who was at the door, a member of the Campus Ministry, inviting her to a Bible study!

"I couldn't believe it. At first, I just stared at her, then I said I'd think about it. I guess she noticed I had been crying, and she asked if she could help me. So, I found myself telling her everything. When I told her how hopeless my life seemed, she told me about Jesus." Tears streamed down Beth's cheeks, and she brushed them away. "Suddenly, I knew He was the answer I had been searching for all my life. I knew that He was the only one who could deliver me from the demons that were destroying my life. I prayed to accept Him as my Lord and Savior, and renounced my involvement in the occult. Naturally, Satan doesn't let his servants go without putting up a fight. I experienced some heavy demonic attack from time to time, but I learned how to rebuke the demons in Jesus' name. Eventually, they left me alone."

Silence filled the room. Matt was shaking his head. "Wow...that's some story," he finally said.

"So, I'm living proof that the spirit world is real. It's very dangerous to disobey God's Word and get involved in the occult."

"So, you really think the spirits you contacted were demons?" asked Matt. He was thinking more and more about the thing he had seen earlier in class, which had seemed pretty darn real.

John asked him, "What do you think they were?"

Matt was silent. The whole thing sounded so crazy. But he knew that Beth wasn't crazy; she and John were two of the most well-adjusted people he knew. Even though they were deeply religious, he couldn't really say they were fanatics. He wanted to say that Beth had imagined everything, but something told him that it really happened. Yet, he wanted to deny it.

"Well?" John's voice broke in on his thoughts, and he knew he had to say something.

"I don't know. I mean, if there are such things as demons..."

"There are," John insisted. "The Bible says—"

"Look, John, I'm not sure I can believe everything the Bible says." Suddenly, Matt wished he hadn't come here tonight. He had never let John draw him into talk about God or religion before, but lately that had changed. It was starting to bother him.

John apparently decided not to push it. He looked at Beth, and gently brushed a strand of hair away from her face. "You okay, sweetheart?"

"I'm fine." She smiled. "It's just a hard thing to relive." She looked at the timer above the stove. "I think dinner's ready." She kissed John on the cheek, then got up to open the oven.

"This stuff is starting to scare me," Matt said suddenly. "I mean, how do I get out of this spirit-guide crap? If they really are demons, I don't want to get near them with a ten-foot pole! But what should I do?" He didn't want to tell John about his experience earlier that night, but he definitely wanted some kind of advice.

"Well, I can tell you what I did when I was forced to take the course at work. Whenever they had us doing meditation or visualization, I focused on a verse from Scripture. I prayed to Jesus, asking Him to protect me from any demonic influences. Naturally, I refused to participate in any activity that was overtly occult. I was reprimanded for insubordination a couple of times, but God protected me. I never got fired, probably because I had just gotten tenure before the course started."

"I think that was the hand of God," Beth remarked, and John nodded.

"So, that's it?" Matt asked. "All I have to do is pray for protection?"

John frowned. "Well, it's not quite that simple. Praying won't do much good if it's not backed up by genuine faith."

"I do believe in God, you know."

"Maybe so, but did you know that the Bible says that even the devil believes in God? Believing that God exists isn't the same thing as having a trusting relationship with Him. For example, you believe that the President of the United States exists, but do you have a relationship with him? If you met him on the street, would he even know you? Of course not. In the same way you can know about Christ without knowing Christ. The only way to have real protection from demons is by accepting His gift of salvation. His shed blood is what protects His people from the forces of evil. Nothing less will do it. Now, if you'd like to accept Jesus' gift of eternal life—"

Matt rolled his eyes up. "John, we've been through this before. Why are you always trying to convert me?"

"Because I happen to care about you."

Beth placed the tray of ziti on the table. Steam rose from the browned cheese on top, and Matt's stomach growled. Why couldn't Gina make a nice meal like this once in a while? "Well, if you really care about me, you'll let me start eating some of this delicious food. I'm starved!"

They ate in silence. Matt didn't like what he had heard tonight, especially after that weird encounter he had. He didn't like the fact that he was beginning to believe what John had told him about the Bible. He wished he could shrug it off, but he knew he couldn't anymore.

* * * *

After John had returned from taking Matt home, he found Beth washing the dishes. He walked over to her, gently putting his hands on her shoulder. "I know how hard that was for you." He thought of the times she woke up screaming in the middle of the night, the sheets bathed in sweat. The insidious presence of evil which made her tremble uncontrollably. He remembered all too well. No, the demons certainly didn't give up their prey without a fight.

He hugged her closely. "Just remember, it's over."

"I know, I just wish I could forget."

John spoke gently. "You have to put it out of your mind." He shook his head suddenly. "I guess this is my fault. I should never have let you relive that nightmare."

"No, Matt needed to hear it. I just have to learn to let go of the past." She sighed. "I just wish I knew how."

"Just keep praying about it." He grabbed a greasy dish and ran it under the hot water. "I think that's something we'll be doing a lot of, especially if things go in the direction they seem to be heading." He was silent for a moment. "I'm starting to wonder if that's enough, though."

"What do you mean?"

"I was just thinking about some of the things Matt was saying earlier. You know, about how people like us are part of the problem. Things have gotten bad. They're going to get worse if this new constitution is ratified. And, we haven't done a single thing to stop that from happening."

Beth looked puzzled. "But you just told Matt that Christians shouldn't get overly concerned about politics."

He sighed. "I know what I said. But that doesn't mean I'm not concerned."

"What's gotten you so worried suddenly?"

"It's something else Matt said tonight. I think it's time we started talking about how the new constitution is going to affect our future."

"I guess you're right."

"You remember that UN Treaty on Children's Rights that was ratified in Europe? I heard it's been used in some countries to take children away from Christian parents. They're calling it 'reeducation.'"

Her eyes widened in horror. "John, if we adopt the UN Constitution, that can happen here! It can happen to us!"

His eyes met hers. "We have to be prepared."

"What will we do, John? What if we have children, and the government tries to take them away?"

"Look, there's no way of knowing if that'll ever happen. We just have to trust God, but be prepared for the worst. That is, if we even decide to have children."

Tears filled her eyes. "But how can we ever be prepared for something like that? I can't believe we're even having this conversation!"

He wished he could tell her that everything would be all right, that nothing bad would ever happen to them, or their children. But he couldn't make such a promise. That's what killed him. It sometimes ate away at him, waking him up in the middle of the night. He had promised to love and protect her, but he might not be able to protect her if things went in the direction they seemed to be heading.

"I'm scared, John," she told him.

"I know," he said softly. "I'm scared, too. But we have to trust Jesus. You know He'll get us through anything that happens. Even if the government does take our children away, God can still take care of them."

"I know that, John. But that won't make it any easier if it happens. Maybe we shouldn't even have children." Her tone was resentful.

He reached for another dirty dish. "Is that what you want?"

"You know I want children. But not if we're going to lose them."

John frowned as he scrubbed the casserole dish with a soapy sponge. He wished he hadn't had to bring the subject up. He hated to do anything to cause Beth unhappiness, but he felt he had no choice; the issue had been troubling him for quite a while now, and it was time they both faced their fears—and got beyond them. Just last month, a couple they were friendly with at church had a baby; John had seen the longing in Beth's eyes when she held the baby for the first time. He knew then that they had to discuss this matter soon.

He turned to face her, his tone gentle but firm. "Beth, we have to trust God. How do you know that our children won't be God's witnesses during the coming persecution? If we do have children, we have to put them in God's hands."

"I don't know if I can do that, John."

"Well, until you feel you can do that, we should hold off on having children. Remember the parable of the king who wanted to go to war? Well, we're probably going to be involved in some heavy spiritual battles soon. If we're going to remain faithful to Christ during these difficult times, we have to count the cost."

"You're right. But losing our children...how could we ever face something like that?" Her voice sounded so sad that John almost felt like crying himself. "Now I understand why Jesus said the tribulation will be hardest on women with small children." She brightened suddenly. "But maybe we won't have to worry about that. If the Rapture comes first—"

"I'm not sure we should be counting on that, Beth."

She cocked her head to one side. "What do you mean?"

"Well, it bothers me that so many Christians are depending on that escape route. How sure are we that it's going to happen? And, what if it *doesn't* happen?" His eyes were downcast. "How many believers will lose their faith?"

She turned away with a shudder. "It *has* to. God's Word promises..."

"Where, Beth? Where does the Bible actually say that Jesus will return secretly to remove all Christians from the earth, *before* He comes a *third* time to judge sinners?"

She groped for the answer. "I think in Matthew. Didn't Jesus say something about one being taken, while another would be left?"

He considered this. "Hmm. That *could* refer to the Rapture. Or, it could simply mean the separation of saints and sinners at the last judgement. And look at 2 Thessalonians. It clearly says that the 'man of lawlessness' will be revealed *prior* to our being gathered to meet Christ in the air."

She folded her arms. "I just can't believe God would allow His people to live through the reign of the Antichrist!"

"Why not? He allows Christians all over the world to be tortured and murdered for their faith." A heavy silence settled between them. "There's something even more serious to consider."

"What's that?"

"We need to decide what it is we're putting our faith in. Is it our Lord Jesus, or the so-called 'promise' of the Rapture?"

He could see by her expression he was getting through to her. "I never thought of it that way."

John started drying some of the clean dishes, passing them to Beth, who put them in the cabinet. "Besides, even if the Rapture does come before the Tribulation, we may still face some heavy persecution before that. I've been facing some at work lately."

"You too?"

"Yeah. I was going to tell you before, but Matt called, and I got distracted. Something interesting happened at work today."

"What happened?"

"I was reprimanded for keeping a Bible on my desk."

"What? I can't believe this!"

"Well, it's true. I've been ordered to keep it 'out of sight.'"

"But why?"

"Apparently the chairman was scared by some news reports about Christians being sued by their colleagues for 'harassment.' In one case, all the harassment amounted to was encouraging a bereaved coworker to trust in God. It hasn't happened where I work, but you know how it is. People are leery these days."

"But why should your chairman care if you get sued?"

"He says he doesn't want any strife at the workplace. It's insane. The Bible is the world's most renowned work of literature, and I can't even keep it on my desk in the English Department! Next thing you know, they'll be calling it hate literature or something. You know, I'm starting to wonder if Matt's right. Maybe we should try to stop this, if there's even a chance."

Beth sighed. "I don't know. Remember what Perry said last week at the Bible study?"

"I know, I know. He said that part of being salt and light means we have to submit to whatever government happens to be ruling us, no matter how evil it is."

"Do you think Perry's wrong?"

He shrugged. "Last week, I thought he was right. Now, I'm not so sure. Is it possible for Christians to oppose tyranny without losing their priorities?"

"It's hard to say. What if the apostles had decided to fight Roman oppression instead of spreading the gospel? Where would the church be today?"

"There would be no church." But he was thinking again about what Matt had said, about how people like John were part of the problem. Usually he didn't get defensive, but that comment had bothered him. He tried to put it out of his mind.

* * * *

Matt was sitting on the couch with the Bible in his hands. Since the nightmares began, he had been reading it from time to time, usually late at night when he couldn't sleep. He had read enough to believe that many world events now unfolding could be signs of Christ's return. What scared him were the things that would happen first. He remembered Beth once saying something about Jesus coming to take people to heaven before the Tribulation. At the time, he thought it was a ploy to get him to convert. But what if it *did* happen? Would he be among those left behind? And if it *didn't* happen, what then? What if he became a Christian, and still had to live through all the suffering and persecution he had read about in Revelation? He shuddered at the thought.

He believed that Jesus was the Son of God, the Messiah, and all that. But John had told him it wasn't enough simply to believe; you had to make a commitment—you had to make Jesus Lord of your life. Matt sighed; he just didn't think he was ready for that. He had too many other problems to deal with right now. And he knew that Gina would think he was nuts; she already thought John and Beth were fanatics.

Why did it have to be so hard? Why couldn't God just accept him the way he was and not demand change? He didn't want to "take up the cross," to give his all to Jesus. He would have to be willing to give up everything. He shook his head. Much too hard. He knew that at least right now, he couldn't cut it. He wasn't like John and Beth. He had recently read the parable about the rich young fool, who couldn't bring himself to follow Jesus because of what he would have to give up. *Maybe I'm like that.* Obviously not rich, but maybe selfish. Like his parents always said. For a long time, he had resented the accusation. But since he had started reading the Bible, he was starting to see things about himself that he could never face before.

When his father had lost the business, Matt remembered thinking, "Now what the hell am I going to do with my life?" It wasn't until after he had agonized over his own feelings of loss that he had even considered what it had done to his father, who had poured his money and blood and sweat into the business for over thirty years, only to see it go under.

He heard the door being unlocked, and Gina walked in carrying a large paper bag. The smell of fast food wafted through the apartment. "Matt, I'm so sorry!" She put the bag down on the kitchen table.

He got up and followed her into the kitchen. "Yeah, you're always sorry. Well, guess what, Gina? I'm sick of hearing it." He saw that she was unpacking the bag of food. "Nice try, but I already ate."

"Don't you want a little?"

"No, I had a huge meal at John and Beth's."

"Fine." She stuffed the wrapped burgers back into the bag.

"Aren't you going to have some?" he asked.

"Actually, I really don't feel like eating."

"So why did you waste your money on that garbage?"

She rolled her eyes, a habit which had always annoyed him. "Because I wanted...forget it. Just forget it."

From her tone he could tell something else was bothering her, and he felt bad for being so hard on her. "Look, I'm sorry I overreacted. Are you okay?"

"No, I'm not okay. I just went through hell covering a riot where I was assaulted by some thug."

His eyes widened. "What? Why didn't you tell me?"

"I didn't want to upset you. Anyway, I wasn't seriously hurt. The cops came just in time."

He put his arms around her and pulled her close. "I'm sorry for being such a jerk. I had no idea what you had gone through."

They brought the food into the living room and sat on the couch as she told him about the riot. He was startled when she told him she was dragged into the middle of it. "See? See how important it is to be able to protect yourself? I wish you'd carry that pepper spray I got you."

She sighed. "Maybe I should. But I don't like the idea that it's illegal."

"What difference does that make? Isn't your own safety more important than obeying some stupid law?"

"Maybe. But I could get in trouble if I use it."

He laughed. "You know, that just proves how screwed up this country is. *You* can get in trouble for defending yourself against some monster who's trying to kill you. Right is wrong and wrong is right. This country has gone off the deep end."

"Well, a lot of things don't make sense. You know, the police wouldn't come until I threatened them with a front page story about their refusal to protect those poor people who were being harassed." She dug into her cheeseburger while Matt debated whether he should tell her about his conversation with John and Beth. Well, it couldn't hurt.

"You know, I had kind of an interesting evening myself," he told her.

"At your brother's? What could be interesting about being over there?"

"Very funny." He knew that Gina didn't think very much of John and Beth. Not that she actually disliked them, she just felt she had nothing in common with them. Matt had always wanted her to get to know them better, so he once suggested she go out to lunch with Beth. Afterwards, Gina complained that Beth had tried to convert her. Like Matt, she had always hated having religion shoved down her throat. The world would be a lot more peaceful if people just kept quiet about religion, she often said. He couldn't deny he felt the same way.

"So, what happened tonight that tops my story?" she asked when Matt was silent.

"You're probably not going to believe this," he began.

When he had finished, Gina said flatly, "You're right, I don't believe it."

"Look, I know it sounds crazy, but I know she wouldn't lie about something like that. And I don't think she imagined it."

"What makes you so sure? After all, you said she was seeing a shrink. Maybe she had schizophrenia."

He leaned back against the sofa, looking at her cautiously. They were treading on dangerous ground. "Gina, don't you believe in anything supernatural?"

She stared absently at her plate. "I guess so, to a point. I do believe in some sort of Supreme Being, if that's what you mean."

"Do you believe in Jesus?"

The question seemed to startle her. Matt had never mentioned Jesus before. At least, not to her. "Why do you ask?"

"Just curious. You were brought up Catholic, so I kind of assumed you believe in Him."

She considered this. "Well, I believe He once walked this earth and died on a cross. I guess I'd say He was a great teacher. But I don't understand why some Christians, like John and Beth, go to such extremes. I mean, what's the big deal?"

He shrugged. "I don't know."

"Anyway, why did you bring this up?"

He was looking away from her. "I don't know. I guess talking with John and Beth got me...thinking."

She laughed nervously. "I hope that doesn't mean they converted you."

He smiled. "Yeah, right. It'll take a lot more than a spooky story about demons to do that." He wanted to lighten the mood, but he still felt awkward. Why was it so difficult to talk to his wife about such an important subject?

* * * *

He was dreaming again. He was in an open field, surrounded by dozens of people. Some of them were friends he had lost touch with, or acquaintances from work. It was like some kind of strange reunion. He was about to ask what was going on, when suddenly they all vanished. For a moment he just stared. Where had they gone?

On the ground where they had been standing he saw huge, black holes. Gray smoke rose out of each hole, and an awful sound of crying and moaning drifted upward from the blackness below. He thought he could even hear screaming.

A hole began to open up beneath him, and he knew that he too would be sucked down into the blackness. Just before the hole had opened up all the way, he fell, landing with both his feet on the edge of the hole, his hands on the opposite edge. All he could see beneath him was blackness. Icy terror gripped him; he knew that if he fell in, there would be no way out...not ever.

He tried desperately to hold on, but felt himself being drawn into the pit. Somehow, he knew that it was there for him. The voices seemed louder now, and he thought he saw a trace of red or orange far below. *What the hell is happening?* He was growing tired of holding on, could feel his legs buckling. *Can't...hold on...much longer.* From somewhere down below, he heard raspy, inhuman laughter. They were waiting for him...

He awoke just as he was about to fall in. Breathing heavily, he looked around the room, flooded in dim moonlight. *It was only a dream,* he told himself. The back of his neck felt clammy with perspiration, and his heart was beating rapidly. He was shivering, even though the room wasn't cold. *What the hell is happening to me?* This wasn't normal. He looked over at Gina, lying in the shadows, her graceful arm stretched across the pillow between them.

He wished he could tell her his fears. But she wouldn't understand. To her, hell was just a myth conjured up by preachers to scare people into going to church. For many years, he had tried to convince himself she was right. But deep inside, he feared that hell was real. He couldn't deny it any longer.

There were a lot of things in his life he'd have to change if he ever wanted to get serious about God. Though he hadn't cheated since he and Gina were living together, he still felt tempted. He hadn't realized to what extent until that bizarre encounter during Gail's class. From time to time he bought pornographic magazines, which he hid in the bottom of his junk drawer. He hoped Gina never opened it.

He often told himself that these weren't serious offenses. After all, it's not as if he had ever killed anyone. Still, he couldn't shake off the fear his dream had aroused—the fear that if he died tonight, a descent into eternal darkness awaited him.

He pulled the pillow over his face, and tried to get back to sleep. It was a long time before sleep finally came.

CHAPTER 6

Gina stood in Ken's office, holding a copy of the morning edition in her hand. He was having a hard time meeting her gaze. "Who the hell wrote this garbage?" she demanded.

He fidgeted with some papers on his desk. "Look, Gina, I know this isn't the story you expected to see—"

"You bet it isn't! I'd like to know which re-write idiot is responsible for this white-washing. I can't believe you let anyone get away with this. You know this isn't what I phoned in last night."

He realized he would have to be firm with her. "Gina, I want you to sit down and listen to me," he said. She sat down on a chair opposite his desk.

"I don't like this anymore than you do," he told her. "But things are different here now. There's a new publisher, and he wants things done a certain way. If I printed the story the way you gave it to me, he wouldn't like it."

"Why not? I was just reporting what happened."

Ken sighed. "I know that. Unfortunately, the truth doesn't matter to a lot of people—their political agenda is more important. That's especially the case with many of the people who own newspapers today. Even the language you used in the story was objectionable, by the owner's standards. Remember that memo I sent out the other day?"

Gina frowned. "I was hoping it was a joke."

"I wish it were. But it came right from the publisher." The memo listed over fifty "offensive" words and phrases prohibited from use in reporters' stories or articles, and even in advertisements. Most of the words didn't seem the least bit offensive to Ken or the rest of the staff, and he knew they all wondered how they could avoid using them when reporting the news. "Conspiracy" and "government cover-up" were listed among the objectionable words. "If you want to look for a job at another paper, where they do things the way you want them done, I'll write you an excellent recommendation. But if you want to stay here, you'll have to abide by the new policies. I'm sorry, but that's how it is."

"But this story is nearly a total lie—all the important details were left out!" she exclaimed. "It's worse than censorship!" He almost cringed at that.

"Gina, both our jobs are on the line. Don't you think that I'd fight this if I could? The owner would fire me in a minute if I refused to print a story the way he wants it printed. I don't blame you for being upset. In fact, I'd understand completely if you wanted to leave. I'd leave, if I thought I could find work at a newspaper where things were different. But the only independent newspapers around anymore are the village weeklies, which pay next to nothing, and it's just part time work. I hate to put it this way, but all I can say is: like it or leave it."

She looked depressed. "I guess I don't have much choice. I need this job, too." With that, she walked out of the office.

It was time for her break, and she was glad. For once, she didn't feel like working at all. She sat in the employee lounge, reading the story about last night's riot, buried somewhere on page twenty-five.

VICTIMS OF RELIGIOUS BIGOTRY FIGHT BACK

Right-wing fundamentalists were the target of a protest last night at an evangelical church in Long Island, where Father Patrick Flannery, a radical Neo-Nazi, was scheduled to speak. The protestors, a majority of whom were oppressed minorities, appeared to be reacting to violent rhetoric addressed to homosexuals and Jews by Flannery, who was charged with hatecrime after a riot he allegedly started in Eisenhower Park last month. The group's spokesperson...

She couldn't even read the rest of it. Most of the details were omitted, and there was no hint of how peaceful the victims were or how dangerous the "protestors" were. Not even a word about their attacking a reporter! Her interviews with Angelina Martinez and the pastor had been scrapped. But what bothered her even more was the biased language. Even though she didn't share Father Flannery's views, she knew he wasn't a Neo-Nazi. But labeling him as such was the perfect way to discredit him, she realized. And of course, labeling those thugs as "oppressed minorities" would elicit sympathy for them. She couldn't believe that this could happen at her paper. She thought about the way Matt always complained about political correctness. For the first time, she understood how he felt. She let out a heavy sigh. *This could have been a great story*, she thought dismally. Perfect for the front page. She took the paper and crumpled it up, tossing it into a wastebasket. She might as well not have covered it.

"Having a bad day?" Gina looked up, and saw a friend of hers from another department standing in front of her table. Her name was Cheryl Hendricks, and she usually covered stories from Manhattan. Although they didn't see eye-to-eye on everything, Gina couldn't help admiring her. Unlike the rest of their colleagues who refused to challenge the new editorial policies, Cheryl had actually filed a grievance against the company, charging them with censorship.

Gina forced a smile. "I guess you could say that. I covered a great story last night, and it was cut to pieces."

"You're lucky it was even printed. I covered a big story last week, and Ken said he couldn't print it unless I changed it. But I didn't feel like distorting the facts, so it didn't get printed."

"Sit down and tell me about it."

"I was driving around the city, listening to my police scanner, and I heard something about a gun-shot fatality on the lower east side. A woman had shot and killed an intruder who was planning to rape her. She called the police, and—get this—she was arrested, and wasn't let out of jail for over twenty-four hours!"

"But didn't the police know she killed the guy in self-defense?"

Cheryl shrugged. "I don't think that matters anymore. There was a big to-do over whether or not the gun was illegal, and they claimed they had to keep her in jail until they had done a thorough investigation. I still don't even know whether the gun was illegal, but they confiscated it and when they finally released her, she had to agree to undergo a mandatory psychiatric evaluation and counseling." Her blue eyes flashed with anger. "It's sick, the way the government wants women to be unarmed and defenseless. She had every right to shoot that monster."

"So, why did the story get canned?"

"Evidently, Whitaker thought it was too controversial, and would make the NYPD look bad."

"So what?"

"Ken said it's bad P.R. At least, that's what he was told." She put special emphasis on the last word, arousing Gina's curiosity.

"What do you mean? You think there's another reason it wasn't printed?"

Cheryl brushed a stray lock of blonde hair away from her face. "Ever since the paper changed hands, this kind of stuff has been happening all the time. You and I aren't the only ones. It seems that freedom of the press has gone up in smoke here. I'm trying to find out why."

"How?"

"I've been taking notes on stories that have been canned or distorted, trying to see if there's a pattern." She lowered her voice somewhat. "I'm also curious about this Damien Whitaker. I plan on doing a little digging into his background." Damien Whitaker was the new publisher. She looked at Gina cautiously.

Gina understood her friend's concern. "Don't worry. I'll keep my mouth shut. I'd like to get to the bottom of this myself."

"I'll keep you posted." Cheryl downed the rest of her coffee and went back to work.

Gina reflected on what Cheryl had said. Could Damien be running the paper according to some secret agenda? And why would he want to censor a story about an attack on a church? She was beginning to sense that the newspaper business was a world of dark secrets that she could hardly fathom.

* * * *

Damien Whitaker didn't want to be late for his first meeting of the United Nations Arms Control and Disarmament Agency, which convened at nine o'clock sharp. He arrived a few minutes early and sat down.

Jack Denning, the President's National Security Advisor, was there, along with Attorney General Joyce Spencer and the newly appointed Director of the U.S. Arms Control Project, Arlene Hollister. The UN's Secretary General, a well-built man in his early fifties, sat at the head of the table, going over his notes. There were a few foreign dignitaries Damien didn't recognize.

He sat unobtrusively at the farthest end of the table, trying to follow everything and feeling overwhelmed in such a prestigious assembly. Oren had invited him to the meeting, which was evidently to be an initiation of sorts. It was time he learned more about the inner workings of the Council, Oren had said, and this meeting would be the ideal way to show him.

At the moment, Arlene Hollister was speaking. Her ash blonde hair was cut in a bob, and her blue eyes had an intense expression. "Our goal is nothing less than total civilian disarmament. Therefore, the United Nations must support any initiative related to disarmament, such as the seizure and destruction of weapons, including weapons turn-in programs in member nations." She glanced at her notes. "I am pleased to acknowledge that the United States has been a leader in such efforts, specifically in Africa, Eastern

Europe, and Latin America, where the U.S. military has assisted in the destruction of weapons stockpiles among private citizens. Unfortunately, the United States still lags behind the rest of the international community in curtailing the possession of firearms among its own citizens, mostly due to efforts of extremist pro-gun lobbying groups. However, once the U.S. military comes under the control of the UN, our task will become much easier." She looked over at Joyce and frowned. "Ms. Spencer, I understand you recently met with the President to discuss this matter."

Joyce cleared her throat and adjusted her eyeglasses slightly. She had short, dark hair and a stocky build. "Yes. Although the President insists on trying to appease the gun lobby with his flag-waving rhapsodies on the Second Amendment, he's actually on our side." It was no secret that the conservative-leaning President had chosen a radical liberal as his Attorney General, to fulfill his promise to create an administration that reflected "the diversity which made this country great." Damien imagined that the two must clash on a number of issues, and wondered how they could possibly work in harmony.

The Secretary General cut in, and Damien noticed his thick Russian accent. "With all due respect, madam, I find that hard to believe. Isn't it true that he was elected President with the full backing of your country's gun lobby?"

"That doesn't mean anything," Jack Denning said. "Those fools will finance just about any Republican candidate simply because they know that none of the third-party candidates who support their right-wing agenda have even a remote chance of getting elected. Since the Republican Party has traditionally championed the private ownership of firearms, however ill-advised, any candidate who runs on the Republican ticket knows he has to give lip-service to the gun lobby. It's all part of the game. But be assured, Mr. Secretary, that the President fully supports our cause."

Joyce nodded vigorously. "That's exactly the assurance I received in our recent meeting. The President is no fool. He knows that if he were to publicly support the type of gun-control legislation necessary for world order, he would risk alienating millions of armed Americans who could pose a serious threat to our plans. We cannot afford to agitate these people. Our best strategy is to lull them into complacency. Instead of focusing our efforts on new legislation, we would be wise to deal with those who refuse to obey existing gun-control laws."

"The best way to approach that problem is through the media." Oren looked at his brother-in-law. "That's where you come in, Damien. We need the media to promote the ideal of total personal disarmament, to the point where owning a firearm becomes socially unacceptable, even dangerous."

Damien was startled at the sudden attention. "Well, I've already been working on that—"

Oren cut him off. "Good, but we need to see more of an effort on your part. Use your imagination—if you have any. You might start by running full-page ads with the BWC's 1-800 number to report illegal gun owners." The BWC, or Bureau of Weapons Control, was a more militant offshoot of the Bureau of Alcohol, Tobacco, and Firearms.

"That's an excellent idea," Arlene chimed in.

Damien was about to make a retort when Oren looked over at the Secretary General, who appeared to be half listening to Oren's conversation. "Mr. Secretary, perhaps you can let us know some of the plans the UN is working on in this area."

He pulled on his moustache and glanced at some papers in front of him. "The UN has plans to implement gun buy-back programs in all of the member nations. People will have the opportunity to turn in their guns for VCRs, DVD players, and concert tickets, or even food and clothing. These programs will be modeled on our pilot project in Albania, which was aimed at the voluntary surrender of firearms by civilians in exchange for community development assistance."

"Good." Oren looked at Damien again. "We need to play this up in the newspapers. In fact, you should run some editorials promoting the programs as a great success."

"But what if they aren't?" Damien asked. "Do you honestly believe that violent criminals and druglords will turn in their weapons just to get a few handouts?"

Oren shook his head disdainfully. "Damien, haven't you learned by now that this meeting is not about disarming petty criminals? We need to get guns out of the hands of those who could stand in the way of our plans for world order. That includes all people who have excessive loyalty to their religion, families, or country—or who cherish the selfish and out-dated notion of individual liberty. Those are the people most likely to resist us."

Joyce wore a determined expression. "It's time Americans got over their pathological obsession with guns! During our meeting, the President and I consulted with the director of the Bureau of Weapons Control. We're planning on starting an amnesty program for those willing to turn in unlicensed handguns and semi-automatic assault weapons. At the same time, I'll have the Justice Department crack down on those who refuse to turn them in voluntarily."

Oren appeared satisfied. "Good. People who are illegally stockpiling guns need to see what happens to those who get caught. If all goes well, by the time the new constitution is ratified, the majority of Americans will be disarmed."

"I wouldn't be too optimistic if I were you," Arlene put in. "There's no way of knowing how many people are in possession of unregistered firearms."

"There are ways of finding out," Joyce said. "But we have to be patient. That new mandate handed down by the National Board of Education should help."

"What mandate?" Arlene asked.

Jack smiled knowingly. "The one which requires all schools to have every student fill out a questionnaire on violence in the home. The students are asked whether anyone in their family owns a firearm."

Arlene looked pleased. "Will the BWC have access to the answers?"

"Of course," Joyce replied. "The Bureau has been in the process of creating a national database of firearms owners for some time now. Those questionnaires are being used in identifying people who own unregistered firearms, and we will simply add their names to the database."

"And once the new constitution is ratified," Oren said, "we can go after legal firearms."

The Secretary General frowned. "It's a shame that the disarmament treaty was not ratified by your Senate. Then we wouldn't have to do this so slowly. Private ownership of firearms would already be illegal in America."

Joyce's eyes flashed with anger. "We can blame that on the gun lobby! The Senate just caved in to their pressure. I can't wait to put those gun nuts out of business!"

"We may just yet," Oren said. "If the Lobbying Reform Act goes through, all lobbying groups will have to register with the federal government, which then will have the power to decide which lobbies can receive licenses. But, we have to be very careful in how we proceed with our disarmament strategy. It's essential to make the gun nuts, as Ms. Spencer so aptly called them, look like villains. That's where the media comes in." He sipped his coffee. "I'm sure they'll do an excellent job."

An indignant voice broke in on them suddenly, startling everyone in the room. "You mean like they did in Texas when government agents murdered more than a hundred gun owners and their children?"

Oren turned slowly, looked at the figure standing in the doorway, and smiled coldly. "Ross...what a surprise," he said smoothly. *Perhaps too smoothly*, Damien thought. "We thought you weren't coming."

Senator Ross Meyers frowned. He was an unassuming man in his early sixties, slight of build, with sallow skin and receding gray hair. "I'd like to know why I wasn't informed of this meeting." Damien glanced at his membership roster. Sure enough, Ross was a member of the Arms Control Project—as well as the Council for Global Unity.

"I'm sure it was an oversight. In any case, now that you're here, please sit down."

"Thank you." Ross looked directly at Oren. "I believe you were discussing the media."

Tension filled the room. A few people shifted uncomfortably in their chairs. Damien watched, fascinated. Ross had committed an egregious blunder. Yet Oren remained composed. "Yes...we were stressing the media's vital role in promoting personal disarmament. I'm sure you realize that private ownership of firearms poses a great threat to public safety, and is also an obstacle to achieving world peace."

Before Ross could respond, Arlene spoke up. "We need to eliminate violence everywhere—in our own communities as well as across the globe." To Damien, her words sounded mechanical and rehearsed.

Ross's face flushed. "Is that why the government murdered innocent women and children in Texas?"

Joyce scowled at him "Those people were hardly innocent. They were armed and dangerous!"

"Really? Tell me, Ms. Spencer, were those children armed and dangerous? Those children who were first gassed and then burned to death—"

"Those fanatics started the fire themselves," Joyce retorted.

"Oh? You're telling me that pumping CS military gas—banned by international treaty—into the building and then ramming a tank through the walls had nothing to do with the fire? CS gas is highly flammable in confined spaces. Any official responsible for that massacre must have known that."

Arlene's expression softened. "Those people had plenty of opportunities to give themselves up. It didn't have to end that way, Ross. Our government did what it had to. Those people had to be stopped. They were stockpiling assault weapons. They were abusing their own children."

He pulled a manilla folder out of his leather briefcase and slammed it onto the table. "That's a lie! If you want to know the truth, take a look at these FOIA files."

Damien strained to see the papers Ross spread out on the table. Some pages were completely blacked out. Most weren't.

Ross thrust a sheet into Arlene's hands. She glanced down at them, her brow furrowed. Puzzled, she turned to Oren. "It says here that the cult was cleared of the child abuse charges before the attack. I wasn't aware of that."

Ross nodded triumphantly. "Most Americans weren't. That's why they supported the atrocity." His eyes narrowed as he looked at Oren. "Fortunately, the Freedom of Information Act is still in effect. A reporter gave me these files. I must say, they are very enlightening."

Oren appeared unruffled. "Oh?"

"I believe the people who perished in that fire were deliberately murdered," Ross said.

Oren shook his head, his expression sympathetic. "Now, Ross, I certainly can't deny that the episode may have been mishandled. But to suggest murder—"

"Look at the facts. Since the FBI had cut off the church's electricity, the families inside were forced to use lanterns."

Arlene raised an eyebrow. "A fire could start very easily under such conditions."

Ross nodded sadly. "The government also cut off the building's water supply, making it impossible for the inhabitants to put out the fire. The FBI refused to allow any fire trucks to come through once the blaze started. On top of all that, the illegal weapons charges were based on a fraudulent search warrant. More recent evidence indicates that the government actually used incendiary devices against the helpless individuals who were trapped within the church's walls."

Jack Denning's lips twisted into a sneer. "What a dramatic story, Ross. Too bad only conspiracy theorists will believe it."

Ross shook his head. "It's not a story. It's the truth. An ugly truth that our elected leaders have swept under the carpet." Ross scanned the faces at the table. "Some of you may think you want what's best for humanity. You may have convinced yourselves that the end justifies the means. The families who died as a result of our government's actions were known to profess politically incorrect views. They were singled out for that reason."

Jack pulled out his pipe and pushed it between his teeth. He fumbled for a book of matches. "They were scum. People like that pose a direct threat to safety and order. They got what they deserved."

Ross stared at Jack. "How can you say that?"

Oren spoke calmly. "Ross, I understand your compassion over the fate of those children. However, we must keep in mind that protecting the public good involves sacrifice. Some individuals must be sacrificed for the cause of peace. Often, this involves making unpleasant decisions. You knew that when you decided to help us implement our plans for world order. Do you wish to renounce your commitment?" He looked around the table, and his voice took on a distinctly harsh note. "Do *any* of you wish to forsake our cause?"

Damien noticed that Arlene had lowered her eyes.

Oren looked at Ross with a fixed gaze. "Well, Ross? What's your answer? Will you be leaving our ranks?"

Ross blanched. "No, of course not. When I joined the Council, I was totally committed to its vision of world peace. My commitment has never wavered. It's just that—"

"What?" Oren asked him quietly.

He took a deep breath, but said nothing. He appeared to be having difficulty concentrating.

"Are you feeling well?"

He stared. Someone in the room coughed. He blinked, regained his composure. "Yes, I'm fine," he said absently. "Just a little tired." He looked at the people seated around the table. They were all staring at him. He glanced at this watch. "I think I should leave now."

Oren smiled. "That's a good idea. Perhaps you've been working too hard."

"Yes." Ross mumbled an apology, turned and left the room.

Damien just sat there, wondering what had happened to Senator Meyers.

* * * *

David could smell the liquor on his mother's breath the minute he got near her. Of course, she had hid the bottle of vodka behind the cleaning supplies in back of the cabinet under the sink, as if he didn't know. She swayed slightly, holding onto the kitchen counter for support. David felt sick.

"Where were you all afternoon?" she demanded.

He looked at her, startled at how tired she appeared. She was a short woman with long black hair worn in a bun, and a pale, haggard face. Her faded blue jeans had holes at the knee.

He took off his denim jacket and tossed it onto a coat peg on the wall.

"Out."

She looked at him suspiciously. "Where?"

"At...Mike's house."

"Oh, really? Then why did Mike call here asking if you were home?" Her words were slightly slurred. "You were at Grandpa's, weren't you?" He didn't answer. Her voice rose, shrill and hysterical. "I thought I told you never to go there again!"

"Come on, Mom, he stopped by my school at dismissal today. What was I supposed to do, tell him to get lost? He's my grandfather! And he's *your* father. Can't you forget what happened? He didn't mean any harm." He walked past her into the kitchen, putting his school books down on the table. His mother followed him.

"Didn't mean any harm? How can you say that? He wants to give you a gun, a violent weapon, and you say he didn't mean any harm! What if Josh got it into his head that *he* wanted to play with the gun, and somehow got hold of it? What do you think would have happened?"

"Nothing," David said sharply. "Because Grandpa doesn't keep any of his guns loaded, and the bullets are in a place Josh wouldn't find them. Grandpa would never let Josh near his guns."

"David, he's just a little boy! He can't possibly know enough to keep away from guns. You know how kids are—they're curious about things that are off limits. Do you know how many children are killed each year playing with guns?"

David sighed. "No, I don't know. But Grandpa says that more kids are killed in car accidents than playing with guns. Does that mean we should ban cars or keep kids from riding in them?"

"You're comparing apples to oranges."

"Oh? Then what about knives? Josh has much easier access to your kitchen knives than to Grandpa's guns—"

She slapped him across the face. "Don't you talk back to me!"

Stunned, David turned away. He didn't want her to see the tears that stung his eyes. But he couldn't give up; he had to convince her that his grandfather didn't pose a threat. After losing his dad, he couldn't lose his grandfather too. "Mom, if parents are responsible and take the proper precautions with their guns, then I'm sure their children won't play with them. Didn't Grandpa own guns while you were growing up?"

She shrugged, looking down at the floor. "Yeah. But that doesn't mean we have to."

"But the point is, he was always careful with them, right? I mean, he never let you near them while you were a little kid, did he?"

"No. Not until I was in my teens. He took me target shooting a few times." She sat down at the table and put her head in her hands.

"Then why do you hate guns so much?"

"Because...I've learned how dangerous they are."

"Really? You grew up in a household with guns and managed to survive." His tone was sarcastic, but he didn't care anymore.

"Don't talk to me that way!"

"Mom, I just don't get it. I mean, you grew up around guns. What made you so afraid of them?"

"If you must know, it was my political science professor at Berkeley. He said that if you give someone a gun, it's like giving him a drug. Eventually, he gets addicted. I don't want to see that happen to you."

"You sure don't have very much faith in me."

"Look, I didn't mean it that way. I just want to protect you. No son of mine is going to own a gun. As far as I'm concerned, only the police and the military should have guns. The world would be a lot safer then."

"But, Mom—"

"David, I don't want to discuss this any further!"

"Okay, but why punish Grandpa? All he did was show me the gun. He promised not to let me see it again, right? We can't keep him out of our lives forever."

She looked at him sadly. "Did you tell him you can't see him anymore?"

David frowned. "I didn't have the heart. Mom, I love Grandpa. Ever since Dad left, he's the closest thing I have to a father. Why don't you want me to see him?"

She looked down at the table. "You just don't understand. He knew how I felt about guns, but he just didn't care. I don't like the idea of you hanging around Grandpa's apartment, with all those guns he owns. It just isn't safe."

"But he keeps them locked up!"

"I don't care. I don't want you near them. If he's willing to get rid of them, then I'll reconsider. But until then, you're not to go there anymore." She got up from the table. "I'm going to start supper. Do you have any homework?"

"A little," he said glumly, looking down at the floor.

"Then you'd better get started on it," she said. David gathered up his books, and went into the bedroom he shared with his brother Josh. He had a project to do for the Student Unity Corps, and was hoping to make lieutenant this semester.

Josh was sitting on his bed, looking dejected. His favorite cartoon, "The Planet Guardians," was on now, but he didn't even have the TV on.

"Hey, what's the matter, kid?" David asked.

"Something happened in school today. I think I'm gonna get in trouble." His large brown eyes were wide with fear.

David sat next to him on the bed. "Want to tell me about it?"

Josh shook his head, hugging his knees against his chest. "I don't wanna talk about it."

David got up from the bed and patted Josh on the head. "Well, I'll be at the desk doing some homework. If you change your mind, let me know."

"Thanks." Josh reached over and grabbed a comic book from the night table.

David looked at the outline for the project he was planning. The Student Unity Corps was open to all students from grade school through high school. Students who joined the group got extra credit for participating in activities or projects that promoted world peace. The higher you moved in rank, the more credit you received. David had just applied for membership this month and hoped to make captain by the end of the year. He read the suggestions listed under the section, "Drama and Role-Playing." Each suggestion had a specific threat to world peace, with directions to write and produce a skit illustrating how he would solve that problem. He considered the first problem. "A group of violent, fundamentalist Christians carrying guns have barged into your classroom. They force you and all your classmates to stand against the wall. They promise to spare your lives only if you convert to Christianity. How would you respond to them? Write a short skit illustrating how you would try to persuade them that they are wrong to force you to become a Christian." That sounded interesting. He was sure he could write a good script for such a skit. He knew that a lot of his friends would be interested in taking part in it.

David wasn't really sure what a fundamentalist was. He knew one or two students who went to church, so he supposed they were Christians. But he wouldn't call them "fundamentalists." He had a vague sense that fundamentalists were intolerant, fanatical, and ignorant, that they hated Jews and anyone else who didn't share their beliefs. But he had no idea what they actually believed.

His thoughts were suddenly interrupted by Josh. "David, can I ask you something?"

He turned around. "Sure, kid, go ahead."

"Is Grandpa bad?"

The question startled him, but then he figured that Josh must have been listening to his conversation with their mother. He sat on the bed, putting his arm around Josh's shoulder. "No, of course not," he said gently. "What makes you ask such a thing?"

"My teacher says that people who own guns are bad. And Mom won't let us see Grandpa anymore because of his guns. So, that means that Grandpa's bad. Right?"

David thought about how to respond. "Hm. Do you think Grandpa's bad?"

"I don't know."

"Did he ever do anything to hurt you?"

"No."

"How does he treat you?"

"He's always nice to me."

"Now, would a bad person be nice to you?"

Josh shrugged. "I guess not. But why doesn't Mom want us to see him anymore?"

"Because she's scared. She's afraid of guns, and she doesn't want us to be around them."

"Then why won't Grandpa get rid of them?" Josh asked.

"Well, he thinks he might need them someday. You see, bad people aren't the only ones who use guns. Sometimes, good people use them for protection when a bad person tries to hurt them. If a bad guy breaks into your house, and you don't have a gun, you can't defend yourself. That's why Grandpa owns guns. For self-defense."

"What if the police found out he had guns?" Josh asked.

David frowned. "I'm not sure. Grandpa says it's very complicated to own a gun nowadays. You need a permit, and I don't think Grandpa has one."

"Will he get in trouble if anyone finds out he has those guns?" Josh asked anxiously.

"He might get into some kind of trouble. He'd probably have to pay a fine or something."

"Would he go to jail?"

David smiled. "I doubt it, kid. They wouldn't put a harmless old man like Grandpa in jail."

Josh seemed relieved. "Good."

"Well, I'm going back to my project." He was glad that his talk with Josh seemed to help. But he wondered why Josh was so concerned that the police would find out about their grandfather's guns.

CHAPTER 7

"You're sure you don't want to come?"

Ben glanced up at Elsie, who was standing by the door. A black raincoat was draped over her shoulders. His eyes went to her small, delicate hands. The Bible she held looked worn; it was black with faded letters across the front. Pieces of paper stuck out between some of the pages, probably notes from her Bible study. He smiled. "No, not tonight. I'm a little tired."

Elsie looked somewhat disappointed, but she smiled. "I'll see you sometime around ten." She bent over and kissed him on the cheek. "I love you."

"I love you, too."

"Don't forget to take your medicine."

"How can I forget, with you nagging me all the time?" But he smiled as he watched her leave.

He settled down into his easy chair, put on his glasses, and reached for the book on the coffee table. The light was dim; to conserve electricity, tenants weren't allowed to keep more than one light on after dark. Someone went around and checked, and if more than one light was on, you got a summons. People grumbled among themselves, but no one bothered to do anything about it.

With a sigh, he flipped through the book, a mystery. He didn't feel like reading. His mind was still filled with questions about the Bible, Elsie's Bible, which he had just recently started reading. But he didn't feel quite ready to go to her study. Somehow he felt he would be out of place. Still, why should he? After all, they were studying Isaiah, from the Hebrew Scriptures.

He thought back to the night Elsie had read the Bible to him. It seemed as if he were hearing it for the first time. They were sitting up in bed reading. She had been to the Bible study, but Ben didn't feel like hearing about it.

"Can I read you something?" she had asked gently. He saw that she had the Bible in front of her, and he figured she'd read him something from the New Testament, about *her* religion.

"All right, go ahead," he had said wearily. As he had expected, it was nothing new; it was about Jesus. Something about His being despised and rejected, and crushed for the people's transgressions. He had heard it all before.

After Elsie had finished, she turned to Ben and asked whom the passage was describing. He had thought the question silly. Obviously she was reading about Jesus, from the New Testament. Who else could that be? But he was shocked at what she told him. "I wasn't reading the New Testament. I was reading from the *Old* Testament, from the prophet Isaiah."

Startled, he took the Bible and read it for himself. He didn't want to hurt her feelings, but he figured her Christian Bible had probably twisted the words around, to make it sound like Jesus. But the next day, when he looked through his own copy of the Hebrew Scriptures, he was startled to find that the meaning was essentially the same, though the wording was slightly different. Something seemed to come over him as he read those words he may have heard years ago but had forgotten. He didn't quite understand, but somehow all the anger, all the bitterness he had felt toward God since those terrible years in Germany began to melt away. Since then, he had done a lot of thinking about this Jesus. He had even skimmed through portions of the New Testament, something he had vowed he would never do. In spite of his initial fears, he remembered something his father had told him: "Never be afraid to search for truth." Perhaps if Hitler's followers had been willing to search for the truth, millions of lives would have been saved.

Could Jesus be the Messiah? The question had haunted him day and night, though he was almost afraid to consider that possibility. But there was something in the pages of the Gospels that spoke to him as nothing else ever had. He recalled a passage he had read, about the disciples' hearts burning within them as they listened to the words of Jesus. Eventually Ben could no longer deny that His words were having the same effect on him.

He still had some questions, and had even confided in Matt about his growing interest in Christianity. After all, Matt and Gina had invited him and Elsie to their apartment last Christmas Eve for some sort of special dinner. But evidently, the two weren't practicing Christians. Matt had gotten very quiet when Ben tried to ask him about Jesus. So, he decided to keep his mouth shut. But he still had questions that Elsie didn't seem able to answer.

It was all that talk about forgiving your enemies that Ben had found most difficult to accept. How could he forget the horrors he had endured in the camp where he and his family were sent when he was a young boy? He still remembered standing for hours in the freezing cold to be counted, the humiliating jeers of the guards, the constant and gnawing hunger. He also remembered his father's continual lament: "Why did we give up our guns? Why did we let those devils disarm us?" After his father became ill and could no longer work, he was shipped to Auschwitz where he died, most likely in the gas chambers. When Ben learned of his father's death, he vowed that he would never allow the same thing to happen to him. He would never give up his life without a fight. So the idea of "turning the other cheek" was quite a stumbling block.

Still, he couldn't allow hatred and bitterness to consume his life—which might have happened if he hadn't met Elsie. He almost hadn't married her because she was a Gentile. But he couldn't seem to resist her. She was kind and warm-hearted with a quick laugh and an easy smile. She hated what the Nazis had done to the Jews and to all others who had resisted. Her own father had been imprisoned for speaking out against the Nazis, and the pastor of her parish had been sent to a concentration camp because he condemned the Nazis for their crimes against the Jews. But most of the Protestant clergy had gone along with the insanity. It was the only way to survive, they reasoned. Ben knew that Elsie shared his aversion to any form of tyranny. Yet, while Ben had taught her how to use his revolver, she often told him she could never take another life, not even to save herself. Probably because of the nonsense she was learning at her church.

He still didn't understand why she had suddenly started going there after all these years. When he first met her, spiritual things hadn't seemed to matter to either of them. Now, she was almost obsessed. She read the Bible every night and even wanted to give money from her pension to missionary work when they were barely getting by themselves.

As Ben sat staring at the book in his hand, he suddenly realized how tired he felt, not so much physically, but emotionally. A weariness in the depths of his spirit had plagued him for years now. The darkness of the small living room oppressed him. He wished he could turn another light on. Looking out the window, he saw rain drops glistening against the pane.

He got up from the chair and turned out the living room light. The long hallway leading to the bedroom was in total darkness, yet Ben fancied he saw strange shadows moving about. "Just my imagination," he muttered, and the sound of his voice almost startled him. A little rest was all he needed. As he sat down on the king-sized brass bed with its patchwork quilt, he could feel his heart throbbing, and he reached for the small plastic bottle on his night table, took out a single white pill and swallowed it. *That should help,* he thought.

But it didn't. He felt a strange uneasiness which he couldn't seem to shake. He was reminded suddenly of the night the Nazis came to take him and his family away, and he vaguely remembered similar feelings of apprehension then. An eerie silence had hung over the neighborhood when he got home from school that afternoon, and he noticed that some of his neighbors were looking at each other furtively and talking in hushed tones. He had sensed that something was dreadfully wrong.

He tried to banish the memory from his thoughts. *This is silly*, he told himself. *All I need is some rest.*

* * * *

Matt was in the kitchen, reheating some leftover pizza in the toaster oven. He opened a bottle of Killian's and sat down at the table, turning on the radio. The pizza would take a while to heat, since the toaster was on its last legs. They wanted to get a microwave, but couldn't seem to save enough to buy one. He vaguely remembered a time when just about everyone had a microwave. But those days had ended a year ago.

He was barely listening to the radio, until something caught his attention. "...about to initiate a nationwide program allowing citizens to turn in illegal firearms for food vouchers, electric appliances, or other items. Anyone who takes advantage of the program will be granted complete amnesty. Other efforts to protect the public from violence have also paid off. In New York, local police departments have offered monetary awards to those who report anyone owning illegal firearms. Already, over one hundred arrests have been made. In Washington..."

Matt turned off the radio. *The country's gone insane!* He remembered what Ben had told him about how it was in Nazi Germany with people being encouraged to inform on their neighbors and friends, even their own relatives. Now, it was happening here. *What's next?*

He ate his pizza quickly, hardly tasting it, and finished his beer. Gina often complained that he wasted so many debits on alcohol, but he didn't care; it was one of the few pleasures he still had left. He missed so many things he had enjoyed before the insanity had started. Target shooting was one of the things he missed most. He remembered all the fun he used to have at the shooting range in Calverton. But he no longer went because of the new law that required surveillance cameras at all shooting ranges. They even required you to sign in and list any weapons you had brought! That was too much. The last thing he needed was to have the government find out that he owned weapons.

He remembered the time he had gone to the range with Ben, about six months ago. That was the last time he had gone shooting with anyone. He had been amazed to find that Ben was an expert shot; he had to be at least seventy years old, maybe even in his eighties.

Ben had told him he practiced at the range every week, for over forty years.

"I feel sorry for anyone who tries to break into your house," Matt had said with a smile.

"Yeah, they wouldn't know what hit 'em," said Ben, laughing. "I hope I never have to use my freedom teeth to defend my life, but if I ever do, I'll be ready."

Matt threw away some uneaten pizza crust and decided to take a shower before Gina got home. He didn't know how long she'd be; she was out covering a story. But it was after nine already, so he figured she wouldn't be much longer. He turned on the radio again, switching to WBAB, a loud rock station. He made it a habit to keep loud music on whenever he was in the shower, or out late in the evening, in order to discourage burglars.

* * * *

Ben was dozing off, the blanket draped partially over his legs. He had been reading through the book of Psalms which Elsie kept on her night table. He thought of getting undressed, but the effort seemed too much at the moment. He smiled contentedly. Soon Elsie would be home, and all would be well.

Just as he was about to drift off, he was startled by a tremendous banging. It sounded like someone—or something—was banging on the front door. Stumbling out of bed, he could feel his heart thudding violently, and he had to take a deep breath to calm down. He dimly became aware of another sound, somehow familiar, but in his grogginess he couldn't quite place it. Then, a sickening feeling hit him as he realized what it was—the sound of splintering wood. Someone was breaking down the front door, of course! That's why it sounded familiar—the intruders were using a battering ram; he knew the sound from his experience with the Nazis. He had to think fast if he wanted to survive. Instantly, he turned off the light and rushed to his closet where he kept his rifles. By now, the intruders were inside the apartment; he could hear furniture being knocked over and glass breaking.

He grabbed his Ruger mini-14 and rammed a clip into it, shoving a few more into his pockets. Next he took hold of a "block-buster" bomb standing near the wall, an old fused relic from the war, and lowered it to the floor. It was nearly five feet long with 3/8 inch steel walls. Even though empty, it weighed well over a hundred pounds. He rolled it into position about fifteen feet from the door—it would make an excellent bullet shield for him. Actually, he had laughingly suggested such a use for it when Elsie had chided him for wanting to buy such a large and ugly decoration for the bedroom. Thank God he hadn't listened to her then!

He tried to think clearly as he struggled to keep his breath. He wasn't sure who the intruders were, but he strongly suspected they could be BWC agents; burglars didn't usually break down your door with a battering ram!

The realization hit him. He probably wouldn't come out of this alive. Agents of the Bureau were known for breaking into homes and beating gun owners to death with clubs. But the thugs were never held accountable for these murders; the mere presence of firearms in the victims' homes was enough to justify their actions, according to the courts.

Ben realized he had two choices: give up or go down fighting. If he gave himself up, he would be arrested on an illegal weapons charge. He doubted he'd get a fair trial with gun owners being vilified by the media. If the intruders were burglars, how would they respond if Elsie suddenly walked in on them? Would they shoot her? He suddenly thought of Danny Cheever's wife. All she had done was open the front door to let her husband inside, and an FBI sniper had shot her in the head. *I can't let that happen to Elsie!* He knew he had to act quickly.

His only chance was to surprise them. He was grateful for the long hallway that separated the bedroom from the rest of the apartment. It could give him a slight advantage. Listening to the men's voices, he could tell they had entered the kitchen. He could confront them, or wait until they came to him. He decided to wait for them. If he went out to them, they might hear him.

Very quietly, he went to the door and unlocked it. If they found it locked they would know someone was inside and he would lose the advantage of surprise. For all they knew, the house might be empty. He returned to the shelter of his block-buster, lay down behind it, and took aim at the door.

Waiting in the darkness, he prayed that Elsie would be delayed somehow.

* * * *

"Thanks for the ride." Elsie got out of the beat up Ford that had pulled up in front of the apartment building.

"Don't mention it." The woman who dropped her off was in her early forties with brown hair spotted with patches of gray. She smiled at Elsie. "If you want, I'll pick you up next time."

"But it's out of your way. I can take the bus."

The woman frowned. "I wouldn't, if I were you. It's dangerous for a woman to be out alone at night, even just walking to the bus stop."

Elsie nodded. "Yes, you're right," she said with a feeling of resignation. "Ben keeps saying the same thing. Well, thank you for your kind offer—I guess I'd be foolish to refuse."

"Good—then I'll see you next week."

"Okay—I hope this time I can convince Ben to come. So long!"

Walking to the front entrance, she fumbled in her handbag for her keys. By now, the rain had become a light drizzle, but the air felt raw. She was looking forward to getting inside and having a nice cup of tea.

* * * *

Moving into the living room, his M-16 aimed in front of him, a tall man wearing a ski mask barked orders at the men behind him. They scanned every inch of the room, yet they saw no one stirring. Bodies taut, they held their machine guns ready, prepared to fire at anything that moved.

* * * *

Elsie stared wide-eyed at the door broken off its hinges. She was about to rush to a neighbor's apartment to call the police. Then she thought of Ben. He was in there! She couldn't waste any time. Suddenly, she remembered the handgun that Ben kept in the desk drawer, right in the foyer. If she could get to it before the intruders became aware of her presence, she'd have a chance. Very slowly, she crept inside the apartment.

Elsie grabbed the handgun from the drawer. Clutching it in her shaking hands, she made her way toward the living room.

* * * *

From inside his bedroom, Ben jumped as the roar of a fully automatic M-

16 rifle thundered through the apartment. *What was going on?* He strained to make sense out of the confused voices that followed.

"Who the hell was that?"

"I don't know—must be his wife," came the indifferent reply.

Elsie!

Ben flung open the door and fired three quick shots at the figure directly in front of him. The man reeled backwards, dropping his rifle. He was dead by the time he hit the floor. Ben's steel-tipped M-855 ammunition could penetrate all but the strongest body armor. He looked at the man's black uniform and ski mask. His suspicions had been right—these *were* government agents!

"Stand guard outside!" Ben heard someone yell. "Make sure no one else gets in." Another agent rushed at Ben with a burst of machine gun fire.

Ben dove to the floor, firing back. A burning pain ripped through his shoulder—a bullet had grazed his skin. He fired madly at the agent in front of him and managed to shoot him in the leg. Incapacitated, the thug fell to the floor. Ben fired again, killing him instantly with a head shot.

He jumped up off the floor and ducked into the bathroom to reload as a third agent ran toward him from the living room. Machine gun fire ripped through the hallway as Ben jammed another clip into his rifle. Crouching low, he stepped half through the doorway and began shooting at the agent, who was already firing at him. Ben got a lucky shot through the man's shoulder just as the last agent, the one guarding the door, lunged into the hallway and opened fire.

* * * *

Matt had just gotten out of the shower and wrapped a towel around his waist. He wanted to blow dry his hair, but he was wondering about all that banging he had heard during his shower. Beads of moisture glistened down his back and he shivered in the chill of the evening; he had forgotten to turn up the heat. Just as he was reaching for his robe, he nearly jumped out of his skin. *What the hell...?*

At first, he couldn't believe what he was hearing. He stood listening, and he heard it again. Machine gun fire! He threw on his robe and ran toward the front door, trying to figure out where it was coming from. Horrified, he realized it was coming from the Weiss's apartment right next door! He called 911, his hands shaking as he pressed the numbers on the touch-tone phone. When he got the police on the line, they asked him a million questions. "My neighbor's in trouble! Just get over here!" he said desperately. Just then he heard another blast of machine gun fire and what sounded like a rifle.

"Sir, we can't send anyone over until we have the necessary information," came the toneless response.

"Are you deaf? There's a gunfight going on in my neighbor's apartment! Now get the hell over here before someone gets killed!" At that instant, a bullet whizzed past him, shattering the lamp on the corner end-table, and he threw himself onto the floor for cover. "If you don't get here soon you'll be talking to a corpse!" he shouted into the phone.

Finally, they agreed to send someone, but they wanted to keep Matt on the line so they could get his social security number. Exasperated, he hung up. He had to do something. There was no telling when the police would arrive. He could hear people running down the hallway toward the elevator exits—probably tenants fleeing in panic. He ran into the bedroom and pulled on his underwear and a pair of jeans, then grabbed his shotgun, the only gun which he had a permit for. Although he knew he wouldn't be a match for anyone using a machine gun, he felt he had to do something to help Ben and Elsie. He knew they had guns, but he also knew that Ben had a weak heart. And he was worried about Gina. What if she came home and heard the gunfire? She was just the type to stick her nose into an armed confrontation if it meant getting a good story!

Cautiously, he opened the front door and slowly walked out into the corridor. He was surprised that none of the neighbors had decided to check things out. *Guess they're not as crazy as I am*, he thought. He figured most of them were probably hiding under their beds—and who could blame them with machine gun blasts ripping through the walls of the Weiss's apartment! It was sheer luck that bullet didn't hit him, he realized.

As he neared Ben's apartment, he noticed that the gunfire had stopped. His eyes widened as he saw the door ripped off its hinges. A figure dressed in black was bending over something on the floor. The man's back was to him, and Matt observed a strange symbol on the back of his jacket, some sort of globe with a pyramid shape inside it. He also saw that the man was holding an M-16 rifle and wearing a ski mask. Could he be a gang member? But what was he bending over? From this angle he couldn't see what it was. As he got closer, he drew back in horror. It was a body. Then he saw the crimson stain spreading underneath a black rain coat, and Elsie's white face framed by disheveled gray hair, her eyes staring out in front of her. For a moment, he stood there frozen in horror. Then, he realized that the man bending over her was taking off her jewelry and shoving it into his pockets. It suddenly hit him—this monster had murdered her! With a fury unlike anything he had ever known before, he aimed his gun at the stranger. "Put your hands up!" he yelled savagely. The stranger stood up, whirled around, and saw Matt's shotgun aimed at him. He dropped his gun and slowly put his hands up. "I wouldn't do that if I were you," he said, looking at Matt with contempt.

"Get over in the corner, you bastard!"

"Listen, you fool," he said coldly, "I'm an agent of the Bureau of Weapons Control. I can show you my I.D." Just as he was reaching for his badge, Matt heard two other men approaching from behind. "Drop your weapon!" they shouted. With the cold barrel of a gun pressed against his naked back, he dropped his gun. A feeling of numbness seemed to spread through him, and his legs felt like jelly.

"What the hell is going on here?" Matt shouted when he had found his voice. His mouth felt like cotton, and he couldn't seem to stop shaking. And where the hell was Ben?

"Don't ask any questions!" he was told. "Do you have a permit for that shotgun?"

"It's...it's in my apartment." He felt as if he were in a daze.

"Then you're under arrest," the back-up agent said coldly.

Before he could protest, the two agents pinned his arms behind his back and handcuffed him. "Wait a minute! Why am I under arrest? I didn't do anything! I thought this guy was—"

"Shut up!" shouted one of the agents who had handcuffed him. "Let's go."

"Wait—aren't you supposed to read me my rights?"

"I told you to shut up!" Something heavy hit his left shoulder hard and he fell to the floor, his shoulder throbbing with pain. He looked up at the agent and saw that he was holding a heavy club, and smiling maliciously.

"Take him away," said the agent whom Matt had confronted.

"Wait—tell me one thing," Matt insisted. "Where's Ben? What have you done to him?"

"Oh—so you're a friend of this criminal? I'll make a note of that. Anyway, it's none of your business." The agent spoke coldly, his face expressionless. To Matt, he hardly seemed human; he was more like a robot.

"Let's go," said one of the back-up agents. They pulled Matt to his feet and dragged him out of the apartment.

CHAPTER 8

Matt stared at the bare concrete walls of the cell. He couldn't believe this was happening. They had strip-searched him, taken his watch, belt, socks, shoes, even his wedding ring. Then, he was fingerprinted and locked in this cell.

Wearing only his jeans, he shivered in the dampness. A foul stench came from the dirty toilet. He refused to touch the musty, moth-eaten blanket rolled up in the corner of his cot.

He had demanded his right to a phone call, but the officers had only laughed at him. No one had told him whether he was even being charged with any crime.

As he sat on the lumpy cot, his mind went to Gina, and a dull ache rose in his throat. Why wouldn't they let him call his wife? And how long would he remain here? Nothing made sense. As far as he was concerned, he had done nothing wrong. He had thought the BWC agent was a burglar, a member of a gang. The black leather jacket with its strange symbol, the heavy boots and ski mask. How could he have known the man was a government agent?

A warden came and handcuffed him. "This way," he said, and pushed Matt ahead.

"What's going on? Am I being charged with something?"

"Beats me, I just follow orders."

Matt was escorted to a small, bare room with a long table and a few chairs. Two men dressed in dark suits were seated at the table, and a single light bulb was screwed into the ceiling.

The warden removed his handcuffs and shoved him into a metal chair. "Who are you?" Matt asked the two men seated at the table.

One of them, a middle-aged man in a dark navy suit with a sallow complexion, looked at Matt coldly. "I'm afraid we're the ones who will be asking the questions, Mr. Lanyon."

"But—"

"You'd better keep your mouth shut or we'll have the warden take you right back to your cell," the second man said. He wore a charcoal gray suit and had a slim build.

Matt refused to give in. "Listen, I don't know who you people think you are, but I know my rights! Now, the Constitution says—"

"The Constitution doesn't apply here," the first man interrupted him.

"What do you mean, it doesn't apply?"

"I'm not authorized to answer any questions." He looked at Matt with a bored expression. "The sooner you cooperate, the faster you'll get out of here. Now, it is exactly—" he looked at his Rolex watch "—seven fifteen a.m. Yes, you've been here all night. If you want to stay longer, that's fine with us. We can have the warden take you back to your cell, and you can stay there another night. It's up to you."

Matt scowled at them. "What do you want?"

"We'd like to ask you a few questions."

"I'm not saying anything until I speak to a lawyer!"

"Very well. You can spend another night in jail."

Matt thought of Gina, and what she must be going through. *She's probably worried sick by now!* "All right, go ahead," he said wearily. He was anxious to get this over with.

The men's voices seemed to drone on endlessly, and he often swayed with exhaustion as he tried to listen.

"How long have you owned your shotgun?"

Matt shrugged. "I'm not sure. A few years, I guess."

"Why were you carrying it without your permit?"

"I heard gunshots in my neighbor's apartment! I didn't have time to look for it."

"Do you own any other firearms?"

He hesitated. "No." He didn't want to lie, but he decided it was best not to mention his carbine, since it wasn't registered.

"Does anyone else in your family own any firearms?"

"What does that have to do with anything?"

"Just answer the question, Mr. Lanyon."

"I don't know, I'm not very close with my family."

"Why do you feel it's necessary to own a firearm?"

"For defense."

"Defense against what?"

Matt was tempted to say, "From people like you." But he merely said, "Intruders."

He answered the first few questions without protesting too much; he wanted to get this over with. Then the questions got more personal. "Do you belong to any groups that have lobbied to overturn gun-control laws?"

"That's none of your business," Matt objected.

The man in the navy suit glared at him. "Just answer the question, Mr. Lanyon."

"What if I don't?"

"That's your prerogative, but we recommend that you cooperate with us. We can make your life very unpleasant if you don't."

Initially, the questions were about firearms. But then they began to ask him about his job, his family, even his religious beliefs. He was asked what kind of books he read, what bumper stickers he had on his car, what political party he belonged to, whether he or any of his relatives had ever received psychiatric treatment, what television shows he watched, even what newspapers he read. Whenever he refused to answer a particular question, he saw one of his interrogators mark something in a small black book.

By the time they had finished, Matt felt drained. They must have been questioning him for hours. His legs were stiff when he got up off the chair, and his mouth was dry and parched. To his dismay, they returned him to his cell. "When can I go home?" he demanded.

"After we've processed your answers," came the response.

He couldn't tell how many hours had passed. A guard was telling him he was free to go, his wife was waiting for him. They returned his belongings, with the exception of his shotgun.

When he asked about his shotgun, the officer told him it would be held as evidence. "Evidence for what?" Matt asked. "You haven't charged me with any crime, have you?"

"This is just standard procedure."

Matt hardly said a word to Gina when he met her near the main desk; his ordeal had drained him. He saw the bewildered, frightened look in her eyes, but just didn't know what to say. When she tried to hug him, he stiffened. He merely took her hand and said, "Let's get the hell out of here."

* * * *

Matt and Gina entered the apartment in silence. Matt obviously was in no mood to talk.

"Why don't you lie down?" Gina asked as she hung up her jacket.

He almost fell into the easy chair. "In a little while," he mumbled. He leaned back and closed his eyes.

"I'll make you some breakfast." She headed into the kitchen. She opened the refrigerator and took out a carton of eggs, some bacon, and American cheese. Then she started to brew some coffee.

She had tried to get him to confide in her as they drove home, but he had simply stared out the car window. Something in his eyes had frightened her. They were cold and lifeless.

She was mixing the eggs with a fork when she heard a terrible crash from the living room. She rushed into the room. "What happened?"

"Nothing." Matt grabbed a German beer stein from one of the shelves and flung it across the room. It smashed into the glass doors of the china cabinet, shattering them and sending shards of glass across the floor. Gina stared in disbelief as Matt grabbed another stein and threw it against the wall.

"Those dirty bastards! Murderers! That's what they are!" In a blind rage, he was shouting and throwing things—anything he could get his hands on.

"Stop it!" Gina choked back a sob. She rushed toward him and grabbed his arm.

He pushed her away. "They murdered Ben and Elsie!" Tears ran down his cheeks. "Those monsters are just like the stinking Nazis!" Gina almost winced at the pain she saw in his eyes. "I saw her, Gina. I saw Elsie...right after they murdered her. She was lying on the floor in a pool of blood...and one of those bastards was ripping off her jewelry!"

He picked up a cream-colored Lenox vase from the coffee table—a wedding gift from Gina's parents—and flung it as hard as he could. It shattered against the wall.

"Matt, please! Stop it!" She had never seen him like this before.

His voice was filled with savage hatred. "Why should I?"

"Because I love you. And I can't stand to see you destroy yourself with this anger!" She ran to him and threw her arms around him, but he pushed her away again. She lost her balance, falling where some glass had broken. She scrambled to her feet, and he saw that her hand was bleeding.

The sight of her blood seemed to jar him. "Gina...I'm sorry." Gently, he took her hand in his and looked at the deep cut on her palm.

"It's not bad, really."

His voice was filled with tenderness. "Come on in the bathroom and we'll take care of it."

After he had washed and bandaged her cut, he pulled her into his arms. "I'm so sorry, babe." He held her against him and stroked her hair. "Can you forgive me?"

"Of course I can." They returned to the living room and sat down on the sofa together.

"Would you feel better if you talked about this?" Gina asked him.

"Why don't we talk over breakfast. I'm starved."

* * * *

Matt showered and changed, then joined Gina in the kitchen. But he could hardly touch the plate of bacon and eggs she had prepared. He nibbled on some toast, then told her the whole story. He sat back, silent, waiting for her reaction.

"I can't believe this!" she said when she finally found her voice. "Ben and Elsie were murdered by *government agents?*"

"Why does it surprise you? Don't you realize that this kind of thing is the natural consequence of gun control?"

"But if Ben hadn't owned all those illegal guns, he and Elsie would be alive right now. I just don't see how it was worth it. You'd think that after living through a concentration camp, he wouldn't take any foolish chances. Besides, we don't know everything that happened. Maybe Ben provoked them somehow. If they wanted to arrest him for illegal gun possession, he should have gone along peacefully. You know Ben. He probably refused to give up his weapons."

"But people in a free country shouldn't be forced to give up their God-given right to own weapons. The Constitution is supposed to guarantee our right to keep and bear arms so that we can defend ourselves against a tyrannical government, if necessary."

"I'm not sure that right applies to individuals," Gina said.

He rolled his eyes. "Oh, really? Then who does it apply to?"

"The military. I was taught in school that the Second Amendment applies to a well-regulated militia, or the National Guard, not individuals."

"Gina, that doesn't make sense. Why would the military need an amendment in order to carry weapons? It's ridiculous! You know, ever since I started discussing all this with Ben, I've been doing some reading on this subject, and our Founding Fathers always said that the militia includes all able-bodied adults capable of bearing arms."

"That may have been true back then. But we can't always interpret the Constitution literally—or apply the writings of our Founding Fathers to this day and age. We have to apply the Constitution to contemporary society.

Now, maybe at the time the Bill of Rights was written, individuals needed to be armed. After all, there was no police force as we know it today. But I don't think Thomas Jefferson and George Washington envisioned a society of violent criminals and teenage gang members who are better armed than the police."

"Gina, did you ever stop to think that if more law-abiding citizens were armed, they wouldn't be at the mercy of violent criminals? After all, if you were planning to commit a violent crime, wouldn't you think twice about attacking someone who might be armed?"

"Maybe," she said grudgingly. "But some criminals are crazy and don't think rationally. Don't get me wrong, Matt. I'm sure Ben felt he had a good reason to own all those guns. But you can't just go around breaking the law. What would happen if people just stopped obeying laws they didn't like? We'd have chaos."

Matt was silent for a few moments. "But you have to draw the line somewhere. I mean, what if the government passed a law that you believed was evil? Would you obey it?"

"I don't think gun control is evil."

He was beginning to think it was pointless to even discuss this. "Maybe if you were a Jew living in Nazi Germany, you would. Okay, let's say you lived before the time of the Civil War, when it was illegal to hide fugitive slaves. What would you do if a bunch of slaves came to you asking you to hide them? Would you turn them in to the authorities?"

She looked indignant. "Of course not! How could you even think I would do something like that?"

He smiled faintly. "Well, it looks like you just proved my point—not all laws should be obeyed. And that's what's wrong with this country! We've been putting up with all sorts of laws which violate our freedom—gun control, environmental laws, zoning laws, roadblocks to check your license and registration, laws which tell us what we can and can't eat, cameras on highways and in public places. I just don't know where it's going to end."

He put his face in his hands, exhausted and irritated from lack of sleep. Why couldn't Gina see the truth about how dangerous the government had become? What kind of a future did they have together if they couldn't even agree about the basic, most fundamental issues of life? He sighed deeply.

"What's wrong?" she asked.

"I think we're witnessing the end of America." *And it was made possible by people like you*, he thought bitterly. "Maybe America died a long time ago, but no one thought of having the funeral."

* * * *

Matt stared silently at the empty apartment. He walked to the rolltop desk in the foyer, where Ben and Elsie's family photos were displayed in ornate silver frames. With a heavy sigh, he reached for their wedding picture and held it up to the light. A young, vibrant couple smiled shyly at the camera. Elsie was draped in a sea of lace, and Ben stood with an arm around her waist, his eyes filled with love.

Matt shuddered as Elsie's white face swam before him, her eyes vacant and staring. He dropped the portrait. A cold, sick feeling spread through him, and he wanted to sob uncontrollably. *What's happening to me?*

He regained his composure and opened the top drawer. He rummaged through the papers and other junk, then grabbed Ben's address book.

His heart thudded violently as he dialed Anita's number. No answer. There was also a cell phone number. Taking a deep breath, he dialed it.

A sad, tired voice picked up. He told her his name. "I'm trying to reach Anita, Ben and Elsie's daughter. Is that you?"

She sounded wary. "Yeah. What's this about?"

He told her he was there that awful night and didn't know if her father had survived.

A long silence. "He...survived." Her voice broke. "But he's not expected to live."

Matt's legs went weak as Anita described Ben's condition. He was in a coma, brought on by the bullet to his head. He hadn't moved since his arrival at Nassau County Medical Center.

"Can I see him?"

"I guess. But he won't even know you're there, he has no brainwaves. Nothing."

"I understand. I just want a chance...to say goodbye."

He tried not to lose it as he scribbled down the room number she gave him.

Just as he was about to leave the apartment for the last time, the phone rang. Not knowing what else to do, he picked up.

"Uh, is this the Weiss residence?" asked a startled voice.

There was a heavy silence as Matt groped for what to say to the man. "Yeah, but, um, something...happened. Are you a friend of theirs?"

"I'm their son."

Matt had to sit down.

* * * *

The two men raced down the corridor to ICU, and Matt prayed they would reach Ben in time. This would be his last chance to see the son he hadn't spoken to in over twenty years.

Anita stood in stunned silence when they entered the room. "What are *you* doing here?" she asked her brother when she finally found her voice.

"I'm here to see Dad," he said in a soft voice. "There are some things I need to tell him." He wiped away the tears that glistened in his eyes. "Things I've been trying to say for years."

"Well, I certainly don't have to listen," she said. She got up from her chair and walked past them toward the door.

"Anita, wait—"

She was shaking. "Forget it, Jordan. You didn't have to pick up the pieces when you broke his heart!" She almost collided with the nurse who stood near the doorway.

Matt hardly recognized Ben. His face was gray and sunken, and tubes protruded from his body, hooked up to machines. Matt's eyes went to Ben's wrist, handcuffed to the bed. He shook his head in disbelief. *As if he could try to escape.*

They both sat down next to the bed. "Go ahead," Matt whispered to Jordan.

"I've got a lot to say. Maybe you should go first."

He took a deep breath, trying to fight back the inevitable tears. "Hey, Ben, it's me. Matt." No response. He turned to the nurse, his voice hopeful. "Is there any way he can hear me?"

She shook her head sadly. "I'm afraid not." She pointed to one of the machines. "He has no brainwaves."

Matt said a stilted goodbye, then turned to Jordan. "Too bad he can't hear us." He didn't know what else to say.

Jordan ran his fingers through his thick black hair, streaked with flecks of gray, then leaned close to Ben's face. He grasped his father's hand, which lay limply on the bed.

"Hi, Dad," he said in a soft voice. "It's me, Jordy. I'm probably the last person you want to see right now. But I had to come." He heaved a deep sigh. "I know how much I've hurt you, and I'm sorry. I wish there was some way to make it up to you. But there isn't. All I can say is, I love you." He wiped away the tears that ran down his face. "I've been wanting to tell you that for years, Dad. Every time I called."

He smiled sadly. "I don't blame you for hanging up on me, after what I've done. And I certainly have no right to expect you to forgive me. Anyway, maybe you don't want to hear this right now, but there's someone else who loves you. Someone who changed my life. It's Jesus, Dad. He loves you so much, more than you could ever imagine. If he can love a worthless sinner like me, think of how much He loves you!"

Matt felt a chill run through him as he saw Ben's eyelids flutter. He was moving his lips, as if trying to speak.

The nurse rushed toward the bed, her eyes wide with amazement. She pointed to one of the machines. "He can hear you!" she exclaimed. "He's got brainwaves. He can hear everything you're saying!"

Tears poured down Matt's cheeks as Jordan spoke to his father about the love of Jesus, who had given His life to save him. "It's never too late to come to Him, Dad. I know that firsthand." Then he spoke about the thief on the cross. "He was like me, Dad. He knew how worthless he was, but Jesus accepted him anyway."

Matt saw the blankets stir under Ben's hand. His fingers tightened around Jordan's. He opened his mouth, straining to speak, but no sounds came forth. A single tear trickled down his cheek.

"You can go to Jesus now, Dad. He's waiting for you."

Ben opened his eyes for the last time. They were gazing at Jordan with love and compassion. Then, his eyes closed, and his grip on Jordan's hand loosened.

* * * *

Matt watched Anita Weiss during Ben and Elsie's memorial service. Her face was pale, and she appeared dazed and bewildered. His heart went out to her. She had no one to turn to for comfort; her little boy clung to her, his face buried in her dark coat. David stood apart, his eyes red with tears.

He was still thinking about what had transpired between Ben and his son. Matt hadn't told anyone about it, not even Gina. A part of him longed to tell her. But she would never understand.

After the service Matt tried to find Anita and offer his condolences, but she was nowhere in sight. Then he noticed a commotion outside. He looked in the direction of the hubbub. Anita's car was surrounded by reporters; they swarmed around her like vultures, shoving microphones into her face and clicking their cameras at her. Though they were a distance away, Matt could hear the reporters firing questions at her.

"How did you feel when you discovered that your father was a terrorist?"

"Did you know he was stockpiling illegal assault weapons?"

"How has all of this affected your children?"

"Have you told them their grandfather was a terrorist?"

She tried to push through the crowd to open the door to her car. Josh had begun to cry, and immediately a camera was shoved in front of his face. Anita pulled him away. She fumbled for her keys, but her hands were shaking so badly, she dropped them. Reporters pressed against her so tightly that she couldn't even bend down to pick them up. Tears streamed down her cheeks and she looked as if she might pass out. "Leave us alone!" she sobbed. The cameras were clicking madly.

"You heard the lady—leave her alone!" Matt began shoving the reporters out of the way. They glared at him, outraged. "If you don't stop harassing her, I'll call the police!" he added.

Anita and the children were able to get into the car. Disappointed, the reporters turned to leave, but they all gave Matt dirty looks as they departed. Anita smiled a little through her tears, clearly touched by his concern. She rolled down her window. "Thank you!" she exclaimed. "I think I saw you at the hospital. I'm sorry, but I don't know your name."

"It's Matt—Matt Lanyon." He turned and pointed to Gina, who was just approaching. "That is my wife, Gina. We...were neighbors of your parents."

"We're so sorry about what happened," Gina said.

"Thanks," Anita murmured.

Matt wondered if he should tell her anything about his own conflict with the BWC that night. Would it upset her more? He knew the newspapers and TV networks were doing their best to portray Ben as some kind of terrorist, a dangerous radical who was plotting against the government. He just couldn't believe all the stories in the papers. According to one account, Ben had attacked the BWC agents with a grenade, and they had fired at him in self-defense. Matt knew that was ridiculous. There was no sign of any explosion, and he knew he would have heard a grenade go off. Besides, the entire apartment would have been demolished.

The media claimed that the BWC agents had gone to the Weiss's apartment to investigate a Zionist terrorist group, of which Ben was allegedly a member.

These so-called "terrorists" were supposedly stealing machine guns and grenade launchers from military installations, and converting semiautomatic "assault" rifles into fully automatic machine guns. The news reports also kept mentioning that Ben was a conservative Jew, as if this was somehow "proof" of his involvement with terrorists. In addition, they hinted that the group had ties with the "religious right," including fundamentalist Christians. The ultimate goal of the group, reporters speculated, was to prevent the World Constitution from being ratified.

Matt noticed that just about every news story mentioned that Elsie was a Christian fundamentalist who went to Bible studies every week, and that Ben was a Zionist who believed in "government conspiracy theories." To Matt, the media's goal was obvious: they wanted to discredit Christians, conservative Jews, gun owners, and patriots—all in one fell swoop. *And of course, the government agents were portrayed as heroes*, Matt thought with disgust. He wanted Anita to know the truth; he just couldn't allow Ben and Elsie's memories to become tarnished in the eyes of their daughter.

"Listen, don't believe all those lies about your father," he told her. "We both knew your parents very well, and they were two of the nicest people we've met."

"Thanks," she said, fighting back tears.

"And if you ever need anything," he added, "don't hesitate to call." Gina took out a pad and pen and scribbled their names, address and phone number on a sheet, which she tore off and gave to Anita.

* * * *

When Anita and the boys arrived home from the memorial service, Josh ran into his bedroom and slammed the door. From behind the door, David and Anita could hear muffled sobbing.

Anita was concerned. "He's taking this so hard," she said to David. "Do you think he understands what's being said about Grandma and Grandpa?"

David's tone had a savage edge to it. "*I* don't even understand it. And I don't believe it—I don't believe any of that crap!" He was close to tears, and Anita put her arms around him. But he shoved her away.

A few moments later Anita knocked on the bedroom door. "Josh? Can I come in?" she asked softly. He said something she couldn't quite hear, but she opened the door anyway. She stepped inside and sat on the bed, gently stroking his hair. "I understand how you feel, honey," she told him.

"No, you don't." His face was buried in his pillow. "This is all my fault!" A heart-wrenching sob escaped him.

Anita was startled. "What on earth are you talking about? Of course this isn't your fault. How can it be your fault?"

He sat up and looked at her, his face pale, his eyes wide and frightened. "I'm afraid to tell you."

Now she was even more concerned, and determined to get to the bottom of her son's puzzling sense of guilt. "Josh, you've got to tell me what's bothering you. I can't help you unless you tell me the truth."

She could see the torment on his face, as if he were being pulled in two different directions. "But I *can't* tell you. My teacher told me not to."

"Your *teacher*?" Now Anita was alarmed. "Josh, you have to tell me the truth. Why do you think this is your fault, and what does your teacher have to do with this?"

"I'm not supposed to tell," he whined.

"Josh, your teacher won't find out that you told me," Anita assured him.

"You won't tell her?"

Although Anita didn't want to make such a promise, she felt she had to if she was ever going to get Josh to tell her the truth. "No, I won't."

He wiped the tears from his face. It was clear he really did want to tell Anita the truth, in spite of his fear. "They made us answer questions. Like a test."

"In school?"

"Yeah—the teacher said everyone had to fill it out. There were a lot of questions."

Anita became wary. "What kind of questions?"

"I can't remember them all. There must've been over a hundred! They asked us what religion we are, what TV shows and movies we watch, and how we get punished when we're bad."

"Josh, those questions are personal," Anita told him.

"I know, but the teacher said it was real important for us to answer them. She said it was for our own good."

This just didn't sound right at all. "Okay, now, tell me what these...questions...have to do with what happened to Grandpa and Grandma."

Seeing how scared he was, she wished she could shield him from all the evil in the world. That's why she had tried to keep him away from her father's guns; she had been taught in college that guns were a dangerous evil, that children had to be protected from them at all costs. But now, she was beginning to suspect that her son had been exposed to a more insidious evil. She recalled some of the things her father had told her about the schools in Nazi Germany, where children were told to give detailed accounts of their parents' personal lives and habits.

"It was one of the questions they asked us," he said falteringly.

Anita almost held her breath. "What was the question?"

"They asked us if anyone in our family owned guns."

The words came like a deathblow. Her heart was pounding wildly, and she shuddered. "Did you answer the question?"

Josh looked miserable. "I didn't know what to do at first. Something told me I shouldn't write anything, but I know I'm supposed to do what the teacher says, so I answered it. I wrote yes. The next question said to write the names of the people in our family who own guns, and how many guns they own. Did I do a bad thing?"

Anita felt betrayed and violated. How dare they ask her child questions like this! She had entrusted her children to the public school system and they had betrayed that trust! Still, she had to show Josh that it wasn't really his fault. He didn't know any better. Anita sighed. "Honey, you were trying to do what you thought was right. But you know, sometimes it's better not to tell strangers everything they ask you, especially if they ask personal questions."

"There's something else, too," Josh said suddenly.

"What?"

"Well, a few days after we answered the questions, the teacher sent me down to one of the offices." He began fumbling with the blanket. "There were some men there who asked me a lot of questions. The teacher gave them my journal, and they were asking questions about it."

Anita felt numb. Journal? "What journal?"

"We all have to keep a journal in school," he replied. "We're supposed to write down all our thoughts and feelings about things that happen to us. They were asking me about the fight you had with Grandpa. You know, the day you called him on the phone and yelled at him about his guns. They wanted to know how many guns he had, and if I ever saw any of them. They also asked if I knew where he kept them."

"Did the men tell you who they were?"

Josh shook his head. "They just said I shouldn't be afraid of them, and they wanted to help me."

Anita couldn't help rolling her eyes up. "Yeah, right," she said under her breath. A feeling of rage was building up within her, and she fought to control it. She didn't want to upset Josh more than he already was. "Josh, from now on, I don't want you to answer any more personal questions or write about your family in your journal. I'm going down to see your teacher next week and—"

Josh panicked. "But, Mommy—you promised you wouldn't tell my teacher! I'll get in trouble. My teacher said we're not allowed to tell our parents about the questions or the journal."

For the first time in ages, Anita wished she had a husband to confide in. She just didn't know what to do. Never before had she felt so alone. There was no one she could talk to about this. Both her parents were dead, and she had no brothers or sisters, or any friends she really felt close to. Then she thought of the Lanyons. They had seemed so eager to help. Still, they might have just been trying to be polite. And she didn't want to burden them with her problems—she had always prided herself on her independence. She put her arm around Josh. "All right," she said. "I won't say anything—for now. But promise me that if the teacher gives out any more private questions, you'll tell me about it. Okay? And don't answer them."

He wiped away his tears. "Okay," he said, sniffling a little. Anita gave him a tissue, then left him alone to read his comic books. She sat down at the kitchen table, her head throbbing. *It just can't be*, she kept thinking to herself. It seemed as if a trap had been set for her father, through his own grandson! How else could the BWC have learned of his weapons? None of them were registered. He had never applied for a permit for any of them, and had bought them all through private individuals who required no paperwork. She knew that local police departments were bribing people to inform on their neighbors who owned illegal firearms, but she knew how cautious her father was. Only the most trusted friends and family members had known he owned guns. And she certainly didn't believe all those stories in the papers about his being a terrorist! Even though he always had very strong beliefs, she knew he would never harm an innocent person, especially after what he had been through with the Nazis. And he was always willing to listen to other points of view—he had enjoyed a good debate. Even when she came home from Berkeley condemning him for owning guns, he had been willing to discuss the issue rationally. She remembered the sadness in his eyes when she told him she would never go target shooting with him again, and that she resented him for being "a threat to society." Tears streamed down her cheeks as she thought of how she had hurt him, refusing to let him see his own grandsons.

Now, it was too late; she could never tell him how sorry she was.

She glanced around the room. "David!" she called. Then she saw that his jacket was gone; he must have gone out. She got up from the table and opened the cabinet under the sink. Reaching far into the back, she pulled out a bottle of vodka. She stared at it for a long time before removing the cap. Then, pouring some into a tall glass, she began the slow process that would push her haunted thoughts into oblivion.

* * * *

Although Ken had not assigned Gina to interview the BWC officials responsible for the raid, she decided to take the initiative and visit their local field office. Something was terribly wrong—and she wanted to find out what. Up until now, she had not considered herself "anti-government" in any way. In fact, she often felt disturbed by Matt's distrust of government, which seemed to border on paranoia as far as she was concerned. He couldn't seem to understand that it was often necessary for the government to restrict people's freedom for reasons of public safety. Yet since Ben and Elsie were killed, questions had flooded her mind—questions she could no longer ignore.

Showing her press card, she was escorted inside. To her surprise, she was given the red-carpet treatment, and she wondered why everyone was so accommodating. It was certainly not what she had expected.

When she spoke to the official in charge, she was immediately turned off by his unctuous, ingratiating manner. She also got the impression that everything he said had been rehearsed. Whenever she asked a direct question, he tried to steer her away from the topic. He seemed especially uncomfortable when she asked whether he had any concrete evidence that the Weisses were members of a terrorist group. He mumbled something about their names being on a list of some sort, but when she asked where the agency had gotten the list, he said that was "privileged information," and he wasn't authorized to disclose it.

"So, in other words, you can't provide the press with any definite proof that the Weisses were terrorists?"

"We do have proof." His tone suddenly lost its oily politeness. "But that's extremely sensitive information. It's too dangerous to disclose at this time."

"There's another question I'd like to ask. When I saw the Weiss's apartment after the shoot-out, I noticed that the door had been broken completely off its hinges. Can you tell me how that happened?"

153

"According to the report I received from the two agents who survived the shoot-out," he said, "that occurred as a result of a hand grenade that was thrown at them by Mr. Weiss."

Gina looked puzzled. "But wouldn't the entire apartment have been demolished?"

"The entire apartment *was* demolished."

"Oh, really? That's very interesting. I spoke to a witness who saw the inside of the apartment immediately after the shoot-out." She didn't mention that the witness was her husband. "He says that the door was off its hinges, but that the rest of the apartment was intact. Can you explain that?"

He hesitated. "Perhaps the grenade only hit the door," he said coldly.

"Then there would have been fire, smoke, and blast damage to the hallway walls and door frame. There wasn't any. That also contradicts what you just told me. You told me that the entire apartment was demolished. Now you say it wasn't. If you're not sure about that, how can you be certain that the Weisses were terrorists?"

"I told you, their names were on a list."

"But you can't seem to tell me anything about that list. For all I know, it could have been a grocery list!" She realized she was putting him on the defensive, and reporters were not supposed to do that. But she was certain that Ben and Elsie weren't terrorists. And she wasn't going to let this smug bureaucrat get away with lying about two of the most decent people she had ever known!

Now the man's voice took on an indignant tone. "I think we had better terminate this interview." He pressed a button, and a uniformed guard appeared from outside the door. "Please escort Ms. Lanyon to her car," the disgruntled official told the guard.

Although disappointed that the interview had ended so abruptly, Gina felt a sense of exhilaration; the man was hiding something!

Back at the newsroom, Ken wasn't too pleased when he received a phone call from the BWC informing him of Gina's visit. The official who called him advised him to be "careful" about sending Ms. Lanyon on such sensitive assignments in the future. Fortunately, the official hadn't thought of speaking to the publisher. Damien had warned Ken not to send any "upstart" reporters to cover stories dealing with the government.

When Ken called Gina into his office for a reprimand, she was indignant. "Why should government officials be immune from public scrutiny? If he had nothing to hide, then he wouldn't have terminated the interview. He also lied to me—don't you want to get to the bottom of this?"

"Gina, I never even assigned you to interview anyone from the Bureau of Weapons Control," he reminded her. "You can't just take it upon yourself to interview whomever you feel like. Besides, since the Weisses were friends of yours, I'm not certain how objective you can be about what happened to them."

But she saw the pained look on his face, and realized he was going through some inner struggle. She knew if he had his way, he would have assigned an investigative reporter to find out what was going on if there was any question about a government cover-up. But since the paper changed hands, the only type of stories to which investigative reporters were assigned included exposés on people who refused to recycle their garbage, pet shop owners who neglected their animals, and "right-wing" patriot groups who opposed the new constitution.

Gina was beginning to suspect that Matt could be right. Maybe the government was getting out of control. She thought of Cheryl, and wondered if she would find out anything suspicious about Damien Whitaker, the new publisher. He definitely wanted the paper to tow the government line. But why?

* * * *

"Anyone who owns a gun today has to be out of his mind. It's just not worth it," Tom was saying to Gina.

Matt tensed as he entered the living room. Gina got up from her chair, forcing a smile. "Guess who stopped by?" she asked a bit nervously.

"Hi, Tom." Matt tried not to show his disappointment. He was in no mood to deal with Gina's father tonight. The last thing he needed was another lecture on how he was wasting his life at the factory instead of going to college and "making something of himself."

Tom got up from the couch. "Sorry to drop in on you like this." Matt realized immediately that this wasn't a social call. Something was up. "Anyway, I'll get right to the point. Gina told her mother about your little run-in with the Bureau of Weapons Control. As soon as I heard about it, I wanted to come over and find out just how much trouble you've gotten yourself into."

He wanted to tell Tom to mind his own business. But he saw the anxious look on Gina's face, and he forced himself to remain calm. "Mind if I put down this pizza?" he asked as patiently as he could.

"Are you hungry, Dad?" Gina asked.

"No, thanks, I had dinner before I came over. But you two go ahead and eat."

"I'll get some plates," Gina said.

"Forget it," Matt said. "I kind of lost my appetite."

"Matt, you have to eat."

He glared at her. "I said forget it. Don't you listen?"

He saw her startled expression, and felt sorry. Lately he found himself increasingly impatient with her, snapping at her when she asked him simple questions and frequently losing his temper. Ever since the murder of Ben and Elsie, he had felt a strange resentment toward her that he couldn't quite understand. Now, he was beginning to realize that he almost blamed her for what had happened to them. He tried to tell himself how irrational this was, but his anger persisted. To him, people like Gina, with their endless rambling about the common good, had allowed the government to grow into the monster it had become. He also resented Gina's refusal to face reality. Whenever she was confronted with an ugly fact that contradicted her own comfortable little ideas, she closed her eyes to the truth. Matt believed that this refusal to acknowledge harsh and frightening realities was slowly destroying America.

Putting these thoughts aside, he turned his attention to Tom. "So, you wanted to lecture me about the BWC," Matt said as he sat down on the couch. Immediately, he knew he'd said the wrong thing.

"Look, I came here because I thought I could help you," Tom said defensively. "I figured you could use a little legal advice. But apparently you don't appreciate my concern."

"I'm sorry. I was out of line. It's just that, well, I'm still pretty upset about what happened, and I'm not anxious to re-live the experience. I'd rather just forget it."

Tom nodded, his expression sympathetic. "I understand that. But I think you need to discuss this situation with someone who knows the law. Now, you can consult an attorney who'll charge you an arm and a leg, or you can talk to someone who won't charge you anything. I can leave right now, if you want."

Matt considered Tom's offer. He sighed. "Maybe you're right. There are some things I'm confused about."

"Listen, I just got the story second hand," said Tom. "Why don't you tell me the whole thing, right from the beginning?"

"In that case, I'll need a beer."

Gina went and got him a McSorley's. When she returned with it, Matt began his story. After he had finished, Tom sat quietly, as if weighing everything Matt had told him.

"And they didn't charge you with any crime?" he asked.

"I specifically asked them that, but they refused to tell me. But they did tell me they had to keep my shotgun as 'evidence.' If you ask me, the whole thing makes no sense." Then, he remembered something else, something that had puzzled him the most. "There's another thing. When they started questioning me, I insisted on calling a lawyer first, but they wouldn't let me call anyone, not even Gina. I told them they were violating my constitutional rights, but they said the Constitution didn't apply in my case. Does that make any sense to you? I mean, how can the Constitution not apply?"

Tom rubbed his chin thoughtfully. "It depends on a lot of factors."

"But isn't the Constitution supposed to protect my rights of due process?"

"Well, the Constitution doesn't apply in all cases," Tom said. "For instance, it doesn't apply in civil cases, and people who attempt to use constitutional defenses in civil disputes wind up losing their case."

"I don't get it," said Matt.

"You need to understand the nature of commercial law. You see, Matt, contracts always supersede the Constitution. In other words, if someone enters a contract, that contract becomes a binding legal agreement, even if the provisions of the contract cause him to waive his constitutional rights. For instance, let's say you're a professional ball player, and your coach says he saw you out after ten on the night before a game, and you owe him ten thousand dollars which he's going to take out of your pay. You say, 'Wait a minute. What about my rights of due process? You can't take my money.' But then, he shows you the contract you signed, and it says right there that any player who stays out after ten the night before a game has to pay a fine of ten thousand dollars. So, you claim it wasn't you, that the coach made a mistake. But he shows you your contract again, and it says if the coach says he saw you the night before a game, then you've gotta pay the ten thousand dollars—if he says he saw you, then he saw you. Now, if you took the coach to court, and used the Constitution in your defense, do you think you would win? After all, the guy's trying to steal your money. He's violating your rights."

"But if I signed a contract agreeing to those terms, I wouldn't have a leg to stand on."

"Exactly. You entered a voluntary, binding agreement with the coach. Therefore, the Constitution wouldn't apply in that case."

"But I still don't understand why the Constitution didn't apply in my case. I mean, I never entered into a contract with the Bureau of Weapons Control."

"Are you sure about that? Many people enter into contracts with the government without even realizing it. They could be signing away their constitutional rights, and they don't even know it."

Matt was fascinated. "I never realized all this. But if I had signed a contract with the government, wouldn't I know about it?"

"Not necessarily," Tom said. "The government doesn't like to spell things out too clearly. For instance, most churches in America are incorporated. When a church—or any business, for that matter—becomes incorporated, it receives certain privileges from the government, like limited liability. But in exchange for those privileges, the business has to abide by certain government regulations. Becoming incorporated is the equivalent of entering into a contract with the government. If a church is incorporated, any donations it receives from its members are tax-deductible. That's the benefit it receives from the government. So, people are more likely to join an incorporated church. But there's a catch."

"What is it?" Matt asked.

"An incorporated church is not allowed to endorse political candidates, or criticize any, for that matter," said Tom.

Matt couldn't believe it. "But that's crazy! I mean, what if someone like Hitler were running for president? A pastor couldn't tell the congregation not to vote for him?"

"Not if he belonged to an incorporated church. If he did that, he would risk losing the church's tax-exempt status."

"But doesn't that violate the First Amendment?" Gina asked.

Tom shrugged. "Well, if a church voluntarily becomes incorporated, it agrees to accept certain limitations on its First Amendment rights in exchange for the privilege of having its donations tax-deductible. It's a way to attract new members. After all, wouldn't you be more agreeable to donating money to a church if you knew you'd get something in return?"

"Sounds like a racket to me," Gina remarked.

"Well, it is, in a sense," Tom admitted.

"But I still don't see how *I* could have had a contract with the BWC," Matt said.

Tom's face had a knowing look. "Didn't you apply for a permit for your shotgun?"

"Well, yeah, but—"

"You had to sign some papers, didn't you?"

"Of course."

"Do you remember what you were agreeing to when you signed those papers?"

Suddenly, things were becoming clear to Matt. He hadn't realized before that when he signed those papers, he was probably agreeing to abide by the policies of the BWC. "Man, I feel so foolish—so I really did sign a contract with them. This is so unfair! If I hadn't gotten the permit, I'd be breaking the law. But they never told me it was a contract."

"Right, and you broke the law when you violated your end of the contract," Tom said. "Didn't you agree not to carry your shotgun without your permit? And didn't you agree to accept the consequences of breaking that agreement when you signed your name to those papers?"

It took him a few moments to absorb the full implication of what Tom was saying. He was a pawn in the hands of the BWC, and so was anyone else who applied for a firearms permit. "But they never explained any of this," he said.

Tom almost laughed. "You expect the government to explain these things to you? Boy, do you have a lot to learn!"

"So, what you're saying is that somewhere in those papers I signed, there's a provision that allows the BWC to arrest and confiscate the weapons of permit holders who break their rules?"

"It probably didn't say so explicitly in the papers you signed. I've dealt with one or two cases like this before. You probably signed a vague statement agreeing to abide by the policies of the BWC. Those policies are stated in some intricate code of law that they hope you'll never see, kind of like the Internal Revenue Code."

"I can't believe this!" Matt exclaimed. "So, when I applied for a Firearms Owner Permit, I signed away my constitutional rights?"

"At least pertaining to any dealings with the Bureau of Weapons Control," Tom said.

"Wait a minute! How can the government make a law requiring you to sign away your rights? How can they legally force me to sign such a contract?"

"That's more of a gray area, and I'd rather not get into that right now." But his expression was troubled.

"Is there any way I can get my shotgun back?"

Tom looked grim. "I wouldn't even try, if I were you. If you make an issue of this, they're going to go after you. They like to make examples of people like you. The smartest thing you can do is to forget about ever owning a gun again. Now that they have your gun, they may leave you alone. That's probably all they were after."

Matt got up from the couch. He decided not to tell Tom about his carbine—which wasn't registered. *And never will be*, he decided. "But this is wrong!" he cried. "Can't you see what they're doing? They want to disarm us, and they're using these registration laws as a means of doing just that. If all firearms wind up in the hands of the government, then we'll have a police state. Is that what you want?"

Tom didn't answer right away. The lines around his mouth made him appear much older. In the heavy silence, Matt had the impression that his father-in-law was trying very hard not to see something which he had been denying for many years, but which he could no longer deny. When Tom finally spoke, he sounded defeated. "Maybe we already have one," he said quietly.

Matt was startled. He had never heard Tom say anything like that before. He had always expressed his faith in "the system" and had nothing but contempt for people who believed in civil disobedience. He wondered what had happened to change his attitude. "If you really feel that way, then why don't you do something about it?"

Tom got up from the couch. He was scowling and obviously upset. "Let's just drop this subject."

"Why? Are you afraid to face the truth?"

Gina got up and put her hand on Matt's shoulder. "Honey, I think it's time we changed the subject," she said tensely.

"No, this is important," said Matt. "The future of our country is at stake. Don't you two think this is something we *should* talk about?"

"I told you, I don't want to talk about this," Tom said through clenched teeth.

Matt sighed. "Fine, just keep your head in the sand. Like everyone else in this stupid country."

"I think we've both said enough," Tom said. "And if we're not careful, one of us is going to say something we'll all regret. So, I think I'll leave now." He reached for his overcoat.

Before leaving, he turned to Matt, and his eyes had a glint of understanding.

"Look, Matt, I think I know how you feel, and I respect those feelings. You feel like your rights have been violated, and maybe they were. But you'll just make things worse if you try to fight this. Believe me, I know what I'm talking about." He kissed Gina on the cheek. "So long, hon," he said abruptly before leaving the apartment.

She closed the door behind him and looked at Matt, who was deep in thought. "What are you thinking about?" she asked.

"I'm just wondering what your father's so afraid of," he said quietly.

CHAPTER 9

Oren Reinhardt entered a Lincoln Town Car parked by the tree-lined sidewalk of Park Avenue. Sitting in the back seat, he opened his briefcase and pulled out a video cassette. He stared at it for several moments, then dialed a number on his cellular phone. "Judge Reynolds, please." There was a pause. "Reinhardt here. I need a favor. I believe you have a Father Patrick Flannery awaiting trial in your district for starting a riot. He's out on bail now. Recently he was involved in another riot. See what you can do to get him back in prison—permanently." Another pause. "Yes—double the usual amount."

* * * *

Father Patrick Flannery glanced at the paper in his hands, a knowing smile on his face. "So, it's come to this. I should be glad, actually. It means they see me as a threat. I must be doing something right!"

Nathan Dalton got up from his checkered easy chair and looked anxiously at his friend, dressed in a pair of brown slacks and a jersey instead of his priestly garb. The pastor of his parish had asked him not to wear it anymore, since he had "dishonored" the priesthood. "The meeting is tomorrow night," said Nathan. "What are you going to do, Patrick?"

Patrick looked him squarely in the eyes. "I won't be intimidated. But if I'm going to be arrested for exercising my constitutional rights, I want to make sure it gets in the papers."

Dalton hesitated. He admired Flannery's courage, but the determined look on his face made him wary. "Maybe it would be better if you kept a low profile."

"It's too late for that. What if George Washington, Thomas Jefferson, and Patrick Henry had kept a low profile when the British were trampling the colonists' rights—burning down their churches and breaking into their homes? I tell you, we must stand up to the government. We have to fight these injustices. If we don't, who will?"

"Maybe it's too late to change things," Dalton said quietly.

"Perhaps you're right," Flannery conceded. "But even if it is too late, even if we are fighting for a lost cause, I'm not giving up. The colonists didn't know for certain whether they'd win. But they were willing to stake their lives on the fight for freedom. Anyway, ultimately, our side will win. Revelation promises that. But remember: evil has a clear path to victory whenever those on the side of goodness fail to stand in its way."

Nathan frowned. "I just wish more Christians were on our side. So many have bought into the concept of world peace through world government. And many others, sadly, would gladly trade their freedoms for a promise of security. It's amazing how far a country can fall in only a few generations."

"It's because people don't know the Scriptures. That's one of the problems I have with some of my Catholic brothers and sisters. Many of them view the Book of Revelation in completely allegorical terms. But I suppose I can't blame them; after all, that's what's being taught in the seminaries these days. I was taught that the Book of Revelation has nothing to do with the actual end of the world, it was 'resistance literature' written to encourage Christians to remain faithful during Roman persecution." He smiled knowingly. "And of course, the Beast was the Emperor Nero."

"That interpretation is becoming popular even among some liberal Protestants." Dalton adjusted his spectacles. "Scripture predicts that a brutally evil dictator will take over the world in the last days. To paraphrase the prophet Daniel, 'By peace he shall destroy many.' Those who support the New World Order need to undermine that prediction. The only way they can is to insist that it's allegorical."

Flannery sighed deeply. "Well, in any case, we know that this battle is a spiritual one. The people who want world government, no matter how well-intentioned, are really pawns in the hands of Satan, who's been planning this for a few thousand years. To paraphrase Saint Paul: 'Our struggle is not against flesh and blood, but against the rulers and powers of this dark world and against the forces of evil in the heavenly realms.'"

"I still think you should be careful," Dalton said. "The CGU is very powerful. Not to mention the fact that they practically own the federal government. You remember the last time you were arrested. What if it happens again? You may not be released this time."

"Well, then it will be worth it. If these videos we show wake up just a few people to the truth, I'll gladly spend the rest of my life in jail."

"I wish all Americans felt that way. But they're so wrapped up in their own lives and their own petty concerns, they don't even see what's happening. As long as they can keep their few luxuries—their VCRs, cars and television sets—they don't seem to mind giving up their freedom."

Flannery picked up his coffee mug from the corner table. "Not only that, but they get carried away with sensationalism in the news." He sipped his coffee thoughtfully. "They love reading about scandals involving celebrities or the latest murder, but they won't read the Constitution. That's why the country's in this mess."

"Do you really think that video is going to make a difference? After all, we don't have much time before the Convention."

"It's hard to say. But it does contain some eye-opening information about the UN. It also exposes the International Coalition of Churches and the CGU, and their connection with the federal government. It's all documented. Anyone can verify the information in that video."

Dalton shook his head. "But some of it sounds so incredible. I mean—that plot to infiltrate the Catholic Church with socialist priests! It sounds like something out of a spy novel."

Flannery nodded gravely. "I wouldn't have believed it myself, if I hadn't seen the evidence. But no one who's been a priest as long as I have can deny that appalling changes have taken place within the priesthood and the Church in general. I visited a few seminaries just to confirm what Bill told me, and he was right. Instead of learning the great truths of the Catholic faith, they're being trained to indoctrinate their congregations to accept world socialism! And it's not just the Catholic Church. Bill told me that mainline Protestant denominations have also been involved in this deception."

"Have you heard from him lately?"

"He called me a few weeks ago saying he had some new information, something about the FBI, I believe. We were supposed to meet, but he never showed up. And every time I call his number, I get his machine. I'm starting to worry about him."

"How long was he investigating the ICC?"

"I'm not sure. It started with an interview he did for *The New Yorker* on one of the leaders of the CGU. Something the man said didn't sit right with Bill, so he decided to investigate the group. He discovered they were donating huge sums of money to the International Coalition of Churches. So, he did some more digging, and found out that the same people who founded the CGU were instrumental in establishing the ICC. When he read about the attempted suicide of one of their priests, he paid the poor fellow a visit."

"And?"

"The priest confessed the entire plot; he was tormented with guilt, apparently. He'd been a staunch communist, and an atheist. But through some kind of miracle, he came to believe the Gospel and repented."

"Well, I'm no socialist. But I can understand how Christians could be taken in by the ideal of socialism. After all, socialists claim that they want to help the poor and needy, to make sure everyone has equality."

"True—but they want to use force and coercion to make everyone equal. The problem is that few people—even conservatives—understand the evil premise upon which socialism is based. It's not a noble ideal," said Flannery. "It seeks to make the individual a human sacrifice for the 'god' of the common good. It destroys incentive, self-reliance, the sense of individual responsibility. As long as man has a sinful nature, socialism can never work. The early Christians tried it, and some able-bodied believers stopped working, assuming the Church would support them. Finally, Saint Paul told them that whoever refused to work, would not eat."

Reverend Dalton sat down again, curious. "By the way, what made Bill get in touch with you?"

"He happened to read an article I had written about the ICC in *The Long Island Catholic*, and he thought I'd be interested in what he found out about them. Since he's been blacklisted in the newspaper business, he figured the only way to get the truth to the public was through a religious publication."

He was gazing out the window at a group of school children playing on the lawn, a faraway look in his eyes. "If it weren't for Bill, I wouldn't have learned the truth about what's been happening in the Catholic Church over the last two generations. The whole spiritual plot ties in with the political conspiracy I've been studying all these years. I just hope he's all right." He finished his coffee. "The information in the video is well-documented, and I think most patriotic Americans will be concerned. But I'm not sure the message will get through to the average, apathetic American. Most of them will fail to see the dangers of world government, no matter how well the facts are presented. Unless they believe they face real, imminent danger, few people will be concerned." He smiled. "Well, it's time I made a phone call to a reporter I know. I want to make sure she gets a front-row seat tomorrow night."

* * * *

Gina and Cheryl were sitting at a corner table in the cafeteria. Gina sipped her coffee quietly while Cheryl complained about another story which had been censored.

"You've been pretty quiet today," Cheryl commented after a moment or two of silence. "Is everything okay?"

Gina forced a smile. "Sure, I'm just tired." But in truth, she was worried about Matt. Something was wrong, but whenever she tried to get him to confide in her, he mumbled that she wouldn't understand. He spent much of his time in a local bar after work and often collapsed into bed long after Gina was asleep. Feeling hurt and resentful, she became more involved in her work, and they hardly ever saw each other.

Cheryl sipped her coffee. "Did you check your e-mail today? Whitaker scheduled another one of those diversity workshops. What a waste of time!"

"I don't think they're so bad. Actually, I find them inspiring." Although Gina certainly didn't like his editorial policies, she couldn't deny that Damien Whitaker was devoted to the cause of world peace. He was on the board of directors of one of the great charitable foundations, the Carney Endowment for World Peace, and often spoke in pious tones of "social justice" and the brotherhood of man. He frequently held "consciousness-raising" seminars with the staff, during which he extolled the virtues of equality and sacrifice for the common good.

"Well, they don't inspire me," Cheryl said. "Maybe if I thought he was sincere, I'd feel differently. But when Whitaker expounds on the need to redistribute the world's wealth more equitably, I doubt he intends on giving up any of his own wealth. I mean, the man comes to work in a limousine and wears Armani suits! And have you noticed that his attacks on wealth are confined to the 'affluent middle class'? I don't know about you, Gina, but I'm part of the middle class—and I'm not very affluent these days. If my taxes get any higher, my take-home pay will be less than what the welfare recipients are getting now."

Gina couldn't help smiling. "You sound like Matt," she said.

"Really? Does he have a brother?"

"Yeah, but he's married."

"Rats."

When Gina and Cheryl returned from their break, Gina noticed a message from Father Flannery. "I better get back to him," she told Cheryl. "The last time he called he had a juicy story for me." She made a wry face. "But, we both remember how that turned out."

"The story I've been working on will probably see the same fate," Cheryl said grimly.

166

Gina was curious. "That good, huh?"

Cheryl lowered her voice; they both knew that Damien had his snoops. "This is big. I may have to go freelance, maybe even put it on the Internet— which is probably the only free press in America now. Actually, I'm looking into starting my own website—you know, for stories that get canned."

"That sounds exciting."

"I suppose it is." She looked thoughtful. "Still, it's only a matter of time before the government starts regulating it. I just hope I can get my story on the Net before that happens."

* * * *

Matt's steps were steady and deliberate as he and Gina made their way toward the little white church which had been the scene of that terrible riot just a month earlier. He didn't like the idea of coming here tonight, but he wasn't about to let Gina come alone after what had happened.

Entering the foyer, Gina and Matt found a wooden staircase which led downstairs. In the large meeting room groups of people were milling about. Some were standing at a table where coffee and doughnuts were set up, others were sitting on hard metal chairs talking in earnest tones.

Gina turned to Matt as they sat down. "That's Father Flannery," she said, pointing. Matt looked over at the priest who was standing in a corner surrounded by several people with intense expressions. He caught a little of what the man was saying. "—not a bit worried. Remember, it's all in God's hands."

"But what if you do get arrested?" a middle-aged woman asked.

"Well, what if I do? That's a chance I have to take. After all, the Apostle Paul was arrested on a number of occasions. And he wrote some of his best letters from prison!" They all chuckled, but to Matt their laughter sounded somewhat forced.

Gina got up. "Come on, I'll introduce you to him," she said.

Father Flannery smiled when he saw Gina approaching. She introduced him to Matt.

"It's hard to believe this is the same place where that riot broke out," Matt said.

An elderly gentleman standing next to Father Flannery shuddered. "Yeah— it was awful! Were you here that night?"

"No, but my wife was there—she covered it for *Island News*."

"No kidding? Wasn't much of a story in the paper. You sure she was at the same riot?"

Matt forced a smile. "Doesn't seem like it, does it? Well, she was pretty upset herself, but her editor claimed he had to tone it down."

Father Flannery frowned. "Sounds more like censorship, if you ask me."

"Yeah, well, you know how it is—everyone wants to be politically correct these days."

A few minutes later, Matt heard someone calling everyone to sit down, so he followed Gina to a front row seat. He wanted to reach out and hold her hand, but he felt strangely awkward with her. He felt guilty for the way he had been treating her, blaming her for something that wasn't really her fault. On a few occasions, she had tried to reach out to him, had asked him to open up to her and tell her what was troubling him. But he felt tired, sick and tired of rehashing the same old argument. It had gotten to the point now where he hardly even resented her any more; he was beginning to feel a weary indifference toward her. And that's what disturbed him the most. In the past, he had actually enjoyed their sparring; it had seemed to lend excitement to their relationship. Now, he wished they had more in common. Sometimes, he even wondered if he had done the right thing by marrying her. Although he was aware of her liberal views then, he'd tried to tell himself that their differences shouldn't matter as long as they loved each other. He had also been strongly attracted to her, and much of their relationship had been physical. All his friends kept telling him what a catch she was, that he shouldn't let her get away. Now, he wondered if he had married her just to impress them. Captivated by her striking looks, he had ignored some of the nagging doubts in the back of his mind. Still, he couldn't imagine his life without her. And he believed he loved her. Even though he didn't say it all that much. But sometimes he wondered if she really needed him. After all, she was an intelligent, well-educated, capable career woman. What did she see in him?

The room had become silent. As Father Flannery approached the podium, Matt was struck by his peaceful expression. No one would guess that he had just been threatened with imprisonment if he dared to speak in public again! Matt sat back expectantly as the priest began to speak. "Let's pray, shall we?" Father Flannery's soft brogue intruded gently upon the heavy silence of the church. Matt watched as the priest bent his head and folded his hands together. "Heavenly Father, we gather here tonight in Your Son's Name, as intercessors for our nation, standing in the gap against a tide of evil. Lord, we ask You to grant us the wisdom we need to expose the works of darkness which threaten to engulf this nation. We ask You to show us Your will, and to bring the enemies of freedom and righteousness to repentance." He paused, allowing his words to sink in, and Matt felt something stir within him. It had been a long time since he had last thought about God, and he wondered if the emptiness inside him was something that perhaps only God could fill. And yet...something kept holding him back.

The priest continued. "We pray that their eyes may be opened to Your truth, and that they may come to know Your Son, who died to give us the greatest freedom of all—freedom from our bondage to sin." Matt glanced at Gina to see if she was as moved as he was, but saw her grimace at the word "sin." He sighed, once again reminded of the gulf between them. Deep in his heart he was beginning to feel he needed Jesus, but Gina would never understand. He forced himself to concentrate on Flannery's prayer. "Lord, we thank You for that most precious gift—the gift of eternal li—" A loud pounding reverberated through the room. Father Flannery froze, his face pale. Pastor Dalton jumped out of his chair, knocking it to the floor. A threatening voice shouted, "Open the door—this is the police!"

Gasps and murmurs rippled through the congregation, and people began getting out of their seats, seized with panic. In an instant Gina had her camera out and was speaking into her tape recorder, describing what was happening. Matt noticed vaguely that a child had begun to whimper.

Though Father Flannery may have been panicked for one brief moment, his face was set in grim determination as he moved cautiously toward the door. He raised his voice so he could be heard above the anxious muttering of the congregation. "Do you have a court order to come in here?"

The words of the officer were met with cries of dismay. "We're looking for Patrick Flannery. We have a warrant for his arrest!"

With the look of a frightened sparrow, Pastor Dalton was at Flannery's side, murmuring anxiously in a low voice. "It's all right, Nathan," Matt heard the priest saying. "We were both expecting this. Perhaps if I go peacefully, there won't be any trouble." He was about to say something else to the officers outside, but they began pounding on the door again, trying to break it down. Gina rushed forward and began taking pictures.

Father Flannery was becoming impatient. "Just hold on! I'll come peacefully if you'll just—" Everything was happening so fast that Matt could hardly absorb it all. The officers must have broken through the door, they were charging down the steps before Father Flannery could get his words out.

"All right—everybody get back!" the superior officer barked. His fellow officers—well over a dozen—moved around the room, eying everyone suspiciously. To Matt, it seemed as if an entire SWAT team had invaded the church! Yet they didn't appear to be ordinary police officers. They were dressed completely in black, wearing ski masks—just like the BWC agents Matt had encountered in Ben's apartment that awful night. And they had the same emblem on their jackets that the BWC agents had worn. They even carried M-16 rifles! Matt wondered if perhaps they were connected to the military somehow. He strained to make out some badge numbers, but couldn't see any badges.

The leader scowled at Flannery, who stood before him without flinching. "Are you Patrick Flannery?"

"I am," the priest said steadily.

The superior officer approached the priest and grabbed his arms, but to Matt's surprise, Father Flannery pulled back slightly. "Just a moment," he said. "May I see your warrant?" At that, the officer shoved him to the ground, pinning his hands behind his back. Two men from the congregation rushed forward, shouting in protest. Matt stood stupefied, a feeling of deja-vu came over him, and a sort of dissociation—as though this were somehow unreal. He saw five of the figures in black surround the two men, kicking and beating them with clubs. Both men collapsed onto the floor, moaning in pain, one of them bleeding. Some of the women were screaming.

Then, through the corner of his eye, Matt saw Gina being dragged across the floor by one of the officers, a tall, husky man built like a football player. On the floor her camera lay smashed into pieces. As the officer twisted her arm behind her back, she cried out in pain. That snapped Matt out of his mental inertia and almost instinctively, he ran forward, grabbed the officer by the arm and tried to pull him away. "Leave her alo—" Matt shouted. The next thing he knew, he was flying through the air—or so it seemed. Like a sack of flour, his body slammed into a shelf which stood against the back wall. He landed on the floor, dazed, his entire back throbbing in pain.

* * * *

After being pushed to the floor, Gina lay there silently, afraid to move. Never before had she felt so vulnerable. She saw Matt lying several feet away from her, and she tried to move toward him. A voice barked orders at the crowd. "Everyone down on the floor—face down! Put your hands behind your head! Anyone who moves will get their brains blown out!"

The people mutely obeyed. Gina tried to move her arm up, but a burning pain shot through her shoulder and radiated down her arm. That officer had injured her somehow. Someone kicked her in the side, yelling, "Get your hands behind your head!" Gina looked up at the officer through a blur of bewildered tears. "I can't," she said, her voice trembling. "My arm—"

The officer bent down and pulled her arms behind her back, and she screamed out in pain. Then she felt the cold muzzle of a gun against her head and went numb with terror. "Shut up or I'll kill you," she was told. Biting her lip to keep silent, she tasted blood.

The officer who appeared to be in charge was pushing Father Flannery ahead of him. "All right—let's go!" he shouted to the rest of the team. He pointed to the two men whom they had assaulted. "Cuff 'em," he told two of the officers. The men were pulled to their feet and handcuffed, so battered they had to be dragged out of the place. Gina noticed that neither of the officers read the men their rights. She suddenly feared they would try to arrest Matt. *God—please let them leave him alone*, she pleaded silently. Then, before she even realized what she was saying, the words came to her lips in a whisper, "Jesus, please help him."

She lay there for what seemed like an eternity, hardly aware of the cold wooden floor, hardly daring to breathe. Her one concern was Matt. She wanted to get up and run to his side, to hold him in her arms. *What if he's seriously injured?* she thought, her heart pounding in fear. She thought about that seemingly endless night when she had no idea where he was, or even if he was alive, and she suddenly realized how much she loved him.

* * * *

As Matt lay sleeping in their king-sized bed, Gina watched the gentle rhythm of his breathing. His face looked so peaceful that she hated to wake him. *Guess I'll let him sleep some more*, she thought. But she really wanted to hold him close and tell him she loved him. She looked at his bandaged wrist and arm, and sighed. He had sprained his wrist when he fell, and his arm had gotten cut by pieces of broken glass which had fallen out of the shelf. His entire back was a mass of purple bruises. Still, it could have been worse—much worse. She shivered as she thought of the two men who had tried to help Father Flannery and had been brutally assaulted. Her instincts as a reporter told her she should be writing all of this down. But right now,

Matt was more important.

She had insisted on taking him to the hospital, but they had waited hours in the emergency room because the staff was short-handed. Though she had always been a champion of nationalized health care, she couldn't deny that waiting lists and long lines at emergency rooms had become the norm since Congress had voted to adopt a government-funded public health care system. Although Matt was not seriously injured, the harried doctor had advised him to stay in bed for the next couple of days. Gina had seen the dark lines under the doctor's eyes and felt sorry for him. She had heard recently that a new wave of drug abuse and alcoholism had invaded hospitals and government clinics; work-related stress in the medical field had become nearly unbearable.

She felt sick when she thought about what had happened at the church. It was too much to absorb—too much to believe. *How could something like this happen?* She had known of corrupt police officers, had known that the government abused its power at times. But she had never witnessed anything like this before. Sitting in the darkness of her bedroom, she went over the entire experience in her mind once more, and it felt as if she were looking back on a nightmare. They had smashed her camera and confiscated her tape recorder. She had also seen them remove the video tape and smash the VCR that had been set up in the center of the room. What was it they were so afraid of? What on earth was on the tape that Father Flannery had planned to show? She had called the courthouse to find out where Father Flannery had been taken, and was disturbed to learn that was "classified information."

"What's going to happen next?" she wondered aloud. She leaned over and kissed Matt on the cheek, then quietly left the room.

CHAPTER 10

In the shadows of a back alley, Senator Ross Meyers moved cautiously among garbage cans and debris. The distant streetlights barely illuminated the ground in front of him. He fought to keep his breath even, his mind calm. He knew it was dangerous, perhaps even insane, to walk through this deserted alley so late at night. But he had no choice, he couldn't afford to be seen.

He thought he heard a noise behind him, something rustling among the garbage. Turning sharply, he moved his hand toward the pistol he had hidden in his coat and peered down the alley. Nothing. Must have been a rat. He shivered, pulled his coat more tightly around him. A mild drizzle made the concrete slippery. He picked up his pace and glanced at a tall brownstone apartment building in the distance. If he could just make it there without being seen.

* * * *

Cheryl Hendricks paced nervously up and down her sparsely furnished living room. The man she was about to meet tonight could hold the key to the conspiracy of silence she had almost stumbled upon looking into Damien Whitaker's background. Having learned that Whitaker was a member of an elite and little-known group called the Council for Global Unity, she did some research. Several congressmen who had been investigating the Council had died days before they were supposed to testify about some of the group's more questionable activities. Two were killed in mysterious airplane crashes, the third was the victim of a car bomb. Fortunately, Cheryl had been able to track down someone involved in the original investigation who remained alive, and who had recommended that the Council be cleared of all charges due to lack of evidence. Although he wouldn't tell her anything about the Council, he did tell her that a New York senator by the name of Ross Meyers had recently paid him a visit asking similar questions. When she found Meyer's name on the Council's membership roster, she knew she had struck gold.

But would he be willing to talk? And if he told her what he knew, would that put her in danger? Besides, if this group were as powerful as she suspected, how would she ever be able to get the truth out to the public?

She almost jumped at the sound of the bell, and took a deep breath before she opened the door.

The man who greeted her looked more like a retired English professor than a politician, and she wondered how someone so innocuous in appearance could be involved with a group as formidable as the CGU. She offered him a drink, and he asked for a Scotch and soda. Cheryl poured herself a cup of Earl Gray tea and joined the Senator in the living room.

After a bit of small talk Cheryl looked at him intently. "I was surprised you agreed to meet with me, Senator. What was it that changed your mind?"

"I've been doing a lot of soul-searching lately, I guess. The truth is," he said heavily, "I've come to hate myself...because I've betrayed my country. I couldn't admit that, not even to myself, until recently. That's what fear does to people, Ms. Hendricks. It makes them unwilling to see the truth, even when it's staring them right in the face."

"What are you afraid of?" she asked in a soft voice.

"Have you ever been in a position where you knew that if you did the right thing you would lose absolutely everything? If I were to tell you what I know about the group you're investigating, it would mean the end of my career." He shook his head in amazement, as if he were hardly able to believe he had the guts to go through with this.

"Then why did you come here tonight?"

"Because I had to. I can never again look myself in the mirror if I allow my country to be destroyed without doing something—anything—to stop it. So, I suppose I'll begin at the beginning."

As Cheryl listened to Senator Meyers describe his involvement with the Council for Global Unity, she could hardly believe that her suspicions about her new boss would lead her into such a web of treachery and intrigue. For the next two hours, the Senator confided everything he knew about the Council—their control over the State Department, education, the news media, their hidden agenda known only to a select cadre within the Council, and their role in influencing U.S. foreign policy.

"What is their agenda?" Cheryl asked. "I mean, what exactly are they after?"

"They'd like people to think that their goal is world democracy. But what they really want is control...and what better way to control the world's masses than through a socialist one-world government? Of course, not everyone who belongs to the Council is aware of its anti-American agenda, though it's become increasingly difficult to keep that a secret anymore." The Senator smiled ruefully. "Believe it or not, we even have a handful of conservatives and 'patriots' on our membership roster—for protective coloring, of course. They only get invited to certain meetings, though. Not the ones where policy decisions are made."

She sipped her tea. "What makes people want to join?"

"Most people join because it's good for their careers, others foolishly believe that the Council really is committed to world peace. After I graduated Harvard and failed to show any promise as a lawyer, my father arranged for me to be invited to join the Council. I was young and impressionable, so at first I was almost intoxicated by the power and privileges I had access to through my membership. Women, money, even luxury cars were dangled in front of me like a carrot...as long as I did their bidding, of course. Once assured of my loyalty, the Council proceeded to build my entire political career, donating vast sums of money to help me get elected and reelected. They built my image, wrote my speeches, even told me how to vote." He shook his head again. "And now, I'm about to expose them!"

She thought of the congressmen who had paid with their lives for attempting the same thing. "Do you know of anyone else who tried to expose them, Senator?"

He sighed. "It's hard to say. I know of at least three congressmen who tried, and I suspect that they may have been murdered."

Cheryl asked him to elaborate, but he didn't seem to want to go into much detail. "Wasn't there another investigator?" she asked.

"Ah, yes. I always wondered why he dropped the investigation so suddenly, especially after the suspicious deaths of his colleagues. So, I recently paid the fellow a visit. He told me about an interesting thing that happened to him at a party in Washington the night before he was planning to go public about the Council. Someone at the party gave him a drink, and he had a blackout. But this was no ordinary blackout. He woke up in a hotel room hours later with no recollection of what had happened after being handed that drink. The next morning when he arrived in his office he found a manilla envelope filled with compromising photos of himself with a very young woman, probably not more than thirteen or fourteen, he said." He sipped his drink and smiled sadly. "You can fill in the rest of the details yourself."

There was a long silence. "So, no one else has attempted to expose the Council?"

"There have been other attempts, mostly by a few isolated ex-members who dropped out when they learned the Council's true goals. But no one's been able to expose us on a large scale."

"Why not?"

"Because the media and academia have brainwashed most Americans into having a knee-jerk reaction to 'conspiracy theories.'"

Cheryl smiled, thinking of some of her colleagues. She recalled that Gina was especially disdainful of such theories. But if Ross were telling the truth, perhaps they weren't "theories" at all. "So, basically what you're saying is that the Council for Global Unity is involved in a conspiracy against the American people?"

He appeared to be mulling this over. "I'm not even sure it can be called a conspiracy at this point. At least, not any more. The Council has become much more open about its goals, now that they feel confident that they have the support of most Americans. But their methods have been completely underhanded. They keep saying, 'The end justifies the means.' That's how they hook you. Hmph! It's all a lie. They don't give a damn about world peace, with all the wars they've promoted."

Cheryl was puzzled. "Why would a group like the Council for Global Unity want to promote wars? Isn't that the opposite of what they want?"

"It's part of an old formula. Create a crisis, then offer a solution—which consists of more government control or promotes some other sinister agenda. You see, without wars people wouldn't perceive a need for a one-world government...would they?"

Cheryl was appalled, yet fascinated. She went back in her mind over all she had learned in her research, starting with her discovery that Damien was a member of the CGU—along with the owners of the twenty-five major newspapers in the country, as well as the board members of the three major news networks. She knew it was a powerful group—but to believe that its members would deliberately promote wars to achieve their goals, well, she'd need evidence before she could believe *that*.

Evidently Ross saw her skepticism. "Sounds a bit far-fetched, does it? Perhaps you wouldn't think so if you knew that the CGU gave Hitler the financial backing he needed to go to war...which amounted to millions of dollars. Did you know that the Reinhardt bank, under a deal cooked up by the Council, loaned twenty million to I.G. Farben?"

Cheryl knew that I.G. Farben was a big chemical company, but that was it. "So?"

"I.G. Farben supplied over forty percent of the funds which got the Nazis elected in 1933. Farben also manufactured explosives for Hitler's war machine. Not to mention the Zyklon gas which was used to kill the Jews before cremating them."

Though startled by this information, Cheryl was not completely convinced. "But that doesn't prove that the CGU deliberately promoted the war. Maybe they didn't know what I.G. Farben was going to do with the money."

"You can believe that if you want," Ross said. "But, even after the war had started, the Reinhardts and other founding members of the CGU kept doing business with Farben. In fact, the Reinhardt's oil company sold millions of dollars in aviation fuel to Farben, knowing that this fuel would be used in Nazi war planes—against American soldiers! You can check this with U.S. War Department records, if you don't believe me. They did an investigation after the war. Want to know what they concluded?"

By now Cheryl was on the edge of her seat. "What?"

"They said that without Farben's facilities, Germany never could have gone to war! Their economy was in ruins, hyperinflation was killing them. And I.G. Farben would never have been able to give Hitler any financial backing without the support of American bankers and businessmen—the same ones who founded the CGU!"

Cheryl was baffled. "But I still don't see what they gained. They didn't achieve a one-world government after the war."

Ross downed the rest of his drink. "Maybe not right away. But, they got one step closer. The Senate approved America's entrance into the UN. Those bastards knew that if they couldn't get a one-world government directly, they could use the UN's treaty-making power to do an end-run around America's sovereignty. In fact, those are the exact words of an article written in our publication, *Global Affairs*, many years back. You see, it had to be done piecemeal, until one day, Americans would be prepared for the final stage—the abolishing of the U.S. Constitution and the adoption of a world constitution. This debit-card system we have in place now is also part of the plan. Do you think the recent world-wide financial collapse happened by accident? No, it was engineered to make the people so desperate for a solution that they were willing to surrender their financial privacy under the World Debit-Card system...which will make it possible for a totalitarian government to enslave every single person on this planet. What better way to control people than to keep track of what they buy and sell? Not only that, but through the World Debit Card the UN and its agencies will have the capability to collect taxes on a global scale—and no one will be able to resist."

She was shaking her head. "It sounds so...so unbelievable. I mean, how could a depression of such magnitude be planned?"

He adjusted his glasses. "Did you know that back in 1913 a congressman by the name of Louis T. McFadden warned his colleagues that if they voted to pass the Federal Reserve Act, depressions would be scientifically created? After the crash of 1929 he was quoted as saying the Depression 'was not accidental,' that it was 'a carefully contrived occurrence.'"

"Really?"

He nodded. "By deliberately contracting the money supply, the Federal Reserve *caused* the very thing it had been created to prevent." His tone was ironic. "Naturally, the Federal Reserve Board was kind enough to warn its member banks to get out of the Stock Market with their profits intact before the crash of '29. However, they neglected to warn the rest of the country. As a result, most of the nation's wealth wound up in the hands of just a few thousand people. And history has just repeated itself...only on a much larger and more devastating scale." He put his face in his hands. "And, I knew about it. I knew what was going to happen yet I remained silent. That makes me an accomplice."

"But how did you know?"

He had the expression of someone in hell. "I was warned. During a secret meeting closed to the press, Oren Reinhardt warned those of us in the CGU's inner circle to get out of the Stock Market before it crashed. Within a month, billions of people lost their livelihoods, life savings, businesses, homes, dreams...but I was spared, along with the rest of the traitors." His tone was bitter.

She was jotting all this down on her pad. "I still don't see how the Federal Reserve can have so much power."

"Because it's not accountable in any way to the American people. It's actually a private corporation, owned mostly by foreign bankers."

"Are you sure? I thought it was a government agency."

He chuckled. "The Federal Reserve System is no more 'federal' than Federal Express. It also happens to have been the single most effective tool in undermining America's sovereignty as well as driving the nation into its current state of bankruptcy."

"In what sense?"

"Because the Federal Reserve Act usurped from Congress the power to coin money and regulate its value, giving that power to private domestic and foreign bankers which now practically own the United States government.

And these same bankers have grown incredibly wealthy off the interest payments on money they loan to the U.S government, money that they create out of nothing! And who pays the interest? Why, the American people, of course." He smiled ruefully. "And guess what? The Reinhardt family has been on the Fed's Board of Governors ever since it was founded.

There was a long silence as Cheryl tried to digest everything she had learned in the past several hours. In some strange way, though, none of it really seemed shocking. It was as if missing pieces of a puzzle had been filled in. Her father had been an intelligence officer in the miliary and had often hinted of terrible secrets he had learned about the U.S. government which he could never reveal to anyone without endangering his family. The question was: who would believe all this? And there was absolutely no way Damien would ever allow these revelations into the paper he owned! Unless Ken had the backbone to sneak them in without Damien's knowledge, the truth would remain hidden. And if Ken did agree to print it, they would both be out of a job...or worse. Of course, she could always try one of the news magazines she freelanced for—or even publish it on the Internet. Maybe she could try Cablevision's Public Forum Channel if all else failed.

She was startled out of these thoughts by something Ross Meyers was saying. "So you see, Ms. Hendricks, everything necessary for world domination is almost in place. Only one thing stands in the way...a sovereign nation called the United States of America, which was founded upon the sacred principles of individual liberty. Once Americans give up their sovereignty, there will be one completely ruthless government ruling the entire planet." He poured himself another drink. "Life, as we know it, will never again be the same, my dear. Just wait and see."

* * * *

Cheryl watched Ken's expression as he read through the exposé she had placed on his desk the following morning. Although he raised his eyebrows now and then, he really didn't look all that surprised. When he had finished reading, he opened his desk drawer, took out a bottle of Whiskey, and poured a shotful into his coffee mug. After taking a swig, he looked at Cheryl. "You want some?"

She shook her head. "Well?"

"Well what?"

"Aren't you going to say something about this report? I mean, this is big!

179

This is like, the story of the century."

He sighed. "What do you want me to say?" He seemed to be having a hard time looking her in the eyes.

Then it dawned on her. "You knew about all this! This is no revelation to you, Ken. How long have you known? And why the hell haven't you told the truth to the American people??"

He quickly got up and closed the door. "Cheryl, it's a lot more complicated than it seems. The people you want to expose, they're extremely powerful—"

"Of course they are! And if someone doesn't try to stop them, they're going to have total control over our country—and the entire world. Doesn't that matter to you, Ken?"

"Cheryl, they already *have* control over our country. Do you really think there's anything we can do to stop them?"

She felt like she had been thrown up against a wall. "So, that's it? We just give up?"

"What else *can* we do? Damien will never allow this story to be printed. He'll have us blacklisted—"

"Well, *I'm* not giving up." She got up from her chair and walked toward the door.

Ken stood in front of her. "Cheryl, don't do anything foolish!"

"You mean like telling the truth?"

He shook his head. "You'll be fighting a losing battle."

"Really? That's what a lot of people thought the colonists were doing when they tried to break away from England." She went to open the door.

"You're forgetting something." He went to his desk and got her report.

She looked at him sadly. "You can keep it. I have extra copies. I'm sure someone will be interested in the truth." She was even thinking of running a full-page ad in *America Today*, one of the news magazines she freelanced for. And thankfully, the CGU didn't control the Internet. At least, not yet.

* * * *

Ken took one last look at Cheryl's report before he turned off the news. His head throbbed from all the vodka he had been drinking the last several hours, but his hands wouldn't stop shaking.

When he heard the news of Cheryl's death, he felt as if he had been hit in the stomach. It happened as she was walking through the parking lot of the newsroom to her car; no one had seen the sniper at the window of the apartment building across the street, sighting his crosshairs at her. She died instantly. Later Ken discovered that a fire had demolished her apartment just hours after her death.

On the news, Cheryl's death was reported as another random sniper attack, and commentators called for more gun-control laws. But Ken knew better. He knew that few people who tangled with the CGU ever lived to tell about it.

He stared at Cheryl's report for a long moment before doing what he knew he had to do. Holding it over a large ashtray, he lighted it on fire. As he watched the paper crumple into embers, he took another swig of Vodka.

* * * *

When Ross had finished speaking, there was a long, awkward silence as he looked at all the blank faces before him. Of all the reactions he had imagined, that had been the farthest from his mind. He gripped the arms of his chair tightly. The back of his shirt was drenched with sweat. He had called the top journalists of the Beltway as soon as he arrived in Washington, knowing he didn't have much time after what had happened to Cheryl. Now, as he sat uncomfortably in his luxurious office, he wondered if he had done the right thing.

A woman's patronizing voice finally broke the silence. "So, you're saying that this—this conspiracy—has existed since before World War II?" She looked incredulous, and he heard a few people snicker.

He cleared his throat. "Well...yes. That's what I've been trying to explain." He realized with burning shame that he probably sounded like an idiot to most of them. Or worse, a madman. Still, there had to be those among this group who knew, or at least suspected, the truth about the CGU. And those who knew the truth and were a party to it would ridicule him the loudest.

Another journalist, a seasoned reporter for *The Washington Post*, looked confused. "I don't understand. I mean, even if what you're saying is true, what's the big deal? It's no secret that the Council for Global Unity is committed to world peace. If they've been promoting a one-world government all these years, so what? A lot of organizations have been doing that. Does that mean they're all part of some sinister conspiracy?"

Ross tried to fight off the panic rising inside him. "You just don't understand. These people are not committed to world peace. What they want is control...world domination, to be precise! And they will stop at nothing to get what they want. What really concerns me is the control they have over our government. You can check the facts for yourself. Don't you find it disturbing that so many top government officials, including the President, his Cabinet, his National Security Advisor—not to mention the entire State Department—are all members of the same organization? Look at our last thirteen CIA directors. They were *all* members of the CGU. And every Secretary of State since Roosevelt's administration was a member. For Pete's sake, every president, with maybe one or two exceptions, has belonged to the Council since it was founded! Doesn't that make you the least bit suspicious?"

He realized he was very agitated, and he could see that some of the journalists were starting to feel nervous. One of them spoke in a conciliatory tone. "Senator Meyers," he said, his face a mask of kindness over his obvious feelings of disdain. "You of all people shouldn't find it unreasonable for government leaders to join a group such as the Council for Global Unity. After all, it does help their careers, and at the same time, they have the chance to devote themselves to worthy causes, like the environment and the quest for world peace. I really don't see what the problem is. Doesn't it make sense for people with similar careers and backgrounds to belong to the same club?"

Ross stood up suddenly, desperate to convince them of the truth yet knowing full well this was a truth that none of them would ever dare to acknowledge; attempting to expose it would almost certainly mean the end of their careers. But he couldn't give up; he had to try to get through to at least some of them. "It's not just their pushing for world government that bothers me—it's their vicious methods! They destroy anyone who gets in their way. Do you think that sniper attack on that Long Island journalist yesterday was just a random shooting? It wasn't! The night before I had told her everything I knew about the CGU—I was at her house for over three hours. She had been investigating the Council and was planning to expose them, the next morning—wham! And she's not the first. Congressmen who were trying to expose them have also paid the price, including that congressman who went down in flight KAL-007. The list is long. And it doesn't end there. They actually work to create strife and problems in our country in order to bring about the changes they want. Look at what's been happening to our country—*your* country—since that blasted Council was founded! Our nation's been plagued by racial strife, crime, inflation, and debt. Not to mention a failing educational system. Most high school graduates have never even heard of the Bill of Rights, and many can't even find the United States on a world map. Yet they're being trained to see themselves as *global* citizens. They may not know how to read, but they sure as hell care about saving the whales and the rainforests! And all the while our freedoms have gradually eroded to the point where our Constitution is essentially dead. Our economy collapsed as a result of a sky-rocketing federal debt. To get us out of that hole, the President pushed us into a global monetary system which has further undermined our sovereignty and has destroyed our right to privacy. No one can make a move without the government knowing about it. There's no place to hide. Do you think this is all a coincidence? If you do, then you're a pack of fools! I can assure you, it's no coincidence. I was a part of it all, I helped plan it! Do you want to know what Oren Reinhardt said at one of our private meetings, years before the economy collapsed? He said that the best way for the government to monitor and control every American citizen would be to establish a cashless monetary system. Is it a coincidence that he got what he wanted? Is it a coincidence that we went bankrupt? Is it a coincidence that every single foreign policy decision made since the founding of the CGU has brought us closer to a one-world government? And you—if any of you believe me and write a story attacking the CGU—do you really think your editors or publishers would allow it to be printed? Why not? Control! Intimidation! Suppression of truth. Do we even have a free press anymore?"

He stopped, breathless, and the room was silent. The journalists were no longer looking at him; most of them were staring at the floor or looking at their watches. He was certain that some of them, at least, believed what he was saying. But they could not afford to admit it. Their careers would be destroyed.

He felt completely defeated. One or two reporters guffawed as they walked past him to leave. Most had avoided looking at him.

Two days later, he received a phone call from one of them, saying he had approached his editor with Ross's information, but his editor was ordered not to print it. Ross wondered if the same thing had happened to any of the others.

For a few days, he closely examined the newspapers and news shows, hoping for some mention of his story. Nothing. Not a word. Now, it was only a matter of time. He wondered how they would get to him and whether he would see the same fate as other government officials who had dared to defy the Council, and had paid with their lives.

He was afforded no such luck, however. On a bright morning in early December, within a week after his meeting with the reporters, a front page story in one of Washington's top newspapers dealt the deathblow to Senator Meyer's career. The story accused him of racism, which was anathema in Washington's atmosphere of political correctness. The story was also picked up by the three major news networks. What really frightened Ross was that on one news segment, there was a video clip showing him denouncing various minority groups. Another clip showed him talking to a Ku Klux Klan leader. But Ross had never said any of those things, and had never met with a Klan leader in his life! After his shock wore off, he realized what had happened. It was a computer imagery technique called morphing, used in movies to create events that never happened. He remembered seeing the technique used in *Forrest Gump*, where the main character appeared in scenes with John F. Kennedy and Lyndon Johnson. At the time, he thought it was amazing. It really looked like Gump was talking to the late presidents! Now, as Ross stared at his television screen, watching himself saying things he had never said, he reflected on how easily technology could be abused.

His wife, a prominent attorney who had gained a distinguished reputation for her efforts on the behalf of minorities, left him. His children, who had never cared much for him to begin with, now despised him. Not because of any repugnance for racism, he realized, but for the humiliation he had brought them.

As Ross sat in his expansive living room with its cathedral ceiling and luxurious furniture, he realized that he had nothing. Absolutely nothing. For all the years of compromise, of distorting the truth, of betraying his country, he had gained nothing. In pursuing his political career at the expense of his integrity, he had lost everything. A phrase came to him suddenly, a saying he had heard somewhere long ago. *What good does it do if a man gains everything, but in the process he loses his soul?* Ross wasn't sure where the saying came from. He only knew that he was a man who had lost everything, possibly even his soul.

CHAPTER 11

Matt and John walked along the edge of a stagnant, murky pond surrounded by tall reeds and willow trees. "You've been pretty quiet this morning," John commented. They had just finished a late breakfast at the Country Kitchen up the road and had decided to go for a walk.

"Yeah, well, I kind of have a lot on my mind," Matt muttered. He had called John on the spur of the moment because he desperately wanted to talk about everything that had happened recently, especially the murder of Ben and Elsie, but he felt annoyed because he had no one else but his brother to turn to.

His friends at work were pretty superficial; usually, their conversation centered on sports, television shows, and the women they were scoring with. Whenever Matt tried to talk about serious issues, like the dangers of big government, they either laughed off his concerns or said they didn't want to hear about it. All they cared about was having fun. Matt couldn't seem to talk to Gina without blowing up at her or making some kind of sarcastic comment. But it was difficult for him to admit that he needed John's help.

"You want to talk about it?" John asked.

"About what?" Matt snapped.

John smiled, shaking his head. "About whatever it is that's bothering you."

"Oh, and I'm sure you have all the answers, don't you?"

John kept his cool. "Matt, I don't claim to have all the answers. If I did, I wouldn't need God."

"Man, that's all you ever talk about! Every time I try to have a conversation with you, you have to drag God into it. Do you have any idea what a turn-off that can be?"

"I'm sorry if it offends you," John said quietly.

Matt softened. "Look, I'm sorry I snapped at you. It's just that—well, something happened that's got me pretty upset, and I guess I took it out on you."

"What happened?"

He pointed to a nearby bench. "I think we better sit down," he said slowly.

John listened in silence as Matt related what had happened to Ben and

Elsie. He also told him about the raid at the church. By the time he had finished, he felt his insides churning; it was awful having to relive that nightmare. He was waiting for John to make some kind of preachy comment about the need to accept God's will. But he was surprised by what John actually said. "Things are worse than I thought," he said. "Unfortunately, I'm afraid this is only the beginning. It's going to get a lot worse. Still, it's hard to believe something like this can happen in America."

"Yeah, I'm having a hard time believing it myself. Would you believe I trashed the apartment? That's how upset I was."

John nodded sympathetically. "Can't say I blame you."

"I just wish there was something I could've done to help Ben and Elsie. If I'd gotten there a few minutes sooner, maybe I could've gotten a couple of those bastards before they murdered them!"

John looked troubled. "I'm not sure violence is the answer."

Matt rolled his eyes. *Here we go again.* "Oh, and what would you suggest? No, don't tell me—you'd quote the Bible to them! Yeah, I can just see it: while government agents are pumping lead into your neighbors, you'd be reading the Bible. Yeah, that would work brilliantly!"

John sighed. "You just don't understand—"

"Wait a minute. What makes you so sure *you* understand everything? I mean, you may know a lot about the Bible, but you don't seem to understand what's happening in your own government. We are heading toward a police state, and all you can do is preach against violence! Have you ever thought about how all this is going to affect you and Beth?"

He looked away. "Yeah, I've thought about it. And I pray about it constantly."

"Well, maybe you should try doing something about it for a change. It's people like you that are making all this possible, who sit around doing nothing while the government is raping the country!"

He shrugged, a helpless expression on his face. "What would you suggest I do? Go down to the local Bureau of Weapons Control and shoot up the place?"

"Of course not. But have you tried any peaceful means of changing the government? When was the last time you even voted?"

"It's been a while," John admitted. "I guess I haven't voted since they abolished the Right to Life Party in New York. There just haven't been any candidates worth voting for since then. I used to like the Republicans, but they've pretty much abandoned their pro-life platform. They also supported that law which forced Christian radio stations to give equal time to secular humanists and New Age gurus. It's gotten to the point where they hardly seem any different from liberal Democrats."

"Look, I know where you're coming from." Matt smiled. "What was it Dad used to call both parties? The Demopublicans? Or maybe the Republicrats."

"That sounds like Dad," John said. "He always said there's very little difference between them. Which is why it seems pretty pointless to vote."

"Yeah, I see your point. No matter which party controls the White House, we always seem to get higher taxes and bigger government. But that's because the dumb sheep in this country keep voting the same kind of worthless candidates into office. And Christians who don't vote or get involved in politics are part of the problem. You all love to whine about the fact that prayer is no longer allowed in public schools, but what are you doing about it? Why don't you Christians try doing something for a change instead of sitting on your butts praying? If you don't like the candidates that are running, there are things you can do about it."

John looked skeptical. "Like what?"

"Well, you could support candidates you do like, and collect signatures to get them on the ballot."

He shrugged. "I don't know. I don't think it would make much of a difference in the long run."

"Why not?"

"Because God puts all political leaders in power. It doesn't matter who we vote for, it's all up to God."

"Yeah, right. So, what you're saying is that whoever happens to be in power was chosen by God?"

"It's in the Bible, in Romans 13."

Matt was incredulous. "Wait a minute. If that's true, then that means God put Hitler in power! Is that what you believe?"

He hesitated. "I guess there are some Christians who believe that."

"But do *you* believe it?"

"I honestly don't know. All I know is that Christians should live the way Jesus would want us to. So, while I may not be sure if God would ever put someone like Hitler in power, I do know that we should respect and obey our leaders, no matter how evil they may be."

"So, if our government leaders are liars and traitors, we should respect them?"

"The Bible tells us to honor the king."

Matt shook his head in disbelief. "So, where would you stand on assassinating some monster like Hitler or Stalin?"

"Matt, violence can never solve anything. Besides, the Scriptures say not to be overcome by evil, but to overcome evil with good."

"You've got an answer for everything, don't you? Okay, let's see if you have an answer for this one. Now, assuming the Bible has the answers, like you seem to think, what does the Bible say you should do when your neighbor is being attacked?"

He seemed to be mulling this over. "Hmm. When Jesus was being arrested, Peter tried to save Him by attacking the high priest's servant. But Jesus reprimanded him. He also said, 'Whoever takes the sword dies by the sword.'"

Matt considered this. "Okay, but Jesus' arrest and crucifixion were part of God's plan, right? So, Peter was interfering with God's will by trying to prevent His arrest. Am I right?"

John smiled. "Guess you have me there. But I'm still not sure that justifies using violence against the government."

"The Bible says to love your neighbor, right?" Matt asked.

"Of course."

"Am I showing love for my neighbor if I don't take any action to save his life when government thugs are trying to kill him?"

There was a long silence as John groped for an answer. Matt jumped in again. "What if Beth were being attacked? What would you do then?"

The question seemed to jar him. "Whatever I had to," he said.

"Would you kill her attackers, if that was the only way to save her?"

He nodded, his expression grim.

"What if they were government agents?"

"I'd kill them," he said in a low voice. "But only if I had to." His eyes had an intensity that Matt had rarely seen before.

"You don't honestly believe that God would hold that against you, do you?"

"I'm not sure. I know some Christians who would say killing is never justified, not even in self-defense. I don't know if I'd go that far, though."

Matt couldn't believe this lunacy. "But if God gave us the gift of life, wouldn't He expect us to defend it when it's under attack? Wouldn't He *require* us to defend the lives of our loved ones? If we didn't, we'd be shirking our responsibilities." When John didn't respond, Matt added, "Besides, in the Old Testament God seems to make a distinction between murder and justifiable killing. Didn't God command the death penalty for murderers?"

John raised his eyebrows. "Why, Matt—you've been reading Scripture," he said in a tone of mock surprise.

Matt chuckled. "All right, my secret's out. But don't go converting me yet. Actually, I read that shortly after Ben and Elsie's murder. You know what else I read?"

John smiled at Matt's eager expression. "What?"

"That it's okay to kill someone who breaks into your house."

"Where does it say that?" he asked doubtfully.

"In Leviticus, smarty. Only it says you can't kill the intruder after daybreak, when it's light enough to catch the guy."

John brightened. "You know, you're right. I remember that now. Still, some things changed with the New Testament. Those who follow Jesus aren't supposed to seek revenge, they're supposed to turn the other cheek."

"But what exactly does that mean? Does it mean we can't use justifiable force to defend our lives and property from armed intruders? I don't know about you, John, but I don't think self-defense is the same thing as revenge."

"Yeah, but what if the intruder isn't intending to kill you? What if he just wants to rob you? Should you kill him then?"

"Hey, if a guy's armed, I'm not taking any chances. And I don't care what the Bible says."

They got up from the bench and walked through the dry grass along the edge of the pond.

Matt hadn't been out this way in quite a while, and he enjoyed the peace and quiet. Parts of Suffolk County reminded him of the country. He and John had grown up in Oakdale, in a house bordering the woods. There was a lake nearby and a canal connecting to the Connetquot River. Enclosed by the woods was a swamp the boys and their dog loved to explore. Whenever Matt came to this part of the island, he yearned for the carefree days of his past.

"How are you and Gina getting along these days?" John asked suddenly.

Matt was startled out of his reverie. "Not as well as I'd like. Guess it's partly my fault. I get so angry with the government, and I take it out on her. In a way, I see her as partially responsible for all this—'cause she's always supported big government. You know—gun control, welfare, quotas. I guess it's pretty unfair of me to blame her."

"Well, I can understand how you feel. In fact, I've been struggling with anger myself lately."

Matt chuckled. "*You*? You're probably the most even-tempered person I know."

"I try to be. It isn't always easy, though."

"So, what is it that makes you angry?"

He dug his hands into his pockets. "My job, for one thing. Lately I've been getting a lot of heat about sharing the gospel at work. Like the other day, a friend of mine happened to ask me a question about the Bible. Well, I started to answer him, and my chairman walked by." He shook his head.

"What happened?"

"He called me into his office and accused me of harassment."

Matt was incredulous. "What?!"

John nodded. "It's because of some new regulation. According to a recent Supreme Court ruling, simply talking about religion in the presence of an atheist amounts to harassment."

"Well, if you want my opinion, you're directing your anger at the wrong person. You should be mad at the government, not your chairman."

"I don't think getting angry at the government will solve anything," John said.

"But doesn't it bother you that your freedom of worship is being attacked?"

"Of course it bothers me. But I try to keep it in perspective."

"How?"

"By reminding myself that God's in control."

Matt looked at him intently. "What about our other freedoms, like the right to keep and bear arms? Doesn't it bother you that the government is attacking our Second Amendment rights?"

He thought about this. "I guess that's not so important to me."

"You still own a gun, don't you?"

"Yeah—I still have the .22 Dad gave me. As far as I know, it's still legal to own a rifle."

"But what if the government suddenly made it illegal? Would you turn it in?"

"I guess I wouldn't have much choice, would I? Anyway, like I said before, guns aren't very important to me at this point in my life. I used to enjoy target shooting, but I haven't gone in ages. So, I wouldn't have a major problem with having to turn it in."

Matt picked up a small, gray stone and tossed it into the pond. "You know, the Second Amendment isn't there to protect our right to go target shooting—or even hunting. It's there to protect us from the government."

John looked wary. "Oh?"

Matt nodded. "Before Ben was murdered, he gave me a little history lesson—the stuff you don't learn in the public schools...or should I say, government schools? Anyway, what most Americans don't realize is that the purpose of the Second Amendment is to prevent government tyranny. As long as citizens are armed, they have the means to resist tyranny. Right now, the government's trying very hard to disarm us, so they can create a police state. But a police state can never happen in a country where private citizens can fight back."

John shook his head in disapproval. "What you're talking about is armed rebellion. That's not God's way."

Matt threw his hands up in exasperation. "Look, we're talking about the real world here, John. A world where monsters like Hitler can murder six million Jews! A world where your next-door neighbor can be gunned down in the middle of the night by his own government. You know, if the Jews in Nazi Germany had been armed, they would've had a fighting chance. I just can't believe that God would expect us to sit back and let the government kill innocent people. Is that what the Bible says—to sit back and let the government murder your neighbors and loved ones?"

"Matt, the Bible says that we should submit to the governing authorities."

"But what if the authorities are evil? Should we obey evil men?"

"Not if they command you to do something that's contrary to God's will. The Bible does say that whenever man's law conflicts with God's law, we should obey God's law. But, that doesn't justify taking up arms against the government."

"But you just admitted that if Beth were being attacked by government agents, you'd kill them if you had to. Isn't that taking up arms against the government?"

John looked unsure of what to say. "I guess it is," he admitted after a moment or two.

"Anyway, it wouldn't even have to come to that, if more of you Christians got involved in politics."

"But there's a lot more to all of this than mere politics," John said earnestly. "We're talking about a spiritual battle, a battle between the forces of Christ and those of the Antichrist. That's what it's going to come down to. And eventually, you're going to have to decide whose side to be on."

They walked in silence. Though he had never believed in conspiracies, Matt was beginning to suspect that there were forces behind the scenes pushing America toward the New World Order. But to believe that Satan was involved seemed to be stretching it. Why would God allow Satan to have such power? It didn't make sense, nothing made sense anymore. His entire world had turned upside down, and there was nothing he could do about it. He had written letters to newspapers, to his congresswoman and senators, about the brutal murder of his neighbors by government agents. None of the newspapers had printed his letters. His representatives had responded with vague promises "to look into the matter." Maybe John was right, maybe it was pointless to change things politically.

He often fantasized about barging into the local Bureau of Weapons Control and tearing the place apart. But that would accomplish nothing, except to land him in jail.

"Say, you've gotten pretty quiet," John said suddenly. "You okay?"

"I don't know," Matt said quietly. "I feel like...like I don't know anything anymore. I don't know my wife, I feel like an alien where I work. Nothing makes sense anymore. Man, I just can't stop thinking about that night." He shivered. "I keep seeing Elsie's face. Just staring up at me. And the blood—it was all over her. All over the carpet. It's so unfair! I mean, what did she ever do to anyone?" Tears sprung to his eyes. He wiped them away, embarrassed. "You know, sometimes I get so angry it actually frightens me." There was a long silence. Matt was grateful that John wasn't preaching to him just now. He didn't think he could take that. "Well, I shouldn't keep dwelling on this. I'll go crazy if I do." He was eager to change the subject. "By the way, how's Beth doing?"

"She's doing okay. I worry about her, though."

"Why? Is something wrong?"

"No, she's fine. I just worry about what's going to happen to us in the future, during the coming persecution. I mean, things are bad now, but they're going to get worse. A lot worse. Especially for Christians. Lately, we've been talking about having children. But we're both afraid that the government could take them away someday. I don't know if Beth could handle that."

"If you're so worried about her, you should hold onto your .22. You might need it to protect her someday."

"Well, I hope I never do."

"There's no guarantee that you won't. Eventually, the government will start going on door-to-door searches for firearms. After what happened to Ben and Elsie, I wouldn't be surprised. Have you thought about how you'd protect Beth without your rifle?"

He shuddered. "That's not something I like to think about."

"Well, you better start thinking about it, and soon. They took my shotgun that night. Did I tell you that? I still haven't gotten it back."

"Was that your only gun?"

"Heck, no. I still have that carbine Dad gave me when I graduated from high school. And I plan on keeping it, even if it gets banned. Not that I expect you to agree."

"It's your decision," John said.

They headed back toward John's light blue Plymouth Reliant. Matt smiled at the bumper stickers plastered all over. Most of them contained Bible verses, and a couple were pro-life. Once they got into the car, Matt said, "Listen, thanks for putting up with my attitude before."

John smiled. "No problem. I'm used to it."

"Well, I realize I'm not very easy to live with these days."

"Guess I'm lucky I don't have to live with you." They both laughed.

"Yeah, well, depression does that to a person, I guess."

"Anyone would get depressed after...seeing what you saw."

He nodded. "But it's not just that—I mean, I feel terrible about Ben and Elsie. But what really yanks my chain is that the people who killed them aren't going to be held accountable. I mean, our government is literally getting away with murder! Doesn't it bother you that evil people can get away with things so easily?"

"It's funny you should ask that. Just this morning, I was reading a psalm about that very subject—Psalm 37."

"What did it say?"

"Just a minute." He reached into his glove compartment and pulled out a small, worn copy of the New Testament and Psalms. He flipped through the pages, then began to read. "'Do not fret because of evil men or be envious of those who do wrong; for like the grass, they will soon wither, like green plants they will soon die away.'"

"I'd like to believe that," Matt said wistfully. "But it's not easy."

"It's not easy for me, either. But we can trust in the promises of God. He never promised that life would be easy, or that we'd never face any trials. But He did promise to protect us during our trials, as long as we follow Him. And ultimately, His side will win." He looked at the page and continued to read. "'A little while, and the wicked will be no more; though you look for them, they will not be found. For the Lord loves the just and will not forsake His faithful ones. They will be protected forever.'"

"That's beautiful," Matt said softly. There was a long pause. "Maybe I should learn more about the Bible. I have been reading it, but there's a lot I still need to learn."

"Well, why don't you come to our Bible study sometime?"

Matt smiled. "Maybe I will," he said—much to his own surprise. But what would Gina say? He decided not to mention it, at least for the time being.

* * * *

"Are you okay?" Beth asked John as she started to get dinner ready. She had just put a pot of water on the stove to boil and was reaching into the cabinet for a box of Ronzoni shells.

"I just have a lot on my mind," John said absently.

"Like what?"

He didn't want to worry Beth, but he had to be honest with her. "It's...kind of complicated. It had to do with something Matt told me today."

"Is he still worrying about adopting the new constitution?"

"No, it's—more than that," he said falteringly. He found himself wondering what he would do if someone tried to hurt Beth. He pushed the thought from his mind.

Now she looked concerned. "John, what's wrong? Did something happen to your folks?"

"No, nothing like that."

"Then what is it?"

He sighed. "Matt's neighbors were murdered. By our own government! Not only that, but he and Gina were attacked by a SWAT team during a government raid on a church."

Her mouth dropped open. "What?"

"I think we better sit down," he said. He told her everything Matt had told him, and then they sat there in silence.

"I guess he's taking it all pretty hard," she remarked after a few moments.

"Yeah, and I'm afraid I was pretty insensitive about it," John said.

"What makes you say that?"

"I don't know. For the first time in ages, he comes to me with a problem, and what do I do? I start preaching to him. I should've just listened."

"Is that what you think the Lord wanted you to do?"

"I don't know. After talking to Matt, I'm not sure what God would want me to do, especially if things continue the way they seem to be going." He shook his head. "Maybe we've been wrong for not being involved in politics. Maybe if more Christians had been politically active, things wouldn't have gotten this bad."

"I'm not so sure. What if God's allowing these things to bring judgement upon America? If we try to stop it, we could be interfering with His will."

"That could be. Still, what if it's God's will to save America? If He wanted to save America, maybe He'd do it through people like us. That is, if we were willing to get involved."

"Involved in what?"

He shrugged. "I don't know exactly—but maybe we should be doing something to protest all this. Before it's too late."

"Too late for what?"

"Too late to do it peacefully," he said grimly.

"I don't like the sound of this. You're not actually considering using violence—"

"You know me better than that," he told her. "I hate violence. But look at the Bible. There are plenty of times in the Old Testament when God commanded His people to use force against evil men who were opposed to His will."

"But that's different—they weren't fighting their own government! I thought Christians were supposed to submit to authority, not rebel against it." She was clearly frightened by the way John was talking.

"But Beth, look what we're dealing with here. A government that doesn't even obey its own laws, that kills innocent people. Is that legitimate authority?"

"I don't know. I don't like to think so, but the Bible does say that God puts all governments in power, and Christians have to submit to them."

"I'm not so sure anymore." His tone softened then. "Look, I don't want any bloodshed, believe me. I'm just saying it may come to that if we don't try to stop this peacefully while we have the chance."

"What do you mean?"

"Well, there are still a lot of people in this country who don't want a one-world government. People like Matt. The media may be ignoring them, but they're out there. They may not take this lying down. We may be heading toward a civil war."

"John, you're scaring me!" She was close to tears now, and he wished he could just drop the whole subject. But he knew they had to face these harsh realities sooner or later.

"I'm sorry, Beth," he said gently. "I don't want to scare you. But we can't ignore these problems—we have to be prepared."

She recovered her composure. "Maybe you're right. But what can we do? If the powers that be want world government, we'll probably get it with or without a constitutional convention. Besides, even if we succeed in opposing this one-world government, what good will it do in the long run? Our own government will do whatever it wants to, anyway."

"Not with an informed electorate." He got up from the table. "You know what Matt told me today? He said I may know a lot about the Bible, but I don't know much about the government. Well, maybe I should change that. You have a bunch of American history books, don't you?"

She frowned. "The ones from my school aren't much good. They're more like revisionist history books. But I have some old ones put away, *The Federalist Papers* and some others that I never got a chance to read."

"Wait a minute. You were a history major and you never read the *Federalist Papers?*"

She smiled wryly. "Would you believe no one ever assigned them? Actually, I don't recall being assigned to read the Constitution, for that matter."

"You're kidding!" He shook his head. "Boy, no wonder we're in this mess."

"You're starting to sound like your brother." She laughed.

John chuckled. "Yeah, and he's starting to sound like me. Would you believe he was quoting Scripture to me earlier today?"

Her eyes widened. "Really?"

"Well, not verbatim, but he does seem to be showing more of an interest in what the Bible says."

"That's a good sign!"

"I suppose."

She cocked her head to one side. "You don't sound very enthusiastic."

"I just don't think he sees the significance of it all. Like today, he seemed to be using Scripture to validate his own preconceived ideas about things."

"Well, some Christians do that, too."

"I wonder if maybe I was doing that with Matt today. Anyway, the good thing is, he agreed to come to the Bible study sometime."

Her eyes lit up. "Really? That's wonderful!"

"Yeah, but I wonder how Gina will react."

"I don't think she'll be too thrilled. Do you think we should invite her to come?"

He smiled. "I don't think she's ready for that yet."

* * * *

Gina sat at her desk in one of the many glass-enclosed cubicles that lined the back wall of the newsroom. She jotted down some notes for an interview she had to do later. The Convention was less than a month away, and the entire newsroom buzzed with excitement. Yet for Gina, the festive air seemed strangely ironic. Her faith in the government had been shaken, and she found herself wondering if things were going to get worse instead of better under the UN Constitution.

"Mrs. Lanyon?" Startled out of her thoughts, Gina looked up to see a man and woman standing before her desk. The man looked familiar—oh, yes, now she remembered. Reverend Dalton, Father Flannery's friend. The woman was somewhere in her late forties, dressed in a somber gray suit. Her face looked careworn, and there were dark circles under her eyes.

Gina rose from her chair. "Yes—what can I do for you?"

"I'm Maggie Rorke," the woman said, shaking Gina's hand, "and this is Pastor Dalton. I understand you did a story on my brother, Father Flannery."

"Yes, that's right."

"Pastor Dalton tells me you were at the church when they arrested him."

"Yes, I was. I'm so sorry about what happened."

"Thank you," Maggie said softly. "I'm here to ask you if you'd be interested in doing a story about my brother and the injustice that's being done to him. The people have a right to know what's happened to him."

"Please sit down." Gina indicated two chairs. "Can I get you some coffee, or tea?"

"No, thank you," said Maggie, and Pastor Dalton shook his head.

Gina sat behind her desk and turned on her tape recorder. She also got out her pad so she could jot down some notes. "Tell me what's happened."

"As you know, my brother was arrested several weeks ago. But he hasn't even been allowed out on bail!"

"Why not?"

"It's very complicated," said Maggie. "Basically, it has to do with a video he made—the one he was planning to show at the meeting you went to. You see, he's been charged with domestic terrorism."

"Terrorism?"

At that, Dalton broke in. "According to the counter-terrorism law that was passed in 1996, distributing or disseminating information that's critical of the government is now considered a crime. Domestic terrorism, to be exact."

"I can't believe that!" Gina exclaimed.

Maggie took something out of the briefcase she was holding. It was a large, thick book of some kind. To Gina, it looked to be at least a thousand pages. "This is a copy of the law." Maggie opened to a page that was marked. "Read it for yourself."

Gina took the book and read the paragraph that was marked. "This is insane. What about the First Amendment?"

Dalton's expression was sad. "Yes—what about it indeed?" It was a rhetorical question.

"But how can they get away with this?"

"Because most Americans don't know—or care—about what's happening in their own country," Maggie said heatedly. "And because we have a controlled press."

"What's going to happen to your brother? Is he actually going to be tried for domestic terrorism?"

"So far, no trial date has even been set," Maggie said. "They won't even give him a probable cause hearing. The judge won't let him out on bail because he claims he's a threat to the government. You see, Patrick was given a summons barring him from appearing in any kind of public forum. The judge who issued it claims he did so because of the riots my brother was involved in—the one at Eisenhower Park and the one at the church. So, he's actually being charged with two crimes—ignoring the summons and disseminating information against the government. Not to mention the earlier charge of hatecrime." Her voice trembled in anger. "And they're treating him worse than any murderer! They only let him out of his cell once a week for ten minutes—just to take a shower. They took his clothes and gave him nothing but a flimsy paper blanket to wear. There's no heat in his cell, and he's freezing." She was nearly in tears.

"This is outrageous!" Gina cried.

"It certainly is," Dalton agreed. "And the charges are completely false. Not once in that video does Patrick advocate violence against the government."

"The judge did say he'd let him out on one condition," Maggie said.

"What's that?"

"He has to sign a statement admitting that he's part of a conspiracy to overthrow the government," said Dalton.

"What?!" Gina was flabbergasted.

"That's right," said Maggie.

"But why?"

Dalton ran his fingers through his thinning hair. "They want to discredit him. A lot of those videos have gotten out, and people are outraged. Patrick's radio show had a big following among conservative Catholics, and they've been writing their state representatives asking them to call off the Constitutional Convention. The Patrick Henry Society is spearheading the effort, and they've been mass-producing the videos. You see, Mrs. Lanyon, that video tells the truth about the UN Constitution—and our own government's involvement in a conspiracy to make sure we ratify it—at any price. The video proves that we're living under an outlaw government, which is determined to destroy our sovereignty. I think the Council for Global Unity is hoping that if Father Flannery gets convicted of conspiracy, people won't pay attention to him anymore—or maybe they'll be afraid to be associated with the video in any way."

"I think they want to make an example of him," Maggie added.

Gina remembered Ken's reluctance to make the group look bad in the paper, and was curious. "Wait a minute. What does the CGU have to do with this?"

"It's rather complicated," said Dalton, "and to most people it sounds far-fetched."

"What does?"

"The fact that the Council has been part of a conspiracy to create a one-world government," Dalton replied.

"Look, it's no secret that the CGU has been promoting world peace. But to say that it's a conspiracy—" Gina broke off in mid-sentence, shaking her head. "I just don't buy that."

"Why not?" asked Maggie.

She shrugged. "Let's just say I don't believe in conspiracy theories."

"Neither did I," said Reverend Dalton, "until I started talking to Father Flannery. He's been researching the conspiracy for years now. His video documents it all. He quotes from the Council's own writings, as a matter of fact."

"I'd like to see this video," Gina said.

"We have a copy right here." Maggie handed one to her. "My brother is the narrator, but members of the Patrick Henry Society helped him with it.

He's been a member for the past few years. My husband and I are also members."

Gina was taken aback at the mention of the Patrick Henry Society. "But isn't that a right-wing terrorist group? I've heard that they're in league with the Klan, as a matter of fact."

"That's what the media want people to believe," Maggie said. "The Society is merely trying to preserve America's freedom and sovereignty. In fact, one of our local chapter leaders was instrumental in helping to convict some Klan members who were terrorizing minorities in his neighborhood."

"Interesting." Gina looked at Maggie. "Is there any way I can see your brother? I'd like to interview him again, if possible."

Maggie's face clouded. "It doesn't look like that's possible. He's being moved to a maximum-security prison tomorrow, and can't have any visitors once he gets there. Not even family members." Now there were tears in her eyes.

Gina handed her a tissue. "I'm sorry," she said softly.

"I just hope you can let the public know what's happened to him. If it can happen to my brother, it can happen to anyone."

"Well, I hope not." Gina suddenly had an idea. "Maybe I can still get in to see him today."

Reverend Dalton shook his head. "They won't let any reporters in to see him."

"There might be a way to get around that. My father's a lawyer and may have some connections. Maybe he can help me."

"I guess it's worth a try." Maggie stood up. "We really shouldn't keep you any longer."

Dalton rose from his chair. "Let us know what you think of the video," he said. Gina asked for their phone numbers in case she had to get in touch with them.

When Gina went to Ken with the information she had, he was silent for a moment. Then he shook his head. "Oh, boy. Things are even worse than I thought. Look, Gina—I'd like to run this story. But Whitaker's a member of the CGU. Do you really think he's going to authorize a story that'll make his own organization look bad?"

"Forget the CGU. Don't you think the public has a right to know that this domestic terrorism law is violating people's rights?"

"Of course I do. But people like Damien don't want the public to know about such things."

"Why not?"

"Because people will lose faith in the government. You know Damien, he loves big government."

"Ken, Pastor Dalton says the CGU is part of a conspiracy. Do you believe that?"

Ken shuffled through some papers on his desk. "I don't know." He avoided her eyes. "I do know they have a lot of power and influence. But as far as a conspiracy goes, I just don't know. Anyway, if you want to find out what Flannery has to say, go ahead. But I can't make any promises about printing it. We're all still on probation. Remember?"

Gina sighed. "Whatever happened to freedom of the press?"

"I don't know. I just don't know."

* * * *

After she had left, Ken got up and stood looking out the window. It was rush hour, and a steady stream of cars moved sluggishly along Northern Boulevard, their headlights twinkling in the darkness. He wondered how many of the drivers realized they were living in a police state. *Funny how you can live in one for years without even knowing it.* He was frightened, too. He feared for his job—and most of all for his family. He often wished he could just walk out and never look back. But he had his family to consider. Although his wife worked full time, they could never get by on just one salary. So, he was trapped. Trapped in a job that he couldn't stand anymore. Sometimes he wondered how he even got through the day.

He sighed, and walked over to his file cabinet. Opening the bottom drawer, he reached in the back and took out a bottle of whiskey. Lately he had gotten into the habit of taking a swig from time to time when the pressure of his job became unbearable.

He stared at the bottle for a long time. Then, he thought of his father. "No," he said quietly, and slowly put the bottle away. After Gina left his office, Ken thought about his father's old friend who had tried to expose the CGU without any success. Still, at least he had tried. But what did he get for his efforts? Nothing—and his career went down the toilet. *That's what I'd have to look forward to,* Ken thought. Besides, it wasn't as though he were printing outright lies. He was simply avoiding controversial issues. Most editors did that now. But he knew that the public had the right to know the truth. And he was keeping it from them. That made him a part of the conspiracy.

His father had once hinted about it, years ago. He had warned Ken about powerful "insiders" who manipulated and controlled politicians for their own gain. "You'll learn about them soon enough, once you become a journalist," he had told Ken. "They like to control the press as well. Just don't let them control you. Stick to your principles, son."

He thought about Cheryl Hendricks, and was grateful his father couldn't see him now. He had compromised his integrity, his honesty, everything his father had taught him, just to keep his job.

A job he despised more and more each day.

* * * *

Late in the afternoon, Gina finally managed to see Father Flannery, thanks to her father, who knew someone who was good friends with the judge. But Tom had thought it best not to mention that she was a reporter—he had said she was a member of Flannery's parish who had to discuss some business with him before he was transferred to the other prison. Separated by a glass partition, they spoke to each other through a phone. She could see that his experience had taken a toll on him; his face was pale and drawn, and he had lost a great deal of weight. His voice was subdued and tired. But he smiled thinly when he saw her.

"Congratulations," he said. "I thought I was off limits to reporters—and just about everyone else."

She wished he hadn't said that. She knew their conversation was bound to be monitored, but that was a chance she had to take. "I'm not here as a reporter," she said in a low voice. "Not officially. As far as everyone knows, I'm just a member of your parish. Your sister told me what's been happening. I just can't believe it."

"It is hard to believe this can happen in America. Essentially, I'm a political prisoner. But I'm sure I'm not the first person this has happened to."

"But there has to be someone who can help."

"I think only God can help at this point. Unless He does a miracle, I'm afraid America is finished, and things like this are going to become the norm."

"Do you have a lawyer?"

"Yes, but the judge is giving him a hard time. My attorney has threatened to file a civil action suit on my behalf, but I don't think it's going to do any good. Under the current law, the judge does have the authority to withhold bail if he thinks I'm a threat to society."

"But this whole thing is a violation of your first amendment rights—your right to freedom of expression!"

"Unfortunately, those rights don't mean very much in America today. And it's going to get worse if the UN Constitution is ratified."

She still wanted to hope for the best. "Maybe it won't be all that bad. After all, the UN is always promoting human rights. Maybe they'll be able to stop some of this insanity."

"My, you are trusting. Do you really believe the UN cares about human rights, after what they did in Katanga and Somalia? After they had a conference on the rights of women in Beijing, where all those students were murdered? And if they really cared about human rights, then why have they welcomed brutal communist dictators into their ranks?"

She didn't answer. He asked her if she'd had an opportunity to watch the video.

"I caught part of it earlier today."

"And?"

"It was...interesting. I admit, I did learn a few things I didn't know before."

"Such as?"

"Well, I was surprised to learn that America isn't a democracy. I always thought it was."

"That's right. Our Founding Fathers didn't trust democracies. They knew that in a pure democracy, the individual's rights could easily be taken away by the majority. That's why they established a republic, which put strict limitations on the power of government. They believed that rights come from God, and that the proper role of government is to protect those rights. The Constitution was framed to contain and limit the power of the federal government, so that we would remain a free people. The problem with the UN Constitution, by the way, is that it does just the opposite. It's based on the premise that rights come from the government, not God, and that we can have only those rights that the government decides to give us. And, the government can take away those rights any time it wants to."

"Well, time will tell."

Father Flannery shook his head, but he smiled nevertheless. "The incurable optimist."

"Look, it's just hard for me to swallow all of this. All my life, I've been told that the UN is the world's last, best hope for peace. I look at the planet and I see war, poverty, pollution, racial strife—and I think, 'Wouldn't it be great if we could put an end to all this?' It's just hard to believe that something I was putting so much hope in can be so evil."

"I understand how you feel, Gina. Most idealists think as you do. But what you don't understand is that many of the people who want world government are using war, chaos, poverty and racial strife to control people. For instance, the UN claims it wants to eliminate poverty. A noble goal, indeed. But in order to do so, they claim they need to redistribute the world's wealth—in other words, steal money from those who have earned it and give it to those who haven't. We tried that here, and look what happened. After spending over five trillion dollars on the Great Society, poverty became worse and the government went bankrupt. Do you really believe that the people who want a one-world government, the 'insiders' I referred to in that video, are motivated by their concern for human rights and social justice?"

"I'll admit, their methods may be a bit underhanded. But did it ever occur to you that they simply may want what's best for humanity?"

He made a wry face. "I'll bet Hitler would have said the same thing. What the UN wants, along with its sister organizations like the International Coalition of Churches and the CGU, is a one-world, socialist government...and ultimately a global religion that would abolish traditional Christianity."

"Father Flannery, have you ever considered the possibility that that might be a good thing? It would put an end to much of the strife and intolerance in the world."

He raised his eyebrows. "Really? And how do you suppose the UN plans to get millions of Christians, Muslims, and other people who are committed to their beliefs, to abandon those beliefs and accept a one-world religion? Through tolerance? What about the millions who will absolutely refuse to convert? Will the UN respect their choice? If you believe that, then you haven't been watching world events. The UN has no tolerance for those who oppose it or its programs. In the past the only thing that kept it from forcing its will upon all nations was its lack of power. But, that's changing now. That roadblock will be removed once our country ratifies the new Constitution. Tolerance can be good to a degree, but today it is the battle cry of the enemy. You see, Gina, I believe there is a greater ideal toward which mankind should strive. That ideal is truth."

"You know, that's the problem with all you religious people—you all claim to have a monopoly on truth. I was brought up Catholic, but I believe there's truth in all religions."

"Gina, think about it logically for a moment. Can religions, which make vastly different claims about the nature of God and the means of salvation, all be true? That just doesn't make sense. For instance, if Christianity is true, then other religions must be false. And if you're truly a Catholic, you must believe that Jesus is the Son of God, that He *is* God. If Jesus is God, and if His claim to be the only Way to the Father is true, then there can't be other ways to God." There was a long pause. "Do you believe in Jesus?" he asked in a soft voice.

She suddenly remembered the last time she had prayed to Him and how her prayer had seemingly been answered. But she didn't want to think about that right now. "I just don't know." She looked at him, curious. "By the way, what did you mean by 'the battle cry of the enemy?' Which enemy were you talking about?"

"I was referring to Satan. Or Lucifer, if you prefer."

She rolled her eyes at that. "You know, that's the one thing that turned me off about your video—when you mentioned that Satan is behind all this."

"Oh?"

"Yes—it weakens your credibility. I just can't believe that all the people who belong to these groups are working for Satan. It's ridiculous."

"Most of them may be doing so unwittingly. I've been studying this conspiracy for years now. The one thing that would seem to defy explanation is the way the conspiracy has lasted from generation to generation, even from century to century. The drive for one-world rule is almost as old as man. The first attempt at a one-world government was the tower of Babel. Then came the Roman Empire. Later during the Middle Ages, a number of secret societies formed for the purpose of creating a one-world government. But none of them lasted. Then, in 1776 Adam Weishopt of Bavaria founded the Order of Illuminati. Hardly anyone has ever heard of it. Yet many of the world's great political leaders, scholars, and educators have come from its ranks. Weishopt developed a plan for creating a one-world government. This plan involved the creation of a number of tightly knit groups of one-worlders who would infiltrate the governments and universities of every Western nation. The plan also involved getting control of the press in each country, and fomenting wars and crises that would be used to sell the concept of world government to the ignorant masses. To make a long story short, generations of power-hungry men, many of whom belonged to the Illuminati, have been implementing this plan for over two centuries now. After one generation of these men died out, the next generation carried on. The strange thing is, most of them had to realize that their goal of world dominance could never be attained in their own lifetime. Yet they still worked at it with an almost single-minded dedication. How would you explain that, Gina?"

"Maybe they weren't in it for the power," she said after some thought. "Maybe they just wanted a better world for future generations."

"Then why all the secrecy? Why not be open about it? And if their intentions were so noble, why were they willing to foment wars to achieve their goals?"

She was silent.

"I think there's another explanation," Father Flannery said. "What if there were some supernatural power behind it all? Some power which had been organizing this plan for all these centuries? Satan is the most power-hungry being who ever existed. He wants to be like God—he wants to rule the entire planet. Couldn't Satan be using these evil, power-hungry individuals to accomplish his own purpose?"

She shifted uncomfortably in her chair. "It doesn't make sense. If there is a God, He wouldn't let this happen. He'd stop it somehow, wouldn't He?"

"You're forgetting that the God of the Bible loves us enough to respect our freedom. He's given us free will to follow Him or reject Him. The freedom to accept His government or man's government. Unfortunately, Americans today seem to want man's government. They've turned away from God and have turned to government to supply their needs. This is a philosophical and spiritual battle as well as a political battle. America was founded on two basic beliefs—faith in God and individual responsibility. Individuals were not to look to government to supply their needs; they were to trust in God and use the abilities He gave them to provide for themselves. They were to accept responsibility for their own lives. But over the years, Americans rejected God, and with Him the ethic of individual responsibility, perhaps because they no longer believed in a God to whom they would ultimately be held accountable. But they were free to do so. If God were to take away our freedom and force us to follow Him, we'd be nothing more than mindless robots."

His words stirred her. She told herself to remain clear-headed and not get carried away by religion. But she was just too curious to let this drop. "Your video mentioned that the Bible predicts a one-world government ruled by the Antichrist. If that's true, then ultimately there's nothing we can do to stop this. So, why bother trying?"

His next words made her bristle. "That's a convenient way to absolve yourself of any responsibility, isn't it?"

"What's that supposed to mean?"

"I've spoken to a lot of people about the conspiracy," he said. "And I've found that most of them tend to have one of two reactions. The first is, 'That kind of thing can't happen here. After all, this is America.' The second is, 'We can't do anything about it anyway, so why bother fighting it?' I've even heard some Christians use that as an excuse for not opposing the World Constitution. They say that since a one-world government is predicted in the Bible, we're going to have one whether we like it or not. So, why fight it? Why not just let history take its course?"

"What's wrong with that?"

"It's an abdication of personal responsibility. By convincing themselves it's hopeless to change things, too many Christians are trying to justify their non-involvement in the political process. And God will hold them accountable for allowing evil to have its way."

"Well, I don't think that's fair." Something inside her warned her to steer clear of a discussion about God. "But let's get off the subject of religion. I'd like to ask you about the charges against you."

"Go right ahead."

"Was it something specific you said in the video that prompted the charges?"

"Not that I'm aware of. I don't even see why they consider me a threat to society. After all, I haven't advocated violence against the government—or anything that could threaten society in any way. But under the anti-terrorism law, any criticism of the government is considered subversive. They claim that if you don't like what the government's doing, then you could be planning a terrorist act against the government. It doesn't matter if they have no evidence."

"So—how do you plan to fight this? Does your lawyer—"

At that moment, a uniformed guard suddenly approached Father Flannery and pulled him to his feet. "Time's up," he said gruffly, and handcuffed him.

Gina got up from her chair. She was about to say goodbye when someone grabbed her shoulder. "Don't go anywhere yet, Ms. Lanyon," a stern voice said. She turned around, bewildered. Two guards were standing there.

"But why—"

"Just follow me," one of them ordered.

She did what she was told, but her mind raged with questions. What did they want with her? Did they find out she was a reporter? She suddenly remembered the speakerphone. Someone must have listened in. Both guards were stone-faced and spoke in monosyllables. They refused to answer her questions.

Momentarily, they escorted her into a small, dreary, windowless room. The door closed behind her, and she was left alone.

CHAPTER 12

Gina was startled to hear the door open suddenly. She had been alone in the locked room for over an hour now, and she was scared. The guards had refused to tell her anything, and she expected the worst.

She got up from the hard metal chair when the door opened and looked anxiously at the three men who entered. They were dressed in business suits and did not appear threatening, but she still felt wary. To her surprise, one of the men greeted her cordially and asked her to sit down. He even offered to get her a cup of coffee. He introduced himself as Mr. Dawson; the other two men said nothing. Mr. Dawson looked to be about fifty or so, and had light gray hair. He held a beige folder, which he placed on the table. The other two men were somewhat younger, clean-shaven and impeccably dressed. One carried an attaché case, the other held a clipboard.

"What's going on?" she asked Mr. Dawson when they sat down at the table opposite her. "Am I in some kind of trouble?"

Dawson cleared his throat. "Not at the moment."

"Then why am I here? Why did—"

"Please, Ms. Lanyon," he said in a courteous tone, "if you don't mind, we prefer to ask the questions."

"But—"

He smiled benevolently. "The sooner you cooperate, the sooner you will be out of here."

She felt relieved at the thought of getting out, even though she objected to his condescending way of addressing her. "Then I'm not under arrest?"

"Not at all," Dawson said pleasantly. "All we need is your cooperation in answering a few questions, and then you can go." He opened his folder and seemed to be reading something. Then he smiled again, as if to reassure her. "As you may be aware, the man you visited is very dangerous. He has been charged with hatecrime and terrorism. He may even be guilty of conspiracy against the United States government. In any event, it is crucial that we know what it is he has discussed with any of his visitors. A security precaution, you understand." He nodded to one of the men, who took out a pen. "Now, Ms. Lanyon, please tell us what you talked about with Father Flannery."

She hesitated, wondering if she should admit the truth. They were bound to find out, anyway. But then she thought of her father. This was the one time he had really come through for her, the one time he had put himself on the line for her. He could get into a lot of trouble if she told them she was a reporter, and that her father had lied to get her in. Hoping against hope that they hadn't caught Father Flannery's comment about her being a reporter, she said, "I'm a member of Father's parish—I'm a member of the parish council actually—and I had to discuss some business with him."

She was talking very fast and her mouth was very dry. One of the men was writing something on his clipboard.

"I see. What kind of business?"

"Uh, well, we're having a fund raiser next month and Father was supposed to be in charge of it. Since he won't be around, I needed to discuss plans to find a replacement for him."

Dawson smiled almost indulgently. "I see." He nodded at one of the men, who opened his attaché case. He took out a small tape player, put it on the table and pressed the play button. Gina felt a stab of fear as her own voice filled the room. "I'm not here as a reporter. Not officially. As far as everyone else knows, I'm just a member of your parish. Your sister—" Dawson nodded again, and the recorder was turned off. "I think we can drop the charade now," Dawson said mildly. "You are a reporter, aren't you?"

She felt strangely light-headed. "Yes." Her voice sounded very far away.

"That's much better. Now, you don't really need to tell us what you talked about to 'Father,' as you referred to him, because we have the entire conversation on tape. It was foolish of you to lie to us. And unfortunate, I might add." Though he continued to speak in a refined and subdued tone, his expression had hardened. The other two men looked on impassively, their faces devoid of all human expression.

"I want to see my lawyer," she said.

He ignored this. "We could give you a summons right now. In fact, we could give your father one as well. After all, he lied to get you in to see that criminal. And the fact that he lied to a judge wouldn't help his career in any way, would it, Ms. Lanyon?"

She couldn't seem to find her voice.

"Actually, we could even go so far as to arrest you—and your father—if we wanted to."

"But you said—"

"Of course, if you cooperate with us, that won't be at all necessary."

She looked at him coldly. "What do you want?"

"It would be most unfortunate if those paranoid delusions of Father Flannery made it into the newspapers. Although I find it hard to believe that a paper with the reputation of *Island News* would print such trash, we can't take any chances. And if the newspaper you work for doesn't print this, uh, colorful fantasy that Father Flannery has dreamed up, we wouldn't want you going somewhere else with it. This kind of story is very damaging to society, you know."

Her voice shook with anger. "What about freedom of the press?"

Dawson scratched the back of his head. "Really, Ms. Lanyon, you must know that when national security and public safety are at stake, the First Amendment does not apply. I'm sure they told you that at journalism college." He rose from his chair. "Thank you very much, Ms. Lanyon. I trust you will take our advice."

She couldn't believe what she was hearing. "Advice? It sounded more like a threat to me."

He smiled broadly. "Now, there's no need to use such strong language. After all, our only concern is the welfare of society. Unfortunately, that sometimes necessitates the sacrifice of certain freedoms. I'm sure you understand that."

"I think I'm beginning to," she said with a trace of sarcasm.

* * * *

She didn't get back to the newsroom until late that evening, past the deadline for the morning edition. Ken was still in his office, and she told him what had happened.

"I don't like the sound of this at all," he said with a look of consternation. "If they don't want you printing Father Flannery's story, then—" He broke off, shaking his head.

"I know. This is more than just some wacko conspiracy theory. Some very powerful people are going to a lot of trouble to keep Father Flannery silent. That's probably the real reason he's in jail."

"I wouldn't be surprised. Are you all right?"

"Oh, sure. I love being threatened by government agents."

"FBI?"

She threw her hands in the air. "Who knows? They never even bothered to tell me. So, I guess this is one story we won't be printing," she said dismally.

"You mean you're not even going to try to talk me into it?"

"Not if it means getting my father in trouble. He took a big risk for me. I just can't let him down."

"Well, I can understand that," he said sympathetically. "Besides, you can bet Whitaker wouldn't let us print this."

"You're probably right. You know something, Ken? I'm actually scared. I'm scared about what's going to happen to all of us if this World Constitution gets ratified." It was something she would never admit to Matt. "I mean, if those people who questioned me at the jail are the kind of people who'll be in charge—" She broke off with a shudder.

"I'm not sure it's going to make much difference, either way," he said in a tired voice.

"What do you mean?"

"I think we lost our freedom a long time ago. We all sat back and let it happen."

She was surprised. "You sound a lot like my husband."

He shrugged. "You may as well get going. You've had quite an ordeal today. Go home and get some rest."

She forced a smile. "Thanks."

* * * *

Gina opened the door to see two men standing outside the apartment, their faces grave. One of them looked to be somewhere in his late forties or early fifties; the other appeared to be in his mid-thirties. He dug his hands into his pockets, looking anxiously at Gina. The older man was carrying a heavy briefcase. He took a deep breath, then exhaled slowly. "Are you Gina Lanyon?" he asked.

"Yes. Can I help you?"

The older man replied, "My name is Hank Jennings. I'm a retired FBI agent. I'm sorry to intrude on you like this, but we need to speak to you about a rather urgent matter."

At the mention of the FBI, Gina felt her heartbeat quicken. What would the FBI want with her? Did it have something to do with her visit to Father Flannery a few days ago? Maybe they knew she had a copy of his video.

Matt came to the door. "What's going on?" he asked.

"This guy says he's from the FBI," Gina said, her voice trembling.

Hank corrected her. "I used to be. But I retired." Gina noticed his expression of distaste. He gestured to his friend. "This is Bill Rodriguez. He used to write for *The New Yorker*."

"I'm a friend of Father Flannery's," Bill put in. "I spoke to his sister earlier today, and she suggested I get in touch with you."

"Really?"

"Yeah. I can verify some of the information in his video."

Gina ushered them into the living room. "I'm sorry I was reluctant to let you guys in. It's just that, well, I had an unpleasant run-in with some government agents recently. They might have been with the FBI, but I'm not sure."

She noticed that Bill and Hank exchanged glances, but said nothing.

"I don't know how much Father Flannery told you," Hank said when they were seated. "Bill here has been filling me in on what he and Father Flannery have been able to piece together. I believe it's all in his video. That video's been banned, by the way."

"What video?" asked Matt.

"The one they were going to show at that meeting—where Father Flannery was arrested." Gina looked at Hank. "Have you met Father Flannery?"

"No, but I wish I had. He sounds like a true Christian patriot."

Bill smiled. "It's funny, but if it weren't for Father Flannery, Hank and I never would have met."

"How did you two meet?" Gina asked.

Bill smiled. "Ever heard of the Patrick Henry Society?"

"It sounds vaguely familiar," Matt said.

"You mean you haven't heard it's the scourge of our age?" Bill's tone was mildly ironic. "Anyway, that's what the government wants people to think. I always heard that only bigots and right-wing extremists would belong to such a group. But Father Flannery, who was trying to help me get some articles published in *The Long Island Catholic*, recommended the Society as a good source of information. I thought he was some kind of radical for even suggesting it, but it turns out he was right. A lot of what I heard at the meeting squared with some of the things I had found out in my own investigation. But what Hank told me nearly blew my mind." He chuckled. "I wanted to dismiss it all as the ravings of one of those conspiracy nuts with an over-active imagination. But he has proof—an entire briefcase of government and military files, which document the planned destruction of this country. He showed them to me when we got together to compare notes."

"Man, if I were you I'd send copies of those files to the editors of every major newspaper and all the major news networks in the country!" Matt blurted out.

"Do you really think they're going to be willing to expose the entire establishment, to which they themselves belong?" Hank asked. "Did you know that when the assistant producer of ABC tried to expose the truth behind the government's involvement in the Oklahoma City bombing, he was fired?"

Matt shook his head in amazement. "You're kidding!"

"Let's not jump to conclusions," Gina said. "There could have been a legitimate reason for his getting fired which had nothing to do with the story on the bombing."

"Ordinarily I'd agree with you," Bill said. "But I've seen too many examples of censorship in the national news media to dismiss something like that."

"That bad, huh?" Matt asked.

"Yeah. You wouldn't believe how widespread it is. An old college buddy of mine who works for an NBC affiliate upstate told me that hundreds of stories coming over the wire services go unreported, especially those which expose government corruption and wrong-doing."

"Have you seen Father Flannery's video, Mrs. Lanyon?" Hank asked suddenly.

"Please, call me Gina. And yes, I have seen it. Maggie, Father Flannery's sister, gave me a copy. But I had no idea it had been banned."

Matt furrowed his brow. "Why didn't you tell me about that video, Gina? I'd like to see it."

Hank cut in. "What do you think, Gina? Did you believe what Father Flannery said?"

She gave Matt a guarded look. She wanted to dismiss the video's contents as paranoia. If she admitted that what Father Flannery said was true, then she'd pretty much have to admit that Matt had been right all along about the UN Constitution. Why was that so hard to do? "His claims did seem a bit far-fetched, but he presented some evidence that was pretty hard to refute. In fact, I did some checking of my own after I visited him. He was right about members of the Council for Global Unity financing communism. And the Reinhardt family has done a lot of business in the former Soviet Union. So, it seems as though some of the super-rich capitalists of this country have been in bed with the communists. It may sound far-fetched, but evidently it's true."

Matt was shaking his head. "This is really something!"

"It may not sound all that crazy if you think about it logically," Hank said. "The Reinhardts hate competition. Back in the 30s and 40s they had a monopoly in steel and oil. They also have a monopoly in banking today. Now, what's the best way to ensure a monopoly?"

Matt smiled. "Eliminate your competition."

"Which is exactly what communism does," Bill put in.

"Under the Constitution for Federation Earth," Hank said, "there'll be no more competition—because the free market will be effectively eliminated through global regulation of the economy—which began with NAFTA and GATT, by the way. The world government will have total control over all industry—and the inner circle of the CGU and its sister organizations will control the government. Pretty convenient, huh?"

Gina was getting impatient. "This is all very interesting, but what does it have to do with what you came to tell me about? You said it was urgent."

Hank looked grave. "Yes, it is. We've taken a big risk in coming here tonight, but we really have no place else to turn. We were hoping that as a reporter, you could get this information out to the public."

Gina sighed. "It may not be all that easy. My publisher is a member of the CGU."

Bill looked disgusted. "Oh, great!"

"Well, then we'll have to find another way. Maybe start an underground newspaper." Hank turned to Gina. "Would you be willing to get involved in such an endeavor?"

This was all happening too fast. "Before I commit myself, I'd like to find out about the information you've uncovered."

He took a deep breath. "It's a long story. It started when I participated in a government raid on an innocent American family in rural Michigan. The Cheever family."

"Weren't they a bunch of white supremacists?" asked Gina.

Hank shrugged. "Who knows? They were tried and convicted by the national media long before Danny Cheever ever got to court. He was set up by the government on a false weapons charge. When he failed to show up in court, they sent a bunch of us agents out there to take him into custody. Funny thing is, it turned out he'd been given the wrong court date. The summons he received told him to appear a month later than he was supposed to. He may not have even been a white supremacist, by the way. But he did belong to several groups which were critical of the federal government. And, he owned quite a few firearms. Not exactly a healthy combination these days. The government pressured him to spy on fellow patriots in his community, and when he refused, the bastards decided to entrap him. Anyway, I was part of a federal SWAT team—the FBI's Hostage Rescue Team, to be exact—sent to take him into custody. Only things went a little crazy." He rubbed his hands together nervously. "We were told that this family was dangerous, that they were planning to overthrow the government. Our superiors told us to bring Danny in—dead or alive. And, we had orders to shoot to kill any armed persons on sight. Like a good little field agent, I didn't question my superiors.

"When we got there, things were pretty quiet. We went in through the woods and surrounded the house. They didn't know we where there at first. Then, their dog found us. He started barking, and suddenly some kid— couldn't have been older than twelve or thirteen—came running out into the woods, holding a shotgun. Obviously, the boy thought we were intruders. One of our agents shot the dog just as the boy came into range. He stopped for a minute, just staring at us, dumb-founded." Hank paused, a sick look on his face. "We were all dressed in black, with ski masks on, aiming high-powered rifles at him. A twelve-year-old boy!" There was a slight tremor in his voice. "All of a sudden, he turned and ran away. Just as I was about to call out to him, I heard a shot ring out. He fell to the ground, shot by one of our snipers! I couldn't believe it. Anyway, that's when all hell broke loose. Someone else was in the woods, I think it was the kid's grandfather. He started shooting at us. He killed two of our agents before we wounded him. But he managed to make it into the house. Within the next thirty minutes, federal marshals and helicopters surrounded the house. There were maybe a hundred armed agents in the area. It was insane. Eventually, Danny surrendered. But not until after one of our agents killed his wife. The guy claims it was an accident. Danny had snuck outside to retrieve his son's body, but one of our snipers saw him. He ran back toward the house, and his wife opened the door to let him in." He shuddered. "That's when a sniper— I think it was the same one who killed the son—shot her in the head. She died instantly."

There was a long silence as Gina and Matt tried to absorb the horrifying story. "You don't seemed convinced it was an accident," Gina said finally.

Hank rubbed his hands over his forehead and sighed heavily. "I don't see how it could be. The guy who shot her was a sharpshooter. He bragged that he could hit a quarter at a hundred yards. He must've had her in his scope. How do you make a mistake like that? Anyway, a friend of Danny's, a highly decorated Green Beret soldier who served in 'Nam, intervened and got him to surrender. Ironically, when his case went to trial, he was acquitted of the false charges. But the FBI got off scott-free. That's when I decided to retire, but not until I did some investigating of my own. I wanted to find out why we were ordered to commit this...atrocity." His eyes flashed with anger. "Anyway, there were a number of things about the whole incident that were pretty fishy."

"Like what?" asked Matt, who was practically on the edge of his seat.

"The sniper who killed Cheever's wife and son, for one thing. He wasn't one of our regular agents. No one on the team had ever seen him before."

"That's strange," Matt said.

"Could he have been one of the federal marshals?" Gina asked.

"No. The marshals didn't come in till after the initial shooting. Besides, he wasn't wearing a marshal's uniform. Anyway, I have a contact in the CIA, someone who has a lot of connections in the intelligence community. I was trying to find out who gave the shoot-to-kill order, which inevitably led to the murders of Cheever's wife and son. But it seemed the FBI leadership was keeping it a secret."

"Why would they keep it a secret?" asked Gina. "Besides, isn't it reasonable to expect FBI agents to shoot people who are armed and dangerous?"

Hank shook his head vigorously. "The orders we were given were *not* reasonable. In all my years as a field agent, I had never gotten an order like that. It practically guaranteed the death of anyone in the Cheever household who happened to be carrying a firearm, even in self-defense...and I should have realized that before the raid. But I guess at that point I still didn't want to acknowledge how lawless the government had become—the same government I was working for. We were actually *encouraged* to shoot these people, even if they didn't pose a direct threat. Someone had changed the rules of engagement, and I wanted to find out why." He paused. "What I found out pretty much blew my mind."

"What did you find out?" asked Gina.

"That the order to kill the Cheevers may have come from the UN, not from the United States government."

"What?" Gina couldn't believe it.

"My contact told me that the man who gave that order is unofficially working for WorCEN, an enforcement arm of the UN. It stands for World Crimes Enforcement Network, and just about any type of a crime falls under its jurisdiction—money laundering, ecocrimes, you name it."

"What's an ecocrime?" asked Matt.

"It's a violation of an environmental regulation. Like building on a wetland, even if it happens to be on your own property...and it doesn't even have to be wet, according to the most recent federal regulations. Anyway, before he left office, President Conlin issued a secret executive order authorizing government agencies like the FBI and the CIA to take orders directly from WorCEN."

Gina was puzzled. "But what did WorCEN have against the Cheevers?"

"WorCEN hates the idea of private citizens owning firearms. If they had their way, they'd go on blanket door-to-door searches here for firearms, but they can't because there'd be too much opposition right now. So, they have to be selective—they can only target certain individuals. People like the Cheevers, who were known for their politically incorrect views, and who wouldn't get much sympathy from the press. Anyway, my contact seems to think that WorCEN may be working with people in the FBI and BWC to go after American citizens who own firearms. It's possible that WorCEN may even be trying to 'liquidate' opposition to the UN government before it officially takes over."

Gina got up from her chair. "I just can't believe that," she said flatly.

"Maybe you just don't want to believe it," Bill said softly.

Hank looked thoughtful. "When the federal government murdered nearly a hundred people in Texas, including about twenty children, most Americans believed that the government had a good reason. I guess it's because people don't want to believe that their own government would kill innocent people. Who knows? Maybe that's why there are still people who deny that the Holocaust took place. Anyway, if you don't want your comfortable beliefs about the government disturbed, I can leave right now. If you want to hear me out, I'll stay. It's up to you."

Gina sat down again. "I do want to hear what you have to say. I'm sorry if I seem skeptical, but it all sounds so crazy! I mean, I thought Father Flannery's video was far-fetched. But this is even worse!"

"I know where you're coming from, Gina," Bill said. "I once felt the same way. But I've seen the evidence. Heck, I was almost a victim myself!"

"What do you mean?"

"I mean the government tried to kill me after they froze my debit account. They sent a bunch of snipers after me in a helicopter. I barely escaped with my life!"

Gina was shaking her head. "This all sounds like something out of a spy novel."

"Well, I can assure you, it's all very real," said Bill.

"But why were they after you?"

"They must have found out I was planning to go to the press with the information Hank gave me, which Maggie suggested I give to you."

Matt looked concerned. "I hope *you* won't be in any danger now," he said to Gina.

"We're all in danger. Anyone who has loyalty to anything besides the UN is going to be in danger if that constitution is ratified." Hank looked at Gina. "Is there any chance that your editor would be willing to stick his neck out and print any of this stuff?"

"Are you kidding? He'd get fired. We're not even allowed to use the term 'government cover-up' in any of our stories."

Bill shook his head. "Man, this country's gone off the deep end," he muttered.

"Well, give it a try anyway," Hank said. "If he won't print it, maybe we'll try the Internet."

"Tell us more about WorCEN," said Matt. "Did you say they've been working with the BWC?"

Hank nodded. "My contact says they've gone on weapons sweeps in public housing projects under orders from WorCEN, without any search warrants. They tend to single out areas that are known for drug rings. That way, there's less public outcry. By the way, you can tell someone's a WorCEN agent by the emblem on his jacket—it has a picture of a pyramid with the all-seeing eye inside a globe."

"Hey, I've seen that!" Matt said excitedly. "It was the night of the shoot-out at Ben and Elsie's." He related what had happened, then said, "One of the bastards was wearing a jacket with that emblem on it. And I think those government thugs who arrested Father Flannery were also wearing it."

Gina perked up then. "I've seen it, too. During the riot at Pastor Dalton's church—some of the rioters had that emblem on their jackets."

"Are you sure?" Hank asked sharply.

"Yeah."

"Then they may not have been ordinary rioters. In fact, WorCEN people may have staged that riot. One of the things I've been able to piece together is that WorCEN's been recruiting street gangs to do their dirty work because they won't have any loyalty to the American people. It's not all that easy to get ordinary military recruits to fire on their fellow countrymen. I have a friend in the military. He's an intelligence analyst who's trying to expose this stuff. Anyway, he said that the reason so many American troops are being sent abroad is to make sure they won't be around to defend American citizens from the UN Army."

This sounded a little far-fetched to Gina. "You really think that's the reason?"

Hank took a file out of his briefcase. "Take a look at this." He handed her a sheet of paper. "My friend in the military got a hold of this—it's a questionnaire they give to new recruits."

Gina glanced over the paper. "So?"

"Look at question fifteen." Matt moved closer to Gina and read the question with her. It read, "The U.S. government declares a ban on the possession, sale, and transfer of all firearms. A thirty-day amnesty period is permitted for firearms to be turned in to the local authorities. At the end of this period, a number of citizen groups refuse to turn in their firearms. Consider the following statement: I would fire upon American citizens who refuse or resist confiscation of firearms banned by the federal government."

"That's terrible!" Matt turned to Gina with a look of incredulity. "You really see nothing wrong with that?"

She shrugged. "It depends on the circumstances. I mean, what if the people who refused to turn in their firearms were dangerous? I don't know about you, but I sure don't like the idea of a bunch of violent dissidents having access to firearms."

"Then you wouldn't have liked our Founding Fathers," Matt said dryly.

Hank leaned forward. "Gina, you may be interested in knowing that the recruits who answer no to that question are being sent abroad. And many of those who answer yes are being put into special UN units stationed here in the U.S. According to my friend, nearly a million UN troops have been training to take over American towns and cities. Fortunately, there are still a lot of patriotic Americans in the military, but they have to keep a low profile."

Gina was thoughtful. "About those street gangs being recruited by WorCEN, why would they be ordered to stage a riot at a church?"

"Who knows?" said Hank. "It depends on what the riot accomplished."

Gina thought about how the riot was used to justify the injunction against Father Flannery, which ultimately led to his arrest. She got up from her chair. "I don't know about you guys, but I could use a drink. Would anyone else like one?" Bill and Matt both asked for a beer. Hank asked for a soft drink.

She returned with two cans of beer. "All we have is Red Wolf and Killians," she said to Bill. "Matt likes the darker stuff."

"A man after my own heart," Bill said with a grin.

Matt laughed. "You like the dark stuff, too?"

"Yeah, but my favorite is amber. The best place to get it is an Irish pub in D.C, right near Union Station."

Gina poured herself a glass of White Zinfandel and handed Hank a can of ginger ale. "It's interesting," she said suddenly. "A few months ago, I started an investigation on debit-card abuses. But after the paper changed hands, Ken killed the investigation very abruptly." She frowned. "He never explained why."

"He was probably ordered to," Hank said. "The debit-card system is part of the plan to keep all citizens under control. What better way to monitor people than to keep track of what they buy and sell?"

Bill added, "Yeah, Father Flannery thinks the next step is to implant some kind of microchip under the skin—either the hand or the forehead—to be used in place of the debit card. It's already being tested in other countries and on military bases here in the States."

"Well, it kind of makes sense," said Gina. "After all, it would ensure against loss or theft."

Matt's eyes widened suddenly. "Hey, that's in the Bible!"

Gina stared at him. "Huh?"

"In Revelation, where it talks about the Antichrist. It says he's going to force everyone—young and old, rich and poor—to get some kind of mark, on the hand or forehead. And no one will be able to buy or sell without it."

"Oh, come on," said Gina. "You don't believe that superstitious nonsense, do you?"

Hank sighed. "We seem to be heading in that direction. That kind of a system would be the next logical step in maintaining total control over people." There was a pause. "You know, that's the thing that disturbs me the most. These events seem to be biblically foretold."

Matt perked up at this. "You believe in the Bible?"

"I was brought up to. But you know how it is. After a while you kind of outgrow your childhood beliefs." He leaned back in his chair. "Lately I've been reexamining some of those old beliefs, though. I guess it's because I'm not sure how much time I'll have left if things continue in the direction they seem to be heading. If we want to stop this, we don't have a lot of time to waste." He looked at Gina. "So, can we count on your help? We could use a talented journalist on our team."

She hesitated. Everything was happening so fast, she could hardly absorb it all. She wanted to help. Yet something inside her pulled back, warned her not to get drawn into something dangerous, and perhaps fatal to her career. She remembered her father's motto, "To get along, you have to go along." She hadn't really understood the meaning of those words until now. But this time, going along would mean participating in a government cover-up, assuming that what Hank said was true. Could she do that? Well, it couldn't hurt to bring the information to Ken. That much she could commit to, and still feel "safe." Beyond that, she wasn't prepared to go just yet. "I don't know. I'd really need to confirm all this, before my editor would even consider printing it."

"That might be difficult," said Hank. "I'm sure you realize much of what I've told you is classified. But, I could get you in touch with my friend in the military. He may be able to confirm what I've told you about new recruits— off the record, of course. But that stuff about WorCEN—that's top secret. *I'm* not even supposed to know about it."

"To tell you the truth, I find it highly unlikely that *Island News* would print any of this, even if it can be confirmed. Damien must be a part of it all, since he's a member of the CGU."

"Not necessarily," said Hank. "They seem to have an inner circle, a group of core members who are controlling the Council. In fact, many of the members may not even know the true purpose of the Council. They've also recruited some patriots and conservatives for protective coloring."

Gina frowned. "Damien's no conservative. He's even more liberal than I am."

"Is that possible?" Matt asked. She looked at him and suddenly found herself laughing, releasing some of the tension she felt. It was the first time they had laughed together in ages, she realized sadly.

Hank sipped his soda. "If you ask me, the distinction between liberals and conservatives is pretty superficial. If you look at the way they vote, they *both* tend to want a lot of government control, just for different purposes. Liberals want the government to prevent people from owning guns or doing what they want with their own land, and support forced wealth redistribution. But conservatives want the government to control other areas of our lives, like what we watch on television, what magazines we buy, what drugs we use. It seems like they're both working toward the same goal, increasing the power of the state, maybe without even realizing it. Most haven't bothered to follow their beliefs to the logical conclusion, which is a very large, powerful and intrusive, even dangerous, government. They never really get the big picture because they fail to learn from history. Compounding the problem is the fact that there are forces within the establishment that are manipulating both conservatives and liberals, trying to influence them to push for an expansion of the government's power. I think that's what the War on Drugs is all about, by the way."

"What do you mean?" asked Gina.

"Whenever you criminalize something," said Hank, "whether it's drugs, cigarettes, or alcohol, you immediately create a black market for it. People who want the product are forced to pay astronomically high prices for it because it's illegal. Those who can't afford the price tag may be willing to steal or even kill for it, depending on how desperately they want it. If they're addicted, they may try to get others hooked to support their habit...maybe even school children. Now when you have a situation like that, the average Joe is willing to sacrifice some of his freedom and privacy to put a stop to it. But it can't be stopped through legislation. Look at Prohibition. What happened when the federal government tried to ban alcohol? Did people stop drinking?"

Gina thought of all the "bootleggers" of the period. "No, I guess they didn't."

"In fact, there was more of a demand for alcohol. Statistics show that alcoholism actually increased during Prohibition. Forbidden fruit is always more attractive, isn't it?"

Gina couldn't believe she was hearing this from a former FBI agent. "Do you really want to end the War on Drugs?"

Hank gave her a probing look. "Tell me something, Gina: what do you do with a war that can't be won? Fight forever? It's insanity. Innocent people are murdered in the crossfire simply because they happen to be at the wrong place at the wrong time. Ruthless druglords are protected by our own government while first-time offenders are sent to prison for thirty years. Look at how drug prohibition is being enforced. Thanks to the so-called 'War on Drugs,' we have DEA agents seizing innocent people at airports and forcing them to defecate over wastebaskets, just because they happen to be the '*wrong*' color or appear too affluent. According to the Supreme Court, these agents have the authority to seize anyone they suspect of drug possession, even if they have nothing more than a 'hunch' to go on. Probable cause is no longer necessary, and the burden of proof is on the suspect, not the government. I've also known narcotics investigators who told me that certain individuals in the CIA and the State Department were providing protection for South American drug cartels. The investigators, who were seeking the arrest and prosecution of the druglords, kept getting their cases dismissed. They were harassed by their superiors and subjected to an attempted frame-up, all because our own government was protecting the cartel, enabling them to sell illegal drugs in America at astronomically high prices."

Gina was mystified. "But why?"

"There could be a lot of reasons," Hank said after taking a sip of ginger ale. "Maybe some people in the CIA and the State Department were getting a cut. I'm sure you're aware that our government, specifically the CIA, has used drug-running money to finance illegal military operations. Now I certainly don't condone the use of illicit drugs or any mind-altering substance, for that matter. But I certainly don't think someone who is simply *suspected* of using drugs should lose everything trying to win a court battle that the government can appeal again and again until the poor guy runs out of money. That's what the War on Drugs is all about. It's a scam to nullify the Bill of Rights and increase government revenue. It brings out the worst in humanity. It corrupts everyone it touches, from school children to street cops to judges and even presidents."

There was a long silence as Gina pondered Hank's words. What Hank said seemed to make sense. But the idea of legalizing something that could destroy lives disturbed her. "Don't you think ending the War on Drugs would tend to legitimize them?" she asked. "What kind of a message would it send to kids? It would tell them it's okay to abuse drugs."

Hank considered this. "Cigarettes are legal. So is alcohol. Both are potentially lethal. Do you think banning them would stop young people from abusing alcohol or smoking cigarettes?"

"I'm not just talking about kids. Let's face it. Some people *are* like children. They need laws and regulations to prevent them from doing things that are destructive to themselves and others."

Hank seemed to be mulling this over. "Sounds to me like you're talking about a parent. Now, if you think the government should play the role of a parent, where do you draw the line? Once you allow the government to tell people what drugs or medicine they can use, where will it stop? Eventually, we'll see laws dictating what we can eat, where we can live, even what kind of work we can do, the way it is in communist countries. It's a slippery slope. Once the government is allowed to intrude into one area of life that should be private, what's to stop it from intruding into every area? It's the nature of power. Most people today want the government to take care of them, and because of that we now have a government that's totally out of control."

"But if the government didn't take care of those in need," asked Gina, "who would?"

"It used to be that private charities and churches did," Hank said. "But with government stealing so much of our hard-earned money, people have very little left over to give to those in need. Besides, socialism and forced wealth redistribution have never worked. They destroy incentive and keep people dependent. And that's what they're designed to do. Remember: communism, which is essentially the same thing as socialism, is part of a bigger conspiracy that has nothing to do with equality. Communists claim to want a classless society, but look at every communist country on earth today. They're all ruled by an elite, which has all the power and privileges, while the people are left subjugated and in poverty. Communism is about power— and greed. Why else would people like the Reinhardts spend millions of dollars to finance the Bolshevik Revolution? You can bet *they* didn't want a classless society."

Gina said, "I admit that in practice, communism's been pretty awful. But don't you think that as an ideal, communism is best for people? I mean, if everyone worked according to his ability and was willing to receive only according to his need, we'd have a better society."

"Yeah, right," Matt muttered.

"You can't deny that in theory, communism has a certain appeal," Gina insisted.

Hank pulled on his moustache. "That's why communism has duped so many well-meaning people. In theory, it appeals to some of our most noble instincts—the desire for equality, brotherhood, social justice. But it can never work, because it's diametrically opposed to human nature. Think about it. Is the childless woman going to be willing to take home a smaller paycheck than a mother of four, simply because the mother 'needs' a bigger paycheck? Will people work to the best of their ability when they know they'll be given only what the government says they need? Will inventors be motivated to design the best products they can if they're not free to charge more than what the government says they need for their products?"

"I suppose not," Gina admitted. She felt eager to change the subject. "So, what are your plans now?"

"I guess we're going to do whatever we can to get the truth out to the American people," Bill said. "We've been trying to get full-page ads about all this published in major newspapers, but so far no one's been willing to print the truth. As Hank may have mentioned, we may even try to start an underground newspaper, possibly through the Internet."

"By the way, how are you getting along without a debit card?" Gina asked.

Bill smiled ruefully. "It ain't easy. But Hank's been kind enough to let me stay with some friends of his who give me room and board in exchange for doing odd jobs around their house. We've also joined up with a group of people who have their own underground economy, kind of like a resistance group. They use the barter system as well as gold and silver."

"I'm glad there are some people willing to oppose the government's insanity," Matt grinned. "In fact, I wouldn't mind being part of a resistance group myself. Heck, I'd probably fit right in!"

Gina looked at him, alarmed. "Matt, this isn't a game," she said quietly.

"Gina's right," Hank said. "The people we're up against are extremely dangerous."

"They'll try to destroy whoever gets in their way. It's best to play it safe until you've thought about how much you're willing to risk in the fight for freedom," Bill added.

Gina saw Matt shudder then. She wondered if he was thinking of Ben and Elsie.

By the time Hank and Bill left, it was almost midnight. Yet both Gina and Matt were too keyed up to go to bed. They sat in the kitchen drinking hot chocolate and rehashing everything Hank had told them. "I guess you're going to say 'I told you so.'" Gina stared into her mug of hot chocolate. It was white with little figures of teddy bears on it.

Matt sounded annoyed. "Is that all you're worried about?"

"Of course not. I'm just wondering...do you think everything they told us is true?"

"Well, it wouldn't surprise me. Not after what happened to Ben and Elsie. Nothing the government would do would surprise me anymore."

"I don't know...it sounds so crazy. How can we be sure Hank wasn't exaggerating? You know, you have to be careful about these anti-government types."

He sneered. "Oh, we do, huh?"

"Look, I know the government's done a lot of harm to some people. But don't you think distrust of the government can be just as harmful? I mean, maybe if the Cheevers hadn't been so paranoid about the government, they wouldn't have been viewed as a threat."

"I can't believe what I'm hearing. Are you saying they asked for it?"

"No, of course not. But the kind of paranoia they had, well, it breeds suspicion and distrust. If they hadn't joined all those anti-government groups, maybe the government would have left them alone."

"You know what I think? I think you just don't want to believe any of this. You're just looking for an excuse to dismiss everything we heard tonight."

"Matt, that's not fair!"

He shook his head. "The sad thing is, you can't even be honest with yourself."

"What's that supposed to mean?"

"It means that ever since I've known you, you've always believed what you wanted to believe. Probably up till now, you've viewed the Cheevers as a bunch of white supremacists who got what they deserved, and now you can't admit you were wrong."

"Okay, maybe I *was* wrong." She lowered her eyes. Why was that so hard to admit?

* * * *

"The Plan is proceeding according to schedule," Oren Reinhardt said to the figure seated across from him in the dimly lighted room. "As long as the media continue to keep the public preoccupied with meaningless events and trivia, we should be able to get the World Constitution ratified without any formidable opposition."

The other man spoke in a thick Italian accent. "What if the delegates vote against it? Then what?"

"Don't worry, my friend. Most of them can be bought, I'm sure."

"And if they can't?"

Oren's eyes narrowed. "Let me assure you, Eminence, that this constitution *will* be ratified." He smiled complacently. "The Hegelian principle works quite well."

The man brightened. "Hegel was a wise man, and his influence has had a tremendous impact on the course of modern civilization. Marx and Lenin recognized the brilliance of his ideas, as did Hitler."

"Fortunately," said Oren, "most Americans are completely ignorant of philosophy." He sneered. "The pitiful sheep have no idea that by begging the government for solutions to the latest 'crisis,' they are being herded further into the pen. First it was the War on Drugs, then the War on Guns. With each new crisis, the poor sheep beg for new laws designed to enslave them."

"Thesis, antithesis, synthesis. Three simple words which, when combined, yield great power."

"Indeed," Oren said. "Never underestimate the potential of a government-created crisis. Through each new crisis, we produce clay that can be molded more efficiently." He raised his wineglass to his lips. The dark, red liquid had the color of a wound. He looked at his friend expectantly. "I trust all is being prepared at the Vatican?"

The man's eyes became alert, as though he suddenly remembered the reason he was here. "Yes. We have all read over the papal speech and have found it satisfactory. Shortly after the constitution is ratified here in the States, that speech will be heard by the entire world. Do not worry. We have been planning this for decades. This is a time for celebration, my friend. The Vatican is ours!"

"He can be controlled?"

"But of course. Didn't your president bow to our will?"

"Only too eagerly. But I'm not so sure of this new Pope. He is not completely one with us, and so there is potential danger. Are you absolutely certain of his allegiance, should he discover our ultimate goal?"

"I wouldn't worry. Soon he will be of no further use to us. We can easily get rid of him, as we did with his predecessor."

"I still would have preferred someone fully committed to our cause. It seems we're leaving much to chance, and I don't like that."

"If we wait for someone else, the Teacher's coming will be delayed. Now is the time to act." He looked at his watch. "I'm afraid I must leave you now. I have some business with the International Coalition of Churches."

Oren nodded. "Thank you, Eminence, for taking time out of your busy schedule to meet with me."

The Secretariat of Vatican State rose from the table. "It was my pleasure. I will keep you informed of any new developments. Thank you for updating me on the progress your own organization has made. I am looking forward to sitting in on some of your meetings."

CHAPTER 13

The small auditorium reminded John of the one at his old elementary school. The hard linoleum floor was covered with scuffmarks and the wooden stage up front looked ancient. He glanced around uneasily. Somehow, he had expected more of a turnout. He counted. No more than twelve people in all; a few were just coming in from outside. Their expressions were tense, their voices hushed. He sat down in one of the hard metal chairs. *Hope I'm doing the right thing.*

Just last night, he happened to glance through an old church bulletin and had seen an invitation to a meeting of Christians for Constitutional Liberties. After debating it, he had decided to come. But he had mixed feelings about his decision. For one thing, he wasn't sure it would do any good in the long run. After all, a tyrannical one-world government might be just what Americans deserved for violating God's laws. To John, it looked as if Americans were following the same path as the Israelites of the Old Testament and were now reaping the consequences. So, if the essence of America's problems was spiritual, he reasoned, then no amount of political involvement would solve them. But did that mean Christians should stay out of politics altogether? His research had convinced him that America's past greatness stemmed from Christians who were deeply involved in the government and whose voices had shaped its laws. He also realized that he saw this battle in terms of either-or: either trust God or the political process. But what if he was wrong? What if God wanted to bring about His will through the political process? The biblical precedent was there. He sometimes performed miracles but John couldn't deny that God often used people to accomplish His will. *How is politics any different? People work out politics. God works through people.* There it was. How had he failed to see this for so many years? Still, he told himself to be careful with this group—he didn't want to lose his way. He had heard they were pretty extreme.

"So, you're new here, huh?"

John looked up suddenly. A middle-aged man with stooped shoulders sat down next to him.

John nodded. "Yeah, this is my first meeting. Doesn't look like much of a turn-out, though."

The man's face clouded. "We had some trouble recently. I think it may've scared some people off. That's why it's nice to see a new face—we could use all the help we can get."

John frowned. "I'm not exactly sure if I'll be joining you guys at this point. I heard about the meeting at my church, and I just wanted to see what you're all about."

The man smiled warmly. "Well, I'm glad you decided to come. My name's Chris, by the way."

They shook hands. "I'm John. Nice to meet you."

"The meeting should be starting soon." He sipped some coffee from a paper cup. "There's coffee over there if you want it."

"No thanks. So, you've been coming here long?"

"Since the group started. It's a shame, though—a lot of people dropped out recently. Guess they couldn't take the heat we've been getting."

"Well, I can understand that. Besides, I can see how some Christians would have problems with this type of a group."

Chris looked curious. "Oh?"

He nodded. "Yeah, I have my own reservations about the concept of Christians for Constitutional Liberties."

Chris smiled good-naturedly. "Why? You don't believe in constitutional liberties?"

John was taken aback; he certainly hadn't meant it that way! "No, it's not that. I just happen to think that there's a more important kind of liberty than constitutional liberty. What I'm talking about is the spiritual freedom that comes from trusting in Christ."

"Of course that's more important," said Chris. "None of us would argue with that. But we think the two aren't necessarily incompatible. In fact, our constitutional liberties are what helped make it possible for Christians to share the gospel all these years."

John shrugged. "You may be right. I guess that's what I'm here to find out."

The meeting began within the next few minutes. A frail-looking man named Pastor Dalton led the opening prayer. His expression was troubled, and John noticed that his hands seemed to be shaking slightly. He wondered if it was a physical condition or just nerves. After the prayer, the pastor introduced the guest speaker, a woman named Maggie Rorke. Wearing a pale blue dress with a small strand of pearls, the solemn-looking woman approached the podium. He dark hair was pulled back, and she looked tired and a bit washed out.

"Thank you, Pastor Dalton." Her voice sounded surprisingly strong and resonant. She looked out at the audience, and for an instant John thought she was about to cry. But she cleared her throat and began to speak. "I know you're all concerned about my brother, Father Flannery; all I can say at this point is, he's holding up. They moved him to a maximum-security prison, and he's allowed no visitors. They've taken his Bible." She paused, and her eyes glistened with tears. She hastily brushed them away. "They won't let him make any phone calls, and they seize all his mail. Since he's been there, I got one letter. I suspect he wrote more, but they won't send them out. He said he's keeping his mind fixed on Jesus—I think that's the only thing that's kept him going. He told me in his letter that he tried singing some hymns, but they told him that's not allowed."

"Is there anything we can do to help?" one woman asked.

"Just keep praying for him," said Maggie. "And keep writing those letters." She glanced at her notes. "As some of you know, we're trying to get the judge to grant my brother a probable cause hearing. They're supposed to give one within forty-eight hours of an arrest, but the judge hasn't allowed it in my brother's case." Her eyes glimmered with sorrow. "The only reason my brother's in jail is because he loves his country. He also loves Jesus. Today, that's a dangerous combination. Christians and patriots are going to be under heavy attack in the upcoming weeks—because they're the only two groups in this country that are standing in the way of one-world government. I'm here today to urge you not to give up the fight." She smiled. "Those of you who know my brother might say that he's a dreamer. Saving America may seem like an impossible dream at this point. But it may still be possible. If we can get the truth out to enough people, if we can break through their apathy, we may have a chance. Ultimately, though, it's up to God. That's why we have to keep praying." A few people in the audience shouted "Amen," and John nodded in agreement.

Maggie's eyes grew luminous. "Our nation was founded by people who believed in the Bible—in the sovereignty of God over nations and individuals. They believed that rights come from God, not from governments, and that only God has the authority to take our rights away. At the moment, we're living under a government that has become completely contemptuous of our rights, and we're heading toward a one-world police state. But we can't give up. Our Founding Fathers designed a system of limited government that has lasted longer than any other on the face of the earth—because they based that system on godly principles—the same principles found in the Bible: respect for human life, private property, and the dignity of each individual. James Madison said, 'We have staked the future of this country, not on the Constitution, far from it, but on every individual's ability to govern himself according to the Ten Commandments of God.' So, while we may lose in the long run, we can't give up; we have to keep trying. We owe it to our Founding Fathers, who fought and died to give us this nation under God. Thank you."

The room thundered with applause. One by one, people rose from their seats, clapping and cheering. Deeply moved, John stood up with them.

The rest of the meeting focused on how to stop the Constitutional Convention. A heavy letter-writing campaign and door-to-door petition drive were in the works. The group had recently joined forces with the Patrick Henry Society, which had local chapters all over the country. Along with Father Flannery's video, the Society was producing and mass distributing several other videos and pamphlets warning Americans of the dangers of the UN Constitution.

After the meeting, most people remained for coffee and cake. John approached Pastor Dalton and introduced himself.

"I'm glad to meet you," the pastor said, shaking his hand.

John shook his head. "I just can't believe what's happening to Father Flannery—it's outright tyranny!" He was actually surprised by his own outrage.

Dalton nodded gravely. "You're right. I just wish more people were as concerned as you. Unfortunately, too many Christians have their heads in the sand. They don't want to acknowledge what's happening, I guess."

"I suppose so. Actually, I have to admit that I really haven't been involved much in politics over the last few years. I'm starting to realize that may have been a mistake."

Pastor Dalton looked sympathetic. "A lot of Christians make that mistake. I'm not sure why. Perhaps they feel politics is, oh, unspiritual somehow."

John sipped his coffee. "That's pretty much how I've felt."

"And why do you suppose you felt that way?"

He thought about it. "I think it's because I was afraid of putting too much trust in the political process. I thought it would mean I wasn't really trusting in God."

Dalton took a bite of pound cake. "Well," he said after swallowing, "there is that danger. You *can* put too much trust in the political system. But that doesn't mean we shouldn't be involved in politics at all. After all, as Christians, our job is to be the light of the world and the salt of the earth. But are we being salt and light if we stay out of politics?"

"I guess we need balance," John said after a moment.

"Indeed we do. I've found that our Christian duty is perfectly compatible with our civic duty. As Christians, we need to be witnesses for Christ, and as citizens we need to vote and participate in the political process. If we fall short in either area, the consequences can be serious."

There was a pause. "Mind if I ask you a question?" asked John.

"Not at all."

"Well, I know you people are trying to take this country back, and it seems to me that you want to do it peacefully."

"That's correct."

"But what if you can't do it peacefully? Would you ever resort to violence?"

Dalton looked startled. "As a group, we do not endorse violence," he said firmly.

"Then, you would agree that Christians shouldn't take up arms against the government?"

Dalton rubbed his chin. "As a general principle, I would say no, Christians should not use force against their own government—provided their government is operating within God's authority."

"What do you mean, 'as a general principle'?"

"Let's just say that I don't believe it's wrong for Christians to use force to oppose tyranny—if there are no alternatives left. But that's not the same thing as rebelling against legitimate, God-ordained government."

"But doesn't Romans 13 say we have to submit to the governing authorities, and that he who rebels against the authorities is rebelling against God?"

Dalton reflected. "Imagine that you are a Christian living in Nazi Germany, and you have the opportunity to assassinate Hitler. Would you do it?"

John was taken aback. Then he remembered that Matt had asked him practically the same question recently. Somehow, things didn't seem so clear anymore. "That's a tough question."

"Is it? Romans 13 says we should submit to the government. Wouldn't your answer be clear?"

"Yeah, but we're talking about someone who was murdering millions of Jews. I read that at the concentration camps, newborn babies were being burned alive in bonfires!" He shuddered. "Hitler was a monster."

"So, are you saying that as a Christian, you might have considered assassinating Hitler?"

John shook his head. "I just don't know. I mean, I think of all the lives that I might be saving, and—" He broke off, completely at a loss.

"Dietrich Bonhoffer faced that dilemma," Dalton said quietly.

He was startled. "You mean the great Christian minister who was imprisoned by the Nazis?"

Dalton nodded. "Few people are aware that he was imprisoned for being part of the assassination attempt against Hitler."

John was speechless.

"That's right," said Dalton. "But he agonized tremendously over that decision. It was something he really struggled with. Anyway, that's why I believe the New Testament does not directly encourage Christians to take up arms against an evil, oppressive government. I think it's because God wants that to be a decision they really struggle with before reaching the conclusion that force is the only way. However, you may be interested to know that in the Old Testament God commanded His chosen people to oppose wicked and ungodly rulers through the use of lethal force."

John was stunned. "So, you really believe that it would be acceptable for Christians to fight their own government?"

"Only if they had exhausted every peaceful means of changing the government. And there is a biblical basis for such a position. Genesis says, 'Whoever sheds the blood of man, by man shall his blood be shed.' I believe that applies to governments as well. You see, when a government gets to the point where it has gotten completely contemptuous of human life, then and only then would Christians be justified in using force against it. But it's something that individual Christians must pray about and struggle with first."

"This sounds incredible, coming from a pastor."

"Perhaps," said Dalton. "But we're dealing with two biblical principles here: the value of human life, and obedience to the government. Sometimes, biblical principles clash with one another. When that happens, you have to decide which is the higher principle. For instance, if you were hiding Jews from the Nazis, and the Nazis asked you if there were any Jews in your house, what would you do? Would you tell the truth?"

"Of course not! I'd be signing their death warrants."

"So then, you'd be willing to disobey God's command against lying in this situation."

"Look, we're talking about human lives here!" John said passionately.

"Exactly," said the pastor. "I think we would both agree that the value of human life takes precedence over the value of truth-telling."

"Of course."

"Well, then, perhaps we should apply the same test to using force against an oppressive, murderous government. In other words, which is the higher value—submission to the government, or saving human lives?"

John thought about what had happened to the Weisses; and he suddenly wondered what he would have done if he had been there. Would he have felt it was his duty to defend them—even if it meant shooting at the government agents who were trying to kill them? He just couldn't be sure at this point, but he was beginning to understand why Matt felt so passionately about the right to keep and bear arms. "I see what you mean," he said.

Dalton continued. "You also have to remember that our own Declaration of Independence states that the people have the right to change the government, by force if necessary, if it becomes too oppressive." He smiled. "So, have I answered your question?"

John shook his head. "Actually, I think you just confused me even more."

"Well, if you're looking for simple answers," said Dalton, "you may find that you're often disappointed."

John nodded. He was beginning to see how true that was.

* * * *

John smiled as he saw Matt getting out of his car in front of the home of Perry Kendall, the leader of the weekly Bible study. "Hey, you made it," John said as he and Beth approached Matt, who was even carrying a Bible.

Perry, a kindly widower in his late forties, opened the door to them, and John introduced him to Matt. "Hello, Matt. I'm so glad you decided to join us in studying the Word."

Matt smiled. "I almost didn't make it. It was unbelievable—everything kept going wrong today. It was like some weird conspiracy to keep me from coming here tonight."

A plump woman named Helen was just approaching the door with her husband, Carl, a heavy-set man with a florid complexion. They were both in their sixties. Though Helen had some sort of degenerative disease and walked with a cane, she smiled radiantly. "That's the enemy, always trying to keep us away," she said.

Matt looked puzzled. "What enemy?"

John coughed, a little embarrassed. He realized that Matt wasn't used to this kind of talk. "She means Satan," he muttered.

"Oh, him." Matt chuckled. "Well, even he couldn't keep me away tonight. It sounds like an interesting topic."

After hanging up their coats, Perry led them all through the foyer into the living room—an inviting little nook, which held two over-stuffed sofas, an easy chair, and a few hard-backed cane chairs. An immense bookshelf dominated the wall opposite the picture window. Andrea, a microbiology major from nearby Stony Brook University, was sitting on one of the sofas, tuning her guitar. Her straight, dark hair was tied back in a ponytail. She smiled at Matt as he approached, and John introduced them.

After they all sang a few gospel tunes, Perry invited people to mention their prayer requests. Audrey, John and Beth's downstairs neighbor, spoke first. She had short, thick hair that was always dyed a different shade of red, and was somewhere in her late thirties. "It's my daughter, Kelsie." John saw the anxiety in her face. "She came home very disturbed about something that happened in school today."

Perry looked concerned. "What happened?"

"She was a little confused about what it was exactly. She said the teacher made them all lie down on the floor. She didn't remember everything the teacher said, but after a while Kelsie felt like she was floating, like she was out of her body. She said it was scary. She could actually look down and *see* her body! What really upset me was that the teacher told them not to tell their parents about the experience."

"That sounds like astral projection," Matt said. "They tried to get us to do it where I work. A lot of the people who tried it said it *is* scary. You feel like you have no control."

Beth looked alarmed. "That's because you're in an altered state of consciousness. It also happens to be demonic."

Audrey's eyes widened in fear and disbelief. "Really?"

Beth nodded. "It's a way of opening up your consciousness to spiritual forces. You kind of suspend your own will and allow those forces to take over. Most people don't realize that demonic forces are involved. It's supposed to be a relaxation technique, but it's really much more sinister than that."

"But I just can't believe a first grade teacher would make the children do anything demonic," said Audrey. "You must be thinking of something else."

John said firmly, "No, Beth's right. The schools are trying to get the kids ready for the New Age, which will probably be ushered in with the World Constitution. Beth's been telling me that at her school, they're trying to put a wedge between the children and their parents. What better way to accomplish that than to get the kids into the occult, make them think they have powers—"

"What kind of powers?" asked Audrey.

"The power to alter reality," said Matt. "That's what they were telling us at work—that existence is an illusion, and we can make our own reality. It all goes back to Hindu mysticism." He looked thoughtful. "You know, a lot of the people who are into the New Age are heavily supporting this World Constitution. In fact, a New Age guru who's been teaching an awareness course at my job claims that the 'Ascended Masters' from other planes of existence have been urging the people of our planet to unite under a one-world government. She even said something about ushering in the coming of someone she calls the World Teacher, who's supposed to be the reincarnation of Jesus Christ."

John perked up at this. "Hmm. That sounds like it could be the Antichrist."

Audrey looked startled. "Really?"

Andrea had put her guitar away and was leaning forward in her chair, fascinated.

Perry cleared his throat. "Well, I think we're getting a little carried away here." John recalled then that Perry tended to avoid controversial topics. "But we will keep Kelsie in prayer. Anyone else with a prayer request?"

After praying, Perry looked around benignly. "We left off in the Gospel of John, chapter fourteen, verse twenty-seven." He glanced at his Bible. "'Peace I leave you, my peace I give you. I do not give it as the world gives it.' What did Jesus mean by this?"

John listened intently. With all the talk of the UN and world peace lately, he wasn't even sure about the meaning of the word anymore.

Andrea wore a dreamy expression. "I think He was talking about the inner peace that comes from a relationship with the Father. That's certainly not the way the world views peace."

Helen grinned. "If you think about it, Jesus and His followers certainly didn't exude peace by the world's standards. They were always stirring up trouble." She giggled. "Rabble rousers! That's what we might call them today."

Matt perked up. "Really?"

She folded her arms and nodded. "Jesus was a master at subversion. He turned the whole world upside down!"

Perry was smiling. "Very true, Helen." He glanced at the yellow legal pad on his lap. "What else did Jesus say about peace?" He looked around the room. "Does anyone here recall the Beatitudes?"

Beth raised her hand, and Perry nodded. She looked down at her Bible. "'Blessed are the peacemakers, for they will be called sons of God.'"

"So, God's Word calls us to be peacemakers," Perry said. "What does that mean?"

John was thinking of what Pastor Dalton had said. "It depends on how you look at peace. I think the world views peace as the absence of war and conflict. If that's the case, it may not be what we should be striving for. As Christians, we often have to enter battle, especially when defending the faith."

Someone named Mitch spoke up. He had silvery hair and blue eyes, and looked to be about forty-five. John recalled that he tended to be pretty conservative. "Hmm. That makes me think of the communists. You know what their definition of peace is? No opposition to communism. That's not my idea of peace."

"I understand your point, Mitch," said Perry. "But to have lasting peace in the world, wouldn't there have to be an end to war and armed conflict?"

"Yes," Mitch said, "but that wouldn't necessarily produce a peace that I'd want to live under. Prisoners in a concentration camp have 'peace' in that sense. They have no weapons and make no war. In many communist and totalitarian countries today that's the sort of 'peace' the people have. A hopeless and repressive peace, knowing that their brutal governments would kill them in an instant if they voiced any opposition."

John had never thought of it that way before. "Good point, Mitch! Peace has to be more than just the absence of conflict. In fact, Jesus told His followers He didn't come to bring peace. He said He had come with a sword, that He would even turn family members against each other."

"Boy, is that true." Matt shook his head. "You should've seen my wife's reaction when I told her I was going to a Bible study. She nearly freaked out!" John wasn't surprised. He had expected this to be a source of contention in their relationship.

"Doing the will of God won't always bring peace into our lives," Perry agreed. "Very often it does the exact opposite. Can anyone think of another example where Jesus' definition of peace would differ from the world's?"

Helen chimed in. "Look at how he dealt with the Pharisees. He really insulted them! I think He called them children of the devil."

Mitch scratched his head. "Our Lord sure didn't pull any punches. He actually used violence against the money changers in the Temple."

"I don't get it," Matt said. "Didn't Jesus say to turn the other cheek?"

"Good question!" Perry glanced around. "Now, how can we reconcile all this? On the one hand, we have a Savior exhorting us to be peacemakers, who went like a lamb to the slaughter. But we also see Him embroiled in conflict with people. How can we make any sense of this?"

Mitch rubbed his chin and frowned. "I think it goes back to what Andrea said about peace coming from a relationship with the Father. By the world's standards, Jesus certainly wasn't at peace with the Pharisees. He wasn't at peace while He was dying on the Cross. His peace came from being in the Father's will."

"I have a question." Everyone looked at Matt expectantly. "If Jesus' idea of peace is different from the world's definition, then how should Christians view the World Constitution? Will it guarantee the kind of peace Jesus was talking about?"

Mitch looked like he was about to say something, but Perry responded. "God's Word never promises genuine peace through any earthly government. Not until Christ returns to establish His Kingdom will mankind ever see lasting harmony. However, that doesn't mean we shouldn't strive to work for peace among the nations of our world. Would anyone else like to voice an opinion on this issue?" Silence filled the room. "Will a world constitution give us the kind of peace our Lord promised?"

"Well, I think it's a step in the right direction," Audrey said firmly.

"That's one thing I don't understand about a lot of Christians," said Carl. "Some of the most vocal opponents of the World Constitution are Christians. I mean, how can you claim to be a Christian and be against world peace?"

Mitch frowned. "I don't think it's a matter of being against world peace. For instance, I for one am not in favor of world government, but I'm certainly not against world peace. Before I'd embrace the UN Constitution, I'd want to be sure it wasn't offering the kind of 'peace' I mentioned earlier—"

Audrey looked confused. "But don't we need a one-world government in order to have world peace?"

"It may not be the kind of peace you're thinking of," said Matt.

"What do you mean?"

"Well, doesn't the Bible predict a very evil one-world government during the end-times?" he asked. "I mean, how can we know that the UN's government is going to be a benevolent one? If you ask me, it'll bring nothing but trouble."

"Look," said Carl, "I never said I thought the UN was perfect. But at least they're making an effort. Besides, the tribulation may not come for another hundred years, for all we know. I think that as Christians, we have a duty to support any effort toward world peace."

Matt looked startled. "*Any* effort? Even if it leads to a dictatorship?"

"I have to agree with Matt," said Mitch. "Now don't get me wrong. As a Christian, I do think we have a duty to work for peace. But we also have to work for justice. Unfortunately, the UN hasn't had a good track record in that area. They've always supported brutal communist dictators and have bullied smaller countries which rejected communism. And look at their stand on abortion and population control. They even support infanticide. I'm sorry, but I just don't think any Christian should support a government headed by the UN. In fact, I think we should be opposing it."

John noticed Perry's troubled expression. "How do you feel about the UN, Perry?" John asked.

"Well, I certainly don't approve of everything the UN has done over the years. But I do think we need the World Body in today's world, where nations can destroy each other at the touch of a button."

"What about a world constitution?" asked Matt.

Perry rubbed his chin. "Hmm...I don't think it would hurt to have some sort of system of world law, if for nothing else than to put an end to the threat of nuclear war. I certainly don't think it's God's will for nations to have the capacity to destroy one another—and the entire planet as well."

John didn't want to get into a heated debate right now, especially since Matt was still pretty new to the study. But it bothered him to hear Perry gloss over the potential dangers of the UN Constitution and the loss of American sovereignty. "I understand how you feel, Perry. But there are a lot of things about the UN that have me very concerned as a Christian. Things that are too serious to ignore. Have you heard of the UN Children's Rights Treaty? It's been used in France and several other countries to take children away from Christian parents. And we're going to be forced to adopt these kind of anti-family policies if we ratify the World Constitution—which was written by the UN."

Audrey narrowed her eyes and frowned. "Wait a minute. What's wrong with children's rights? I happen to believe very strongly in the rights of children. Abused children should be taken away from their parents. I just don't see how anyone could be against such a treaty."

"But the treaty has nothing to do with child abuse," Beth put in. "They want to take children away from parents whose views are politically incorrect. That could include all of us sitting here. In fact, the treaty grants children freedom of religion and conscience. That means they could take our children away if we make them go to church. Even without that treaty, our own federal government has gotten extremely invasive where families are concerned. The National Board of Education would just love to take children away from Christian parents—"

"I don't believe that," Audrey said flatly. "If the government has taken children away from their parents, there must have been a very good reason. I've been a social worker, and I've seen plenty of people who had no business being parents."

Perry coughed. "I think we're heading into the realm of political debate, and this really isn't the place for it. Now, I realize that many of you have legitimate concerns about our government and about the UN, which could very well become our government in the near future. But I think we have to remember that bad government is very often a judgement from God. When God gave the Law to Moses, He promised that blessings would come to the Israelites if they obeyed the Law, but they would receive curses for disobedience. One of the curses mentioned was oppressive government. So, if it seems that the federal government has gotten more intrusive over the years, that could be the consequence of our own disobedience as a nation. Besides, the one-world government predicted in the Bible isn't necessarily going to be used by the Antichrist in its early years. And if the UN is as much of a threat as some of you believe it to be, it may be part of God's judgement on America to put us under a UN-controlled government. If that's the case, then perhaps we shouldn't be opposing this."

"I'm not so sure I'd go that far," said Mitch. "Using that line of reasoning, someone could argue that the Holocaust was God's way of judging the Jewish people, so it was wrong for Christians to oppose Hitler."

"You guys are probably going to hate this next question," Matt said, "but I might as well ask it. Is it wrong for Christians to oppose government tyranny by force? In other words—would it have been wrong for Christians living in Nazi Germany to fight the Nazis?"

John smiled inwardly. He was wondering when that question was going to come up. Well, Matt always did love to stir things up.

Mitch chuckled. "Boy, you sure opened up a can of worms with that one!"

Matt grinned. "I like to keep things lively."

"That's a tough one all right," Andrea agreed.

Perry was thoughtful. "Well, let's consider what the Scriptures have to say about that question. Does anyone know of a Scripture passage which sheds light on this issue?"

"Didn't Pastor Bradley preach on that topic a few weeks ago?" asked Carl.

Mitch's wife Carol spoke up. "That's right. I think he used Romans 13 as his text." Her short blonde hair was parted to the side, and she was wearing a heather gray sweatshirt over faded jeans.

"All right, then, let's turn to Romans 13," said Perry. "Would someone like to read the verses for us?"

"Which verses?" asked Mitch.

"One through five, I believe."

"I'll read it," said Mitch. "'Everyone must subject himself to the governing authorities,'" he began, "'for there is no authority except that which God has established. The authorities that exist have been established by God. Consequently, he who rebels against the authority is rebelling against what God has instituted, and those who do so will bring judgement upon themselves. For rulers hold no terror for those who do right, but for those who do wrong. Do you want to be free from the one in authority? Then do what is right and he will commend you. For he is God's servant to do you good. But if you do wrong, be afraid, for he does not bear the sword for nothing. He is God's servant, an agent of wrath to bring punishment on the wrongdoer. Therefore, it is necessary to submit to the authorities, not only because of possible punishment but also because of conscience.'" He looked up. "Should I continue?"

"No, I think that covers the issue we're dealing with at the moment." Perry looked around at everyone. "So, what is Paul telling us here?"

"To obey the government," said Audrey.

"And why should we obey the government, according to Paul?" asked Perry.

Everyone glanced at their Bibles. "Because God established it," Helen replied.

Matt looked at Perry. "I have a question. Does that mean God established every single government in existence, or did He just establish the institution of government?"

John was impressed. "That's a good question."

"Well, would anyone like to venture an answer?" asked Perry.

Mitch scratched the back of his head. "To me, the only thing that makes sense is that God established the institution of government. I mean, if God established every government that ever existed, then we'd have to say He established Nazi Germany, the Soviet Union, and Communist China, where millions of His people are being tortured and killed for their faith. I just can't believe that a just God would establish evil governments like those."

"That's a good point," said Perry. "Does everyone agree?"

Carol looked thoughtful. "Well, I don't think God actually wills evil governments into existence, if that's what you mean. But I do believe that God allows evil governments to exist, just as He allows other forms of evil to exist. Maybe an evil government is simply the natural consequence of rejecting Christ."

"But it's not that simple," Andrea put in. "Look at all those Third World dictatorships, where the people are horribly oppressed. In many of those countries, people never even have a chance to hear about Jesus."

"Okay, let's say God does allow evil governments to exist for some obscure purpose," Matt said. "Does that mean we can't use physical force to defend ourselves—and our friends and families—from an evil government? For instance, let's say the government tries to murder my next-door neighbors. Am I supposed to sit by and let my neighbors get killed? Or would I be justified in shooting at the government agents who are attempting to murder them?"

"But what if it's God's will for your neighbors to die?" Audrey asked. "If you try to save them, you could be interfering with God's will."

John was shocked by her statement. "You'd really be willing to take that chance with your neighbor's life?"

"All I know is that I could never take a human life, even to save someone else. God said, 'Thou shalt not kill.' It's right in the Ten Commandments."

"Actually," said Mitch, "God said, 'Thou shalt not murder.' The literal translation of the original Hebrew in the verse is 'murder,' not kill. So, that means killing in self-defense or to save someone's life could be acceptable. Remember, God also said, 'Whoever sheds the blood of man, by man shall his blood be shed.'"

John perked up at this—the exact words Pastor Dalton had used! Could God be confirming what Dalton had told him?

Audrey folded her arms. "I don't know. I just couldn't do it."

"Even if someone were attempting to kill your husband—or your children?" asked Matt. "I mean, we expect the police to kill violent criminals if they have to in order to protect us. Why shouldn't we be willing to do the same thing in order to protect ourselves or our loved ones?"

"I think we're getting off the question at hand," said Perry. "Killing in self-defense isn't the same thing as armed insurrection."

"So, then it's okay for a Christian to kill in self-defense?" Matt asked.

"I think that's a matter of conscience," Perry replied. "I realize that some of you may disagree with me, but I don't believe a Christian should ever engage in violence—even if it means submitting to an assault."

This sounded extreme even to John, who had always considered himself a pacifist. "But what if it's the only way to save your wife or children? Don't we have a duty to protect our loved ones?"

"Yes, but our primary duty is to represent Christ to a fallen world. Striking out at our enemies with violence—even to save our loved ones—is hardly Christ-like, in my view. And remember—an intruder who is killed in an armed confrontation will never have the chance to repent. So, in the case of saving another person's life, I would have to say that force should be used only as a last resort—and only if you can stop the attacker without actually killing him. Now, let's get back to the question Matt addressed—whether it's acceptable for Christians to oppose government tyranny by force."

"Isn't that what our Founding Fathers did?" asked Matt.

"That's right," said Mitch. "And they were Christians, weren't they?"

"No, they were deists." There was a distinct note of disapproval in Perry's tone.

John smiled. "Actually, most of them *were* Christians, according to their writings."

Beth looked at him, surprised. "They *were?*"

He nodded. "I've been reading up on American history—about what our Founding Fathers actually wrote and said. They were men of great faith. In fact, I believe George Washington said that our Constitution would work only for a moral and religious people, and that no one could govern rightly without God and the Bible."

"Wow, I never knew that," Andrea said in amazement.

"Yeah, they never taught us that in the public schools," Carol said.

Beth looked sad. "They don't even teach that in some Christian schools."

"I still don't like the idea of overthrowing your own government." Carl sounded a bit disgruntled. "When Paul wrote his letter to the Romans, he was living under a pretty oppressive government. And he told the Christians to submit to it. I don't care what our Founding Fathers believed, I still say it's wrong to overthrow the government."

Audrey nodded in agreement. "That's right. Any government is better than no government."

John raised an eyebrow. "Really? Even a government that puts Christians to death or condones human sacrifice?"

"Yeah, what if the government is violating God's laws?" Andrea chimed in.

Mitch leaned back against the sofa. "I believe the Bible says we should obey God rather than men."

Perry agreed. "Yes, it does. As Christians, we are never obligated to obey laws which conflict with God's laws. But that's not the same thing as outright rebellion."

Mitch was frowning. "Our government's been violating God's laws for years."

"But where do you draw the line?" asked Matt. "I'm no Bible scholar, but I think I have a pretty good idea of what the Bible teaches. Look at the Ten Commandments. One of them says, 'Thou shalt not steal.' But the government is now stealing nearly 70 percent of our hard-earned money. They steal money from one group of people and give it to another group of people. Or they spend it on things that aren't exactly good causes—like abortion or obscene art. So, why should I let the government steal my money?"

Perry shook his head disdainfully. "I'd hardly call taxation stealing. And verse six of Romans 13 says we should pay our taxes. Besides, the government has a moral obligation to provide for those in need."

John was thoughtful. "Isn't that the church's role, though? I mean, the Bible says, 'Don't steal.' It doesn't say it's okay to steal as long as it's for a good cause—or as long as you give the money to someone who needs it."

"I think we're getting a little silly about this now," said Perry. "Taxation is not stealing. The government couldn't function without the income tax."

Mitch smiled at that. "Actually, the federal government functioned very well without it for over a hundred years—and there was always a surplus in the treasury. Excise taxes and tariffs provided more than enough revenue to run the country. We didn't even have a national debt until the government started all those entitlement programs—which cost over five trillion dollars and did nothing to end poverty."

"But aren't we all supposed to take care of those in need?" Audrey asked.

"We are, as the Body of Christ on earth," Mitch said. "But Jesus told individuals to help the poor; he never told them to ask the government to do it. Remember the rich young man? Jesus told him to sell his possessions and give to the poor. He didn't tell him to vote for welfare programs for the poor.

Besides, when we expect the government to take care of everyone, we're forcing the government to assume God's role."

"But what if people refuse to help those in need?" Beth asked. "Should we take that chance?"

Mitch was emphatic. "If we want to be obedient to God, yes."

"But what about people who can't work because of a disability or illness?" Andrea asked.

"That's a good question," Perry said. "The Bible tells us to love our neighbors. But are we loving our neighbors if we aren't willing to be taxed in order to take care of their needs?"

John thought about this. "The Bible commands God's people to care for widows and orphans. I suppose that would include all those who can't provide for their own needs."

Audrey looked confused. "I still don't see how that's different from the government doing it."

"It's different because God never authorized the government to take care of people's physical or material needs," Mitch said. "Don't you see the danger in that, Audrey?"

"Not really."

"Well, once the government starts providing for everyone's needs, people will start looking at the government as their god. That's not what God wants. He wants people to trust in Him, not the government."

"I don't know. What you're saying does make sense, but..."

"But what?" he asked.

"Well, it just seems wrong. It seems heartless not to want the government to take care of those in need. I used to work for Social Services, and I've seen women whose husbands walked out on them struggling to raise their children on minimum wage jobs. Those jobs just don't pay enough, Mitch. Some women have no choice but to go on welfare."

"Maybe the problem is that it's just too darn easy for a husband to walk out on his wife," Mitch said.

"You're right," John agreed. "If a guy knows the government will take care of his family if he doesn't, it's a whole lot easier for him to shirk his responsibility to them."

"So, what do you want, John? You want single mothers and their children to end up in the streets?" Audrey was clearly getting upset.

Mitch spoke gently. "None of us want that, Audrey. And it's not what God wants, either. But He doesn't want us to demand that the government do what He hasn't authorized it to. Not only that, but the government has a miserable track record in getting entitlement monies to the intended recipients. Did you know that out of every dollar ear-marked for entitlement programs, only twenty-five cents gets to the intended recipients? The other seventy-five percent is eaten up by administrative costs—and sometimes downright fraud. Churches and private charities have done much better."

"Well, my heart tells me I'm right," Audrey said flatly. "And when I feel this strongly about something, I know I can't be wrong."

Perry looked troubled. "I understand your concern for the needy, Audrey, but we need to be careful about relying too much on our feelings. Remember— the Bible says that the heart is deceitful above all things."

Now she sounded angry. "Look, no one's going to change my mind about this. I've always believed that the government should take care of those in need, and I always will. I don't care what the Bible says!"

Carol broke in then. "I'm not sure that's wise, Audrey. We can't reject God's Word every time it doesn't conform to our feelings."

"Maybe if you knew what it was like to be homeless or out of work, you'd understand how I feel."

Mitch spoke diplomatically. "Audrey, we do understand. You obviously have a great deal of compassion for the needy. But allowing the government to take care of everyone can have serious consequences—and can ultimately destroy the very people such a philosophy aims to help. The ancient Romans tried it, and it destroyed their civilization. It got to the point where everyone was on the government dole, and no one was working. Eventually, the entire economy collapsed. Now, that certainly didn't help the poor, did it?"

Audrey chuckled. "I thought Beth was the history teacher," she said in a playful tone. But John wondered if that was her way of dismissing an argument she simply couldn't refute.

Perry grimaced. "Well, be all that as it may, we still have a moral obligation to pay our taxes."

"Look, I'm not saying we shouldn't pay taxes at all," said Matt. "But what if our tax dollars are being used to do evil?"

Perry thought about this. "If you don't like the way the government is spending your tax dollars, then you should pray for the government. Ask God to give our leaders the wisdom to do His will. And search the Scriptures. Never do anything that's contrary to the Scriptures. And remember, Jesus said, 'Render unto Caesar what is Caesar's.'"

John skimmed through the passage again, and something caught his attention. "The wording in this next verse is interesting. It says, 'Give everyone what you owe him: if you owe taxes, pay taxes.' But what I'm wondering is—do we owe taxes to an evil government? For instance, say you live in a country like Nazi Germany, and you know the government is collecting a tax to build concentration camps for Jews. Should you pay the tax?"

"That's a good question," said Mitch.

"Believe me, I'm not advocating tax evasion," John said. "But this Scripture passage seems to be talking about a government that's fulfilling its proper role—keeping the peace, punishing evil—in other words, administering justice. But what if the government isn't doing those things? What if the government is perverting justice? Are we under the same obligation to submit to its authority?"

"In all things that don't conflict with the will of God—I would have to say yes. There's another Scripture passage that deals with this same issue. Let's see." Perry turned to his Bible. "I believe it's 1 Peter, chapter two. Verses 13-17. Would someone like to read?"

"I will," said Carl. "'Submit yourselves for the Lord's sake to every authority instituted among men; whether to the king, as the supreme authority, or to governors, who are sent by him to punish those who do wrong and to commend those who do right. For it is God's will that by doing good you should silence the ignorant talk of foolish men. Live as free men, but do not use your freedom as a cover-up for evil; live as servants of God. Show proper respect for everyone: Love the brotherhood of believers, fear God, honor the king.'"

Perry was smiling complacently. "Seems pretty clear, doesn't it?"

To his surprise, John found himself annoyed at Perry's tendency to gloss over a complex question with a tidy little verse from Scripture. He was beginning to see that these issues were much more complicated than Perry wanted to admit. "But what if the government *isn't* punishing those who do wrong and commending those who do good? What if it's doing the opposite— persecuting innocent people and rewarding the wicked?"

"As I said before, in that case we should pray for the government. I believe Chronicles says, 'If my people will turn to me and pray, and seek my face, I will heal their land.' That's a paraphrase, but I think it's pretty close." Perry frowned. "One of the things I've sensed among Christians today—especially those who are opposed to the World Constitution—is an excessive concern with political freedom rather than our spiritual freedom in Christ. Many of you fear that under a one-world government, you'll lose some of your political freedom—your so-called 'rights.' But that's not the kind of freedom that should concern us. Remember, we have no rights in Christ. Our main focus should be on the freedom that comes to us through salvation in Christ."

Mitch looked troubled. "That's true. But one of the concerns I have is that we'll be prohibited from witnessing under the new constitution. You know, the UN isn't exactly fond of us Christians. They could ban witnessing— they might call it hatespeech or something. If that happens, then it'll be pretty hard for us to bring people to Jesus. The political freedom we've had in America has made it a whole lot easier to share the gospel."

Helen, who had been pretty quiet during most of the discussion, suddenly spoke up. "Yes, Mitch, but look at the first Christians. They were living under a very oppressive government, and they still managed to share the gospel. No matter how oppressive the government gets, God's still going to be in control. No government can stifle the Holy Spirit."

"You're right about that," Mitch agreed. "But I'm not sure we should be willing to give up our sovereignty to the UN so easily. I believe God gave us this nation, and I don't think He'd want us to just sit by and let it be taken over by a godless organization like the UN. And I don't believe we should allow our God-given rights to be stripped away by God's enemies—which is exactly what'll happen if we give up our own Constitution and adopt the UN's—which is based on the Humanist Manifesto, by the way."

Perry spoke mildly. "I realize that feelings about these issues run deep in all of us. Some of you are very patriotic, and that's admirable. But remember— patriotism can be carried too far. It can blind us to the evils in our nation, and give us a false sense of superiority over other nations. After all, nationalism has caused war and strife in most parts of the world. We shouldn't allow our love for our country to stand in the way of peace."

It was Matt who spoke next. "So, you're convinced that the World Constitution will give us true peace?"

Perry seemed to be reflecting. "I think we all need to realize that only Jesus can give us true, lasting peace. No constitution or earthly government can guarantee peace. But I don't believe it's God's will for nations to be at war. A world constitution may not be the ultimate answer. But I think it's a step in the right direction." He glanced at his watch. "Let's see—it's going on nine thirty. In closing, I'd like to look at one more Scripture: John 14, verse 27. Matt, would you like to read it?"

Appearing somewhat startled, Matt looked up the verse, and began to read. "'Peace I leave with you; my peace I give you. I do not give to you as the world gives. Do not let your hearts be troubled and do not be afraid.'"

"Many of you seem very troubled about the future. Especially in light of recent political developments." Perry spoke gently but firmly. "But we must put our trust in God. Remember—He's in control. For those of you who fear that adopting a world constitution will threaten the civil liberties we've been blessed with, keep in mind that the greatest liberty of all is freedom from the bondage of sin. As long as we have Jesus, we never need fear what man can do. In light of what Matt said earlier: yes, the Bible does predict a satanic empire in the last days ruled by a dictator known as the Antichrist. And I know a great many Christians who are opposed to the concept of world government for that very reason. They fear that any attempt to create a one-world government will usher in the reign of Antichrist. But they forget that God will allow the Antichrist to rule this planet, however briefly, for one reason only: to show mankind the consequences of rejecting Christ. If that's the case, then world government is inevitable; there's nothing we can do to stop it. We can't change what God has already ordained." He looked around. "Mitch, would you like to close in prayer?"

"Sure." He folded his hands and bowed his head. "Heavenly Father, we thank You for this time we've had together, and we thank You for the opportunity to gather in Your Son's Name to worship You and study Your Word." His voice took on an earnest note. "Lord, we ask that You make it possible for us to continue to worship You in this country, no matter what government is ruling us. Please bless the delegates to the Constitutional Convention, give them Your wisdom. Protect us from government oppression, and help us to be Your witnesses during any persecution that may await us. Lord, no matter what happens, we ask that Your will be done, and that Your Name be glorified. In Jesus' precious Name, Amen."

Perry disappeared into the kitchen and returned with a tray of coffee and cookies, placing them on the sideboard in front of the living room window. Paper plates and napkins were set out, along with coffee mugs and tea bags.

Mitch approached Matt with a smile. "So, did you get an answer to your question?"

"I'm not exactly sure." Matt lowered his voice a bit, but John caught what he was saying. "Perry seems dead-set against any kind of violence, even in self-defense. I just don't buy that. I mean, does God want us to be helpless victims? Is that what turning the other cheek is about?"

Mitch frowned, rubbing his chin. "I don't think so. That verse about turning the other cheek has to do with reacting to an insult, not an intruder trying to kill you. In biblical times, slapping someone on the cheek was considered the worst kind of insult. Turning the other cheek means you're not supposed to seek revenge for an insult. It doesn't mean we can't defend ourselves against violence. I've never owned a gun myself, but I do believe using force to defend yourself or your loved ones against intruders is justified."

"What if the intruders are the government?"

Mitch laughed. "Boy, you sure love to ask tough questions!"

"Actually, I'm asking that question for a specific reason." He hesitated, and John noticed he was having difficulty keeping his voice steady. "My neighbors were murdered by government agents who broke into their apartment looking for guns. Of course, the 'official' story was that my neighbors were terrorists. But I know that can't be true. They were probably well into their seventies. The guy was a concentration camp survivor. All he wanted was to be left alone. He never registered his guns because that's how the Nazis were able to disarm the Jews in Germany. He probably fought back when they broke into his apartment. But I'm also convinced that he would never use his gun unless he felt he had to."

Mitch looked shocked. "I can't believe something like that can happen here!"

"Where've you been for the past ten years?" Matt's voice rose. "This has been happening since the early 1990s. Remember that religious cult in Texas? And the Cheever family?"

"Yeah, but those people were crazy," Mitch said. "They were extremists."

John could see the blood rising to Matt's cheeks. "And so were my neighbors, in the eyes of the government. Did that give the government the right to murder them?"

Mitch looked concerned. "Hey, take it easy."

"Why should I?"

John was just about to intervene when Perry approached them, a coffee mug in hand. "Because hatred isn't the answer," he said.

"That's easy for you to say," Matt retorted. "Look at what's been happening lately. Our own government is trying to disarm innocent civilians. And there's this group called WorCEN which is going around killing people who are opposed to the UN Constitution—"

"I'm familiar with conspiracy theories." Perry wore an expression of mild distaste. "Frankly I think those theories have done more harm to this country than our own government has. Those theories do nothing but spread paranoia."

"And I suppose the Jews in Germany during the 1930s were paranoid for worrying about Hitler," Matt said sarcastically.

Perry spoke cautiously. "I'm not saying our government has done no wrong in recent years. But extremism isn't the answer. Hatred isn't the answer."

"So what are you saying?" asked Matt. "That we should just ignore what the government's been doing?"

"I'm saying that we can't fight evil with evil. There's a very thin line between righteous anger and hatred. Now, I'm certainly not condoning some of the horrendous things our government has done in the past. But I don't think it's healthy to dwell on these things, Matt. You shouldn't let your anger consume you."

"I don't think fighting evil is evil, but I am trying to control my anger," he said with a slight edge of resentment in his voice.

John put a hand on his shoulder. "It's getting late. Maybe we should get going." He could see how upset Matt was getting, and he didn't want him to lose his temper. He knew that if Matt were pushed too far, he could really lose control.

Matt sighed. "Yeah, all right." He forced himself to be polite to Perry. "Well, I hope I haven't stirred things up too much."

"Not at all," Perry said mildly. "I hope you'll join us next week."

Matt grinned. "You sure about that?"

Perry only smiled.

Mitch patted Matt on the back. "Well, I sure hope you will. It's nice to know there are still a few patriots left. I was beginning to think we were an endangered species!"

John walked Matt to his car, while Audrey chatted excitedly to Beth about a new recipe.

"So," John said cautiously, "what did you think?"

Matt smiled. "Well, I'll say one thing—it was interesting."

"Does that mean you'll be coming back again?"

"Maybe. Actually, I think I will."

John was surprised. "Really?"

"Well, *someone's* gotta set Perry straight."

They both laughed. But as John watched Matt drive away, he felt deeply disturbed about what had transpired that night. These were issues that could really divide people, even Christians. He wondered if the church could withstand such division. A divided church, he knew, was vulnerable to attack.

CHAPTER 14

"I'm telling you the truth! Cheryl Hendricks was murdered because of a story she was planning to write on the CGU!"

Ken sat silently, uncertain of what to say. Gina stood near his desk, going over some last minute details of a new assignment when Ross Meyers had barged in and demanded to talk to the managing editor.

Ken took a deep breath, then exhaled slowly. "Do you have any evidence?"

Ross sighed impatiently. "No. But I can tell you everything I told her about the CGU. Maybe that will convince you that there was enough of a motive for them to kill her!"

Ken got up from his chair and spoke in a patronizing tone. "Look, Senator Meyers, I'm a very busy man. Now, maybe you think that by smearing the Council for Global Unity, you'll deflect attention from the charges that have been brought against you, but—"

He spoke through clenched teeth. "Those charges are false! I'm not a hatecriminal. I've never had anything to do with the Klan!"

"I saw the news reports."

Ross was becoming more agitated. "All lies! They must've been faked or something. I never said those things, and I never even met the person they showed me talking to." He looked at Ken with a helpless, pleading expression. "Please, won't you listen to what I have to say? I may not be able to prove that Cheryl was murdered. But I can tell you the truth about the CGU—and get it out to the public before it's too late."

Ken could hardly look at the man. "I'm sorry, Senator. But my hands are tied. This paper is practically owned by the CGU. Even if what you're telling me is true, I couldn't print it."

"Won't you at least try?"

He looked away. "I'm sorry. There's nothing I can do."

Ross Meyers nodded, his face etched with sorrow. "It seems they've gotten to all of us, haven't they?" He turned and walked out of the office.

Gina looked at Ken incredulously. "I can't believe you wouldn't even listen to what he had to say!"

Wearily, Ken sat back in his chair. "What would be the point? We're under Damien's fist."

"Oh, come on, Ken. You could print it without his knowing about it. He doesn't check everything, you know. You could slip it in somewhere—"

"And then get fired the next day? No, thanks. I need this job."

"More than you need your integrity?"

"I don't see *you* standing up to Damien. You've gone along with this as much as I have. The only one who ever stood up to him was Cheryl—" He broke off, ashamed. If what Ross said were true, then Ken was now guilty of trying to cover up her murder. He sighed. "It's more than just this job," he said slowly.

"What do you mean?"

"Last week, Damien wanted me to print some lies about a New York assemblyman opposed to the World Constitution. I told him that's where I draw the line. Twisting the truth is one thing. But printing bald-faced lies, well, that's something I just won't do. I told him I'd rather quit than do that."

"And what happened?"

"He threatened me."

"With what? Getting fired?"

"If that's all it was, believe me, I'd be outta here. No, it was a little more detailed than that. He told me he'd make sure I never work again—and that my sons will never work once they graduate college. He even threatened to use his influence to get them kicked out of college."

"What!"

"You heard me. So, when I said my hands are tied—well, they really are tied." He got up from his chair and began pacing the floor. "This job's making me crazy! I can't even sleep any more." He pounded his fist on his desk. "I feel like an animal in a damn trap!"

"I know the feeling. What do you think about that news clip of Meyers? You think it was faked, like he said?"

"It's possible. They have the technology to do it. I think it's called morphing."

"Kind of like what they did in *Forrest Gump* with President Kennedy?"

"Yeah, they get a film clip of someone and do a voice-over, make it look like they're saying things they never said, change face and features. It's all done with computers."

"It's kind of scary, isn't it? I mean, if they could do it to Senator Meyers, they can do it to anyone. Even to you or me."

"I guess we're all potential targets these days. But we don't have the guts to do anything about it. We're so used to being comfortable and secure, that we're afraid to take any risks." He smiled ruefully. "I think it was Thomas Jefferson who said, 'Those who are willing to give up liberty for security deserve neither liberty nor security.' I don't think he'd like me very much."

Gina sighed. "Well, there's some good news. Some of the delegates to the Convention are reconsidering whether or not they should go. People like Father Flannery and groups like the Patrick Henry Society seem to have gotten the public shaken up about the UN Constitution."

Ken was thoughtful. "Hmm," was all he said.

She eyed him curiously. "What are you thinking?"

"I don't know. I just find it hard to believe that the one-worlders are going to give up that easily. They're too close to let America slip through their fingers now."

"So, what are you getting at?"

"I'm sure they have some kind of contingency plan. Something that'll guarantee America goes one world, with or without a constitutional convention."

* * * *

A horde of dark beings swarmed above the Manhattan skyline like locusts. They swooped down through soaring skyscrapers and office buildings, moving effortlessly through steel, glass and concrete, and descended upon the Grandview Hotel. Their swords gleamed against the evening sky, their faces contorted with hate.

They were watched by another contingent of heavenly beings who stood near the hotel. Their swords were drawn in readiness.

"Can we stop it?" a tall, luminous being asked his Commander.

The Commander surveyed the warriors who clung to the hotel like leeches, grinning and cackling and sneering. He sadly shook his head. "Our purpose here is to protect the one with our Lord's seal upon her forehead. We can do nothing else. The people of this land will never learn to resist the Dark One until they choke under his rule. They must be made to see the price of their allegiance."

"Can we protect the children?"

The Commander cast a regretful look at the building. "No. Their parents belong to the prince of this world. But most have not yet reached the age of accountability, so the Dark One has no claim on their souls"

He pointed to a woman getting out of a taxicab. "There!" He nodded to the others, who moved alongside of her, covering her with their broad wings. "Don't let her out of your sight!"

Gina felt something brush against her shoulder as she exited the cab. She whirled around.

Nothing.

Traffic moved slowly down Fifth Avenue, coming to a near standstill in front of the hotel, where a stream of taxicabs and limos edged toward the curb. Shivering as the wind whipped their coats about them, elegantly dressed men and women hurried through the revolving doors of the lobby.

Gina looked around in awe. Balloons in every color of the rainbow floated high above the Grand Ballroom. A huge banner with the words, "WORLD PEACE THROUGH WORLD LAW," was spread across the dais. Exquisite tapestries covered the gilt walls, and a magnificent crystal chandelier hung from the ceiling.

In just a few more days, the Convention would begin in Philadelphia. Almost every major celebrity who supported world government was here to arouse last minute support for the World Constitution. Numerous government officials were also present, including the Mayor of New York City. The Governor had arrived earlier, but had been called away on a family emergency. All the major networks would be broadcasting live. Some had already started.

Although she was beginning to have reservations about the UN Constitution, it was impossible not to get caught up in all the excitement. Matt had shown nothing but disdain about the whole affair. When she asked if he planned to watch the telecast, he told her he'd probably kick the TV set in if he did.

Wearing a red-sequined dress with a full, georgette skirt, which she had been lucky enough to find at a Goodwill Store, she stood near the entrance to the ballroom and snapped pictures of celebrities as they made their way inside. She scanned the crowd for members of the CGU, but saw few she recognized. She glanced at the Council's membership roster, which she had obtained earlier via e-mail. After Senator Meyer's startling revelation, she wanted to learn more about this group.

The Mayor of New York City approached the podium. Smiling into the cameras, he spoke a few words of welcome, then gave a rousing speech in support of the World Constitution. Gina had her pocket tape recorder going, so she barely listened since she had heard similar discourses so frequently. Then he introduced the Speaker of the House, who had flown in from Washington for the event. Curiously, both men excused themselves immediately after, saying they couldn't stay because of family obligations. Hoping to ask them a few questions about the upcoming Convention, Gina, along with a hoard of other reporters and photographers, approached the two men as they hurried away. But both men wore strained expressions and spoke brusquely. After they rushed out of the ballroom, Gina remembered that both were Council members.

The next person who spoke was a famous actress well-known for her thousand dollar seminars on Transcendental Mediation and visualization. The crowd cheered as she denounced Christian fundamentalism and flag-waving patriotism as the two greatest evils of modern society. Listening to her impassioned speech, Gina moved uncomfortably in her chair. The woman was mocking people like Father Flannery, who had convictions and was not afraid to assert that there was ultimate truth. A few months ago, Gina would have got up and cheered herself. But now, she had a cold feeling inside as she listened to words that sounded strangely hollow to her. *What's happening to me?*

Gina nibbled on a bit of quiche as she sat through yet another speech. She looked at her watch. *How long can these people ramble about the same topic?* Few speakers actually said anything positive about the World Constitution. They mainly attacked those who opposed it, denouncing the United States Constitution as the product of Bigoted, Oppressive White Christian Males (they all seemed to phrase the words in capital letters). Surprisingly, the most vehement attack against traditional Christianity came from religious figures. A Protestant minister and a nun both spoke out against fundamentalist Christians who opposed world government.

The minister passed by her table, and Gina rose from her chair to ask him about his speech.

Smiling congenially into the cameras, Reverend Glenn Harrison, known for the many books he had authored on "possibility thinking," took a sip from his champagne glass. Suddenly, as if on cue, he adopted an expression of grave sadness as he spoke to reporters.

"It's unfortunate that traditional Christians have misinterpreted Christ's message," he said. "Once we adopt the World Constitution, I think we'll start to see some major changes in the Church. It's going to happen. It has to. The only way the people of this planet can remain united politically is to unite spiritually. I never was a big fan of Catholicism, but this new pope has been saying a lot of the same things. He really seems to understand the problem. I think he's going to be a big force for the spiritual union of this planet."

The cameras panned away in search of other faces, and Reverend Harrison was left alone. Gina approached him and introduced herself. "I was surprised to hear you say Christianity is an outdated religion," she said. "Aren't you a Christian minister?"

"In a manner of speaking, I suppose. What I mean is that traditional Christianity, like our current mode of individual governments, is going to have to change in order to keep up with all the cultural and social changes that have taken place during the last millennium. Mankind is about to make a jump to the next phase of evolution. We're going to see a great advance in spiritual, or what I like to call planetary, evolution. But it's something that most 'traditional' Christians aren't ready for yet. Their outmoded interpretation of Christianity will have to change if they're going to fit in."

Gina was intrigued. "What exactly do you mean by a jump in evolution?"

"It's really a shift in consciousness, on a planetary, or global level," he said in a didactic tone. "Over the centuries, we've been evolving on a massive scale, becoming more advanced intellectually and technologically with each new era. We seem to have reached the limit of biological evolution. So, the next phase is spiritual evolution. Humans will inevitably evolve into a more benevolent, spiritually enlightened species. The fact that we're this close to putting an end to war proves it. We're going to see a change in the entire face of the earth! It's very exciting. In fact, my own congregation has reacted with great enthusiasm when I preached about this subject recently."

She had never heard a minister speak like this before. "What does your church believe about Christianity?"

"The Church's primary mission is to help the individual to achieve self-actualization. If you think about it, Jesus was simply a great man who had totally fulfilled his potential. In other words, He had reached self-actualization. Which basically means getting in touch with the divine in each of us. Yes, Jesus was divine, but we *all* are! Spiritual evolution is about achieving our own godhood. In fact, some people are going to become so spiritually advanced that they'll be able to perform miracles! You know, that's really the only reason Jesus could perform miracles, because He recognized and used the divine power within Him. We could all do the same if we had His awareness."

Gina had mixed feelings about the minister's words. On the one hand, she liked the image he presented of Jesus. Definitely non-threatening. But what he said about spiritual evolution and the divine within, as appealing as it sounded, just seemed wrong somehow. She thought about Father Flannery and his concern with evil. His reference to Satan. "What does your church teach about good and evil?" she asked.

He smiled broadly. "Oh, we don't believe in evil."

She was startled. "Why not?"

"Evil is simply a figment of our minds. The eastern mystics have taught us that good and evil are really two sides of the same coin. Good could not exist without evil, just as heat couldn't exist without cold. We need to have balance in everything. We also know that what's evil for one person may be good for another."

Gina was troubled by his words. The ideas weren't totally new to her; she'd heard much of the same at the Catholic college she had attended. At the time she had embraced such thinking. But now, it all struck her as terribly wrong. She wasn't sure why. She had never considered herself a traditional Christian by any means. And yet, something deep inside her was offended by what Reverend Harrison was saying. "So, in other words, if some guy rapes me, that may be evil for me, but good for him?"

An amused, condescending smile played across his lips. "That's not exactly how I would put it. But evil depends greatly on our own perception. For instance, traditional religions train us to think of suffering as evil. However, suffering is actually good, because it allows us to atone for wrongs committed in a previous lifetime." Gina noticed that he didn't use the term, sin. "As a result, we advance to a higher spiritual state in our next life. And ultimately, to a higher plane in our own spiritual evolution. So, I would have to say that if a woman is raped, that experience is somehow necessary in order to help her soul rid itself of some bad Karma."

"So, in other words, she's being punished for something she did in a past life?"

"I don't like to use the word punishment," he told her. "I would prefer to call it a learning experience."

"I doubt a rape victim would see it that way," Gina said. "Anyway, there's one thing I don't get—how can suffering in this life help us spiritually when we don't remember our past lives?"

"Actually, we do remember on an unconscious level. And there are ways to bring those dim memories to our conscious awareness. One method is through hypnotic regression, which is utilized in Past Lives Therapy. If you're interested, I can recommend an excellent therapist in that area."

She didn't feel like hearing any more of this nonsense. "No thanks. If you'll excuse me, there are some other people I need to speak with."

The orchestra started to play some Christmas music; the tune of "Silver Bells" mingled with the laughter and chatter of the guests. Someone was saying it was almost time for the children to perform.

* * * *

In the back alley of the hotel, a U-Haul truck pulled to a stop, its tires moving soundlessly over a thick layer of slush. Inside were over a dozen armed men, wearing black masks over their faces. Dressed in fatigues and combat boots, they looked straight ahead, their eyes devoid of expression. Someone gave a signal, and they filed out of the truck, carrying black machine guns, and blending smoothly into the dark alley.

* * * *

A man dressed in a Santa Claus costume weaved among the guests, handing out brightly wrapped packages. A striking-looking couple dressed as the sun god and moon goddess danced around the ballroom, accompanied by chanting and the beating of drums. The celebration of Winter Solstice ended in a rousing rendition of "Let it Snow."

Gina stood near the dais watching the children as they lined up in front of the dais to sing their song. The very young children, those no more than six or seven, laughed and giggled, tugging at and pushing one another. The older ones stood quietly, looking around in awe.

Suddenly she froze, her heart beating rapidly. Something was wrong. *This is silly. What's the matter with me?* But she felt somewhat light-headed. *Maybe too much champagne?* She took a deep breath.

In every corner of the ballroom invisible shadows loomed menacingly, their fangs dripping a foul substance. But they couldn't get near the one who wore the seal.

The luminous beings had formed a hedge around her that nothing could penetrate.

* * * *

Matt strained to see the road as his wiper blades sliced through the layer of snow that clung to his windshield. A sickening feeling of dread had come over him, and he couldn't figure it out. It started on the drive to Oakdale. Navigating the icy roads, he told himself it was just the poor visibility and treacherous road conditions. On Idle Hour Boulevard he took the many turns on the winding road very slowly and carefully after skidding into a curb a mile or so back near the flat bridge. Fortunately, the car wasn't damaged. But even as the snow finally began to let up a bit, the feeling persisted.

When he arrived at his parents' dilapidated apartment, he tried to sound cheerful. It wasn't easy. Old newspapers were piled up against the wall. A pitiful looking Christmas tree stood in front of the window, with a few glittering bulbs hanging from its sparse branches. The shades were pulled down, covered with a thick layer of dust. There were no curtains. Matt's father sat in front of the black and white TV set wearing only a worn-out old bathrobe. He didn't acknowledge Matt's entrance at all. Occasionally he took a swig of beer.

Matt walked into the tiny kitchen and offered to help his mom in the dinner preparations.

She looked at him sadly, then forced a smile. "It's okay, hon. You just relax. Have some cookies. I made your favorite."

He grabbed a molasses cookie still warm from the oven. "You remembered." He lowered his voice. "Mom...how long has he been like that?"

Mom brushed away a strand of hair, a mixture of ash blonde and light gray, and shrugged. "It's hard to say. I guess it's been building up, little by little. Since he lost the business. It's like, he lost all hope." Her voice was filled with sorrow. "Like he's got nothing to live for no more. I try to keep the place tidy, but it's getting harder and harder. I can't do very much myself, but I try. I sweep up and vacuum from time to time." She chuckled. "I try to work around the clutter as much as I can. But he don't seem to want the place to look nice. He won't let me throw stuff away. I don't know..." Her voice trailed off, and Matt could see she was trying not to cry.

"Are John and Beth coming?" he asked, trying to get her mind off her troubles.

Her face brightened. "Oh, yes, and Beth's bringing her famous eggnog cheesecake."

"Oh, that fattening thing with a million calories? I remember having it at their place last New Year's Eve."

She laughed. "Yeah, I think it has three packages of cream cheese, two sticks of butter and two cups of whipping cream. Not to mention a ton of confectioner's sugar and the eggnog." She looked hopeful. "Maybe that'll perk your father up. He always did have a sweet tooth."

Matt noticed with concern that she seemed to be coughing a lot. He asked her if she was sick.

"Oh, I'm sure I'm fine. Probably just a touch of the flu. I don't want to bother with the doctor. I'd just wait for hours and then be in and out in less than fifteen minutes. It's just not worth it. Even if it is free." Her voice had a touch of sarcasm.

John and Beth arrived shortly. They both greeted Matt's father, who merely grunted and then turned his attention back to his show.

"I swear, sometimes I'd like to throw that thing out the window." Their mother was shaking her head.

"Hey, Mom, do you know if Dad's got any cigarettes around?" asked Matt.

John looked surprised. "Didn't you quit?"

Matt shrugged. "Yeah, but I'm feeling kind of uptight. Thought maybe a cigarette would help."

Beth smiled. "Oh, yeah, I'm sure that nicotine is just what you need to calm down."

John looked at him curiously. "What's got you so uptight?"

"I don't know. I think maybe I'm getting paranoid." His mom handed him a steaming mug of hot chocolate.

He shivered. "I just can't shake this creepy feeling." He turned his attention to the telecast of the ball. A group of smiling children was lining up in front of the cameras. Their tiny voices rose in song, as the band played softly in the background.

Something made him think of Gina.

"Dinner's ready!" Mom called from the kitchen.

They gathered at the table, and their mother asked John to lead them all in prayer. John was about to begin praying, when Matt broke in. "I think we should pray for Gina," he said. He wasn't sure why, but something told him it was important.

* * * *

Gina's head throbbed painfully, and a wave of nausea hit her. She rolled her eyes. *Perfect timing.*

She dashed out of the ballroom and down the hallway, looking for the ladies' room. Gratefully, she pushed open the door and ran toward one of the stalls. The queasy feeling was lessening now, but she still felt dizzy and her head hurt. She decided to sit in the ladies' lounge on one of the pink velvet chairs until the dizziness passed.

* * * *

The three desk clerks of the Grandview Hotel were slumped over on the floor behind the front counter. A big, husky security guard lay sprawled across the carpet, his glassy eyes wide open. He had managed to get off one shot with his .38 Special that wounded one attacker, but nobody heard due to the high level of noise from the celebration. Four armed men stood like sentinels near the elevator; the front entrance was also guarded.

* * * *

Gina splashed some water on her face. She looked in the mirror. A blotch of mascara ran down her cheek. She fumbled in her purse for a tissue, and pulled out a wad of crumpled up paper. *You never have a tissue when you need it*, she thought, mildly annoyed.

She was reaching into her pocket when a sound unlike anything she had ever heard before shook the entire room. She reeled backward and almost fell. *Gunfire!*

At first, she thought it was coming from somewhere in the room. But the gunshots were coming from outside the lounge.

The steady burst of gunfire seemed to shake the entire building. *Machine guns!* Her heart pounded violently and her legs shook like jelly. In the distance she could hear people screaming and glass shattering. *The ballroom!*

Shaking violently, she forced herself to think clearly. She held her breath, afraid that any sound would give her away. *What if they come in here?* She shuddered as she realized that any gunmen taking over a building would definitely check the bathrooms!

Frantically, she looked around the room for a window to escape through. No windows! Then, she noticed the ceiling. It was made of panels. She pushed open one of the stalls, put the lid down and stood on top of the toilet seat. This was her only chance of escape! She almost slipped in her red satin pumps. She pulled them off and placed them on the tank, reached up and pushed at one of the panels. Her heart leaped as the panel moved. It was very light. She pushed a little harder until it came loose, then slid it over to the side. Pushing her arms up into the opening, she held on and tried to hoist herself up. Then she remembered her shoes and her bag. She grabbed them and tossed them into the opening. *Can't leave any clues.*

She had just made it through and was replacing the panel when someone kicked the door open and burst into the lounge. With shaking hands she slid the panel back in place. A loud, threatening voice thundered below. "Come on out!"

Her entire body stiffened and she drew in her breath. *He's seen me. He's going to kill me!* Lying in the darkness, she thought of the pepper spray in her evening bag. Her only means of defense. But what good is pepper spray against a machine gun? Her heart sank as she realized the complete hopelessness of her situation. She was trapped. For the first time in her life, she wished she had a handgun. Then she'd at least have a fighting chance.

She lay very still, hardly daring to breathe. Underneath her, she could hear the gunman kicking open the doors of the stalls. Soon he was right beneath her. She could feel her dress clinging to her body, damp with perspiration. She held her breath, afraid to make even the slightest noise. She listened. In an instant, he was at the next stall. Her body relaxed only slightly. How would she ever get out of here?

The blast of machine guns continued. Suddenly, her reporter's instincts took over. She realized that the lounge was adjacent to the Grand Ballroom. If she could crawl directly above the ballroom, she might be able to open a panel and get a photo of the gunmen; she still had her camera around her neck. Any photos she took could be of help to the police. Groping around in the darkness, she found a ceiling beam. *Perfect.* She began to climb across it toward the ballroom.

CHAPTER 15

Matt stared at the television set, his mouth open in disbelief. Over a dozen armed men had burst into the ballroom, shooting at everyone in sight. Hundreds of people stampeded toward the doors, clawing each other and screaming in terror. A mangled pile of bodies lay in a heap, drenched in blood.

The camera panned to a middle-aged woman pushing the children to the floor. Bullets ripped through her and she crumpled to the ground, her eyes glazed and staring. Survivors crawled along the floor, trying to hide under tables.

Matt wasn't sure how long the spectacle continued. He could hear the startled exclamations of his family, but couldn't find his voice. The ballroom started spinning, then all he could see was the ceiling. The camera operator had been shot.

The gunfire slowly subsided to intermittent bursts, then stopped. Matt could hear people screaming and moaning. The screen went black. A stilted male voice said, "We are experiencing technical difficulties. Please stand by."

Moments later, an attractive woman appeared on screen. Her voice sounded very far away. "Terrorists have taken over the Grandview Hotel in downtown Manhattan. Police are on the scene..."

Gina! Matt turned to John. "I've gotta get over there!" He ran to the closet to get his coat.

John put his hand on Matt's shoulder. "Matt, you'll never make it. The roads are bad enough, there'll be a million cars trying to get through—"

"*My wife is in that building!* I have to get over there."

His mother rubbed her hands together. "Hon, there'd be nothing you could do. The police are over there—"

"*Screw the police!*" He almost spat the words. He softened when he saw her stricken face. "I'm sorry, Mom. But I've just got to get over there. I can't sit here doing nothing. I just...need to be there."

"Then I'll drive you. You're in no state to drive, anyway." John turned to Beth. "You stay here and keep the folks company, okay? We'll call once we know what's happening."

The two men threw on their coats and rushed out into the darkness.

* * * *

The roar of gunfire was deafening as Gina reached the ballroom. Slowly she lifted up the panel right beneath her and peeked through the opening. Men and women spattered with blood lay sprawled on top of one another. Tables had fallen over on people, shattered glass was strewn across the floor.

She looked toward the dais. The children.... She squeezed here eyes shut. A choked sob threatened to give her away.

The gunmen were still shooting!

Steeling herself against the emotions that threatened to overwhelm her, she tried to position herself to get a good shot of the gunmen, or at least one of them. She set the shutter speed for one thirtieth of a second to compensate for the low lighting conditions. Fortunately, she had a silent camera and was using ASA 200 film, so she didn't need a flash. She snapped as many pictures as she could, hoping that no one would notice her. If anyone did, she'd be dead in an instant.

* * * *

Matt listened to the car radio in a dazed silence as John fought his way through the heavy traffic on the Long Island Expressway.

Some of the hotel guests, those few who weren't at the banquet, tried to dial 911 when they heard the shooting. But all the phones were dead. No one dared leave his room. Some guests had hidden in closets, others had crawled under their beds. They weren't sure where the shooting was coming from, but they all feared that the gunmen would eventually be coming for them.

By the time police had entered the building, a few dead bodies lay in the hallways, staining the beige carpet crimson. All three desk clerks were dead.

The radio report continued, "The first police units to arrive on the scene were met with machine gun fire and some sort of self-propelled incendiary device—leaving the cars flaming wrecks. These devices were fired from various nondescript cars placed in strategic positions at all four intersections near the hotel, with four other cars two blocks away but within sight— obviously as backup for the terrorists. By the time the police arrived in force, seven patrol cars were burning and the gas tanks of four had exploded— showering the road and nearby buildings with burning gasoline. It was a scene no one will ever forget. By this time the terrorists had made their escape. All roads out of Manhattan are closed and roadblocks are being set up at nearly every corner."

Matt wanted to turn off the radio, but something compelled him to keep listening. The entire city was in a panic, knowing that terrorists were on the loose. There was talk of the National Guard, backed by UN peacekeeping troops, being called into the city.

The report went on to say that Oren Reinhardt, the big tycoon who owned the hotel, was notified immediately. Vacationing in Zurich, he had boarded his private jet and would be home the next day.

* * * *

Gina stumbled out of the lounge, her dress torn and streaked with dirt, her hair disheveled and matted with sweat. Feeling numb and slightly dazed, she clutched her camera tightly. Immediately surrounded by police, she shoved it into her purse.

* * * *

Matt and John couldn't get near the hotel at all due to the roadblocks, so they parked the car and half-ran, half-walked the twelve blocks there. It was out of the question to take the subway; it was closed by order of the NYPD. When they finally arrived at the Grandview, total chaos greeted them. Reporters and TV news vans circled the hotel like vultures, demanding entrance to the building.

"We'll never find Gina in this confusion." Matt looked desperately at the hotel. "She's just got to be alive!"

They managed to find someone in authority, who told them that all the victims had been taken to the nearest hospitals. Matt dialed several from a corner phone booth. He cursed. The lines were all busy. After several tries he gave up.

John was waiting in front of the building. "Couldn't get through?"

Matt shook his head, trying to shake off the despair that nearly overwhelmed him. By now he feared the worst. He fought back tears as he recalled their fighting in recent months and his coldness toward her. Now, all he wanted to do was hold her in his arms and tell her he loved her.

He stood at the fringe of the crowd, which was just starting to disperse.

With the victims taken to the morgue or the hospital, there wasn't much left
to see. John had just suggested that they head over to the closet hospital,
when Matt suddenly heard a familiar voice, filled with elation, calling his
name. "Matt! Is that you?"

He looked up, stunned to see Gina a few yards in front of him, waving.
Wordlessly, he pushed his way through the crowd, hardly daring to believe
his eyes. In a moment they were in each other's arms.

"*Gina!*" They held each other tightly. "I can't believe you're alive!"

"Neither can I," she said almost breathlessly.

He just couldn't seem to let her go. "I love you, Gina...so much!"

Tears streamed down her cheeks. "I love you, too." Her voice sounded
small and frightened, almost child-like.

Matt held her silently, thanking God from the bottom of his heart.

* * * *

During the drive back to Oakdale, Gina told Matt and John everything
that had happened. After the gunmen fled, she had remained in her hiding
place until she could hear the police and paramedics searching for survivors.
She soon learned that the FBI Hostage Rescue Team had arrived, and her
guard went up because of what Hank had told her about their involvement in
the death of Danny Cheever's wife and son. When she saw that the agents
were searching all the survivors, she popped out her film and hid it inside her
bra. It was uncomfortable there but at least not visible. Fortunately, she'd
used up the roll.

Well over an hour passed before Gina managed to leave the building. The
survivors were detained for questioning by the FBI agents, who arrived on
the scene immediately after the police. The first thing the agents did was to
confiscate all cameras. To Gina, it seemed the agents were treating the
survivors like criminals, not victims. Unlike the police, the agents showed
little compassion for anyone. Even those survivors who were dazed and grief-
stricken at having lost loved ones during the shooting were treated with cold
efficiency.

Getting out of the city was no small feat; traffic was jammed because of
all the roadblocks, and every car was searched. By the time they arrived back
at the home of Matt's parents, it was well after two in the morning. Mrs.
Lanyon suggested that Gina and Matt spend the night in the spare bedroom
instead of driving all the way back to East Meadow at that hour. Somewhat

reluctantly, they agreed; they were both physically exhausted and emotionally drained, and didn't feel up to another long drive.

But Gina was up fairly early the next morning; she wanted to get her story in as soon as possible. Besides, she couldn't sleep, even after taking an over-the-counter sleeping pill. Scenes of last night's carnage haunted her. It was something she would never forget. She had called Ken before she went to bed; he had watched the telecast and was amazed and relieved to learn that she was unhurt.

Mrs. Lanyon was frying eggs and bacon when Gina walked into the kitchen; the aroma seemed to fill the apartment. Fresh coffee was brewing, and Gina was tempted to stay for a hearty breakfast. But she couldn't afford to waste a single minute.

Just as Gina was leaving, Mrs. Lanyon turned on the TV. Gina froze as she listened to the words of the newscaster. "...have just claimed responsibility for last night's massacre at the Grandview Hotel in Manhattan. They call themselves the American Patriot Army, an outgrowth of the citizen militia movement of the 1990s. Although citizen militias were banned under the Counter-Terrorism Act, many went underground, storing up a stockpile of assault weapons and ammunition. It is believed that the American Patriot Army is an alliance of these former militia groups. Made up of paranoid conspiracy theorists and anti-government zealots, the group is demanding cancellation of the Constitutional Convention, scheduled to begin on January fourth, as well as the abolishment of the Council for Global Unity—two members of which were killed in the massacre. If the Convention is not cancelled, they say, other sites will be targeted.

"A federal emergency has been declared, and the President has issued an executive order calling for a mandatory nationwide curfew. Interstate travel has been prohibited until further notice, and all airports in the New York metropolitan area have been shut down in an effort to prevent the terrorists from escaping to other parts of the country. Joining me in the studio this morning is Edward Jenkins, Deputy Director of FEMA, the Federal Emergency Management Administration, which was established in 1976 to deal with such a crisis..."

Gina felt increasingly disturbed as she listened to the rest of the newscast. Matt soon entered the kitchen and stood next to her, watching silently, his face grim. Somehow, it occurred to Gina suddenly, it just didn't feel like Christmas.

Mrs. Lanyon sounded perplexed. "I just can't believe that a group of patriots would do something so terrible."

"Maybe they weren't real patriots," Matt said quietly.

Gina was startled. "What do you mean?"

"Well, now the one-worlders have just what they need to discredit their opposition—a horrible atrocity committed by their opponents. Pretty convenient, don't you think?"

"Are you saying the one-worlders were responsible for the shooting?" Gina asked.

He shrugged. "Maybe. Maybe not."

Gina was putting on her coat. "That's crazy. I better get going. Are you coming?"

"I'll walk you to the car. But I'd like to stick around and have breakfast with the folks. John can drive me home later."

They stood outside, shivering in the cold, crisp air. In spite of the cold, it was a bright sunny day, and the wet, slushy streets glistened with the reflection of the sun. "Come home soon." Matt pulled her close to him. She leaned her head against his chest as he kissed her hair. "I can't believe how close I came to losing you!"

"I have a hard time believing it myself." She shuddered. "I was lucky I happened to be in the ladies' room when it happened." It was then that she told him about her strange feeling of dread and the queasy feeling that had made her leave the ballroom just moments before the shooting.

"Isn't that the strangest thing?"

Matt's eyes grew wide with amazement. "This is incredible! I had a premonition, too. I kept thinking that something terrible was going to happen at the ball—that you were in some kind of danger. In fact, when I told John about it, we all decided to pray for you."

"Really?" In spite of her usual religious skepticism, she found herself strangely moved. Could their prayers have been responsible for saving her life? She didn't know. She only knew that she was alive, while many others were dead. It was definitely something to think about.

* * * *

Ken sat in his office watching the U.S. Attorney General's press conference. Promising swift action against the terrorists, she blamed those who opposed the new constitution for creating "the climate of hatred and fear" which had instigated the shooting. "These zealots with their fixation on the outdated United States Constitution are a threat to national security and public safety. They cannot be allowed to intimidate us!"

Ken shook his head. The news of the shooting was barely out when the media—along with government officials on the left and the right—began denouncing patriots, constitutionalists, and "gun-nuts" as a threat to society; anyone opposed to world government was branded a potential terrorist.

Ken recalled the President's words in a televised speech to the American people in the wake of the shooting. "On Christmas Eve, a time that people across our world gather together to celebrate peace and goodwill, terrorists struck our nation with a cowardly act of violence. Sadly, this is not the first time America has fallen victim to terrorism. We now live in a world where twisted individuals are seeking to impose their will through vicious crimes against the innocent. It's time for the people of the world to unite like never before in our commitment to peace. We cannot give in to these monsters. If we give in to their demands, then all terrorists will think they can dictate their will to us. If we reject this opportunity for world peace, the terrorists will have won. We cannot let them win!"

But Ken was beginning to think that the real terrorists were those who were running the government. He knew of dozens of stories coming over the wire services which were simply not being reported—of innocent people being arrested without a search warrant and held without bail; most were leaders in the patriot movement or had written letters opposing the World Constitution to their representatives. A conservative radio talk show host in Colorado Springs was arrested in his own studio as he reported warrantless searches and seizures against leaders of several grassroots organizations, including the Patrick Henry Society and several gun rights groups. Ken also learned that an entire segment of C-Span devoted to these arrests had been blacked out by order of the director of FEMA, who was authorized to take such action in the event of a national emergency.

Ken turned to the papers strewn all over his desk; he knew he had to get some work done. But he couldn't seem to concentrate on anything these days. He felt sick about the tragedy and the fact that it was being exploited for political purposes. A poignant memorial service for the victims of the Grandview Hotel shooting was televised by satellite across the nation. During the service, which focused primarily on the children who had died, tearful parents and grandparents expressed their shock and disbelief that anyone could do something so horrible to innocent children. "Is the United States Constitution worth all this?" one woman sobbed. "Is it worth killing children over?"

With the FBI failing to turn up any leads, the latest issue of *Time* magazine proclaimed, "The FBI appears inadequate to protect U.S. citizens from the threat of terrorism that has become a crisis of epidemic proportions. Since terrorism is a global problem, it requires a global solution: a supranational police force under UN authority." That very week the President announced that the UN's World Crimes Enforcement Network (WorCEN) would join forces with the FBI in the quest to apprehend the terrorists. *Great*, Ken thought, remembering what Gina had recently told him about WorCEN. *We have a group of terrorists investigating terrorism. That's just wonderful!* Of course, Hank's allegations would be difficult to confirm—and very dangerous to investigate. He thought of Cheryl Hendricks; if Senator Meyers was right, then she had paid the ultimate price for being willing to tell the truth. Ken was ashamed to admit it, but he wasn't sure it was a price he was willing to pay.

He was thinking this when Damien suddenly barged into his office. "What the hell were you thinking, Hughes?" he demanded.

"What are you talking about?"

"That editorial you were planning for page 17a. This is a newspaper we're running—not a tabloid for conspiracy theorists."

Ken rolled his eyes up. He should have expected that anything hinting at a government cover-up would never get past Damien's scrutiny. At a recent meeting he had warned the staff that it was dangerous to print anything that could stir up "anti-government sentiment" right now. When Ken had alluded to some of the puzzling aspects of the shooting and the way it was being investigated, the publisher gave him a stern lecture about pandering to "paranoid extremists" who are disaffected with the government. But this time, Ken stood his ground. "Look, Damien, I think there's more to this shooting than meets the eye. One of my reporters was there, and she noticed something strange. Not one government official was there when the shooting began. They had all left. Except for two low-ranking members of the CGU. In fact, both had only recently joined the group, and both were known to be conservatives—not at all like the majority of members who have leftist leanings. It's as if.... Well, never mind that. Anyway, she also found out that the cops assigned to watch the building during the celebration had been called away on a wild goose chase that night. Don't you find that just a little bit strange?"

"It's purely a coincidence," Damien said icily. "And if any of your reporters insist on calling it more than that in the paper, you'll find yourself looking for another job. And—I'll see to it that you never work at another newspaper for the rest of your life. Is that clear?"

Ken looked at him, unflinching. "It's clear, all right. It's clear that this is no longer a free press."

Damien raised his eyebrow. "I'm warning you, Mr. Hughes." His tone was deceptively civil. "You're treading on thin ice. Another comment like that, and you're out of here. And if you don't like the idea of early retirement, you'd better cancel that editorial." With that, he turned on his heel and left.

Ken sat at his desk, shaking his head. He wondered how much longer he could stand working here.

* * * *

It was the eve of the Constitutional Convention, and Matt was watching the news, which had interrupted the regularly scheduled program. "The UN has just had a major breakthrough in its investigation of the shooting," the newscaster said excitedly. "WorCEN forces have successfully raided the compound where most of the terrorists were in hiding, and the UN is confident that the remaining terrorists will be apprehended and brought to justice. Apparently they had escaped from the hotel in black helicopters, flying without lights, which had landed on the roof of the building. The choppers managed to escape detection by flying below radar."

Moments later, the President made an impassioned speech about America's debt to the UN. "The United Nations has proven itself the only law enforcement body capable of protecting Americans from the threat of terrorism," he said in a televised address from the Oval Office. "Thanks to the UN, Americans may once again walk the streets in safety, free from fear." He paused dramatically, allowing his words to sink in. "Tomorrow morning, delegates from across the nation will begin the Second Constitutional Convention in this nation's history. I realize that some of you may feel uneasy about that. You wonder what we may be giving up by adopting a world constitution. But rest assured, we will be gaining far more than we can imagine. Imagine a world free of fear. A world where war, aggression, and terrorism have been blotted out forever. This is what world governance can offer us! The Bible has given us a vision of world peace, where 'swords have been beaten into ploughshares.' That is the vision of the UN, a vision that will become a reality only if we have the courage to cast aside our fears. The time of rampant nationalism is over. It's time now for a new order, and a new constitution. A constitution that grants us the same privileges and protections we now have under our own Constitution, but with the added protection of world law. In adopting the Constitution for Federation Earth, we have nothing to lose and everything to gain!"

Matt turned off the TV.

After tossing and turning for hours, he had finally gotten out of bed...just to hear this garbage. He went to the kitchen for some milk and cookies—he definitely needed some comfort food tonight. After he had finished nearly the entire box of Keebler Chips Deluxe—something he rarely did—he sat down in the living room and thumbed through the Bible, looking for a comforting verse. But the page he happened to open to—from the Book of Isaiah—was hardly comforting.

"'Their deeds are evil deeds, and acts of violence are in their hands.

Their feet rush into sin; they are swift to shed innocent blood. Their thoughts are evil thoughts; ruin and destruction mark their ways.

The way of peace they do not know; there is no justice in their paths. They have turned them into crooked roads; no one who walks in them will know peace.'"

With a shudder, he closed the Bible. *Are these the kind of people who will rule America in the near future?*

Somewhere he had a stash of cigarettes. He rummaged through a drawer till he found an old pack of Marlboros and a book of matches. His fingers trembled as he tried to light the cigarette.

He leaned back on the sofa and took a drag. *It's been a long time.*

Gina would kill him if she knew he had started smoking again.

But right now, that was the least of his fears.

PART 2

DARKNESS PREVAILS

"We look for light, but all is darkness; for brightness, but we walk in deep shadows. Like the blind, we grope along the wall, feeling our way like men without eyes. We look for justice, but find none; for deliverance, but it is far away."
(Isaiah 59:9-11 NIV)

"I fled Him, down the nights and down the days;
I fled Him, down the labyrinthine ways of my own mind; and in the mist of tears
I hid from Him..."
Francis Thompson, "The Hound of Heaven."

CHAPTER 16

Sitting on a bench in Battery Park, Ross Meyers gazed across the harbor at the Statue of Liberty. A single tear trickled down his face. Fireworks burst into the air as hundreds of people gathered for perhaps the biggest celebration in America since the signing of the Declaration of Independence. A steady stream of confetti blanketed the park, jammed with revelers of all ages and ethnic backgrounds. Mounted police officers weaved through the crowd, their faces flushed with excitement.

Ross pulled himself up from the bench. He took one last look at the statue, then walked slowly toward the Bowling Green subway station.

When he arrived at his Fifth Avenue apartment, he poured himself a cup of his best, single-malt Scotch. He took it out to the balcony, but didn't drink any, just stared at the amber liquid for a long moment.

He put his face in his hands. America, land of the free, was no more.

"I tried to stop them," he said in a feeble voice. *But not soon enough.*

Some might say he was lucky. The charges against him had been silently dropped. He was completely forgotten, even by his enemies. He was no longer a threat. Just a pathetic drunk, scorned by his peers and shunned by his family.

In all likelihood they wouldn't kill him. His story was no longer credible. After he had contacted the press in Washington, killing him would have aroused suspicion. He shook his head. Clever scoundrals. By destroying his reputation, they were able to discredit him and have their revenge as well. He shook his head. *Serves me right.* For decades he had known of the Council's plans to destroy his country, and had done nothing. Because of his silence, and that of many others who knew the truth but refused to come forward, America—the America that so many patriots had fought and died to preserve—was lost forever.

He gazed down at the streets below, and a chill ran through him. A shadow seemed to loom over the entire city, darkening everything in its path.

A single tear trickled down his cheek. "I tried," he said feebly. But no one had listened. He had risked everything. But what good had it done? Only one person had been willing to listen, and she had been murdered.

For the first time in his life, he had cared about something beyond himself, about his country. Once a beacon of hope in a world marred by tyranny and oppression, now gone...destroyed by people like himself. People who stood by and did nothing in the face of evil.

"Goodnight, America.... Goodnight," he said quietly, and slowly fell forward over the balcony.

* * * *

Patrick Flannery stumbled into the packed courtroom. The guard who pushed him laughed. "Time to enter the lion's den!" he said.

He sat alone on a hard, wooden bench. The Catholic attorney who had taken his case had been disbarred. He had refused to pledge an oath of loyalty to the United Nations. Patrick sighed heavily, then reminded himself that God would never forsake him, no matter the outcome today.

He surveyed the room. The American flag was gone. The words, "In God We Trust," replaced by the UN emblem and charter.

The room was beginning to fill with reporters and curiosity seekers. Few wanted to miss the first major trial to take place in Earth Region #5, once the United States of America, under the World Constitution.

He listened quietly as the prosecutor read the charges against him: hatespeech and domestic terrorism. With the jury system abolished under the World Constitution, he had little hope of receiving anything even remotely resembling a fair trial. Especially having been branded an enemy of society, a member of the dreaded "religious right." Of course, the same journalists who vilified him for his faith in God said nothing about the forced abortions in China, or about the gulags and torture that other totalitarian regimes used against their own people. It was okay to force a woman to undergo an abortion against her will, even to be forcibly sterilized. It was perfectly fine to allow a newborn infant to die in a trash can, to burn "religious fanatics" alive in the name of the public good. But to claim there were definite standards of right and wrong, to insist there was one God who would hold all people accountable to Him, was unpardonable.

Speaking in a low monotone, the head judge asked, "Now that you have heard the charges against you, how do you wish to plead?"

Patrick looked him squarely in the eyes. "I'm not going to enter a plea."

"But you have to." He cleared his throat. Clearly he hadn't expected this. The other two judges looked on, dumb-founded.

"May I ask why, your honor?"

"Because, well, it's just proper procedure," the judge stammered.

"Then I'm afraid I cannot comply."

"And why is that?"

"I don't believe I have committed a crime."

The head judge looked confused. "Then, why not simply plead innocent?"

"Pleading innocent would be an acknowledgement that the actions for which I'm on trial are criminal. But I don't believe they are. I was arrested for exercising my inalienable right to freedom of expression. If I plead innocent, I would simply be saying that I didn't take such actions. It's a catch-22."

The judge stared coldly at him. "I don't think you realize the serious nature of these charges. Are you aware that the penalty for hatecrime is a minimum sentence of ten years, and that the minimum sentence for domestic terrorism is twenty years to life?"

"I am."

Another judge spoke in a conciliatory tone. "Every defendant must enter a plea. If you don't enter one, then we have the authority to enter one for you."

"But I don't recognize your authority."

A murmur went through the crowd. The head judge jumped out of his chair. "*What* did you say?"

"I don't recognize this court's authority. I don't believe a UN court has any right to try me."

The head judge almost stuttered. "How dare you say such a thing? Who gave you the right—" He broke off, shaking his head, uncertain of how to proceed.

"My rights," said Patrick, "come from God. Neither you nor anyone else has the authority to take them away. I haven't damaged anyone's property, nor have I committed aggression against another. My rights can be forfeited only if I infringe on those of others, if I harm another person's life, liberty, or property. But I haven't done so. Therefore, this court has no right—"

"What is at stake here," the judge said icily, "is the public good, not your so-called rights. As a priest, surely you must recognize that the public good supersedes the rights of an individual."

Patrick looked in the direction of the spectators, and hoped that his words might get through to some of them. "That belief is the philosophical foundation of totalitarianism. Every totalitarian regime—whether Nazi, Fascist, or Communist—has demanded the sacrifice of the individual for the so-called public good. For the Nazis and the Fascists, it was the nation; for the

Communists, the state or collective. For the UN it's the 'international community' or the 'global village.' However, without individual rights there can be no public good. The public is composed of individuals, and when governments abuse individuals, they are abusing the public."

The head judge banged his gavel. His eyes blazed fiercely. "You've said quite enough!"

Patrick held back an impulse to smile. *I'll bet I have.*

"You may be seated," the judge said wearily. He turned to the bailiff. "Call in the first witness."

"Your honor?" Patrick asked.

"What is it?" the judge snapped.

"Will I have the opportunity to question the witnesses?"

The judge sneered. "You forfeited that privilege when you refused to accept counsel."

"I had good counsel, but he was unlawfully disbarred."

The gavel hit the table. "You keep quiet or you'll be held in contempt of court!"

Patrick sat down. Actually, he had expected as much. His former attorney had told him that as of now, all lawyers worked for the United Nation's International Court of Justice and were forced to put the interests of the World Court ahead of their clients'. And Patrick had no intention of deliberately putting himself under the UN's jurisdiction by accepting their counsel. He only hoped that the reporters watching would recognize the inherent injustice of a court which called itself a court of "justice" refusing to give the accused the chance to confront the witnesses against him!

He sat quietly while the prosecutor questioned the witnesses, who sounded as though they were reading from a script.

One of the few witnesses who did not appear to be acting was Senator Conlin. "Never in my life have I heard such pure, unadulterated hatred. He even went so far as to advocate genocide against unbelievers, including homosexuals and lesbians!"

Gasps and murmurs rippled through the courtroom, and the judges' gavels thundered against the bench.

A number of "experts" in the field of psychology and social behavior were asked to render judgement, based on the video, as to whether the priest posed a threat to society.

"The level of paranoia manifested in the video indicates a mindset prone to violence, pathological hatred, and possible criminal behavior," one woman testified. She wore a gray suit and her blonde hair was cut short, pushed back behind her ears. Her colleagues concurred that in their clinical judgement, Father Flannery posed a serious threat to society.

Finally, the testimony wound down; it was Patrick's last chance to say anything in his defense. "If I may, your honors, I would like to call a witness of my own."

The judges looked stunned. "You have a witness?" the prosecutor asked.

"Yes, your honor, I do."

"But...I thought you weren't going to enter a plea."

"I'm not. But I still reserve the right to call in a witness who can testify as to what really happened at that riot."

The judges looked at one another warily, like rats in a sinking ship. The prosecutor broke their awkward silence. "I'm afraid we cannot allow you to call in your witness until you enter a plea."

"I see. It's becoming obvious that this court intends to railroad me into a conviction, so it would be pointless for me—"

"Enough! You either enter a plea or you sit down and shut up! We'd like this case handled expeditiously."

"But not judiciously!" Everyone started at the loud voice which came from somewhere in the back of the courtroom.

The judge glared. "Who said that?"

Patrick held his breath as Mike Casey stood up. "I did. I'm the witness, and I demand to be heard!"

The crowd murmured excitedly. People jumped from their seats, straining to look at Mike.

The judges banged their gavels repeatedly. "Order! Order! Order in the court!"

Hope surged through Patrick. He said a silent prayer of thanks for this brave young man who had called his lawyer last week offering to testify on his behalf. The scene was bound to be reported in the news with this many journalists present. If the judges refused to let Mike speak, they risked public censure.

"Young man, you are out of order," the head judge told him gruffly, "and you are causing a disruption of these proceedings. Now, sit down and be quiet!"

"No—I won't be quiet. If all those other people can testify, then I should be able to testify."

"We'll decide who is allowed to testify. Now, I want you out of this courtroom, and if you do not leave quietly, we'll have you arrested for contempt of court."

"But it's not fair! Those witnesses you had on the stand before were lying! I was at the riot, and Father Flannery never said any of those things—"

The gavel banged down on the table. "You are in contempt!" The head judge turned to an officer standing nearby. "Arrest him!"

The courtroom erupted into pandemonium as Mike was handcuffed and dragged away. "This is a set-up! Those witnesses were lying!"

The judges shouted over the din. "Anyone else who speaks out of order will be arrested immediately!"

They retired to their chambers to deliberate. When they returned less than half an hour later, Patrick was hardly surprised by the verdict. "We find the defendant, Patrick James Flannery, guilty of hatespeech and domestic terrorism. He is hereby sentenced to life imprisonment, with no possibility of parole, at a maximum-security facility in Alaska." The gavel echoed in the heavy silence of the courtroom.

Patrick stopped briefly to say goodbye to Maggie and Reverend Dalton, who were standing not far from Gina Lanyon. Maggie's face paled at the mention of the Alaska facility. She tried to hold back her tears as she said goodbye to her brother. "I can't believe they're sending you there!"

"Don't you go worrying now." He spoke as cheerfully as possible under the circumstances. "Remember, God works all things for good, for those who love Him."

"I know, but—"

"No buts. And no tears. My life is in God's hands. We either trust Him, or we don't."

One of the guards started to pull him away. "Let's go," he said in a monotone.

* * * *

Gina caught Father Flannery's glance as he was led away. There was so much she wanted to say to him. She wanted to tell him he had opened her eyes to a world she had never imagined.

He smiled at her reassuringly, then disappeared through the large wooden doors of the courtroom, escorted by armed guards.

She stood there silently, trying to absorb everything that had happened in the last few months. So many things she had believed in were crumbling into dust. If this was world government, she wanted no part of it. But she had no choice; world government was here, whether she wanted it or not. An old proverb came to mind: Be careful what you wish for, you might get it.

She hurried to catch up with Maggie and Reverend Dalton.

"I'm so sorry about your brother," she said.

Maggie forced a smile. "Thank you, Gina."

"Are you going to appeal?"

"Why should we bother? We won't get any justice from the UN!"

"I understand your feelings, but you can't just give up—"

"I don't think you understand," Maggie said. "The United Nations would destroy my brother in a heartbeat. They don't care about justice. All they care about is control. That's why they target people like my brother. He was railroaded because he's a man of convictions who believes in ultimate truth and isn't afraid to defend it. Don't you see, Gina? The United Nations despises all those who are courageous enough to challenge their power structure, which is subject to moral relativism, not the immutable criterion of justice."

The three of them were now walking down the corridor toward the lobby. "Would you mind if I asked you a question?" Gina asked.

"Go ahead," she said wearily.

"Do you know anything about the Alaska facility where your brother's being sent?"

"I'm not sure you'd believe it if I told you."

"Try me."

She sighed. "Essentially, it's a concentration camp."

Gina just stared at her. "Are you sure?"

"Don't take my word for it. Ask some of the people whose loved ones have died there—from starvation, disease and overwork! The Patrick Henry Society and some other grassroots organizations have received letters from families whose relatives were sent there as political prisoners."

"I'm sorry. It's just hard to believe—"

Dalton cut in suddenly. "Hard to believe what? That those kinds of things can happen here? Have you forgotten that the U.S. government sent innocent Japanese Americans to detention camps during World War II? What makes you think it can't happen today?"

There was nothing she could say.

Maggie spoke gently. "I understand how you feel, Gina. Most people feel the way you do—they don't *want* to believe that their own government can send innocent people to concentration camps. Do you think ordinary citizens of Nazi Germany wanted to acknowledge what was happening to their neighbors who suddenly disappeared in the middle of the night?"

Gina thought about Ben and Elsie, and how she had sought some justification for their brutal murders. "You're right. People tend to look away when the truth gets too ugly."

They were now standing in the parking lot. The late afternoon sun glinted on the metal fence that surrounded the sprawling lot. "Does the Society have any plans to fight these injustices?" she asked after a brief pause.

"It's been trying." But Pastor Dalton didn't sound very hopeful. "Even under our old constitution it was hard. Now it's nearly impossible. The UN doesn't recognize our right to freedom of expression, nor our right to petition the government for a redress of grievances."

"But doesn't the World Constitution say we have those freedoms?"

"Oh, sure," Maggie said sarcastically. "It also says that those freedoms are subject to limitations 'as prescribed by law.' What that means is that the government can take away our 'rights' whenever it wants to. And a right that can be taken away isn't really a right; it's a privilege. You have to remember that even the Soviet Union had a constitution that 'granted' certain rights to the people. And that's what the problem was. Any government that claims to grant rights can also take them away."

* * * *

The following day dawned with hardly a word of the controversial events surrounding Father Flannery's trial. Not a single paper mentioned Mike's outburst and arrest or the priest's condemnation of totalitarianism, even though the courtroom had been packed with reporters and TV cameras. The story Gina had written was censored.

A week passed, and she wondered why Mike wasn't back at work. She asked Ken about it. "Mike's been fired," he said.

"Why?"

He made a face. "Take a guess." He sounded completely disgusted.

"Maybe I should give him a call."

"Don't bother, he's still in jail. And it looks like they're not in a big hurry to release him."

"This is outrageous! We should do something—"

"Don't mess with them, Gina. You'll lose everything, and it won't do any darn good." There was a hardness in his voice that she had never heard before.

"What's happening to you?"

He laughed bitterly. "Can't you tell? I'm losing my soul."

"Maybe we all are," she said quietly. "I mean, this was the first major trial to take place under the jurisdiction of the world government. A world government I supported and campaigned for! How could I have been so naive? My love for peace made me lose sight of justice." She shook her head. "Why couldn't I see that before?"

She returned to her desk to check her e-mail. A message from Hank Jennings immediately caught her eye.

It had to do with the picture she had taken during the shooting, an amazingly clear shot of the face of one of the terrorists, whose mask had come off during a scuffle with one of the victims. The photo, which accompanied the front-page story of the shooting, stirred a wave of controversy. The FBI had barged into Ken's office, demanding the photo and the negatives. When Ken asked to see their search warrant, they threatened to arrest him, so he gave them what they wanted. He didn't tell them that as a precaution, he had made copies of the negatives. The issue had sold over a million copies, easily their most popular issue in years.

Her mouth dropped open as she read Hank's message. This was big—probably the biggest story of her career. It could change everything!

Then, her heart sank as reality hit. This was one story that would never be printed.

* * * *

"Well, it looks as if all your fears were unfounded." Perry spoke in a mildly ironic tone. "The World Constitution has been ratified, and none of us has been rounded up by the police yet."

The Bible study had ended, and Perry had just brought in the refreshments: a pot of steaming mulled cider and a tray of shortbread cookies Audrey had brought. Matt couldn't wait to dig in; he hadn't had time to eat supper.

John merely smiled. "The key word is yet."

Matt almost did a double-take. He certainly didn't expect such a statement from John.

Carl rolled his eyes. "Don't tell me you two still view the UN as a threat? Look at how they saved us from those terrorists. Our own government certainly wasn't doing any good. If it hadn't been for the UN, they would probably still be at large, and there would've been even more bloodshed."

Matt forgot all about his hunger as he recalled what Gina had just told him. It had nearly blown his mind, but in a way it made sense. "I don't know. It seems there's more to that than we're being told."

"What are you getting at?" asked Carl.

"My wife is a reporter, and she's learned things that the newspapers simply refuse to print. In fact, there's evidence that the federal government may have been involved somehow—or, at the very least, is covering up the truth about who was responsible. Who knows? Maybe the UN was in on it, too. Gina recently told me some horror stories about the UN that would shock most of you, and she's always been a staunch supporter of world government."

Mitch frowned. "Matt, I'm no fan of the UN, and I don't trust the federal government, for that matter. But to suggest they had something to do with that shooting, well, that sounds a little extreme."

"Yeah, that's getting paranoid," Carl agreed.

Perry shook his head in disdain. "The whole idea is preposterous."

Matt sipped his cider. "You might not think so if you knew what my wife found out. You want to hear it all?"

"I wouldn't mind." John actually sounded intrigued.

Perry wore a look of disapproval. "Surely you can't believe that the federal government was involved in that massacre."

"Look, there are a lot of things about that night that just don't add up," Matt said. "My wife was assigned to investigate the shooting. In fact, she was there when it happened—and was one of the few people to get out alive."

By now, all eyes were on Matt. Andrea broke the silence. "What did she find out?"

"First, the cops guarding the hotel were sent on a wild goose chase right before the shooting. Not only that, but almost all the government officials who were there that night left well before it happened. They wouldn't even stay to answer reporters' questions. Gina said they seemed tense, very unusual at an event like this. Anyway, not one of any importance was around when it happened. Lucky for them, huh?"

"None of that proves anything," Perry insisted.

"Maybe not," Matt admitted. "But get this. A couple of the cops she interviewed said they were specifically told not to answer any questions about the shooting, or they'd be fired!"

"That does sound kind of suspicious," Mitch agreed. "Why wouldn't the police department want reporters to know the truth?"

Perry waved his hand. "We're dealing with a terrorist investigation here.

In such cases, national security is at stake."

"There's something else. The detective who was investigating the shooting was thrown off the case very abruptly. He didn't like the way the FBI was handling it, and when he decided to pursue his own investigation, he was told in no uncertain terms to stop. At least, that's what he told my wife—off the record, of course."

Carl looked dubious. "Yeah, then how come none of that was in the papers?"

"Because we no longer have a free press. My wife's getting a lot of heat for the stories she's been trying to pursue. Her editor is dying to print what she's uncovered, but he can't, he told her he'd get fired if he even attempted it. She said all the reporters have been walking on eggshells since the paper changed hands—apparently it was bought out by someone with a lot of power and influence in the government. Her editor said it's like that with all the corporate newspapers these days."

"I find that hard to believe," said Perry. "Surely there are some editors who are willing to print the truth."

"Maybe there are—but what good is it if they get fired for doing so?" Matt asked. "Anyway, I've been saving the clincher for last. Do you all remember the picture of that terrorist's face in the newspaper? He's been identified."

"So?" said Carl. "Most of the terrorists have been caught by now. What's so special about him?"

"Well, prior to the Grandview attack he was working for the government." Everyone gasped.

"That's ridiculous!" said Perry. "How do you know that?"

"My wife's been in touch with a retired FBI agent who's been trying to get the truth out to the press. He told her that several people he knows in the intelligence community recognized the gunman in that photo as someone who was hired by the NSA!"

Helen put her hand to her mouth. "You're kidding!"

Mitch's jaw dropped. "This is unbelievable!"

Audrey cocked her head. "What's the NSA?"

Beth looked stunned. "The National Security Agency."

Perry was just staring at Matt with a doubtful look on his face.

"Hey—this is all true. Gina's source told her that the guy in the photo was a zealous Marxist who had actually joined a communist cell which endorsed the use of terrorism. Their goal was to overthrow the U.S.

government and replace it with a one-world, socialist government. To gain access to classified information, he applied for a job with the FBI. He was turned down because of his terrorist connections. He was also arrested several times but let off by leftist judges. But get this—the NSA hired him, even though he never passed the FBI's background check!"

"That's impossible," Perry said. "How could someone like that ever get security clearance?"

Mitch rubbed his chin. "Hm...maybe the NSA isn't interested in national security?"

"What do you mean?" Carl asked.

"A friend of mine who worked for the government once told me directors of intelligence agencies had their own secret agendas, often at odds with the best interests of the American people, not to mention national security." Mitch frowned. "At the time I thought he was getting a little carried away with conspiracy theories. Now, I'm not so sure."

Carl snorted. "Look, did it ever occur to you that the guy in that photo might have had a look-a-like? They say everyone has a double. Besides, there's no way I'll ever believe our own government would be involved in something like this."

"It may not be the entire government," Matt said. "Could be some cadre within the government that wanted the United States to ratify the World Constitution, at any price."

Matt looked around the silent room at the astonished faces and felt oddly elated. He seemed to be getting through to them. "Anyway, Gina went to her editor with this information and begged him to run the story, but he refused. He said he couldn't print a word—because the owner wouldn't let him. I hate to say it, but the press in our country today is no better than *Pravda*. It's strictly monitored and controlled, and the people never get the real truth."

Everyone seemed to be taking in Matt's shocking revelation.

After a moment or two Carl broke the silence. "I'm still finding all this very difficult to believe."

Audrey made a face. "Me, too. Why would the government murder innocent people, when it's their job to protect us?"

"Governments have done a lot of evil, Audrey," Mitch said. "In this century alone they've murdered millions of innocent people—mostly their own. Why, all we have to do is look at the former Soviet Union or Red China, even Cuba, not to mention the radical Islamic countries where Christian converts are murdered . If you think such things can't happen here, you're very naive."

Helen rubbed her frail hands together. Her lips quivered. "But why would the government want to kill all those people? What did they gain by it?"

"Exactly what we have now," John said.

Mitch ran his fingers through his hair. "I believe it's something called the Hegelian principle."

"I don't get it," said Audrey.

"It's how the Nazis came to power," he said. "It was developed by a philosopher named Hegel, a collectivist who practically worshipped the state."

Carl looked impatient. "So what does he have to do with all this?"

"Hegel developed a three-step process for making sweeping political changes that most people would normally resist. The first step creates a crisis, a problem. Then you generate fear and hysteria, so the people demand a solution. That's where the third step comes in. The government offers a so-called 'solution' to the problem created in step one, usually more government control or even an outright dictatorship. Hitler knew the German people wouldn't give him total control unless there was some reason to justify it. So, he had the Nazis set the Reichstag Building on fire, and he blamed it on the Communists. The Nazis were voted into power by a landslide, and the people gave Hitler dictatorial control to deal with the so-called Communist threat, as well as other crises." Mitch looked thoughtful. "I'm sure Hegel never anticipated that his ideas would inspire a monster like Hitler to come to power."

"Well, you know what they say," John said. "The road to hell is paved with good intentions. We need to remember that ideas have consequences."

Carl threw his hands up. "But you're talking about something that happened over sixty years ago, in another country! What makes you think the same thing can happen here?"

Helen clutched his arm. She looked lovingly and sadly into his harsh-set eyes.

"There are plenty of things that have happened here lately that would shock you. Would you believe my wife and I attended a church meeting that was raided by police? They arrested a priest who was planning to show a video exposing the truth about our government and the UN." Matt described the event in detail.

Gasps and shouts of outrage echoed through the room. Perry was silent, taking everything in. Carl just folded his arms and scowled.

"So, do you still believe our government wouldn't be involved in that shooting?" Matt asked.

"Look, I'm sure there was a good reason for arresting that priest," Carl said. "You may not know all the facts."

Matt felt the blood rush to his cheeks. "Oh, really? Did the police have a good reason for throwing me up against the wall when I tried to protect my wife?"

Once again, John surprised Matt. "Our government's been doing some vile things, Carl. Matt's elderly neighbors were murdered by agents from the Bureau of Weapons Control. And look at Danny Cheever's wife—she was shot in the head by an FBI sniper while holding her baby! Surely you can't defend such actions."

"There had to be a reason," Carl muttered.

Matt wanted to bang his head against the wall. "You know something, Carl? You would've made a good Nazi!"

An awkward silence settled in the room. Carl glared at Matt in stunned indignation.

Perry spoke firmly. "I think this conversation is getting out of hand. Matt, I understand your concern over the possibility that our government may have been involved in that shooting. But nothing has been proven. These allegations are all based on hearsay. Not only that, but your continual harping on the subject is disrupting our study. So, I'll ask you to please drop this before someone says something we'll all regret."

"Why are you so afraid of the truth, Perry?" Matt asked.

Perry frowned, then turned to Audrey. "I've been meaning to ask you, Audrey—how are things going with your daughter?"

She looked disgusted. "Not good. I just don't know what to do anymore."

"Then maybe we should pray for her," Perry suggested.

"That might be a good idea." She sighed. "I'm just so confused. The school keeps saying they have her best interests at heart, that *they* know what's best for her. But what about me? I'm her mother, for crying out loud! Don't I count for something? They won't let me take her out of those awareness classes, and I know they're not good for her. She's been having nightmares and crying a lot. She's also gotten very defiant lately. Whenever I reprimand her, she says that her teacher told her it's okay for children to disobey their parents, as long as they're willing to accept the consequences."

"You're kidding!" Matt exclaimed.

"I wish I were. I even called her teacher to discuss Kelsie's disobedience. You know what she said? She said it's 'healthy' for children to disobey their parents—it teaches them autonomy."

"Have you thought of calling the principal?" Beth asked.

Audrey shrugged. "I did, and he just brushed me off. He said it's over his head—the superintendent is the one to talk to."

"So, maybe you should talk to him," Beth suggested.

"Mike told me not to. He says if we make an issue of this, things will just get harder for Kelsie. He says we're going to have to learn to go along with things we don't like if we want her to survive in this world."

"So, he's into conformity, huh?" Matt asked.

Audrey nodded. "He just doesn't understand how all this is harming her."

"Well, let's put all our needs in God's hands," Perry said, and everyone gathered in a circle to pray.

Feeling like an outsider, Matt bowed his head while the others took turns praying out loud. *How can Carl and Perry be so blind? How can they trust a government that committed so much evil? And if it's bad now, how much worse will it get under the rule of the Antichrist?*

Images of Christians being martyred swam before him. Yeah, that was definitely holding him back. John had once told him you have to count the cost. And right now the cost just seemed too high.

CHAPTER 17

Matt was staring absently at the TV in the employee lounge. His fifteen-minute break had just started, and he was attempting to drink his coffee from a flimsy paper cup without burning his hand; styrofoam had been outlawed under some UN environmental treaty a few years ago. The women were watching a soap opera, and he didn't feel like asking them to change the channel.

He was just about to get up and go for a walk outside when the soap was interrupted by a news bulletin. The women started whining. Matt sighed. *What now?*

But he froze when he heard the newscaster. "A rebellion is brewing across the West. Right-wing extremists in Montana, Wyoming, Colorado, and Texas refuse to recognize the World Constitution and have drafted illegal sovereignty resolutions. As we speak, the dangerous radicals are banning together in armed militias and preparing for war. They claim secession rights and are demanding recognition as a sovereign nation. Some of these anti-government zealots have taken over government buildings and are holding people hostage. This could very well erupt into civil war! Stay tuned to this station for further developments."

Matt felt something wet on his leg and noticed that he had dropped his coffee cup.

The women began talking at once.

"This is terrible!"

"Civil war? I can't believe it!"

The door jerked open and some of the supervisors and foremen rushed inside. Their eyes were fixed on the television. A few shook their heads in disbelief.

Matt's supervisor Lloyd broke the silence. "Boy, this is just great! We finally have a chance for world peace, and some right-wing nuts have to ruin it. I hope they get what they deserve!"

"I wonder," Matt said quietly.

Lloyd glared at him. "Don't tell me you're defending those lunatics?"

"Look, all we know at this point is what some talking heads are saying. We have no way of knowing what's really happening out there."

"Starting in with your conspiracy theories again, huh, Lanyon?" Lloyd asked.

"All I'm saying is I've seen a lot of stuff on the news that turned out to be bald-faced lies. I should know, my wife works for a newspaper."

No one commented, and Matt shook his head. *Why don't they care about the things that really matter?* Whenever he tried to get through to them, they shrugged off his concerns or told him he was paranoid. The few who believed him insisted things were so hopeless there was no point in trying to do anything.

He looked around. "So, none of you would consider the possibility that the news could be lying about this?"

"That's ridiculous," said Lloyd.

A tall redhead smacked her gum loudly. "Why would the media lie?"

"To promote their own agenda." Matt suddenly remembered something his dad had told him years ago. "Any of you heard about the Gulf of Tonkin attack?"

They all looked at him blankly.

"It's the battle that got us into the Vietnam War. Well, guess what? It never happened. The entire battle was fabricated to get us into Vietnam!"

Most of them were rolling their eyes. "Yeah, right," somebody muttered.

Lloyd nodded in agreement. "Another conspiracy theory."

"Look, it's not a theory, it's a fact. Admiral James Stockdale wrote a book exposing the whole thing."

Lloyd folded his arms. "Oh, yeah? Who the hell is he?"

"He happens to be a Congressional Medal of Honor winner," said Matt. "He also ran for vice president once."

Lloyd was unimpressed. "Yeah, so what makes him such an expert on this Gulf of Tonkin thing?"

"Because he was there when the attack was supposed to have happened. He said the whole thing was a fraud! And, the film clips on the major news networks was actually footage from World War II. If you don't believe me, check out his book in the library."

"No thanks." Lloyd sneered. "I have better things to do with my time."

"I'm sure you do," Matt said sarcastically.

"Listen, you better be a little more careful about what you say around here, Lanyon."

He rolled his eyes. "Oh, and why is that?"

"You mean you haven't heard about the reports that have been filed on you?"

Matt was getting uneasy. "What are you talking about?" He was aware of the policy of keeping written reports on employees who exhibited "problematic attitudes," a vague term that encompassed everything from a short temper to racial prejudice. "Why would anyone report me? And isn't that something I should know about?"

"Well, it's really not my place to say anything." Lloyd smiled maliciously. "Have a nice day." With that he turned and left.

Matt leaned back in his chair and stared at the ceiling. *Man, I don't need this.*

* * * *

Gina had just returned from an assignment when news of the rebellion came over the wire services. Shock waves shook the newsroom as the editorial staff scrambled to get the story ready for the front page of the morning edition. Everyone was on edge, wondering if the volatile situation would erupt into full-scale war.

By mid-afternoon there was no longer any question. According to government reports, the "extremists" had set buildings on fire and were rioting in the streets. Federal troops, backed by UN peace-keeping forces, moved in to put down the uprisings with tanks, air support, and heavy artillery. Martial law was declared and reporters barred from the scene, at least for the time being.

Gina and Ken were sharing a table in the cafeteria. It was well past noon, but this was the first chance they had to grab a bite in the rush to meet their deadlines. "It doesn't make sense, Ken. Reporters were present at the bloodiest military operations in Eastern Europe, not to mention the Middle East. Why keep us away from the conflict out West?"

Ken nibbled on his burger. "You mean you haven't figured it out yet?" he asked between bites.

"You think the government is hiding something?"

"What else is new?"

She picked at the blueberry muffin she had ordered. "I'd love to find out what's really happening out there."

* * * *

The phone woke Gina in the middle of the night, and she turned on her side to pick up. Ken's voice made her spring to life. "How soon can you have your bags packed and get to the airport?"

She bolted out of bed. "What's up?"

"They've lifted the ban on reporters. I want you to be the first to get the inside scoop."

* * * *

Matt and Gina were standing in the Delta terminal at LaGuardia. It was just a little after 6 a.m., and Matt had to be at work in two hours. But he had insisted on driving her to the airport, even though she could have easily taken a taxi.

"I'll be fine," she said. "Don't worry."

"I'll try not to."

He stood stiffly, his hands in his pockets. He made no attempt to hug or kiss her goodbye.

Once again, they had drifted apart. Gina had hoped things would be different after the Grandview shooting. But with the adoption of the World Constitution, Matt had withdrawn. The night it was ratified, he had staggered into the apartment and collapsed onto the kitchen floor. Gina had cleaned him up and put him to bed.

She gave him a quick, awkward peck on the cheek, then picked up her carry-on bag and left him standing in the terminal. For all appearances, they might have been strangers.

* * * *

When Gina arrived in Wyoming that afternoon, the first thing she noticed was the unusually heavy security at the airport. Federal troops patrolled the lobby, randomly stopping travelers to search their luggage. Surveillance cameras were everywhere, even in parking lots. Over a dozen military helicopters swooped overhead, and the roads leading to the airport were lined with police vehicles, tanks, and soldiers toting submachine guns. Gina wondered if all this was meant to protect people or to frighten them.

She rented a car and drove north on I-25, past Cheyenne and Laramie, to the town of Wheatland, the site of a federal "reeducation center" where many of the "zealots," as the media referred to them, had been transported by trucks or railroad.

She arrived at the facility late in the afternoon, along with a horde of journalists from all over the country. Beyond the hillside dotted with evergreens and pines, soaring mounds of snow-covered granite gleamed in the bright sunlight. The network of buildings resembled a school campus, except for the guard house, which looked something like an airport control tower, manned by a uniformed soldier. A chill went down her spine as images of concentration camps came to mind. She tried to remind herself that the people inside were violent dissidents.

Security was tight; a line of cars was backed up for nearly a mile to get through the six-foot wrought-iron gates at the entrance; each car was admitted one by one, and only after the guard in the security booth thoroughly checked everyone's press card and ID.

The journalists were escorted into a huge amphitheater and addressed by a tall, broad-shouldered African American man wearing a highly decorated military uniform with the UN insignia. He introduced himself as General William Travis, Special Assistant for Internal Security Affairs. "This is not a press conference," he told them in a cultivated, resonating voice. "I am not here to answer questions. You will listen to what I tell you, and if you have any questions, you are to direct them in writing to the Executive Council for Global Governance.

"The people in this facility are terrorists," he said. "They have taken up arms against their own government, and in so doing have threatened the very fabric of our society."

Gina watched the other reporters scribble frantically on their pads as General Travis heaped condemnation upon the "right-wing extremists" who "refused to be subject to authority." But he didn't give many details about what they had actually done.

After Travis had left, the director of the center addressed them. He had a kindly, benevolent face, and appeared to be somewhere in his fifties. "I realize that you all have been led to believe that this is a federal detention center. However, we prefer to think of it as a rehabilitation center. According to government directives, the people here are not to be treated like criminals; they are to be rehabilitated. Cured, if you will."

Gina raised her hand. "Cured of what?" she asked when he nodded to her.

"Of the destructive attitudes that brought them here," he said. "They are not criminals, my dear. Merely poor, frightened souls unable to adapt to a peaceful society. For years, they have been conditioned to think in terms of the old order of nationalism and individualism and other such destructive notions. Now, they must learn to live within our global community. Their minds must be...reconditioned, so to speak."

She didn't like the sound of that. "How will that be done?"

He smiled. "Our methods are quite humane, I assure you. We don't believe in punishment here; only rehabilitation. We have an excellent staff of psychotherapists, the best in the country. I'm confident that all of the inmates will learn to overcome the destructive thought patterns that brought them here."

She made some notes on her pad, then raised her hand again. "Would it be possible to interview some of them?" she asked.

He looked startled. "I'm afraid that's out of the question."

"Why?"

His expression took on a sudden hardness. "Security reasons."

Other reporters fired questions at him, but he said they were out of time. He cleared his throat. "The security officers will show you all out."

He started to leave. "Wait a minute," said Gina. "You mean to tell me that none of us can question any of the people involved in the uprising? They're *all* off-limits?"

The director smiled. "It's for their own good. We wish to shield them from unpleasant publicity."

"But don't they have the right to tell their side of the story?"

"I'm afraid that's not for me to decide. Now, if you'll excuse me..." His voice trailed off, and he hurried away.

The reporters were talking excitedly among themselves, but didn't seem concerned that the prisoners were off-limits to the press. They seemed perfectly satisfied in reporting whatever they were told by the government's spokesmen. *What's wrong with them? Am I the only one here who wants to know the truth?*

Frustrated, she headed toward the door. So, this was it. This was the big story she had flown across country to cover? She could have simply gotten this off a press release.

Once outside, she felt someone tap her on the shoulder. She turned around to see one of the guards holding a piece of paper. "You dropped this, ma'am," he said in a western drawl. She was about to say he was mistaken, when he said in a very low voice, "Don't read it here." The look in his eyes told her to shut up and keep it.

"Thank you," she said. He nodded and walked away.

She shoved the piece of paper into her handbag. *Looks like I may get a good story out of this after all.* As soon as she had exited the gate and was driving back to town, she took the paper from her purse and read it. "The truth? 9:00 p.m." It gave an address.

Curiouser and curiouser, she thought. The beauty of the mountains and the strangeness of her situation made her feel like Alice in Wonderland. She just hoped to keep her head in the end.

CHAPTER 17

Gina checked the address again to make sure she had the right place. Then she pushed open the heavy oak door and walked inside the church.

The place was deserted.

She looked at her watch. Not quite nine yet. She sat down in one of the pews and surveyed her surroundings. Brilliant stained-glass windows lined the walls, and a breathtaking mural of a waterfall with snow-capped mountains in the background hung behind the altar.

She heard footsteps behind her and turned around. The guard from the facility approached her. He was tall and powerfully built, with short, reddish-brown hair. He couldn't have been more than twenty, but the harsh set of his jaw made him appear much older. He walked purposefully and deliberately. "Let's go," he said.

"Where?"

He nodded for her to follow him. "This way."

They walked down a long corridor that led to a staircase. It was so dark he had to use a flashlight. "Why are all the lights out?" she asked.

"You'll understand in a minute," he said tersely.

At the bottom of the stairs they came to a doorway. The guard knocked four times. "It's Randy," he said. "Open up." Someone unbolted the latch and let them in.

Gina stared at the sleeping bags and cots sprawled throughout the room, which was the size of a small auditorium. Men, women, and children were huddled in blankets and spoke in hushed tones. Cartons of MREs lined one of the walls, and her eyes widened at the ammo boxes stacked in a corner. Several men armed with machine guns were posted strategically near the door.

She turned to Randy. "What is going on here?"

Before he could answer, a middle-aged man sporting a beard and wearing jeans and a red flannel shirt ran over to her. He vigorously shook her hand. "Hello, and welcome," he said with a gentle smile. "I'm Pastor Jack. You can just call me Jack."

"I'm Gina Lanyon." She looked around at all the people. "Who are they?" she asked.

"Part of our rescue mission," Jack said. He bubbled over with excitement. "I can't tell you how thrilled I am that someone from the media is willing to tell the truth to the American people! This is an answer to prayer!"

Randy coughed. "Jack, she doesn't know yet."

He looked bewildered. "But I thought—"

"Never mind." He turned to Gina. "I think I better start at the beginning," he said.

They sat cross-legged on a blanket as he explained their operation.

"Basically, we highjack the trucks that transport the prisoners. I sneak into the computer and access the routes. Then I tell our men where to go. A friend of Jack's owns a helicopter and airstrip. Our pilots fly below radar to bring the people to safety. Some of 'em are brought here. But we have other safe houses, too."

Gina was writing furiously on her pad. She pictured the military trucks snaking up the high mountain roads, covered with a thick layer of ice. Randy always made sure his men were armed with the M-16 rifles and machine guns he stole from the armory.

Her eyes fell on a young woman holding a crying baby. She looked around apprehensively, as if she feared the cries would give away their hiding place. An old woman sat in a corner, her eyes vacant and staring. A few women huddled close to their children, who clung to them with bewildered and frightened faces. Gina shook her head. These were the "terrorists" who threatened the fabric of society?

"These people have lost everything," Randy told her, as if reading her thoughts. "All because of their love for freedom and their loyalty to the United States Constitution." He looked down at the floor. "And I played a part in it all."

"What?"

His eyes filled with pain. "Nothing," he said quietly.

"Why were they arrested? I mean, what exactly did they do?"

"It depends. Everyone here was on one of three lists. The red list is top priority. They get arrested first. To be on that list, you got to be a leader in the patriot movement, or at least well known. The government sees them as the biggest threat. Then there's the blue list. They're kind of in-between. Not leaders, but known to be involved in the freedom movement. Usually they belong to groups like the Patrick Henry Society or Christians for Constitutional Liberties. Now, there are some people here who were on the green list, but most ain't."

"Why not?"

"Because there's no rush to arrest them," Randy said. "They're just suspected of having 'anti-government sentiments,' mostly because they wrote a few letters opposing the World Constitution."

"This is unbelievable," Gina said.

"It gets worse," he said in a soft voice.

"What do you mean?"

He lowered his eyes. "The people in the facility." He called to Pastor Jack. "Hey, Jack! Get me a beer, will you?"

Jack looked at him disapprovingly. "Randy, that's not the answer. You can't numb your pain with alcohol."

He shrugged. "I sure as hell can try." He got up from the blanket. "Want a beer?"

"Actually, I wouldn't mind a cup of coffee," she said.

He returned in a few moments with a can of Bud, a mug of coffee, and a few packets of creamer and sugar from one of the MREs. "My own private stash," he said, indicating the beer. "Jack don't approve, of course, but he can't very well tell me what to drink."

He took a gulp, and his face blanched. Gina wondered if perhaps he would need something stronger. She waited for him to continue.

"They're killing people at the facility. Injecting 'em with stuff."

Her eyes grew wide. "Are you sure?"

"I've seen it with my own eyes! Hell, I've seen the body bags thrown into the furnace!"

She just stared at him for several seconds. Nothing could have prepared her for this. She sat mutely as he described dazed, incoherent men and women who drooled like infants, their minds destroyed by psychotropic drugs or forced injections that sent them into convulsions...and worse.

She put her face in her hands. "Dear God," she said. America had become like Nazi Germany!

He nodded toward the people in the room. "You can talk to them, if you'd like," he said softly. "I'm sure they're eager to tell you their stories."

Gina settled on a cot next to a youngish woman from Colorado. Two little boys sat on the floor in front of her, playing with some action figures.

"My husband was stationed at Fort Carson," she said, brushing a strand of dark hair from her eyes. "He had circulated a sovereignty petition. One night he called me and told me to pack a bag and take our boys into the mountains where my folks lived. He hung up before I could say anything. I did what he said, but by the time we got out to the car, our house was surrounded by UN troops." Tears ran down her cheeks. "They forced us into a truck filled with other prisoners..." She groped for a tissue. "I never saw my husband again."

For several hours Gina listened to similar stories. She even met a few government officials who had signed sovereignty resolutions.

A member of the Montana Legislature sat cross-legged on a sleeping bag. He was in his mid-forties, with a roundish face and dark creases under his hazel eyes. "After we declared sovereignty from the United Nations, UN forces stormed the capitol and arrested everyone who had signed the resolution, even our families! They rounded us up like cattle." His eyes blazed with anger. "Of course, we were prepared for something like this. We even asked the state militia to be ready in case of violence. They managed to kill a few hundred of the thugs, allowing some of us to escape. But how do you fight against the World Army? Once the UN's reinforcements arrived, it was pretty much over."

He raised his eyes toward the ceiling and took a long, deep breath. The fair-haired woman sitting next to him clasped his hand tightly. He turned to her and smiled. "My wife and I are two of the lucky ones. If we hadn't been rescued, we would've been separated and sent to federal work camps...or worse."

Sitting on a wooden crate, Gina jotted this on her pad. "So, other than the militia, did anyone else try to resist?"

"I wouldn't doubt there was some house-to-house fighting." He smiled ruefully. "After all, it *was* Montana. I'm sure there were plenty of patriotic Americans who wouldn't submit to those *peacekeeping* brutes without a fight. The thing is, we're completely outnumbered. Last I heard, there were more than a million UN troops stationed on American soil in preparation for an event like this. Most of them are foreigners with absolutely no loyalty to the American people."

Gina recalled what Hank Jennings had said, and a chill ran through her. So much for conspiracy theories. Matt would have a field day with all this. It was bad enough he had gotten her to admit the government was covering up the truth about the Grandview shooting. But this...

All the months of fighting...*and he was right!* She put her face in her hands. *Oh, God, he was right.*

She felt a strong, firm hand on her shoulder, and she started. Randy was squatting on the floor beside her. His eyes glimmered with understanding.

"You okay?" he asked in a soft voice.

"I'm not sure I'll ever be okay again. I think of everything I believed in...and this is where it led." She shuddered. "Why didn't I listen? Why couldn't I see it?" She felt ready to cry.

"Don't be too hard on yourself. I've been there, too," he said.

She was suddenly conscious that he was gazing deeply into her eyes. Her face reddened. She regained her composure as another thought occurred to her. "Aren't you afraid of being discovered here, Randy?"

Pastor Jack broke in on their conversation. "We're trusting in the Lord to protect us. He can easily hide us from our enemies. I once heard of a pastor who smuggled Bibles into Romania. The Soviet police stopped him dozens of times to search his car, but they never found any Bibles, even when they opened the trunk, which was crammed with hundreds of them. 'Where are you hiding your Bibles?' they asked. The pastor looked a little puzzled and said, 'They're right in front of you. Can't you see them?' 'Stop playing games with us!' they said. 'There are no Bibles here!' With that, they let him go." He paused, waiting for Gina to comment.

"It's a nice story," she said. "But pretty far-fetched."

He smiled at that. "It's no more far-fetched than the fact that God has always existed, or that He made the universe out of nothing. Or that Jesus is God's one and only Son, who was born of a virgin and died for the sins of mankind."

She was about to jump in and argue, but his next words grabbed her. "And—Christianity is no more far-fetched than atheism, which maintains that matter and energy have always existed. But where did they come from?"

She groped for an answer, but couldn't think of one.

"You know what's *really* far-fetched?" he went on. "The idea that biological machines more complex than anything man can make today evolved by random chance over the years." He shook his head in amazement. "Now *that* takes a leap of faith!"

She drew back in surprise. "But isn't evolution a proven fact?"

"You think so? Okay, Gina, tell me how you would go about proving it?"

"Well, I guess I'd look at the fossil record..."

"And what would that prove?"

"It would show how one species evolved into another."

Jack was smiling. "In other words, you'd look for transitional forms."

Now, she had him. "Exactly."

He rubbed his fingers across his beard. "How many are there?"

She shrugged. "Hundreds, maybe thousands."

He laughed so hard he broke into a coughing fit, and Randy had to hit him on the back. "What's so funny?" Gina asked.

"Can you name *one*?"

"Of course I can." Thinking, she stared up at the ceiling. "There's Neanderthal Man."

"Just an ordinary human being with rickets. And, his brain was larger than ours."

She listed as many "missing links" as she could think of. Jack debunked them all. At first, Gina wanted to dismiss his arguments as fundamentalist drivel. But she couldn't deny that he seemed to have the facts of biology and anatomy on his side. And not once did he even mention the Bible.

"There are so many holes in the theory of evolution, it isn't even funny," he said. "For example, scientists have determined that a single cell is more complex than a major city like Manhattan. If even one part of this incredibly intricate biological machine isn't working properly, the cell will die. One scientist named Behe pointed out that a single flaw in a cell's protein transport system is fatal. Unless the entire system came into place at the same time, our ancestors would have died. But if you buy into evolution, you have to believe that the human body, in all of its complexity, came into being in a step-by-step, random process. It *couldn't* have happened that way. Science proves that. In fact, any mathematician will tell you that the mathematical odds against life forming by random chance are staggering!"

Jack looked at her expectantly. She fidgeted with her pen. "So, you still think miracles are far-fetched?" he asked.

"I suppose...anything is possible."

"Let me ask you another question, Gina. If God did create the universe out of nothing, and if He created *you* in His own image, what does that mean?"

Her defenses shot up. "Look, just because the theory of evolution has a few holes, that doesn't mean everything happened the way the Bible says."

His fixed gaze made her uncomfortable. "Why are you so afraid to believe what the Bible says, Gina?"

She looked away. "I'm not afraid. I'm just open to possibilities."

A woman's voice chimed in suddenly. "Be careful, hon. Some people are so open-minded, their brains fall out!"

Randy, who had been strangely quiet during Gina's conversation with Jack, chuckled at that. "Good point, Charlene!" He grinned at Gina. "She's a riot!"

"Well, someone's gotta lighten things up around here once in while. Get me a cigarette, will you?"

Randy reached into his pocket and handed her a pack of Marlboros.

Jack shook his head. "Now, Charlene, we're in a confined space here."

She made a face. "Oh, all right. I suppose I should cut down, anyway. It's a nasty habit." She laughed. "But it's sure hard to break it at my age!"

The woman, who looked somewhere in her sixties, extended her hand to Gina. "Name's Charlene O'Darby." Her dancing brown eyes and warm smile immediately put Gina at ease. She pointed to an auburn-haired woman about Gina's age. "This is my daughter, Linda."

Linda smiled. "Nice to meet you." She gave a nod to a little girl curled up in a sleeping bag. "That's Mary Katherine, my daughter."

"She likes to be called Katie these days," Charlene said.

Gina asked what brought them here.

Charlene's eyes flared. "Would you believe we were arrested at our church?"

"Actually," Gina said ruefully, "it might not surprise me as much as you'd think."

Linda described how UN troops had stormed their church during an evening worship service. "We were on our faces praying for the nation. The next thing we knew, armed troops had burst through the doors and were dragging people out of the building, including the pastor and all the Sunday school teachers!"

Gina was mystified. "But why? I mean, you were only praying. How is that a threat to the government?"

Charlene smiled knowingly. "For a government under the control of Satan, prayer is the most dangerous threat of all."

Linda nodded in agreement. "Our pastor was also very outspoken against the New World Order. He often warned against giving up our sovereignty to the UN." Her eyes saddened. "But Mom's right. Prayer can make a tremendous difference in the course of a nation. God's Word promises that if His people pray and turn from their sins, He will heal their land. If more of His people had been praying for America, I'll bet none of this would have happened."

"Where is your church?" Gina asked, eager to change the subject.

"Albuquerque," Linda said.

"You were taken to Wyoming all the way from New Mexico?"

Linda nodded. "First they put us on a train, then we wound up on one of those trucks." Her blue eyes grew luminous. "That had to be the hand of God. Otherwise, who knows what would have become of us?" She looked at Randy with an expression of gratitude, but he turned away, embarrassed.

Gina was wondering about something. "I take it you're fairly religious. On the outside chance this place does get raided, what will you do? Submit peacefully, I suppose?"

Linda's eyes registered surprise. "Are you joking? No way!"

Gina wasn't buying this. "So, you'd fight back?"

"Why not? We've got plenty of weapons here. My mom and I both know how to shoot, and so do most of the other people here, including Jack. Even some of the kids know how to use a gun."

Charlene piped up. "Linda's been in the Air Force, and she's an expert shot!" She swelled with maternal pride.

"I don't get it. Aren't Christians supposed to be against violence?"

Linda smiled playfully. "So, basically, you think Christians are a bunch of wimps?"

"I didn't mean it that way," Gina said, a bit flustered. "It's just that, well, aren't you supposed to love your enemies? You know, turn the other cheek?"

Jack said firmly, "The Bible says we have to love our own enemies. It says nothing about having to love God's enemies."

"In fact," said Linda, "The Psalms say we're supposed to hate those who hate God. I'd say the UN falls under that category." She brightened as another thought occurred to her. "And, did you know that Jesus once told His disciples to carry swords? Or that Nehemiah had armed guards posted during the rebuilding of the Temple?"

"The Bible is filled with instances where God authorized the use of lethal force against ungodly men," Jack added.

"I never knew that," Gina said.

"A lot of Americans don't," said Linda. "It's why we're in this mess." She looked downcast. "We've fallen so far. From a group of ragged colonists who dared to defy the world's greatest empire, we've become a nation of sheep at the mercy of godless tyrants!"

Charlene screwed up her face. "It's sickening!"

Randy finally chimed in. "And it happened because most Americans were brain-washed into fearing guns more than they fear tyranny." His eyes blazed, and she suddenly thought of Matt. He had been trying to tell her this stuff for years, and she had never bothered to listen. Maybe their marriage would be better today if she had listened.

"Boy, you've all given me a lot to think about," Gina said after a moment or two. She turned to Randy. "I'm curious, though. Why me? What made you approach me with the truth?"

The look in his soft brown eyes made her feel self-conscious. "Because...you were different from those other reporters. I got the sense you could think for yourself."

For the first time in her life, she wondered how much truth there was to that.

"We're counting on you to get the truth out to the public," Jack said with an earnest look in his eyes.

Randy nodded. "The only way we can win is by getting the American people on our side."

"Wow...that's a lot to expect right now." She went on to explain the situation at *Island News.*

"There's got to be a way," Randy said. "I mean, we may not be able to win a war against tanks and missiles. But we *can* win a war of ideas."

Jack suggested they all pray together about it.

"Jack, you know I ain't the praying type," Randy said.

"Well, maybe it's time you changed that," Jack said. "Look around, Randy. We're in a desperate situation. *America* is in a desperate situation. You really think we have a chance against the entire might of the World Army without God on our side?"

His tone was like acid. "You know what I'd like to know, Jack? Where was God when *I* needed Him? Where was He when I lost the only woman I ever loved?" He got up and stormed out of the room.

Jack sighed regretfully. Then he looked at Gina. "Would you like to join us in prayer?"

She folded her arms and looked around uncomfortably. "You go ahead." She glanced toward the door. "I think I'll see if he's all right."

She found him sitting on the front steps, gazing up at the starlit sky. She sat down next to him and looked toward the heavens. Never before had she seen such a sky. Hundreds of stars twinkled in the vast darkness, and she was amazed at how bright they appeared.

"Sure is a pretty night," said Randy, as though reading her thoughts.

"Yes, it is," she agreed.

He grasped her hand. Instinctively, her fingers tightened around his. A tingling like electricity shot through her. She couldn't remember the last time Matt had held her hand.

"You want to talk about it?" she asked.

He had a dreamy, faraway look in his eyes. "Her name was Jenny. I was crazy about her."

"Things didn't work out?"

His face clouded. "She died of leukemia."

"I'm sorry," she said softly.

"Me, too. I married her right after high school. We had almost a year together..."

"You must miss her a lot."

He nodded. "Especially now. There are times when I wish..." He broke off with a shrug. There was an awkward silence.

"How about you?" he asked suddenly. "Have you ever lost someone you loved?"

She thought of Matt, and what he was like before everything changed. She could see the boyish smile playing across his ruddy face, could feel his strong, rugged arms that used to make her feel so safe. Tears shimmered under her eyelashes. "I think...maybe I have," she said quietly.

Randy looked at her with tenderness. Slowly, he leaned toward her and closed his eyes. His lips brushed hers, very softly.

She jerked away from him. "I have to go," she said, jumping up from the steps.

He got up and put his hands around her waist. "You're trembling," he said, his voice like a whisper.

"It's cold out," she said. "I better go back inside." She almost stumbled into the church door.

She sat in one of the pews, her heart thudding like a jackhammer. *What was I thinking?*

She had to get home to Matt.

* * * *

The narrow highway snaked between jagged boulders and pines that stretched toward the darkening sky. Gina hoped to get to the airport before the snowstorm hit. She moaned. Flecks of white spiraled onto the windshield. She dreaded the thought of driving back to the motel in a blizzard. And she didn't relish the prospect of sleeping on a bench in the terminal. *Maybe I should turn around.*

Tires screeched and a small, black truck zoomed past her, cutting right in front of her. She slammed on the brakes and nearly lost control of the car. Her heart pounded as she glared at the truck, careening wildly across the road.

Her eyes widened. A man was dangling precariously out of the back. Someone was on top of him, pummeling him relentlessly. She reached for her cell phone to call the police. Then, her jaw dropped as she caught a glimpse of the victim's face. It looked like Randy!

She pressed her foot on the gas and sped closer. The truck looped around a curb, just missing a boulder that jutted out of the mountainside. She gaped at the UN insignia emblazoned on the back door swinging from side to side.

She opened the window and stuck out her head. "Randy!"

He punched his attacker in the jaw. The thug tumbled backwards into the truck. Randy shot a desperate glance at Gina, who was closing in. "Jump!"

In the next instant he was sprawled across the hood of the car. Gina threw it into reverse, then turned the wheel as hard as she could. "Hang on!"

The car skidded on the slippery road that was beginning to ice up. Randy almost lost his grip. Gina pressed the button to open the passenger-side window, and he climbed inside.

The truck had turned around and labored up the steep incline behind them. The subcompact Gina was driving shot ahead at forty miles an hour. She wouldn't risk going faster in the snow.

The back windshield shattered as the truck gained on them. Gina ducked. "They're shooting at us!"

"Keep going!"

She drove blindly into the storm.

* * * *

High above the swirling snow, dozens of luminous figures moved into position. They descended from the sky and surrounded the little car, holding it securely on the road. Six of them, more than seven feet tall, hovered in front of the truck. Another squadron darted toward the darker hoard that swarmed above the car and surrounded the truck.

* * * *

"We're losing them!" the driver of the truck shouted. He turned to his partner, who was sighting the car in is scope. "Blow a hole in their tires!"

He cursed. "I can barely see anything in this blizzard!" A purple welt was puffing up under his eye. "This wouldn't have happened if we had just shot the bastard in the first place!"

"We had orders to bring him in alive." He gripped the steering wheel tightly as they rounded another curve. "We need backup." He grabbed his CB. "We're in pursuit of a red Toyota, license plate..." He strained to make out the numbers.

A blinding flash of light exploded in front of the windshield. The two men covered their eyes as the truck spun out of control.

* * * *

Gina glanced in the rearview mirror, and her mouth opened in amazement. The truck slowed considerably, then slid across the ice in a 360-degree turn. Smashing through the guardrail, it plummeted over the edge of the mountain.

* * * *

"We won't be able to get much farther in this blizzard," Randy said as the car slowed to a crawl.

"I know." Gina strained to see the road. A dense fog surrounded them, and everything was white. "We have to pull over somewhere."

"They might have people looking for us. We'd have to hide the car." He fumbled with the map Gina had bought at the motel. "There's got to be some back roads around here."

"I can't even tell where we are. How could we even see another road?"

"There!" He pointed to a small route sign. "Try that one."

A thick layer of slush crunched under the tires as Gina turned off the main highway. She eased off the gas as the car went into a skid, then lightly pumped the brakes.

They drove another few miles through the isolated countryside, dotted with pines and evergreens blanketed with ice crystals. The wiper blades barely made a dent in the snow that clung to the windshield.

Turning around a bend, Gina saw something big and red in the distance. A barn! She pointed. "Look!"

Randy let out a whoop.

The road had become impassable, so they had to get out of the car and push it the rest of the way. They yanked open the massive wooden doors and shoved the car inside the barn.

Gina leaned against a mound of hay and took a few deep breaths to calm down.

"You okay?" Randy asked her.

Her legs were still shaking like jelly. "Actually, I should be asking you that." A mass of bruises covered his handsome face, and a long, jagged cut ran across his cheek.

"I'll survive."

"There must be a first aid kit in the car."

They sat down on a worn quilt that Randy had found, and Gina applied antiseptic cream to his cut. Then he told her what happened.

"They ambushed me on the way back to town. Hit me over the head, then dumped me in the truck. When I came to, I heard 'em talking." He shuddered, his face pastey white.

She caught her breath. "Were they planning to kill you?"

His expression was grim. "Worse. They were going to torture me till I told them everything." His eyes blazed. "I couldn't let that happen. Not after...what I've done." He looked away.

"What did you do?" she asked in a soft voice.

He put his face in his hands. For a long moment he didn't say anything. When he finally looked at her, she saw the face of a man tormented by guilt. "I followed orders," he said. He shook his head, incredulous. "Just followed orders like a stinking Nazi!"

"What do you mean? What orders?"

Tears glistened in his eyes. "I flew a helicopter with infrared tracking equipment. I had orders to track down a group of patriots hiding in the woods at night, so our troops could ambush them. At the time, I thought I was doing the right thing...that I was on the side of peace. What a joke!"

"But Randy, how could you know?"

"I saw the whole thing, Gina. They were trapped. Men, women, children...massacred. Because I was following orders!" He was shaking. "After it was over, their bodies were thrown into a mass grave." There was a long silence. "I was ordered never to tell anyone."

For a moment she just stared at him. She didn't know what to say.

He lowered his eyes. "I wonder how my Jenny would feel if she knew what I've done."

"You can't hate yourself forever," Gina said quietly. "And, you're doing the right thing now. You're helping people—"

"So, that makes it okay? Are you telling me that makes it okay?" He was trembling uncontrollably, and she moved closer to him, gently putting her hand on his shoulder.

"How could you know what was happening? The government's been lying to all of us."

"But don't you see, Gina? I'm a part of it all! I helped make it possible. Without people like me, who blindly follow orders without question, the government couldn't have killed all those people. Sometimes I can't even look in the mirror. I think of all those people..." He broke off with a shudder.

Instinctively, she put her arms around him. "It's okay," she whispered. "Think of all the people you've been helping, at such great risk. How many others would do the same?"

He gazed deeply into her eyes, and a soft smiled played across his lips. "You're very sweet, Gina." His voice was barely a whisper.

The next thing she knew, his lips were on hers; to her own astonishment, she was kissing him back.

"We shouldn't do this," she whispered. But he continued to kiss her, and she closed her eyes in surrender.

* * * *

Gina lay on a bail of hay in the corner of the barn, while Randy slept fitfully on the quilt. It had stopped snowing, but would take awhile for the roads to clear.

She stared up at the rafters for what seemed like an eternity, sickened by what she had done.

How could I have let this happen? She put her face in her hands and let the tears slide down her cheeks.

Adultery! The word screamed at her, and she felt a strange stab of fear. As if something dark and hideous was in the barn. Watching her.

Her head was throbbing, so she rifled through her purse for some headache pills. Her heart nearly stopped when she grabbed the pocket-sized New Testament Jack had given her. An inexplicable urge made her open it. She flipped through the pages. Her eyes fell on a verse in the book of Romans.

"For the wages of sin is death..."

She shuddered as the words blazed into her heart.

Crouching beside her, several dark beings whispered into her ear.

She slammed the book shut.

CHAPTER 18

Gina's knees were shaking as she scanned the crowd outside the terminal. Her stomach lurched when she saw Matt's face. Hesitantly, she waved to him. His eyes brightened and he walked toward her.

"Welcome back," he said.

She dropped her carry-on bag and melted into his arms. "I missed you." She buried her head in his shoulder. "More than I ever thought possible."

He pulled her close. "I missed you, too, babe."

Her heart ached with remorse. Not just for what happened in Wyoming, but for everything else.

He looked at her with concern. "You okay?"

She shook her head. "You were right, Matt. About everything."

His eyes registered surprise. "What do you mean?"

She heaved a sigh. "There's a lot I have to tell you."

* * * *

Matt sat wide-eyed at the pizza place where they had stopped as Gina finished her story. "This is unbelievable!" he blurted out.

She sipped at her soda. "Everything you said was true, Matt. I was too much of a fool to listen." She smacked her forehead. "How could I have been such an idiot!"

"Gina, don't be too hard on yourself. A lot of decent people have fallen for government lies. That's how Hitler took control of Germany."

She played with a piece of pizza crust. "I'm surprised you haven't said 'I told you so.'"

"What would that accomplish? The main thing is, you've recognized the truth."

"But why did it take so long?" she asked. "I mean, it was staring me right in the face. Ben and Elsie's murders, the attack on Father Flannery. Why couldn't I see it then?"

"Maybe you didn't want to," Matt said softly.

Then it hit her. All her life, she had believed what she wanted to. If the facts didn't fit her preconceived ideas, she simply rationalized them away. "I think you're right," she said.

His eyes were shining, and suddenly she saw the boyish man who had stolen her heart so long ago. "Let's go away together," he said suddenly.

She drew back in surprise. "What?"

He reached for her hand. "You heard me. It doesn't have to be for long. Maybe just a weekend."

She smiled. "Where did this come from?"

"Things haven't been right between us for a long time, Gina. I want that to change."

"You think a weekend getaway is the answer?"

He shrugged. "I don't know. I just know that I need you. I need our marriage to work." His eyes saddened. "There's not a whole lot I can count on anymore."

She understood. He had lost so much. Ben and Elsie. The construction company. Even his country.

"It might be difficult for me to get away for awhile..."

"Well, just give it some thought."

She forced a smile. "Okay." But guilt and fear pierced her heart.

* * * *

Ken was chewing on the end of his pencil as Gina played the tape she had brought back from Wyoming. She had asked him to meet her after hours at an Irish pub on Old Country Road. It was rumored that Damien had private detectives spying on employees he didn't trust, and she wouldn't put it past him to keep tape recorders hidden.

She pressed stop, then looked Ken squarely in the eyes. "Well?"

For a long moment he didn't say anything. Finally he spoke in a low voice. "I kind of suspected things weren't what they seemed. But *this*..." He broke off with a shudder.

"The American people have the right to know, Ken."

He rubbed his forehead. "Come on, Gina. Do you honestly think Damien will let us print something like this? And if we run it without his permission, we'll both be out of a job."

She stared at him. "Ken, don't you think getting the truth out is more important than keeping our jobs?"

"I'm not just worried about our jobs. We could be killed if we try to print this! Has that thought even occurred to you?"

"Look, we have to do *something*. We can't just let the government get away with this."

He picked at his corned beef sandwich. "There's something I think you should know. Remember the Grandview shooting?"

"How can I forget?" she asked ruefully.

He looked embarrassed. "Oh, right. Sorry. An old friend of mine, Congressman Dobson, who had recently joined the CGU, paid me a visit a couple of weeks after it happened."

"Dobson? The name isn't familiar."

"He was a low-ranking freshman, not too well known. He was fairly conservative, actually. Probably useful for protective coloring, if you get my point. Anyway, he told me he was at the banquet, but a high-ranking friend of his in the Council talked him into leaving early."

She raised an eyebrow. "Oh really?"

"Dobson didn't think much of it until after the shooting. He also said that he wasn't the only member told to leave early that night. Some were even called away on emergencies."

"Did Dobson know who told them to leave early?"

His voice was low. "He heard it was Oren Reinhardt."

"The big tycoon? I don't get it. Why would he—" Her eyes grew wide. "Wait a minute. He's chairman of the CGU!"

Ken's face had a knowing look. "Which means he had a lot to gain from the shooting. He also happens to be Damien Whitaker's brother-in-law."

Her jaw dropped. "You're kidding!"

"There's something else. When Dobson started asking questions, he was told to keep his mouth shut and just be grateful to be alive."

She shook her head. "This is incredible!"

He looked grim. "It gets worse. Three days after he confided this to me, he was dead!"

She stared at him. "How did he die?"

"His death was ruled a suicide. But when I questioned the paramedics who had arrived on the scene, they told me he was shot in the *back*."

"Interesting suicide. Either he had some kind of unusual gymnastic ability, or..."

Ken nodded. "We have to be *careful*. These people are deadly. They'll stop at nothing to keep the American people from learning the truth. Look what happened to Cheryl."

"So, Senator Meyers was telling the truth?"

He nodded. "Cheryl wrote a twenty-page exposé on the Council for Global Unity. She showed it to me the day before she was murdered."

A chill ran down her spine.

"Cheryl's not the first to pay with her life for telling the truth about the conspiracy. Ever hear of James Forrestal?"

"I'm not sure."

"He was our first Secretary of Defense during World War II. He was also one of the most outspoken enemies of international Communism. At the time of his death, he was planning to expose Soviet spies who had infiltrated the U.S. government. He was going to buy *The New York Sun* to get the truth out to the American people."

"So, I take it something happened to him."

"You guessed right. He died in the psychiatric wing of Bethesda Naval Hospital. He had been there for months, even though his own doctor insisted that there was nothing seriously wrong with him. According to hospital officials, he leaped from the window to his death. A bathrobe cord was tied in mid-stream around his neck. It looked as if he had attempted to hang himself, then changed his mind and jumped out the window instead."

She frowned. "That does sound fishy."

"Interestingly, Forrestal was supposed to be discharged the very next day." He clenched his fist. "If only there were some way to print your story anonymously."

Her eyes lit up suddenly. "I think I know a way to do this! But I'll need some help. Isn't one of your sons an Internet guru?"

He nodded, puzzled.

She smiled. "I need you to ask him a favor."

* * * *

She arrived at Penn Station late in the afternoon. Walking casually toward the Eighth Avenue exit, she gave a quick, nervous glance at the many security cameras mounted on the walls, then looked straight ahead. The over-sized briefcase she was carrying knocked against her leg. She gripped the handle tightly, trying to ignore the strange tightness in her chest. Her scalp itched slightly under the long blond wig she was wearing, and her tinted sunglasses bathed everything in an amber hue.

Once she reached the street, she hastened her steps and headed toward the New Yorker Hotel on Eighth Avenue at 34th Street. A tall building with a large, sprawling lobby and grand ballroom reminiscent of the 1920s, it had fallen into disrepair after the crash and had never quite recovered, like many hotels in the metropolitan area. Still, it would suit Gina's purpose, and that's all that mattered.

At the front desk she asked for a room. When the clerk asked for her debit card, she looked around furtively, then pulled a shining, four-ounce gold coin out of her purse. "I'm sorry, I forgot debit card," she said, adopting a fake accent. "Would you accept gold coin instead—it should cover day's stay, including local phone calls I make."

"I can keep it?" he asked in a low voice, almost in disbelief. The coin was worth well over a thousand dollars on the black market. She nodded, and he took it eagerly.

Inside the hotel room she pulled a laptop computer out of her briefcase and placed it on the desk. She was taking a huge risk, but was fairly confident she could pull it off. Her heart beat rapidly as she realized the significance of what she was about to do. By the time she left here tonight, the truth about what had happened out West would be sent to every e-mail address on the Internet!

The plan was simple enough. Ken's son had loaned her an online service disk, including one week of free Internet access, which he had purchased with cash before the debit card system had been instituted. The disk couldn't be traced. He had also obtained an underground, general broadcast program from a friend of his who was also an Internet guru. The program, which Gina had loaded in before she left home, would allow her to send her message automatically to every e-mail address in every country world-wide.

Once she had the computer set up, she plugged the phoneline into the modem jack on the computer, and ran the online service program. The computer hummed quietly enough, yet to Gina the sound filled the entire room. She glanced at her watch. Better make this quick, she told herself. Using a phony name, she typed the user information and password, logging onto the online service. She perused the icons, looking for something that would indicate the Internet. One of the icons had the letters INT inside a small, blue globe. There! She clicked twice on the icon, and she was in.

Her hands moved feverishly at the keyboard, her body taut with excitement—and more than a little anxiety. She couldn't believe how far technology had come; to be able to send a message to everybody in the world with an e-mail address just boggled her mind. Of course, if the government caught the message in time, they could force certain online services to delete it from the e-mail storage area before all their users could download it. Still, millions of people would get the message; the government couldn't possibly delete it from every e-mail address in the world! But while the government couldn't trace the disk, they could trace the message to the telephone line, and that's where the danger was. She had to send her message as quickly as possible and then get the hell out of there before it was traced. With today's sophisticated phone surveillance technology, the government could trace the call in a matter of seconds.

Once she had finished typing her message, she drew in her breath, then clicked on send. Her hands were shaking and her legs felt abnormally heavy. But she couldn't leave yet. She pulled off her wig and the bulky, over-sized sweater she was wearing, along with her baggy sweatpants, and shoved them into a plastic bag she had brought with her. Underneath she wore a pair of skin-tight leggings and a different colored top. Hastily she packed up her laptop and left the room key on the dresser.

She glanced up and down the corridor before heading toward the elevator. If the phoneline had been traced, the building would soon be swarming with government agents.

Outside, a light, wet snow was falling, making the sidewalks slick. Now at the height of rush hour, the sidewalks were jammed with commuters heading back to Penn Station. She was just crossing the street when she heard a siren. She whirled around, her heart thudding nervously. She shook her head, relieved. Just an ambulance.

She pushed her way through the crowd at Penn to track sixteen and just made her train before it pulled out of the station. As the train sped through the darkened tunnel she leaned back in her seat and let the tension drain from her body. She had made it!

* * * *

She looked at the headline in disgust.

INTERNET HOAX THREATENS GLOBAL GOVERNANCE

The Internet has been the target of a vast, right-wing conspiracy to discredit global governance. The perpetrators are believed to be paranoid anti-government zealots...

She couldn't even read the rest.

When she saw Ken later, their eyes met briefly in silent understanding. But neither said a word. The message had been seen by her colleagues. She heard some of them discussing it in hushed voices. The editorial page was filled with impassioned pleas calling for strict regulation of the Internet.

The stories calling her message a "hoax" hadn't even bothered to refute her message. The media had simply labeled it a "conspiracy theory" concocted by "right-wing, anti-government extremists."

That was what most people wanted to believe. Gina couldn't really blame them; she understood how difficult it was to believe that your own government could be capable of such evil. But she had learned that history was filled with the grim lessons of people who had trusted their governments, only to be rewarded with betrayal and murder.

CHAPTER 19

John looked into his rearview mirror again and frowned. The police car had been following him for two blocks now. Still, he wasn't speeding and had been observing all traffic laws. Maybe the cop just happened to be going in the same direction.

"You're awfully quiet," Beth commented as John turned onto Route 25, a scenic road which wound its way through lush, wooded areas and charming Victorian homes. He checked the mirror again. Sure enough, the cop was still following them.

He and Beth were on their way home from a meeting hosted by Christians for Constitutional Liberties, which had been called to address concerns over the new luxury tax that the UN had proposed, to be introduced in the next legislative session of the World Parliament. Since the U.S. had voting privileges, it was still possible to oppose some of this lunacy. At least, that's what John was hoping. Local government officials had been invited to the meeting, but most failed to show up. The few who did come had denounced those organizing the meeting as "right-wing extremists" afraid of progress and unwilling to pay "their fair share." At one point John had stood up and accused them of selling out their country. Beth had nearly freaked out when they demanded to know his Social Security Number, but he had refused to give it. Could that be why the cop was following him?

He didn't want to scare Beth, and so far the cop hadn't flashed his lights. Maybe he was worrying for nothing. "Yeah. I was thinking about the meeting," he said, trying to forget about his apprehension. "You know, I can't believe how many idiots are in favor of this tax. Especially people who call themselves Christians."

"You're thinking of Pastor Bradley, aren't you?"

"I still can't believe he actually supported this so-called 'luxury tax' in his sermon last week. He sounded like he was quoting from the *Communist Manifesto!*"

She raised an eyebrow. "Don't you think you're exaggerating?"

"I don't know, Beth. Somehow I doubt that paying a yearly luxury tax on cars and homes was what Christ had in mind when He spoke of being poor in spirit. I just can't believe our own pastor would promote something like that."

"I'm sure he's just concerned for the poor. Shouldn't we all be?"

"Of course. But it's the church's job to take care of them, not the government's. Besides, I don't think this new 'luxury' tax on Western countries has anything to do with helping the poor. I think the UN wants to bleed us dry so we have nothing leftover to spend on anything that poses a threat to their ungodly agenda, like sending missionaries overseas to spread the gospel."

Beth looked troubled. "You really think that's what this is all about?"

He nodded. "It's about control. The less money people have, the easier they are to control. Besides, our recent take-home pay is proof enough that redistributing people's wealth simply makes everyone equally poor. Matt used to tell me that all the time, and—"

"I'm not sure you should be listening to everything Matt says," Beth said with a distinct note of disapproval in her voice. "In fact, I think you've been letting him influence you far too much lately."

He was taken aback. "What's that supposed to mean?"

"I'm just not sure how healthy it is to dwell on all these things. Look at Matt. He's consumed with bitterness. I don't want to see that happen to you."

"So, you'd rather keep your head in the sand and pretend nothing's wrong? Is that the way to deal with problems?"

She sighed. "No. But I don't want to see you go off the deep end."

"Beth, I don't think being concerned about tyranny and injustice is going off the deep end. I think it's a legitimate concern of all Christians. Anyway, once the UN starts enacting 'luxury taxes' on cars and homes, what's next? Maybe they'll want to slaughter our newborn children like they do in Communist China."

She shuddered. "What a terrible thought!"

"I don't think it's that far-fetched. In fact, I've heard on the news recently that the UN is considering a luxury tax on newborn children to curb overpopulation. The next step might even be to limit the number of children people can have, which wouldn't be all that surprising since the UN's 'model' for population control is Communist China."

"Well, hopefully it won't come to that," she said.

"Don't be too sure." He had been so engrossed in their discussion that he was startled to hear the siren. *Oh, great.*

"What's wrong?" Beth asked nervously. "Were you speeding?"

"No, of course not." The officer was signaling him to pull over.

"What's the problem, sir?" John asked politely after rolling down the window. "I didn't think I was speeding."

The tall, imposing-looking figure eyed John suspiciously. "You've got some questionable bumper stickers on your car. One might even say dangerous. Are you trying to cause a disturbance?"

John stared at him, dumb-founded. "With my *bumper stickers?*" He couldn't understand it. Though politically incorrect, his bumper stickers certainly didn't seem dangerous. One was pro-life, another had a Bible verse on it. The third one read simply, "*No Jesus, no peace. Know Jesus, know peace.*"

"Let me see your ID," the officer said. "And your license and registration."

"Why? I wasn't speeding and I haven't committed any crime."

"John, just do what he says," Beth pleaded.

"I think I have a right to know why he wants to see my ID." John tried to remain calm. He turned to the officer again, and spoke in a mollifying tone. "Sir, I don't want to cause any trouble. I just want to know why you need to see my ID. Have I done something wrong?"

"Just show me your ID card, license and registration."

"But—"

"If you don't cooperate, I'm going to have to arrest you."

He couldn't believe what he was hearing. "*Arrest* me? For what?"

Beth was nearly in tears. "John, *please*, just do what he says!"

To appease Beth, John gave in and showed the officer his identification card, along with his license and registration. But that didn't satisfy him.

"You were at that town meeting tonight, weren't you?" he asked in a slightly menacing tone.

"Yes, as a matter of fact, we were. Do you have a problem with that?"

"You two go to church regularly?" It definitely wasn't a friendly question.

"Yes. We're both Christians."

"What's the name of your church?"

"Why do you ask?"

"I need that information for my report."

"Your *report?* What report?"

"Look, just give me the name of your church—and your pastor as well. I also need to know what religious denomination you are."

This was too much. "What is this, Nazi Germany? It's none of your business where we go to church. And you have no right to fill out a report on us with such personal information!"

"I'd advise you to cooperate, mister. If you don't, I'm going to have to take you in for questioning." The officer sneered. "There are a lot of religious groups spreading hate and it's my job to make sure you bigots don't harass innocent people. Now, tell me the name of your church and the name of your pastor."

John had heard of religious profiling being done on groups that the government planned to target for surveillance. A few people from Christians for Constitutional Liberties had mentioned some FBI report called Project Meggido which was being used to convince law enforcement agents that Christians who believed in the Second Coming of Christ posed a serious threat. John wasn't about to give this officer any ammunition. "I told you, that's personal. And right now *you're* the one who's doing the harassing."

Beth was almost hysterical. *"John! Please!"*

But this time, he just couldn't back down. "Sir, as a police officer, you took an oath to uphold the United States Constitution—"

The officer cursed at him. "Just answer the question!"

"But the Fourth Amendment says—"

"I don't give a damn about the Fourth Amendment! We have a new constitution now! So, get out of the car with your hands behind your head. Move!"

John had no choice but to comply. He looked over at Beth, who was sobbing quietly. He felt outraged that she was being put through such an ordeal. Although he knew he could have prevented it simply by telling the officer what he wanted to know, he believed that a greater principle was at stake. He just couldn't give in to this type of intimidation anymore. "I'm sorry, Beth," he told her gently. She wouldn't look at him.

He was handcuffed and pushed into the back of the squad car.

* * * *

John tried to ignore the cold, contemptuous stares of the prison guards as he was roughly thrown into his cell. All he could think of was Beth. He could only imagine what she was going through. He knew this was something she just couldn't deal with. And he had allowed it to happen!

Sitting on the cot in his cell, he put his face in his hands. *Maybe I should have just given in.* But where would it have ended? How many more personal, intrusive questions would the officer have asked him? As far as he knew, he hadn't even been charged with any kind of a crime. And he certainly hadn't been read his rights. When he mentioned that to the officer who had taken him in, the man had laughed at him. John was convinced he had to take a stand. He couldn't give in to tyranny and intimidation. Not anymore.

He wasn't sure how much time had passed when he was transferred to a dimly lit room where he was told to sit down behind a metal desk. The guard stood in a corner, watching John carefully.

The door opened momentarily. John looked up to see a woman, somewhere in her fifties, with a short, severe haircut, and harsh lines around her mouth. "Mr. Lanyon, I presume?" Her voice was cold and businesslike, and she wore a white clinical jacket over a drab, brown skirt.

He nodded, uncertain of what to expect.

"I'm Dr. Renfield. I'm here to ask you some questions." She sat down across from him and adjusted her eyeglasses.

"Wait a minute. Before I answer your questions, I'd like to ask a few of my own."

"I'm afraid that won't be permissible," she said firmly.

"Why not?"

She glanced at the papers on the desk. "As a clinical expert in religious hate, I'm here to determine to what extent—"

John was taken aback. "Religious *hate*? What's that?"

Her tone was filled with cold civility. "Under the Criminal Code established by the Council for Global Governance, religious hate is a dangerous brand of hatecrime that poses a serious threat to public safety and morals. I'm here to assess to what extent it is manifested in your psyche, and whether rehabilitation is necessary. Now—" she glanced at her notes again "—do you believe that the Bible is the infallible Word of God?"

Why would she ask him that? "Of course. I'm a Christian."

The questions continued, following the same theme. Was he opposed to abortion? Had he ever donated money to anti-abortion groups? Did he believe in the Second Coming of Christ? John welcomed this opportunity to share his faith, so he didn't mind answering them. After all, Jesus had told His followers that they would be brought before kings and rulers for His sake.

"Do you attend any Bible studies?"

"Yes, I do. But I think I have a right to know why you've been asking me all these questions."

She jotted something on her pad, then looked up at him and smiled condescendingly. "Religion, like all drugs, affects people in different ways. Some religions are quite benign. Others are deadly. They have led to the slaughter of millions of people and wiped out entire cultures. Those who have been led astray by such belief systems need clinical help, much as a drug addict needs help in overcoming an addiction. I'm here to give you that help, Mr. Lanyon."

John's muscles tensed, but he fought to remain calm. He sensed she was baiting him, hoping to arouse an angry confrontation. Silently, he asked the Lord for help.

Don't be angry, John. She's given you an open door.

He looked at her earnestly. "I appreciate your concern, Dr. Renfield. Sadly, I have to agree that many terrible atrocities have been committed in name of religion."

She raised her eyebrow. "I'm surprised you would admit that."

"Why should I deny the truth? Religion *can* be addictive. So can food. So can work. So can anything that becomes an idol."

She stared at him, her mouth open. Clearly, she was not expecting such a response.

John continued. "History is filled with demented, greedy men seeking power through selfish ambition. Many of them have hidden behind religion to justify any means to get what they want. And what is religion, anyway? Just another *man*-made institution that keeps God in a box to oppress the people. It doesn't matter what denomination or label it's been given."

Dr. Renfield frowned. "But you're a Christian. Christianity is a religion."

He shook his head. "To be a Christian is far more than a religion. It's a personal relationship with the one, true God, the Creator who sees all and knows all. He loves us so much that He chose to die that we might live." John happened to glance in the direction of the guard, who was listening very attentively.

Dr. Renfield appeared to be at a loss for words. John said in a soft voice, "Those who know Jesus understand that His grace and His love are not motivation for killing others. You see, Christianity differs from all other beliefs in one significant way. We cannot earn our way to heaven. We can give nothing to God through our service. All we have to do is have faith that what He says is true. We don't need a church, a religion, a minister, or pope. All we need is Jesus. Pretty radical, huh?"

She seemed to be mulling this over. "I must admit, I've never heard such a perspective before. I've always thought..." She shook her head, confounded.

"What?" he asked gently.

"Well, it seems to me that most people who profess to be Christians are always rallying against some group or activity they don't like. I have a cousin who's like that." Dr. Renfield drew back her shoulders. "She even criticized me for serving champagne at my daughter's wedding!"

John spoke in a gentle tone. "Well, not all Christians are that legalistic. After all, Jesus turned water into wine, and He drank wine at the Last Supper. He also said that it's not what goes into a person that makes him unclean, but what's already inside. Unfortunately, there are some Christians who think that God's standard isn't good enough. They want to impose a higher standard, usually one that *they* find easy to live up to."

She eyed him skeptically. "And you're saying that *you've* never done that?"

John pondered this. Could he have been doing that with Matt? "Hmm. Jesus told His followers to search their own lives for weaknesses before pointing out the flaws of others. You've just reminded me how important that is. Sometimes, I forget."

"Then, why not put that teaching into practice? Why can't you all just leave people alone, instead of pushing your beliefs on others?"

John smiled. "That's a good question, Dr. Renfield. Let me ask you this: are we truly showing love by leaving people alone? Think about it. If your neighbors were trapped in a burning building, would you leave them alone? Of course not. You'd try to save them. The fact is, Jesus loves *you* too much to leave you alone. He wants you to be everything that He created you to be. Most importantly, He wants to have a relationship with you."

She arched her back "And what if that's not what *I* want?"

"That's your choice, Dr. Renfield. You're free to choose a life-giving relationship with the One who created you, and who died to save you, or you can go your own way."

She grimaced. "And what happens if I decide to 'go my own way,' as you put it? Will I burn in hell?"

John hesitated. This was always difficult to discuss. "God doesn't want you to go there, Dr. Renfield. He wants you to be with Him for eternity."

"But I *will* go to hell unless I embrace what you believe. You can dress it up in a lot of nice words, but ultimately, that's what you believe, isn't it?"

He spoke softly. "This is what I believe, Dr. Renfield: 'For God so loved the world, that He gave His one and only Son, that whoever believes in Him shall not perish but have eternal life. For God did not send his Son into the world to condemn the world, but to save the world through him.'"

"And if I choose not to believe, I'll perish. Do you *like* that idea, Mr. Lanyon? Does it give you pleasure to contemplate my eternal suffering?"

He didn't answer right away. He realized that without the power of God's Spirit, someone like Dr. Renfield would never understand why hell had to exist. God was indeed a God of love, but also of justice. No one who went to hell would ever be happy in heaven. He suddenly remembered that the beginning of Dante's *Inferno* said that *love* had created *hell*. What a paradox!

John prayed silently that his words would convey Christ's love for her. "Hell wasn't made for you, Dr. Renfield. It was made for the devil and his demons. God doesn't want any human being to go to hell. That's the good news of the gospel. You won't ever have to go to hell if you accept Christ's gift of eternal life. Think about it. Jesus loved you enough to *die* for you. He longs for you to be in heaven with Him someday."

Dr. Renfield was silent for a long moment. She looked at what she had scribbled on her pad. Finally, she spoke. John could hardly believe what he was hearing. "It is my assessment that you suffer from a type of mental disorder known as religious hate, characterized by paranoia, intolerance, and sociopathic hatred of unbelievers—"

"Hold on a minute. Did I say *anything* to indicate that I hate unbelievers?"

"Your hatred is implied in your belief system," she stated coldly. "It's impossible to profess such beliefs without becoming obsessed with hatred for those who believe differently. Based on my assessment, I recommend that you undergo counseling." She handed him a sheet of paper. "These are the names and addresses of excellent counselors in this area."

He looked at her in disbelief. "You want me to get counseling because I'm a Christian?"

"A cultist would be a more accurate term."

"A *cultist*?"

She opened a booklet and began to read from it. "According to the United Nations Report on Religion and Public Safety, a cultist is one 'who has a strong belief in apocalyptic religious literature; who believes that those who deviate from fundamentalist religious dogmas will suffer eternal punishment; who professes to being against a woman's right to choose; who homeschools his/her children; who believes in stockpiling assault weapons and hoarding survivalist foods; and who distrusts government authority. Any of these may qualify a person as a cultist but certainly more than one of these would cause this person to be viewed as a danger to society, and his family as being in a risk situation that might qualify for state intervention and assistance.'" She looked at him pointedly. "It would appear, Mr. Lanyon, that you do exhibit at least some of the characteristics of a cultist."

He found himself laughing at the insanity of it all. "I can't believe this," he muttered. "So, what if I don't agree to go for counseling?"

She pursed her lips in regret. "Since this is your first offense, you would have to pay a fine, an excessive one, I might add. However, I strongly urge that you comply. After the second offense, you will face mandatory counseling and incarceration. If you cannot learn how to overcome your hatred and intolerance, you may become a danger to society."

He still couldn't believe what he was hearing. "Can't you see what the real danger is? I've just been arrested for my *beliefs*. Doesn't that frighten you?"

She glared at him. "I'd be careful, if I were you. You may not get off so easily in the future." She nodded to the guard, who handcuffed John and led him back to his cell.

Before departing, the young man glanced around furtively. Then he said hesitantly, "Uh, I couldn't help hearing that stuff you were sayin'. You know, about having a relationship with God." He looked down at the floor. "I think that's somethin' I need. My life's pretty messed up."

"What's wrong?" John asked quietly.

He sighed. "My wife just walked out on me." His eyes filled with sadness. "Can't say I blame her. I ain't so easy to live with. Always puttin' her down. I ain't so good with the kids, either."

"Do you want to change?"

"Yeah, sure. But I've tried. Went to counseling and everything. Even took some 'anger management' class. What a waste!"

"God can change you. He can make you a new creation."

The guard's eyes brightened. "Really? You really think there's hope, even for someone like me?"

"God's grace can do amazing things."

The man smiled. "Yeah...like that old hymn. 'Amazing Grace.' Used to sing that in church years ago. Okay, so what do I do?"

"It's simple. You admit you're a sinner, and ask Jesus into your heart. If you'd like, I can lead us in prayer together."

A smile lit up the man's face. "I'd like that," he said softly. John bowed his head, and began to pray.

* * * *

"What would you have suggested I do?"

John sat at the kitchen table, annoyed and frustrated. Emotionally drained, he had hardly touched his dinner. After his interrogation, he had been locked up in his cell, where he had remained for the next twenty-four hours. On top of everything that had happened to him, Beth wasn't giving him an ounce of support! He was bitterly disappointed. If only he could make her understand what was at stake. For the first time in all the years of their marriage, he felt a huge gulf between them. He didn't know what to do about it.

"You should have answered the officer's question," she said, as though stating the obvious. "Would that have been so difficult?"

"Beth," he said wearily, "you don't understand."

"Oh, I understand, all right. I understand that all you care about now are your political rights!"

He couldn't believe she could say such a thing. "Beth, you know that's not true."

"Well, that's what it looks like to me."

"I was trying to do what I thought was right. How could you expect me to do otherwise?"

She looked at him in disbelief. "You really think you were doing the right thing?"

"Of course!"

"Then you've changed, John," she said sadly. "Your priorities have changed."

"What do you mean, my priorities have changed? I was standing up for what was right. That's what I've always tried to do, it's what we've both tried to do."

"No, John, you were standing up for your political freedom. Not for the Kingdom of God."

He felt hurt and indignant. "Oh, really? Then what was I doing while I was being grilled about my faith in Jesus? You know, if I hadn't been brought in for questioning, I never would've had an opportunity to lead the guard to the Lord."

"Maybe," she conceded. "But look at why you were there in the first place. You weren't there because you wanted to share the gospel. You were there for trying to assert your rights."

"And what exactly is wrong with that?"

"It shows that your priorities are all wrong. You're more concerned about political freedom than you are about the Kingdom of God."

"You're starting to sound like Perry," he muttered. Still, he understood

Beth's distress. After all, his political beliefs had completely turned upside down. Ever since he became a Christian, he'd had definite, fixed beliefs about what his priorities should be. The Kingdom of God would always come first. But did building God's Kingdom mean His people couldn't oppose an evil, oppressive government? No. He was increasingly convinced that Christians had a duty to oppose evil in all its forms. He just wished he could convince Beth. "Beth, our political freedom comes from God. Do you really think He wants us to relinquish it so easily?"

"I think God wants us to be more concerned with exalting the Name of Jesus than defending our rights. When you were arguing with that cop, you certainly didn't seem to be doing it in the Name of Jesus!"

He sighed. "I was opposing something I believed was evil. I think that's what God would have wanted me to do."

She was close to tears. "John, what if you had wound up in jail indefinitely? Did you ever stop to think about that? Did you ever once stop to think about the possibility that we might never see each other again?" Her voice broke, and John suddenly understood why she was so angry about what he had done. "I was scared, John! I was terrified. I didn't know if I was ever going to see you again. With everything that's been happening lately, the way the government murdered those people out West who were resisting, I was terrified that I was going to lose you!"

He got up from his chair and held her in his arms. "I'm sorry, sweetheart. I'm sorry I put you through all that."

She wiped away her tears as he sat down beside her. "I'm the one who should be sorry. I shouldn't have said all those things to you."

"You were upset. That's understandable."

"But I shouldn't have accused you of not caring about the Kingdom of God. That was a terrible thing to say."

He looked at her intently. "Beth, I need to know. Is that what you really believe? Or were you just saying that because you were angry?"

"I just don't know." She looked confused. "Sometimes I don't know what to believe anymore. You say our rights come from God, but people like Perry say that we shouldn't be concerned about our rights."

"Well, Perry could be wrong, couldn't he?"

She shrugged. "I suppose. But don't you think it's spiritually dangerous for Christians to get too concerned with their political rights?"

"I don't know. Maybe you should ask Christians who have lived under Communism, or Nazism, or Fascism. Ask people who are being tortured for their faith, or whose children are taken away from them because they're Christians." He eyed her curiously. "Didn't it bother you that we were pulled over by a cop simply because of our bumper stickers, or because we attended a meeting he didn't like? Don't you think that's wrong?"

"Of course I do. I'm just not sure it was worth getting arrested over." She sighed. "Maybe we shouldn't have even gone to that meeting."

"Beth, we can't just sit back and allow the government to run rough-shod over us. For a long time we both stood by while this country literally went to hell. Sure, we prayed, but that's about all we did. The Bible says we have to be salt and light. I'm convinced that means being involved in the political process and trying to wake people up to what's been happening. We both heard from Matt what Gina found out. Innocent people are being murdered by our own government. It's going to get even worse if people like us just stand by doing nothing. We have to do *something*."

"What good would it do? Unless *everyone* gets involved in changing things, it's not going to do any good."

"I don't buy that, Beth. Only a small percentage of the colonists, like maybe four or five percent, were involved in the American Revolution, and they made a big difference. They changed the course of history."

She smiled wryly. "Sometimes I think you know more about American history than I do."

"Well, you can blame your teachers for that," he said with a smile. "So, are you still mad at me?"

"No, I guess I was just scared, more than anything else."

"Then maybe you should pray for courage. Because we may be in for a lot worse."

After his ordeal, he felt like a soldier preparing for battle. He only hoped he had chosen the right one.

CHAPTER 20

"I don't like it, Oren. Something like that just shouldn't have happened." Frank Maguire fidgeted nervously at the far end of the conference table.

"It was handled effectively," Oren said evenly. "Our people in the media did an excellent job at diffusing the situation. Everything is under control."

"Maybe. But for how long? How long do you think we'll be able to maintain control when more and more people start telling horror stories like the one on the Internet? We can't let this happen again!"

Oren looked at him with disdain. The Master didn't like cowards in his ranks. "I wouldn't waste my time worrying about that idiotic drivel on the Internet," he said in a slightly placating tone.

Serena glared at Frank. "We have more important matters to focus on now. There are still preparations to be made for the arrival of the Teacher. The people must be prepared to hail him as their messiah."

"Which may not be easy, if the religious right has anything to say about it." Reverend Zachary Clayton, the director of the International Coalition of Churches, did not appear confident. A Catholic by birth, he had embraced secular humanism after entering the seminary. Then he had been drawn to the New Age Movement, which filled the spiritual void in his life without forcing him to believe in a God to whom he would one day be held accountable. At least, this is what Oren had been able to surmise through their many discussions.

"Perhaps if your people in the ICC had been doing their job, the religious right wouldn't be a problem." Madeline San-Savage wore a slightly arrogant smile. An ordained Protestant minister steeped in the arts of Wicca, she had drawn many well-intentioned souls to Luciferic Initiation; Oren found her very useful indeed.

Before Zachary could respond, Oren broke in. "Please, we mustn't fight among ourselves," he said testily. "We must make the transition as smooth as possible. One false move, and everything could fall apart." He smiled. "Fortunately, we have allies in a very strategic place."

Jack Denning looked doubtful. "You mean the Vatican? Well, I don't trust them." He glowered at Clayton. "I don't trust anyone who's mixed up with religion."

Oren smiled indulgently. "I understand your reservations, Jack. But I can assure you that the Master can make excellent use of organized religion, as he has for thousands of years. Look at the Crusades and the Inquisition, and the so-called '*holy*' wars in the Middle East. Indeed, many of our allies have entered the clergy simply to be in a better position to serve the Master and help implement his Plan." He paused dramatically so that his next words would sink in. "No, our enemy is not that merely *human* institution, organized religion. Our enemy consists of all those who follow the Nazarene."

They all drew back as if Oren had spoken a word that was anathema, and he was satisfied to have achieved his desired effect. If there was one thing that would unite this contemptible group he had to work with, it was their common hatred—and fear—of the Nazarene. "We must all remember that this is a spiritual war to win the hearts and souls of all humanity," he continued. "Therefore our strategy must involve an appeal to the deepest spiritual longings in every human being. Through organized religion, the Master will draw all people to himself."

Jack looked frustrated. "But how?"

Oren smiled cunningly. "You shall see," he said cryptically. "Soon the Teacher will be revealed, and when he takes his rightful place as the prince of this world, no one will be able to oppose him. Or *us*, his servants." He took a sip of cognac and sighed contentedly. "Now, shall we begin our ritual?"

Each person disrobed, then pulled on a long, black, hooded cape. His eyes gleaming, Oren held a golden chalice up to the light. Serena took out a silver-handled dagger, placing it in front of Oren, who fingered it reverently. "Is the sacrifice ready?" he asked, his face a mask of hate.

* * * *

"Did it start yet?" Gina ambled into the living room, where Matt was sitting on the sofa.

"I think it's about to."

"I still don't see why you're so interested in this." Gina sat down next to him. "You're not even Catholic."

"I'm surprised you're not more interested, growing up Catholic and all."

"Well, I suppose I should listen to it." She had to admit, this Pope did have a certain appeal. The media described him as "a breath of fresh air," an "innovative leader working to bring the Church into the 21st Century." Previously an obscure cardinal, he had been narrowly elected to become the most popular Pope in all history, largely through his efforts to expand the ecumenical movement and relax some of the Church's more stringent moral standards. He spoke often of the need to follow one's conscience, and urged his flock to respect beliefs that were different from their own, even if those beliefs seemed to contradict traditional Catholicism.

In an effort to find common ground with Protestants, he had signed a rather controversial document called "Protestants and Catholics United." Signed by hundreds of Protestant leaders all over the world, the document contained a common statement of faith to which Catholics and Protestants agreed to subscribe. The controversy concerned a statement in the original document that the Pope had insisted on deleting. The statement, which claimed that personal salvation could be achieved only through faith in Jesus Christ, seemed "too rigid" to the broad-minded Pope. Concerned for the future of the ecumenical movement, most mainline Protestant leaders agreed to delete the statement. Many evangelical Protestants objected, refusing to sign the document. Gina recalled how the media had condemned them as being backward and narrow-minded. The Pope, on the other hand, was lauded for his "spirit of tolerance and inclusiveness." It was in this spirit that he often warned Catholics of the dangers of "fundamentalism," and narrow, literalist interpretations of the Bible which "could only lead them astray." Gina had to agree.

She vaguely remembered that there had been some sort of controversy surrounding his election, but couldn't remember what it was about. To her knowledge, no pope had spoken *ex-cathedra* in decades. As the Vicar of Christ, the Pope's words would be considered infallible. Indeed, the entire world awaited his message. No one knew what he was planning to say.

She turned up the volume and leaned forward expectantly. The Pope began to speak from Saint Peter's Square in Rome. "Today I am addressing the world," he said in English, "as the Vicar of Christ on Earth. What I have to say concerns the very future of this planet. God has given His humble servant a new revelation, one that is meant to bring everlasting peace and happiness to all mankind. As many of you know, in 1917 the Blessed Mother appeared to three children in Fatima, Portugal. During the course of her appearances, she confided three secrets to the children, two of which have already been revealed. Nearly a century has passed since then, and the world is now ready to learn the final secret of Fatima.

"Ever since the time of Christ," he said after a dramatic pause, "the world has been progressing toward a state of spiritual unity. The purpose of

Christianity was to teach humanity to live in peace and brotherhood. Sadly, the Church has not always been successful in promoting Christ's message of peace. But now, things are different. We have entered a New Age. We have seen the virtual end of the nation-state, an end to imperialism, nationalistic chauvinism, and selfish individualism. Never before have we been closer to attaining Christ's ideal of world peace and universal brotherhood." He paused again, looking into the camera with gentle benevolence.

"Through the Blessed Mother, our Mother Mary, God has revealed that the return of Christ is imminent. The final secret of Fatima could not be revealed until our civilization was advanced enough to understand it. For more than two millennia, mankind has been evolving physically and mentally. Now, we are ready for the next stage of evolution, our spiritual evolution. This leap could not have been made until humanity as a whole was ready. That time is now. The message is this: Christ's return will occur when people and nations have put aside their petty differences, and learned to live in harmony—when they have beaten their swords into ploughshares, as the Bible foretold. We are almost there, my friends. We have taken the first step— the adoption of a world constitution. The significance of this step cannot be underestimated, for we now have the political unity to make Christ's vision of world peace a reality. But something more is required—spiritual unity. Yes, our Lord will be coming soon. But we must prepare the way for him. We must show him that we are ready to unite spiritually as well as politically. There is only one way to do that—through a united religion of mankind. Now, I realize that may sound like a startling proposal to some of you. No doubt some adjustments will need to be made. But it is the only way. If we fail to advance to the next stage in evolution, if we cannot learn to live in spiritual harmony, we will be destroyed. Destroyed by our own fear, divisiveness, and hatred. We cannot allow that to happen. We must give peace a chance!"

Gina listened in amazement as he continued in a slightly ominous tone. "Unfortunately, there are those among us who are not spiritually evolved enough to embrace God's plan for peace; these 'fundamentalists' are part of the Old Order of darkness and division, and are standing in the way of peace and enlightenment. They will try to prevent us from entering the new stage in our evolution. They are enemies to peace, and a threat to our very civilization. They could be your friends, your neighbors, your coworkers. If you want to live in peace, you must resist them. You must reject their false teachings of intolerance, hatred and division. That is not God's way."

Gina looked over at Matt, whose brow was furrowed. The Pope continued on a more positive note. "In order to facilitate the creation of a united religion of mankind, I am proposing that the world's religious leaders meet for a summit to be held here in Rome next month to begin the formation of a World Parliament of Religion. I realize the challenge that lies ahead of us. But as long as we recognize that we are all God's children, and that God lives within each one of us, every religion will have a voice. No one will be left out. For there are, indeed, many roads to God." He raised his hands in a gesture of blessing. "May the God who lives in each of us bless you and keep you," he said.

"This is incredible!" Gina blurted out. She could hardly believe it. A Catholic Pope actually proposing a one-world religion! But before she could get caught up in the euphoria, she suddenly remembered what Father Flannery had said about the one-worlders' plans to create a global religious system to further expand their power. She had to wonder. Matt sat quietly, his expression troubled. "What's the matter?" she asked.

He seemed preoccupied. "Hm? Oh, I don't know, something about that speech just...didn't sit right."

She was surprised. "Really? How so?"

He seemed to be trying to make light of it. "If you must know, it has to do with some stuff I heard from John and Beth. You know how they love yacking about that end-time crap."

She was curious. "What did they say?"

"You wouldn't believe it, probably."

"Try me."

"They said a lot of this stuff is a sign that the Antichrist may soon come to power."

She rolled her eyes. "Yeah, right."

He shivered, and she realized then that he felt more than a little disturbed—he was actually frightened. She put her arms around him. "You can't let fear get the best of you," she told him.

He leaned his head against her shoulder. "I just wish..."

"What?"

He gazed into her eyes with an expression of profound sadness. "Sometimes I wish I had what John has. None of this scares him, Gina. He has this peace about the future that I can't even fathom."

She was amazed at how Matt was opening up to her. But she felt a bit wary that he seemed to be taking this religious stuff seriously. "I guess everyone needs something to believe in," she said.

Matt looked at her intently. "What do *you* believe in, Gina?" he asked in a soft voice.

At one time she would have answered the good of humanity. But she had seen enough to know that was a lie. "I wish I knew, Matt. I wish I knew."

* * * *

Gina entered Saint Patrick's Cathedral and made her way toward one of the front pews. She couldn't help feeling a sense of awe. The gleaming marble floors, Corinthian columns, and majestic arches reminded her of a palace. The scent of incense filled the air, and the soft glow from the candles that burned on the small altars in niches along the walls had a soothing effect. A few people were kneeling down in the intricately carved wooden pews. Some were praying the Rosary.

Gina felt like an intruder in a world where she didn't belong. Her eyes were drawn to the wooden crucifix suspended high above the altar. As she gazed at the frail-looking body, arms outstretched upon the narrow wooden beams, a strange uneasiness came over her. She wasn't sure if it was guilt or fear. Christ's head hung downward, the eyes closed.

She looked away suddenly, wondering why the crucifix had held her interest so long. A terrible ache rose in her throat and she felt as if she might cry. There was something about the Cross that seemed to beckon her, but was somehow out of reach.

She sat down in one of the pews near the front. Next to her, an old woman, slightly hunched over, sat with her eyes squeezed shut and her lips moving in prayer, barely audible. At one time the sight would have filled Gina with scorn. She had always detested traditional Catholicism, and all of orthodox Christianity, as repressive and intolerant. Now, she felt a strange sense of reverence that she couldn't understand.

She looked around, waiting for the Archbishop to make his appearance. A chill ran down her spine as she caught the words of the old woman's prayer. "*Forgive us our trespasses...*" Gina drew in her breath. Forgive us our trespasses. How long had it been since she had said those words?

Tears glistened in her eyes as the memory of that night in Wyoming flooded back to her, ugly and repulsive and sickening. She had tried to convince herself that what she and Randy had shared was beautiful. It just couldn't be wrong. Whenever she recalled Randy's tender kiss and gentle touch, their desperate need to find comfort in each other, her heart ached with longing. How could a God who had allowed the Holocaust condemn her for something so trivial?

She thought of Randy often and wondered if he was safe. The morning they parted, he was planning to hitchhike to Colorado, where he hoped to find safety with a band of patriots Jack had been in touch with. Sometimes she awoke in the middle of the night, her heart pounding, wondering if Randy had been captured.

She was roused from these thoughts by the entrance of the Archbishop of New York City, Cardinal John J. O'Donnell. Gina had been assigned to cover a speech he was about to make in response to the Pope's proposal. She had requested the assignment because she was curious about what he would say and no longer trusted the news media.

Televised worldwide via satellite, the Pope's speech had rocked the world. According to the columnists, anyone who wasn't overjoyed by the Pope's call for a global religion was some kind of hatemonger. That appeared to be the consensus among the Church's leadership as well. While Catholic bishops who supported the Pope's proposal were paraded on television as often as possible, those who had the slightest misgivings were completely ignored. Although Gina did find the concept of a universal religion appealing, she remembered Father Flannery's warnings about it and wondered if he could be right. After all, she had been wrong about the World Constitution. How could she be sure that a one-world religion would be any better?

The Archbishop approached the pulpit. Gina leaned forward expectantly, holding her pocket tape recorder ready. Beloved of conservative Catholics and respected by evangelical Protestants, he had often incurred the wrath of the liberal media for his uncompromising stand on moral issues. He had even received a few death threats in his day, Gina had heard. She was struck by his almost grandfatherly countenance, perhaps it was his white hair, or the lines around his face. Yet she saw the resolute expression in his eyes, and realized that beneath his tame exterior was a will which could not be bent.

She pressed record as he began to speak. He opened with a prayer, then got down to business. "I realize that all of you are eager to hear my opinion of the Holy Father's—er— rather startling proposal. In order to make a proper, *Christian* response to such an idea, I think we need to clarify some issues that should help us to put it in its proper context. One of those issues is spiritual evolution, which appears to be the foundational doctrine, so to speak, of this so-called united religion of man. In order to accept spiritual evolution, however, we must first accept physical evolution. Now, I realize it's fashionable, even among Catholics, to believe in evolution, and has been for quite some time. But that does not change the fact that evolution, spiritual or physical, is a lie that has been used to justify and promote the most horrendous of evils. The Nazis used it to justify the murder of Jews, Slavs, the handicapped and other so-called 'undesirables' who stood in the way of Hitler's plan to create his 'master race.' The Communists have used it as a means of indoctrinating generations of children with atheism. Time does not permit me to catalog the mountain of scientific evidence against evolution—such as the fossil record, the laws of probability, and the Second Law of Thermodynamics. Suffice it to say that adherents of evolution, including Harold Urey, a Nobel Prize winner in Chemistry, have admitted that there is absolutely no scientific evidence for the theory and it must therefore be taken on faith. They continue to believe this lie because it's all they have to rationalize their belief in a Godless universe."

Gina sat there in amazement as she recalled what Pastor Jack had told her. All her life, she had been taught that evolution was an established, scientific fact, even by her parents and her Catholic theology professors. It sounded almost insane for someone to stand up in front of a crowd of people and say it was a lie!

She vaguely recalled John and Beth trying to tell her the same thing, but she hadn't bothered to listen. Could it be that they were right? No, no it couldn't be. How could any educated, intelligent person believe that God had created the world in seven days, as the Bible claimed? That had to be a myth, dreamed up by primitive minds.

But she listened intently as the Archbishop continued. "Not surprisingly, many of those who ascribe to physical evolution also embrace spiritual evolution: the belief that mankind is ascending to a state of god-like perfection, not just physically, but morally and spiritually as well. This, my friends, is the ultimate lie, it's the Great Lie that Satan told Eve in the Garden of Eden: that if she and Adam ate of the forbidden fruit, they would be equal to God. There's something else to consider: If we're all evolving toward godhood, then we don't need a Savior, do we? And if that's the case, then Christ's death on the Cross was meaningless. This is a monstrous lie! It is a direct attack on the Person and mission of Jesus Christ."

Gina looked around to observe people's reactions. She noticed that many were nodding their heads in agreement. A man sitting in back of her said, "Amen!" She jotted some notes down on her pad, then turned her attention back to the Archbishop.

"Contrary to what the Pope said in his speech, Christ did not come to teach us how to live in harmony. He did not come to establish a one-world government or a global religion founded upon New Age feel-good slogans. He came to bring us salvation. In this light, we need to clarify the Church's mission. The primary mission of the Roman Catholic Church, and all Christian churches, for that matter, is to proclaim the Gospel of Jesus Christ. That mission has never been easy, nor popular. But it is a mission which we cannot neglect, even if it is politically expedient to do so—or even if it appears to be in the best interests of 'humanity' or the so-called 'global village.' The Church was not established to serve humanity; the Church was established to advance the Kingdom of God. Jesus said that His kingdom is not of this world.

"Today, however, we are witnessing an attempt to build an earthly kingdom—a one-world government—in the Name of Our Lord. Based on God's revelation in the Scriptures, the Pope's proposal can only serve to further the cause of the New World Order, a cause which I believe is inherently evil. Throughout history, there have been many attempts to build a New World Order. The first attempt was the Tower of Babel, which was condemned by God in the Bible. Then there were the Empires of Persia, Babylon, Greece, and finally the Roman Empire, each one as godless as the other. And of course, there was the Third Reich, perhaps the greatest culmination of evil in all of history. But, I fear the worst is yet to come. Uniting the religions of the world under the banner of a one-world government will pave the way for the most horrendous apostasy since the time of Noah, and is something that the Mother of Christ would never endorse, by the way. That proposal could never have come from her, in spite of the Holy Father's claim. An attempt to merge Christianity with those religions which deny the Word of God as revealed in Sacred Scripture can only result in heresy. My friends, there is no room for compromise when it comes to truth. I realize that in today's climate of political correctness, these words may sound rather intolerant." He smiled. "Well, this may be hard to accept, but Jesus was very intolerant at times. He was intolerant of sin and evil, of all the things that separate us from God. But His invitation to eternal life is open to all people who turn to Him in repentance, with a humble and contrite heart. Jesus said, 'I am the way and the truth and the life. No one comes to the Father except through me.' How can we be true to the gospel if we welcome heretics and pagans into our ranks, without offering to them the salvation that comes only through faith in the Lord Jesus Christ?"

Some people in the audience started heckling him. He had to raise his voice to be heard. "Saint Paul said that we do not belong to the night or to the darkness. He also said that there is one faith, and one Lord. As Catholics, and as Christians, we must resist this satanic attempt to follow those who walk in darkness. While we must always offer to unbelievers the truth of the gospel, we must never become yoked with them. Our Lord was very clear on that point—"

He stumbled backward as something hit him in the face. Gina stared in disbelief as she realized what it was. *Tomatoes*. People were throwing tomatoes. In the hallowed grandeur of St. Patrick's Cathedral, people were behaving like barbarians! She ducked suddenly as something nearly hit her— it looked like a beer can.

"Please!" The Archbishop held up his hands. "Please, stop this! Someone may get hurt."

In the next instant, the cathedral erupted into pandemonium. The rioters were shoving people into the aisles and began kicking and stomping them as they screamed in terror. Gina had to fight a wild desire to run from the church. Speaking into her tape recorder, she forced herself to remain calm. "St. Patrick's Cathedral is in chaos today as rioters—"

She stopped in mid-sentence as nearly a dozen black-garbed men burst into the cathedral. Wearing ski-masks and brandishing machine guns, they rushed toward the altar where Cardinal O'Donnell was standing. They ignored the rioters, who were scrambling for the exits. The team leader shouted at the bishop as the agents pushed their way through the crowd. "Don't move— you're under arrest by order of the UN Task Force on Religious Hate!"

A pregnant woman stumbled to the floor, falling right in the path of the SWAT team. "Get out of the way!" One of them kicked her viciously. She cried out in pain, struggling to get up but unable to do so. "I said MOVE!" the man shouted at her.

The Archbishop rushed forward. "Leave her alone!"

"Stay where you are!" the leader warned him. "Or we'll charge you with resisting arrest."

"But that woman may be hurt!"

Outraged, Gina ran down the aisle toward the woman, who was moaning in pain and clutching her side where the thug had kicked her. "Stay back!" one of the officers barked at Gina.

"Are you some kind of monster?" she asked him, incredulous. "That woman needs help!"

"Sit down and shut up, or you'll be under arrest, too," he told her.

Gina looked down at the woman, whose face had turned white. "Please...help me," she whispered to Gina. Then she lost consciousness.

Horrified, Gina noticed a pool of blood underneath her. "Oh my God! She's hemorrhaging! Someone call an ambulance!"

One of the officers bent down to look at the woman. He turned to the leader, his voice urgent. "She's right! She *is* bleeding."

"That's not our concern," the leader muttered.

By now, half a dozen of the officers had surrounded the Archbishop, but he pleaded with them, "That woman could be miscarrying! Please, I know first aid. Maybe I can help her!"

"Someone else can help her," the leader said, grabbing him by the arm.

Suddenly, the Archbishop broke loose from his grasp and started to run down the aisle where the woman lay bleeding. The leader hit him across the back with a club.

He fell to the floor, face forward. The officer got on top of him. His knee pressed against O'Donnell's back, the leader pinned his hands behind him and cuffed him, then dragged him to his feet. "Let's go," he muttered, pushing the Bishop ahead of him.

Several of the officers got on either side of the Bishop, aiming their M-16s at him. Gina watched, stupefied, as he was dragged out of the cathedral.

She kneeled down next to the injured woman. The woman's long brown hair was disheveled, her pale face drenched with sweat. She was in shock, so Gina draped her coat over her to keep her warm.

A few other people gathered around, asking if they could help. "Does anyone know first aid?" Gina asked.

They all shook their heads sadly.

An erie stillness filled the cathedral. Most people had fled in terror when the SWAT team arrived. Someone had called an ambulance. Gina could hear sirens piercing the silence. She watched helplessly as the paramedics lifted the woman onto a stretcher.

By now, all the camera crews had packed up and left. Gina looked around, appalled by the sight. Broken pieces of stained glass, tomatoes, beer cans and other debris were strewn all over the marble floors. Statues had been overturned. She knew she should immediately go to the newsroom to get started on this story, but somehow, her heart wasn't in it. *No, I can't be this way*, she told herself resolutely. The public had a right to know about what happened here today. Steeling herself, she walked down the aisle and out the heavy, wooden doors.

* * * *

"What's wrong?" Matt asked when Gina slammed the door shut.

"I guess you didn't watch the news yet." She draped her coat over one of the kitchen chairs and sat down in the living room.

He looked concerned. "No. What happened?"

The image of the pregnant woman being brutalized by government agents made her feel sick. It was like something she would expect in Nazi Germany, not in America! "Something terrible." She could hardly stand to think about it.

Matt sat down next to her and took her hand in his. "Hey—you're shaking."

"I'm sorry," she muttered.

"Don't be sorry. I'm your husband. Remember?" He smiled reassuringly. But his very tenderness reawakened the memory of her betrayal, which loomed like a shadow between them. She just couldn't feel close to him as long as she was keeping this terrible secret from him. She wondered if she should tell him. Could she go on keeping this secret forever?

"I'll make you a cup of tea and you can tell me what happened." He headed toward the kitchen.

The phone rang, and she waited for the machine to pick up. She was in no mood to talk to anyone right now. But she was surprised to hear Ken's voice. "Gina, are you there?" A pause. "If you're there, pick up. Gina? It's about your story."

There was something about his tone that told her this was important. Very important. She picked up the phone. "Yes, Ken?"

He sounded relieved. "Thank God I got you! Listen, put on channel twelve right now."

"Sure, hold on." She got up and turned on the TV. What she saw shocked her.

Matt had just put the kettle on and stood next to her. "Wow," he said, looking at the TV. "Looks like some bishop is freaking out."

Gina saw it, but she couldn't believe her eyes. Or her ears. "There's going to be a religious war," Cardinal John J. O'Donnell was raging, "and I won't rest until all those who embrace the Pope's diabolical scheme are destroyed! This calls for a direct attack against the heretics and pagans who are trying to create a New World Order, even if that means the murder of Jews and other 'undesirables' who walk in darkness." The camera cut to the anchors, who explained that police had to be called when the crazed Archbishop assaulted a member of the audience who had tried to reason with him. The scene shifted to a close-up of the pregnant woman moaning in pain.

Matt turned to Gina. "What is it?" he asked. "You look as if you've seen a ghost."

She was still staring at the TV screen. "That's not what happened," she said, after finding her voice.

He looked stunned. "Huh? You mean you were there?"

She nodded. She went over and picked up the receiver. Ken was still there. "Ken, you have to believe me. I was at that riot and I'm telling you that's not what happened!" He told her he had no choice but to pull her story. She slammed down the receiver and burst into tears. Was she going insane?

"What the hell is going on?" Matt asked. She told him everything, and he sat down next to her, shaking his head in amazement. "Look, if what you saw on TV didn't happen, there's only one logical answer. The film was doctored."

Of course! Why hadn't that occurred to her? Probably because she had never experienced anything like this before. Then, she suddenly remembered Senator Meyers, and the news footage of him saying things he claimed he never said. *Morphing!* That was it. The film had been morphed! It suddenly hit her that some of the Bishop's actual words had been spliced into the video. Very clever, indeed. And very frightening. Someone, or some people, had gone to a great deal of trouble to discredit Cardinal O'Donnell. The question was: why?

She called Ken and urged him not to pull the story. "Ken, I have an audio tape of the entire incident, including the part where those UN goons wouldn't let O'Donnell help that pregnant woman and threatened me with arrest when I tried to help her. I'll even sign an affidavit if you think it's necessary. I'll scour the city and find eyewitnesses who will verify what actually happened. In fact, I'd like to go down to every news station which showed that doctored film and play my tape. We can't let the media get away with this!"

"Gina, come on. That scene with the Archbishop was on every major news network tonight. Unfortunately, no one will believe your story. They'll think you're crazy—and that *Island News* is crazy for printing it."

"You're wrong Ken," she said, resolutely. "There *are* people who will believe my story—the ones who were there!"

"So, what are you planning to do—round them all up and get them to verify your story?"

She looked at her watch. "It's not too late. I'm going to make some phone calls. There's bound to be someone connected with Saint Patrick's who saw what I saw today."

"But, Gina, even if you do get people to verify your story—even if you get a hundred people to back you up—do you have any idea of what we'll be up against if we decide to print it?"

"Ken, what do you think is going to happen if we keep letting these people get away with all these lies? Do you think things are going to get any better if we keep letting them win?"

He didn't answer. She said, "At some point, you have to make a stand. You can't just sit back and let evil triumph."

"Gina, these are dangerous people. Going up against them could mean much more than just the end of our careers."

A point well taken. Still, if being a journalist meant covering up the truth, she didn't want any part of it anymore. "Ken, think about the reasons you went into journalism in the first place. Think of the ideals you once had. Do they mean anything to you anymore?"

When he didn't answer, she said, "Look, Ken, just do what you think is right. I'll get back to you after I make some calls."

* * * *

After Gina hung up, Ken sat staring at the phone for what seemed like a very long time. As usual, he felt as if he were between a rock and a hard place. If what Gina said were true, that meant that every major news network in the metropolitan area was participating in one monstrous lie. There had to be a reason for it. There had to be some greater power orchestrating the whole thing, and that's what really scared him. He also knew there were ways of verifying Gina's story. He could call the news networks and question the reporters who had covered the speech. Maybe some of them would crack under the pressure and confess the truth. He wondered how many of them had refused to go along with the lie and had been fired. His entire future, and perhaps even the future of his country, depended on what he would do in the next few hours. The choice was very clear. He could act in his own self-interest and protect his own hide, or he could do what was right and stand up for the truth. And perhaps lose everything in the process.

"What's wrong, sweetheart?" He looked up, startled, to see his wife Estelle standing before him.

"Hmm. Nothing," he muttered. He was afraid to tell her what had happened, afraid to let her know how bad things had gotten. Even more, he was afraid of the danger they would both be in if he did what he thought he should do. He didn't really care what happened to him. But he couldn't bear the thought of anything happening to Estelle—or the boys.

She tousled his hair with the playfulness he had always found so endearing. "Do you want me to fix you a snack?" she asked. He always enjoyed a sandwich whenever he stayed up working late.

"No thanks." He looked into her loving eyes, and realized he couldn't make this kind of a decision without asking her opinion. "Sweetheart," he said, "there's something we need to talk about..."

* * * *

Gina couldn't sleep that night. The last time she heard from Ken, he still hadn't made a decision. But she had spoken to over a dozen people who had witnessed the riot and the arrest of the Archbishop and were willing to back her up. It wasn't easy. The first person she spoke to was a priest, and though he had witnessed everything, he was reluctant to come forward. While he didn't say it in so many words, she got the distinct impression that he was under pressure to keep quiet. But he did give her the phone numbers of other people whom he had seen in the cathedral during Cardinal O'Donnell's speech. Some of them had been so outraged by what they had seen on the news that they even offered to come down to the newsroom themselves and give a sworn statement to the paper. "That may not be necessary," she told each of them. "But if it is, I'll be in touch."

She lay on her side, struggling to get to sleep. Suddenly, she was jarred by the sound of Matt thrashing around in bed next to her. He was moaning again in his sleep. "Matt...Matt, wake up." This was the third nightmare he'd had this week.

He sat up suddenly, and she was startled to see tears in his eyes. Instinctively, she put her arms around him. "Matt, what's wrong?"

He hastily wiped them away. "I don't know," he said, slightly disoriented. He was shaking.

"Was it a nightmare again?"

"I'm...not sure." But his eyes had a sadness that seemed to come from the depths of his soul.

"*Something's* wrong," she insisted. "Why can't you tell me?"

He lay back against the pillow, a faraway look on his face. "Do you ever feel as if...life has no meaning?"

She shrugged. "Sometimes, I guess. But everyone feels like that at some time or another. Don't they?"

"But does it have to be that way?" His voice was filled with despair. "I mean, I just don't see why it has to be that way."

She didn't know what to say. "Maybe you should try getting back to sleep," she suggested.

He looked at her earnestly. "Gina, don't you ever feel like there has to be more to life than this?"

"Than what?"

He shrugged. "I don't know, just living day to day, I guess. Just getting by. Don't you ever hope for more?"

Tears welled up in her eyes. She did long for more, but every time they came close to getting it, something snatched it away. "Sometimes," she said quietly, stroking his hair. She snuggled up next to him, and he put his arm around her.

He sighed heavily. "Sometimes I wonder if I'll ever feel secure again. I mean, I look at what's happening in this country and I wonder what kind of a future we're going to have. We've already lost so much. I thought it was bad losing the house and all our savings. But I think we may lose much more than that. And that's what scares me."

At that moment Gina realized she could never tell Matt the truth she had been hiding. Everything he had ever counted on had been lost to him forever. His future with the construction company. All his savings. The house they had bought. And now—his country. She wasn't sure if he could take another major disappointment. She could never bring herself to hurt him, not even to ease her own conscience.

His next words startled her. "Promise me you'll never leave me," he whispered.

"I won't." Tears spilled down her cheeks, and she wished she could ease her conscience and tell him the truth. But it would destroy him. So she remained silent, hoping against hope that he would never find out.

CHAPTER 21

"Do you have any idea what you've done?"

Damien's voice, usually icily polite, seemed to cut through the walls of his glass-enclosed office.

"Yes, I know what I've done," said Ken. "Something I should've done a long time ago. I've finally printed the truth!"

The publisher of *Island News* looked at Ken with contempt. "Are you *insane*? Who cares about the truth when the future of this paper is at stake?"

Gina looked at him coldly. She and Ken were both seated on the charcoal gray sofa opposite Damien. "We do," she said, "And the public does. Eventually, they won't put up with these lies anymore. And they'll stop buying your precious paper."

"Oh, really? And what paper will they buy instead? This is the only newspaper on Long Island."

"There are always the underground papers," she replied, thinking of Hank and Bill.

"Those papers are illegal," he huffed. "And they are saturated with lies and hatespeech."

Ken shook his head in disbelief. "And *Island News* isn't? How many lives have been destroyed by the lies you've printed, Damien? How many reputations has this paper tarnished in order to promote your anti-American, globalist agenda?"

Damien glared at him. "That's enough! How dare you insult the integrity of this paper—"

Ken cut him off. "How dare *you*, Mr. Whitaker? How dare you even mention that word when you force your entire staff to disseminate your lies— and threaten them when they have the integrity to stand up to you?"

Damien's face turned red. "You're fired! Both of you. I want your desks cleared out by 5 p.m. this afternoon." He smiled complacently. "And, don't count on a recommendation from this paper. In fact, if I were you, I wouldn't count on ever working in this field again."

Ken wore a satisfied smile. "That's fine with me, if it means I won't have to be associated with scum like you."

He looked incredulous. "Get out!" Gina laughed as Ken wiped the man's spittle from his eye.

"Let's go," said Ken, feeling strangely liberated. "I'll buy you a cup of coffee." They left the office without looking back.

* * * *

"I wonder how Damien's going to explain away my story," Gina commented as they sat in Starbuck's coffee shop, the one in the Barnes and Noble bookstore on Northern Boulevard, just east of Shelter Rock Road.

"He'll think of something. People like Damien always seem to land on their feet."

She sipped her latte. "You know, I expected you to be more—well—disconcerted about losing your job. You're taking it awfully well."

"Funny, isn't it? Losing this job was my biggest fear, and now that I've been fired, I actually feel relieved."

"Why do you think that is?"

He took a bite of the Italian breakfast bread he had ordered. "Well, I guess a burden's been lifted. I don't have that fear hanging over my head anymore. And, it's nice not to feel like a moral coward anymore."

"Don't you think you're being a little hard on yourself?"

"It's what I was, Gina. I was compromising all my principles just to keep this lousy job. I didn't realize just how cowardly I was being until I confided in Estelle about it. You know, all along, I tried to tell myself I was somehow protecting her and the boys by going along with the lies. But she convinced me that I had an obligation to print the truth. No matter what the consequences."

"How did she manage that?"

He smiled. "By telling me that part of why she fell in love with me was my commitment to the truth. Of course, I warned her that whoever's responsible for this lie might try to retaliate, possibly by harming her and our sons. But that didn't matter to her. Doing the right thing was more important to her than her own safety."

"She sounds like an unusual woman," Gina remarked.

"She is. She told me that I couldn't go on living a lie, and as long as I continued to print lies, that's what I'd be doing."

"She's right. It's a terrible thing, living a lie."

Ken noticed her haunted expression. "Hey, are you okay?"

Her smile seemed forced. "I'm fine. So, do you have any plans, now that you're out of a job?"

He shrugged. "Well, after today, I really don't expect the get another job in the newspaper business. But, I'll get by somehow." He smiled ruefully. "I'm sure the government will take care of me, if it comes down to that."

"Surely some paper would be willing to hire an editor with your principles."

He almost spit out his coffee. At least he could still laugh. "No. I've seen this happen before, Gina. It's over. I think you should face that, too," he said grimly. "Our journalistic careers ended the moment we decided to stand up for the truth."

"What a sad commentary," she reflected. "Isn't that a journalist's job: to stand up for the truth?"

He sighed, thinking of his father. "Maybe at one time. But now, journalists are taught that their job is to mold opinions and influence people, in other words, to spread propaganda. It doesn't matter what the facts are."

She looked at her watch. "Maybe we should get going if we want to hit those news studios before rush hour."

"Right," he said. They had decided to confront the producers of the networks which had shown the doctored film of the speech.

"You think it'll do any good?" she asked him.

"Well, I don't think we'll get them to come clean, if that's what you mean. But at the very least, it'll show them that there are people who won't sit still for that kind of thing."

* * * *

As it turned out, Ken was right. Most of the producers acted as if they thought that Ken and Gina were crazy.

"I can produce at least ten eyewitnesses who will sign affidavits swearing that what they saw on your news program isn't what happened at that riot," Gina insisted. But no one was willing to admit that the film had been morphed.

There was one producer who didn't laugh at them or tell them they were crazy. But he wouldn't admit the truth, either. He simply said that they would be wise not to ask questions or pursue the matter any further.

"Why?" asked Gina.

He then said something that sounded very familiar to Ken. "'Some of the biggest men in the United States, in the field of commerce and manufacturing, are afraid of somebody, are afraid of something. They know that there is a power somewhere so organized, so subtle, so interlocked, so complete, so pervasive that they had better not speak above their breath when they speak in condemnation of it.'" He would say nothing further.

Gina appeared startled by the revelation, but Ken wasn't. Driving back to Long Island, he told her that someone else had said those exact words nearly a hundred years ago.

"Who?" she asked.

"President Woodrow Wilson."

* * * *

John sat at the kitchen table drinking his morning coffee, the newspaper spread out in front of him. The events of the past several weeks had him very concerned. Just last night he and Beth had watched the news coverage of the latest riots in New York City and L.A., which were said to have been incited by the Archbishop's speech. Watching the broadcast, John felt increasingly depressed; the riots were being used as an excuse to attack Christians and discredit everyone opposed to the idea of a global religion.

"Once again, UN police forces are mobilizing to suppress this latest threat to peace. Fueled by religious hate, crazed fundamentalists who took the Cardinal's words to heart have torched churches and synagogues which have endorsed the united religion movement, and have burned crosses on private residences of individuals who have given public support to the Pope's proposal. Most of the perpetrators belong to extremist religious cults that are possessed of a rabid intolerance..."

John had turned off the TV in disgust. As usual, the media was telling only one side of the story. Very conveniently, they neglected to mention what was being reported by Christian news organizations on the Internet: evangelical and conservative churches were being raided by agents of the UN's Task Force on Religious Hate, and pastors who condemned the united religion were being thrown in jail. After what Matt had told him about the government's probable role in the Grandview shooting, John wondered if the rioters might actually be *agents provocateur* employed by the UN. Anything was possible in such times as these.

He turned the page, and his eyes fell on something near the bottom. "Colorado Springs, CO— Another important step in the disarming of private citizens took place in a city in Colorado yesterday. Colorado Springs, home to the Air Force Academy and NORAD (North American Air Defense

Command)—both of which are now under UN command—is known for its right-wing populace and fundamentalist churches, many of which have expressed fierce opposition to the united religion movement. Just days ago, the new Sonic-Infrared (SON-IR) technology, developed by the British in Northern Ireland to detect IRA terrorists, revealed that numerous residents of the city were in violation of the new law requiring that all firearms be registered with the United Nations. Fearing an outbreak of terrorism, the United Nations Arms Control and Disarmament Agency (UNACDA) has initiated a peacekeeping mission to disarm the criminal element which has refused to turn in these unregistered firearms."

The story went on to describe several violent confrontations between UN troops and residents who refused to turn in their weapons, including the shooting death of a radio talk show host who had illegally broadcast the events on short-wave radio, which had recently been banned. According to the report, the man had been well-known for his "extremist religious views" and "paranoid ravings about the end-times and the Mark of the Beast."

John continued reading, and his eyes widened in disbelief. The sale, transfer, manufacture, or possession of an unregistered firearm was now punishable by life in prison. "This is insane!" he exclaimed.

"What's insane?" He looked up to see Beth puttering around at the kitchen counter; he had been so engrossed in the story he hadn't even heard her come in.

He pointed to the article, and she skimmed through it. Instead of getting upset at what John considered to be blatant tyranny, Beth condemned the Colorado Springs residents who were being victimized by the government. John couldn't believe it. "UN troops are breaking into people's homes and raiding evangelical churches. Innocent people have gotten killed! How can you condone something like that?"

"But John, those people were breaking the law! And I still don't understand how anyone who calls himself a Christian would want to own a gun."

His voice was low. "In case you've forgotten, *I* own a gun. Remember the .22 that Dad got me? I still have it. And it isn't registered. At least, not with the UN."

She looked like she was going to be sick. "So that means...?"

"Exactly," he said grimly. "I still haven't decided what to do about it."

"You've got no choice! You have to register it!" She sounded almost hysterical.

"I'm not sure that would be wise, Beth."

"How can you say that?" She was shaking, and he got up to put his arms around her. But she pushed him away.

"Beth, you've got to get a hold of herself." He was actually starting to feel annoyed at her. "Once people start registering their firearms with the United Nations, the UN will be able to confiscate them. Now, the only chance we have of stopping this monstrous one-world government and restoring righteous government is for people like us to hold onto our firearms. Don't you see? If we turn them in, we'll never be able to get our freedom back. We'll be at the mercy of the UN for the rest of our lives—and so will our children. Is that what you want?"

"I want to be obedient to God. And I don't see how we can do that by breaking the law."

"Really? Did you know that Benjamin Franklin said, 'Disobedience to tyrants is obedience to God.'"

"Well, Benjamin Franklin doesn't carry the same authority of Scripture, as far as I'm concerned. And I find it very disturbing that you'd put more stock in what our Founding Fathers have said than in God's Word."

"Okay—where in the Bible does God forbid His people from defending themselves against godless tyrants who are murdering innocent people?"

"Romans 13 says we should submit to authority."

"Does it say we should submit to ungodly authority? I don't know about you, Beth, but I can't believe that tyrants represent legitimate authority. Ephesians says our battle is against the powers and the authorities of this dark world and the heavenly realms. If that's the case, then I don't think we're expected to submit to rulers who are enemies of God."

She threw her hands up in frustration. "John, that passage is talking about spiritual warfare. You're taking it out of context."

He thought of something else. "Shortly before His crucifixion, Jesus told His followers to buy swords. I never understood why. Now, I'm wondering if it was for self-defense. And Nehemiah commanded the Israelites to have armed guards posted during the rebuilding of the Temple."

She folded her arms and scowled. "So?"

"Those are just two instances in Scripture where God authorized His people to carry weapons. He must have expected them to use them. Besides, we both know that throughout the Old Testament, God commanded His people to defend themselves against their enemies—with lethal force, if need be. Remember when Lot was kidnapped? Abraham used armed force to rescue him." He looked at her earnestly. "Do you really believe God would condemn us for doing the very things He commanded the Israelites to do?"

She shook her head, incredulous. "I can't even believe we're having this conversation!"

"Do you think this is easy for me, Beth? I hate violence. I've always been a pacifist. But things are different now. I'm not sure pacifism is an option during times like these. The Bible says there's a time for peace and a time for war. Now, maybe—"

"I can't listen to this anymore!" She ran past him out of the kitchen, and he followed her.

"Beth, we have to talk about this. We can't make this problem go away by ignoring it—we've done that for far too long already."

"What do you mean?"

"It's like I said before—we both sat by doing nothing while our government went to hell. And now we're reaping the consequences of our failure to act peacefully while we had the chance."

She looked at him pleadingly. "Maybe it's not too late. Maybe if we write letters—"

He sighed. "I've done that already. I showed you the letters I wrote to our representatives in the World Parliament after what Gina found out. Do you want to know what they said?"

She nodded grudgingly.

He walked over to the desk in the corner of the living room and rummaged around in one of the drawers. When he found the letter he began to read it aloud.

"*'Dear Mr. Lanyon:*

We understand your concern over alleged abuses of authority by UN peacekeeping forces, as reported on the Internet by dubious, unverified sources from the extreme right-wing. While such reports are highly exaggerated, please be assured that whatever military actions UN troops took against the terrorists who have refused to recognize world law were for the protection of the public good. Indeed, citizens who obey the law have nothing to fear from the United Nations or its agents. Unfortunately, threats to public order often require drastic and swift action. In this light, the anti-terrorist tactics which you condemned in your letter are regrettable, but often necessary, in dealing with extremist groups who pose a serious threat to public safety, welfare, and morals.'"

He put the letter aside. "So, no-knock searches and shooting people to death in the middle of the night are 'regrettable but necessary.' This is the kind of government we're living under now, Beth."

"But John, he was talking about extremist groups—"

"He was talking about people like us!" He couldn't believe she didn't see that. "Matt told me that Christian pastors and some Sunday school teachers were arrested by UN peacekeeping troops, probably for speaking out against unrighteous government. Don't you see? In the eyes of our current government, people like us—Christians who believe in God's Word—are extremists unworthy of life or liberty. Do you think the government will simply leave us alone if I turn in my rifle? That's just what they want us to do, Beth—they want us unarmed and helpless when they come to break down our door in the middle of the night."

"That's not going to happen!"

"How do you know? We have to be prepared—"

"Whatever happened to turning the other cheek?"

He should have expected her to bring this up. It was a question he had been agonizing over, too. For years he had taken Christ's exhortation that His followers love their enemies to mean that violent self-defense was simply not an option for Christians. Now, he wasn't sure that was the case. "That verse has to do with revenge, Beth. I'm not sure that's the same thing as self-defense. Do you honestly think Christ meant that Christians should passively submit to every kind of brutality and never defend themselves or their loved ones?"

"It's what Jesus did. He submitted like a lamb being led to the slaughter. What about the early Christians, who submitted to torture and death for the Kingdom of God? What about all the Christians in communist countries who don't fight back against the most horrible brutality and oppression?"

He had to admit, she had a point. He was more than willing to die for his faith, if it came down to that. He knew that many of the Old Testament saints had been willing to die for their faith, even though God often had commanded them to fight their enemies. Daniel had been willing to die in the lion's den; he hadn't used force against the government leaders who were threatening to kill him. Suddenly John wasn't sure what course God wanted him to take; he only knew he wanted to do God's will, whether through pacifism or armed force. "You're right, Beth. Jesus *was* a pacifist when He died for our sins. But He used violence to run the money-changers out of the Temple. Remember? According to the Book of Revelation, He'll use violence again when He returns to destroy His enemies and establish His Kingdom. It's interesting. Most Christians do see Jesus as a pacifist. They tend to overlook those passages in the Bible where He's pictured as a warrior."

"But that still doesn't mean Christians can use violence."

"Hmm. Maybe it depends on the circumstances. We know that God's plan for our salvation required Jesus to be a pacifist, to submit to the most horrible of all deaths. Jesus submitted to a violent death because it was God's will to save us. But in different circumstances, Jesus used violence against the money-changers in the Temple. In both instances, He was doing the will of God."

She looked puzzled. "So what's your point?"

"It's simple. If we choose pacifism, God will bless us through it. But I'm starting to believe there are times when it's okay to use justifiable force for a godly cause. Look at World War II. If America hadn't intervened with force against Germany, how many more Jews would have died in the Holocaust?"

"But if your primary goal is to win souls for Christ, isn't pacifism a better witness?"

He thought about this. "Well, look at our Founding Fathers. They weren't pacifists when they broke away from England. They were warriors fighting for freedom. Because of their war against England, America came into existence, sending missionaries all over the globe to win millions of souls for Christ. There's no other country in the world that has sent so many missionaries overseas."

"And you're saying that justifies taking up arms against the government?"

"That's not what I'm saying. If you'd just think about this logically—"

"I don't want to think about it, John. I don't even want to talk about it!" She ran into the bedroom and slammed the door.

He opened the door and sat next to her on the bed. She looked up at him, her eyes brimming with tears. He reached for her hand, but she pulled it away. "Beth, don't let this come between us," he said gently.

"You're the one who's letting this come between us," she said through a choked sob. "Do you have any idea of the danger you're putting us in by holding onto an unregistered firearm?"

"And do you think turning it in will make us any safer? What if someone breaks into the apartment and tries to kill us?"

"We'll call the police. It's their job to protect us."

"Beth, the police can't be everywhere. They usually don't come until after a crime has been committed, when it's too late. That's why we have to be responsible enough to protect ourselves."

She looked at him as if he were a stranger. "What's happened to you, John? You never used to talk like this."

"Maybe I'm finally waking up."

* * * *

"All of the things that we see happening in the world are part of God's plan. So, we shouldn't get all shook up; we must remember that God is in control." Perry's voice, soothing and reassuring, broke in on the discussion John was having with Carl and some of the others about the government's latest crack-down on religious groups which had voiced opposition to the united religion movement.

John sighed. If only it really were that simple. "I know that, Perry. But you make it sound so easy. Like all we have to do is sit back and let God's plan take its course. But what about all the people who are being abused, and even murdered, by the government? Like those people out West, who were rounded up and sent to detention centers. Remember what Matt's wife found out? The government is experimenting on them, Perry. That's downright *evil*. Shouldn't we be actively opposing such things?"

Perry spoke mildly. "John, we have no proof that any of that happened. After all, none of the newspapers have corroborated your sister-in-law's story—which is rather far-fetched, to say the least."

Matt broke in suddenly. "Are you calling my wife a liar?"

Perry looked embarrassed. "Matt, I certainly didn't mean to imply that. But perhaps she received misleading information. From what I've heard, these kinds of stories are usually circulated by paranoid extremists who have an almost fanatical distrust of the government."

Matt rolled his eyes up. "So, you're saying that anybody who doesn't trust the government is paranoid?"

"No, but I don't think excessive distrust is healthy. Now, it's very easy for us to go around criticizing the government. But sometimes we forget that we have a responsibility to the government."

At this point, everyone present was listening to the exchange between Matt and Perry.

Matt's eyes blazed with anger. "Don't tell me what my responsibility to the government is. I've seen the government at work. You're forgetting that two of my neighbors were murdered by government agents!"

Perry looked at Matt with pity. "I'm sorry that happened, Matt," he said quietly.

Matt shook his head in disbelief. "Is that all you can say? You're sorry?"

"What else *can* I say?"

Matt threw his hands up. "Doesn't it bother you that the government is murdering innocent people?"

Perry spoke in his most diplomatic tone. "It may be that you don't have all the facts. Now, if your neighbors violated the law——"

Matt inhaled deeply as he struggled to remain calm. "Ben and Elsie were in their seventies or eighties, Perry. They were two of nicest people I've ever known. There's no way I'll ever believe that they did anything that justified what the government did to them. I even saw one of the scumbags ripping off Elsie's jewelry, right after they killed her!"

Mitch, who had been listening closely, looked shocked. "That's outrageous!"

Helen shuddered. "It's just...awful." Carl put his arm around her, and John noticed that for the first time he was at a loss for words. Maybe the truth was finally sinking in.

Perry looked around uneasily at the frightened faces in the room. "I'm not sure this is the time or place to discuss this," he said quietly.

"Why not?" asked John. "Are you saying you don't want people to know the truth?"

Beth spoke in a firm voice. "John, I'm sure that's not the case."

Matt said, "I wish everyone knew about what monsters we have in government. Heck, I'd like to shout it from the rooftops!"

"Matt, that's not the answer," said Perry. "Anti-government sentiment can only lead to extremism...and violence."

"Look, I'm not advocating violence. But when you're dealing with evil monsters, sometimes you have to be a little extreme. After all, our Founding Fathers would probably be considered extremists by today's standards."

"I wouldn't hold them up as paragons of virtue," Perry said dryly.

"Well, what about Jesus and the Apostles?" asked Matt. "They were considered extremists in their day, weren't they?"

"That's different," Perry said. "They were advancing the Kingdom of God."

Mitch frowned, his brow furrowed. "But shouldn't we oppose evil in all its forms? Even if it means being labeled as extremists?"

Carl suddenly chimed in. "I think extremism is dangerous. Now, maybe the government has overstepped its bounds, but that doesn't mean we need to go crazy—"

Frustrated, John sighed. "Look, all Matt wants is for people to know the truth about some of the evil things the government's been doing. And I don't understand why some of you have such a problem with that. After all, wasn't it Jesus who said the truth shall set us free?"

Perry looked at John with disapproval. "Yes, but we need to be careful about taking God's Word out of context. And as far as the truth is concerned, I think we need to realize that we don't always have all the facts. Besides, even if we have legitimate reasons to find fault with the government, we shouldn't give in to feelings of anger and suspicion. That only breeds terrorism and anarchy."

Matt bristled. "You calling me a terrorist? I'll tell you who the terrorists are—they're the ones who are in charge of the government. The ones who murdered my neighbors!"

"Maybe we shouldn't talk about this anymore," John said quietly. He didn't want Matt to lose his temper.

But Matt wouldn't back down. "No, I think we should talk about it. This is something that's gonna affect all of us—and it's something all Christians should be concerned about. You guys call yourselves Christians, but what does that mean? Does it mean we should look the other way when innocent people are being murdered? I mean, we're talking about people's basic human rights here. Shouldn't they count for something?"

Perry looked at Matt intently. "Matt, I understand your concern. It's easy for us to get all fired-up about our so-called 'rights.' But nowhere in the Bible does it say we were born with any 'inalienable rights.' That notion came from men, not from God. According to the Bible, the only 'right' any of us have is to be classified as sinners in need of redemption. Anything else we may receive, whether it's life or liberty, is ours only by the grace of God, not because it's our 'right.' As I said before, in putting too much emphasis on what we think of as our 'rights,' too often we forget that we have a responsibility to the government."

This was too much. Unable to remain silent, John turned to Perry. "When are you going to wake up, Perry? When government agents break down your door and start shooting at you? Just look around. We're living in a police state! I'm not sure what Bible you were referring to when you said that we have no rights, but in my Bible God condemns murder. Period. If individuals are forbidden to commit murder, then I don't see why governments should be permitted to do so. As far as I know, God never authorized governments to kill innocent people or haul them into jail without a trial or due process of law. Now, maybe the Bible doesn't specifically mention the concept of inalienable rights, but I think it's implied in the Ten Commandments."

Perry spoke in a low voice. "John, I think you're reading something into God's Word that isn't there."

"Am I? Then maybe we should look at what God says about the proper role of government." With that, he opened his New King James Bible and read from the Book of Proverbs, which he had marked just last night. "'It is an abomination for kings to commit wickedness; for a throne is established by righteousness.' Sounds pretty clear, doesn't it? The government isn't supposed to abuse its power." If you look at Romans 13, you'll see that civil government has a mandate to render justice. That's the only reason it bears the sword: to punish the wicked and protect the innocent. Is that what our government is doing today? Not as far as I can see. Now, you say we have a responsibility to the government. Well, what about our responsibility to our children, and to future generations? When your grandchildren are living in slavery, and they come to you and ask you why you didn't do anything to prevent it, what are you going to tell them? 'I was more concerned about my responsibility to the government'?"

He broke off, startled to find that everyone was staring at him. No one at the Bible study had ever spoken out so vehemently before. He took a deep breath to calm down. "I'm sorry if I was rude. This is just something that's been building up in me for quite some time."

"I can see that." Though Perry said it good-naturedly, John could tell by his expression that Perry still just didn't understand.

Once the others had turned their attention away from John, Beth gently put her hand on his shoulder and spoke to him in a soft voice. "Are you okay, sweetheart?"

He looked into her eyes, filled with love and concern, and saw everything he so desperately longed to protect. "I'm fine," he said quietly.

At that moment Audrey called her over to talk about a new sale at Macy's.

Matt approached him, grinning. "Way to go, man!"

John smiled wryly. "What is this, a football game?"

"Look, I'm just glad to see you're willing to stand up to that idiot," Matt said once Perry was out of earshot.

"Perry's a good man." John frowned. "I think we just have a different philosophy of government. He's always seen the government as a force for goodness. I think it's hard for him to admit that it can be capable of so much evil."

"Then he's gotta ignore most of the world's history."

John shrugged. "You're right about that."

Mitch approached them suddenly. "I believe it was Santayana who said that those who fail to learn from history are condemned to repeat it." His expression was grim. "Unfortunately, I believe that may happen to a lot of people very soon. Especially God's people. There's another verse that expresses the same idea as the one you quoted in Proverbs, by the way." He opened his NIV and skimmed through it. "Here it is. 'Can a corrupt throne be allied with you—one that brings on misery by its decrees? They band together against the righteous and condemn the innocent to death.'"

Matt perked up. "That's just what's happening today!"

"You're right," John said. He noticed that Perry was signaling him, so he followed him into the kitchen.

"I think we need to talk." Perry looked grave. John sat down in one of the walnut-colored chairs. Perry ran his fingers across the back of his head, as if groping for the right words. "John, don't misunderstand me. I am not condoning government wrongdoing, by any means. But I just hope your priorities aren't getting mixed up."

John was about to say something, but Perry held up his hand. "Please, let me finish. Obviously, your brother is terribly concerned about the way the UN has been dealing with these anti-government dissidents—"

He was incredulous. "Anti-government *dissidents*? That's what you call patriotic Americans who have refused to recognize an ungodly, totalitarian government?"

Perry cleared his throat. "I hardly think it's patriotic to attempt to overthrow God-ordained authority, however much we may suffer under it. God has called us to be peacemakers. As such, we may have to endure terrible evils and heartaches. But we can't take matters into our own hands. Now, don't get me wrong. By no means am I trivializing what has happened to some of those misguided folks who have run afoul of the government. They deserve our compassion and they need our prayers. I can certainly understand why you would share your brother's concerns over their plight. But, can I give you some advice?"

He shrugged. "Sure."

"Don't let this become an obsession with you, like it is with Matt."

"But don't you think Christians should be concerned about government tyranny? Think about those who are suffering at the hands of the government.

Think of all the people whose lives have been destroyed by government decree. Shouldn't their lives count for something?"

Perry spoke earnestly. "The Bible tells us not to fear those who can kill the body, rather to fear him who can destroy both body and soul in hell. Besides, if these things have been ordained by God, we shouldn't be opposing them. Scripture does seem to predict a satanic, apostate government during the end-times. But Christ will emerge victorious. And, we could be interfering with God's will if we try to oppose what He has already ordained."

John just couldn't accept such a fatalistic perspective. "Well, if it is the will of God, then nothing we do will stop it anyway. But the Bible shows us that God works through His people. Look at Moses, and Joshua, and David. Isn't it possible that Christ could delay His judgement if enough Christians get involved in restoring America to righteous government?"

"I suppose it's possible," Perry said grudgingly. "But I'm more concerned about what our priorities should be. I'm afraid that these so-called Christians who are illegally stock-piling weapons and actively opposing the civil government have put too much emphasis on politics and not enough on the Kingdom of God. Our weapons against evil, whether it's government tyranny or some other kind of evil, should be spiritual, not carnal. Remember, John, the ultimate solutions to evil aren't political, they're spiritual."

"I know that, Perry. But you seem to be saying that Christians shouldn't be involved in politics at all, that we should just stick our heads in the sand."

"That's not what I'm saying. But I think it's dangerous for Christians to get too consumed by political battles. Our main focus should be sharing the gospel, not fighting for our political rights."

"You don't think we can do both?"

Perry sighed. "I'm not sure. For instance, when your brother criticizes the government, I get the sense that he's not doing it in the Name of Jesus."

"Maybe not. But I still don't see what's wrong with being concerned about government oppression. Isn't that a legitimate concern for Christians?"

"Not if it causes you to misplace your priorities. Every battle we fight should advance the Kingdom of God."

"But can't we fight evil for its own sake, like Mitch said? Look at Nazi Germany. There were plenty of Christians who opposed the Nazis. Maybe they weren't directly advancing the Kingdom of God in the way you're talking about, but I believe they were doing God's will. They were helping their fellow man. Remember the story of the Good Samaritan? He may not have been preaching about the Kingdom, but he was doing the will of God."

"You have a point," Perry admitted. "But I just don't want to see Christians neglecting the gospel because of their concern over what they perceive as their political rights."

"I understand that," said John.

"Do you?"

"Of course I do. What makes you think I wouldn't?"

He rubbed his chin, looking a bit uncomfortable. "Beth told me about your arrest, John. She called me right after it happened. I guess she didn't know where else to turn. Obviously, she was pretty distraught."

The memory of Beth's ordeal filled John with pain and regret. "I can imagine," he said softly.

"Being arrested for sharing the Gospel is nothing to be ashamed of, John. It happened to the Apostle Paul on a number of occasions. But getting arrested simply because you're unwilling to obey legitimate authority is quite another matter."

"Is that what Beth told you?"

"She told me that you refused to answer questions posed to you by a law enforcement officer. Frankly, I'm very concerned. You've been arrested once, and I'm sure I don't have to tell you what that did to your wife. I'm afraid if you continue down this road you're on, it can only end in disaster and heartache. Is that what you want for Beth?"

He was silent for a long moment. He certainly wasn't eager to put Beth through another ordeal like that again. But could he ignore his conscience, and everything he thought was right, simply to spare Beth pain? Is that what God wanted him to do? He just wasn't sure. "Of course that's not what I want for her. I'd do anything to protect her." He sighed, completely frustrated. "I just want to do what's right. No matter what you may think, Perry—no matter how much you and I may disagree on the proper, Christian response to an ungodly, unjust government—I just want to do what's right."

Perry got up from his chair. "I hope so."

John looked up at him. "Wait a minute, Perry."

He stopped. "Yes?"

"Will you pray with me? I feel like I'm being torn in two directions. I can really use God's guidance right now."

Perry sat down, and they folded their hands and bowed their heads in prayer.

* * * *

"How was the Bible study?" Gina asked when Matt got home. He was surprised to see that she was still up.

He smiled, remembering the fireworks between John and Perry. "Interesting." He proceeded to tell her all about it.

"I've never seen John so passionate about anything before, other than the Bible. It was great! You know, maybe if other people start to feel that way, we'll have a chance to turn things around."

She didn't look convinced. "You really think so?"

"Sure. Why, don't you?"

"I'd *like* to think so. But I'm not counting on it. Besides, don't John and Beth think that this is the end of the world or something?"

Matt sat down on the sofa next to her and unlaced his work boots. He pulled them off and settled back against one of the cushions. "Yeah, they call it the 'end-times.' But there's no way to know for sure if this is really the end. The Bible says we can't know the day or the hour. We may have another hundred years for all we know." But he wondered if they really had that long. Probably not.

"Well, I hope you're right." She yawned, then looked at her watch. "I might as well go to bed."

"Yeah, it's late for you, isn't it?"

She shrugged. "It's not as if I have much of a reason to get up early."

Matt put his arm around her. "You'll find something."

"I'm not so sure."

He understood. Under the government's new job search program, the government automatically placed those who were unemployed in jobs that were supposed to be suited to each person's ability and background. But Matt had heard stories of people sitting behind a desk all day doing nothing, and college professors known for their politically incorrect views cleaning toilets. No wonder she wasn't eager to register.

"Did you go through the mail?" he asked, hoping to get her mind off things.

"Oh, I forgot. Are you coming to bed?"

"Nah, I'm feeling kind of keyed up. Guess I should've had decaf tonight."

She kissed him on the cheek. "Well, good night."

Her sad tone troubled him. "You okay?"

She forced a smile. "I'm fine. As long as I have you."

He smiled. "Don't worry. I plan to stick around."

"Good." She got up from the sofa.

"'Night, babe." He watched her disappear into the bedroom, then he reached for the pile of mail on the coffee table. Same old stuff, he thought as he recognized the usual junk mail. Absently, he tore them all open with the scissors Gina used to clip coupons; he never could seem to find the stupid letter opener.

He stopped suddenly. One of the letters he had opened was addressed to Gina. But they often opened each other's mail, so he figured she wouldn't mind. He had the letter in his hand and was about to put it back in the envelope when something caught his eye. It was a sentence near the end of the letter.

He stared at it in disbelief. Suddenly, he wanted to tear it up and forget he ever saw it. But he couldn't. He had to know what the rest of the letter said.

After he had read it, he wished to God that he had never opened it. He sat there, frozen in horror, as the sickening truth slowly sunk in. Gina had cheated on him...she had slept with another man.

He put his face in his hands. "Gina...how could you do this to me?" He felt like his insides had been ripped apart. He recalled his recent struggles against temptation, and how he had remained faithful. He fought back the tears that sprang to his eyes. *What a fool!*

Reading the letter again, he burned with rage as he pictured Gina in the arms of the man who had written it. He jumped up from the couch and ran to the bedroom to tell her what a disgusting tramp she was.

He stood in front of the door, his heart pounding. He just couldn't face her. He didn't want her to know how much she had hurt him. The thought of her pity humiliated him. It was more than he could take right now.

He tore the letter into little pieces and burned them over the kitchen sink, then tossed the charred remains into the garbage pail. Then he put on his denim jacket and walked out into the cold, dark night.

CHAPTER 22

Matt took a deep breath before opening the door to the apartment. For the last two nights he had slept on a friend's couch, unable to face Gina. He needed some time to cool off.

Gina threw her arms around Matt the minute he walked in the door. He stiffened, trying to resist the urge to push her away.

"Where were you?" she asked as he tossed his jacket onto a chair. "I was worried sick!"

He reached into the refrigerator for a Killian's. "Lighten up," he muttered, hoping his voice didn't give him away. If he let her know how much she had hurt him, she'd just pity him. He couldn't take that right now.

"Matt, what's wrong? Why did you take off like that in the middle of the night? And where were you the last two days? I called your job, and they said you were out sick."

He almost slammed the bottle of Killian's onto the kitchen table. "Look, I just needed to get away from things for awhile," he said as he sat down.

"What things?" she persisted, her voice filled with concern.

"You know how I get when I'm in one of my moods. Sometimes I just have to take off ."

He expected her to yell at him, to tell him how inconsiderate he was. But she simply looked sad. "I'm sorry you felt that way," she said softly. "I wish I could have been there for you."

She leaned over and kissed him gently on the cheek. He took a swig of beer. Suddenly he wished with all his heart that he had never seen that blasted letter.

* * * *

Matt stared at his plate of lukewarm scrambled eggs and bacon as he told John what had happened. They were sharing a booth at Friendly's on Montauk Highway in Sayville. Nearly a week had passed since Matt had read that awful letter, and he finally had to talk to someone. Whenever he was home, he wanted to slam his fist through the wall. Or even slam Gina around. So far, he hadn't acted on his inclination. But if he didn't let it out of his system, he feared he might.

There was a long silence as John sat there with his mouth wide open. "Wow," he said after a moment or two. "I'm really sorry, Matt. I had no idea you were going to tell me anything like *that*."

"Yeah, life is just full of surprises."

John stirred some sugar into his coffee cup. "So, what are you going to do?"

Matt shrugged. "I'm not sure. At first, I wanted to get even with her. I picked up a woman at a dive bar. We got a room at the East Meadow Motor Inn." He lowered his eyes. "I couldn't go through with it. Man, I felt like such a jerk! That woman must've thought I was crazy or something."

"What stopped you?" John asked.

"At first, I wasn't sure. Then, it hit me. I still love her." He shook his head and laughed. "How's that for stupidity?"

"It's not stupid to love someone," John said softly. "You did the right thing. Revenge never solved anything."

He pushed his eggs around the plate with his fork. "That's easy for you to say."

"Are you going to tell her you know?"

"I'm not sure." For some reason, he was afraid to tell her. Maybe because it might force her to make a choice he wasn't sure he wanted her to make right now.

"You're not planning on divorcing her, are you?"

"I thought about it, believe me. I'm still not sure I can forgive her. But I don't think I want a divorce right now. I'd rather just make her miserable for awhile."

"Matt, if you want your marriage to work, you're going to have to find a way to forgive her."

"Well, what if I can't?" he snapped.

"Then you're going to be miserable for the rest of your life. Your anger's going to eat away at you and destroy any chance for happiness you and Gina still have left."

"Well, don't blame me. She's the one who was unfaithful!"

John shook his head in amazement. "Aren't you forgetting something?"

"What?"

"You haven't been completely faithful to Gina yourself, if I recall correctly."

Matt scowled. It was just like John to throw that up in his face. "That was different. We weren't married then."

"But weren't you engaged at the time?"

He shrugged. "Maybe. It's still not the same thing."

"Oh? Would Gina have felt that way, if she knew the truth?"

He remembered how desperately he had feared her learning the truth. That's why he had been forced to confide in John all those years ago. He had needed an alibi, and the only person who came to mind was John. There was no one else he felt he could trust. Mostly, he had been afraid of losing Gina. But he also didn't want to hurt her. He wondered if she had similar fears right now. "I don't know what to think anymore," he said after a moment or two.

They ate in silence for awhile. "Will there be anything else?" They both looked up suddenly as a tired-looking waitress stood in front of their table.

"No, thanks, just the bill." John reached into his wallet for his debit card. "It's on me," he told Matt.

John suggested they go for a walk, and Matt agreed. He smiled wryly as they walked along the beautifully manicured lawns of Union Cemetery in back of the restaurant. "This isn't exactly what I had in mind," he said.

John grinned. "Why? Don't you like cemeteries?"

"Look, not everyone is as weird as you. When you suggested going for a walk, I thought of a park or something. Not *this* place."

"Don't tell me you're *afraid* of cemeteries?"

"Come on. Don't you find them just a little bit creepy?"

"Not at all. In fact, I find them quite peaceful."

Matt looked around. Maybe John had a point. The golden haze of the early morning sun spilled across the lush green lawn, and the trees were covered with bright yellow blossoms. Just a few short weeks ago they were completely bare. Now they were beginning to grow leaves. Spring was finally here after a long, harsh winter.

"'Nature's first green is gold,'" John said suddenly.

The words sounded vaguely familiar. "What was that?"

"It's from a poem by Robert Frost. The scenery here brought it to mind."

"I think I read that in high school," Matt said. "What's it about?"

"Oh, you know...the beauty of nature, and how quickly it fades." His eyes had a faraway, dreamy expression. "It makes me think of life, how fleeting it is. We're here for such a short time, really." He almost seemed to be talking to himself.

"That's a depressing thought," Matt commented as they continued walking.

"Why?"

"Well, I don't know about you, but I'm not exactly in any hurry to die."
John smiled. "*I'm* not afraid to die."

"Not even just a little?"

He shook his head. "The only thing that would worry me is how Beth
would take it. Believe it or not, in a way I'm actually looking forward to it."

Matt looked at him as if he were crazy. "How can you be looking forward
to it?"

He smiled softly. "Because I know I'm going to be with Jesus."

Matt didn't say anything, and they walked on in silence. Cemeteries gave
him the creeps. They were filled with the aura of death. He remembered
walking through a cemetery on a dare once, it might've been on Halloween.
He had pictured the wrought-iron gates as the entrance to hell, and the gnarled
trees had looked like evil spirits. Definitely not his favorite place to be.

"*There* it is," John said, startling Matt out of his reverie. He was pointing
to a tombstone.

Matt looked at the writing engraved on it. He couldn't see anything special
about it at first; it belonged to a husband and wife, apparently. Then, he
noticed the epitaph inscribed beneath their names: "*Until the day breaks,
and the shadows pass away.*"

"That's my favorite gravestone," John said.

"Yeah? How come?"

"I love the epitaph." He spoke softly. "I think it's from the Bible." There
was a pause. "Isn't it beautiful?"

"It is kind of pretty," Matt admitted.

"Yeah. It reminds me of eternity."

"Is that all you ever think about?" Matt asked, trying to lighten the mood.

"It's comforting to think about eternity at times like these. Whenever I
start getting depressed about life or the evil in the world, I remind myself
that this life is temporary."

"And that helps?"

"It sure does. Think about it. What if this life were all there is?" John
threw his hands in the air. "What if there was nothing after this? Wouldn't
that be depressing?"

Matt shrugged. "I suppose. But isn't the thought of dying depressing?
The thought of leaving this world and everything you love?" With a stab of
regret, Matt realized suddenly that there was little in this life that he loved
anymore.

"Not to me. I see a world that's getting more twisted and evil, even though people are attempting to make it better through manmade solutions. Look at all the technology we have now, and how we're abusing it. Like everything we know about genetics. Are we using that knowledge to save lives and cure diseases? No, we're using it to *create* diseases and plagues. To wipe out whole populations." He shuddered. "Germ warfare. What's next?"

"But doesn't all that depress you?"

"It saddens me. But I try to put it in perspective."

"How?"

"By looking at it from God's perspective. Nothing earthly can last forever. Not even the greatest country in the world. I try to remind myself that what really matters, ultimately, is being with God for eternity."

"Well, I'd like to enjoy life on *this* side of eternity. But obviously, that's not what God wants."

John spoke softly. "You know something, Matt? God wants more for you than you can ever imagine. He has a wonderful plan for your life, but you just keep getting in the way. Do you have any idea how much He loves you?"

Matt threw back his head and laughed. "That's a good one! If God loves me, He sure has a funny way of showing it. First, He takes the construction company, my house, and my life's savings. Then, He lets the whole country go to hell and doesn't do a thing to stop it. Just when things are finally on track with Gina, *Whamm!* He takes that away." He was fighting back tears. "Yeah, God must be having a good laugh screwing me over! You know what galls me the most? I was actually trying to be a decent person for a change! I was reading the Bible, going to a Bible study, and trying to make my marriage work. And how does God reward me? With a kick in the teeth!"

"Matt, I understand how you feel. You've lost a lot of things you were counting on. But think of what Jesus suffered for *you*. He was betrayed, spat at, beaten to a bloody pulp and crucified to save your soul...because He loves you."

There was a long silence as Matt gazed upon the rows of tombstones that stretched before them. "What if it's all a lie, John? What if it's a fairytale made up by a few crazy fishermen?"

John looked him squarely in the eyes. "Would *you* give your life for a lie? The apostles laid down their lives rather than forsake their faith in the Resurrection of Jesus."

Matt dug his hands into his pockets. "What if they were mistaken?"

"There's no way they could have been mistaken, Matt. The Bible says that Jesus appeared to five hundred people at once after He had been raised from the dead."

"Yeah, but they already believed in Him. What does that prove?"

"According to the Bible, Jesus also appeared to people who doubted Him, including His own brother James. Both Roman and Jewish historical sources confirm that His tomb was empty. Positive evidence from a hostile source is considered the strongest kind of evidence. Besides, even if it *is* a lie, what have I really lost? My relationship with Christ has given tremendous meaning to my life. If the Resurrection is a lie, I haven't really lost anything. But if it's true, think of what I've *gained*!"

"You make it sound so easy," Matt said. "There's just too much I have to deal with right now."

"The Bible says the day of salvation is now."

"Maybe I'm just not ready. Not with everything I have to deal with."

"You mean you're not ready to start living for someone other than yourself. That's it, isn't it?"

He didn't feel like arguing anymore. "Maybe. But in any case, it's a decision I'll have to make for myself, isn't it?"

CHAPTER 23

Gina stared at the slice of leftover pizza she had just reheated in the toaster oven. She didn't seem to have any appetite. All afternoon she had poured through the classifieds, depressed at having to settle for a clerical job after being blacklisted. If only there were some way she could get back into journalism without having to compromise her principles. But that was impossible.

The doorbell rang suddenly. She was startled to see Bill Rodriguez standing there.

"I hope this isn't a bad time," he said as she hung his coat up in the closet. He was brushing snow off his hair. "I would've called, but I don't trust the phones these days."

"I know the feeling," she said. "So, I take it it's still snowing?"

He rolled his eyes. "Yeah, can you believe it? It's supposed to be springtime, for crying out loud. This morning it was thirty-two degrees!"

"I know. This weather's crazy. Can I get you some coffee, or maybe some hot chocolate?"

"Hot chocolate sounds great," he said as she led him into the kitchen.

"I'm so surprised to see you," she told him as they sat down. "How is Hank doing?"

Bill's face clouded. "Not so good."

"Why? What happened?"

"Well, it's kind of a long story. You remember that shooting at the Grandview Hotel?"

"Actually, I was there. I was covering the banquet for *Island News*."

"Oh, right. Hank told me." He shook his head. "Wow! How'd you manage to get out alive?"

"Either I was very lucky, or God had something to do with it. Take your pick, I still haven't made up my mind." She suddenly remembered the information Hank had e-mailed her about the gunman whose photo she had taken. She asked Bill if Hank had mentioned anything about it.

He nodded. "He mentioned it, all right. But that's just the tip of the iceberg. Hank was very suspicious about that whole shooting. The timing was just too convenient, if you get my drift. And he's not the only one who felt that way. Someone he knew from the FBI also got suspicious, and the two of them decided to do a little investigating."

"What did they find out?"

"More than they were supposed to." Bill looked grim.

She raised an eyebrow. "Oh?"

"It looks as if the government had prior knowledge about the shooting—but did nothing to stop it!"

She was fascinated. "Really? What makes you say that?"

"Well, it seems that every government official who was there left well before the shooting. That's what made Hank's friend suspicious. It was as if they had been warned or something. Of course, none of the major news networks seemed to pick up on that little fact."

Gina couldn't contain her excitement. She told Bill about the congressman who had been warned to leave the hotel early that night and wound up dead when he asked too many questions.

Bill rubbed his chin thoughtfully. He didn't look all that surprised. "Hmm. It seems this shooting is leaving more and more bodies in its wake."

"What do you mean?"

"You know the gunman in your cover story? The guy showed up dead within weeks of the shooting!"

She stared at him. "Really?"

"Yeah, but it was kept very quiet."

"I wonder why," she mused.

Bill wore the expression of a little boy who knew a secret. "Probably because he was a WorCEN operative."

"Are you sure? I mean, Hank said he worked for the NSA—"

"Remember Hank's contact in the CIA? Well, he confirmed that the gunman was transferred to WorCEN shortly before the shooting. In fact, Hank suspects that the shooting was orchestrated by WorCEN. They're a bunch of terrorists! That gunman was probably killed because his picture was all over your front-page story. If he got caught by any bona fide federal investigators, then he could have blown the whole thing."

"Well, if all this is true, then the government's going to do everything it can to keep the truth from coming out."

Bill looked rueful. "Tell me about it. That's why Hank's been arrested."

Her voice rose. "Arrested? Why didn't you tell me?"

"Sorry, I kind of got side-tracked." He pounded his fist on the table. "You know, it really galls me that a decent guy like Hank is rotting in prison just because he tried to find out the truth about the monsters that are running the government! But it ain't over yet. Not by a long shot."

"What do you mean? You're not considering the use of violence?"

"Believe me, Gina, there's nothing I'd like more than to take out as many government terrorists as I could. But that wouldn't solve anything. I'd just wind up in prison...or dead. Either way, I'd be useless. What we need to do is wake up the American people to what's really happening. If we can get the truth out to enough people, especially those in law enforcement and the military, we may still be able to turn things around. Actually, that's why I'm here."

"Oh?"

"Yeah, I thought you might be interested in helping us. See, I happened to notice your story in the paper recently—the one about that riot at Saint Patty's—"

She groaned. "Don't remind me. You know, I got fired over that story."

"That doesn't surprise me. You totally contradicted the entire news media in the metropolitan area." He grinned. "I'm surprised they didn't lynch you!"

She smiled. "I think my publisher wanted to. Ex-publisher, I should say."

"After I read that story, I figured you might be out of a job pretty soon. I thought maybe you'd like to write for our underground paper."

"Does it pay anything?"

He laughed. "Are you kidding? We're lucky if we don't get arrested!"

"Boy, that's a very tempting offer," she said, laughing.

He became serious then. "All we want is to get the truth out to the public. And we really could use the help of a talented journalist like you."

"Thanks. Actually, I think I'd enjoy writing for an underground paper. At least that way, I'd be able to print the truth and not worry about getting fired."

"Exactly," he said with a smile.

She frowned. "I just wish more journalists felt that way."

He nodded. "Maybe if more of them had, things would never have gotten to this point. Too many of them were willing to sell out the truth for their careers." He handed her a slip of paper. "Anyway, this is the name of your contact. He'll be stopping by sometime next week with an assignment for you and some other information about our set-up. It's kind of difficult, but we can't really meet as a group because under the new constitution, our paper is considered hatespeech. Matter of fact, I checked the Internet recently, and the paper's on WorCEN's list of terrorist publications."

"I'm not surprised."

"Yeah, now that all newspapers are totally controlled by the government, there's a whole list of topics that are totally off-limits. One of the stories we plan to pursue is that so-called 'pacification' effort in countries which haven't ratified the World Constitution."

"I'd like to know more about that myself. The news reports have been pretty vague about it."

He nodded. "Big surprise. What exactly have you heard?"

She shrugged. "Nothing very specific. Just that a number of countries have still refused to ratify the world constitution, and that supposedly makes them a threat to peace."

"Did the reports mention how this so-called 'threat' is being dealt with?"

She tried to recall the most recent report. "They said something about efforts being underway to assist these countries in making the transition to 'peaceful coexistence in our global society.' But they never explained how this would be done."

He smiled. "Gee, I wonder why? Could it be that they don't want us to know?"

"Something tells me you know more about this than I do. Well? Are you going to keep me in suspense?"

Bill's expression became serious as he explained. "According to the UN and the World Parliament, no country should be allowed to stand in the way of peace. So, the UN has decided to disarm any country that refuses to ratify the world constitution—mostly civilians, of course. Those who resist are being murdered. Of course, the UN may encounter some difficulty in a country like Israel, where practically the entire civilian population is armed. Even the teachers carry firearms to protect their students from terrorists." He sipped his hot chocolate. "Maybe the UN will think twice about going after the Israelis."

"What about the Arab countries?" Gina asked. "The UN could be in for quite a showdown considering the nuclear capacity some of them have."

"Yeah, you're right. That's why the UN is being pretty selective about which countries they're targeting. They're mainly going after the ones that are opposed to their big government, totalitarian agenda. Arab countries are hardly bastions of individual liberty."

"That's for sure." She shook her head sadly. "I think of the poor people who suffer under those repressive regimes...women being stoned to death for exposing an inch of flesh! That's part of the reason I supported the UN

Constitution. I thought it would put a stop to all that."

Bill let out a heavy sigh. "Ironically, the UN has actually financed some of those regimes, and so has our own government. Not only have we given foreign aid to state sponsors of terrorism, but we sold biological warfare agents to at least one country that we later went to war with, and those agents were used against our own troops."

She stared into her mug. "It's all so...senseless."

"It seems that way, but the people behind these acts know exactly what they're doing. They train here for years, and our own government just looks the other way. Hank told me that there are at least a thousand terrorists in this country, and they're very well connected. He also told me about FBI informants who've warned our government of multiple terrorist plots, only to be ignored. Then—bam! Something horrible happens, thousands of people are killed, and those who remain are so desperate for security that they give up more and more of their freedoms." He rolled his eyes. "I heard of an airline passenger whose pen was confiscated because it could be used as a weapon!"

"That's insane!"

"This whole country's gone insane, Gina." A look of anger crossed his face. "There's something else about these radical terrorists that most people would never guess."

She was beginning to wonder if anything would surprise her again. "Try me."

"Supposedly, they're motivated by religious fanaticism. I mean, that's what we've been led to believe, right?"

She nodded.

"That may not be the case. From what Hank told me, something other than religion has been influencing these groups."

"What's that?"

He clasped his hands behind his head and leaned back in his chair. "Can you imagine the power that a group of people would gain by infiltrating the world's fastest-growing religion and manipulating it for their own twisted purposes? Throughout history, organized religions have been co-opted and used for sinister designs. It happened during the Crusades. Think about it, Gina. What if the one-worlders found a way to gain control of Islamic governments? Think about the power they'd have. There's also the added advantage of being able to orchestrate terrorist attacks against a superpower like the U.S. without a direct confrontation."

She shook her head. "It sounds startling, but it is plausible." A brief silence fell between them. "Come to think of it, the Soviets have exerted a lot of control over some of those regimes."

Bill snapped his fingers. "Exactly! And contrary to what the mainstream media says, communism isn't dead in Russia. The so-called 'former' Soviet Union is as committed to world conquest as ever. They've just adopted a new strategy. By lulling the West into complacency, they've been able to build up their nuclear arsenal while getting foreign aid. It's something that Lenin had once suggested, in fact."

She cupped her mug in her hands. "It's actually very clever," Gina said.

Bill nodded. "There's so much going on behind the scenes of world politics that the average person would never dream of. Hank once hinted about some Anti-American coalition, comprised of former communist regimes and other countries hostile to the U.S. If we hadn't adopted the World Constitution, they probably would have gone to war against us."

Her heading was spinning. "Wow.... So, do you have any *good* news?"

His eyes brightened. "Actually, I do. Some UN soldiers are starting to see the light, and they've refused to obey their orders. American peacekeepers are deserting the UN army and have managed to get the truth to the underground. Their desertion has stymied the UN's so-called 'peacekeeping' operations in some of these countries."

"That's a good sign."

"Still, our job won't be easy, even with people coming forward with the truth. If you decide to write for our paper, you'll be taking a huge risk."

"I guess the possibility of being charged with hatecrime isn't something to take lightly."

"It's more than just that. Writing or disseminating anything critical of the UN or the World Constitution has actually been deemed terrorism, punishable by the death penalty!"

She was stunned. "*What?* Who decided that?"

He shrugged. "Who knows? It may have been the Executive Council for Global Governance, or some other agency."

"You know what I'd like to know?" she asked suddenly. "Who's really running things? The World Parliament is supposed to be the main legislative body. But if that's true, then why do we have this Executive Council and all these agencies giving so many 'directives'?"

"Because that's how government thugs control people." He shook his head. "Man, I can't believe how naive I used to be about this stuff. I supported every big government agency in existence, the EPA, HUD, OSHA, BWC. I thought they were there to protect us. Now, I realize they were out to control us. You know, Hank told me that the World Parliament doesn't have any real power, even though its members are directly elected. They're the window-dressing. I guess most people think that as long as they can still vote, they're free."

Gina was puzzled. "I don't get it. If the Parliament doesn't have any real power, then who's in charge?"

"The real power is in the hands of the Executive Council, which is unelected. Kind of like all those Washington bureaucrats governing every aspect of our lives. It's really nothing new, just on a larger scale now."

"You know, I used to think we needed a law for everything. I always supported gun control, environmental laws, quotas, you name it. But now, I'm starting to see that these types of laws just give the government more control over people."

He nodded. "Make enough laws, and you can keep the people in line through fear and selective enforcement. Think about it: at any given time, you and I could be breaking any one of hundreds, possibly thousands, of laws, and we wouldn't even know it."

"You think so?"

"Definitely. Did you know that last year alone Congress passed twenty thousand new regulations? And it's getting worse under the new constitution, especially where gun control is concerned."

"I know. I think Matt's pretty concerned about that new registration law."

"Yeah, well, it's even worse than that," he said gravely.

"What do you mean?"

He took a sip of hot chocolate before he continued. "Well, it seems that WorCEN has begun door-to-door searches for unregistered firearms and other weapons. They've been confiscating any weapons that aren't registered with the UN—and arresting the owners."

Her heart skipped a beat. Matt's carbine wasn't registered. "Are you sure about this? I haven't heard anything about it."

He made a wry face. "Why would you expect to? You think the government's going to advertise this?"

"But it hasn't been happening around here yet, at least, not as far as I can see."

"They may not be doing it in highly populated areas just yet, they don't want to start a panic. I think they're afraid if they move too fast, too many gun owners will be prepared and may try to resist. So, they're doing it piecemeal. From what I've heard, they're doing it mainly in rural areas and smaller towns. Places that are more or less isolated. Or in high-crime areas where people have come to expect that sort of thing and actually welcome it. So, I doubt they'd try something like that in a suburban apartment complex. At least, not yet. They seem to be targeting specific groups, so it may be a while before they get to the population at large. But eventually, they will. I'm sure those Nazi thugs are just looking for an excuse to ban firearms ownership outright. They could just be waiting for the right cause that will generate enough public support."

"What groups are they targeting?"

"Mostly people they see as a threat. You know, patriots, survivalists, even fundamentalist Christians."

"Why Christians?"

"Think about it, Gina. Dictators don't want subjects with divided loyalties. They want subjects whose first, and preferably only, loyalty is to the government. Based on what Father Flannery told me, Christians owe their first allegiance to God. So, they may not be as compliant as most other people. Besides, they're a convenient scapegoat. That's what every tyrant needs. There's a lot of anti-Christian sentiment right now, since many evangelicals are opposed to this 'united religion.' They're being portrayed as a threat to peace, along with gun owners and others who won't bow to the government. By the way, I think you should tell your husband what's happening. He needs to be prepared."

"What if he turns in any unregistered firearms? Will they leave us alone?"

He frowned. "I wouldn't count on it. In most cases they don't even bother to check whether or not the guns are registered, they just take whatever weapons they can find."

"This is scary," she said.

"Oh, yeah? You don't know the half of it."

"You mean there's more?"

"A lot of innocent people are being murdered during these door-to-door searches."

Her eyes grew wide. "Really? Why?"

"Well, some of them have refused to turn in their weapons, and they're being shot on sight! Of course, there are always a few who manage to get in a few shots before—"

She didn't want to hear anymore. "Look, spare me the lurid details."

"Sorry. I thought you wanted to know what was happening."

"Of course I do. It's just very upsetting." She suddenly remembered something. "You know, I think I did see something on the news recently about guns being confiscated. I heard they belonged to criminals or terrorists."

He shook his head. "Of *course* the government's going to say that, Gina. In their view, anyone who owns a gun is a criminal or a terrorist. And that's what they want everyone else to think, too. You know, one of the people killed during these searches was a woman who was six months pregnant. A bunch of WorCEN agents had machine guns aimed at her, and they told her not to move. Her kids started crying, and when she turned to comfort them, one of the bastards shot her, just like that. Of course, they didn't put *that* on the five o'clock news! Come to think of it, I did see a news story like the one you mentioned. It reported that an arsenal of weapons was confiscated by police during a sting operation out in New Jersey somewhere." He laughed and rolled his eyes.

"What's so funny?"

"They showed the 'arsenal' on film. It was nothing but two shotguns and a deer rifle!"

"You know, everyone who was promoting this constitution kept saying we wouldn't have to worry about losing any of our freedoms. I'm sorry to say that even I fell for it."

He looked sympathetic. "Well, it was something you really believed in. I mean, who doesn't want world peace? The question is, what price are we willing to pay for it?"

"Good question. By the way, how long has Hank been in jail?"

"A couple of months, I think. Would you believe he hasn't even been charged with anything? There was no arraignment, no indictment, nothing! His wife's completely distraught. She's made appeals on every level, but all she's gotten is the run-around. She's even being harassed by the government. One of their kids has been tested for drugs at school without her consent, and she's been brought in to some agency for questioning. Social workers come to the house on a weekly basis to see if her children are 'at risk.' Now she's afraid she's going to lose custody of them."

"That's just awful! Do you have any idea what's going to happen to Hank?"

"It doesn't look good. They'll probably keep him locked up indefinitely without a trial, like other political prisoners. Or, they may have him killed in prison."

"Can they get away with something like that?"

"Gina, they can do whatever the hell they want, now that we've adopted their constitution. The protections we once had under the Bill of Rights no longer apply to any of us."

She felt a chill run through her. "It's just hard to digest all this—like the concept of having political prisoners."

"Well, it's nothing new, really. Look at Father Flannery. America's had political prisoners for decades now. It's just been covered up."

"I guess that could happen to any of us. Especially if we're involved in writing for an underground newspaper."

His eyes twinkled. "Hey, you're not chickening out on me, are you?"

She smiled. "Me? A reporter who was willing to contradict the entire establishment media?"

He grinned. "Yeah, I have to admit, that took guts."

"You think so? Well, you don't know the half of it." She then told him about her little escapade on the Internet.

He looked amazed. "That was *you?*"

She nodded, and he shook his head. "I don't know whether that took guts or plain insanity, but I'm glad you'll be on our team."

She chuckled. "Thanks—I think." Her eyes were downcast. "I just wish the media hadn't called it all a hoax."

"Well, what can you expect? But don't feel bad. You may have gotten through to more people than you think. A lot of people were talking about that story...and asking questions."

"Maybe, but I'm not sure enough people believed it, especially after it was labeled an anti-government conspiracy."

He shrugged. "Look, all we can do is try. We can't get through to everyone. But if we get the truth out to enough people, maybe we can make a difference."

"I hope so," she said.

Bill looked at his watch. "I gotta go." He smiled. "Thanks for the hot chocolate."

"Don't mention it."

After he left, she turned her attention back to the classified section, but somehow her heart wasn't in it. How could she focus on such a mundane task when the whole world had gone mad? Though she certainly wanted to expose the truth, she wondered how much difference it would make. How many people would listen?

She knew from her own experience how easy it was for people to delude themselves when faced with an ugly reality. Most people were all too willing to embrace the lies of tyrants in exchange for the promise of peace and safety.

* * * *

She woke up in the middle of the night, her eyes filled with tears. They streamed down her cheeks and onto her pillow, and she had to stifle a sob that came from the depths of her soul. She didn't want to wake up Matt, who had staggered in drunk just a few hours ago. Gina had cleaned him up, undressed him, and put him to bed. It was becoming a regular routine.

At first she thought she had been dreaming of him. He was planning to leave her, and she was begging him to stay. She tried to recall the rest of the dream, and suddenly it dawned on her: she hadn't been dreaming about Matt. She had been dreaming of her high school sweetheart, reliving the night he had broken up with her.

She remembered it so clearly now. He had invited her to a Bible study, and she had gently teased him about becoming one of those "Jesus freaks" they both used to make fun of. That's when he dropped the bomb on her. He told her he had to make a choice, and he had chosen Christ.

She couldn't believe it. How could he throw away everything they had together because of some outmoded religion?

His answer had filled her with resentment. *"Jesus said that He came to divide people, Gina. Even family members. Mother against daughter, father against son. He said that anyone who loves his family more than Him isn't even worthy to follow Him. Don't you understand? I have to make a choice, and I've chosen to follow Jesus."*

She told him she would never understand.

She could still remember his answer. *"Maybe someday you will. Maybe someday, you'll find what I've found in Jesus, and you'll realize it's worth any sacrifice."*

Her heart burned with anger, not just at her boyfriend, but at the God he had chosen to follow. What kind of a God would ask people to sacrifice their loved ones, to turn their backs on those who mean the most to them? It just didn't make sense. Ever since then, she had despised Christianity and had wanted nothing to do with it.

That's why she had been so afraid when Matt began to show an interest in the Bible and Christianity. She feared he would become a religious fanatic like her former sweetheart and ultimately reject her.

But strangely enough, it bothered her that Matt had stopped going to the

Bible study. She couldn't figure out why. Earlier, she had feared and resented his newfound interest in God. Why would that change?

On some level she sensed that Matt needed to believe in something, some Higher Power, at least. Maybe that's what had kept him from falling apart during these dark times. The question was, how do you maintain that kind of faith without losing everything that matters to you? How do you find God without losing yourself?

* * * *

Gina arrived at the small, white church off Route 6 in the quaint little town of White Mills, Pennsylvania. As she pushed open the heavy oak door, the irony of her assignment struck her: no matter how hard she tried to avoid it, she always seemed to find herself inside a church! A weird thought hit her. Was God trying to tell her something? She shook her head. Probably just coincidences.

She was greeted by an elderly gentleman of slight build and white hair who led her to the rectory adjoining the church. "Your Eminence," he said with a little bow to the man who was seated in the sparsely furnished room. "There's a young lady here to see you."

The man looked up, shook his head and smiled. "Gerry, how many times do I have to tell you not to use that stale old title? When I left Rome, I left all that behind me."

The old man looked crestfallen. "Sorry, Father. But it's just not right, you worked so hard—"

The priest put up his hand in protest. "It's all right, Gerry, it was my choice to leave. Remember?"

The old man shrugged. "It's not right," he mumbled as he left the room.

Standing up, the priest smiled at Gina. "Gerry's having a hard time adjusting to my step down. I suppose it's because he knew me when I first became a cardinal, back in Philadelphia. I take it you're Gina Lanyon."

"That's right." She extended her hand in greeting. "Father Malachi, I presume?"

They shook hands. "I must admit our phone conversation certainly piqued my curiosity. But please, can I offer you something to drink? Some coffee, perhaps?"

"No, I'm fine, thanks."

They both sat down and the priest immediately got down to business.

"So, Gina, how can I help you? As I recall, you said something about an article on Vatican politics."

"Actually, there's more to it than that, but I wasn't sure I could get into it over the phone. You see, I write for one of the underground papers."

He raised his eyebrow. "Ah! That explains why you were so reticent on the phone."

"I was told you might have some insight into the death of the previous pope. Evidently there are those who suspect foul play."

"And you're wondering if I'm one of them," he surmised.

She nodded, and he was silent for a long moment. Then he said, "Let's backtrack a little, shall we? First of all, do you know anything about the circumstances surrounding the current Pope's election?"

"I heard there was a lot of controversy involved. Is it true that there was widespread opposition to his election?"

"As a matter of fact, a significant number of cardinals resigned in protest after his narrow election."

She was surprised at this, especially considering the Pope's tremendous popularity, even among Protestants and non-Christians. "But why?"

He appeared to be mulling over his answer. "Well, it's a bit complicated, if you're not up on Vatican politics. You see, the Sacred College of Cardinals has the responsibility of electing a new pope. Unfortunately, the College has become corrupt in recent years. Too many cardinals are seeking political power, rather than the will of God. Not all of them, mind you. But enough of them to have created a corrupt influence in the College of Cardinals, and even in the Vatican as a whole. When the former pope died, these more worldly minded cardinals saw an opportunity to elect the kind of pontiff they wanted, who wouldn't allow any 'old-fashioned' religious convictions to stand in the way of what *they* perceived as the natural progress of humanity toward a united, global society. One which they hope to control."

She thought about what Father Flannery had said about the ICC, but she made no comment as Father Malachi continued. "I stayed on in Rome hoping to be a positive influence in the Vatican, but I soon realized that any influence of mine and others with a genuine commitment to Christ would be undermined by the more pernicious influence of the globalists, who greatly outnumbered us. After the new Pope was elected, those of us who opposed the New World Order were reassigned to trivial posts, preventing us from having any real influence on Vatican policy. I even tried to appeal to the newly elected Pontiff directly, but it was no use; he's basically a pawn." Father Malachi shook his head, his eyes downcast. "The sad thing is, he doesn't even realize it. He's not an evil man, really. Just misguided. But that's dangerous for someone who's *supposed* to be the Vicar of Christ. The cardinals who resigned after his election feared that his humanist leanings and denial of supernatural truths would threaten the very survival of the Church. Obviously, they were right. His vision of a so-called united religion had to be conceived in the mind of Satan."

"But didn't the Pope say it came from Mary? That's why I don't understand how some Catholics are having a problem with the idea." She recalled her father's complaint that the Pope's vision of a united religion had nearly split the Catholic Church.

Father Malachi's answer puzzled her even more. "Hmm. You might be surprised to learn that not all Catholics believe the idea came from Mary, at least not the *real* Mary."

"What do you mean?"

He sighed deeply, as if troubled in spirit. "I fear a great delusion has come upon the Church, starting in the early twentieth century and accelerating in recent years with multitudes of people all over the world, including non-Catholics and even occultists and New Agers, claiming to have seen apparitions of Mary."

"You don't believe in the apparitions?"

"Oh, I believe people have been seeing someone who calls herself the Mother of Jesus. I'm just not certain that's who she really is. At least, not anymore."

"But if it's not Mary, then who is it?"

Father Malachi sighed. "That's a question I've been agonizing over lately. A few years ago, one of my parishioners showed me a book written by an occultist. It described a 'spirit guide' who calls herself 'Mother Mary' and claims to be an Ascended Master from a higher plane of existence. Evidently, many New Agers have been channeling this entity. She said she was sent to guide the spiritual evolution of mankind. Even more disturbing, she claimed that Jesus Christ was also an Ascended Master who had reached the highest level of human evolution, and that we could all be like Him if we only recognized our divine potential. This is a blatant contradiction of the Scriptures, which leads to only one conclusion: this entity who calls herself Mother Mary is an evil spirit masquerading as the Mother of our Lord to deceive multitudes into rejecting the God of the Bible."

Fascinated, she leaned forward in her chair. "But how can that be possible?"

"Saint Paul wrote that Satan disguises himself as an angel of light. What better way to deceive Christians than to masquerade as the Mother of Jesus and present to the world a 'peace plan' that merges Christianity with paganism and denies the truth of the gospel? What I find particularly disturbing is that the pictorial form in which this 'Mother Mary' is represented in occult literature is strikingly similar to the way the Virgin Mary has appeared in so-called Catholic visions and apparitions, particularly in the last few years."

She shook her head. "This sounds bizarre!"

"If you think that's bizarre, you'd be shocked at what the former pope had uncovered about the Vatican. I believe it marked him for death."

She was on the edge of her seat. "What was it?"

"He discovered that some powerful individuals in the Church Hierarchy have had ties with Satanists, and that Satan worship actually has been going on in the Vatican for years now."

Her mouth dropped open. "*What?*"

He nodded gravely. "Just before he planned to go public, the pope died of a heart attack. A journalist from a prominent Catholic newspaper was assisting him in his research. Guess what? He perished in a fire that destroyed his computer and all of his files, which contained incontrovertible evidence that Satanists had infiltrated the Vatican. They've been exerting a powerful influence on the new Pope and may very well have persuaded him to endorse this Satanic 'peace' plan."

"Do you have any evidence of this?"

He nodded slowly, and his face paled slightly.

"Why don't you go public with it?"

He rubbed his forehead. "That's something else I've been praying and agonizing over. First of all, a revelation like this could destroy the Catholic Church. But there's an even bigger reason I've held off going public. If I reveal what I know, innocent people could be murdered, including a young woman who once came to me for help." He shuddered. "She had been kidnapped and used for ritual sacrifices."

Gina sat there in stunned silence. "I can't believe it," she said when she finally found her voice. "How could something like that happen in the Catholic Church?"

"The Bible predicts a great apostasy, or falling away, in the last days. I'm sure this is part of it. You also have to remember that the Catholic Church, like all churches, is made up of fallen, sinful people. Just because someone happens to be a pope or a priest, or even a minister, doesn't mean he can't fall into temptation. In fact, I'm sure religious leaders are the very people Satan hits hardest."

Gina recalled Father Flannery's description of an age-old conspiracy to control the world, orchestrated by the Prince of Darkness, which had seemed ludicrous to her. But she couldn't deny that what Father Malachi was saying supported such a scenario, as incredible as it sounded. Matt had said something about biblical prophecies concerning the end of the world and the rise of the Antichrist. At one time she had dismissed such talk as religious superstition. Now she wasn't sure. "Tell me something, Father. Do you believe we're living in the end-times?"

He nodded. "I believe we are, Gina. Or, at least, we're very close."

"Is that what Christians mean when they talk about a Great Tribulation?" She remembered John and Beth using that phrase on more than one occasion.

"It does indeed. You see, Gina, the Bible predicts the rise of a powerful world leader known as the Beast, or the Antichrist, as he's referred to in the letters of John. Most Catholics today don't buy the concept of a literal Antichrist, but there are those of us who do. And the Satanists who have infiltrated the Vatican have dedicated themselves to paving the way for his rise to power. This completely degenerate man will have religious power as well as political and economic power. Once he assumes power, Christians will be the most endangered species on earth."

"Then why would anyone in his right mind want to be a Christian?"

"That's a good question, Gina. I guess it boils down to what Jesus said to His followers. He said that anyone who wants to keep his life will lose it, but whoever loses his life for the Lord's sake will find it. It's a paraphrase, but I think it's close."

Something stirred within her. In the past, she had resented being preached to. But somehow, this seemed different. Still, she didn't feel ready to hear a whole lot about religion right now. "That's a comforting sentiment," she said politely.

His eyes grew luminous. "It's more than a sentiment, Gina. It's the only assurance we have in a world that's plunging further and further into darkness." He looked at her intently. "What about you? Do *you* have that assurance, Gina?"

She cringed as she remembered that awful night in Wyoming. "I'm really not sure what I believe."

"Are you Catholic?"

She nodded. "But I'm not a practicing Catholic, if that's what you mean."

He smiled. "I'm not sure that matters as much as you might think. You can be a so-called 'practicing' Catholic and not know God from a hole in the wall. The same thing can be said for 'practicing' Protestants. What counts is having a relationship with the Living God. Have you found that yet, Gina?"

She decided it was time to change the subject. "What you told me about the cardinals in Rome is very startling. It's hard to believe that with all their religious training, they would become so depraved."

"Well, if you knew anything about what's being taught in the seminaries these days, it might not be all that surprising. Would you believe I have a nephew who entered the seminary a devout Catholic, only to become an atheist by the time he left?"

Gina thought about her own experience at a Catholic college. Her theology professors tended to rationalize any reference to the supernatural and the miraculous. One had claimed that the burning bush Moses saw was a natural phenomenon and that he had simply *imagined* that God was speaking to him. Another instructor made the startling statement that the entire Old Testament, including the Passover and parting of the Red Sea, was derived from pagan myths. They supposedly had some vague, spiritual significance that her teacher never seemed able to explain.

At the time, she felt relieved at not having to take the Bible literally. Now, she found the memory strangely disturbing. A couple of students had tried to argue with these professors but were ridiculed for their 'blind' faith and simplistic thinking. She told Father Malachi about the experience.

"At the time, I felt superior to the students who believed in the Bible. I thought they were naive and unsophisticated, while I was so broad-minded and tolerant." She shook her head, ashamed at her own arrogance.

He nodded sympathetically. "Ah, yes. Today everyone wants to be *open-minded.*"

"You think that's bad?"

"Not necessarily. We all should strive to be open to truths that we may not have considered before. But not so open-minded that our brains fall out!" He chuckled.

She smiled, remembering that Charlene O'Darby had said the same thing. Again, the thought occurred to her. *Was God trying to tell her something?*

Then he said something that disturbed and troubled her. "Could it be, Gina, that *you* were open-minded in that sense, so completely uncritical of humanist philosophy because it made you feel comfortable, because it's what you wanted to believe?"

At one time she would have been outraged by such a suggestion. But she had learned the danger of putting her faith in ideals which appeared comforting on the surface but were based on lies. "Maybe," she conceded. She would say no more. Evidently Father Malachi decided not to push the matter. She looked at her watch. "I guess I should get going. Thank you so much for seeing me, Father."

He smiled. "Don't mention it. Did I tell you everything you wanted to know?"

She nodded. "More than I even expected."

CHAPTER 24

"Are you sure you want to go through with this?"

Ken smiled in response to his wife's question. They had just left Penn Station and were about to hail a taxi. "We've come this far," he said. "I might as well see it through. Besides, I was invited. Remember?"

"Well, that was awhile ago, before you—"

"Before I developed a backbone. Anyway, the Press Club hasn't revoked my invitation. At least, they haven't said so. So as far as I'm concerned, I'm still welcome at their dinner."

Estelle's smile was ironic. "They'll probably throw you out by the end of the evening, if you do what you're planning tonight."

He shrugged. "I've been thrown out of much better places."

As they settled themselves in the backseat of the cab, Ken felt exhilarated. For nearly a year, he had been struggling to hold onto a job that he despised. Now, he was free. He still couldn't believe the sense of liberation that had come from standing up to Damian Whitaker. Although he and Estelle were struggling financially, he could now look at his father's portrait without feeling guilty. He smiled, thinking how proud his father would be if he knew what Ken was about to do tonight. It was risky, though. Telling the truth these days could be dangerous. He wondered if Estelle realized just how dangerous his plan could be.

"What's the matter?" she asked, sensing his anxiety.

"They could call this hatespeech," he reminded her. "Could you handle it if I had to go to prison?"

Her face clouded at that. "Ken, what can I say? Of course, I don't want you to go to prison. But even if you don't go through with this, we could both wind up in prison eventually for something else. It could happen to anyone now. The only chance we have to get our freedom back is if people like you are willing to tell the truth about those who have been selling us out, whether it's the government or the media."

"You're right, Estelle. People have to start standing up for the truth."

But as they entered the Grand Hyatt Hotel where the New York Press Club Dinner was being held, he didn't feel all that confident. Even after they got past the usher who was checking invitations. It wasn't until he and Estelle

THE SHADOWS OF BABYLON

were sitting at their table and sipping champagne that he started to relax somewhat.

He was glad to see Damien seated way up front. The last thing he needed was for Whitaker to notice him and have him thrown out right away. That would ruin everything. Fortunately, Damien appeared totally preoccupied with trying to impress the people seated at his table. "The pretentious little toad," Ken muttered to Estelle.

"Now, now," she said with a smile.

The dinner progressed rather tediously. The keynote speaker rambled on and on about the role of journalism in raising public consciousness and effecting social change, citing the adoption of the Constitution for Federation Earth as an example. "That was journalism's finest hour," she said solemnly. Ken didn't know whether to laugh or cry.

Finally, the dinner was winding down and the master of ceremonies was saying good night. It was then that Ken seized his opportunity. He walked up to the dais, asking permission to address "this fine assembly of journalists." He was amazed at his ability to keep a straight face. No one stopped him. It wasn't until he began speaking that he saw the expression of horror on Damien's face, but by then it was too late. His former boss usually didn't make a scene in public. He was too afraid of what people would think.

Ken's legs felt like jelly as he spoke into the mike. "Ladies and gentlemen of the press, I would like to share with you a discovery I have made that has profoundly changed my life. Over the years, something has been slowly dawning on me, though my mind has rejected the conclusion because of its abhorrence. But now I can no longer deceive myself or deny the fact that there is no longer any such thing as an independent press in America. You know this and I know it. Not one person among you dares to utter the truth. If you did, you know beforehand that it would never appear in print. During my entire career as a journalist and an editor, I was paid to keep the truth out of the newspaper for which I wrote. You too are paid for similar services. When I finally had the courage to do so, my career was over. If any of you would be so foolish as to print the truth in the newspaper you work for, you'd be out on the streets looking for another job."

He looked out at the audience and saw the shame etched across their faces. A few nodded in agreement. Most were looking down at the floor.

He continued. "It is the duty of the journalist to lie, to distort, to ridicule, to grovel at the feet of Mammon, to sell out his country for his daily bread. We are the mindless slaves of the rich behind the scenes. They pull the strings and we dance. Our time, our talents, our capacities are all the property of other men. We are intellectual prostitutes."

For a long moment the room was filled with stony silence. Most people averted their eyes, others coughed nervously.

Finally, someone in the audience stammered, "Is this some kind of joke?"

A middle-aged man in the front row blurted out, "This is an insult! You owe us an apology!"

"If you think I owe all of you an apology," said Ken, "then perhaps you should ask the person who originally made this speech, which I modified somewhat, to apologize. Unfortunately, that may be a little difficult, since he delivered the speech early in the twentieth century and probably isn't alive anymore."

Ken was startled by the voice that piped up. "It was at the New York Press Club Dinner. Sometime in the 1920s, I believe. Charles Swinton, if I'm not mistaken?"

Ken looked in surprise at the elderly, white-haired gentleman seated in the back. "You're right. He was chief of staff of *The New York Times*."

The crowd stirred. Damien stood up, his face red with anger. "I think you've said quite enough, Mr. Hughes. Now, get out of here before—"

"Shut up, Whitaker," the elderly man said wearily.

Ken suddenly recognized him as Edward Harrington, owner and publisher of a prominent New York City newspaper.

"Why are you telling *me* to shut up?" Damien pointed his finger at Ken. "*He's* the one who's telling lies—"

Harrington stood up. He had the lean, haggard face of one who has seen too much ugliness for much too long, and has finally had enough. "No, Mr. Whitaker. *We're* the liars—you, me, and everyone else in this room. We've all sold out to the powers that be, and you pack of jackals know darn well that it's true, but you're all too gutless to tell the truth, which is why what I've just said will never be seen in print!"

Ken couldn't believe what he was hearing. He had never expected anyone, least of all Ed Harrington, to agree with him.

"You mean to say you agree with that ridiculous speech?" Damien stammered in disbelief, forgetting his usual decorum.

"I'm saying that I've grown tired of the game we've been playing on the American people. Frankly, I find it disgusting, and I, for one, won't play it anymore." He looked at the crowd with an expression of contempt. "I don't know how you people live with yourselves." He turned and left the room.

A sickening, awkward silence ensued.

"Well," Ken said into the microphone, "I guess I've said everything I wanted to say. Have a good night." Without another word, he made his way toward the exit, where Estelle was waiting for him. Clasping hands, they walked out the door. Ken never looked back.

* * * *

Ken stared at the front page of Harrington's newspaper in disbelief. Charles Swinton's speech was printed in its entirety. A lengthy editorial on journalistic ethics followed. Elated, Ken showed it to Estelle. "Isn't this great!" he exclaimed. "Harrington's on our side. He's getting the truth out to the public!" The emotionally charged scene at the banquet had gone unreported, in spite of all the news crews he saw at the dinner. But this was even better.

"It's wonderful," Estelle said in a cautious tone.

"What's wrong?"

"I just hope they don't crucify the man."

"Gee, I hadn't thought of that. He could face a lot of harassment over this. But he can't get fired or anything, he basically owns that paper. It's been in his family for decades. Maybe I ought to call him, though, and give him my support."

"That's a good idea."

For the next few days Ken tried unsuccessfully to get through to Harrington. Eventually he learned that the man was in the hospital, but no one would tell Ken why. He decided to stop by the local newsstand and see if there was anything about Ed's hospitalization in the papers.

He felt heartsick when he read the headline. It said that Edward Harrington had gone insane and had been committed to a mental institution.

"Honey, it's not your fault," Estelle told him later that evening. He was sitting on the couch sipping a glass of whiskey. All the lights were out, and he could barely discern Estelle's shadowy figure in the doorway of the living room. "You only did what you thought was right—"

"And look what happened," he said bitterly. "A man's life has been destroyed!"

* * * *

Ken sat in Ed's room at Creedmore Psychiatric Hospital. He had to surmount a mountain of red tape, but he finally got in to see him.

What he saw shocked him. The man was sitting on a rubber mattress, wrapped in a straightjacket, his eyes wide and vacant. "What have they done to you?" Ken whispered.

It was almost too much to bear, but he had to try to get through to him. Hesitantly, he approached the man who had once been a distinguished figure in the field of journalism. "Edward, do you recognize me?" he asked earnestly. "Do you remember me from the Press Club Dinner?"

Slowly, Edward turned his face toward Ken. There wasn't even a glimmer of recognition in his eyes. His mouth hung open, and a thin line of drool ran down his chin.

"He doesn't even recognize his own family," said the rotund nurse who had escorted Ken into the room. She shook her head sadly.

Ken turned to her in anger. "What have you people done to him?"

She blinked. "Excuse me?"

His voice rose sharply. "This man was perfectly sane just two weeks ago, and now he's a blathering idiot! You want to explain that to me?"

She started to back away. "Look, these things happen—"

He laughed bitterly. "Yeah, and I was born yesterday. Have they been drugging him? Is that it? What is it, psychotropic drugs? Or maybe electroshock treatment?"

"I'm not allowed to discuss the patient's treatment with anyone," she said nervously. "Now, if you don't calm down, I'm going to have to call security."

"Don't bother. I'm not going to waste my time trying to find out the truth at a place like this." He stormed out of the room.

He decided to visit Harrington's wife. It wasn't something he was eager to do, but he felt he had to. He wanted to find out if there had been any indication that Harrington was actually insane.

She shook her head. Her large, brown eyes filled with tears. "They just came and took him," she said in a shaky voice.

"Who? Who took him?" Ken asked urgently.

"The men from the hospital. They just barged in here and took him."

"Did they say anything?"

She nodded. "They said he was mentally incompetent and for his own safety they were taking him to a mental institution. They also injected him with something." She blew her nose. "I'm sorry. It's just so hard..." Her voice trailed off.

"I know," he said softly. "I hate to make you relive this, but maybe if we can prove that your husband wasn't insane when they—"

Her voice rose shrilly. "You *saw* him, didn't you? There's no way anyone would believe he's sane now. He's practically a vegetable. He doesn't even recognize me!" She put her face in her hands and wept.

"So, he wasn't like that when he was admitted?"

"No! Of course not. He was as sane as you and I."

"Have you considered taking this to court?"

"The damage has already been done," she said wearily. "Even if I could prove he was sane when they brought him in, do you think he'll ever be normal again?"

Ken couldn't answer. "Look, we have to try something—"

"And you think I haven't? I've spoken to my attorney, and he doesn't think we have a chance. Apparently some law allows the government to institutionalize people they suspect of being mentally unbalanced. It's been happening to a lot of people lately, and no one's been able to fight it. Besides, some people in high places have signed affidavits testifying that Ed is unbalanced and poses a threat to society."

"A few affidavits from some influential people and that's it? You're trapped in an institution for the rest of your life? That's insane!"

There was a long silence as Ken struggled to think of something he could do to help, but nothing came to mind. As someone who had run afoul of the establishment, his own testimony would be worthless. "So, that's it? You're giving up?"

She put her face in her hands again. "I just don't see what I can do. The court fees could wipe us out financially, and there's no guarantee that we'd win. I just don't know what to do!" She sobbed quietly into her handkerchief.

Ken wouldn't give up. "Look, Ed was a prominent journalist. Maybe if we arouse enough public outrage—"

"It's no use," she said, sniffling. "Did you see that speech he printed in the paper, the one by Swinton?" Ken nodded, almost hating himself for his role in all this. "Ed made a lot of enemies over it. Some very powerful people in the media, and even the government, were pressuring him to print a retraction. But he refused. So, I don't think the media will have much sympathy for him."

He sighed, completely discouraged. "You may be right," he said. There didn't seem much else that he could say, so he finally left, telling Mrs. Harrington to call him if she needed anything. As he walked to his car, he cursed himself, furious at his own miserable helplessness.

CHAPTER 25

Audrey, Beth and John settled into a cozy little booth in the corner with their coffee and pastries. They had just left the Sunday evening service and had decided to stop at the coffee shop up the block from the church.

Beth picked at her muffin and sipped her coffee in silence. She really didn't feel like joining in the heated discussion that John and Audrey were embroiled in. In fact, she was beginning to wish John would just keep his mouth shut. They were discussing a recent news program promoting a UN proposal to license parents.

"Audrey, you're a mother," John was saying. "How can you support something like this?"

"Because I happen to love children," Audrey said emphatically. "As a Christian, I'm surprised you're against it. After all, it will put an end to unwed pregnancies and child abuse."

He shook his head. "Audrey, can't you see that's how they're trying to justify this? That's how the government enslaves people—by brainwashing them into thinking it's for their own good, or for the children, or some other seemingly benevolent purpose. If you ask me, this whole thing is a scheme to make sure that only the sheep who blindly obey the government will be allowed to have children."

Audrey looked mystified. "Don't you care about children, John? Don't you want what's best for them?"

"Of course I do. But forcing parents to get a license from the state won't guarantee their children's well-being or happiness. It will only make it easier for the government to stick its nose into every family's business. The UN has actually suggested that expressing the 'wrong' religious and political beliefs could disqualify some parents from getting a license. They seem particularly concerned about Christian fundamentalists, by the way."

Audrey tossed her head. "All I know is, something has to be done. We can't allow abusive, violent people to become parents. Children's lives have to count for something!" She raised her voice, and a few people turned and stared. "I've seen the consequences of child abuse, and it's not pretty. Maybe if you saw battered and bruised children on a daily basis, you'd understand why we need this law. After all, I used to work for social services, remember?"

John kept his voice even. "Look, I understand how you feel. But think about it: whoever has the power to license parents also has the power to deny licenses, or to seize children from parents who don't qualify for one. What if that happens to you? What if the government decides *you* don't qualify?"

"How can you even think that, John? You know what kind of a mother I am." She looked as if she were about to start crying.

Beth felt she had to intervene then. She knew how sensitive Audrey could be. "John didn't mean to imply that you're not a good mother, Audrey. He was just trying to make a point," she said gently.

"Well, he didn't have to insult me."

Beth could see that John was determined to get through to her. "Audrey, the UN has said on more than one occasion that parents have no right to indoctrinate their children with their religious views. What if the government doesn't like your religious beliefs? What if they refuse to issue you a license because you're a Christian—and decide to take your child away?"

Beth shuddered at the thought. Why did John keep harping on this depressing subject? She played with her muffin, wishing she were somewhere else.

"That wouldn't happen," Audrey stated flatly.

"How do you know?" John asked.

"I just don't believe it. The government would never do something like that."

John looked incredulous. "Are you kidding? Look what the government did to Matt's neighbors—gunned them down in their own living room!"

Audrey started fidgeting with her napkin. "Maybe it was an accident—"

He threw his hands up in the air. "An *accident*? An elderly couple are machine-gunned to death by a government SWAT team and you're telling me that's an accident?"

Beth looked around uncomfortably. They were certainly attracting a lot of attention. An elderly couple in the next booth were staring at them, their expressions etched with concern. Beth thought she recognized them from church.

Audrey looked flustered. "I don't know. Maybe it was a case of mistaken identity."

He rolled his eyes in frustration. "This would be comical if it weren't so sad."

"You know what I think? I think you've been listening to that hot-headed brother of yours too much," Audrey said. "With all his talk about government conspiracies, he's gotten you paranoid. Well, I don't think that's healthy. I think we have to trust the government to do what's best for us. Otherwise, there's no point in even having one."

"The government is supposed to have a very limited role in our lives, Audrey," John said. "That's what our Founding Fathers believed, and guess what? They got their ideas about government from the Bible. And as far as I can tell, God's Word never authorized the government to decide who can and can't have children. People who want their political leaders to have that much power are guilty of idolatry. They want their government to be their god. They're giving our leaders the power to decide the most basic, fundamental issues of our lives." He looked at her intently. "Can't you see that's wrong?"

There was a long pause as Audrey stared into her coffee cup. "I don't know.... When you put it that way, it does sound wrong. It's just hard to believe that the government would take away our children just because we're Christians."

Beth was surprised at her friend's naivety. "It's been happening to Christians in communist countries for about a hundred years now, Audrey. What makes you think it couldn't happen here?"

"I don't know," she said in a low voice. "Maybe I just don't want to believe it."

John said, "Audrey, we can't make reality conform to our beliefs. As Christians, we're supposed to love truth. When we deny reality, we're rejecting the truth. It may be painful sometimes, but sooner or later, we all have to face it. Remember, Jesus said that the truth would set us free."

For a few moments, Audrey didn't say anything. Then she looked at John with a tired, hopeless expression. "Can we not talk about this anymore? Can we just not talk about it anymore?"

They finished their coffee in silence.

* * * *

"You've been pretty quiet tonight," John said as he and Beth walked into the living room. Cleo was wagging her tail and looking as dopey as ever.

Beth kneeled down and patted the dog affectionately. "Hi, sweetie," she cooed. "Do you need to go out?"

"Beth, I think that can wait."

She reached for Cleo's leash. "Maybe I need to get out of the house," she said.

"You're mad at me, aren't you?"

"I'm not mad at you, John. I just wish..." She broke off with a frustrated sigh.

"What?"

She sat down at the kitchen table. "I wish you could just leave things alone sometimes. You really had Audrey upset."

That's just what he had hoped. "Good. Maybe she needs to get a little upset. Maybe that will open her eyes to what can happen when the people allow the government to overstep its bounds."

She looked at him for a few moments without saying anything. But he could tell from her knitted brow that she was deeply troubled. He sat down next to her. "Something else is bothering you. This isn't just about my argument with Audrey, is it?"

She stared down at the table. "When I hear you talk like this, it scares me. I'm terrified you're going to do something drastic." She looked up at him, fighting back tears. "I don't want to lose you, John."

He wished he could promise her that she didn't have to worry, that everything would be fine. But he knew that he couldn't. He also wished she would be stronger. He couldn't stand the thought of how she would react if something really did happen to him. He put his arm around her. "Look, I'm not planning on joining a militia or anything. But I'm convinced that all Christians have an obligation to help restore righteous government to this country. When our elected leaders become the agents of Satan, it's our duty to do everything in our power to resist them. Now, that may not mean going up against them in an armed confrontation. But it could mean speaking out against them publicly or refusing to obey their unjust, ungodly laws. If we do that, we're bound to make enemies. As Christians, don't you think that's a risk we have to take?"

"Of course, when you put it that way." She leaned back against her chair. "It's just hard to believe this can be happening. I mean, how did we ever get to the point where we have to fear our own government?"

"I'm afraid it's our fault." He sighed. "We Christians pretty much handed the system over to Satan when we stopped getting involved in politics. Now, we're reaping the consequences."

"Do you think there's any chance of turning things around?" He could tell by her expression how desperately she wanted to believe this. But he couldn't give her false hope.

"Well, nothing is ever hopeless where God is concerned. He could always do a miracle, bring revival to the land. But I think we may have passed a point of no return. Since most Americans accepted this ungodly one-world government, and the Church pretty much did nothing to oppose it, judgement may be inevitable. I think God's enemies are going to hit us with everything they have. There won't be any place to hide."

She looked alarmed. "What do you mean by that?"

He hesitated. "There's something I found in the car last week, a microprocessor under the hood. Right in the engine, actually. I've heard about them, but I never thought I'd find one in *our* car. I didn't want to tell you about it because I was afraid it would scare you."

"What's a microprocessor?"

"It's a tracking device of some sort."

Her mouth dropped open. "Are you sure?"

"Well, I wasn't at first. See, I've heard of these things, and I've seen pictures of them, but I never actually saw one. So I checked with an old buddy of mine from Suffolk Community College. He's now an engineer, got his Ph.D. at Stony Brook."

"Well, I guess he'd know. But how did it get in our car?"

He shrugged. "Your guess is as good as mine."

"Could someone have planted it?"

"I don't know. It could have been installed by the manufacturer, for all I know. I've read about these devices in *Popular Mechanics*. They were being promoted as a possible deterrent to car theft. The idea was that if someone stole your car, the thief could be tracked down. But if it can be used to track car thieves, what's to prevent the government from using it to track the owners?"

"This is really scary. To think that our every move could be traced—"

"That's nothing. I've heard that some hospitals are considering implanting biochips in newborn children, supposedly so they can be found if they run away from home or are abducted. They've been doing it with animals for years now. So, the government now has the technology to keep track of every single citizen. Which means that we're getting closer and closer to Revelation 13, and the Mark of the Beast. It may only be a matter of time before the Antichrist is revealed."

"Don't say that, John!"

"Sweetheart, I know this is upsetting. But we both know that there is a bright side to all this."

"What's that?" she asked sullenly.

He smiled. "We're that much closer to the return of Christ. Aren't you excited about that?"

"Of course I am. But I don't want to be around when the Antichrist comes to power and initiates his reign of terror."

He reached for her hand and squeezed it reassuringly. "God will take care of us. He'll protect us, Beth, even during the darkest of times. Satan can't do anything to us unless our Lord allows it."

"I know. But that doesn't make it any easier." Tears streamed down her cheeks as she gave vent to the deepest longings of her heart. "I just want a normal life, with children, and the man I love. I want to grow old with you, John. I want to see our children grow up and get married. I want to see our grandchildren, if possible. Is that too much to ask?"

In the next moment she was in his arms, and he was gently stroking her hair. "There are millions of Christians who never got to enjoy any of those things, Beth," he said in a soft voice. "But it's going to be okay. Whatever happens to us, whatever we have to suffer for the Kingdom of God, Jesus will be there with us. He'll never forsake us. And that's all that really matters, when you get down to it."

She wiped away her tears. "You're right. It's just hard to believe that all the time."

"I know."

"I'm in my thirties, John. If we want to have children, we can't wait forever. But if we do have children, we could lose them. Especially if the government starts licensing parents. I just don't think I can handle that."

"Sweetheart, we've been over this before. If we do have children, we're going to have to trust God to take care of them. Even if we can't. Even if the government does take them from us. After all, everything we have comes from God. Everything we have belongs to Him, really. We have to be willing to give it back to Him, if He ever asks us to. That includes any children we may have."

"You make it sound so easy." She sounded almost resentful.

"It's not easy, Beth. Look at Abraham. Do you think it was easy for him when God asked him to sacrifice his only son? But he was willing to do it, because he trusted God completely. He knew that God could raise Isaac from the dead. That's how *we* have to trust Him, Beth. We have to trust our Lord to do whatever is best for us and our children, even when things appear hopeless."

"I just don't know if I can do that," she admitted.

"Then maybe you should ask God to give you the grace you need to trust Him in those circumstances."

"Maybe we just shouldn't have children. I mean, Jesus did say that it will be hardest for pregnant women and nursing mothers in those days."

"That's true."

She put her face in her hands. "I just don't know what to do, John."

"Pray about it. Ask God what He wants us to do."

"Do you want us to have a baby?"

"I want whatever God wants," he told her. "If it's God's will for us to have a baby, then that's what I want."

"But how will we know?"

He thought about it. "I guess when you come to that point when you're totally at peace about it, then we'll know it's His will."

She smiled through her tears. "I think that'll take a miracle."

* * * *

Audrey looked pale and haggard when John and Beth arrived to pick her up for the Bible study. She ushered them into the living room. "I don't think I should go tonight." Beth noticed dark creases under her eyes. "Something's wrong with Kelsie."

"Is she sick?" John asked.

Audrey shrugged. "I'm really not sure."

Beth drew in her breath. A sickening sense of oppression permeated the room. The presence of evil. She knew it all too well from the sinister forces unleashed during her involvement in the occult. Her eyes darted around the room. Something was moving behind one of the chairs! She grabbed John's arm and pointed.

"What's wrong?" John asked her.

She blinked. It was gone.

"It's...nothing."

"You look like you've seen a ghost," Audrey said.

"Just my imagination playing tricks on me." She looked at Audrey. "What's wrong with Kelsie?"

"Well, it's very strange. Last night she woke us up, hysterically crying. We found her in the living room, squirming around on the floor."

John's voice rose. "On the floor?"

Audrey nodded. "She must have been sleepwalking or something. Mike and I tried to wake her up, but it was almost impossible. Her eyes were glazed over. She kept saying, 'Don't let them take me away!'" She shuddered at the recollection. "After we managed to get her to snap out of it, she said she thought that *something* was trying to get inside her head. She said they were trying to take her away from us. Mike thought maybe some monsters on TV had scared her."

Beth felt a chill run down her spine. "Has she ever done anything like this before?"

"Well, she's been having a lot of nightmares lately. But she never acted like that before. It has me very disturbed. I'm wondering if I should take her to a psychotherapist or something."

"Hmm. I'm not sure I'd advise that," said Beth. "It may even lead to more problems."

"Really?"

Beth nodded. "I had a few sessions with a therapist back in college when I was into drugs and the occult. I was an emotional wreck and thought I was going insane. But the psychologist I saw only encouraged the mindset that had messed up my life to begin with. Essentially, my problem was sin and rebellion against God. But the therapist told me that I wasn't really responsible for my immoral behavior because I was driven to do whatever I was doing by the traumas I had suffered during my childhood. Instead of telling me to repent, she told me the answers I sought were within me and all I needed was more self-esteem."

Audrey looked frustrated. "So, what should I do?"

Beth suddenly recalled the occult activities that Kelsie was being exposed to in school. She couldn't help wondering if there was a connection. Could demons be responsible for Kelsie's strange behavior? She didn't want to frighten Audrey, but she realized that was a distinct possibility. "You know, it may be that Kelsie's problems are spiritual, not mental or even emotional."

Audrey looked puzzled. "What do you mean by that?"

"You mentioned that she's been exposed to some eastern, New Age practices at school awhile back. Do you know if that's still going on?"

She shrugged. "Kelsie's been kind of tight-lipped about school lately. She used to come home all excited about what she was learning, but she hardly says anything now. I practically have to drag things out of her. She almost doesn't seem to be the same little girl that she used to be."

"Do you have daily devotions with her?" John asked.

"I used to read her Bible stories every night, but lately she gets very agitated when I try to read them. She'd rather play this mystical adventure game that she learned in school."

"What kind of game?" asked Beth.

"I read about it in Kelsie's language arts book. It's make-believe. The kids imagine they're going on a quest in a canyon filled with spirits. For awhile Kelsie kept insisting that she saw a little boy who would tell her secrets about the spirit world. I thought she was just pretending, but she seemed convinced that he was real. I've actually seen her carrying on conversations with this imaginary child." There was a long pause. "Do you really think that Kelsie's problems are related to what she's learning in school?"

Beth took a deep breath. This was worse than she had thought. It sounded like Kelsie was being taught how to summon a spirit guide. "Audrey, Kelsie is being exposed to the occult and Eastern mysticism, which inevitably leads to an altered state of consciousness. That could make her vulnerable to demonic influences."

Audrey quivered. "That sounds so extreme!"

"What sounds extreme?"

Everyone turned around as Mike entered the room. He looked as if he hadn't slept much recently. There were circles under his eyes and his complexion looked sallow.

"I thought you were taking a nap." Audrey turned to John and Beth. "Mike and I haven't been getting much sleep lately with Kelsie's nightmares and all."

Mike searched their concerned faces. "What's going on?"

"Audrey was telling us about your daughter's problems," Beth said. "We're sorry you guys are going through such a rough time with her."

He ran his hand across the back of his dark, receding hair. "I'm sure it's nothing to worry about. All kids go through night terrors."

Audrey sounded annoyed. "Mike, I think it's more serious than that. What happened last night wasn't just 'night terrors.' Her eyes were glazed over, for crying out loud!"

"If you think it's that serious, Aud, then why don't we have the school psychologist take a look at her? After all, it's free. We've got nothing to lose."

She rubbed her hands together nervously. "Maybe that's not such a good idea."

"Why not?"

"Beth seems to think that Kelsie's problems may be spiritual."

His voice rose sharply. "What's that supposed to mean?"

Beth and John looked at each other awkwardly. They knew that Mike wasn't into "all this Jesus stuff," as he usually phrased it.

Beth considered her words carefully. "Mike, I know this may sound a little strange, but it could be that Kelsie has been under the influence of certain, uh, forces that were unleashed through some school activities."

He folded his arms. "What kind of forces?"

She fumbled for an answer. "Well, it's kind of hard to explain. We're dealing with the spirit realm, and—"

Mike rolled his eyes and smirked. "So, Kelsie's being tormented by Casper the Friendly Ghost? Doesn't sound like anything to worry about."

Anger rose in her when she considered the danger that Kelsie was in. "Look, I don't know how else to say this, Mike, but it could be that demons are involved."

Mike glared at her. "Oh, really? That's what you think?"

"Look, we can't be sure at this point," John said. "But you really should take this seriously. With all those New Age practices at her school—"

Mike groaned. "Not this again." Apparently, Audrey had discussed this issue with him before. "I just don't understand you people. Anything that's the least bit different is demonic or something. I thought that kind of thinking went out with the Dark Ages!"

Audrey looked hurt. "Mike, that's not fair. John and Beth are just trying to help."

"Well, we don't need their help."

Beth knew that Kelsie's soul could be in mortal peril. "Mike, there are spiritual forces here that you can't even begin to fathom. As a teacher myself, I know that there are highly organized forces in the education establishment trying to draw innocent kids into demonism under the guise of meditation and Eastern mysticism. If you care about your daughter's eternal destiny—"

"Don't tell me what's best for my daughter!" Mike snapped. "You're the ones with the problems, always trying to shove your religious views down people's throats. You just can't deal with anything outside the realm of your primitive religious ideas."

Beth realized there was no getting through to him, at least not now. "Maybe this is something you two should work out on your own." She looked at Audrey. "We should be heading over to Perry's, hon. Are you coming?"

"I'm sorry. I just don't think I should leave Kelsie tonight."

"I think that's best." Mike looked at Beth and John apologetically. "Listen, I'm sorry if I was rude. But we've both been under a lot of stress lately."

"That's okay," said John. "We understand."

Beth squeezed Audrey's hand. "We'll pray for Kelsie," she said reassuringly.

"Thanks," said Audrey. She tried to smile, but still looked very uneasy.

* * * *

Audrey awoke from a fitful sleep, her heart pounding. She looked at her watch. Just a little after eleven. Mike's side of the bed was empty; he must be up late watching TV.

The vague sense of apprehension earlier was beginning to give way to dread. Something just didn't feel right. *Oh, I'm just worried about Kelsie.* She tried to shake off her fear.

She sat up in bed suddenly as she heard some sort of rustling. Footsteps? Maybe Kelsie wanted to come into bed with her. "Kelsie? Honey, is that you?"

No answer. *Must be the wind blowing through the trees outside.* She leaned back against the pillows, breathing deeply and wondering why her heart was still pounding. She shook her head, embarrassed. *How silly!*

Another noise. She strained to listen. *Voices!* They seemed to be coming from down the hall, where Kelsie's room was. Could someone be in her room? Maybe it was the television.

"Mike!" she called shrilly. He didn't answer.

She bolted out of bed and stepped into the hallway. A feeling of stark, cold terror grabbed hold of her. She turned on the hall light. Strangely, the hall didn't appear any brighter. Could there have been a blackout?

Plunged into an eerie darkness, Audrey made her way toward Kelsie's bedroom. She stopped suddenly, her heart thudding violently. Something had brushed against her. Whirling around, she thought she saw it moving in the corner of her eye. She couldn't make it out. An intruder?

She drew in her breath and peered into the darkness, but didn't see anything out of the ordinary. If only she had a flashlight! And where was Mike?

"Mike!" Her voice filled her with dread. "Mike, where are you?"

Still no answer. Was it possible that someone had broken into the house and knocked Mike unconscious? She had to call the police! She was about to turn around and head back to the safety of the bedroom when a sense of urgency compelled her toward Kelsie's room.

As she opened the door she froze in terror. No one was in the room with Kelsie, but Audrey could distinctly hear raspy, angry voices, in a language that didn't even sound human! She saw strange shadows hovering over the bed. Kelsie was talking in a terrified voice. "I don't want to play with you anymore! Leave me alone!"

Audrey was almost paralyzed with fright. She heard herself shouting. "Mike! Mike!" She tried to turn on the light, but it didn't seem to be working.

Mike was in the room almost immediately, his face white with fear. "What the *hell* is that?"

"Then you hear it, too?" Audrey was dismayed to learn that she was *not* hallucinating.

He nodded, at a loss for words.

"Where were you?" Audrey asked. "I called you several times."

"I was outside," he said after he had found his voice. "I thought I heard someone, or *something*, moving in the bushes, so I went to check it out." He shuddered as he looked at Kelsie, writhing and squirming on the bed. "What the hell is going on? What's wrong with her?"

Audrey ran to the side of her bed and shook her, trying to wake her up. Although she didn't open her eyes, Kelsie seemed to sense her mother's presence. "Mommy, Mommy! Don't let them take me away!"

The voices became louder and more menacing, dripping with hate.

"Who's trying to take you away?" Audrey asked.

"They're trying to get inside my head! Don't let them take me away! Don't let them get inside me!"

Unsure of what to do, Audrey began to pray. "Dear Lord, Jesus..." Suddenly she fell backwards.

Mike ran over to help her up. "What happened? Why did you fall?"

Audrey was shaking. "I didn't fall. Something pushed me!"

He looked astonished. "*What?*"

"Never mind," she said. "We've got to do something!"

"I'm calling a psychiatrist."

"Oh, so you think Kelsie's crazy? Is that what you think this is?"

He didn't answer.

"Mike, we both hear those voices, don't we?"

He nodded.

"Then obviously this can't be in Kelsie's mind, can it?"

For the first time in their marriage, he looked completely helpless. "I just want to help her! There has to be something we can do." He was fighting back tears. "I don't want to lose my little girl!"

"We're not going to lose her. Call John and Beth."

"What if we wake them up?"

"I think our daughter's more important right now!"

He looked doubtful. "But honey, what can they do?"

"Look, they said this could be a spiritual problem. It sounded like they know what they're talking about."

"But—"

"Just do it! Tell them everything that's happened."

"Maybe you should call them," he suggested.

"I'm not leaving my baby!"

Audrey prayed silently as Kelsie's agitation increased. She looked like a trapped animal, trying to break loose from some invisible bonds. Mike returned in about five minutes, his expression bewildered.

"What did they say?" asked Audrey.

"Well, they said they're coming over to help. But if you ask me, they're nuts!"

"Why do you say that?"

"They started talking about demons again. I think those two are fixated or something."

In a few minutes, John and Beth were knocking on the door.

"The whole thing sounds crazy," Mike said after they had explained what needed to be done.

Audrey had never seen such a determined expression on John's face. "Look, you have to engage in spiritual warfare," he said. "It's the only way to deliver your daughter from the forces of darkness. She's obviously under the influence of demons."

Mike shook his head. He was definitely having trouble accepting all this.

Beth grabbed Audrey's hand. "Audrey, I've been through something like this before. Even after I was saved and no longer involved in the occult, the demons still tried to harass me sometimes. But when I rebuked them in the Name of Jesus, they left. You have to do the same thing to deliver Kelsie. It's the only thing that works."

Audrey put her face in her hands. "How can this be happening?"

"It may be that a door was opened through some of the occult activities she's been exposed to at school," Beth said.

Mike rolled his eyes up. "You two have been watching too many movies."

He turned to Audrey. "*Now* can we call a psychiatrist?"

"You just don't get it, do you, Mike? You just can't accept the fact that there *is* a spirit world, even when the evidence is right in front of you. Even when that world is involved in a battle for our daughter's soul!"

"Don't be ridiculous," he said scornfully. "There's got to be a logical explanation for this."

A sound like the roar of wild animals filled the room. "Oh, really?" Audrey asked.

"You think that's the spirit world?" asked Mike. "I'll tell you what it is. It's the television."

She pointed to the TV set. "The TV isn't even on, Mike!"

He didn't say anything.

"Fine, you can believe what you want. But I won't let you stop me from helping our daughter." Audrey looked at John and Beth. "What do I say?"

"Command the demons to depart in the Name of Jesus," John said. "We can do it together, if you'd like."

She nodded. They both approached Kelsie's bed, shrouded in blackness.

In an authoritative voice, John addressed the demons. "Spirits, in the Name of Jesus, I command you to depart! I rebuke you in the Name of Jesus!"

"This is crazy," said Mike, rolling his eyes up.

The voices rose to a frenzied pitch as Kelsie waved her arms wildly. Gently but firmly, Audrey put her hands on Kelsie's shoulders. "Depart in the Name of Jesus!" she shouted.

They all stared wide-eyed as the bureau began to shake, spilling items to the floor. The lights flickered. A loud buzzing filled the room.

Mike drew back in terror as shadowy, ghostly figures floated above Kelsie's head. Audrey saw their red, glowing eyes and hideous faces in the cavelike darkness.

In the next instant, the voices stopped. The room was silent, and the ghost-like figures receded.

Kelsie opened her eyes and smiled. "They're gone, Mommy. They got scared and went away!"

Mike's eyes filled with tears as he put his arms around them both. "I love you," he told them. He looked at Audrey with an expression of awe mingled with tenderness. "I'm sorry I ever doubted your faith!"

She kissed him, and John and Beth slipped quietly out of the room.

* * * *

"We wanted to clarify some troubling things that Kelsie has been telling her teacher," Dr. Schneider, the school principal, said amiably.

Audrey shifted uncomfortably in her leather chair. "What kind of things?"

"She seems to have been taken with some rather bizarre notions." His pale, blue eyes were mystified. "She's afraid to engage in certain class activities. In fact, she's been very uncooperative. Under Achievement 2000, all students are required to meet certain outcomes in order to receive their certificate of initial mastery. One of those is the ability to cooperate with others. Students who fail to meet the mandated outcomes won't be eligible for their certificate. The consequences are quite serious, I'm afraid. Without her certificate, your daughter will not be allowed to go on to college or even apply for a job."

"But that's crazy! She's only in elementary school."

"I understand your feelings, Mrs. Richards, but we're trying to prepare our children to become productive members of our newly emerging global society. Cooperating with others is absolutely essential to meet this goal. I'm sure you can understand that."

She certainly couldn't argue with that. But she didn't like the idea that Kelsie was being forced to participate in activities that frightened her, especially after her recent trauma. "I'd like to know what activities Kelsie is so afraid of."

"Every morning the teacher engages the class in a relaxation exercise. Your daughter has refused to participate during the last few days."

"What exactly do you mean by 'relaxation exercises'?"

"It's a type of meditation."

Audrey knew she should remain calm, but it was difficult. After all, the principal was discussing the very activities that had nearly destroyed her daughter! "Before we continue, may I ask a question?"

"Certainly."

"Is prayer allowed in the public schools?"

His face registered distaste. "Of course not!"

"Then why should meditation be allowed?"

"Meditation is different—"

"It's different, all right. It can be dangerous, for one thing."

He laughed good-naturedly. "Surely you don't believe that?"

"Look, all I know is that ever since my daughter started these so-called 'relaxation exercises' she hasn't been the same person. She's convinced that spirit beings have been trying to control her. The teacher called them spirit guides, but Kelsie's terrified by them. As a Christian, I don't want my daughter engaging in any activities that could put her in spiritual danger. This whole experience has done nothing but wreak havoc in her life. The school has no right to do this to her!"

His eyes flickered with interest. "Hmm. Perhaps that explains what she's been telling her teacher. Have you suggested to your daughter that she's been in spiritual danger?"

"I didn't have to suggest it. It was obvious!"

"Can you explain why you feel this way?"

"I shouldn't have to explain my feelings. It should be enough that I won't allow her to engage in activities that are against my religious beliefs."

"But doesn't your daughter have a right to her own religious beliefs?"

She slowly shook her head. "I don't believe this," she muttered.

"Actually, what really has us disturbed is that your daughter has been suffering from some sort of delusional hysteria. She seems to be under the strange impression that demons were trying to possess her. Is that something *you* told her, Mrs. Richards?"

He was jotting something down on a pad. "What my daughter and I talk about in the privacy of our own home isn't any of your business." But she was beginning to feel wary.

He smiled benevolently. "I assure you, Mrs. Richards, that I only have Kelsie's best interests at heart. Surely you understand that?"

She heaved a deep sigh. "I'm not sure what to believe anymore."

She still felt emotionally drained from the terrifying experience just a few nights ago. As a Christian, she had always believed in the spiritual realm, but to her that realm belonged to God and His angels; she had never given much thought to Satan or his demons. In fact, she hadn't even wanted to acknowledge their existence till now. But she had learned the hard way that Satan was real, and that Christians ignored him at their own peril. Perhaps if she had been more discerning, Kelsie would not have been such easy prey.

Audrey wished she could make Dr. Schneider understand what was at stake here. She believed he was sincere in his concern for Kelsie's well-being. But she also knew that he wasn't a believer, and therefore couldn't possibly understand the ramifications of the occult activities to which Kelsie had been exposed at school.

"You seem very distraught," he observed in a kindly tone. "Perhaps you might want to consider attending some sessions with our school psychologist. A number of parents have taken advantage of this opportunity."

"Why would I want to do that?"

"It could make you a more effective parent, for one thing. It could help you cope better with the pressures of parenting."

She laughed. "Thanks for the offer, but I have my own method of therapy for that. It's called prayer."

"I'd hardly call that therapy," he said disdainfully.

"What would you call it?"

"Superstition."

This was too much. "Wait a minute. If prayer is superstition, then what about all this mumbo-jumbo about *spirit guides* and meditation that Kelsie's been learning in school? *That's* not superstition?"

He leaned back in his chair. "Perhaps to the unenlightened mind it may seem that way. But there's an essential difference between prayer and meditation. You see, Mrs. Richards, prayer is based on the primitive notion that '*God*,' or whatever transcendent being you happen to ascribe to, is somewhere '*out there*,' separate from us. But more enlightened cultures, particularly the Eastern mystics, have recognized the god within. Meditation is simply a means to come in contact with that part of ourselves which is, essentially, divine."

She folded her arms. "So, in other words, we're all gods?"

He smiled. "Exactly. Some of us are just more aware of our godhood than others."

Her sudden boldness surprised her. "Well, I hate to burst your bubble, but that's not what the Bible teaches. The Scriptures teach that there's only one God who created the heavens and the earth. He created each one of us. Someday, we're all going to be held accountable to Him. Guess what, Dr. Schneider? You're going to be held accountable for every child whose mind you've corrupted with idolatrous notions about their own divinity!"

He didn't seem offended. "That's very interesting. You seem to think that I'm corrupting young minds."

"If you're filling them with the lie that they're equal to God, then I'd say yes."

"One might say that you're corrupting your daughter's mind with paranoid notions of a condemning, wrathful God and demons that are trying to possess her." He spoke mildly. "*Some* people might call that child abuse."

She jumped up from her chair. "How *dare* you equate what I teach my daughter about God with child abuse? *How dare you?*"

"There's no reason to get so hostile," he told her in a patronizing tone.

"Remember, I only have your daughter's best interests at heart. But I must say that I'm very concerned about the type of environment you're creating at home for Kelsie. All this talk of demons and the wrath of God is bound to make any child paranoid. It could even lead to mental problems, perhaps even insanity."

She was shaking. "The only insanity is that you have the nerve to criticize the way I'm raising my daughter!" She bent down to pick up her handbag, which had fallen to the floor.

"Please, Mrs. Richards, calm down. I'd like to help you. Now, we have a wonderful parent educator on staff who would be happy to visit you at home—"

"No thank you," Audrey said emphatically. She walked past him and out the door without looking back.

By the time she got to her car, tears blurred her vision. *What am I going to do?* She fumbled in her purse for her keys. The mention of child abuse terrified her. What if he reported her to the authorities and they took Kelsie away?

"No," she said, shaking her head. That just couldn't happen. *It just couldn't!*

* * * *

"Thanks, Lord, for this food we're about to eat..."

Mike spoke somewhat awkwardly. He had never prayed out loud before, at least, not since he was a kid. He vaguely remembered having to learn to recite the Lord's Prayer during Sunday School, which seemed like a lifetime ago. But things were different now. The God he had forgotten about since childhood suddenly seemed real to him. He still didn't fully comprehend what had actually happened that night in Kelsie's room. He only knew that he had seen the power of God, and he would never again be the same. To his own surprise, he had even skimmed through some of the Bible verses Audrey was always nagging him to read. Of course, he didn't feel he was ready to become a fanatic or anything, but he did want to know a little more about this God who had delivered his daughter from the mouth of hell.

While Audrey was clearing away the breakfast dishes, the doorbell rang. "I'll get that," Mike said. He was carrying Kelsie around on his shoulders, and she was giggling and squealing with delight. Gently, he put her down, and she ran off to play.

A tall, dignified woman holding a clipboard was standing on their doorstep. Her mousey brown hair, streaked with gray, was pinned back behind her ears.

"May I help you?" Mike asked.

"Mr. Richards, I presume?" He nodded. Her smile was crooked and unnatural. "I'm Ms. Burnell. I'm a parent educator from your daughter's school."

"Parent educator? I'm not sure what you mean."

"I'm part of the school district's Home Visitor's Program. I've been assigned to conduct a family assessment to determine any factors that may have placed your child at risk."

He stared at her. "What?"

She showed him an official-looking form. "This form authorizes me to make an assessment of your daughter's home environment to determine if there are any risk factors which may inhibit her physical, emotional, or mental well-being."

"Wait a second. You can't just barge in here and stick your nose in our business—"

"Sir, if you don't cooperate, I'm going to have to put that in my report, which could adversely affect any decision that's made."

"Decision about what?"

"About whether your daughter is at risk and needs to be removed from her home environment."

He couldn't believe what he was hearing. "Get the hell out of here!"

Audrey rushed over to see what was the matter. "Mike, what's going on?"

Ms. Burnell spoke with cold efficiency. "If you don't cooperate immediately, I'm authorized to return with an officer of the court to remove the child from the home."

Audrey's face turned white. "*What*?"

Mike felt torn. He didn't want to give in to this insanity, but he also didn't want to take any chances of losing custody of Kelsie. Maybe if they cooperated now, everything would work out. "Look, I don't want any trouble, Ms...Burnell. But I would like to know why this is necessary. I think you owe us that much."

She spoke as if she were reading from a script. "According to the UN Convention on the Rights of the Child, as well as the Constitution for Federation Earth, all children have the right to an emotionally, mentally and physically healthy home environment. If a child's home environment is deemed unhealthy, it is the duty of the state to intervene and ensure that the child is raised in a suitable environment, even if that necessitates removing the child from his/her present environment."

Mike rolled his eyes; the woman sounded like a computer. "Can you say that in English, please?"

Audrey cut in suddenly. "This is about that meeting I had with Dr. Schneider last week, isn't it? He sent you here, didn't he?"

"He did make a referral to my office."

"What gives him the right to send you here uninvited?" Audrey demanded.

"All school personnel are authorized to report any suspicion that a child is at risk to the proper authorities. The standard procedure is to send a parent educator or social worker to the home to assess whether the child actually is at risk, and then to remove the child if necessary."

Audrey looked dismayed. "Remove her? You mean take her away?"

"I realize this can be very upsetting." Ms. Burnell sounded almost human for the first time. "But I assure you that your chances of retaining custody are much higher if you cooperate."

"Really?" Audrey's tone was hopeful, and Mike knew how desperately he wanted to believe this. But he wasn't sure they could trust anything Ms. Burnell said.

She smiled. "Of course."

Audrey looked at Mike. "What should we do?"

He shrugged. "It looks like we don't have much choice." He had a sick feeling in the pit of his stomach as he ushered Ms. Burnell into the living room. He and Audrey sat on the couch while the ice princess nosed around the apartment.

He had expected her to inspect the house for safety features like smoke alarms, but she seemed more interested in some of the religious plaques hanging on the wall. Her eyes fell on a wooden plaque of the Ten Commandments which Audrey had insisted on hanging above the sofa. She frowned. "A major goal mandated by the International Youth Council is to ensure that all children are raised in an environment where they are free to develop their own beliefs and values. Unfortunately, it appears that you may be denying Kelsie her fundamental right to freedom of conscience."

Audrey's voice rose an octave. "I'd never force her to believe as I do. But don't we have the right to raise our daughter according to our own religious beliefs?"

Ms. Burnell smiled reassuringly. "I'm religious myself, Ms. Richards. However, it's best for children to have a number of choices concerning religion. Don't you agree?"

The ice princess turned her attention to the Bible on the end table. Mike saw her expression of distaste. He suddenly felt nervous. "Do you punish Kelsie when she disobeys you?" Ms. Burnell asked.

"That's really none of your business," said Mike.

She jotted something down on her pad. "It's unfortunate that you don't wish to cooperate."

"Now, look here—" Mike started, but Audrey put her hand on his shoulder.

"Mike, please! Remember what she said about cooperating? It's our only chance."

"All right," he agreed with a sigh. He looked at Ms. Burnell. "What do you want to know?"

"Do you ever use corporal punishment?"

"Not very often. Audrey's always been against it." *Which is probably why Kelsie tended to have a slight rebellious streak*, he thought privately.

The woman raised an eyebrow. "But you have used it at least once?"

Mike hesitated. "Well, yeah," he admitted, a little uneasy. "I'm sure every parent must have some occasion to. You know how it is. If a kid's about to do something dangerous, you might have to get a little physical."

"Can you give me an example?"

He considered this. "Well, one time Kelsie tried to put her hand on a hot barbecue grill, and I slapped her hand to stop her. Otherwise, she would've burned herself."

"One might suggest that it wasn't very responsible to allow her to get that close to the grill in the first place," Ms. Burnell said.

He jumped up off the couch. "Where the *hell* do you get off insinuating that we're irresponsible parents?" He was ready to throw her out of the house, but then he saw her write something on her clipboard. He knew he had to control himself.

"You seem easily irritated, Mr. Richards. But I assure you that I'm only here in the best interests of your daughter. I suggest you continue to cooperate without any further outbursts. It will go much easier for you that way." He sat down, shaking his head in disgust. Ms. Burnell glanced down at her clipboard. "Do you own any firearms?"

He almost laughed at that. "No way. If I did, my wife would have made me get rid of them long ago."

"What kind of television shows does your daughter watch?"

"We try to limit her television," Audrey said. "But we do allow her to watch wholesome programs. Unfortunately, there aren't too many, but awhile ago we bought some Bible videos for her. She loves them."

Ms. Burnell wrote on her pad again. "I take it you both believe in the Bible, then?"

"I always have," said Audrey. "But Mike, well, he's never been very religious."

"Do you take the Bible literally, Mrs. Richards?"

"I guess it depends..."

"On what?"

She looked as if she were thinking it over. "Jesus said that the only way to inherit the kingdom of heaven is to be born-again. Obviously, He didn't mean that literally. He was talking about a spiritual rebirth."

"That's very interesting. Would you consider yourself...born-again?"

She nodded. "Definitely."

"And do you believe the Bible is infallible?"

"Of course. It's the Word of God."

"I see." She wrote something else on her pad.

Mike was beginning to feel very uneasy about this line of questioning. "I don't understand why all these questions are necessary. Why do you need to know about our religious beliefs? Isn't that personal?"

"A parent's religious beliefs can have a tremendous impact on a child's emotional and psychological well-being, for good or ill," said Ms. Burnell. "Children need to learn tolerance so that they can appreciate the cultural diversity of our global society. On that note, I'd like to know what beliefs your daughter has been exposed to concerning people who don't share your religious affiliation. For instance, have you ever told her that unbelievers are going to hell?"

Mike shifted uncomfortably. He hoped that Audrey wouldn't give this witch any more ammunition.

"Kelsie's still very young for that type of discussion," Audrey said uneasily.

"But that's what *you* believe, isn't it, Ms. Richards?"

She looked flustered. "I know that Jesus died to save us," she said quietly. "Anyone can be saved, as long as they believe in Him."

"And what happens to people who *don't* believe in Him? Are they condemned to hell?"

Mike saw something in the woman's eyes that almost looked like rage. It seemed incongruous with her coldly clinical demeanor. "Is that the poison you've been feeding your daughter."

Audrey jumped off the couch. "*How dare you say that?*" she stammered in disbelief.

Mike, who had never believed in the devil, suddenly felt as if they were facing one of Satan's most vicious minions. "I think you'd better leave right now," he said, trying to control himself. "And I'd like the name of your supervisor, by the way."

Ms. Burnell smiled sweetly. "I apologize. I was out of line. It won't happen again. Now, if you don't mind, I'd like to discuss an incident which your daughter said occurred just last week."

Audrey and Mike exchanged guarded looks. "Something did happen," Mike admitted. "But it was very upsetting to both of us, and if you don't mind, we'd rather not get into it right now."

"Your daughter seems to be under the impression that she was possessed by demons. Is that something *you* told her?"

Audrey glared at Ms. Burnell. "Of course not!"

"How do you know about all this?" Mike asked suddenly. "Kelsie hardly seems to remember the incident. She hasn't spoken about it since. She's been perfectly fine. Why would she tell anyone at school about it?"

"Evidently your daughter has refused to participate in certain class activities. In fact, she was so fearful of the activities in question that there was cause for concern. Her teacher referred her to the school psychologist, and after one or two sessions—"

Mike was livid. "Wait a minute. Are you saying our daughter was referred to a psychologist without our consent?"

"I can assure you, Mr. Richards, that was done in your daughter's best interests."

He got up and walked toward the phone in the kitchen. "This is insane! I'm calling my lawyer!"

Ms. Burnell was unperturbed. "You'd be wasting your time, I'm afraid. There is plenty of legal precedent that supports such intervention if it is deemed to be in the best interests of the child. And after what your daughter revealed during hypnotic regression—"

Mike almost lost it then. "Hypnotic regression? You mean to say the school had my daughter *hypnotized*?"

"Mike, calm down," Audrey said in an urgent voice.

"Calm down? We just found out that Kelsie was put under hypnosis without our consent and you're asking me to calm down?"

"Mike! We've got to cooperate if we want to keep custody of Kelsie."

He could see that Audrey was close to tears. Feeling completely helpless, he sat down on the couch again and put his face in his hands. What were they to do? It didn't look good at all. He felt like he was going to be sick. Audrey sat next to him and reached for his hand. After a moment or two, he looked up at Ms. Burnell. "What did Kelsie say while she was under hypnosis?"

The woman took a deep breath, then exhaled slowly. "What your daughter described, Mr. Richards, was an exorcism. She said that demons were trying to take control of her, to get inside her head. According to her recollection, you and your wife fed her paranoid delusions by performing what can only be described as an exorcism! Frankly, I find that disgraceful."

"Our daughter was not imagining things!" Audrey retorted. "And neither were we. You can ask our neighbors in the apartment upstairs. They saw everything."

Ms. Burnell was shaking her head in disbelief. "And you actually believe that demons were responsible for what was happening to your daughter?"

"How else would you explain invisible voices and furniture moving by itself? It had to be something supernatural," said Audrey.

"Did it ever occur to you that what was happening could have been a manifestation of Kelsie's internal fears, which you instilled in her through your paranoid religious beliefs?"

"That doesn't even make sense," Audrey said.

"Wait a minute," said Mike, "you mean you actually *believe* that stuff happened?"

"The issue is not whether I believe you," Ms. Burnell pointed out. "The issue is whether or not your religious beliefs are creating a harmful environment for your daughter."

"That's ridiculous!" said Audrey. "How can raising a child to believe in Jesus be harmful?"

"The image of Jesus that fundamentalists have conjured up is a manifestation of primitive psychosocial beliefs rooted in fear, hatred, and paranoia, which are extremely detrimental to a young child's development." Ms. Burnell sounded as if she were reading from a textbook. "Exposure to such beliefs can result in severe psychological trauma. Apparently, the incident which occurred here last week was a manifestation of such trauma."

"So, what are you saying?" Mike asked angrily. "That Kelsie's 'at risk'?"

"I can't make that determination immediately. I have to make a full report to my superiors. They'll contact you as soon as a determination has been made."

"Oh, how nice of them," he said sarcastically. Audrey looked like she was going to be ill.

After Ms. Burnell had left, Audrey nearly collapsed in Mike's arms. "Mike, what'll we do? *What'll we do?*" She was almost hysterical.

He held her, not knowing what to say. He wanted to tell her that everything would be all right, but he knew he couldn't make such a promise in a world gone mad.

* * * *

Audrey jumped when she heard the doorbell ring. Everything seemed like a blur. A strange numbness came over her as she realized what was happening. Someone was reading something from a form; several police officers were present. She heard the word "cult" repeated several times. She put her face in her hands. *This can't be happening.*

Her cries fell on deaf ears. "Please, you can't take her! She's my baby!"

Kelsie looked up from her coloring book. "Mommy, what's the matter?"

The police officers restrained Audrey as a middle-aged woman approached Kelsie and held out her hand. "You'll have to come with me now," the woman said coldly.

"Where are we going?" Kelsie asked, bewildered.

"To a place where you'll be safe," the woman said with a forced smile.

"Is Mommy coming?"

"No, she can't come."

"Then I won't go!" Kelsie said stubbornly.

The woman grabbed her by the hand, but Kelsie pulled away. "I'm not going anywhere without my mommy!"

The woman tried to pick her up, but Kelsie pushed her away and ran to her mother's side. "Mommy, Mommy, don't let them take me away!"

Audrey felt as if she were in a daze. The officers' hands were clamped tightly on her arms and she couldn't pull away. "Why are you doing this?" Her face was streaked with tears. Their only response was a cold, stony silence.

"This is for your own good, dear," the woman told Kelsie. Audrey watched helplessly as she injected Kelsie with a tranquilizer. Her eyes rolled back and she collapsed in the woman's arms.

Audrey tried to struggle free from the officers' grip. "*You can't do this! You can't take my baby!*" She sunk down onto the kitchen floor, sobbing.

That's where Mike found her when he came home.

CHAPTER 26

Sitting in the hard, wooden pew, Mike looked around awkwardly. He wished Audrey had come, but she had totally withdrawn into herself. He had come here only because he simply didn't know what to do.

He had consulted a lawyer who had said it could wipe them out just to pay the court fees for a custody battle, and the chances of winning were slim to nothing. "Under the UN Convention of the Rights of the Child," he said, "just about anything can be considered child abuse, and grounds for loss of custody. Unfortunately, the law is being used to target Christians in particular. The judges who decide these cases tend to be biased against Christians. They don't even allow the defendants to bring in their own witnesses."

Feeling he had exhausted every human resource, Mike did something he normally didn't do. He prayed. Then, something told him he should go to church.

During the service Mike felt awkward and out of place. He had a hard time focusing on the sermon because he kept thinking of Kelsie. The baby dedication had nearly torn his heart out.

If God were as loving and merciful as Audrey always said, then how could He allow a little girl to be taken away from her parents? He thought of Kelsie's nightmares, and how he used to rock her back to sleep after she woke up crying. Who was going to hold her now? Who was going to tuck her into bed at night and read her a bedtime story? Who was going to say her prayers with her? Sometimes, he actually had to walk away from his desk at work because he didn't want his boss to see him crying.

The service finally ended, and Mike made his way out of the pew. He rolled his eyes. *What am I doing here?*

He felt a gentle, yet firm hand on his shoulder, and he turned around. A frail-looking man who appeared to be somewhere in his sixties or seventies stood behind him.

"You look like you could use a friend," he said in a tone mingled with reassurance and concern.

Mike almost laughed at the man's simplistic greeting. "I could use a lot more than a friend," he said, a little gruffly. "I could use a miracle. But it seems God's not into that sort of thing anymore."

"What makes you so sure?" the man said with a smile.

"Look, I'd rather not talk about it, if you don't mind."

The man looked unperturbed. "Suit yourself. But remember, God can take care of your daughter, even if you can't. She's not alone, my friend."

Mike stared at him. "What did you just say?"

He smiled gently. Mike was struck by the infinite kindness in the man's eyes. He had never seen such an expression of love before. "I said that God is watching over your daughter. He loves her more than you can even imagine."

"You must have been talking to my wife," Mike said.

The man shrugged. "Who's your wife?"

"Audrey Richards. She goes to this church."

He smiled again. "Can't say as I've met her. You see, I'm a visitor here."

Mike felt a chill run down his spine. "So, you've never been to this church before? You don't know anyone here?"

"No," he said mildly. "I'm not from around these parts."

"But—" Suddenly, a couple sitting in Mike's pew tried to get past him. He moved out of the way to let them by.

When he looked back to the stranger, he was gone.

With a strange urgency, Mike ran out of the sanctuary and into the lobby, trying to find him. He was nowhere in sight.

Mike returned to the empty sanctuary, mystified. He stared at the huge, wooden cross suspended high above the altar. He recalled everything Audrey had told him about Jesus. He loved the little children, had opened the eyes of the blind, and raised a little girl from the dead. If He could do that, surely He could bring Kelsie back.

He pictured the crown of thorns, the nails that had pierced His hands and His feet. An overwhelming feeling of love washed over him. He shivered. A powerful, resonating, voice, filled with infinite peace and tenderness, spoke to his soul. It came from everywhere and nowhere at the same time.

"*Your daughter is not alone, Mike. She is with Me. I will never leave her or forsake her. That is why I sent my messenger to you, so you would know that Kelsie is safe.*"

Mike dropped to his knees and began to weep. He knew that Jesus was real. "Thank you, Jesus. Thank you!"

* * * *

Audrey was sitting at the kitchen table staring into space. She hadn't gotten dressed that day—or the last few days, for that matter. Sometimes she spent most of the day lying in bed sobbing.

Mike had never felt so helpless. His little girl had been torn from their home, and his wife was on the verge of a nervous breakdown. As a new Christian, his faith was certainly being put to the test. But he couldn't think of himself now; he had to get through to Audrey somehow.

"Why don't you come with me to the Bible study tonight? Everyone's been asking after you, and the fellowship might do you some good." Mike had attended the study last week with John and Beth and had found it very comforting.

"The only thing that will do me any good is getting our daughter back," Audrey said. "And it doesn't look like that's going to happen any time soon!"

"Look, we can't give up. We have to trust Jesus—"

Her voice rose in anger. "Oh, really? Well, tell me something, Mike. Where was Jesus when they took Kelsie away? Well? Where was He?"

"And where is He when millions of Christians are tortured and killed for their faith? Honey, we can't turn away from God just because He's allowed evil and suffering to touch our lives. You saw the way He delivered Kelsie from those demons. He was with us then, wasn't He?"

"Well, what good did it do? Kelsie's gone now!" She said the words bitterly. "Mike, what if we never see her again?" She put her face in her hands and sobbed.

Mike put his arms around her but she pulled gruffly away. "Look, I know this isn't easy," he said, fighting back tears. "Don't you realize that my heart is broken, too? But we can't let this destroy our faith. We've got to trust God to bring Kelsie back to us."

"Well, this is just dandy!" she said sarcastically. "After all these years you finally get saved, and God takes away my little girl. What kind of a God would do something like that?"

He sighed. "I don't know why God has allowed this to happen, Audrey. Maybe we'll never know. All I know is, we have to trust Him, even when His ways don't seem to make sense."

* * * *

"I always thought her faith was so strong." Mike shook his head, then smiled wryly. "I figured it had to be, if she could put up with me. But she fell apart after they took Kelsie away. I just don't get it. I mean, she's been a

Christian for a lot longer than I have. You'd think she could handle this better."

Beth was in the kitchen making coffee. John sat across from Mike on the couch. They had invited him up to the apartment for coffee after the Bible study. Mike hated the thought of leaving Audrey alone, but he could hardly stand to watch what was happening to her. Besides, it wasn't as if he was doing her any good. The more he tried to help her, the more she seemed to withdraw.

"It could be that God is giving you a special grace to trust Him during this time," John said.

"But why not Audrey?"

John shrugged. "Maybe she's not open to God's grace at the moment. Maybe she's too consumed with her own feelings of loss. I think Audrey's problem is that she was totally unprepared for what happened. So, she just can't deal with it."

"But how can you ever be prepared for something like that?" Mike asked.

"It's not easy," John admitted. "But if you look at the signs, you can be somewhat prepared. For instance, Beth and I believe that we're now living in the end-times, because Jesus gave us specific signs to look for. It's clear from God's Word that those times are going to be very hard on God's people. As a matter of fact, that's why we've been putting off having children."

Mike was perplexed. "But Audrey reads the Bible. Wasn't she aware of these signs, too?"

Beth brought in the coffee pot and poured them each a cup. "Did Audrey ever talk to you about the Tribulation before you got saved?"

Mike opened a sugar packet and stirred it into his coffee. "No, not that I remember. She made it sound like Christians have it made. She kept telling me that if I became a Christian, God would shower me with blessings and I'd never have to worry about anything again. But she never mentioned anything about a tribulation."

"I don't think Audrey wants to believe we're living in the end-times," Beth said. "And she certainly didn't want to believe that the government would take her child away. To be honest, Mike, I often got the impression that she never wanted to believe anything negative at all."

Mike nodded regretfully. "That sounds like Audrey, all right. In fact, one of the things that upset her so much about all this is that she was trying to be a good Christian. She keeps saying that something like this shouldn't happen to someone who's been a good Christian, doing everything right, so to speak."

John shook his head sadly. "Well, that's not what the Bible says. Jesus told His followers they would have trouble in the world, but that they should take heart because He had overcome the world. As Christians, we should expect tribulation. It's the only way we can be prepared when it hits us."

He sipped his coffee. "I think that's the problem with most Christians in America today. They expect Christianity to be a walk in the park. They've never had to suffer for their faith, like those in communist countries or the Middle East and Africa. And they don't really understand the Scriptures. They trust the government too much, instead of relying on God. That's why we're in this mess. Too many Christians want the government to be involved in every aspect of their lives. Then, when the government takes away their kids, they can't understand how something like that could have happened.

"I never thought about it that way," Mike said. "I hate to admit it, but I used to be like that. I always believed that the government was responsible for taking care of everyone. But look at how it's taking care of my family! My daughter is God knows where and my wife is falling apart." There was a pause. "I just wish there was something I could do to help Audrey. But I've tried everything I can to get through to her. I just don't know what to do anymore."

Beth spoke in a reassuring voice. "Just keep praying, Mike. After all, she prayed for years for you to come to Jesus. There were times when she wondered if her prayers were doing any good."

He smiled. "I'm glad she never gave up on me." Another thought occurred to him. "Things are going to get worse for us, aren't they, if we're living in the end-times?"

John nodded, his expression grave. "As the saying goes, we ain't seen nothin' yet."

* * * *

Pastor Bradley, a slim, spindly man in his early sixties, looked out at the congregation with an expression of fatherly concern. John and Beth made their way to one of the front pews and sat down. They were both waiting with baited breath to hear what the pastor had to say tonight, and hoped that he shared their concerns.

The sanctuary buzzed with people talking in hushed voices and solemn tones. But it wasn't quite the turnout John had expected. *Where are God's people when they're needed?* He looked around for some familiar faces. He smiled when he saw Mitch and Carol sitting a couple of rows ahead. Perry was there, too. Good. At least someone here would speak out against the insanity which was the topic of tonight's meeting.

After a brief prayer, the pastor brought the meeting to order and addressed the congregation. "As you all know, the purpose of this meeting is to openly discuss our sentiments about the Universal Statement of Faith, which was drafted at the United Religion Summit earlier this week. Now, I realize that the statement has stirred a great deal of controversy, and a number of you have expressed legitimate concerns about it. However, we cannot allow fear to get the best of us. We must keep in mind that hundreds of religious leaders from all denominations have hailed the statement as the ultimate realization of Christ's vision for world peace."

Some disgruntled muttering came from the crowd, but some people were clapping. John could hardly believe it. He raised his voice. "Have you read that statement, Pastor Bradley? Do you know what it actually says?"

The pastor cleared his throat, looking a bit discomfited. "I don't think you're getting the big picture here, John. What the statement says isn't as important as what it represents—a major stepping stone toward world peace. With such a great opportunity before us, we don't want to be perceived as narrow-minded, especially if we want to reach a wider audience with the gospel. Now, I realize there may be problems with some of the wording, but—"

Mitch spoke, incredulous. "Some of the *wording*? If you ask me, that statement is outright heresy! It's totally unbiblical and completely antithetical to the gospel!"

The congregation was in a furor. Pastor Bradley asked everyone to calm down. A number of people hadn't read the statement and were demanding to know what it said.

The assistant pastor, Ray Donovan, approached the pulpit and offered to read it to the congregation. Pastor Bradley looked around nervously. "I'm not sure that's a good idea, Ray. We don't want to get everyone in an uproar over this."

The congregants were insistent. "We have a right to know the truth!" someone said.

A chorus of voices chimed in. "Yeah! Tell us what it says!"

Regretfully, Pastor Bradley turned the microphone over to Ray. John had always liked Ray, a soft-spoken, gentle man somewhere in his fifties who had been a police officer before his conversion to Christianity and whose love for the lost consumed his very life. John and Beth had gone to one of his Sunday School classes on the book of Revelation and had loved it.

John listened, barely able to restrain his outrage, as Ray read from the handout he was holding. Though he had seen an abbreviated version in the newspaper earlier that week, John still couldn't see how any Christian could endorse such a perverted conglomeration of humanism, environmentalism, and pantheism.

It referred to the earth as a conscious, living entity to which all human beings owed their primary allegiance. True morality consisted of taking care of the planet and respecting the diversity of others.

At the next few sentences a murmur went through the crowd. John saw a lot of people shaking their heads in disbelief.

"'We hold that God is a part of the natural environment,'" Pastor Donovan read, "'and that all human beings—regardless of their race, creed, gender, or sexual orientation—have a share in the Divine Consciousness from which we have all evolved.'"

"'Finally,'" Ray continued, "' we renounce all forms of religious intolerance. In order to ensure lasting peace, there can be no claims to exclusivity; we must recognize that all roads lead to God, whatever we hold him or her to be. Therefore, we urge all denominations to declare a moratorium on proselytizing so as not to alienate those of other faiths.'"

Gasps and shouts of outrage erupted. Ray had to pause for a moment. "'For there are many faiths, but one Divine Consciousness which we call God.'"

The last few sentences articulated the primary mission of the United Religion of Mankind: to improve the social and economic conditions of all human beings, rather than distracting people with "'*archaic concepts such as sin and redemption.*'"

Ray turned toward Pastor Bradley and said firmly, "Pastor, this is not a stepping stone toward world peace. This is a rejection of the gospel of Christ!"

John looked around to gauge the reaction of the congregation. He was glad that many were nodding their heads in agreement. Someone sitting behind him shouted, "*Amen!*"

Pastor Bradley looked troubled. "Please, let's not overreact. Surely we can find some common ground with such an *ecumenical* outlook. Of course, we needn't espouse *everything* it says, but I'm not sure it's wise to condemn it at this point. We don't want to get a reputation for being against peace and brotherhood. That could turn people off to the message of the gospel."

"But shouldn't our first priority be truth?" asked Perry, who was sitting in one of the middle pews. "And how can we present the true message of salvation if we're willing to compromise with paganism and pantheism? Besides, the apostles certainly weren't worried about their reputations. Neither was Jesus, for that matter. We must remember that He claimed to be the *only* way to God. If we endorse that New Age, pantheistic sermon, we're calling Jesus a liar."

Someone else spoke up, a woman with silvery hair who looked to be in her forties or fifties. John didn't know her name, but he recognized her as a member of the choir. "Look, there's no way to know for certain that Jesus actually said that. The gospels weren't written down until hundreds of years after the Crucifixion. They were based on an oral tradition. By the time they were written down, none of Jesus' original disciples were alive anymore. Who knows what could have been added to their original accounts?"

"That's not true," Pastor Donovan said emphatically. "The most recent fragments of the New Testament found in the Dead Sea caves have been dated within thirty years after the Crucifixion. And those fragments are virtually identical to several Scripture verses in the gospels of Luke and Mark."

The woman grimaced. "That still doesn't mean we have to take everything in the Bible so literally. Look at the Old Testament. It's filled with myths and inaccuracies!"

Mitch was astonished. "How can you say that? Aren't you a Christian?"

She tossed her head. "Of course I am! And I'm a very *good* Christian. But I also happen to be a science teacher, and I know for a fact that the first two chapters of Genesis are completely at odds with what we know about evolution."

"Actually," Ray said, "evolution has never been proven."

She looked at him as if he had two heads. "Of course it's been proven, Ray. It's an established, scientific fact!"

"You're wrong, Midge," Ray said, gently but firmly. "Evolution contradicts many laws of science, including the Second Law of Thermodynamics and the laws of probability. Besides that, there's not a shred of fossil evidence that evolution ever took place. Evolutionists themselves have admitted as much."

She rolled her eyes disdainfully. "Oh, really? I can show you the evidence in the biology textbook I use. There's Neanderthal Man, for one thing."

A heavy-set man near the back spoke next. "Turns out he was an ordinary

Homo sapiens, just like you and me."

"Then why didn't he walk upright?" Midge asked with a smug expression.

"The poor guy had rickets."

A few people chuckled. John couldn't help smiling. "Sounds like your biology textbook is pretty outdated," he said.

Midge's voice shook with indignation. "I'll tell you what's outdated—it's people of your ilk who want to turn back the wheels of progress and plunge us into the Dark Ages when Christians believed everything the Bible said without question! Never mind what *science* has to say!"

A few voices chimed in, agreeing with her.

"The Bible is perfectly compatible with what we know about science," Pastor Donovan said. "And we need remember that our own understanding of science, of everything for that matter, is limited. Scientists today are saying that the more we learn about the universe, the more of a mystery it becomes. So, how can we presume to know more about science than the God who inspired the Bible? But ask yourself this, Midge: why are you so afraid to believe in creation? Is it because you would have to admit that the same God who created you will also judge you someday?"

Pastor Bradley broke in. "Please, let's not argue among ourselves. We mustn't allow petty differences to divide us."

"But these aren't petty differences," Ray said earnestly. "Evolution is a lie that strikes at the very heart of the Scriptures! God's Word teaches that death came into the world because of sin, and that's why we need a Redeemer. But if evolution is true, then death is part of the natural order and we don't need a Savior. Sin would be an inherited animal characteristic, not the result of the fall of man through disobedience to God. That's a blatant contradiction of Scripture and would make Christ's death meaningless!"

"Not necessarily," a middle-aged man piped up. John recognized him as one of the local university professors. "Higher Criticism has found that the individual books in the Old Testament were compiled by numerous authors hundreds of years after the events described allegedly took place, which means they couldn't have happened literally. But that doesn't mean there isn't some underlying truth to them. As Midge pointed out earlier, the book of Genesis must not be taken literally; it's a collection of myths and allegories handed down from ancient cultures and primitive societies. However, it does contain certain spiritual truths. We need to keep in mind that what it says isn't as important as what it means."

John shook his head. He should have expected this from a liberal philosophy professor. "What nonsense! Higher Criticism was totally debunked by C.S. Lewis. He submitted one of his own essays to a group of higher critics and they claimed it was written by more than one man. He made them look like idiots!"

Pastor Bradley approached the microphone again. "Please, we're not going to get anywhere with this bickering."

Ray nodded. "You're right, that's not what we came here for." He looked out at the congregation, his expression resolute. "I believe we need to draft a rebuttal to that ungodly statement of faith we just heard. We can't let it go unchallenged!"

Claps and shouts of "Amen!" resounded through the sanctuary. Others frowned and shook their heads in disappointment. A few gathered up their coats and turned to leave, including Midge, who was muttering something under her breath.

John couldn't understand it. How could someone who called herself a Christian buy in to so many lies? How could members of an evangelical church, including the senior pastor, condone a statement that amounted to heresy? Then, he reminded himself that he was living in a day of deception, and Christ had warned that a day was coming when even the elect could be deceived...if that were possible.

* * * *

Ray closed his eyes as the steaming water splashed against his tense muscles. This had been a rough week, and he was glad to see it come to an end. He sure had made a lot of enemies after his outspoken opposition to that New Age Manifesto. Not only did he preach against it in a sermon he delivered at the evening service last Sunday, but he had also denounced it publicly at an interdenominational meeting that had been called to address concerns over the statement. The press had been invited, and they heckled Ray when it was his turn to speak.

The following day, *Island News* attacked him and the entire "Christian Right" not only for being "backward and provincial," but for being "enemies of peace, possibly even hatecriminals." He was also ridiculed on the local ten o'clock news. But that wasn't all. Ray's home was vandalized while he and his family were out having pizza; they had come home to find the words "*NEO-NAZI*" spray-painted in red across the front door. His children were even being harassed and intimidated in school.

He took a deep breath, letting the tension drain from his body. Thank God the weekend was here! He could use a little R and R.

He was just drying off when he heard his wife Nancy calling him, hysterical. *Dear God, what now?*

He threw on his terrycloth bathrobe.

He ran downstairs to the front porch, where he found Nancy kneeling over the body of their dead cat. It had been strangled.

He held Nancy in his arms as she sobbed. She had raised the cat since it was a kitten. How would they tell the children?

For the first time since he had become a minister of the gospel, Ray felt like striking out at someone, the monsters who were terrorizing his family. He took a deep breath, asking God to give him the grace to bear the world's hatred.

He couldn't help wondering what else those thugs were capable of. How would he protect his family? He knew he had to be prepared for the worst.

CHAPTER 27

John was a little startled at the reason for Ray's visit the next day. Still, he understood why Ray would want to buy a gun privately, through a trusted member of his congregation. Most firearms dealers had gone out of business after the World Parliament instituted a 2000 percent sales tax on ammunition and raised the license fee for firearms dealers to 10,000 debits. Since it had to be renewed every year, practically no one could afford it. Buying a firearm legally had become virtually impossible.

Beth was out shopping, and John had been grading some English composition papers. The pastor's visit was a welcome distraction. John wasn't sure he could stand to read many more choppy, incoherent essays which sounded like they were written by elementary school students with mud for brains.

No wonder. Instead of learning the basics in elementary and high school, they were taught "lifeboat ethics" and "death education,"designed to teach them that individual lives were of little consequence and could be sacrificed for the good of society. Social engineering had replaced genuine learning.

Ray stretched out comfortably on the couch while John poured them each a glass of lemonade. Wearing faded blue jeans and a red flannel shirt, Ray appeared much more relaxed than he did at the Sunday morning service, where he wore a suit and a tie.

John was shocked at what had happened to the cat. "I can't take any chances where my family's safety is concerned," Ray said. "You once mentioned that you owned a rifle, and I thought you might want to sell it or maybe trade it for something. I have some silver coins I'd be willing to trade. I hear they're pretty valuable on the black market." His blue eyes looked regretful. "I was a fool for giving up my pistol after I left the force, but Nancy didn't like the idea of having a gun in the house. Being a brand new Christian, I mistakenly thought it was the right thing to do. But I've learned a lot since then."

"I see where you're coming from. Unfortunately, I just have the one rifle, and I'd like to hold onto it. But my dad may have an extra one that he doesn't need. He used to have quite a collection. Maybe I'll give him a call."

"Thanks." Ray shook his head, looking almost embarrassed. "I guess it seems kind of unusual, a pastor considering using a firearm for self-defense. I just hope I'll never have to use it. From my experience as a police officer, I know that just the sight of it would most likely scare someone away."

"That's usually how it works." John smiled. "My grandmother once used a starter pistol to scare away a burglar. She didn't even have to fire it, just waved it at the intruder and yelled, 'I'll blow your brains out!' The guy was out of there so fast it made her head spin!" They both laughed, and Ray seemed to relax.

"You know, I used to be in the military before I joined the force," Ray said. "With all my experience, you'd think the idea of owning a firearm wouldn't seem so foreign to me."

"Well, we live in a society that's become very sheep-like, where owning a gun for self-defense is viewed as something extreme. After all," he said sarcastically, "we're supposed to rely on the *government* to protect us." He shook his head. "It's funny. I used to be a complete pacifist, yet recently I've done a 180 degree turn." He was quiet for a few moments, thinking.

"Is something troubling you, John?" Ray asked in a soft voice.

He sighed. "I just wish I knew for sure that I'm right. This whole issue has caused a lot of friction between me and Beth. What if I'm wrong?"

Ray smiled reassuringly. "John, nowhere in the Bible does it say we can't own weapons, or use justifiable force, to protect ourselves and our loved ones. God gave each one of us the right to life. Along with that right, we can assume, comes the right to defend our lives. Did you know that according to Luke's Gospel, our Lord actually told his disciples to arm themselves with swords at one point?"

John nodded. "Yeah, I think I've read that before. But self-defense against intruders isn't the issue I've been grappling with."

Ray looked curious. "Oh?"

John folded his hands together. He wanted to resolve this dilemma once and for all, if that were possible. "What if the intruders are the government? What if government agents break down your door with the intention of killing you and your loved ones?" He had a sense of deja-vu as he realized that Matt had asked a similar question at one of the Bible studies.

Ray sat quietly for a few moments, his brow furrowed. "Hmm. You're talking about resistance to tyranny. Christians have struggled with the same question throughout the centuries. How do we know when it's time to resist an evil government with force? I'm sure a lot of Christians were asking the same question prior to the American Revolution."

"What do you think?" John asked him.

He sipped his lemonade. Then he said, "Well, Pastor Bradley probably wouldn't agree with me. As a pacifist, he thinks the War for American Independence was immoral. But I don't see it that way, at least, not anymore."

"What about Romans 13?"

He looked into space for a few seconds, musing. "Does it seem to you that Paul was describing a tyrannical, murderous government in Romans 13?"

"Not at all. He seems to be describing a government that's operating within the bounds of God's will. You know, keeping the peace and maintaining justice. At least, that's how I see it."

Ray nodded in agreement. "I don't see how a reasonable person could interpret it any other way. But unfortunately, many Christians have interpreted Romans 13 as giving the government carte blanche to do whatever it wants, no matter how evil, and that Christians are obligated to obey such a government without question. It may have something to do with some of the newer Bible translations that have cropped up in recent years. You really have to be careful about them. For instance, one version of the New Testament translates the first verse of Romans 13 as, 'Obey all government leaders because God put them in power. God established every government that ever existed.' This implies that we're obligated to obey any government, no matter how evil it is. But that's not what the original Greek says."

John was intrigued. "What does it say?"

"Well, for one thing, the word for 'government' doesn't appear in the Greek text at all. The actual word used is best translated as 'authority' or power. What the verse really says is that every soul should be subject to the highest authority, and there is no authority but of God. Now, who is the highest authority?"

John smiled. "God," he answered.

"And, since man's highest authority is the Lord, should Christians be subject to an authority which acts in opposition to His Word?"

"Of course not," said John. "But I've spoken to quite a few Christians who think we have to obey the government no matter what, that it's always wrong to use lethal force against the government, even when it's committing terrible evils—like murdering innocent people."

"Yeah, that's a real problem today. I think it has to do with that sheep-like mentality you referred to, especially where the government is concerned. Too many Christians seem to have forgotten that we're supposed to be God's sheep, not the government's. Ministers today are telling us that Romans 13 means you have to obey everything the government tells you, even *evil* government. But what the Scriptures really teach is that we're only supposed to follow leaders who are just. Remember what Peter said when he was arrested for sharing the gospel? 'We must obey God rather than men.' He knew that the only powers that merit our obedience are those that are of God—in other words, those that are operating within His laws."

"So, then, you think it's okay for Christians to overthrow a tyrannical government?"

"Only when the government has gotten to the point where it's taken over every aspect of our lives, where it's totally in opposition to God. It's what our Founding Fathers did, and most of them were devout, Bible thumping Christians, as I understand," he said with a smile. "But they did so only after they had exhausted every peaceful, lawful means to change their government. When you think about it, all they really wanted was for their government to abide by its own laws. You see, John, when a government becomes tyrannical, it's no longer ordained of God. In fact, according to the Old Testament, whenever God's people refused to remove evil leaders from the throne, the people were judged quite severely. So, based on my understanding of the Scriptures, Christians not only have the right to oppose evil government, but an *obligation* to. Anyone who thinks otherwise can read the writings of Martin Luther, John Milton, and other devout men of God who said the same thing."

"Wow! I never thought I'd hear this from a pastor of my own church. It's certainly not a popular thing to believe these days."

"Truth is rarely popular," Ray said after sipping his lemonade. "I haven't always seen things this way, John. While I was on the force, God gave me a revelation that changed my whole way of looking at government."

John was fascinated. "Really?"

Ray ran his fingers through his thick mane of dark hair. "I pulled a woman over for a minor traffic violation, like not signaling. There were no other cars in the area, and she hadn't endangered anyone. But at the time it hadn't seemed to matter. After all, I had a quota to meet. When I approached her to give her the ticket, she didn't say a word, but she was close to tears. I could hear her kids fighting with each other in the back seat. Obviously, she was having a really bad day, and I had made it worse. I couldn't get the incident out of my mind. It was as if God were trying to tell me something. I found myself questioning the whole concept of government I had been indoctrinated with. I began to wonder about the purpose of government. I realized that the lady I gave the ticket to probably thought that the government was here to make her life miserable. After I came to that realization, I did something that I had never done before. I read the oath of office that I'd had to take all those years ago when I joined the force. And you know what? Reading that oath made me feel ashamed of my entire career as a police officer. I had made a promise to protect and defend the U.S. Constitution, which I had never even bothered to read. I felt like a complete hypocrite. As a police officer I was supposed to be the people's servant, not their master. But that's not how I acted while I was on the force."

He went on to describe how he would conduct random searches at checkpoints and how he had once arrested a woman who kept a handgun in her car for self-defense. She had been the victim of a car-jacking in the past, but the judge wouldn't allow the defense attorney to inform the jury of this fact.

There was a long pause. John felt moved by the pastor's realization of what he had become in seeking power over the very people he had promised to serve. "Anyway, that's what ultimately led to my decision to leave the force. Ever since then, I've been studying the Constitution and the writings of our Founding Fathers," Ray said. "I've also been reading what the Bible has to say about civil government. Contrary to what most Christians today have been taught, the Bible teaches that our government leaders are to be our servants and protectors. They're supposed to bless us, not betray or enslave us. As far as violent self-defense goes, all you have to do is read Nehemiah to see that God's people not only have a right but an obligation to defend themselves against aggression." There was a long silence. "Well, I guess it's never too late to learn the truth."

John felt bold enough to ask another question. "Would *you* ever be willing to resist government tyranny with force?"

He hesitated only for a moment. "If I was convinced through prayer and fasting that's what God wanted me to do, I would. And of course, I would have to be certain it was the only option left."

"If only it were clearer. I mean, there are Scripture verses which seem to support pacifism, while others seem to condone self-defense. How do you know which is right?"

"I guess it depends on the circumstances and where God's Spirit leads you. The Bible does say that there's a time for peace and a time for war. I suppose God could have made a lot of things clearer. But the Bible isn't a step-by-step instruction book. You won't always find easy answers in it.

Maybe that's because God wants us to trust Him, even when there are no easy answers. After all, trusting our Lord is more important than knowing the answers to all our questions."

John couldn't deny that was true.

They continued sipping their lemonade and turned toward more pleasant topics, like the Bible study which Ray was hoping to teach next fall. The phone rang suddenly, and John went to answer it. It was Mitch, and he sounded urgent. "Put on CNN!" he said.

"Sure, hold on." Wondering what to expect, John turned on the TV. What he heard shocked him.

"The United Nations has just declared that religious indoctrination is a hatecrime and a violation of civil rights," a female news anchor was saying. "The World Body has urged Parliament to draft legislation which would establish special Human Rights Tribunals to punish those who illegally impose their religious beliefs on others. Punishments would range from community service to excessive fines and/or jail sentences."

At first John and Ray just sat staring at the TV. The anchorwoman went on to say that a toll-free hotline would be established so people could report offenders to the authorities.

"This is insane!" John said when he had found his voice. "They want us to spy on each other and report our friends and neighbors to the government. That's sick!"

"It's what happened in Nazi Germany," Ray said quietly.

"You don't really sound surprised about this."

Ray sighed. "This is what happens when nations turn away from God and allow the ungodly to rule over them. I've heard it said that men who refuse to accept God's rule will be ruled by tyrants. I think we're reaping what we've sown."

* * * *

The Bible study was about to start, and John could see by the dour faces that the stark realities, which many had refused to accept for so long, had finally sunk in. Perry had cancelled the scheduled topic so that they could devote the entire session to prayer and intercession. An uneasy, frightened silence hung over everyone tonight, and to John the atmosphere seemed more like that of a funeral than a Bible study.

Last Sunday a nearby Pentecostal church had been raided by government agents dressed in black Ninja outfits and wearing ski masks. The senior pastor, who had been reported by disgruntled neighbors annoyed by his church's door-to-door evangelistic outreach, had been arrested and was being held in jail without bail or a probable cause hearing. In order to be released, he would have to sign a statement agreeing that his church would refrain from any further proselytizing. That's all anyone had heard since his arrest. His wife had not even been allowed to visit him and they wouldn't let him talk to his lawyer. She and the assistant pastors had called every evangelical church in the vicinity to enlist their support. The Suffolk County jail out in Riverhead had been bombarded with irate phone calls but to no avail. The pastor was being used as an example. The terrifying scene of black-clad, jack-booted thugs barging into a church in the middle of a Sunday service was deliberately calculated to frighten Christians into submission.

Though the two didn't see eye-to-eye on many things, Perry had invited Ray Donovan to lead the group in prayer. Ray cleared his throat and pulled a folded sheet of paper out of his pocket. "Before we pray, I'd like to read something," he said. "Charlie, the pastor who was arrested last week, wrote it in jail. I think it's something all of you need to hear, though many of you won't like it."

He looked down at the letter and began to read.

"'More than 200 years ago, our ancestors came to these shores seeking religious liberty. It was so precious to them that many gave their lives so that their children, grandchildren, and millions born in future generations might worship God freely.'" Ray paused briefly, fighting back tears. "'We are now living in a country where sharing the gospel is a crime. If you invite your next-door neighbor to church on Sunday, you could be arrested and thrown in jail without a trial. How did this happen? How *could* it happen in a nation that once was known as the land of the free? It happened because we allowed it to. Because we esteemed peace and safety more highly than our God-given liberties, we handed this nation to Satan. Now, we're reaping the consequences.'"

John's heart sank at his own role in bringing this disaster upon America through his refusal to be involved in politics. He listened as Ray continued. "'I also believe it happened because too many Christians, who are supposed to rely on the Lord Jesus Christ, were trusting in government to solve every problem and meet every need. Now, God is showing us the outcome of such a path. Is it too late for America? I honestly don't know. What I do know is that ultimately, it depends on God. If we turn to Him in repentance, He *can* heal our land. He can restore what Satan has robbed from us. The prophet Joel assures us that the Lord *will* give back the years that the locusts have eaten. But only if we return to Him with all our hearts. Only if we surrender our lives to Him. *"Return to the Lord your God, for he is gracious and compassionate, slow to anger and abounding in love, and he relents from sending calamity. Who knows? He may turn and have pity..."''*

Ray looked up and spoke softly. "Let's pray, shall we?" He bowed his head and lifted his voice to God. John felt the power of the Holy Spirit filling the room. A chorus of voices joined in prayer. Some people fell on their faces and wept for their persecuted brothers and sisters in the Lord, asking Him to break down the enemy's stronghold in the nation.

Overcome with emotion, John began to cry silently. He was mourning for the loss of America, the only country on the face of the earth founded upon the principles set fourth in the Word of God. And yet, something else was happening here. For the first time in ages, he sensed a genuine unity among his fellow members of the Body of Christ. But what a terrible price to pay for it.

John looked at Perry, who had buried his face in his hands. When he finally spoke, his voice broke. "Forgive me, Lord," he said.

CHAPTER 28

"You're positive?" Astonished, John stared at Beth, who looked almost giddy with excitement.

"That's right. We're going to have a baby! I just found out this morning."

He let out a whoop of joy and picked her up in his arms. "Wait a minute, is it okay to do this?" he asked suddenly.

She laughed. "The baby isn't going to break, you know."

"Wow, I can't believe it!" Then, he eyed her with concern. "You're sure you're okay with this?" The last time they had discussed the possibility of having a baby, she had been plagued with fears and uncertainty.

They sat down together on the couch. Her smile was radiant. "Yes, I am," she assured him. "I want this more than anything in the world."

He pulled her close. "Me, too," he whispered. "What is it that made you so sure?"

Her answer surprised him. "It was shortly after Kelsie was taken away. At first, I thought I could never live with something like that. I figured we'd be better off never having kids if we could lose them someday. But then I started praying about it, like you suggested. I thought about Moses' mother, and how she gave him up to save his life. Despite the heartache that caused her, God used Moses to deliver His people from slavery in Egypt. Besides, there's always the possibility of losing a child. All parents face that risk."

Her eyes had a sad, faraway look. "I once heard about a baby girl who was born with some sort of congenital problem. She lived for only two days. Her parents knew she was going to die, but they gave her all the love they had for those two days. They said that every hour of her life she was in the arms of someone who loved her. Their brief time with her was worth the pain of losing her." Tears glistened in her eyes, and John pulled her close.

"That's beautiful," he said softly. "Beautiful yet so sad."

"We shouldn't let fear stop us from enjoying all that God has for us. I know that I want to be a mother, even if it can only be for a little while."

He thought about Audrey and how she had fallen apart when she lost her daughter. He wondered if Beth really was prepared for such a thing. What would they do if something like that happened to them? What would God want them to do?

"What's wrong?" Beth asked suddenly.

He didn't want to bring up such a gloomy topic right now. They should be discussing happy things, like names or how to decorate the baby's room. Still, he couldn't pretend they had nothing to worry about. "Now that we're going to be parents, there are some serious issues we need to resolve."

She cocked her head to the side. "Like what?"

"Beth, things are going to get ugly. I hate to say it, but we've got to face the truth. The government has made it clear that Christians are an open target. We have a baby on the way. How far should we be willing to go to protect our child from an increasingly oppressive and brutal government?"

Her face paled. "Do we have to talk about this now?"

"We can't brush this under the carpet. We have some major decisions to make before the baby is born."

"What kinds of decisions?"

"First of all, what should we do if I'm asked to turn in my rifle? I'm sure the government is just itching to disarm all Christians and everyone else they hate. What should we do if government agents break down our door demanding we hand over any weapons we have? And what should we do if they try to take away our baby?"

She put her face in her hands. "I don't know. What *can* we do?"

"There are two options, basically. We either give the government whatever it wants, whether it's my rifle *or our baby*, or we can stand on principle and not give in. What do you think?"

Her eyes widened in fear. "John, think about what you're saying. If the government asks you to turn in your rifle and you refuse, you could be killed. We both could get killed. Is that what you want? Do you want our child to grow up an orphan?"

"Beth, once we give up my rifle, we'll be helpless, just like the Jews were in Nazi Germany. The way things are headed, eventually we'd wind up in some kind of prison camp. The government would take our child and it would be raised by the state." He looked at her intently, hoping his words would sink in. "Is our baby worth fighting for, Beth? Or is it just government property to be taken at their whim?"

She sat quietly for a few moments, considering. "I'm willing to fight for our baby, if I have to. I just want to be sure that's what God would want us to do."

He understood. It was a course he never thought he would consider at one time. But a great deal had changed. He now knew what it was like to live under tyranny. He had heard of gun-control advocates who bought handguns after being raped or mugged at gunpoint. Now, he knew how they felt. He was considering something that went against everything he had once believed: defending himself and his family against his own government. "I know how you feel, Beth. But our Founding Fathers did it. Most of them were devout Christians. Do you think they were wrong?"

"No, of course not. But the thought of us doing the same thing...well, it sounds so...so drastic."

"These are drastic times, Beth. You admitted that our Founding Fathers were justified in fighting tyranny. So, you must agree on principle that fighting an evil government can be justified."

"I do, but..."

"But what? Think about it. If you truly believe in something on principle, you shouldn't change your opinion when you apply the same principle to your own circumstances." She seemed to be mulling this over, but she didn't say anything.

"Anyway, it's up to you," John said. "If you want me to get rid of my rifle, if you honestly think that's the right thing to do, then that's what I'll do. Pastor Donovan is interested in it, so if you don't think we should keep it, I'll take him up on his offer."

There was a long silence. He didn't want to push her. He wanted this to be her decision. When she finally spoke, she said something he never thought he'd hear her say. "Maybe you're right. Maybe we should hold on to your rifle."

"Are you sure that's what you want?"

She nodded. "I was thinking about all the children who died in concentration camps during the Holocaust," she said in a soft voice. "And little ones who are being murdered in countries like Somalia and the Sudan today. It suddenly hit me. If their parents had been armed, those poor children could have had a future. Their parents might have been able to protect them." Her eyes met his. "John, I want our baby to have a future. But if we keep letting this monstrous government have its way, what kind of life will our baby have? I just can't believe it's God's will for our child to grow up as a slave at the mercy of a godless, totalitarian government."

He threw his arms around her, relieved beyond words. The gulf between them had closed.

They would fight for their baby's future together.

* * * *

"So, you're gonna be a father!" Matt patted John on the back as he and Beth entered the apartment. Gina had insisted on inviting them over for a celebration dinner. Matt had started celebrating two hours ago at the corner bar. He had just returned with a bottle of champagne. His speech was a little slurred, and Gina hoped no one else would notice.

He grabbed the bottle from the refrigerator. "C'mon, let's have a drink."

"Maybe that's not such a good idea," John said cautiously.

"Why not?" Matt asked in a petulant tone.

John looked a little awkward, and Gina cringed. *He must know that Matt's on his way to getting sloshed.*

"Well, uh, Beth can't have any, in her condition," John said.

Matt laughed. "So? Why should that stop us from having a little toast?"

Gina said quietly, "I think we should wait until dinner." Maybe if he waited until dinner, he'd have some time to recover.

"Can I help you with dinner?" Beth offered.

"No thanks, you just relax. Have a seat in the living room—I put out some appetizers. And there's soda, too—it's caffeine free." She disappeared into the kitchen.

Standing at the counter to slice tomatoes, she tried to hold back her tears, but it was no use. Seeing Beth and John so happy together only reminded her of the emptiness of her own marriage. Now, they were having a baby. Something Matt had wanted for so long. But she had wanted to pursue her career, and now what did she have? No career, no children, not even much of a marriage anymore.

"Are you okay?"

She whirled around suddenly.

"I'm sorry," Beth said awkwardly. "I just came in to get a glass of milk, and—"

Gina brushed away her tears. "It's okay. I guess it's kind of obvious that things aren't going great around here."

"You want to talk about it?" Beth asked gently.

Gina sighed. "I'm not sure you'd understand. You and John seem to have the perfect marriage." She opened the refrigerator and took out a quart of milk.

"Look, there's no such thing as a perfect marriage," Beth said as Gina poured the milk into a glass. "John and I have had our share of problems. But we've always managed to work things out."

Gina handed Beth the milk. "What's your secret?"

"First, we're both totally committed to our marriage. It's the most important thing in our lives, aside from God. And we share a bond that most couples don't have. We're united in our love for Jesus. He's the cord that binds us together."

Gina arranged the tomatoes in a large glass bowl filled with lettuce and shredded carrots. "That sounds nice," she said wistfully.

"Gina, you and Matt can have that, too. All you have to do is commit your lives, and your marriage, to Christ."

"You make it sound so easy."

"Do you want to have a relationship with Jesus?" Beth asked in a soft voice.

Gina shrugged. "Right now, I think I should be concentrating on my relationship with Matt."

"Gina, once you give your life to Christ, everything else will fall into place. Trust me, I know. My life was a mess before I gave it to Jesus. I was into the occult and addicted to drugs. I almost committed suicide. But Jesus changed my life, and He can do the same thing for you and Matt."

"I don't know. I'm not sure I'm ready for that."

"But you've got nothing to lose," Beth said.

No, only myself. "Beth, I know you mean well, but I'm just not like you. I don't think I could ever have that kind of faith."

"Anyone can. Jesus said that even faith the size of a mustard seed is enough—"

"Look, I have enough problems right now without complicating my life with religion," Gina said abruptly. She was already taking enough of a risk writing for the underground paper. To become a "born-again" fanatic on top of that was just asking for trouble, especially now with fundamentalists being attacked so viciously by the government.

* * * *

After dinner John and Matt walked up the block to the video store. John was relieved that Matt had stayed away from the booze—at least for the time being. Poor Gina. She had no idea why her husband was bent on destroying himself.

"So, how's your church dealing with that new hatecrime law?" Matt asked.

"Naturally we're all very concerned. The senior pastor's been walking on eggshells. Some goons are terrorizing the assistant pastor and his family. He even asked if I had an unregistered firearm I was willing to part with."

Matt looked surprised. "Oh yeah? I thought religious types hated guns."

"He wants to be able to protect his family. And so do I. Beth and I had a long talk. We both decided to keep my rifle. If the government tries to take it, they won't get it without a fight." John looked at Matt expectantly. "So, what do you think?"

He was totally unprepared for Matt's response. "If you want to throw your life away, it's none of my business."

"Wait a minute. I thought you'd be all gung-ho for fighting back. As a matter of fact, I was going to ask if you'd be willing to part with some extra ammo."

"I don't have any left."

"What? I thought you had plenty."

"I did. But I turned most of it in. The rest I got rid of."

"You did *what?*"

"You heard me. I got a letter from the BWC. You know that law requiring gun dealers to record the names, addresses and social security numbers of people buying ammo? Well, it looks like I fell into their little trap. They claimed the ammo I bought awhile ago is now illegal, and I'd have to turn it in or go to jail. Since I didn't feel like rotting in prison, I turned it in."

"But you must have ammo that you bought before that law was passed."

"Well, let's just say I'm not taking any chances. Since the government knows I bought some in the past, they may decide to drop by and see if I have any more. If they saw how much I had, they would have arrested me on the spot, maybe even shoot me, for all I know. So I got rid of it. Dumped it into the Long Island Sound."

John was mystified. "But why? You're the one who's always been saying that we shouldn't give in to the government when it violates our rights. I thought you believed in fighting tyranny."

"Why bother? The government's going to win, anyway. If you're right about us living in the end-times, there doesn't seem to be much point in fighting. I might as well stay alive as long as I can."

"This doesn't sound like you. You can't really mean that."

"Why not?"

"Because you're the one who taught me the importance of being willing to resist evil government instead of giving in to it. I can't believe you would just give up!"

"Maybe by giving up, I'll stay alive a little while longer," Matt said quietly.

"But aren't some principles worth dying for?"

"Maybe I thought that at one time. But a lot's changed since then."

"Like what?"

He sighed. "In case you forgot, I don't have a hell of a lot going for me anymore. So, I'd like to enjoy life for awhile. How can I enjoy it if I'm constantly wondering if a bunch of jack-booted thugs are gonna break down my door at any minute looking for guns or ammo?"

"So, that's it? You're just giving up?"

"It looks like I don't have much choice," he said in a sullen tone.

"You do have a choice, Matt. We all do. Just because we may be living in the end-times doesn't mean we should give up and let evil have its way. Jesus could delay His coming if enough of His people pray and work to restore righteous government. Besides, you're just fooling yourself if you think the government will leave you alone as long as you give up your ammo. They'll come after you eventually for something else, and then you'll have no means of defending yourself. It's just a matter of time."

"I'm not about to give them any reasons to come after me. Besides, if they do come for me, being in jail's better than being dead."

John shook his head. "So, better red than dead? That's the philosophy you've adopted?"

Matt looked grim. "It's easy for you to criticize me right now. But what makes you so sure that *you* won't give in when a SWAT team breaks down your door and is ready to kill you if you don't give them what they want? Think about it, John. You'd be up against the full might of an extremely vicious government that couldn't care less about our lives or liberties. There's only one way that could end. You may think you're ready to fight, but how will you feel when some thug has a gun to Beth's head and threatens to blow her brains out unless you turn in your rifle?"

John shuddered at the image. "Okay," he said quietly, "you do have a point. But I still can't believe you'd give up so easily."

"You think this decision was easy? A part of me hated to turn in that ammo. But the thought of losing my life over it, well, it just isn't worth it. Besides, there was a time when you would have approved of my decision."

"I would approve of it if I thought it was based on the strength of your convictions. But we both know that's not true. We both know you're just afraid. That's what this is all about."

His voice was soft and low. "You calling me a coward?"

"What would *you* call someone who throws his convictions out the window because he's afraid he might have to act on them someday?"

Matt's fist slammed into his jaw, sending him sprawling backwards onto the ground. Somewhat dazed, he lay on the grass, the salty taste of blood in his mouth. The next moment Matt was helping him up and apologizing profusely, but not sounding very sincere. He seemed more embarrassed than anything else. "I don't know what got into me, John. Guess I haven't been myself lately."

John took out a handkerchief from his back pocket and wiped the blood from his mouth. "Look, it's okay. I suppose I was a little out of line."

"Let's just drop this whole thing," Matt said wearily. "It's not worth fighting over."

"You're right," John said. He wondered how many others would give in. *If only we had opposed this madness through the ballot box when we still had a chance! Then we wouldn't be in this position.*

But he couldn't deny Matt had a point. Would he lose his resolve if giving in could save Beth and their unborn child? But what kind of a life would they have as slaves to a godless, tyrannical government? Eventually, they would wind up in one of those "detention centers" he had heard about. He believed in his heart that couldn't happen unless God allowed it to accomplish His purpose in their lives. But he hated the idea of being separated from Beth and unable to protect her from evil men. He shuddered as he imagined her alone in prison, possibly at the mercy of sadistic guards willing to torture or even rape her. He reminded himself that he had to submit to the will of God, even if it meant being separated from his wife and unable to protect her. He prayed desperately that it would never come to that.

* * * *

Arriving at her first period Global Studies class, Beth stared in horror at the uniformed officers who blocked the door. They wore UN insignias and the words "TASK FORCE" were printed in large bold letters across their backs. Some of her students were milling about, anxious and concerned. The principal was there too, a look of cold disapproval in her steely eyes.

One of the officers approached Beth with a menacing look in his eyes. "Are you Beth Lanyon?"

Her heart was pounding. "Yes, is there a problem?"

The next thing she knew, she was thrown against the wall spread-eagle with a rifle at her back and one of the officers was patting her down—right in front of her students and the principal! Then he pulled her hands roughly behind her back and handcuffed her as the students looked on in astonishment.

Seized with panic, she started screaming. "Why are you doing this? What did I do?" She couldn't believe this was happening.

The agents refused to answer her questions. "You'll find out later," was all they would say. One of them gave her a push, and she almost fell. She forced herself to walk steadily, thinking of her unborn child. *Jesus*, she prayed desperately, *please help me!*

* * * *

A well-dressed man with cold, dead eyes stared at Beth as she was escorted into a small, windowless room the next morning after spending the night in a musty, damp cell. Her stomach was in knots, she hadn't eaten in over twenty-four hours and hadn't even been allowed one phone call. *John must be sick with worry!*

The man never gave his name, but told her with a self-important air that he was a local Commissioner of the Human Rights Tribunal. Then he said in a tone that was obviously meant to intimidate her, "A parent has accused you of forcing your religious beliefs on her child. Proselytizing is a violation of a student's civil rights. It's a serious violation of the Freedom of Religion and Conscience clause of the Constitution for Federation Earth, and is also a hatecrime. Now, do you deny that you referred to yourself as a born-again Christian during one of your classes?"

She swayed slightly—probably from hunger and fatigue, she realized. "May I sit down, please?" she asked weakly.

"Just answer the question," the Commissioner said in a monotone, his face devoid of expression.

In spite of her physical weakness and sheer exhaustion, Beth suddenly felt angry. "If I told my students I was into witchcraft or worshipped Gaia, would that be a hatecrime?" Before he could answer, she said, "There are plenty of teachers at my school who promote the occult and secular humanism in the classroom, but they don't get arrested. Only teachers who claim to follow Christ get arrested. Besides, how can you accuse me of a hatecrime when I haven't expressed hatred for anyone?"

He scowled at her. "The UN Task Force on Religious Hate has designated

Christian fundamentalism a terrorist-cult. Professing to being a born-again Christian is evidence that you are a member of this dangerous cult. It denotes a belief system which fosters hatred and intolerance of unbelievers, and is therefore a hindrance to world peace."

She could hardly believe what she was hearing. "That's ridiculous! If you ask me, the real hatecrime is arresting Christians simply because of their allegiance to Christ. The only hatred I see here is hatred for Jesus and His gospel."

"You've just given me all the evidence I need to convict you," he said triumphantly. "I've been taping this conversation."

She felt a boldness that surprised her. "Well, I guess you must be proud of yourself. I hope it's worth it when you have to stand before God someday and answer to Him."

"I'd advise you not to use that tone with me, young lady. You should realize that I can put you behind bars for a very long time if I want to."

She was suddenly struck by how pathetic he was. Here he was on this big power trip, thinking he controlled her destiny and having no idea that his own fate was in the hands of the very God whose people he was persecuting. If only she could make him see the truth! "I'm not afraid of going to jail," she told him calmly. "You're the one who should be afraid."

"Why should *I* be afraid?" he asked with an ugly sneer.

"Because you've made yourself an enemy of Christ by persecuting His people, and someday you'll have to bow down before Him and be judged by Him."

"Oh, is that so?" His voice was dripping with sarcasm.

She was amazed that she felt no fear. "Yes. The Bible says that one day every knee shall bow and every tongue confess that Jesus Christ is Lord. Someday, you *are* going to bow down to him, sir. But you have a choice. You can bow down to Him as His vanquished enemy to suffer eternal punishment—or as someone who's been reconciled to Him and washed in His blood, to live with Him in everlasting glory." In spite of the darkness of her circumstances, her heart surged with joy as she recalled what Christ had foretold concerning the end-times: that His people would be handed over to the government and stand before rulers and kings to be witnesses to them.

The Commissioner was silent for a long moment, his expression inscrutable. Yet the deadness in his eyes told her that he was capable of incredible evil. When he finally spoke, it was as if he had given her a death sentence. "I'm sorry to have to make this decision, Ms. Lanyon, but you leave me no choice. You are clearly mentally incompetent and for your own safety you are to be committed to a mental institution where you will receive the proper treatment for your illness." Her mouth dropped open as she saw him reach into his pocket for a large syringe. As he moved toward her, she backed away instinctively. But the two armed guards who had been standing by the door grabbed her and held her still as the Commissioner injected her. The room became a blur and then everything went black.

* * * *

Beth struggled against the despair that threatened to engulf her as she lay tied to the bed. She wasn't sure how long she had been here. A week? Maybe longer. Her mind swam in a black pit of terror. Restrained and injected with drugs, she was haunted by nightmares and hallucinations. John had no idea where she was. What if she never saw him again? What if they kept her here indefinitely? Who would ever know? She could die here for all she knew!

Each time she saw the government-appointed psychiatrist, she begged for permission to call John, but was told that she couldn't have contact with anyone outside because she was seriously impaired and a danger to others. They had taken her clothes and all her personal belongings, forcing her to wear a flimsy paper gown that was practically transparent. She recoiled at the leers of the male guards assigned to her room. What if they tried to rape her? If she reported it, no one would believe the word of someone who had been declared mentally incompetent.

Crying into her pillow, she suddenly heard a soft female voice from the next room. "Don't be afraid. I know how scary this place can be, but you're not alone. God is watching over you."

Beth felt overjoyed at the sound of a friendly voice. "Are you a Christian?" she asked the patient excitedly.

Her answer was a little mysterious. "I am a servant of the King."

"How long have you been here?"

"Don't worry, I'm sure you'll only be here a little while longer," the patient said, almost as if she hadn't understood Beth's question. "You're being prepared for the fulfillment of God's purpose in your life. This is a time of testing."

"What is your name?" Beth phrased the question slowly and deliberately; she had the sense that her neighbor might be from another country and wasn't used to speaking in English.

"It is difficult to pronounce in your language. But that is not important; I'm here to remind you that your God has not abandoned you. He will be with you to the end."

The stranger's words filled her with peace and assurance. In spite of her eagerness to continue conversing with her new-found friend, she found herself drifting off into a blissful sleep...the first decent night's sleep she'd had since being committed.

The next day she asked one of the nurses the name of the patient in the room next-door. The woman looked at Beth strangely. "There is no patient next-door. Both of the rooms next to yours are vacant."

"Are you sure?" Beth asked. "Maybe she checked out this morning."

The nurse shook her head. "Honey, both rooms next to yours have been vacant for over a week."

"But I heard someone in there last night—"

"You couldn't have. Maybe what you heard was some voices in your head."

"Could it have been a nurse?"

"I was the only nurse on duty last night and I sure didn't go near your room." The nurse left the room, shaking her head and rolling her eyes.

But Beth knew she wasn't imagining things. Someone had spoken to her last night, giving her words of comfort that could only have come from God. Tears filled her eyes as she recalled the words of her favorite Psalm: "'For He will command His angels concerning you, to guard you in all of your ways.'"

* * * *

John was nearly out of his mind with worry. When Beth never came home from school last week, he had called the principal and was stunned to learn what had happened. Since then he had made dozens of phone calls trying to find out where she had been taken, but no one seemed to know. Then he got a phone call which made his insides turn to ice.

He listened as the caller described what was about to be done to his wife in the name of "treatment" at the mental institution where she had been for the last week. "We've had to administer psychotropic drugs which have had some rather unfortunate side-effects. We're now considering the use of electroshock therapy," a coldly clinical voice told him. "If that fails to achieve the desired effect, we may have to resort to brain surgery. Her personality would be permanently altered, I'm afraid. She would have to remain institutionalized for the rest of her life."

He felt his knees go weak and actually had to hold on to the edge of the kitchen counter for support. The image of his gentle, loving wife being tormented in a mental institution was almost too much for him. He could hardly even speak. When he did, his voice shook with rage. "That's crazy! My wife is perfectly sane!"

"She's been examined by a competent psychiatrist who has determined that your wife poses a danger to society." There was a long pause, and John waited for the other shoe to drop. "Of course, that wouldn't be a concern if we could be assured that she had no access to firearms once she was released."

So, that's what this was all about. Somehow, the government had found out about his rifle. But how? It wasn't registered as far as he knew. How could they know? Then it hit him. The drugs. If they had given Beth the right kind of drugs, she'd probably tell them anything they wanted to know. "Look, my wife is not violent. Anyone who knows her would testify to that—"

"We're not interested in anyone else's opinion, Mr. Lanyon. We just want your cooperation. If you cooperate with us, you can be assured that your wife will be released."

"What do you want?" John asked in a low voice. This was blackmail, pure and simple.

"We simply ask that you turn in any firearms you may possess."

"What makes you think I have any?"

The voice on the line was filled with scorn. "Please, Mr. Lanyon, there's no use in pretending. Your wife revealed quite a lot while under drug-induced hypnosis. In fact, she revealed enough for the both of you to be designated global terrorists—which is a capital crime, I might add. Fortunately for you, the government is willing to grant amnesty if you voluntarily turn in your rifle and ammunition."

John shook his head in disgust as the phrase "voluntary compliance" took on a new, lucid meaning for him. If all they wanted was his rifle, they could have sent a SWAT team to his home to steal it. But they wanted him to go crawling to them with his tail between his legs. They wanted willing submission, and that's how they got their kicks.

After a brief pause, the caller asked pleasantly, "Shall I give the order to begin your wife's electroshock therapy?"

John felt like a mouse in a huge, steel trap that was about to snap shut. "No, that won't be necessary. I'll give you what you want."

* * * *

When John arrived at the local police precinct where he had been told to turn in his rifle, he was surrounded by a SWAT team dressed in black Ninja suits, helmets and ski masks, all aiming assault rifles at him. They wore no badges. He slowly put down his own rifle, which he had been holding at his side, unloaded, and put his hands in the air. Suddenly they rushed at him and slammed him down onto the concrete. As he lay there wondering what to expect next, he heard one of them bark, "Get your hands behind your head! Now!" He did what he was told. His only thought was to get Beth safely out of their clutches—and he knew the only way to do that was to submit to these bullies. They frisked him, taking his keys and wallet. Out of the corner of his eye he saw one of the goons rifling through it. Then they searched his car. *If their intent is to make me feel like a criminal, they certainly are doing a good job,* he thought ruefully. Or was that for their own benefit? Maybe the only way they could live with themselves was to convince themselves that the people they were victimizing were the criminals, and not the other way around. He only prayed that they didn't throw him in jail; that's all Beth would need right now.

After what seemed like an eternity he was pulled roughly to his feet and led to an ambulance parked in back of the police station. He thought his heart would burst with relief when he saw Beth being escorted out of the back of the ambulance. She looked pale and shaken, and had lost quite a bit of weight. But when she saw him her eyes lit up. She ran into his arms, weeping, and he clung to her as if he would never let her go. His precious gem, the apple of his eye, had been restored to him through the grace and mercy of God! His anger at having been blackmailed into giving up his rifle was forgotten. All that mattered now was knowing Beth was safe.

* * * *

"Isn't there any way we can fight this?" Beth asked the next morning after a fitful night's sleep. She had been severely traumatized by her experience but was afraid to take a sleeping aid because of all the drugs she had been given. Neither one of them even wanted to think about the effect the drugs may have had on the baby. But John told himself that their baby was protected by God.

"There's no justice anymore, Beth," he said sadly, in answer to her question. "At least, not in this world. Isaiah spoke about a time when people would seek justice but wouldn't find it. It looks as if that time is here. I suppose we could talk to a lawyer, but I doubt that would do much good. All lawyers are now under the thumb of the World Court. " He sighed. "Well, the government has us right where it wants us—disarmed and defenseless."

"I'm sorry," she said. She clearly felt terrible at having been used to blackmail her own husband.

"Honey, it's not your fault."

"This is so unfair! This whole thing happened because of a workshop on religious tolerance I had to conduct with my class. The aim was to get the students to be tolerant of other religious beliefs. I guess it was done to promote this one-world religion craze. Anyway, a couple of kids started bashing born-again Christians."

"Really? How come?"

Her hands shook slightly as she raised a cup of herbal tea to her lips; obviously she was still quite shaken from her ordeal. He wondered how long it would take for her to fully recover. "They claimed that Christians are intolerant and standing in the way of world peace," she said.

"No wonder they think that with all the propaganda they see in the movies and on television."

She nodded. "But what really got to me was when they started to attack Jesus. I swear, they sounded like satanists or something! I can't even repeat what they said. Anyway, that's when I said I was a born-again Christian—and I wouldn't tolerate any blasphemy against my Savior in my classroom."

"And that's how you wound up in a mental institution—and how the government got me to turn in my rifle. And now, I won't be able to protect you from those goons."

"Don't let it get to you, John. It could be that God allowed this to happen in order to prevent us from having a show-down with the government, so that we can be His light for those who are walking in darkness. After all, we can't be witnesses for Christ if we get killed in a violent confrontation with government agents. Maybe God wants to keep us alive so we can be His witnesses during the Tribulation."

"You're probably right—and if that's His will, then that's what I want. But at times like these I wish I could be sure I can protect you." His heart swelled with emotion as he thought about how much she meant to him. "Since the moment I met you, all I ever wanted was to love you and take care of you for the rest of my life. And on our wedding day, I made a vow to take care of you forever. But I may not be able to do that now." He remembered her description of being thrown against the wall outside her classroom execution-style with a gun to her back, and it nearly tore him apart inside. He thought of Danny Cheever's wife, who had been murdered by a government sniper while holding her baby. What if some government thug tried to kill Beth? How would he be able to protect her without any kind of weapon? He knew he should be trusting this to God, but it was harder now than ever before.

She took his hand in hers and squeezed it gently. "You don't have to worry, John. Jesus will never fail us." He listened in amazement as she told him about her mysterious visitor. Then she looked at him with an expression of unearthly peace. "Just keep your eyes fixed on Jesus. Look to the Cross. It's all we have to protect us from a world gone mad."

He took her hand in his and drew it to his lips. "You're right," he whispered. "I guess I just have to believe that Jesus can protect you, even when I can't."

CHAPTER 29

When Matt wasn't drinking, he fell into a lingering silence that sometimes lasted for days. He usually came home after Gina had gone to bed and watched late-night talk shows until he fell asleep on the sofa. Whenever he happened to come home early enough to have dinner, he hardly touched his food and avoided Gina's eyes. He rarely spoke to her. After dinner, he sat quietly smoking or nursing a beer.

Tonight Gina decided that this had gone on far too long. For once he wasn't in a drunken stupor, and this might be her only chance to get through to him. "Matt, we need to talk," she said firmly.

He looked up, his eyes expressionless, a cigarette dangling from his mouth. He took it out and squashed it onto the coffee table. "About what?"

"About us. About our marriage. And your drinking."

He scowled. "What if I don't feel like talking?"

"Look, Matt, we obviously have some serious problems—"

"Yeah? So what?"

She sighed. Maybe it would be easier if she just walked out. But she couldn't give up on him. She couldn't just sit back and watch him destroy himself. "I'm your wife. Husbands and wives talk to each other. They work out their problems, instead of ignoring them and letting them fester."

He smiled sardonically. "Wasn't he the guy from the Addam's Family?"

She rolled her eyes. "Why does everything have to be a joke to you?"

"Maybe because that's the only way I can get through the day," he said quietly.

She sat down next to him on the couch and tried to touch his hand, but he pulled it gruffly away. "Matt, what's wrong? What is it that's troubling you?" She looked deep into his eyes, but he just turned away.

"Nothing you'd want to know about."

"How do you know that?"

He laughed bitterly, his eyes cold and lifeless. "Believe me, I know."

She refused to be put off any longer. "Matt, I think we should see a marriage counselor."

"Oh, really? You think this is something a marriage counselor can solve?"

"Look, we have to try. If we want to salvage our marriage, we have to at least try."

"I have better things to do with my time," he said sullenly.

"Better things. Like drinking yourself into oblivion every night or watching mindless drivel on TV?"

"Don't push me, Gina."

Her voice rose an octave. "Push *you*? You've been treating me like dirt for months, and *I'm* the one who's pushing you? That's just great!"

"You don't understand."

"I understand, all right." She walked over to the window and stared vacantly at the streets below. The rain-soaked pavement glistened with the puddles of a fleeting summer storm, and the last rays of the sun painted the sky purple and gold. Soon darkness would descend. Already a couple of fireflies were hovering over the grass.

"I understand you're completely unwilling to do what it takes to save our marriage. You won't talk to me. You refuse to go to a marriage counselor. I don't know what else to do anymore. What can I do, if you're not willing to take any responsibility for saving our marriage?"

He got up off the couch and walked toward her. "So, this is all my fault? That's what you're saying?" There was something about his eyes that frightened her.

"Of course it's your fault. It's certainly not *my* fault. I've done everything I can to save our marriage. You haven't done a thing!"

"You think it's my fault. Well, I'll tell you whose fault it is. It's *your* fault, you lying little tramp."

The words struck her like a physical blow. "What?"

"You heard what I said. And you know why? Because I know the truth about what happened in Wyoming."

A strange, sick feeling spread through her, and she sunk onto the couch. Suddenly it all made sense—Matt's stormy moods and sullen silences, his drinking and staying out all hours of the night, his hopelessness and despair. She had never imagined he would find out.

Before she could say anything, he said, "Don't try to deny it. I saw the evidence myself." Then, with a triumphant and arrogant sneer, he told her about a letter he had read that had been meant for her, but which he had opened by mistake. "So, are you going to deny it?" He was actually enjoying this.

She looked down at the floor, unable to meet his scornful, mocking eyes. "How can I?" She didn't know what else to say.

"Gee, you mean you're not going to beg for my forgiveness? I'm disappointed in you, Gina."

She made no attempt to wipe away the tears that glistened under her eyelashes and slid down her cheeks. But there was something she had to make clear to him, something so important that nothing else mattered. "Matt, I know you're angry and disappointed in me. You have every right to be. I made a terrible mistake. One that I'll regret for the rest of my life. But I never stopped loving you, not even for a moment."

He was incredulous. "A mistake? You call that a mistake? Gina, a mistake is something you do by accident, like adding wrong. A mistake doesn't rip somebody's life apart!"

"Matt..."

"Shut up! Shut up and listen while I tell you what I really think of you." She clutched the edge of the couch as he called her the most vicious names she had ever heard—and could never forget. She wanted to run from the room, but couldn't seem to move. When he had finished, he gave her a withering look that burned into her soul.

He stood waiting for her response, but she didn't say a word. Simply got up and ran out of the apartment.

* * * *

After the door slammed behind her, Matt took a few deep breaths to calm down. He had finally vented all the anger and hatred buried inside for so long. But he didn't feel any better, he actually felt sick. The look in Gina's eyes jarred him. He knew he had hurt her far more than he had ever intended. Suddenly he wanted to run after her and tell her he would forgive her, he didn't mean all those things he had said.

As he grasped the doorknob, he stopped himself. *Why should I go crawling back to her?*

He heard a still, small voice that he had almost come to hate. *Because you love her.*

Matt walked over to the liquor cabinet, yanked open the door, and pulled out a half-empty bottle of vodka. He poured a glassful and took a swig. Soon, he forgot all about Gina.

* * * *

458

"David, what's the matter with you?" Anita Weiss looked at her son with alarm. The expression in his eyes unnerved her. They had the vacant look of an animal.

"Nothing's the matter with me," he said in a mechanical, lifeless tone.

"Don't give me that. You haven't been acting like yourself ever since you were admitted. Now, I realize you've been having problems accepting your grandfather's death, but—"

He said something vile and unrepeatable.

Anita stared at him, shocked and dismayed. "David! How can you talk that way about your grandfather?"

His smile was crooked and unnatural. "It's easy. I just have to listen."

"Listen? Listen to what?"

"My spirit guides," he said simply.

Now she felt even more perplexed. She had read of spirit guides in several women's magazines, and had even bought a book, written by a well-known actress, which hailed such beings as the ultimate source of spiritual enlightenment and expanded consciousness. They were supposed to be *good*, not evil. "What are you saying, David? That spirit guides told you to call your grandfather those names?" It just didn't make sense.

"You should hear what they call you," he said, laughing. But all the while his eyes retained that hollow, distant look, devoid of all human feeling. He then let out a string of four-letter words that almost made her blush.

"That's it," she said firmly. "I'm taking you out of here." When David was admitted to the Lucid Home because of his difficulty accepting his grandparents' death, she had been assured that, through therapy, he would overcome his depression and withdrawal, becoming a more productive member of "our new global society" (the phrase was ubiquitous these days). At first, he did seem to improve; during her first few visits, she had marveled at his increased self-esteem and new enthusiasm, particularly for what he was learning in therapy. He talked excitedly of transcendental meditation, guided imagery, and astral projection, and it seemed to Anita that her son had entered a whole new world in which ordinary human beings had access to the deepest mysteries of the universe. He also began to speak with an eloquence that astounded her. Gradually, though, he began to exhibit a subtle change in demeanor that she couldn't quite pinpoint, but which profoundly disturbed her. And his praise for his therapists seemed so excessive at times that she found herself wondering if her son had joined some mind-controlling cult. Initially, she tried to convince herself that her fears were unfounded, that she had somehow gotten the wrong impression. After all, the people in charge of the home were trained professionals with advanced degrees in psychology and years of experience dealing with troubled adolescents. Surely they knew what was best for David, probably even better than she did. But what she saw today didn't just frighten her; it terrified her. Something dreadful was happening to David, and she wasn't about to let it continue.

"I'm not going anywhere," he said flatly. "And if you insist on telling me what to do, I can command the spirits to tear you to pieces."

She tried to shake off the feeling of horror that was beginning to envelop her. "David, don't be ridiculous. You're talking nonsense."

"It's not nonsense!" His tone was defiant, and Anita could swear his eyes were glowing. "It's power—power beyond anything you could even imagine. I don't need you anymore, do you understand? I don't need other people's approval or acceptance anymore. I can be a god!"

What kind of garbage are they teaching him here? "Oh really? Who told you that?"

"The wise ones. The Ascended Masters who have chosen *me* to be a part of their Plan for the future of this planet."

"What plan?"

"To usher in a new kingdom ruled by those who have discovered the divine light that lives within us all, a light that will soon change the entire world! Don't you see? *I'm* one of the chosen ones!"

In spite of her fears, she found herself strangely drawn by what David was saying. Yet he had spoken of spirits tearing her to pieces. Something was definitely wrong with this picture; it just didn't add up. "What do you mean by that, David? I'm still not sure how you fit into this 'plan.'"

"It will all be revealed soon enough." He sounded as if he were reciting part of a memorized text.

She began to feel a vague sense of apprehension at these words. "When? When will it be revealed?"

He had a faraway, dreamy look in his eyes, as if listening to some inner voice. "At my Initiation."

Inexplicably, the word filled her with dread. An icy coldness spread through her, and she felt like someone on the edge of a precipice. "Your initiation? Initiation into what?"

At that moment the door opened and a staff member, wearing a white smock and smiling amiably, entered the room. "I'm sorry, Ms. Weiss, visiting hours have just ended. You'll have to come back next week."

She looked at her watch. "But there's still over forty-five minutes left."

His expression darkened, and for an instant she thought he would be angry. But in the next moment, the look vanished. "Oh, really?" he said lightly. "Well, I'm sorry to have to cut short your visit, but it's time for David's group therapy session."

Anita raised her eyebrows slightly; it was evident the man was trying to get rid of her. She brushed a lock of dark hair away from her eyes, a nervous habit she'd had since her childhood. "I thought you didn't schedule any therapy sessions during visiting hours."

There was something about his smile that made her uneasy. "Ms. Weiss, you must understand that we here at the Lucid Home have David's best interests at heart, and if he's going to overcome his problems, we must have your cooperation. Sometimes, that may necessitate a certain amount of sacrifice on your part. It also requires your trust. Now, if you insist on questioning our methods, you may undermine the relationship we have with David, which could adversely affect the entire recovery process. I'm sure you don't want that to happen."

"Of course not. But—"

"Good. We'll see you next week, then."

He took hold of her arm, and a strange feeling of oppression came over her. She wanted to pull away, but felt powerless to resist. What was happening to her?

As she was led toward the door, her eyes fell on a book on top of David's dresser, partially covered by a sheet of notebook paper. But she could see the title, and she nearly gasped.

It was a copy of the Satanic Bible.

* * * *

Anita had never believed in the devil, and that posed a problem. How can you fight something you don't believe in? For the three days since her last visit to the Lucid Home, she hadn't had a decent night's sleep. Every little noise made her jump, and whenever she did manage to fall asleep, she would awake suddenly in the middle of the night, her heart pounding. When she tried to drink her morning tea, her hands shook so badly she usually ended up spilling half the cup. Sometimes she stood in front of the liquor cabinet, staring at the half-empty bottles of vodka, whiskey, and rum. She longed for a drink, even just a swig, but something held her back. After all, she certainly couldn't help David in a drunken stupor. But it wasn't just that. She felt directed by some inner voice, a voice so urgent that she couldn't ignore it.

It was this same sense of urgency that finally compelled her to see a rabbi, though she hadn't been to a synagogue in years. Expecting him to express grave concern over David's recent behavior, particularly his possession of the Satanic Bible, Anita was perplexed when the rabbi assured her that there was nothing to worry about. "It's natural for young people to experiment with new ideas and philosophies, even if they may seem unorthodox, if not bizarre, to their parents," he said.

"But he said he could command spirits to tear me to pieces. Don't you find that frightening? I mean, you can't possibly tell me that's normal. If you ask me, it's sick! In fact, it's more than just sick—it's downright evil."

The rabbi smiled broadly. "Well, it seems your son has stirred quite a strong reaction in you. I would say he's accomplished his goal."

She was beginning to feel frustrated by his refusal to take her fears seriously. "What are you saying? That he was just trying to get a rise out of me?"

"That could be. Youngsters his age often like to shock people, especially their parents. They may even act rebelliously at times. But it's all a healthy, normal part of growing up, of gaining autonomy."

Anita couldn't believe this; the man was parroting what she'd learned in her college psychology classes! At one time, she would have agreed with him. But not anymore. She had a sense that something was horribly amiss, not just with David, but with the world, possibly even the universe. Ever since her last visit with him, she felt a deep sense of foreboding, of impending horror. As if she had caught a glimpse into another sinister dimension, parallel to this world, but unspeakably evil. Her own son was being drawn into this eerie dimension, and she felt powerless to save him. Just the thought of returning to the Lucid Home and trying to get David released filled her with dread. But she had to do something.

Recalling her mother's Catholicism, she decided to confide in a priest at the local parish church. To her consternation, she received a response not unlike the rabbi's.

"I think my son's gotten involved in the occult," she told the priest.

"Well, I wouldn't worry." He spoke in a kindly tone obviously meant to reassure her. "For most young people, it's a purely innocent pastime. And, it's natural for them to be curious about such things."

"But isn't there something about demonic possession in the Bible?"

He considered this. "The gospels do have accounts of Jesus supposedly casting out devils. But today we know that those people weren't really possessed by demons; they were probably suffering from some form of mental illness."

"Are you sure?"

He smiled benevolently. "Well, there doesn't seem to be any other reasonable explanation. After all, how can any educated, intelligent person believe in demons in this day and age?"

With nowhere else to turn, she paged through her address book that night frantically searching for someone—anyone—who might be willing to help her. But her search seemed futile. She didn't have many friends, and the few she had would never understand something so bizarre.

With tears of frustration, she tossed the book against the coffee table and it slid to the floor. Tiny pieces of paper flew out of the book, memo pages where she had written phone numbers that she had never copied into the book.

Bending down to pick them up, she saw a name on one sheet that was vaguely familiar. There was also a phone number and address. She stared at it for a long time...and then she remembered.

With trembling fingers she dialed the number. Busy. She waited about a minute, pacing, then tried again. Still busy. She stuffed the piece of paper into her purse and hurried out the door.

* * * *

At first she didn't quite recognize the man who answered the door. Wearing a shabby bathrobe of checkered blue flannel, he gave her a long, angry scowl, swaying slightly as he held onto the door. Uneven stubble covered his haggard face, and his eyes were slightly bloodshot. "What do *you* want?" he grunted.

"Um, I'm not sure if I have the right place. Is—is this the Lanyon residence?"

"Yeah, but if you're looking for Gina, she's gone." He spoke in the tone of an angry, petulant child.

Anita was beginning to wonder why she had even bothered coming here tonight. She still wasn't sure what it was that had prompted her to make the half-hour drive through a dangerous neighborhood of roving gangs at such a late hour; she only knew that she had run out of alternatives, and it was worth a try. "Then you must be Matt," she found herself saying in spite of her misgivings. "I guess you don't remember me. My name is Anita. I met you at my parents' funeral. Anyway, you and your wife seemed so kind...I thought maybe..." In the next instant, she was crying.

She saw a glimmer of recognition in his eyes. "You're Ben and Elsie's daughter," Matt blurted out.

She nodded, and he immediately ushered her into the apartment.

"Here, sit down," he said gently as he led her to the kitchen table.

"I'm sorry." She fumbled in her handbag for a tissue. "This is so embarrassing."

"Look, it's okay. I'm the one who should apologize for being rude. I guess I haven't been myself lately. Can I get you anything? Some coffee or tea?"

She was tempted to ask for a Scotch, but decided against it. "No, thanks. But could I use your bathroom?" She wanted to wash her face, which was smeared with mascara.

He pointed toward a little alcove. "It's the second door on the left."

When she looked in the mirror, she almost drew back at her disheveled appearance—the long dark hair, streaked with gray, that tumbled past her shoulders in disarray, her pale face and the dark creases under her eyes. She hadn't eaten much in the last few days, just nibbled on a slice of toast in the morning. Thank God she wasn't drinking!

After washing her face, she returned to the kitchen. Matt had made her some tea and had poured himself some coffee. "You look like you could use some," he told her.

She smiled weakly. "Thank you. I'm sorry for intruding like this, but I was kind of desperate. There aren't many people I can turn to."

"What's the matter?"

She wasn't sure how to begin, or what to say that wouldn't make her sound crazy. But she had to start somewhere. "Are you a religious person, Matt?"

The question seemed to startle him. "Not exactly. Why do you ask?"

"Well, I'm not religious, either. Religion was always a little confusing to me, since my parents had kind of a mixed marriage in that respect. My mom was kind of a nominal Christian, and my father wasn't religious at all. He felt pretty bitter toward God because of his experience in Nazi Germany."

"Didn't your mom go to a prayer group or something?"

Anita nodded. "But that was pretty recently. My father was *not* too happy about it, either. Anyway, whenever I asked them questions about spiritual things, they told me I should just find 'something' to believe in. They didn't want to influence me one way or another, so they decided to let me make up my own mind." She sighed. "Now, I'm not sure that was such a good idea."

"Why not?"

"Because I don't have the answers I need right now to help David. I even went to a priest and a rabbi, but neither one of them seemed able to give me the answers I need. You see, David had a very hard time dealing with the loss of his grandparents, especially since he was so close to his grandfather."

Matt nodded. "I remember they were pretty close."

"Well, he's been in a home for troubled adolescents. But something happened to him there that has me very frightened."

"What happened?"

She hesitated. "Well, I know this is going to sound crazy, but I think he's been possessed."

Now he really looked startled. "Possessed? You mean by demons?"

She threw her hands up in desperation. "I guess so. I mean, I don't even know what demons are. That's why this is so confusing to me. David talked about spirit guides, and expanded consciousness, but—"

Matt stopped her for a moment. "Wait a minute. Did you say spirit guides?"

She nodded. "Yes. Is that important?"

"It might be." His expression was grim.

"So, then, you know about this stuff," she said hopefully.

"A little. But not much. You see, my brother and his wife are born-again Christians, and they're a lot more up on this spiritual stuff than I am."

"Do you think they'd be willing to help?"

"Are you kidding? They live for this stuff. They're always yacking about God, and the spiritual realm and all that crap. They'd probably eat this up."

She was puzzled. "So, it's kind of a hobby for them?"

He shrugged. "That's one way of putting it. I'll give them a call."

* * * *

The next day, Anita sat in a cramped apartment filled with all the trappings of Christianity that had always made her uncomfortable. A Bible was displayed prominently on the coffee table and several religious plaques hung on the wall, including one of the Lord's Prayer. She glanced at the bookshelves that lined the wall and saw that most of the titles had something to do with religion. The rest looked like English and history books. *What am I doing here?* She felt completely out of place.

Matt had taken Anita over to his brother's apartment so they could talk in detail about David's condition, and decide on a plan of action. But suddenly she was having cold feet. She wondered what she was getting herself into.

John looked grave as Anita related to him everything that had occurred during her last visit with David. When she mentioned the word "initiation," he looked even more concerned. "You've got to get him out of there," he said when she had finished.

"But what if they won't release him?" Anita asked.

"Then we'll just have to pray that they will. We're dealing with strongholds and principalities here." He was talking very excitedly. "We have to pray that the Lord will break down the stronghold of the enemy and deliver David from their grasp."

Anita felt as if John were speaking a foreign language. "I'm not sure I'm following you. Besides, they won't even let me talk to him on the phone anymore. I doubt they'll let me take him home."

Matt's voice was firm. "Be persistent. Tell them you'll camp out there every night until they release him...maybe even threaten them with legal action. And don't go there alone, either. Bring someone with you. If you show up with someone else, they may be more likely to give in. Besides, you shouldn't go there alone anyway, if it's as dangerous as John thinks it is. I'll go with you, if you want me to."

"I think I should go, too," John said.

"Why?" Matt sounded resentful. "Don't you trust me to handle this by myself?"

"Look, there's bound to be some heavy demonic influences over there. That Initiation David referred to sounds like a Luciferic Initiation, which is basically an invitation to worship Lucifer. You shouldn't go there without a Christian present, it's much too dangerous."

"But if he's been reading the Satanic Bible, he's probably already worshiping Satan," Matt pointed out.

"That's possible. But we don't know for certain. Besides, this Initiation will involve more than just worship; it'll probably require an outward sign of allegiance, like a mark of some sort. I've read about these types of Initiations. In fact, the Bible talks about a mark that Satan's followers will receive during the Tribulation. According to the Book of Revelation, anyone who takes the mark will be condemned."

Anita felt heartsick. "So, if David does receive a mark, then there's no way to save him?"

"Not necessarily. The mark in Revelation 13 will be vastly different from anything that came before it. Besides, there's no way to know for sure if David's Initiation will involve such a mark. But we shouldn't take this lightly." He looked directly at Anita, and his voice was very firm. "There's a battle going on for your son's soul, and it's not going to be won through mere human effort. The Bible says our struggle is not against flesh and blood, but against the powers and authorities of darkness and against the forces of evil in the heavenly realms."

Anita felt bewildered and more than a little intimidated by such talk. "But what does that mean?"

Matt sounded impatient. "Yeah, let's stick to English."

John looked at Anita again. "It means that the only way to deliver your son from the forces of darkness is through the power of God and His Holy Spirit. The Bible tells us that the only way to defeat Satan is by taking on the full armor of God. Some Christians call that spiritual warfare."

"I still don't get it," she said.

"Okay, when Jesus died on the Cross and rose from the dead, He defeated all the powers of darkness. Not only that, but His Spirit lives within all those who believe in Him. That means all believers share in His victory. Through Jesus' Name and by the power of His blood, Christians have authority over all the demons of hell. When we rebuke them in the Name of Jesus, they have to obey us."

Anita found all this fascinating. "Really?"

"That's right. But only a Christian saved by the blood of Christ will be able to confront the demons that are holding your son captive. That's why I should go with you. And I think we should bring a pastor as well."

Anita looked at Matt. "Then, you're not a Christian?"

He looked uncomfortable. "Nah, I'm not into this stuff the way my brother is," he said lightly.

Anita started to recall some of the things her mother had told her about Jesus, things she didn't want to listen to at the time. Now, she wished she had paid more attention. She turned to John, grateful at finding someone who could give her some answers. "Jesus cast demons out of people, didn't He?"

John smiled approvingly. "That's right, He did."

She then related what the priest had told her, and John shook his head.

"Why would a priest deny the existence of demons?" Matt sounded surprised.

"Denying the existence of the supernatural is part of the Great Apostasy which the Bible predicted for the last days," John replied. "Nowadays anything in the Bible that makes people uncomfortable is simply dismissed. That's why most people today, including so-called religious people, don't believe in the devil or demons anymore. And that's just one step away from denying the existence of God."

"So, what are we going to do about David?" Anita asked.

"Well, first I'm going to call my pastor and ask him to pay David a visit. But you need to be prepared, Anita: this could get nasty. The pastor will probably have to confront the demons that have your son in their power. If he is possessed, the demons will have to be cast out, and that can only be done by a committed Christian."

"You're talking about an exorcism, aren't you?" Matt asked in a soft voice.

Anita drew in her breath. "I don't like the sound of this. Are you sure it's safe?" Images of her son spewing out blasphemy and writhing around like a maddened animal filled her with dread. What if an exorcism put him in more danger? Could she take that risk?

John tried to reassure her. "We're going to pray that Jesus will send His Spirit before us to remove any obstacles that might be put in our way and to open David's eyes to the truth."

Anita was hopeful. "Do you think it will work?"

John frowned. "Yes, but unfortunately, there's no guarantee that the demons won't come back...unless your son gives his life to Jesus."

"Why is that?" she asked.

"Well, Jesus told His followers that after the house is swept clean, ten more unclean spirits will enter where the previous spirits left."

"I don't understand."

"Okay, even if the demons are cast out, as long as he's not saved by the blood of Christ, they could always come back. Especially if he's been involved in the occult, because that's basically an open invitation to demonic possession."

She felt depressed. "So, why should we even bother?"

"Look, that doesn't mean you have to give up hope," John said. "It just means we should pray for David's salvation. We also need to pray for protection from the demonic forces that are bound to be at that place." He looked at Matt and Anita with concern. "You two are particularly vulnerable since you're not Christians."

"Why?" Anita asked, curious.

"Because Christians are under the special protection of the blood of Jesus. Satan can't do anything to a believer unless God allows it. That's been attested to by former Satanists who later became Christians, by the way. This one guy wrote a book about his conversion to Christianity after being high priest of a satanic coven. He claimed that whenever the coven put a curse on Christians, the curse never worked; it only worked on non-Christians. In fact, whenever the Satanists tried to put a curse on committed Christians, the Satanists wound up being victims of their own curse." He then went on to relate a story about a Satanic cult which had cursed a group of Christians with fire. Within days, the Satanists who did so died in a fiery car accident.

Anita felt a chill run down her spine. "David told me he could command spirits to tear me to pieces. What if he puts a curse on me?"

John asked softly, "Do you believe all the things I told you about Jesus?"

"You mean about His defeating the power of evil and all that?"

John nodded.

She looked down at the floor. "I'm not sure. I—I want to believe it. But I was never a religious person. This is all new to me."

John smiled. "Well, guess what? Christianity is not a religion."

"It isn't?" This didn't even make sense.

"No, it's a relationship. A relationship with the Living God through the Person of Jesus Christ." He then explained to her that all other religious systems taught salvation through good works, but Christianity alone preaches salvation through a personal relationship with Jesus Christ, the Son of God. "Would you like to have a relationship with Jesus?"

"Maybe...someday. But I'm not sure I'm ready for that yet."

"Even if it guarantees your protection from the forces of darkness?"

She shrugged. "I'll have to think about it," she said quietly. She didn't want to become one of those fanatics the media was always railing against.

"I'll give the pastor a call." John disappeared into the kitchen for a few moments, but Anita caught bits and pieces of his conversation with the pastor. She felt dismayed as she realized that he was giving John a hard time about performing an exorcism. This had been her last hope. She put her face in her hands and tried to fight back the sob that rose in her throat.

Matt put his hand on her shoulder and spoke reassuringly. "It'll be okay. I know my brother. He can be a self-righteous pain-in-the-butt, but he's stubborn as hell. He won't take no for an answer."

"Hey, that's my husband you're talking about." Anita looked up at the smiling woman who entered the room. Her auburn hair had dark roots and was somewhat tousled, and she looked a little groggy. Anita noticed her oversized sweatshirt and protruding belly and knew immediately that she was pregnant. But she didn't look well. Her face was pale and drawn, and there were dark creases under her eyes.

Matt looked sheepish. "Oops, looks like I put my foot in my mouth. Sorry, Beth."

"That's okay, I'm used to it." She smiled warmly at Anita and introduced herself as Matt's sister-in-law. "You'll have to excuse my appearance—I was taking a nap. I just got up to get some herbal tea. Would you like some?"

Anita forced a smile. "No, thanks." John hung up the phone and Anita nearly jumped off the couch. "What did he say?"

John was frowning. "He won't do it."

Matt and Anita shouted in unison. "What! Why not?"

"He says that exorcisms went out with the Dark Ages. I tried to get a hold of the assistant pastor—who may be willing to do it—but he's out visiting sick parishioners." He looked grim. "It looks as if I may have to do it. This isn't something that should be put off."

Matt looked skeptical. "Wait a minute. Are you sure you know what you're doing? I thought only priests and ministers could do an exorcism."

"Well, the Bible refers to a priesthood of believers. It means that all those who follow Christ are priests of God. As such, all believers should be able to cast out demons in Jesus' Name. In fact, Jesus told His followers that they would be able to do everything He did, and that would include casting out demons."

Beth returned with her tea and eased herself onto the couch. "Besides, John does have some experience with this sort of thing." Anita was awestruck as Beth described John's success in helping to deliver a little girl named Kelsie from demonic influences.

"That's incredible!" Anita exclaimed. "I've never heard of anything like that. It's like something out of a movie."

"I can assure you it was very real." John sat down on a chair next to the couch. "So, Anita—it's up to you. Do you want me to do this?"

She nodded. "If it will bring back my son..." Tears glistened in her eyes, and she brushed them away.

Beth turned to John. "Do you want me to come with you?"

"No, we need you to stay home and be our prayer warrior. I'm sure you realize how critical it is to have another Christian praying for us. Besides, I don't want you exposed to any direct contact with demons. That's the last thing you need right now."

The four of them bowed their heads as John led them in prayer. Just as they were about to leave, Beth kissed John on the cheek. "Be careful," she said, and Anita noticed that her face had grown even paler.

John pulled her close. "Don't worry, sweetheart. Jesus will never fail us. He's with us wherever we go."

She smiled. "I know. I've learned that we never have to face anything alone, as long as we have Jesus."

As the three headed out toward the car, Beth stood by the open front door. "I love you!" she called to John.

"I love you more," he said with a smile.

Matt rolled his eyes up. "Come on, let's go."

Anita saw the look of tenderness between John and Beth, and she envied them. They seemed to have something that few couples ever found. Well, they certainly were lucky. *Then again*, she thought, *maybe luck had nothing to do with it.*

* * * *

"Are you ready, David?"

He looked up, startled. The High Priest was dressed in the ceremonial black robe, his hooded face barely discernible in the dim light of David's room. Although David knew he was supposed to trust the elders here with his very life, especially the High Priest, lately he felt a slight stab of fear whenever he entered their presence, though he wasn't sure why. "Ready? For what?"

"For your Initiation." The High Priest, who had taken the name of Legion during his own Initiation, looked at David with a penetrating gaze, which made him even more nervous.

"But I thought it was scheduled for next week."

"There's been a change of plans." His expression was inscrutable. "Come with me."

Obediently, David followed. But as his eyes fell on the long, silver-handled knife that gleamed in Legion's hand, a shiver ran down his spine.

Maybe I shouldn't do this. But the voices in his head assured him that all would be well, for he was about to achieve the full potential of his own godhood. The thought was intoxicating. After being shunned and rejected by his peers when his grandfather was branded a terrorist, the idea of becoming a god aroused a sense of power and exhilaration unlike anything he had ever imagined. It was like a drug. During his therapy at the Lucid Home, the elders had revealed to him his true identity: that of a reincarnated Ascended Master, full of divine human potential and spiritually superior to other human beings. After his Initiation, his true powers would be unleashed and there would be nothing he couldn't achieve.

With that thought in mind, he ignored his fears and followed Legion down the hall toward the Meditation Chamber, where the ceremony would take place.

* * * *

John shook his head as he scanned the list of therapists prominently displayed in the lobby of the Lucid Home.

"What's wrong?" Anita asked.

"Notice anything strange about the degrees these people have?" he asked her.

She looked. "Not really. It looks like most of them have Ph.Ds."

"Yeah, but in what field?"

Matt looked, too. "Parapsychology."

"It's the study of the occult," John explained in response to Anita's quizzical expression. "Of course, the word now in vogue is 'paranormal,' but it's essentially the same thing. No wonder your son's been acting like he's under the influence of demons."

"So, what'll we do?" she asked urgently, her voice a whisper. "I'm not even sure they'll let us in to seem him."

"We have to trust that God's in control," John told her. "He'll give us an opening. We just have to follow His leading."

* * * *

David's heart was beating rapidly as he watched the elders prepare for the ritual. He knew he was supposed to make an oath signed in his own blood—that's what the knife was for—but now as he looked at it a sickening feeling of dread washed over him and he wanted to run from the room. But the voices persisted. *You can't turn back now, David, you've come too far.* Their tone was both seductive and threatening. If he tried to back out now, something terrible would happen to him. But the images of murder and mutilation that constantly swam in his head made him tremble. He squeezed his eyes shut and tried to focus on the ritual.

* * * *

John sprinted down the hall, followed by Anita and Matt.

"We don't have much time," he said. "Where did you see that Mediation Chamber?"

"I think it's just around the next corridor," Anita replied. "You really think David's there?"

"Well, you said he likes to spend a lot of time there, and he's not in his room," John said. "Besides, I have a strong feeling that's where he is, especially after hearing your description of it."

"But why?"

"Because it's the typical layout of a witch's coven."

Great, Matt thought. *Just the place to be on a Saturday afternoon.*

"Here it is," Anita whispered, pointing at the entrance.

Matt tried to shake off the horror that suddenly came over him. A mysterious, sinister Presence seemed to surround them. His heart was beating rapidly, and beads of perspiration trickled down the back of his neck and across his forehead. *Man, I don't wanna be here*, he thought.

In a soft voice John began to pray. "Lord Jesus, Son of the Living God, we ask that You give us victory over the enemy, and that your Name be glorified. Please deliver David from the forces of darkness that are holding him captive, and lead him into Your heavenly Kingdom. Show him that You are the Way and the Truth and the Life, that he is eternally lost without You. We ask this In Your precious Name. Amen." He slowly opened the door, and Matt wondered vaguely why no security guards had pursued them yet.

A heavy silence filled the room, along with an almost stifling oppression. At the far end of the sprawling, temple-like chamber hung a plaque. It said, "THE ASSEMBLY OF THE GODS." Strange symbols bordered it, the swastika and the all-seeing eye of Osiris, which Gail had rambled about during the awareness course. Paintings of bare-breasted women, their hair entwined with serpents, covered the soaring cathedral ceiling. Demonic gargoyles were perched on marble ledges in each corner. The intricately woven tapestries on the walls depicted the pagan gods of the ancient world. Matt remembered a few of them from the mythology course he had taken in high school.

One of the statues seemed to look right into his eyes. He glanced at the name underneath, then spoke to John in a low voice. "Who's Moloch?"

"An Ammonite god who demanded the sacrifice of newborn babies. During Old Testament times, some of the Israelites turned away from God to worship him. They burned their children alive."

Matt shuddered. "Man, this place is creepy!"

His eyes fell on the massive oak table in the center of the room. There were thirteen chairs, ornately carved in wood, on each side. Only the chair at each end of the table had arms. "Interesting table. I wonder what it's used for."

"Could it be a banquet table?" Anita asked.

John looked grim. "It's used for a witch's coven. The High Priest sits at one end with the Priestess at the other end."

"How do you know all this stuff?" Matt asked.

"I've done some reading on witchcraft."

Anita looked startled. "Really? How come?"

"A couple of students at the college where I teach had gotten involved in witchcraft awhile back. They thought it was harmless, and I wanted to show them it wasn't. So, I had to do a little research."

Matt still didn't understand why no one had stopped them from entering. Just as he was thinking this, a dark, hooded figure emerged from a door between two of the tapestries. "We've been expecting you." His tone was smooth and confident, and Matt could swear his eyes were glowing.

"Who are you?" John asked.

"I am Legion," he said with a devilish smile. "And today I am going to demonstrate to you the power of Lucifer, the god of this world. That is why you have all been permitted to enter his sanctuary."

"Lucifer has no power over me." John's voice was strong and resolute. "I'm under the protection of Jesus of Nazareth, the Son of the Living God. The devil you serve may be the god of this world—temporarily—but Jesus Christ is God of the Universe."

At the Name of Jesus, Legion shrunk back. "I forbid you to speak that Name in my presence!"

"Where's David Weiss?" John asked.

"Ah, yes, you've come to rescue the poor, wayward child," Legion said in a mocking tone. "Do you really think you can prevent his Initiation into the ranks of the gods?"

Matt shuddered. How could Legion know why they were here? Then he recalled that the woman at the front desk had threatened to call security when Anita and John had demanded to see David; she had probably phoned Legion and alerted him to their presence.

Legion looked directly at Matt and smiled knowingly. "Why should you be surprised that I know your purpose for coming here? I'm a member of the Master's Inner Circle. Do you really think someone as powerful as I would have to depend on a primitive mechanical device for knowledge of the enemy's plans?" Matt stared at him and a chill went down his back. Legion had read his mind!

John seemed unfazed. "If you're so powerful, why are you afraid to let us talk to David?"

"I'm not afraid! David already belongs to the god of this world, and no one can take what is rightfully his."

"Then it shouldn't be a problem to let us see him." His tone was so matter-of-fact that Matt could only marvel at his bother's sense of calm. Just being here was enough to give Matt the willies.

"Oh, you shall all be permitted to see him. But only so you can witness the power of Lucifer, the Prince of Darkness." With that, Legion stepped back through the doorway he had entered.

"I don't like the sound of this," Matt said uneasily.

"Don't worry," John whispered. "Remember, God is in control. Legion is drunk with pride, and God can use that to our advantage."

Matt nodded. "Yeah, it looks like the guy wants a show-down."

"Well, that's exactly what he's going to get."

Legion returned presently, followed by an entourage of hooded people dressed all in black, who seated themselves at the table. Matt noticed that Legion sat at the head of the table.

David entered last, looking around nervously until his eyes fell on the Bible John was holding. An expression of absolute hatred came over his features, and he approached John with an arrogant sneer, mocking Christ and bragging about the power of Lucifer. "I'm about to be initiated into the ranks of the gods. Once I undergo my Initiation, the power of Lucifer will become fully manifest in me." Matt could hardly believe this was the same, down-to-earth kid he had known as Ben's grandson. But Matt also sensed that beneath all his bravado, David was actually afraid.

"Lucifer is a liar." John spoke calmly yet firmly. "Jesus called him the father of lies. He'll betray you as soon as you outlive any usefulness you might have to him. Besides, you're lying to yourself as well."

"What do you mean by that?" David asked defensively.

"I can tell you're afraid. But you won't admit it, not even to yourself."

He looked at John with contempt. "Afraid? Afraid of what?"

"Of what you're about to become. And you've already begun to have doubts about Lucifer. You're not sure you can trust him."

"That's not true!" His eyes flashed with rage, but his face was pale.

"David, once you make this decision, there's no turning back. Satan—the one you call Lucifer—wants you to be his slave. He knows he can't defeat Christ, so he wants to drag you down with him. He wants you to spend eternity in the fires of hell. But Jesus wants to set you free from the power of sin and death. Do you want to be free, David?"

For the first time Legion sounded uneasy. "True freedom is found only in the service of Lucifer."

John said firmly, "I'm not talking to you; I'm talking to David. Well, David? What's it going to be? Freedom from sin and death through Jesus Christ, or slavery and eternal darkness with Lucifer?"

David's confidence appeared to be shaken. "I—I don't know," he stammered.

John held out his Bible. "Will you let me read something to you?"

"Don't open that book!" David shouted. "It's full of lies."

"Why are you so afraid of this book?" John asked quietly.

"He's not afraid," Legion insisted. "Go ahead, read! That book has no power over us."

John opened the Bible and began to read a passage that described Christ's deliverance of a demon-possessed man. As John read the passage, Matt couldn't help noticing the agitation of those seated at the table. A few began to writhe and moan in anguish, while the others cursed and shouted horrible blasphemies against the Name of Jesus. At times, John had to raise his voice over the din, and that seemed to make them even more angry.

Matt had never been so frightened in his life. He had seen movies about demons before, and had found them horrifying yet strangely captivating. But to be in the presence of such raw, unadulterated evil filled him with a terror beyond his worst imagination. His throat tightened, and he could hear the blood rushing through his head. He recalled the dream he once had, in which he hung suspended over an abyss of endless darkness. Beneath him, the mouth of hell gaped open, drawing him downward toward its terrible blackness. He knew that he was standing in the kingdom of the Prince of Darkness, surrounded by the demons of hell. He wanted to scream and run from the room, but invisible hands clamped his legs, holding him immobile.

In the midst of all this evil, John was confident and unafraid. When he finished reading, he looked at David intently. "You'll notice from this passage that the demons recognized Jesus as God. They knew He had authority over them, and they had to obey Him."

Legion laughed wildly. "The Nazarene has no power over us," he said contemptuously.

John ignored him. Looking directly into David's eyes, he said, "Spirits, in the Name of Jesus of Nazareth, Son of the Living God, I command you to come out!"

David's eyes rolled back in his head and he let out a long, angry hiss. "Leave us alone," he said in a low moan, and Matt realized that the demons were talking through him.

John continued undaunted. "In the Name of Jesus the Messiah, come out of him!"

At the same time Legion began to taunt John, spewing the most vicious insults at him. The people at the table chanted praises to Lucifer, their eyes glowing with an eerie, unnatural light.

John began to quote Scripture passages, and the demons inside David shrieked in rage. Then, David spoke in a deep, raspy voice that made Matt's hair practically stand on end. "Do you love your wife, John? Do you want us to hurt her? We know your wife, and we can tear her to pieces. After all, she used to be one of us!"

They're trying to get to him, Matt thought. But John wouldn't let them unnerve him. He raised his voice above David's. "The Lord is my rock and my salvation, my fortress, and my deliverer. I will never be shaken!" He paused, then took a deep breath and continued. "In the Name of Jesus Christ, the Alpha and the Omega, the First and the Last, I command you to come out!"

David staggered backward and fell onto the floor. He writhed and hissed, spitting out horrible blasphemies. "Leave us alone!" the voices inside him screamed, and to Matt they sounded terrified.

"You can't win," Legion told John. "No matter how hard you try, your pathetic faith in a dead Savior is no match for the power of Lucifer!"

"My Savior is alive," John said triumphantly. "After He died on the Cross and defeated the power of sin and death, He rose from the dead and is now seated at the right hand of the Father. And at the Name of Jesus, every knee will bow and every tongue confess that Jesus Christ is Lord. Someday, you're going to have to bow down to Him, too!"

"Never!" he cried. "That will never happen!"

"Then you're deceiving yourself," John said. He was beginning to appear physically and emotionally drained. But he wouldn't give up. With a voice that sounded dry and hoarse, he continued. "In the Name of Jesus Christ, the Redeemer of the world, I command you to depart! You have no authority to stay here—you have to get out!"

"No we don't! Leave us alone!" Then something really weird happened. The demons started pleading with John to let them stay inside David. "We won't hurt him, we just want to stay here. Please, just let us stay and we won't hurt him!" They sounded pathetic to Matt, and he didn't get it. Weren't demons supposed to be fearless and ferocious? But now they actually sounded afraid. What could they be afraid of?

"You can't stay," John said in an authoritative tone. "You've got to leave. In Jesus' Name, I command you to get out!"

Finally, after twenty-five minutes of what could only be described as intense spiritual warfare, it happened. Matt stared wide-eyed as David was thrown through the air and against the wall, landing on the floor with a horrible thud. The entire room echoed with the most awful, blood-curdling screams, as a putrid stench filled the air and gradually began to dissipate. Then the room became deathly silent. Matt turned to look at the robed ones at the table and was astonished to see them sitting petrified in their chairs—a look of abject terror on their faces.

David looked up and blinked. The glassy, vacant look in his eyes had vanished, and Anita wept with relief. She ran to him and threw her arms around him, and he clung to her like a terrified child. Matt remembered what John had said about more demons returning after the house was swept clean, and he wondered how this would turn out. Would the demons come back? The thought made him shudder.

Somewhat dazed, David looked up at John. "Am I...free now?" he asked with effort.

"Almost," John replied. "If you really want to be free from the power of darkness, you need to put your trust in Jesus. If you make Him Lord of your life, Satan can never harm you again."

"No!" Legion screamed, enraged. "I won't allow it!"

Ignoring him, John asked David, "Do you believe that Jesus Christ died to save you from your sins?"

David's eyes glistened with tears. "Yes...I know He saved me."

Matt noticed that Legion had gotten strangely quiet. He then saw that Legion was walking toward the table, his eyes fixed on the blood-red tablecloth. Matt tapped John on the shoulder. "Maybe we should get out of here, John."

Anita's voice was filled with anxiety. "Yes—let's go." She spoke tenderly to David. "Can you get up, sweetheart?"

He smiled weakly. "I think I may need a little help."

"No one's going anywhere!" Legion's voice was dripping with hate. Matt looked toward the door, and saw that two of the hooded figures had blocked it. They were all trapped. His heart raced as he tried to think of what to do, but he felt a blind, mind-numbing panic that bordered on hysteria. "So, you think you can get away with stealing what rightfully belongs to the Master?" Legion snarled.

John scrambled to his feet as Anita helped David up. They all stood together, shivering; a bitter coldness had suddenly descended.

"You can't keep us here," John said. "And you no longer have any power over David; once he gives his life to Jesus, Satan can never touch him again. You might as well let us go."

"And allow you to get away with stealing one of the Master's disciples?"

"Your master is a liar and a destroyer," John said. "And he was defeated more than two thousand years ago when Jesus died on the Cross."

"That's a lie!" Legion almost spat at him. "Soon the Teacher will be revealed, and Lucifer's kingdom will be established on this earth."

"Maybe for a time, but his kingdom won't last. When Christ returns in glory, He's going to destroy the Antichrist—your teacher—and throw him and all his followers into the lake of fire. In the meantime, Jesus' followers will continue to expose the works of darkness and lead people into God's Kingdom. And there's nothing you can do to stop us."

Legion was seething. "So, you're determined to oppose us? You're determined to oppose the New World Order and the kingdom of Lucifer?"

John spoke calmly. "Yes—my life is dedicated to spreading Christ's gospel and proclaiming His Kingdom."

Matt didn't see the knife until it was too late. He heard himself scream as it plunged into John's chest, and he watched, numb with horror, as his brother pitched backward to the cold, marble floor, his face contorted with pain. "Call an ambulance!" Matt shouted at Anita as he rushed to John's side and fell on his knees beside him. But as soon as he saw his blood-soaked shirt and pale, ashen face, Matt knew that the ambulance would never get there in time. *No!* The word screamed at him from the depths of his soul. He couldn't just give up; he couldn't let his brother die. "You've got to hang on," he said, his face streaked with tears.

John looked up at him, and his serene expression revealed the truth that Matt could not accept. He was gasping for air, his chest heaving painfully, as he struggled to speak.

"Don't try to talk," Matt said gently. "Just hang on."

Slowly and deliberately, John shook his head. "It's...time," he said with tremendous effort.

Realizing that there was nothing else he could do, Matt cradled John's head in his lap, trying to make him as comfortable as possible. "Just hang on, buddy," he said, his voice dry and choking.

John closed his eyes. "Tell Beth...I love her," he whispered.

This was almost too much for Matt. "Come on, John, don't you go dying on me!"

"I'm going...to be...with Jesus. He's...waiting for me."

Matt was desperate. "John, please...you've got to hang on!"

John opened his eyes, and his voice seemed to gain new strength. "He is the resurrection and the life...those who believe in Him will live with Him forever." His eyes appeared to be gazing far away into some great distance, and a smile of such radiance came over his face that Matt trembled with awe. Then, his head rolled to the side, and he was still. With great tenderness, Matt held his brother's lifeless body in his arms as blood continued to drain from the fatal wound in his chest.

Suddenly, a terrible, sickening thought came to him: how on earth was he going to tell Beth? "This wasn't supposed to happen," he sobbed. *"It wasn't supposed to happen!"*

CHAPTER 30

The day of the funeral dawned with bright golden sunshine in a deep blue sky, one of those glorious summer mornings that John had loved. With a heavy heart, Matt sat down in the front pew between Beth and his mother, looking around uncomfortably at the many strangers who had gathered here to pay their final respects to his brother. Although he recognized those who regularly attended the Bible study, most were people he had never seen before.

His father couldn't bring himself to come. The news of John's death had hit him hard. Matt figured it was one more blow from a world that had become increasingly devoid of hope. He understood such feelings all too well. John's brutal murder was more than just the tragic loss of his brother. It was the final death of all his hopes, of all that had ever mattered to him. One by one, he had lost everything that had any meaning for him, and as he sat in the midst of these people of faith, he felt an emptiness that was almost unbearable. He also thought of Beth, and his heart went out to her; he couldn't imagine how she would go on without the husband she had loved so dearly, and without a father to raise the child she was carrying.

The pastor approached the pulpit. He introduced himself as Ray Donovan, and said that Beth had invited him to give the sermon. He looked out at the congregation, his expression sad, yet when he spoke his voice was filled with hope and assurance. "Before we begin the opening hymn which you'll find on page two of your bulletin, I wanted you all to know that Beth selected this hymn herself. I believe it testifies to the faith that she and John shared, the faith that led them to find each other and which will one day reunite them in heaven with their Lord and Savior, Jesus Christ."

Matt was startled as he glanced at the title; it was called "Great is Thy Faithfulness." He vaguely recalled singing it in the Lutheran church he went to as a kid. He couldn't understand why Beth had chosen a hymn of such soaring, exuberant hope for her husband's funeral; it just didn't make sense. As he listened to the words, which promised enduring peace and mercy and rejoiced in the blessings of God, he couldn't even bring himself to sing.

Then, he looked at Beth, and his mouth opened in wonder and amazement. With tears streaming down her cheeks, she sang the hymn falteringly, at times choking back a sob. But as she gazed up at the plain wooden cross that hung above the altar, there was something in her eyes—an expression of profound hope and trust—which was beyond Matt's comprehension. How could she continue to trust in a God who had allowed her husband to die a violent, senseless death, which had resulted from his very willingness to do what God wanted? How could anyone continue to trust such a God?

He got his answer during the sermon. At first, he was only half-listening. He kept reliving that awful moment when a psychotic killer had plunged a knife into his brother's heart, viciously stabbing a man whose entire life had been dedicated to Christ, and who left behind a loving, devoted wife...and a child he would never see. That moment was the culmination of all the evil Matt had seen in the past year, and he felt a despair as black as the deepest pit of hell.

He wanted to tune out the small, insistent voice that spoke in the silence of his heart, telling him there was more to life than this. Everlasting peace and fulfillment could be his if only he would make a choice that possibly could end his life. He didn't want to die. Didn't want to suffer or make any heroic sacrifices. Torn in two directions, he wished he could forget the world he had glimpsed through John's eyes, a world where the light of faith was bright enough to dispel any darkness, but where you had to pick up your cross and follow a King who had been crucified.

He caught a phrase of the sermon that screamed for his attention. "Why would anyone continue to trust God in circumstances such as these?"

The words grabbed hold of Matt. "How can anyone put their trust in a God who would allow something like this to happen? The same question was asked over two thousand years ago, and is at the center of a cosmic battle that continues to this very day, the battle between God and Satan for men's souls. It was Satan who asked that very question, and a man named Job found himself on God's proving ground for the answer."

Pastor Donovan opened the Bible and read from the opening chapter of the book of Job. Then, he looked out at the congregation with an expression of great sympathy. "Here was a man whose entire life was dedicated to God, and who experienced tremendous suffering, not because he was evil, but because he was good! Now, Job could have easily turned away from God. After all, anyone would have expected him to. As a matter of fact, his wife urged him to curse God and die. But he wouldn't do that; he remained faithful to his God. This is the ultimate challenge of the ages: how can we trust God in the midst of evil and tribulation? Jesus asked a similar question before He died on the cross: '...when the Son of Man comes, will he find faith on the earth?' In other words, will anyone trust in Christ during the intense period of evil, suffering, and heartache of these last days? *Can* we trust Him in these circumstances?" His voice softened to almost a whisper, and he seemed to be fighting back tears. "Can Beth trust in Christ, even though He allowed her heart to be broken by the brutal slaying of her husband?"

Matt drew back, startled by the pastor's bluntness. "My friends," Ray Donovan said quietly, "there's only one way to trust God in such circumstances: by realizing that this life is temporary, and that we cannot set our hearts on the things of this world, not on our home or possessions, not even on our families and our loved ones. There's only one thing in this life we can depend on—the love of God in Christ Jesus our Lord. Please turn with me to Romans, Chapter 8."

Matt fumbled for the Bible, then silently read the words through a blur of tears. "'Who shall separate us from the love of Christ? Shall trouble or hardship or persecution or famine or nakedness or danger or sword? As it is written: 'For your sake we face death all day long; we are considered as sheep to be slaughtered.' No, in all these things we are more than conquerors through him who loved us. For I am convinced that neither death nor life, neither angels nor demons, neither the present nor the future, nor any powers, neither height nor depth, nor anything else in all creation, will be able to separate us from the love of God that is in Christ Jesus our Lord.'

"My friends, the Bible tells us that we *can* trust God in those times, and that ultimately, only God can sustain us in our suffering. Now, earlier I pointed out that Job was on the proving ground for God's answer to Satan's fiendish taunts. But Job wasn't the only one who found himself on God's proving ground. We all have, all of us who follow Jesus as our Lord and Savior. But we aren't alone. We're in a great company of the saints throughout the ages who learned to trust God in the midst of great suffering, who trusted God even when it didn't make any sense to do so."

Then he turned to the book of Genesis and read about how God tested Abraham by telling him to sacrifice his son Isaac. "Think about this, friends," he said after he had read the passage aloud. "Abraham was ready to sacrifice his only son...simply because he believed it was the will of God. Now I'm sure most people today would think that Abraham had lost it. I mean, how could anyone be willing to sacrifice his own child, especially when that child was the manifestation of a promise that God had made, of a covenant that was supposed to last forever? That kind of faith doesn't even make sense to us, does it? But that's how God wants us to trust Him. He wants us to set our hearts so completely on Him that we're willing to surrender everything else that has value to us. He wants us to trust Him even if He asks of us things that don't seem to make any sense. And that is why, so often in our Christian walk, we find ourselves on the proving ground of God. Yes, my friends, you and I are on the proving ground—Beth is on the proving ground—and God wants to use us as His answer to those who would ask, 'How can anyone put their trust in a God who allows evil and suffering?'"

He looked at the congregation with great tenderness, and Matt felt as if the pastor were talking directly to him. "Perhaps this is a question that some of you have been asking today. Someone you love has died, and his death seems senseless. But you know something? When Jesus died, His death seemed senseless, also. His disciples were devastated, numb with disbelief. After all, they had seen His miracles. They knew He was God! They had even seen Him raise people from the dead. They were probably saying, 'How could this happen? This wasn't supposed to happen!' But they were wrong; it *was* supposed to happen. Jesus' death was ordained from the beginning of time to redeem mankind from the bondage of sin. It was all part of God's plan. And because Jesus died what appeared to be a senseless death, we know that John is alive today, he's alive with Jesus in everlasting glory. 'For God so loved the world that he gave his one and only Son, that whoever believes in him shall not perish but have eternal life.' Jesus is alive, my friends, and because He lives, we can live too, as John lives. As long as we're in Christ, we'll never have to fear death again. We will have tribulation in the world, but Jesus has promised to be with us always, and one day He's going to wipe away all our tears." He paused. "Now, for those of you who are not in Christ, and have been wondering how you can have any kind of lasting, permanent happiness in a twisted world like ours, you need to start putting your trust in Jesus. Ask Him to come into your heart and be the Lord of your life. He's all we can count on in a turbulent, transient world."

Matt was hardly listening to the closing prayer. He was thinking about the words of the sermon, which seemed to burn into his heart. As John's coffin was carried out of the church, Matt could hear the church bells peeling triumphantly. Tears sprang to his eyes as the congregation began to sing another song of unwavering hope and trust, of those who dwell in the shelter of the Most High, abiding in His shadow and finding comfort in His strength. He recalled that early April morning when he and John had walked through Union Cemetery, and how certain John had been of where he would be when he died. And suddenly, Matt knew in his heart that his brother was alive in heaven, with Jesus; he was alive because the Son of God had consented to die a horrible, brutal death on the Cross of Calvary. A strange, unearthly joy surged through him as he pictured the Cross towering above him into the clouds, and he wanted to throw himself on the ground and weep. But he didn't. He couldn't. Not here—not in front of everyone. It wasn't until he was alone that he allowed himself to give vent to the full range of the emotions that swelled within him.

Sitting alone on the balcony of his apartment that evening, he gazed up at the stars, and he recalled how John had loved to stargaze while the two of them were growing up in Oakdale. On summer nights like this his brother often used to lie on a lounge chair in the backyard, listening to the soft trilling of the crickets and staring up at the silent stars. Tonight clouds shrouded many of the stars, but he could still see the brightest of them shining in the darkness.

"The light shines in the darkness..."

Where had he heard that before? Somewhere in the Bible, no doubt.

He thought of the darkness of his own life, of all that he had lost and thrown away, and his eyes filled with tears. He had turned his back on everything good and decent and embraced the darkness of despair. Instead of trying to save his marriage, instead of forgiving his wife for the very thing he had done to her, he had made her feel worthless and degraded and had broken her heart. Instead of putting his trust in the Savior who had died for him, he had drowned his sorrows in alcohol. And now, because of his own pride and selfishness, he had nothing. He was completely alone. The future he had hoped for, the country he had once loved, his marriage, and now his brother— all gone. There was nothing left, nothing that he could count on.

Except Jesus.

The words seemed to spring from the depths of his soul, and he fell on his face, his body racked with sobs. All his life, he had turned his back on Jesus, and now that he had nothing left he realized his desperate need for the Savior he had stubbornly ignored.

He began a hesitant, uncertain prayer. "I guess You haven't heard from me very often. But You know who I am." He wiped away his tears as the words began to pour forth. "Man, I really made a mess of my life, Lord." He choked back a sob. "But I guess that's why You died for me. Anyway, I'm not really sure how I'm supposed to say this, but I need You, Jesus. I've needed You all along, but I didn't want to admit it. I guess I just wanted to go my own way. Please forgive me for that, Lord. Forgive me...for everything. I love You, Jesus. I love You and I want You to be my Lord and Savior." He realized he sounded like a child, but somehow he knew that didn't matter, he knew that Jesus loved him and accepted him totally, in spite of the mess he had made of his life, in spite of his pride and selfishness and complete unworthiness.

For a long time he remained prostrate, basking in the light of God's presence as he spoke to His Lord in the silence of the night. There were a million things he wanted to say, things which he had left unsaid for far too long. Confessions of past sins, prayers of thanksgiving and praise gushed forth from his lips like a fountain, and the emptiness he once felt was consumed with the depth and fullness of God's enduring love. He never knew how long he had stayed there like that; time seemed to stand still as he poured out his heart to the God who had died for him so long ago.

He slowly got to his feet, his face flushed, wondering what to do next. He felt as if he had been released from a cold, dark prison, and his new sense of freedom filled him with an exhilaration that almost made him giddy. There were so many people he wanted to tell. He ran inside and picked up the phone, but suddenly stopped himself; he was about to call John. Shaking his head sadly, he put the receiver back in its cradle. Anyway, he figured that where John was now, he already knew and was rejoicing with the angels in heaven. Actually, right now there was only one person in the world he wanted to see, and that was Gina. All his anger and resentment had melted away in the awesome fire of God's love. He felt terrible as he reflected on how deeply he must have hurt her, and he longed to ask for her forgiveness. Above all, he wanted to tell her about the Savior who had redeemed him, and who wanted to be her Savior, too.

* * * *

"Haven't you hurt my daughter enough?" Tom eyed Matt coldly when he showed up at his in-laws' looking for Gina. It was almost eleven, and his frantic knocking had obviously woken Tom up from a sound sleep. But Matt felt he had no choice; Tom kept hanging up on him whenever he tried to call.

"I know, I'm sorry. You have every right to be angry—"

"You bet I do." He suddenly looked weary. "Listen, Matt, if you can't treat my daughter with any kind of decency, then can you please just leave her alone? She doesn't need any more heartache."

Matt felt terrible as he recalled Gina's arrival at John's wake with a card and some flowers for Beth, and how he had gruffly told her to leave. The look on her face then was more than he could bear. "Believe me, I don't want to hurt her. I just want to make things right."

Looking rather doubtful, Tom told him that she was staying with her aunt and uncle out at Montauk Point for the weekend.

"Can you tell me where they live?" Matt asked urgently. "I've just got to talk to her."

"Well, if Gina's crazy enough to take you back, there's not much I can do about it." Reluctantly, he gave Matt the address where Gina was staying.

* * * *

Early the next morning, Matt began the two-hour drive through the Hamptons to Montauk Point. Along the way he passed the little farm stands where he and Gina used to buy fresh corn and tomatoes during the summer after they had gone wine tasting at the North Fork out in Riverhead. He smiled, remembering the time he and John had driven out to Montauk during a major hurricane. They were probably the only two people insane enough to attempt something like that. He never forgot the tremendous blasts of wind that had nearly knocked them over as they tried to walk through the deserted parking lot toward the rocky cliffs, which led down to the Atlantic Ocean. "Forget this! Let's get out of here!" Matt had shouted at the top of his lungs over the roaring wind.

But John was laughing delightedly, his face flushed with the wind, enjoying every minute of it. He let out a whoop as a gust of wind knocked him off his feet. "This is great! It's like we're flying!" he had exclaimed, his expression filled with wonder.

Matt brushed a tear from his eye as memories of John and the times they had spent together came flooding back to him. But he reminded himself that they would meet again someday.

When he finally reached his destination, a somewhat dilapidated motel near the end of Edgemere Avenue—one of the few places where Gina's aunt and uncle could get work after the depression—he wasn't sure he could face her. What would he say to her? What *could* he say? He wanted more than anything to make things right, but it wouldn't be easy after the way he had treated her. In any case, one thing was certain as far as Matt was concerned: only God could help him make things right with Gina again. He sure couldn't do it on his own. As he got out of his car, he said a quick, desperate prayer, hoping against hope that Gina would take him back.

"I'm sorry, she's not here," said Gina's aunt, a stooped little woman with gray hair, who greeted him at the front desk.

The words filled him with dismay. "You mean she went back to her parents'?"

"Oh, no. She just took a drive up to the Lighthouse. She should be back by lunch time."

He couldn't believe it—that's where he had proposed to Gina! To think that he would find her there of all places. And he realized that it was more than coincidence—this was the hand of God. He was so excited he almost stumbled down the steps.

* * * *

He could see her in the distance, gazing up at the brilliant blue sky above the Atlantic, which seemed to stretch beyond the horizon toward eternity. She appeared to be watching a pair of gulls hovering over the water. Her long, chestnut-colored hair blew gently in the wind that rose up from the sea. She was wearing a pair of faded bluejeans, rolled up to her mid-calf, and as she waded in the puddles of the rocky shoreline below the Lighthouse, she had never appeared more beautiful to Matt. He wanted more than anything to take her into his arms and tell her how much he loved her. But first, he had to seek her forgiveness.

Just as he was wondering how to approach her and what he should say, she turned around. For an instant, she didn't appear to recognize him and she looked at him quizzically as he began to walk toward her. Then, her eyes grew wide and she put her hand to her mouth, nearly staggering backward in her surprise. "Matt?" she asked, her tone bewildered and confused. "Is that you?"

"It's me," he said, his voice dry and husky. Then, she saw the bouquet of daisies he held at his side, and she looked as if she might cry. They were her favorite flowers. Matt had picked them up at a florist on the way.

"What are you doing here?" she stammered. Then she looked worried. "Is there something wrong? Did something happen to my parents?" It obviously had never occurred to her that he was here because he loved her and wanted her back.

He was shaking his head slowly. "No, no, everything's okay," he told her gently, trying to control the emotions that nearly overwhelmed him.

She looked at him coldly. "Then why are you here? Did you think of a few more names you wanted to call me?" He looked into her eyes and wondered what he could possibly say to prove how sorry he was for hurting her. She seemed to soften then. "I'm sorry," she said. "That wasn't fair."

"No, I deserved that." He was fighting back tears. "There's no excuse for the way I treated you, Gina. I only hope that somehow, you can find it in your heart to forgive me."

She looked at him with wonder and surprise. "Of course I can forgive you," she told him, and her eyes glistened with tears. "I just hope you can forgive me." She said the words hesitantly, almost like a child, and he was stirred with great tenderness.

He smiled. "I already have."

She fell into his arms, weeping, as if she had never dared to hope that he would ever forgive her. As the daisies fell to the ground and scattered in the wind, Matt held Gina as if he would never let her go, stroking her hair and murmuring over and over again, "I love you, Gina. I love you so much..." And in the silence of his heart, he said a prayer to his Savior, thanking Him for giving him a second chance.

* * * *

"So, what do you call yourself now? A born-again Christian?"

They were sitting at an outdoor table at Gosman's Dock, a popular restaurant right on Montauk Harbor. Seagulls flew overhead, and every now and then Matt tossed them a piece of bread from their table. They swooped downward like dive-bombers, and Matt laughed delightedly as Gina ducked, afraid that they would hit her. She laughed. "Must you keep feeding them?" But her heart soared with a joy she hadn't felt in years.

"Sorry." He grinned mischievously. "I'll try to be a good little boy from now on."

"You'd better be," she said playfully. "After all, people expect more from a born-again Christian. That is what you'd call yourself, I take it?"

"Actually, this is all pretty new to me. Believe it or not, you're the first person I've told."

She took a sip of the champagne they had ordered to celebrate their reconciliation. "Would you like some?" she asked him. She noticed that he hadn't touched it, even after the toast he had proposed; he had just sipped his water.

He hesitated. "Maybe I shouldn't."

Suddenly she understood, and she was eager to change the subject. "I guess now that John isn't around, you don't have anyone to talk to about these things anymore," she said sadly.

He took her hand in his. "Gina, I want to talk to *you* about the things that are important to me. Don't you see, honey? I want to share everything with you—especially this."

She couldn't believe this was the same man who had been consumed with rage only weeks ago. "I'm glad you feel that way," she said. But she couldn't help wondering if such a sudden transformation could really last. Besides, she wasn't exactly religious. What if Matt had a problem with that? What if he wanted her to change?

Her cautious tone must have told Matt that something was troubling her. "Is something bothering you?" he asked.

"It's—nothing," she said lightly. She didn't feel like spoiling their celebration with any gloomy talk right now.

"Are you sure?" He looked so concerned that she decided to tell him.

"I'm just afraid you might leave me again. I mean, since I'm not born-again—"

He stopped her. "Gina, you don't have to worry about that, believe me. I love you with all my heart, and I'm never going to leave you again. You have my promise."

"But wouldn't you be happier with someone who could share your faith? Besides, let's face it. I haven't been the best wife in the world."

He smiled. "And you think I've been the perfect husband?"

She laughed. "I guess neither one of us is going to get any medals in that department." Still, she wanted to be certain of just where she stood. "But seriously, Matt, now that you're...born-again and all that, don't you think that you'd have more in common with someone who shares your faith?"

"You trying to get rid of me?" he asked playfully.

"No, of course not. I guess I just don't want any surprises down the road. I mean, I have been unfaithful to you, and now that you're a Christian..."

"Gina, there's something I think you should know," he said suddenly. By the look on his face, she already knew what he was going to tell her.

"You've been unfaithful, too," she said quietly.

He looked startled. "You knew?"

"I kind of suspected it."

"Boy, you must think I'm a total jerk. After the things I said to you—"

"That's all in the past now. Besides, I deserved those names." For a long time, she had tried to convince herself that she hadn't, that she had just made a mistake, that these things can happen to anyone. She had even tried to alleviate her guilt by dwelling on her suspicions that Matt had cheated on her while they were living together. But she knew in her heart that she could no longer make excuses for what she had done; she had to face the truth. She had committed adultery. Ironically, it was Matt's vicious words to her that had forced her to admit to herself just what she had done. They had shaken her to the core, and for a long time she had resented him for saying them. But now, she understood. She understood how it felt to be hurt so deeply by someone you loved that all you want is to hurt them as cruelly as they had hurt you.

His voice was filled with remorse. "I had no right to say those things to you, Gina."

She grasped his hand in hers and squeezed it gently. "It's okay, Matt. If you could forgive me, then shouldn't I forgive you?"

He grinned. "Well, if you're willing to forgive me after the creep I've been, wouldn't I be crazy to leave you?"

She thought about her high school sweetheart, and she still wasn't completely convinced. "Maybe," she said quietly.

"Honey, you have nothing to worry about. I *want* to stay married to you. And that's what God wants, too."

"But how do you know that? What if God wants you to find someone else—"

"He doesn't, Gina. He wants me to stay with you, I'm sure of that. Want to know what the Bible says about marriage?" She nodded, and he reached into his denim jacket and took out a pocket-sized New Testament. He was looking something up. "Here it is," he said after a moment or two, and began to read. "'Husbands, love your wives as Christ loved the church and gave himself up for her to make her holy, cleansing her with water through the word, and to present her to himself as a radiant church, without stain or wrinkle or blemish, but holy and blameless. In this same way husbands ought to love their wives as their own bodies. He who loves his wife loves himself. After all, no one ever hated his own body, but he feeds and cares for it, just as Christ does the church—for we are members of his body. For this reason a man will leave his father and mother and be united with his wife, and the two will become one flesh.'"

Her eyes glistened with tears. "I never heard that before, it's beautiful.

How did you know where to find it?"

"I was reading one of the gospels last night and then I just started randomly flipping through the letters of Paul. When I came across this passage, it kind of leaped out at me. And after I read it, I decided then and there that's how I'm going to love you, for the rest of our lives."

She shook her head in amazement. "I can't believe this. It's like, you're this whole new person."

"I am a new person. A new person in Christ. That's what being born-again means."

"Oh, so it's a spiritual rebirth."

"That's right." Matt looked pleasantly surprised, as if he hadn't expected her to show any kind of interest in his experience. Well, no wonder. Usually whenever Matt brought up the topic of religion, she would get uncomfortable or defensive. But somehow, things were different now.

"What was it like?" she asked quietly.

He was silent for a moment, a faraway look in his eyes. "It's hard to put into words. I felt like I was truly free, for the first time in my life. And I felt the presence of God—of Jesus—in my heart." The awe and reverence in his voice almost gave her chills.

"That sounds beautiful," she said.

He nodded, and his eyes glimmered with tears. "It was like nothing I've ever experienced before...and I knew that this was what I had been searching for all my life."

She was quiet for a few moments, taking it all in. To hear Matt talk about God like this was extraordinary. "So, that's what it means to be born-again. I never understood that term before."

Matt nodded. "Yeah, I think it's confusing to a lot of people. I know it was to me, especially after my brother first got saved."

She smiled at his use of this new terminology. "I bet that's a term that gets misunderstood, too."

"You're right," he admitted, and he was smiling now, too. "Some of the Christians I met at the Bible study used to come up to me and ask, 'Are you saved?' As if I'd say no to that question. That's the problem—when you go up to some guy and ask if he's saved, he's not going to say no. Even if he doesn't understand what being saved means."

Gina took a bite of the grilled salmon she had ordered. "I'm not sure *I* understand what that means. Growing up Catholic and all, I always assumed I was saved. I figured as long as I went to church fairly regularly and tried to be a good person, I'd make it to heaven. Then, I met someone who told me I was wrong." She was thinking of her high school sweetheart again, who had experienced the same life-changing transformation as Matt had. But at the time she had wanted no part of it. She decided to tell Matt the whole depressing saga. "Anyway," she said when she had finished, "ever since then I had a really negative attitude toward religion. I guess I always associated religion, specifically Christianity, with rejection. I think that's why I got so paranoid when you started going to those Bible studies. I didn't want to be rejected again by someone I loved."

"Talk about ironic," Matt said with a smile. "It was my rebellion against God that made me reject you, and my coming to God that brought us back together. Anyway, Christianity isn't about rejection, it's about acceptance—complete and total acceptance in spite of our sins. Remember the story of the prodigal son? As a Catholic you must have heard it at some point."

"Oh, yeah. I love that story!" She thought of her own father and all the pressure he had put on her to succeed...and her constant fear of disappointing him. "I always wished my father would love me the way the father in the parable loved his son."

"Well," Matt said in a soft voice, "Jesus loves you that way. He loved you enough to die for you."

She was silent for a moment, watching some of the gulls gliding on the wind. "I wish I could believe that."

"Why is it so difficult?"

She shrugged. "I'm not sure. I always hated the idea of a condemning, judgmental God, so I guess I tried to make up my own God...one who was sort of detached and didn't care much about what human beings did. I convinced myself that God had so many other problems to deal with, like the threat of thermonuclear war and overpopulation, that He didn't care what people did in the privacy of their own bedrooms—or the backseat of a car. That way, I didn't feel guilty whenever I did anything that 'old-fashioned people' would consider 'sinful.' But eventually, I started to feel as if God didn't care about me at all."

"That makes sense," Matt said quietly. "If God is so detached from us, why would He care about us?"

Gina took a sip of champagne, amazed that Matt no longer seemed tempted to drink himself into oblivion. It seemed that his dependence on alcohol had vanished along with his rage. She commented on this, and he smiled.

"Gina, I really feel like a different person. I don't even want to get drunk!"

He shuddered. "Man, I can't believe how much I was drinking. The night John died, I must've put away at least two six-packs. And that's not counting the hard stuff I drank. I kept hoping that if I drank enough, the emptiness inside me would go away. But it only got worse. Until I found Jesus." He smiled. "Or should I say, till He found me."

"That's an interesting way of looking at it."

He looked thoughtful. "I guess I was using alcohol as a substitute for God. You know, I think most people like to make their own gods. They like to believe whatever makes them feel comfortable."

Gina thought about the way many of her own beliefs had recently been shaken. "You're right—I know I've always had that problem. The idea that there could be such a thing as absolute truth was unthinkable to me."

"Do you still feel that way?"

She shook her head. "Not anymore. Not after what I've seen lately. I mean, if there can be such terrible evil in the world, then there has to be some standard of good. Otherwise, how could we avoid doing evil?"

"You're right, Gina. If there's no absolute truth, then truth is whatever people want it to be. Everyone would be free to create their own reality—and morality."

She shuddered as she thought about the many evils perpetrated against innocent people by the government recently—all for the so-called "common good." She said, "Anything becomes okay, no matter how twisted."

"That's what happens when Satan's lies replace God's truth. Anything is justifiable."

"But how do we know what God's truth is? Since human beings are so prone to moral blindness, how can we ever really know what's good, and true?"

"There is a way," Matt told her.

She knew what he was thinking. "Right, the Bible," she said. But she wasn't convinced.

"Think about it," Matt said. "Aren't the Ten Commandments the best standard we could possibly have?"

"I suppose," she agreed reluctantly.

"When was the last time you actually read the Bible?" he asked gently.

She thought of that night in Wyoming, when she had opened the New Testament and read words that burned into her soul. "It's been awhile. I didn't like what it said."

"What did it say?"

She lowered her eyes. "It said...the wages of sin is death."

"Did you read the verse that came after it?"

She shook her head. "I didn't want to read anything after that."

Smiling, Matt opened to the New Testament again. She saw that a portion was highlighted in yellow. "'For the wages of sin is death, but the gift of God is eternal life in Christ Jesus our Lord.'"

Gina perked up. "It says that?"

He nodded. "Puts a whole different light on things, doesn't it?"

"Yeah. I always thought we were supposed to do certain things to get to heaven. Like going to confession. But if eternal life is a gift, then everyone's going to be saved. Right?" She saw Matt frown, and figured she got it wrong.

"I think you missed the part about Jesus," he said gently.

"Why is Jesus so important?"

"He paid the penalty for our sins. When He died on the cross, He was literally taking on the punishment *we* deserved. Jesus died in your place. He died so that you might live. But you need to accept that gift through faith."

She played with a piece of bread. "I don't know, Matt. I'm still not sure I can believe everything the Bible says. I'm not sure how much of it is true."

"Well, if you really want to know whether or not the Bible is true, why don't you start reading it yourself?" Matt suggested. "Find out what it has to say about truth, and goodness, and the God you seem to feel so detached from. See if His Word speaks to you. You might try praying to God to open your eyes to the truth."

"Maybe I will." Then, almost hesitantly, she asked, "Can you tell me where to start?"

He smiled, and she had never seen such love in his eyes.

* * * *

The telephone rang in the middle of the night, waking Matt from a fitful sleep. As a brand-new Christian, he wasn't prepared for some of the things he'd had to deal with in the past few weeks. Like all the heat he was getting at work for sharing the gospel with his coworkers. Just the other day he walked through the parking lot after his shift to find that his tires had been slashed and the words "JESUS FREAK" had been spray-painted across his windshield. He also sensed a terrible spiritual oppression at the factory that he had never noticed before, and he prayed daily for the grace he needed to show God's light to those walking in darkness. But in spite of these challenges, he felt a peace he never had before: the blessed peace of knowing where he would be when he died—with his precious Redeemer in heaven.

He was startled to hear Beth's voice on the phone; she sounded almost hysterical. When he finally got her to calm down enough so he could understand what she was saying, he bolted out of bed. "I'll be right over," he said.

Within forty-five minutes he was sitting in Beth's living room with Gina; she had insisted on coming along when she heard why Beth had called. Beth's hands were shaking as she lifted the cup of warm milk that Gina had just heated for her. "It was terrible," Beth said with a shudder. Matt was horrified as Beth described the phone calls that had woken her up, from voices dripping with the most obscene cruelty. "Your rotten husband deserved to die!" the anonymous callers had told her. "And so do you!" Then they uttered a string of blasphemies and hung up.

Gina insisted on calling the police, and Matt's first instinct was to burst into a fit of rage. But strangely, the feeling passed in an instant, and he felt the peace of Christ wash over him. He knew what Beth had to do first. "You need to bring this to the Lord," he told her gently.

"Why would anyone be so hateful?" Beth asked tearfully.

"You know why, Beth," he said. "It's because you're a Christian."

"Do you think it has something to do with that newspaper article?" she asked.

"It could be." When he first read it, he had been seething with anger and was about to call the paper demanding they print a retraction. Disguised as a news story about John's murder, it was the most vicious slander he had ever read in his life. The story claimed that John had instigated the stabbing by "unlawfully barging into a chapel and disrupting a religious service." The article also accused him of trying to kidnap one of the teenage patients at the Lucid Home, possibly for some sort of cult-sex ritual. But the worst part of all was the way the writer had portrayed John, describing him as "one of those dangerous, over-zealous fundamentalists, who insist that their perverted concept of salvation is the only way to heaven and the rest of us are all going to hell. People like John Lanyon deserve whatever fate they receive when they spew their hateful, bigoted lies at a world that has become more enlightened since the days of the Inquisition and witch-burnings." The article went on to say that Bible-believing, fundamentalist Christians represent the most serious threat of all to the future of this planet. "Indeed, they are not even Christians in the truest sense of the word," the writer remarked. "The true Christians are those who are awaiting the Cosmic Christ of the New Age, who will usher in an era of peace which will be the antithesis of everything so-called traditional Christianity has stood for." The article concluded by calling John's murderer a victim of the "cancer of fundamentalism" and saying, "No doubt fundamentalists will claim that John Lanyon is a martyr. But he doesn't deserve that title. A religious fanatic, he was an enemy of peace and a danger to society. Ironically, the real martyr here is Lanyon's killer, who will have to face the humiliation and anxiety of a murder trial. Hopefully, he will be vindicated by public opinion, and remembered as a martyr for peace." After his initial rage had passed, Matt felt the power of the Holy Spirit calming him and melting away his anger. He knew from the Bible that these things were prophesied. Just the other day, he had read in his King James Bible, "...Yea, the time cometh that whosoever killeth you, will think that he does God service." *Boy, was that true*, Matt reflected. He also knew that the New Age Cosmic Christ referred to in the article was actually the Antichrist. The fact that a mainstream newspaper article, a "news story" no less, had talked so openly of this personage told Matt that the world might be closer to the end than he had realized.

Matt suggested that the three of them pray together, and they all joined hands as Matt led them in prayer. Afterwards Beth offered to make some hot chocolate. As the three of them settled down in the living room with their mugs of cocoa, Beth suddenly remembered something she had been planning to tell them, but had forgotten with the trauma of the phone calls. Matt stared at her, dumbfounded, as she told him what she had heard earlier that day from some parents whose children had been committed to the Lucid Home. The parents had seen Beth's name in the newspaper article and had called her to let her know that her husband was not the only victim of the Lucid Home. Intrigued, Beth agreed to meet with one of the callers. Her name was Marjorie, and they decided to meet at the Country Kitchen in East Setauket.

"I'm telling you, it sounded like something from out of *Mein Kampf*," Beth told him. "Those kids were being brainwashed into believing they were the elite, the 'chosen ones' who would usher in a new super-race of highly evolved beings. I know it sounds bizarre, but Marjorie and some of the other parents seem to think that the Lucid Home is part of an elaborate plan to create a new 'master race.' She said that when her son came home, he was a different person, rebellious, arrogant, and full of contempt for his parents. When she complained to the administration at the home, she was told it was part of a self-esteem enhancement program."

"I'll bet," Matt said wryly. "Sounds more like they're trying to create a bunch of egomaniacs."

"She also gave me the name of a pastor who leads a deliverance ministry for teens in bondage to the occult. He's had success in delivering children who were committed to the Lucid Home. I spoke to him earlier today, and he told me that the brainwashing techniques used at the home are virtually identical to activities listed in the curriculum guide for the United Nations Schools for the Gifted."

Matt vaguely recalled hearing something about the newly established boarding schools on the news recently, but it was all hype. "What kind of activities?"

He and Gina listened wide-eyed as Beth told them what the kids were learning there—witchcraft, goddess worship, sorcery. They had even been encouraged to engage in sexual experimentation with people of the same sex! Almost daily, they watched videos filled with graphic scenes of bloodshed, mutilation, and rape. "The pastor has counseled parents whose kids have gone to those schools," Beth said. "During the first semester, they were ordered not to have any contact with their parents. By the time they came home for their first break, their parents hardly recognized them." Her eyes were filled with sadness. "The worst part is that some of the students actually committed suicide after coming home."

Matt was outraged. "This sounds like it's straight from hell!"

Beth nodded. "Yes—literally. And it all seems to fit into Satan's plan to take control of this entire planet in the last days."

"That's a horrible thought," said Gina, who had been pretty quiet through much of the conversation.

Matt shook his head and smiled reassuringly. "But it's not all that horrible, Gina—not really. Don't you see? This means the return of Christ could be right around the corner!"

"That's right," Beth said. "Jesus said that when we begin to see these things happening, it means that our redemption is near."

"That's a comforting way of looking at it," Gina said, her tone hopeful. Matt was amazed at the change in her; at one time she would have dismissed any reference to Satan as a remnant of the Dark Ages. She was definitely becoming more open-minded about spiritual matters. But she didn't seem ready to commit her life to Jesus yet, and Matt didn't want to push her; she would come when she was ready, just as he had.

* * * *

Just when Matt thought nothing else could surprise him, Beth called him with more startling news. She had received a letter from a Christian named Barry Sommers, who claimed to have been a member of a cult that worshiped Lucifer. After describing his deliverance from Satanism through faith in Jesus Christ, the young man confided that he had vital information about John's murderer that the government was covering up. Beth eagerly agreed to meet with him, and Matt came along, too.

They met at a diner on Flushing Avenue in Queens, not far from where Barry lived. He was a soft-spoken guy in his mid-twenties, with a gentle, easy-going manner, and straight, dark hair, which was neatly combed. *Definitely not the picture of someone who would be into Satanism,* Matt thought. Wearing a faded denim jacket and weathered jeans, Barry greeted them warmly. They found a quiet booth and listened to his story.

"I had no idea what I was into," he told them. "I didn't even know it was Satanism. As far as I knew, we were just a group of fellow travelers on the astral plane, seeking to become one with God. We were into crystals, expanded consciousness, astral projection—nothing that the average person would associate with Satanism. But we did believe that Lucifer was a god, the same way we believed Jesus was a god. We saw them as brothers, actually." He smiled wryly. "Pretty twisted, huh?"

"I'll say," Beth agreed. "It does sound very New Age, though."

Barry looked sad. "You know, the vast majority of New Agers are well-intentioned, like I was. They have no idea what they're really into. They honestly believe that they're seeking God. Or at least, their own version of God. That's what I thought. Yeah, I saw myself as very spiritual. But I felt no sense of accountability to God. Unfortunately, that's the big attraction of the New Age: people can feel like they're spiritual without having to change their lives or repent. They don't have to follow anyone's rules but their own. It's sad, really. They have no idea they're on the path to hell."

"What made you realize it?" Matt asked.

Barry sipped his herbal tea. His expression had clouded somewhat, and he looked as if he weren't eager to talk about this topic. "I met this guy who called himself Legion. He was the High Priest of some powerful coven, and he was invited to one of our meetings to teach us what he called the ancient mysteries." He shook his head. "What he said was incredible."

At the mention of John's murderer, Matt felt his blood run cold. "What did he say?" he asked in a low voice.

"He encouraged us to practice human sacrifice."

"You're kidding!" Matt was horrified.

"Of course, most of us were shocked by the idea. But when Legion explained the rationale behind it, a few of our group actually approved. Anyway, that's when the Holy Spirit began to convict me. I started to see that what I was into wasn't as innocent as I had thought."

Beth looked at Barry intently. "What was the rationale behind it?"

"Legion told us that it was necessary to remove certain individuals from the earth because they're standing in the way of humanity's so-called spiritual evolution. He said that a giant leap in global consciousness was about to take place, but in order for that to happen, we'd have to get rid of those he called the enemies of mankind: fundamentalist Christians, orthodox Jews, patriots, anyone who opposed us."

"And some of the members of your group approved of this?" Matt asked, astonished.

Barry nodded regretfully. "You have to understand the mind-set these people have. They already believe in reincarnation and the law of Karma. In their eyes, people who supposedly have bad Karma deserve to die. Would you believe that there are those who claim that the Jews who died in the Holocaust were being punished for their so-called bad racial Karma?"

"That's hard to believe," Matt said.

"Well, if you believe the lie of reincarnation, what other explanation is there for something like the Holocaust?" asked Barry. "And that's exactly what these so-called 'spirit guides' are telling people who channel them. They're saying that everyone who suffers has chosen that experience in order to gain from it, or that somehow they're being made to atone for wrongs committed in a previous life." He shook his head. "Believe it or not, a professor I had for comparative religion actually objected to laws against murder on the basis that murdering people can help them spiritually."

Matt rolled his eyes. "That doesn't even make sense."

"Of course not," Barry agreed. "But those who hold to the law of Karma believe there is no death. If you kill someone, it simply removes them to another plane of existence—where they continue their journey toward Nirvana. It moves them one step closer to their final destination in the afterlife. So, if you murder someone, you're actually helping them. Anyway, that's what Legion told us. He said the people we sacrifice will be removed to another dimension where they would be given the opportunity to be reprogrammed, to 'unlearn' their destructive ways of thinking."

"How lovely," Beth said in a sarcastic tone.

"So, how does all this tie in with my brother's murder?" Matt asked suddenly.

"Legion is a cold-blooded killer," Barry said. "Your brother wasn't the first person he killed. He's killed before, and he's actually bragged about it."

Matt nearly lost it then. He struggled to control his anger. "Wait a minute. If he's committed other murders, then why the hell isn't he in jail?"

"He was in jail. He was sentenced to life in prison for committing a series of ritual murders as High Priest of a Satanic coven. But the government released him from jail, along with thousands of other dangerous criminals."

Matt was stunned. "The *government*?"

Beth just sat there, a look of disbelief on her face.

"Actually, it might have been one of those quasi-governmental UN agencies. Most of the prisoners were drafted into the World Army to do the UN's dirty work, like breaking down people's doors in the middle of the night looking for weapons. They were the cannon fodder, the useful idiots. But they were told they could keep whatever they felt like taking, so that gave them incentive in spite of the risks."

Beth shuddered, and Matt noticed that her face had gone pale. "Sounds a lot like Hitler's Brown Shirts," she said.

"It gets worse," Barry said. "Legion bragged to us that he and some of the other prisoners—all those who had been in jail for Satanic murders—were recruited for some sort of special government project. He said it was called Project Lucid, or Operation Lucid. Something like that. It stands for Lucifer's Identity."

"So, I take it the Lucid Home somehow ties in with Operation Lucid," Beth said.

"Yeah, it was one of their pet projects."

Matt was curious. "When you say 'their,' who exactly do you mean?"

"Well, Legion wasn't all that specific. But he did hint that there's a secret cabal within the UN and the Executive Council of the World Parliament that actively worships Lucifer and is working behind the scenes to prepare the way for his World Teacher."

"You mean the Antichrist," Beth said, and Barry nodded.

"Anyway," he continued, "the goal behind Lucid is to initiate the youth of the planet into the worship of Lucifer, through a series of so-called 'outreach programs' at local high schools and bogus psychotherapy for troubled teens.

The people behind this project want to create an entire generation of dedicated, obedient Satanists. They want the youth all over the world to be prepared to hail the new Teacher as God and be willing to destroy his enemies, even if it's their own parents."

Matt felt a chill run down his spine. "Man, this is really scary!"

"But it certainly explains a lot," Beth commented.

"There's something I don't get," Matt said. "Why would Legion tell people about this? You'd think he'd want to keep it a secret."

"Because he's arrogant," Barry said simply. "That's one trait that all Satanists have in common. Even most New Agers who aren't into hard-core Satanism have a problem with pride. I know I did. I didn't want to admit I needed a Savior. The New Age told me that I was a god, and I liked that idea. And I sincerely believed I was seeking the truth. But because I was blinded by my own intellectual pride, I didn't recognize the truth. Until I met Legion. When I listened to him that night, I saw the kind of evil that my beliefs could ultimately lead to. It scared the life out of me."

"So, Legion isn't afraid of people finding out about this stuff?" Matt was still having a hard time swallowing this.

"No, he believes he's protected by the god of this world. Besides, Legion perceives himself as very powerful. He talked about many important officials in government who fully support his cause, though he didn't mention any names. He probably thinks no one can touch him. And get this—as High Priest of a Satanic coven, he's had success in actually putting curses on his enemies and he bragged to us that he's been in contact with some very powerful spirit beings."

Matt was shaking his head. "This is incredible—the government has actually been infiltrated by Satanists!"

"Well, it was bound to happen," Beth said. "The Bible predicts that in the end-times, the whole world will worship Satan, all those who don't have their names written in the Book of Life. So, it makes sense to expect that the government would turn to Satanism. Not many people know this, but Hitler and the SS were heavily into the occult, so this sort of thing has happened before."

Matt looked earnestly at Barry. "Listen, would you be willing to testify at Legion's trial? Beth and I are afraid he could get off because the media is portraying him as this wonderful 'peace-maker.' But if you testify that he's a Satanist who's committed human sacrifice, we may have more of a chance to see justice."

Barry nodded, his eyes full of sympathy. "Of course I'm willing to testify. Unfortunately, I'm not sure whether I'll still be around by then."

"Are you planning on moving?" asked Matt.

Barry smiled. "No, but I have a feeling that Jesus is going to be taking me home soon."

Matt was puzzled. "What makes you think that?"

"I've made some powerful enemies now that I've given my life to Jesus. I've also been trying to warn a lot of my friends who are still in the movement, and some of them have come to Jesus. I've already received death threats, and my home has been vandalized." He said this so calmly that Matt could only marvel at Barry's sense of peace.

"These people sound pretty vicious," Matt commented.

"Well, most New Agers aren't like that," Barry pointed out. "Like I said before, most of them have the best of intentions. Some of them even consider themselves to be Christians, believe it or not. But they're following a false Jesus, not the Jesus of the Bible." He shook his head sadly. "It just breaks my heart when I think of the millions of misguided souls who are caught up in Satan's web of lies."

"The New Age is a powerful delusion," Beth remarked, and Matt wondered if she was thinking of her own experience.

"It almost doesn't sound fair," he said. "I mean, how can God condemn them when they've just been deceived?"

"But aren't we all deceived, in one way or another, before we come to Christ?" Beth asked. "There's so much deception we can fall into if we reject God's Word—there's secular humanism, eastern mysticism, pantheism, not to mention evolution which has been the foundation of Nazism, Communism and practically every religious system which rejects the Bible. We can't use deception as an excuse for rejecting God's truth. We have to realize that truth may not always be what we want to hear. Sometimes it may contradict everything else we've ever heard."

"You're right, Beth," Barry said. "God's Word promises that all those who sincerely seek Him will find Him. John's Gospel says that anyone who listens to the Father and learns from Him will come to the Son. The Bible also tells us to test the spirits to find out if they're from God. But New Agers are rarely willing to do so because the spirits are telling them exactly what they want to hear...which is nothing but a lie."

Beth looked thoughtful. "The Bible also says that those who reject the truth will be given a delusion by God—so that they will believe a lie."

Barry nodded. "That lie is the same lie that Satan told Eve in the Garden of Eden."

"You will be as gods," Matt said, recalling something John had once told him.

"That's the heart of the New Age Movement," Barry said.

Matt recalled then what Gail had said about achieving Cosmic Consciousness. Though it had sounded like mystical mumbo jumbo to him, a lot of his coworkers had eaten it up. He wondered if that was the reason for the spiritual darkness at the factory these days.

They continued talking, and Matt suddenly thought of the hateful phone calls Beth had been receiving. He decided to mention them to Barry.

His expression darkened. "Hmm. That sounds like something Satanists would do."

"Really?" Beth's face was a little pale again.

"It's a form of psychological warfare," Barry explained. "You see, Beth, those who are trying to prepare the world for the New Age Christ are viewing this whole thing as a war. Many of the leaders in the New Age have actually used the term 'holy war.' Anyway, Legion said that when someone is sacrificed for the Kingdom of Lucifer, we also need to target their families and loved ones. Not necessarily physically, but spiritually and psychologically. He said their spirits need to be broken, so they won't be able to resist the new leadership which is about to take over the world."

"Do you think Beth is in any physical danger?" Now that John was with the Lord, Matt felt a strong sense of responsibility toward his pregnant sister-in-law.

"Look, there's no sense in worrying," Barry said. "Sooner or later, all Christians will be under attack by Lucifer and his minions, so we have to trust God to protect all of us. And, He can always put a hedge of protection around His people."

Beth tried to put Matt at ease. "I'm not alone, Matt. We both know that. Jesus has promised to be with us always."

"You're right," he said.

"Besides, if it makes you feel any better, Audrey and Mike have been looking out for me."

"How is Audrey?" asked Matt, recalling her near breakdown.

"She's a little better," Beth said. "Hearing about what happened to John seems to have startled her out of her shell. I guess it made her realize that she's not the only one who's had to suffer for being a Christian." She then explained Audrey and Mike's plight to Barry.

"Boy, that's gotta be tough. Where's the little girl now?" Barry asked.

"She's in a children's home," Beth replied. "But the Lord's been merciful. Audrey and Mike have been allowed to visit Kelsie a few times."

"Is the government planning on taking permanent custody of her?" Matt asked.

Her expression clouded. "Well, they claim they want to give Mike and Audrey a chance to get Kelsie back. But there are a few conditions involved."

"Of course," Matt said ruefully.

"Yeah, the people from Social Services have been pressuring them to get 'counseling' on how to overcome their so-called 'religious fanaticism,'" Beth said. "If they agree to get counseling, they'll have a chance to get Kelsie back, but before they can have full custody, they'll have to sign a statement agreeing to refrain from forcing their religious views on their daughter."

"That's ridiculous!" Matt exclaimed, and Barry was shaking his head.

"They're trying to put it all in God's hands. Their big worry is the kind of influence Kelsie might be under when she's away from them." She looked at Barry. "And after what you just told us about Operation Lucid—"

Barry spoke reassuringly. "It sounds like Audrey and Mike are committed Christians, from what you told me. If that's the case, their influence is going to be much stronger than anything else in her life. When Legion encouraged us to reach out to the younger generation, he warned us that there would be children we would probably never reach: those of born-again, Bible-believing Christians. Legion said that no matter how much effort we put into re-educating them, he knew from experience that the children of those 'deluded' people could rarely be swayed. The thought made him sick, but he couldn't deny it."

Beth looked hopeful. "That sounds encouraging."

The waitress brought their bill. They all handed her their debit cards. "Hmm. These will be obsolete pretty soon," Barry remarked. Beth and Matt smiled knowingly.

"Yeah?" The waitress looked intrigued. "How so?"

Grateful for this opportunity to share his newfound faith, Matt briefly explained the system of the mark predicted in Revelation 13. "Sounds great," she said. "It'll be even easier than carrying this card around."

"But the mark will be a sign of allegiance to Satan," Barry pointed out to her.

She looked at him as if he had two heads. "Hey—are you one of them fundamentalists I keep hearing about on the news?"

Matt smiled. "If being a fundamentalist means having your sins forgiven by trusting in Jesus, then I guess we all are."

"Yeah, well, whatever makes you happy," the waitress muttered uncomfortably as she rushed off to another table.

"Now that we know all this stuff about Operation Lucid," Matt said to Beth after Barry had left, "what should we do about it? I mean, we can't just ignore this."

"You're right. We have to do something. I guess we should start by telling other Christians about it."

* * * *

On one of those hot, muggy days in August so typical of Long Island, Matt and Beth, along with a small group of believers from various denominations, met outside the Lucid Home for a prayer vigil. They carried Bibles, printed hymns, and signs that read, "FIND OUT THE TRUTH ABOUT LUCID." Matt had run off a bunch of flyers to distribute explaining in detail what Barry had revealed. But their primary purpose here was to pray for the poor kids who had been led astray by the Lucid staff through no fault of their own. Most of them were there because they had problems that were easily exploited, making them easy prey for the parapsychologists' occultic blend of mind control.

"Well, this is it," Matt said as he and Beth stepped onto the sidewalk across the street from the entrance to the Lucid Home.

They looked around at the people already gathered in prayer. Matt smiled when he saw Anita and David waving. He had kept in touch with them, and had been overjoyed to learn that David had given his life to Jesus, and was now working on getting his mom saved. Matt felt a twinge of sadness as he thought about Ben and Elsie, and how much Ben had meant to him. He smiled. *I'll be seeing them again.*

Beth's voice broke in on Matt's thoughts. "Here we go," she said, a little nervously.

"Into the lion's den," Matt added. Neither of them knew exactly what to expect, but they did know that this was a spiritual battle, and Matt figured that Satan was going to hit them as hard as he could. But he reminded himself that the blood of Jesus protected them, and that nothing could happen to them unless He allowed it. With that thought in mind, Matt crossed the street with Beth and they entered the enemy's territory.

* * * *

Gina waited by the phone for hours, reliving her worst nightmares when Matt didn't come home that night. He had left a little after nine that morning, and had expected to be gone for just a couple of hours. But he did warn Gina it was possible they might get arrested since praying in public had recently been dubbed a "hatecrime."

"Then don't go," she had pleaded. He had tried to explain to her what he believed was at stake, but she simply couldn't understand why he would take such a risk.

It was nearly dawn, and he still wasn't home. She had cried till she didn't think it was possible to shed any more tears, and had called the county jail a dozen times only to be told that it didn't have jurisdiction over "illegal prayer vigils." When she asked who did, no one seemed able to tell her.

He came home just a little past dawn, looking so bedraggled that Gina could only gasp. His face was swollen with bruises, and he stood by the door, swaying a little, his body limp with exhaustion, as Anita and David helped him inside. A huge gash ran across his forehead, and blood trickled down from a deep cut on his lip. She ran toward him and he nearly fell into her arms. She helped him to the couch and he slumped onto it, his eyes so glazed he looked as if he might pass out. "Matt..." she began. She could say nothing else. Anita and David slipped out quietly, as if they understood that Gina and Matt needed to be alone.

He looked at Gina with profound tenderness and gently touched her cheek. He spoke in a weak, tired voice. "Sorry...you have to see me...like this."

Her eyes glistened with tears. "That's okay, darling," she said softly.

He leaned his head on her shoulder, his forehead damp with perspiration, as she gently stroked his disheveled, matted hair.

A few moments later she washed his cuts and put antiseptic on them, and he winced. "I'm sorry," she said, horrified at having to cause him more pain.

"It's okay," he whispered.

Gingerly, she helped him to undress and put him to bed. He slept for over nine hours.

When he woke up, she brought him a light supper and some tea. He told her what happened—the police had come and arrested them all, and he was hauled off to some prison where he was viciously beaten and then locked in a cell, with no food or water for the next eleven hours. Since it was his first offense, he was released, along with most of the others. But they were all warned not to "shove their religion down other people's throats" anymore.

"Why didn't you call me?" she asked. "I would've picked you up."

"They wouldn't let us call anyone—not even after they released us. Would you believe I had to share a taxi with Anita and David?"

"Is Beth all right?" Gina asked, concerned for the baby.

"She's holding up. They made her sleep on the concrete floor of her cell all night, but they didn't hurt her, thank God."

"Where is she now?"

"Someone from her church took her home. Since this is her second offense, they've implanted some kind of a microchip under her skin so they can keep track of her. She's not supposed to leave the house except to go to work. Basically, she's under house arrest."

"For praying in public?" Gina shook her head in disbelief.

Matt nodded slowly, then lifted a spoonful of chicken soup to his mouth. His hand shook slightly, and she was startled at how weak his ordeal had left him. She had never seen him like this before...fragile, vulnerable, almost like a child. It made her feel intensely protective toward him. "I don't understand why God would allow this to happen to you. If this is what being a Christian is all about, then it's not worth it."

He spoke patiently. "Gina, millions of Christians have suffered for their faith. I can't expect to be spared. But I know how you feel, believe me. This was one of the reasons I wasn't too eager to get serious about God in the first place. I knew it meant that I'd have to be willing to get hurt."

She was close to tears again. "But why? Why should you be willing to suffer for doing what's right?"

"Because Jesus was willing to die in my place," he said in a soft voice.

"You really believe that?"

"I'd stake my whole life on it." He smiled. "In fact, I am. You know, it's funny, in a way. Before I gave my life to Jesus, I was terrified of dying, even though my life was so empty. Now, my life finally has meaning, yet I'm not afraid of dying anymore. In fact, I'm actually looking forward to it—because I know I'll be with Jesus."

"Do we have to talk about death?" She was curled up in bed with him, her head propped up against two huge, down-filled pillows.

"Gina, it's something we all have to face, sooner or later. But we don't have to be afraid of it. I know I'm not. At least, not anymore."

"That's what scares me."

He looked puzzled. "It scares you that I'm not afraid of death?"

"I'm just afraid you're going to do something foolish," she said, her voice quivering somewhat. "And I don't want to lose you."

"Gina—"

"Wait," she said earnestly. "Hear me out. We've never been this happy before, Matt. We've never been so in love before, not even when we first got married. I'm not sure I really understand the change in you. But I can't deny that you've changed—for the better. I never dreamed we would ever be this happy together. But if something happens to you...I just don't think I could take it. I just can't lose you again." She was crying now, and he put down his soup and pulled her gently into his arms.

"Gina, you don't have to worry about losing me," he assured her.

"But if what you and Beth believe about us living in the end-times is true, then that means you could be put to death for being a Christian someday. Isn't that true?"

"Yes," he admitted. "But that wouldn't have to separate us forever. Don't you see? If you put your trust in Christ, if you accept His gift of eternal life, then we'll be together with Him through time unending. We'll never have to worry about being apart again. We'll never have to fear anything, because Jesus has promised to be with us forever. Think about that, Gina—there's Someone who will never let you down, Someone who loved you enough to die for you. Jesus died for both of us, and we can both be with Him in heaven someday. All you have to do is trust Him."

She sat there silently, listening to the rain patter against the window, as Matt's words began to sink in. Something stirred within her, a longing buried deep in her heart for many years...that nothing on this earth could fill. Seeing Matt's unshakable peace, she suddenly understood what it was she had been searching for all her life. "Maybe...maybe I do need Jesus," she said, her voice as soft as a whisper.

He smiled the most radiant smile she had ever seen. "Then let's pray." They bowed their heads and clasped hands, as Gina invited Jesus to be her Lord and Savior.

And Matt knew that the angels were rejoicing with him.

EPILOGUE

They sat on a bench under a tall willow tree near the lake and watched Gina as she carried her one-year-old nephew over to the pair of squirrels that had caught his attention. They were fighting over a peanut, but when they saw Gina approaching with Johnny, they scampered away into the woods. The baby looked disappointed until he noticed the ducks bobbing around on the lake. "Come on, let's go see the ducks," Gina said with a smile. Matt watched her, his heart nearly bursting with joy. God had indeed given him all the desires of his heart.

The late afternoon sun glinted through the long, drooping branches of the many willow trees that surrounded the lake. Matt suddenly thought of the old willow tree that had once stood in his backyard so many years ago—and how sad he had felt when it was cut down. Maybe it had something to do with his longing for security and permanence, for something in this life which would last forever. But now, he knew that there was only one thing in life which was sure and lasting: the love of God in Christ Jesus.

Beth turned to him and smiled. "Look at that, she's already acting like a mother. When is the baby due, by the way?"

"November." Matt beamed at the prospect of being a father, and he said a silent prayer of thanksgiving. Still, life was far from easy. He had been called in to see his supervisor recently because someone had overheard him inviting a coworker to a Bible study. Now, his supervisor was pressuring him to get counseling on how to deal with his "intolerance." If he refused, he could be reported to the viciously anti-Christian Human Rights Tribunal. There was also Gina's work with the underground paper, which had become a matter of concern lately. Just last week, WorCEN agents raided the home of one of the paper's writers. They had followed him when he was seen distributing some of the papers around his neighborhood. After being beaten and tortured for hours, he was left to die in his own living room, where his wife and children had found him. Now, Matt and Gina were praying for God's wisdom in deciding whether or not she should continue writing for the paper, especially since she was pregnant. In spite of their concerns, their love for the truth made them reluctant to give up that easily.

"You think John might be watching us today?" Beth asked suddenly, her tone a bittersweet mixture of love and sadness. "He always dreamed of taking his son to the park someday—" She broke off, looking as if she might cry, and Matt touched her shoulder.

"It's okay, Beth," he said gently. "You're still allowed to mourn, you know."

She wiped away the tears that sprang to her eyes. "I know. I know God understands how much I still miss him. I guess I always will."

"Of course you will. But you'll be together again someday."

Her eyes shone with a light that seemed to see beyond this world and into the next. "That's right. I know we won't have to be apart very long, because Jesus is coming back soon. And when Johnny is old enough to understand, I can tell him that his father died for the Kingdom of God." Her voice sounded far away, and he wondered if she was thinking about the outcome of the trial. The thought that John's murderer would be allowed to roam free while thousands of Christians were being jailed and tortured for their faith was a bitter blow to both of them. But the hardest part of all was having to see John's name dragged through the mud at the trial, where he was branded a hatecriminal, and then listen to the media assassinate his character on the nightly news. The trial itself was a farce. Most of the witnesses for the defense were psychologists who claimed that Legion was a victim of some vague, childhood trauma that had left him emotionally scarred for life. Then there were the many character witnesses. They painted such a glowing picture of Legion that the media could hardly conceal their admiration for this "wonderful man of peace," whose only crime had been to cross paths with a "deranged religious fanatic" who posed a threat to everything that Legion held dear. Who could blame him for "snapping" under such circumstances? And all the while, Legion had sat there complacently, showing absolutely no remorse. By the time the panel of judges had reached its verdict, Beth and Matt had been certain that Legion would be acquitted, even if Barry had lived to give his testimony.

They were both dismayed when they heard the news of Barry's death. His car had been found at the bottom of a ravine on the north shore of Long Island, where, the press said, he had run his car off the road in an apparent suicide. None of the newspapers reported the recent attempts on his life or the death threats he had been receiving.

"You two ready to eat?" Gina called to them.

"I'll start the hotdogs." Beth got up off the bench. "You coming?" she asked when Matt didn't get up.

"I'll catch up with you in a minute," he said. She smiled at him and walked over to the picnic area where Gina was setting up the grill.

Southhaven Park was beautiful this time of year. Matt looked around and recalled all the times he had come here with John. Memories of hazy summer afternoons playing ball or swimming in the lake flooded back to him. He smiled as he remembered the time they had attempted to walk around the lake as the sun was setting, only to get lost in the darkness before they had reached the other side.

He watched Johnny crawling in the grass, fascinated by a Monarch butterfly he had spied, and he felt sad that John couldn't be here to see his darling little boy. There were a million things that Matt wished he could say to his brother...so much had been left unsaid.

It's funny how we rarely think about such things until it's too late. At least too late for this world.

But he knew he wouldn't have to wait forever.

"I'll see you again," Matt whispered. "When the day breaks, and the shadows pass away."

A NOTE FROM THE AUTHOR

Although this story is a work of fiction, it incorporates elements of truth. The following publications were invaluable sources of information and research:

Allen, Gary and Larry Abraham. *None Dare Call it Conspiracy*. Rossmore: Concord Press, 1972.

Behe, Michael J. *Darwin's Black Box: The Biochemical Challenge to Evolution*. New York: Simon & Schuster, 1996.

Brooke, Tal. *When the World Will Be as One*. Eugene: Harvest House, 1989.

Griffin, G. Edward. *The Creature from Jekyll Island: A Second Look at the Federal Reserve*. Appleton: American Opinion Publishing, 1994.

Higham, Charles. *Trading with the Enemy: An Exposé of the Nazi-American Money Plot 1933-1949*. New York: Dell, 1983.

Jeffrey, Grant R. *The Signature of God: Astonishing Biblical Discoveries*. Toronto: Frontier Research, 1996.

Jasper, William F. *Global Tyranny Step by Step: The United Nations and the Emerging New World Order*. Appleton: Western Islands, 1992.

Kah, Gary. *En Route to Global Occupation*. Lafayette: Huntington House, 1992.

Luksik, Peg and Pamela Hobbs Hoffecker. *Outcome-Based Education: The State's Assault on Our Children's Values*. Lafayette: Huntington House, 1995.

Marres, Texe. *Circle of Intrigue* Austin: Living Truth Publishers, 1996.

Peikoff, Leonard. *The Ominous Parallels: The End of Freedom in America*. New York: New American Library, 1982.

Perloff, James. *The Shadows of Power: The CFR and the American Decline*. Appleton: Western Islands, 1988.

Zahner, Dee. *The Secret Side of History: Mystery Babylon and the New World Order*. Hesperia, Calif.: LTAA Communications, 1994.

Zelman, Aaron and Jay Simkin. *Gun Control: Gateway to Tyranny*. Milwaukee: Jews for the Preservation of Firearms Ownership, 1994.

I am also indebted to Boston T. Party whose writings provided a wealth of information on the Federal Reserve System and the causes of the Great Depression.

Printed in the United States
791100002B